Hold On

Discover other titles by Kristen Ashley at:
www.kristenashley.net

Commune with Kristen at:
www.facebook.com/kristenashleybooks
Twitter: KristenAshley68

Hold On

KRISTEN ASHLEY

Copyright © 2015 by Kristen Ashley
First ebook edition: September 1, 2015
First print edition: September 1, 2015

ISBN: 0692467459
ISBN-13: 9780692467459

Dedication

At the end of this series—
a series precious to me because it's based where I learned how to be me—
it's apropos to dedicate this book to my readers.
Thanks for going home with me.
Thanks for liking being there.
I tip my Hilligoss powdered sugar, chocolate buttercream-filled donut to
you.
We might be done with this version of The 'Burg…
But here's to many adventures to come.

One

Worth Every Penny
Cher

"I'm stayin'."

"I got this."

"I'm stayin'."

"Go."

"I'm stayin'."

"*Go.*"

Darryl looked at me standing in front of him, his back to the back door, then beyond me into J&J's Saloon.

I knew what he saw and that meant I knew why he wanted to stay.

What I didn't know was how this was going to go. Darryl didn't have a lot going on between his ears, but he was loyal, worked like a horse, was strong as an ox, and, since getting hacked with an ax by a serial killer in order to protect his boss, was insanely protective.

But he knew me. He knew I could take care of myself. Saying that, I didn't know if he knew what I'd be putting myself through, taking on what was right then sitting alone at the bar.

He looked back to me and jerked up his chin, ordering, "Get his ass in a taxi."

"You got it, hoss," I muttered.

1

He opened the door and kept bossing my ass. "Lock this behind me. Code the security for doors and windows."

I rolled my eyes but moved forward so I could do what he said, even though I would've done that anyway.

I'd learned to be smart, to go out of my way to stay safe and not to take any chances.

I locked up, moved to the security panel, coded it, then took a deep breath and moved down the back hall into the bar.

It was after three thirty in the morning. We were closed. The glasses washed and put away. The trash taken out. The fridges restocked. The cash register cleaned out, money in the safe in the office. The bar top and tables wiped down. Chairs up on the tables all ready for Fritzi to come in in the morning and mop the floors as well as clean the bathrooms and stock them with toilet paper, so when Feb got in tomorrow, she could just unlock the doors and start the day.

He was at the side curve to the bar, had his back to me, ass to a barstool, feet up on the rungs. He had his elbows to the bar, and since I'd poured it for him, I knew he was nursing a glass of top-shelf whisky sitting in front of him. Whisky that set him back a whack, more so seeing as he'd had five shots of it along with the seven beers he'd sucked back the last five hours.

When I'd followed Darryl to the back, I'd left the hinged section of the bar open. I rounded it and took the two steps to stand in front of him.

The minute I stopped, Garrett "Merry" Merrick, lieutenant on the 'burg's PD, tall, dark, gorgeous, and the last bastion of good guys available in the 'burg—that meaning he was single—grabbed his glass. He put it to his lips and threw it back.

I watched him do it, my palms itching, my eyes to the muscular cords working around his throat.

He slammed the glass down and lifted his beautiful blue eyes to me.

"I'll call a taxi, Cher."

I didn't say anything even as his hand went to the jacket he'd thrown on the stool beside him.

Instead, I moved to the back of the bar, reached high, and grabbed the bottle of whisky that had stayed at its level for months, seeing as it was fifty bucks a shot, until Merry had brought that level down that night.

I grabbed another glass, put it in front of him, and I knew his eyes were on my hands as I filled both glasses, his and mine.

"On me," I muttered, setting the bottle aside and looking at him.

He tossed the phone he'd gotten out of his jacket to the bar and caught my eyes.

"You know," he stated. His words weren't slurred. Merry could hold his drink. He'd had more than his normal that night, for sure. But he wasn't sloppy drunk. Just, I hoped, feeling no pain.

Or less pain. The kind of pain he was drinking away didn't really ever go away.

"I know," I told him.

And I did. Everyone in the 'burg knew.

The finale to a fairy tale that didn't have a happy ending.

He looked at me a second, then grabbed his glass and lifted it toward me. He didn't wait for me to grab mine. He took a healthy swallow of his. He didn't shoot the whole thing, but he wasn't fucking around.

He set the glass back to the bar.

I wrapped my fingers around mine and leaned into my arms on the bar top.

"She's a dumb fuck, Merry," I said softly.

He didn't look up from his contemplation of his whisky when he replied, "She isn't. But I sure as fuck am."

"That just isn't true," I returned, and he lifted his gaze to me.

It took a lot, but I didn't flinch at the depth of pain and strength of anger burning from his eyes. The bad kind of anger. The worst.

The kind where you're pissed as all hell at your own damned self.

"Got shot of her," he declared. "Fucked around when I knew I shouldn't in gettin' her back. Watched Feb and Colt get it back. Watched Cal get his head outta his ass, find Vi, and hold on. Tanner and Rocky got their shit together, and when they did, Tanner told me. Pointed that shit out to me. Warned me what would happen if I fucked around. Mike nearly lost Dusty, bein' stupid and protecting himself against somethin' good, but he pulled out all the stops to get her back and keep her. All that goes down, what do I do?" He shook his head. "Dick."

He lifted his glass, took a sip, and lowered it.

3

When he did, he muttered to his glass, "I did dick."

"Your ex lives in the 'burg too," I pointed out.

He looked at me, brows slightly pulled together. "And?"

"She also did dick."

It was true. She did.

Mia Merrick did dick.

Which made the bitch the single stupidest female on the planet.

I was not around when they were married. I was not around when they got divorced.

I *was* around when every decent man in the 'burg got nailed down and happily allowed the ball and chain to be clamped around their ankle. And that meant I was around, and Mia Merrick was around, seeing all that and waiting for Merry to make his play to get the wife everyone in that 'burg said he loved more than anything back in his bed.

And now I was around, alone at J&J's Saloon, the bar where I worked, watching Garrett Merrick drown his sorrows because the news made the rounds that day that Mia Merrick got engaged to another man. Not only that, he was a professor, had worked at IUPUI in Indianapolis, but this semester he'd taken a new position down at IU in Bloomington.

So she was getting hitched and leaving town. The FOR SALE sign had gone up in front of the house she'd shared with Merry that very day.

Moving on.

Leaving Merry behind.

"Was my play to make," Merry told me.

"Yeah? How's that?" I asked him.

"Cher, babe," he said gently, "it's cool you're tryin' to be there for me, but you don't know."

"I know she did dick," I shot back.

His lips tipped up in a small, sad smile.

"Was my play," he repeated.

"No," I declared, leaning into my arms on the bar. "That's bullshit, Merry, straight up. You got good, you don't let it go. It lets you go, you hold on. It slips through your fingers, you pull out all the stops to get it back. You got somethin' worth fighting for, you *fight for it*. You do not sit on your ass waitin' for it to come back to you. You show whoever that is they mean something and you go all out on that, and the only way you go down is doin' that shit swinging."

Merry stared at me, which was good since I had his attention and I wasn't done.

"I get you. I been around this 'burg for a while now so I get you, the kind of man you are," I stated. "You think, you got a dick, you gotta do the work. Make the plays. Give the chase. Fight the good fight. But you're wrong. It's not like that woman was not in the know you had some serious history, and the seriousness of that history was the kind that hangs around a while. Your sister sorted out her gig with that because she had a good man at her back who kept her standing and swinging. But that isn't the only way it goes. Any woman worth that kind of devotion, she takes her man's back so he can stay standing. She does not wait for him to sort out his shit and then find her and kiss her ass."

Merry continued to stare at me before one side of his lips bowed up in a small but not sad smile.

"Don't hold back, Cher. Hand it to me straight," he teased.

When he did, I felt it. I felt it like I felt it every time he was in. Every time he gave that kind of thing to me. Every time he gave *anything* to me.

The sting. The sting that made itself known. The sting that was a thorn that lived with me. A thorn I'd had so long that I could sometimes ignore the pain.

A thorn buried deep under my skin. A thorn that was Garrett Merrick.

A man who liked me. A man who laughed at my jokes. A man who smiled at me regularly. Who teased me often. Who shot the shit with me. A man who liked me a lot.

A man who was my friend.

A man who thought of me as a friend.

The man I loved more than breath.

"How long you known me?" I asked.

He just gave a slight shake of his head, his mouth still curled up on one end, making the beauty of his face a playful beauty that felt like a gift from God. A gift I wanted to call mine. A gift I wanted aimed at my son so he had a good man who could make him laugh, make him feel funny, and teach him how to be decent.

A gift that I got just like that, the way he was giving it to me now.

It was there.

But it would never be mine.

"A while," he answered my question.

"I ever go soft?"

That got me a full smile and I knew I should feel lucky.

I never went soft. I was all hard. I'd built a shell around me no one could crack. I had reason. A really fucking good reason.

Problem was, I built that shell so hard, even I couldn't break out of it.

That wasn't exactly a bad thing. It could be considered good. It meant I couldn't open myself up to the likes of Garrett Merrick, or the rest of the male population who were shades or whole freaking strides less than him, to walk all over me.

Still, I should feel lucky because Merry didn't mind the hard. He looked past it to be my friend. A lot of folks didn't.

That was good too. You didn't put in the effort, why would I bother with you?

Merry put in the effort. A lot of folks in that 'burg did when I'd moved there, even after what had happened to make me move there.

Which was why I stayed.

Not for me—for my kid.

Ethan needed people around him like that.

"You aren't drinkin'," Merry pointed out, tipping his head to my glass.

I lifted it and shot the whole damned thing.

Merry burst out laughing.

I slammed the glass down and grabbed the bottle to pour more.

"Only you would shoot a fifty dollar glass of Feb and Morrie's finest Scotch," Merry noted.

I topped his off and poured myself another one.

Then I again shot it.

When I did, Merry burst out laughing again.

Which was precisely why I blew one hundred dollars I could not afford in less than thirty seconds.

Laughter like that coming from Garrett Merrick was worth every penny.

The bed moved and my eyes opened.

I closed them immediately as the sick hit my gut and the throb of pain made itself known in my head.

It took me a few beats, but I heard the noises.

A man was getting dressed and doing it quiet.

Shit. What did I do last night?

It had been a while since something like this had happened. Around about the time I got hooked up with Ethan's dad, thought I'd hit the mother lode, found myself knocked up, and got myself left behind when the asshole evaporated. Hard to live wild and have a good time pregnant. And a single mom at twenty-four, you got your shit together. So, between working to keep my kid fed and in babysitters, I didn't have many shots at living wild.

Ethan, however, was right now at a friend's house. A sleepover.

And expending effort I didn't have in me, considering I was totally hungover and maybe still a little drunk, I remembered that last night, for the first time in years, I'd lived wild.

I'd done this shooting the shit with Garrett Merrick, polishing off a bottle of scary-expensive whisky, chasing that with beer, going all out, putting everything I had into it to do what I could to ease the heart of a brokenhearted man.

Somewhere between polishing off the bottle and moving to a less expensive one, things turned.

We got a taxi.

We came to my house.

We fucked, we did it wild, and we did it for a long, *long* time.

And now it was morning, I felt like I had twenty seconds of sleep, and he was up before me, quietly dressing.

It had been a while, but I knew the drill. I knew those careful sounds he was making.

He didn't want me to wake up. He wanted to get his ass out of there and get home. Get a shower to wash himself clean of me. Get his head straight enough to kick his own ass that he did something as stupid as banging me. And, only since he was Merry and Merry was that kind of guy (other guys wouldn't bother), finding it in himself to determine the right time to make his approach and make it clear where we stood.

We'd fucked.

But nothing had changed.

Friends, even though he knew the taste of me and I knew the feel of him.

I always thought everyone got it wrong, and lying there, eyes closed, pretending to sleep to let Merry have what he needed—a clean getaway—I thought it again.

It wasn't walking out of a house into a taxi or your car in your clothes from the night before that was the walk of shame. You wanted what you wanted, you went after it, you got it, then you left it and went on with your life. There was no shame in that. None.

The shame was lying naked in your own bed listening to a man be quiet while dressing because he woke up next to you not wanting one thing to do with you. It didn't matter how that happened—if you gauged what was going on with him wrong and he was just out for a fuck, or if you both got trashed and things got out of hand when you didn't mean them to.

I lay still feeling the burn of that shame that singed deeper because the man who wanted not one thing to do with me was Merry.

It would be okay. For me, it'd be totally okay.

Okay, right. Not really. That thorn had driven itself deeper, knowing how he kissed—the range of intensity, the level of expertise—not to mention knowing a whole lot more about what Garrett Merrick could do.

But I'd make myself okay to keep him as I had him.

I'd have to work him.

He'd start out cool. Definitely. He'd be cautious with me. He'd see to my feelings. He'd be sensitive in his badass cop way, but he'd still do it.

But he'd be embarrassed. Losing control like that. Stooping so low as to fuck the bartender at his local. The bartender who was a single mom and who used to be a stripper. The bartender who got played by a serial killer.

I'd work him, though. I wouldn't let it slide to awkward. I'd show him it was all good. I'd show him we could be who we were; we didn't lose what we had. It happened. It was good (I hoped for him too). It was a one-time thing. And now…onward.

I kept silent and still, breathing steady so he'd think I was asleep, wanting it to be done. I had shit to do that day. Ethan was going to be gone in the morning, still at his friend's. I had the day off work. It was Saturday. I had groceries to buy. A house to clean. Bills to pay.

And then I would have my son and it would be all about him.

I tried to take my mind off Merry, thinking first up was my hangover cocktail. Then, depending on the time, the grocery store, but only if it was early and I could beat the crowds.

People annoyed me. They were rude. And the more people there were, the ruder they were. They totally did not get that we were all in this game of life together *and* playing on the same team, working toward the same goal. Every single one of us had something to do, and we just wanted to do it without a lot of hassle and eventually get home safe.

Somewhere along the way, people got the idea that whatever *they* had to do was the priority and everyone else could eat shit. So they drove like lunatics. They were impatient in lines. They were assholes to clerks when a clerk could no way memorize the price of everything in the entire store at Walmart so they wouldn't have to inconvenience some jerk to call for a price check. They acted like waiting the whole five minutes it took to get that price check was akin to torture. Then again, the number of folks who ran orange lights that were only a hint of yellow, instead of waiting the whole *maybe* five minutes for the light to change to green, was the same damn thing.

Everyone was in a hurry. Everyone was out for themselves. No one gave a shit about anyone else. Long ago, kindness, courtesy, and civility had taken a hike.

So, yeah.

People annoyed me.

These were my thoughts as I felt the bed move again, and the bed moving freaked me way the fuck out.

So I opened my eyes and got freaked out a whole lot more.

Merry was not sneaking out of my room.

He was instead clothed and sitting on the edge of the bed, chin dipped, dark hair the good kind of hot mess, some of it falling on his forehead, sleepy, gorgeous blue eyes aimed at me.

He also had a hand coming my way, and I tensed when he used it to brush the hair off my neck, then curl it warm there.

God, no man had ever touched me like that.

Not one.

Not in thirty-four years.

"Hey," he whispered.

What was happening?

"Hey," I whispered back, uncertain how to proceed in this unprecedented situation.

"Didn't wanna wake you." He was still talking quietly. "But also didn't wanna disappear on you."

At his words, I felt something weird happening to me. Like the beginning of a release. A release that was both pain and relief, the kind that comes as a splinter is being pulled out.

Or a thorn is working its way out.

"I'm on this weekend," he continued. "Gotta get home, shower, change clothes, get to the station."

That was when something weirder happened to me.

I felt like I was going to cry.

The last two times I shed tears, I remembered.

One was sitting in Mimi's Coffee Shop, listening to Alec Colton be cool to me after what I'd thought was a death blow had been delivered. Not a literal one, but definitely a figuratively emotional one.

The other was when I'd heard that Dennis Lowe was dead.

The first were tears of bitterness, sadness, defeat, and shame.

The last were tears of happiness.

Considering Merry was talking, I realized I had to pull my head together and respond.

So I said, "Okay."

"I'm on all weekend, but we'll talk later," he declared.

I stared into his face, my eyes tipped up his way, not moving my head from the pillow.

I tried to read something, anything that would tell me what was going on in his mind.

He just looked sleepy and kind of cute.

This was shocking.

Garrett Merrick was all man, not all-*cute* man.

He was a cop. He was built, muscular but lean. His tough, sinewy frame, which I knew from my time as a waitress, then a stripper, and finally a bartender, concealed the power packed in his build. He wasn't a hulk, and therefore, you might think you could mess with him when you absolutely could not. I knew this from looking at him. But he'd broken up three bar brawls in my tenure at J&J's Saloon, so I'd also seen it firsthand.

Further, he was handsome in a smooth way that didn't quite succeed in hiding the fact that, under the surface, he was not smooth at all. He was rough.

His sense of humor was wicked.

And his personal sense of right and wrong was razor-sharp (if perhaps a little crazy). There wasn't a lot of gray in the world of Garrett Merrick. There was black and there was white. He had a reputation in that town and I was a bartender in that town, so I knew his reputation. He was a cop for a reason. He was about order and justice. There was just a part of him that was compelled to decide what kind of order there should be and how justice should take place.

He had a good ole boy exterior.

Under that was something else entirely.

I got this. I knew his history. There were several ways to go on with your life after what had happened to his family and none of them were good.

Except the one Merry chose.

So he was not cute.

Not at all.

Until right then.

Sleepy and cute and not even looking a little bit hungover.

"Cher?" he called.

I blinked away my thoughts and muttered, "Sorry, kinda out of it."

He grinned, the cute took a hike, and a miracle occurred.

I had been completely hungover, freaked out, and uncertain.

Witnessing that cocky grin, I was straight up, full-on *turned on*.

He knew what he did to me last night. He knew how much I liked it. He also knew I might have participated fully, but he'd dominated the play and he got off, but he got *me* off spectacularly.

Five times.

My legs shifted and Merry bent closer.

"Rest up," he murmured. "Get some aspirin in you when you wake up. I'll call you later."

I nodded, head sliding on the pillow.

He bent deeper, and I didn't know whether to brace or turn my head just in case he needed a straight shot to my mouth because he intended to give me a kiss.

I found he was giving me a kiss. A sweet one. Brushing his lips lightly along my cheek, he moved his mouth to my ear.

"Never forget last night, babe. None of it," he whispered there, then gave me another kiss, touching his mouth to the skin in front of my ear before he finished, "Thank you for that."

I didn't know what to make of that. It was sweet, but was it final?

Or was it a beginning?

He pulled his head away but slid his hand from my neck to my jaw, where he used his thumb to sweep the apple of my cheek as he caught my eyes.

Another touch no man had ever given me. A simple maneuver, only his thumb moving, but it still felt like it spoke volumes, every word beauty.

"I'll call you."

That said beginning.

Oh God, were Merry and me beginning?

My heart clutched.

"Okay, Merry," I replied.

He grinned. He winked. My stomach curled in a nervous, excited way I almost didn't recognize because I hadn't felt it since I was fifteen years old.

Then he straightened from my bed and walked out of my room.

I did not go back to sleep to get rest I desperately needed (considering I *had* slept about twenty minutes).

I also did not get up to go to the grocery store.

I got up and went to the bathroom.

I brushed my teeth and looked into the mirror, thanking God for the first time that I'd perfected the art of makeup application through my stripper days so that shit would not move unless it was *removed*. The day before, I'd worked a shift with it on. I'd gotten drunk after that. I'd gotten royally laid after that, and it still looked awesome.

Nevertheless, I took it off.

I then went to the kitchen and got my hangover cure-all: two ibuprofen, two migraine pills (caffeine and aspirin), one Tylenol. I sucked that back, then power-slammed a huge glass of cold water. After that, I grabbed a Diet 7UP, made a pot of coffee, and hit the shower.

I did the hair gig. The makeup gig. The clothes gig. The jewelry gig.

Once ready, I called a taxi.

I could walk to J&J's from my house, but I wasn't going to do that, and not because I was wearing high-heeled boots. I could walk a mile in high heels. But the taxi ride would only cost five dollars, and I wasn't doing what I was going to do with the hangover hovering and my energy zapped from hoofing it to the bar.

Or the station.

I sat in the taxi, knowing what I was about to do was a risk. A huge one, and not one I'd taken in years.

Then again, I hadn't let anyone in in order for there to be a risk to take.

Not to mention, even before I built my shell, I'd never known with absolute certainty like I knew right then, that it was a risk worth taking.

I had to do it. I had to make that statement. I had to communicate without delay where I was. I was not going to make the same mistake as the stupidest bitch on the planet.

I was going to share what needed to be shared.

That being, I didn't just like getting laid by Garrett Merrick last night.

I liked *him*.

And if this was our beginning, I was all in.

The taxi let me out in front of J&J's, and since I knew the driver—he drank at the bar and he'd given me a ride more than once—I tipped him one hundred percent on the five dollar ride.

I didn't go to J&J's or through it to get to my car in the back.

I went to Mimi's Coffee Shop.

I bought two lattes and two of her blueberry muffins with the sprinkles on top.

Luckily, my girl Mimi was in the back, baking, so I didn't have to take time to chat. Two of the kids she employed were manning the counter—one who was a cheerleader at the high school, and the yin to her happy-go-lucky, my-life-is-golden yang—one who, this time, had green hair and, if I was right, two new piercings.

I got the stuff, balanced the tray of coffees and the bag, and left.

I hit the sidewalk and headed down the block to the station.

I made it there, climbed the steps, pushed through the door, and saw Kath at the reception desk.

Her eyes got big when she saw me.

"Hey, Cher!" she cried.

"Hey, Kath." I smiled at her and jerked my chin up the stairs that led to the bullpen behind her. "Merry up there?"

She shook her head.

From her seat at the reception desk at the 'burg's PD, she knew it all before anyone but the cops knew it. She also drank at J&J's, so she knew me. And, of course, she knew Merry.

She'd seen me shooting the shit with Merry, so she also knew we were tight.

But more, she knew Merry wouldn't go for me. Merry went for a lot of tail since he'd left Mia; however, I was not the kind of tail he went for.

So she wouldn't have any thoughts about why I was there...at least not the correct ones.

"He's out back," Kath didn't hesitate to tell me. "Mike needs a ride. Think Rees has his truck and Dusty's doin' somethin' and needs hers, so Merry took off to go pick him up."

Shit.

"Left about two seconds ago, so you could still catch him," she went on.

I nodded, turning and moving swiftly back to the front door, calling, "Cool. Thanks. See you later."

"Later, babe," she called back.

I was out the door and hoofing it around the station, taking my shot at catching him before he took off but not thinking I'd get that chance. Merry would go out the back door, which led direct to the parking lot where he'd left his truck last night and walked down to J&J's so he could get hammered. He'd probably be gone by the time I made it around the building.

I was about to turn the corner to the back when I heard a familiar voice that came from a familiar man, this man being Alec Colton, that voice raised and irate, saying, "What the fuck, Merry? Jesus Christ. Did you bang Cher?"

Holy fuck.

How could he know that?

I stopped dead, out of sight at the corner of the building.

"Colt." I heard Merry rumble.

"Feb went in this morning to do paperwork. I dropped her. Cher's car there. Empty bottle of whisky you like on the bar. I get to the station, see your truck in the lot where it was parked yesterday. I walk up to the bullpen, you can't meet my eyes."

Shit.

Cops.

They figured out *everything*.

"Sorry, brother, gotta get Mike. Greetin' you like a happy puppy was not top of my priority list," Merry returned, voice not raised but instead sarcastic and also irate.

"Bullshit. Darryl walked in before I left Feb, said he left Cheryl with you, you drunk, her lookin' to mother hen you. You take advantage of that?"

I peeked around the corner and saw them both in front of Colt's truck. They were in standoff mode. Merry was pissed. Colt was more pissed.

"You need to stand down," Merry warned.

"You take advantage of that?" Colt repeated when Merry didn't answer, and I watched around the corner as Colt got an inch closer to Merry, and Merry's already taut and alert frame got more of both. "You fuck your cares away, Mia gettin' a ring on her finger not yours? You bury that shit in Cher?"

I watched this going down having no clue what to do.

Normally, I would charge right in. Take Merry's back.

But I'd never had anyone but my mom take care of me the way Alexander Colton, his wife, February, and their family and friends took care of me when my life turned to shit. Took care of me. Took care of Ethan. Didn't do it from guilt or pity; they did it out of kindness and then love.

15

In my life, I had a great mom, a shit dad, made an awesome kid, and there was not much else.

Until I hit that 'burg. Until Colt talked me into moving there, working at Feb's bar, and turning my life around.

Then I got it all, worked to keep it good, and handed it right to my boy.

And there Colt was, taking care of me again. It wasn't the first time. It was just that it was new this time, and straight up, even if years had passed, I still wasn't used to it.

No doubt about it, the man had no sisters, but Colt made me one. He did not fuck around doing that. He took care of me. He spent time with Ethan, quality and quantity. He did everything a big brother would do.

I had no idea if this was true. I had no brothers or sisters.

But Colt did everything a big brother would do, the kind of brother you had in your dreams.

"Careful, Colt." Merry's deep voice wasn't a warning now, it was a threat.

"This is Cher we're talkin' about, Merry," Colt fired back. "You know I'm not gonna be careful, a man, he's my brother or not, walks all over her. So you better stand there tellin' me you did not drown your sorrows in her kindness and now you're gonna walk all over her."

"Cher and I are gonna talk it out," Merry replied.

"And how's that gonna go?" Colt pushed.

"Colt, you know Cher knows how it's gonna go. And you know it's gonna be good. She and me, we're tight. Woman she is, she knows. She isn't gonna have a drunken fuck with some asshole who was hung up on his ex-wife and not know how it's gonna go. We'll talk it out and go back to what we had. Fuck, she'll probably be the one who suggests it, thinkin' she's letting me off the hook for kickin' my ass for the exact shit you're spewin' at me right now."

I pulled my head from around the corner and leaned back hard against the stone of the station behind me. It was cold and I felt that cold instantly start seeping through my sweater.

At the same time, I didn't feel it.

I didn't feel anything.

"You take care a' her, man." I heard Colt demand, losing some of the pissed from his voice.

"You know me better than that," Merry returned, still fully pissed. "I get you. I get you're lookin' after her. But you know what she and me got, so when you calm the fuck down, you'll understand that this is a kick in the teeth you wished you didn't deliver because I'm gonna take care of her and you fuckin' know it."

He would.

He'd take care of me like he took care of me by not sneaking out of my house and making me feel like a stupid slut.

Merry would take care of me.

Just not the way I wanted.

Never that.

He could kiss me how he'd kissed me. He could move inside me, his eyes locked to mine, watching his work build, watching it explode. He could sit on the side of my bed and brush his lips along my cheek, wrap his hand around my neck, and tell me he'd call me.

But he'd never give me what I wanted.

I forgot.

I forgot I wasn't the kind of girl who got what she wanted.

Not once.

Not in my whole fucking life.

Yeah, I'd forgotten that.

And as I walked down the side of the station to the sidewalk, heading toward J&J's to get my car, passing a garbage bin and tossing the coffee and muffins in it, I reminded myself of that fact.

Slicking another thick, strong coat on that layer of hard I'd built around me, I reminded myself again.

And I did it in a way that I'd never forget it.

Not again.

Not ever again.

Until the day I died.

Two

IRONIC
Cher

I drove home because, caught up in visions of life actually not sucking for once, I'd stupidly not taken my grocery list with me.

And as I drove to my and Ethan's rental—a crackerbox house on a street that was full of tiny crackerbox houses—I knew that, even if it wasn't yet ten in the morning, my shit day was about to get shittier.

This was because Trent's beat-up, piece-of-shit car was at the curb in front of my house.

Ethan's dad.

He'd bailed on me the day after I told him I was pregnant.

I'd been cautiously excited. He had his problems, but I was young, stupid, and misread the situation (not unusual back then and, apparently, *now*), thinking I saw a decent guy underneath him smoking anything he could get his hands on—pot, meth, crack, whatever.

When you were young, you could go crazy, do stupid shit, then pull your life together, or that's what I'd thought. And people bounced back from that all the time; I'd thought that as well. If they were in too deep, they found reasons to get clean; I'd thought that too.

And I'd been good to him. I was in love with the decent guy I saw underneath, and I was all in to pull that guy together and give him happy. We were young, so I had time to fix whatever was broken in him and build a good life.

18

We'd had great times. I wasn't a nag, not about his drug use, not about anything. I was generous with the money I earned waitressing at a rundown bar since he couldn't hold down a job. I'd thought it was him being a good-time guy, but looking back, he was a full-blown junkie.

And I thought there was no better reason to get your shit together, to grow up, to start your *real* life, than the fact you were bringing a kid into the world, making that kid with someone you loved.

When I'd told him Ethan was on the way, Trent had acted ecstatic. We'd celebrated. He'd gotten loose, doing it saying it was the last time, promising he'd get his shit sorted starting the very next day, and we'd had sex all night before both of us passed out.

The next morning, I woke up and he was gone. I knew it regardless of the fact that he didn't take anything but some of his clothes, the money out of my wallet, and the huge jar of coins I threw all my change in.

I didn't see or hear from him for years.

Not until the shit hit with Dennis Lowe.

I aimed the tires of my car to the two strips of cracked cement that led to an old, one-car, unusable-except-for-storage garage, doing this repeatedly glancing at Trent's wreck, watching him fold out of it and make his way to the sidewalk.

By the time I'd parked and got out, he was at my front stoop.

As I moved toward him, it gave me no joy to know that I'd not been wrong. There *was* a decent guy under all his bullshit.

The problem was, when he got his shit together and got himself a steady job, he'd found himself a steady woman (who was obviously not me), married her ass, knocked her up, and only then did he come clean to her that he had another kid out in the world.

She'd lost her mind. She'd told him he was out on his ass unless he made good with his new kid's brother or sister.

He'd balked at this and they'd gone 'round about it, but when my name hit the news alongside a serial killer, he sought me out.

This was one reason why I'd legally changed my name and moved out of Morrie's old apartment that Colt and Feb had moved Ethan and me in to after Denny Lowe committed suicide by cop. Too easy for all sorts of trash to find me.

Dennis Lowe played Cheryl Sheckle.

Now, me and Ethan were Cher and Ethan Rivers.

I'd thought about doing it up big, finding some fancy romance novel heroine's name and giving it to me and my son. But in the end, that just wasn't me, and I didn't want to do anything that might make Ethan a target for snotty kids at school.

And I liked water. Lakes. Oceans. Rivers. Even streams. I didn't have much calm in my life, but anytime I was around water, I found it.

So Rivers it was.

"Hey," Trent called.

"Yo," I replied, making my way toward him, needing food in my stomach and another cocktail of hangover cure.

I scratched swinging into McDonald's before I hit Walmart on my to-do list as I arrived on the stoop.

I looked up at Trent.

He was good-looking, always had been, but it was better now that he wasn't gaunt and strung out because he'd rather smoke than eat. And I was grateful to him for giving me one thing—or giving it to Ethan—that being sharing with my son all the good stuff he had to give. Thick, dark blond hair, a long, sturdy frame, nice bone structure.

But Ethan got his momma's brown eyes.

"What's up?" I asked.

"You got a second to talk?" he asked back.

I didn't. I didn't because I didn't, and I didn't because I felt shit, and I didn't because my morning was even more shit than I felt, but I also didn't because I never wanted to take a second to talk to Trent.

He might have gotten it together, but he still left me alone, pregnant, and in love with a junkie asshole who, in the end, didn't give a shit about me.

I could hold a mean grudge; it was just how I was.

But on that score, I felt he deserved it.

Of course, him being Ethan's dad and now around, I reined that in when usually I'd let it fly.

Another part of life that sucked.

"Sure," I answered, digging out my keys and moving to the door.

He got out of the way so I could pull open the screen door, and as I did that, seeing as it was late September, I decided it was time for me to get the storm windows from the garage and switch out the screens.

I put that on my to-do list too.

Then I let us in, Trent shutting the door behind him.

I tossed my purse and keys to the couch.

Even though he'd been there before to pick up Ethan, Trent looked around. I didn't. I knew what I'd created for my son. I knew why I did.

It was me and it was comfortable, even if it was more than a little crazy.

It leaned toward boho, something you might not read looking at me, my high heels, my short skirts, my tight tanks and tight jeans.

Then again, you might.

In my living room (and throughout the house), there were some garage sale finds. There were some secondhand store finds. There were also some good, quality pieces I'd saved up for or put on layaway or bought on my card and paid off.

I'd thrown some scarves over ornate lamps. Other lamps had bright shades in pink or turquoise. Fringed, floral throws. A tiger-print ottoman. Whacky-patterned, mismatched toss pillows on equally mismatched furniture. A wicker bucket chair with a round paisley pad cushioning it. Lush potted plants everywhere.

The living room was smallish and painted a muted grape that somehow pulled all the colors and patterns in the room together, giving the whole thing a warm, fruity, cave-like feel. And the walls were chock-full, nearly edge to edge, of everything from prints of flowers to tribal designs to abstracts to cartoonish portraits to beat-up, old mirrors to framed pictures of me and Ethan living our lives.

The house was old, built back in the '50s, so there was no great room. No cathedral ceilings. It was segmented into small rooms that, unfortunately, separated its occupants. But it worked for Ethan and me because it was just the two of us and we liked to hang together.

The renters before me had dogs that didn't behave, so the carpet was new. Not even close to top of the line, but it was still clean and I took care of it so it looked nice.

The hall off the side to the left led to two bedrooms, a utility room, and a bathroom that Ethan and I shared. My landlord had let me paint Ethan's room blue and it was decorated in *boy*. My room was a continuation of the boho feel but super-charged, painted a subdued turquoise and stuffed full of *stuff*, from furniture to knickknacks to pictures.

The door off to the right led to a kitchen that wasn't all that big, but it was big enough to put a relatively nice kitchen table in it, which also worked for Ethan and me. We didn't need a fancy dining room table (or dining room). Not for just him and me.

No one would be banging down my door to beg me to let them take pictures for some decorator's magazine. But I liked it. It was me. It made me feel safe and comfortable and like I'd accomplished something. It surrounded my kid in me, hopefully making him feel the same way, but also showing him he should be himself and get off on that no matter what that was and no matter what anyone thought about it.

I could tell by the look on Trent's face that he was uncertain about *all* of that.

I didn't give a fuck. I'd never been to Trent's house, but knowing his wife, I pictured doilies.

"You wanted to talk?" I prompted, and he looked to me.

"Yeah, you got any coffee?"

Recovering addicts and their coffee.

Shit.

I walked to the kitchen feeling Trent following me and trying not to think of Merry.

I achieved this miraculous feat but only by allowing thoughts of Trent to leak in. How he'd sorted his shit out *after* he left me. How he'd been clean and sober now for nine years, with his woman for eight, married to her for seven, and devoted to her and their daughter and newborn son.

And how he had not given any of that shit to Ethan and me.

Though, now he gave it to Ethan. Coming to me first to "touch base" and "make sure all's good after that crazy guy went on a rampage."

That had eventually led to the disclosure of his real purpose for seeking me out—he wanted to meet Ethan and he wanted Ethan's new little sister to know she had a big brother.

Possibly more than all that, Trent wanted to make his wife happy.

For my part, I did not want anything to do with any of his shit. He'd bailed, he could stay fucked off for all I cared. I went from waitressing at a shit bar to stripping because I needed the money to take care of my kid. I ate shit and paid big with anyone I knew to get them to help me out, watching Ethan when me or my mom had to work. I took money from my buddy, Ryan, knowing that he would never get in there with me, even if he didn't hide it real good that's what he wanted, just because I needed his cash so fucking bad.

And I'd been blinded to a man who treated me right, who made me feel special, who doted on Ethan, a man who I was certain was a good man.

A man who turned out to be a madman.

But it wasn't about me. Trent was clean and sober, had a solid job and a family.

It was about Ethan.

I'd asked my kid. He'd hidden he was over the moon excited at the prospect of finally having a dad.

But I caught it.

So I'd let it happen.

A couple of short meets, attended by me, moved into a couple of dinners, also attended by me.

Then, when it came clear Trent actually had pulled it together, his wife Peggy was an okay woman, and Ethan enjoyed being with them, I let them take him alone. Eventually, this led to him spending the night or entire weekends.

Ethan dug it, albeit cautiously. He'd not had a dad for a long time and he was my boy, so he was smart enough not to go all in.

And he loved the big family he had now, what with me and Mom; Feb and Colt and their kid, Jack; Feb's brother, Morrie, his wife, Dee, and their kids; Feb and Morrie's mom and dad, Jack and Jackie (the J&J of J&J's), as well as all they brought with them. Then there was my girl Vi, her man, Cal, and their kids; Colt's colleague Mike and his woman, Dusty, and all that came with them; Feb's besties, Mimi and Jessie, who'd adopted me right along with everyone else.

In other words, I'd done what I needed to do. I'd traveled a lonesome road paved with shit and snipers aiming at me from each side, but I got my kid what he needed.

A nice house in an okay neighborhood in a small town (mostly) filled with good people. And a big family who gave a fuckuva lot more than a passing shit.

Add Ethan's birth dad and his growing family, and my boy, sweet and social, was in seventh heaven.

I was not.

Ethan never knew that and he never would.

Thinking on this was not much better than thinking about Merry, so I quickly made Trent a cup of joe the way he liked it. I nuked it, since I'd turned off the half-empty pot before I took off to slam my head against the brick wall of my life. When the microwave dinged, I handed him the mug and leaned a hip against the counter across the room from him, leveling my eyes on him.

"What's up?" I repeated my question of earlier.

Trent took a sip and put the coffee on the counter beside him.

Not granite counters. Not marble. No fucking way. There wasn't a granite, marble, or trendy cement counter within a five-block radius.

Mustard-yellow, old-style Formica. This matched the fridge and the stove, both having been in that house since America celebrated its bicentennial.

The dishwasher had bit it and didn't match, which sucked. But all the appliances, cabinets, countertops, and even the old-school linoleum floor were in excellent shape. I'd worked with it, and the kitchen was just as boho eclectic as the rest of the house, with vintage nostalgia thrown in.

I loved it.

I didn't take it in right then, however.

I watched Trent reach behind him and pull something out of his back pocket.

It was an envelope, whatever was inside making it thick, and he set it beside his coffee mug on the counter before picking the mug up and taking another sip.

Only then did he look at me.

"Been savin' awhile, me and Peg," he said.

"Savin' for what?" I asked.

"For that," he answered, nodding his head down to the envelope. "Seein' as I wasn't around and didn't do what I should've for my son, been savin' to try to make that up just a little bit."

Oh shit.

"There's three thousand, five hundred dollars in there," he went on.

Shit.

It was safe to say I was not rolling in it. But Feb and Morrie paid a decent wage; their bar was established and popular so they could. I also made tips, good ones, so I always had cash on hand. And I didn't have to pay for anyone looking out for Ethan. When I moved to the 'burg, Mom got a job and moved there about six months after me. If she didn't look after Ethan while I was at work, Jackie did. Or Feb, if she wasn't working. Or Mimi, since she had a slew of kids herself, one more was no skin off her nose. Vi was always happy to be on call too. Even Jessie took a turn every once in a while. She was a whackjob (a lovable one, but definitely a whackjob) and she didn't like kids, but she liked Ethan.

That list went on and all I had to pay was markers for my friends helping out, something I did whenever they needed me to do it.

But I'd do that anyway.

Even so, three and a half thousand dollars was a lot of cake and I could use it simply because I was the bartending single mother of a growing boy. That was probably my Oreo budget for the year, Ethan's favorite fuel.

It did not scratch the surface of what Trent owed me in a lot of ways.

But he had a job as a janitor, his wife was a part-time assistant for a financial advisor, and they had two young kids at home. I didn't know for sure, but looking at his piece-of-shit car, even though Peggy drove a nice, newish minivan, I had to guess he had less than me.

Saving that money probably cut and did it deep.

"And I got a raise at work," Trent continued. "So Peg and me talked, and we figure we can swing it to give you about a hundred every two weeks to help you out with Ethan."

I stared at him, needing to down more pills and get my ass to McDonald's so I could also down an Egg McMuffin. Being hungover and having a totally shit morning, what I didn't need to deal with was the possibility I actually had to express gratitude to a man I once loved who left me high and dry with a kid growing in my belly and went on to a happy life with another woman.

"Cheryl?" he called when I said nothing.

I continued to say nothing because I had no fucking clue what to say.

Finally, I found it.

"Cool of you," I muttered.

He nodded, looking funny, and I didn't know this new and improved Trent very well, so I didn't get that look. I thought it was disappointment, like he'd hoped I'd decline so he could buy his son a new crib or something.

As I was often in my life, I found out pretty quickly I was wrong.

"Also, Peg and me want you to think about something."

I felt my teeth clench, which made my aching head start to throb.

Trent didn't talk about Trent, not ever. He talked about Trent and Peg. It was like they were one person with one mind, and I got the feeling that mind was all hers. She had the leash on her man, frequently yanked the chain, and he was so devoted, he just panted happily and obeyed her every command.

The okay part about this was that what Peg wanted was good for Ethan.

The sad part about this was seeing a man, any man, much less one I'd once loved and thought I had a future with, brought to heel.

"What do you want me to think about?" I asked when he didn't share any more.

He took another sip of coffee, then put the mug to the counter, his body straightening. Mine straightened with it, automatically bracing.

"We wanna see more of Ethan," he announced.

Fuck.

He lifted a hand. "I know we live in Indy, but Peg and me think Ethan's at a time in his life where he needs more time with his dad."

"Trent—" I tried to get in, but he kept speaking.

"So we want you to consider shared custody. One week with you. One week with us. We won't change his school or anything. We'll get up early, get him to school, arrange for him to be picked up so he can get home. We don't have it all worked out now, but we're closin' in on it."

There were so many things wrong with this idea, my head clogged with them all.

Even in my state, I managed to focus on one.

"You gettin' up early to get Ethan to school means Ethan's gotta get up early," I pointed out.

Trent nodded. "It might be hard in the beginning for him to adjust, but he likes bein' at Peg's and my place. Bein' with his brother and sister. He'll get used to it because he'll dig what he gets out of it. And Peg and me are already lookin' for places on the west side so we'll be closer to the 'burg and can shave off ten, fifteen minutes of the school commute."

Okay.

Right.

No way I could do this now.

Truthfully, I didn't want to do it ever, but there was no way I could do it now.

So I shook my head. "Now's not a good time to talk about this. We'll talk later."

"I figure, you had him all to yourself for so long, never would be a good time. But it still has to get done. He's ten, almost eleven. He's gonna stop bein' a boy soon and needs to find his way to bein' a man. And you can't help him with that."

Okay.

Right.

Trent was going to teach him how to be a man? *Trent*, on Peg's leash, could do a better job with that than Colt? Morrie? Jack?

Merry?

No fucking way.

Now he was pissing me off.

I didn't let on.

I said, "Trent, like I said, now's not a good time to talk about this. I gotta get to the store. I got laundry to put in. And I want to clean the house before Ethan gets home from his friend's."

"I just want you to tell me you'll think about it," he pushed.

"I'll think about it," I lied.

I wouldn't think about it. I might eventually discuss it with my kid, because it was an offer he needed to accept or refuse. But I wouldn't ever think about it because I already knew what I thought about it.

I hated it.

Trent studied me.

He knew I was lying and his tone became wheedling. "Cheryl, this is the best thing for Ethan."

"Just sayin', you're talkin' about it when I just told you that I got shit to do."

He took a step toward me and stopped.

"Think about it," he urged. "A house in a not-so-great neighborhood, just you and him—and most the time you're workin', so he isn't even with you—when every other week he can be with us at our place. A decent pad that's bigger. A brother and sister he can watch grow up. A mom *and* dad to look out for him, there all the time."

He was right. My neighborhood was not so great.

It didn't suck either.

Most of my neighbors were old folk whose kids were assholes and forgot they existed. Some of them were new couples or new families trying to make a go at life. Good folk, all of them.

But there were a couple of rentals that had renters who were sketchy. However, outside the occasional loud party (which got shut down real quick because my kid needed his sleep and I knew every cop in the department, so I didn't hesitate to make a call) or a loud fight, they kept to themselves.

But it wasn't about me feeling defensive about the home I gave my son.

It was his "mom *and* dad, there all the time" bullshit.

Ethan had a mom.

Me.

In other words, he was no longer pissing me off.

I was there.

"You need to stop," I warned.

Stupidly, something they didn't have a program for, so Trent had not in all his years stopped being, he kept pushing. "You think on this, you'll know it's the right thing for Ethan."

It did not sit great with me that he was not letting this go, mostly because it shared how bad Peg wanted it and I didn't get good vibes from that. She was an okay woman and she was also a woman made to be a mom. Not just because she had a lot of love to give, which I figured she did, but also so she could have as many people in her life that she could boss around as she could get.

I tried one more time.

"Back off, Trent."

He pointed at the envelope before looking back at me. "We're tryin' to take care of you too."

"Think I've proved over the last ten years I been lookin' out for Ethan on my own that I don't need someone takin' care of me," I pointed out.

He lifted his chin. "We're doin' right by you."

"Woulda helped, you did right by me when I needed it, not shovin' it down my throat when I don't."

I could see right away that pissed him off.

"Knew you'd throw that in my face," he bit out.

"Trent, for fuck's sake," I snapped. "I'm tellin' you to back off. I told you I'd think about it. And I told you I got shit to do."

"Nice mouth, Cheryl. You talk like that to our son?"

That was when I lost it, and, honest to God, it was a wonder I'd held on for so long.

Leaning toward him, I hissed, "I can talk any way I want to *my* son because I *earned* that privilege by bein' there for him every day his whole fucking life."

"So you do," he returned.

I leaned back, shaking my head. "Of course I don't, you moron."

"Name calling. Nice," he clipped. "You teach our son that too?"

"I'll ask again, can we not do this now?" I requested sharply.

His face changed. It was not a good change.

It was a stubborn, nasty change.

That part of Trent I knew.

"I didn't want it to get to this, but I think it's fair that you know, you don't do what's best for Ethan, Peggy and me are prepared to take you to court. And, just a heads up, she feels Ethan should be with his dad full-time. The shared custody idea was what I talked her into. You push it, she's gonna get pissed and we're gonna go for it all."

At the barest thought of losing my son, I stood in my kitchen while the world collapsed all around me. At the edge of my vision, the walls and cabinets and counters and houses and the town beyond all crumbled to the earth, a cloud of dust rising, obliterating everything but me and Trent staring at each other.

He must have read that on my face because he quieted his voice when he said, "And you know that won't go too good for you, Cheryl."

It happened to me then, and I got it. I got how normal folk got pushed into corners, their loved ones threatened, and the urge came to them, overwhelming them, turning them from humans to animals focused solely on their need to protect. I got how they lost control and lost their minds and viciously attacked their attackers with nothing but annihilation in mind to void the threat.

I got it because that happened to me.

But I'd been kicked when I was down so often, I had just enough in me that morning to hold it in check.

"It won't?" I asked, my voice barely above a whisper. "It won't go too good for me?"

Trent looked like he didn't want to say it.

Still, he said it.

"Dennis Lowe."

I nodded my head. "Yeah. You're right. I fucked a serial killer. He told me he was a cop. He told me he loved me. He took care of me. He took care of Ethan. I was taken in by that shit. Then again, so was his boss. His co-workers. His neighbors. His wife of a gazillion years."

"You were a stripper, Cheryl," he carried on.

"I was because, you see, my methhead, pothead, crackhead boyfriend bailed on me the second he found out he'd knocked me up, and he left me and my boy to go it alone for seven years before *his wife* forced him to do the right thing."

"I'm clean," he bit back.

"And I've never been *not* clean," I returned.

"And I've never given a lap dance," he sneered.

I took two steps toward him, edging his space but not getting into it and also not losing eye contact.

"I did," I said softly. "I gave hundreds of them. And I'd do it again. And again. I'd do it for the rest of my *fucking* life if that money put food in my kid's stomach. If it put a roof over his head. Clothes on his back. If it gave me the opportunity to give him what he needed and as much of what he wanted that I could give him. If it made certain he didn't feel like we were hurting, he was hurting, I was hurting, or him bein' in this world was hurting me."

I got closer and gave him my stripper voice, all coy and tempting, giving the impression he was getting something at the same time giving nothing.

"I'd grind my crotch into a guy, shove my tits in his face, baby. I'd do it with a line forming, give it good to one asshole after another. I'd do it with a smile on my face if it gave me what I needed to give my kid what he needed. And I'd come home bein' proud of that. I'd come home knowin', even though not one soul would agree with me, that I should be up for 'Mom of the Year' *every* year because I'm willin' to eat shit so my boy *won't*."

"There were other ways to give that to our son," he retorted.

"There were?" I asked, stepping back. "You a bitch with a vagina who's got nothin' but a high school diploma and a history of waitressin' who got herself knocked up and her man bailed, stealing four days of tips she had in her wallet and her change jar before he went?"

He flinched, but I didn't let up.

"You a bitch who's got no savings, living in a shithole apartment she can't raise a kid in, desperate to find the cash to set up somethin' good for her baby in a way she can keep it good? You know," I threw out a hand and injected my voice with sarcasm, "outside of buyin' a lottery ticket that hits or turnin' to another profession that's looked down on a whole helluva lot more than strippin'?"

"There had to be ways," he stated.

"Name one," I shot back.

"There are ways, Cheryl."

"Name *one*," I repeated.

"A secretary," he threw out.

"I can't type."

"Grocery store clerk."

"No way in fuck either of those earns more than stripping."

He set his teeth.

"And, just sayin'," I kept on, "you don't get to stand in *my* kitchen passin' judgment on what *I* had to do to take care of *my* son after you got the news you planted a kid in me, fucked me all night as your good-bye, stole my money, and took off not to be seen again until your bitch yanks your chain and makes you be a good boy."

"Leave Peggy outta this," he ground out.

At that, I threw up both hands. "The woman's not already in this?"

"This is about Ethan. Just Ethan."

He was so full of shit.

This was *all* about Peggy. What she wanted. How she felt about me. It was *all* her.

But I decided Trent's current shit was over.

"You fight me, Trent, I'll take you down."

He shook his head, his upper lip curling before he spoke.

"In your wildest dreams, you cannot imagine that a bartender who works nights, barely sees her kid, depends on her mom and friends to raise him, and puts his ass in a shitty house in a shitty 'hood is gonna convince a judge to let her keep her kid. You cannot imagine that same woman, who got paid to shove her tits in strangers' faces and sucked a serial killer's cock while she helped him stalk his prey, is gonna convince a judge to let her keep her kid. And you cannot imagine that a judge is not gonna look at what Peg and me can give him and not hand him right the fuck over."

I didn't hesitate with my reply.

"You push this, we get a stick-up-his-ass judge who wouldn't see that for what it was and let me keep my son, I bet all I own that if Alexander Colton takes the stand and vouches for me, that judge'll think again."

Trent's mouth got tight.

Direct shot.

I didn't let up.

"Put Feb up there, her and Colt bein' that prey Denny Lowe stalked, also bein' my boss, also lettin' me look after *her* kid when she needs me, that judge'll think even more. And they'll do that for me. They won't blink. They'll wanna bury you so bad for fucking with me, they'll do anything they can. And they aren't the only ones, Trent. My girl Violet Callahan and her husband, Cal. Jack and Jackie Owens. Morrie. Dee. Upstanding citizens. Pillars of the fucking community. I'll have so many people's asses tellin' that judge what kind of mom I am, he'll wonder what the fuck is wrong with you that you'd try to take my boy from me."

"You seem convinced," he scoffed.

"I'm not convinced. I'm goddamned right," I shot back. "You're all kinds of stupid, you don't rethink this bullshit. I'll stop at nothin' to keep my boy with me. Do not doubt it. And I'm doin' you a solid in advising you not to take that on. There's been one constant in Ethan's life." I jerked my thumb to myself. "*Me*. No judge in his right mind will look at my history of givin' it all that I got to give good to my kid and then take him away from me. You fight me, it's a battle you're gonna lose. But you fight me, you're gonna lose Ethan, and that shit will *not* be about me takin' you away from him. That shit'll be about him knowin' you're fuckin' with his mom and him not wanting one single thing to do with you."

Indecision flared in his eyes right before he turned, took the step he needed to nab the envelope off the counter, and shoved it in his back pocket.

He turned back to me.

"Seems I'm gonna need this to hire an attorney," he declared.

"Right, good call. Take it. Works for me. Ten years Ethan's been breathin' and you haven't given me a dime to help. I'm down with that. A judge, though, he might not be."

"Screw you, Cheryl," he bit out.

"You already did that, Trent, in a *lot* of ways."

He scorched a glare at me, then walked out of my kitchen.

I stood in it and listened to him slam the front door.

Then I dropped my head and stared at my boots, finding myself breathing heavily.

I was not wrong. Colt, Feb, Vi, Cal, Jack, Jackie, everyone would help me.

Again.

But it'd all come up.

Again.

The stripping.

Lowe.

All of it shoved down Ethan's throat.

It didn't matter his name was Ethan Rivers, his mom's Cher Rivers— that was on our rental agreement; that was on my driver's license. It wasn't like your old identity was washed away when you changed your name. That shit was public record. Which meant, however infrequently these days, fuck-wads and freaks still found me for whatever reason they needed to do that to be close to Denny.

If Trent and Peg took me to court, it'd all come out. It might even hit the news. And it would definitely make Ethan vulnerable.

Fuck.

Fuck, fuck, fuck, fuck...*fuck*.

I lifted my head and turned it, looking at the wall of open shelves over base cabinets, which was stuffed full of retro glasses, multi-patterned, mis-matched bowls, wonky-shaped pitchers, old-fashioned canisters.

I studied my things—the bowls Ethan poured his cereal into, the pitchers I grabbed to make him Kool-Aid—and I felt that thorn dig deeper.

Because if I was a different woman, the kind of woman who could attract a man like Garrett Merrick, get him close, and make him want to stay that way, people would not fuck with me because he wouldn't let them.

Not Trent.

Not Peg.

Not my neighbors who threw wild parties.

Not the occasional person at the bar who looked at me with fanatical eyes, asking me if I was Cheryl Sheckle, *the* Cheryl Sheckle, sidepiece to Denny Lowe.

Not the assholes who phoned me thinking about a movie, a book, a TV show, and wanting me to help them "get in the mind of Dennis Lowe."

I didn't mind asking my cop buddies to shut down parties.

It would suck, but I'd do anything for Ethan, so I would buck up and ask for all the help I could get to keep my son.

And at the bar, Darryl and Morrie dealt with the lunatics who sniffed out the Denny Lowe trail because they were fucked in the head, not only to protect me from that shit, but also to protect Feb and Colt. But that message had been sent frequently, and after all these years, those nutjobs were few and far between.

Like Trent being back in Ethan's life, no one knew about the phone calls. They didn't need to worry about Trent being a part of our lives. And they definitely didn't need the Denny Lowe shit dredged up. And last, I didn't need *yet another* way for people to feel they needed to take care of me.

34

I could take care of myself. I'd done it since I was eighteen, and I knew it was my lot in life to do it until I died. I might have forgotten this that morning for one crazy, stupid, hopeful moment, but then I'd been reminded.

That didn't mean I wouldn't appreciate a man like Merry in my life.

I would.

And I would more than any normal woman because I knew how precious having someone to look after you, someone to share the load, someone who gave even a single *solitary* shit actually was.

Which was ironic, since I was one of those girls.

One of those girls who would appreciate it.

One of those girls who would take care of it.

One of those girls who would beg, borrow, and steal in order to keep hold of it.

And one of those girls who would never have it.

"Would it kill them to stock diet grape soda?" I bitched, staring at the soda shelves at Walmart.

Ethan busted out laughing.

I looked down at my kid.

I'd rearranged my activities that day. Instead of hitting the store, I did some laundry, paid my bills, and cleaned the house before he got home.

This was because he liked going to the grocery store and he wasn't a big fan of cleaning.

I didn't let him totally get away with that. He had chores. He took out the trash, helped me do the dishes when I was home at night, and he had to keep his room picked up.

He got an allowance because I thought it was best he learned that you had to earn what you got. I didn't want to shelter him, then send him out in the world so he could get blindsided about how hard you had to work just to afford decent. I wanted him to know even as I was careful not to bog him down in that crap.

So he got extra if he vacuumed or dusted. More if he took on the bathroom or mopped the kitchen floor. And he needed cabbage for whatever kids needed cabbage for, so he did both, often.

But I didn't want our time together that day, a Saturday that was a full day off for me, to be about laundry and cleaning. I wanted it to be about hanging and doing shit we liked.

I wasn't a big fan of grocery shopping, but Ethan was, so I got the crap stuff out of the way so that when he got home we could focus on the good stuff.

"Somethin' funny?" I asked, feeling my lips quirk, even after the day I'd had and the lingering hangover that I'd had to manage without an Egg McMuffin but with pills and a fried egg on toast.

"Mom," Ethan said through his laughter, sweeping his hand to our cart. "We got diet orange, Diet 7UP, Diet *Cherry* 7UP, Diet Coke, Diet Dr. Pepper, and two different kinds of Fresca. How much diet crap do you need?"

"I have to look after my girlish figure," I retorted.

"Yeah, right," he muttered, putting his hands to the cart and starting to push. "You do that real good with your candy stash."

I didn't look in the cart because I didn't have to. We'd hit the candy aisle already and we were loaded up. My kid liked sweets, but I was a candy junkie. I had some every day, sometimes more than "some."

I had a lot of bad habits.

I could drink my fair share of booze.

I had three drawers of makeup in the bathroom.

I knew I should filter some of the shit that came out of my mouth, but I didn't bother.

I dressed in a way I knew people thought was more than a little skanky, but I liked it. It made me a dick magnet of the extreme variety, but even knowing this, living and breathing it, I still didn't change. I just couldn't bring myself to tone it down. I liked the way it looked—it was *me*—and I'd learned the hard way to be nothing but *me*.

And I ate lots of candy.

I followed my son, sharing my wisdom, "The diet pop negates the candy bars."

"It sucks that that makes sense and is probably true," he muttered, turning the corner into the snack aisle. Another bad habit...for both of us.

"Considering your concern for my nutrition, maybe we should skip this aisle and go straight to the carrots."

He lifted his eyes and gave me a look.

I grinned at him.

He rolled his eyes, the ends of his mouth curling up, and went right to the microwave popcorn.

I followed him, thinking about how in a couple of years, he'd be taller than me. A year or two after that, his voice would drop. A year or two after that, he'd be dating. A year or two after that, he'd be on his way to building his own life.

In other words, this time was precious.

Every moment was precious—I knew that—but this time it was even more.

I'd had ten, nearly eleven years where he was mine. I shared him because I was generous that way.

But still, he was all mine.

That time was more than half over.

Seven more years and…

"Theater style or cheddar?" Ethan asked, breaking into my thoughts.

"Uh…duh," I answered as my phone in my purse rang. "Both."

That was when Ethan grinned full-out at me.

Yeah, Trent had given him good. My boy would be handsome when he got older because he was cute as hell right now.

Though, those were my eyes that were bright with humor, so my genes didn't fall down on the job.

Ethan got both kinds of popcorn and tossed them into the cart.

I dug my phone out of my purse and looked at it.

The instant my eyes hit it, the balm of being with my son disappeared and that thorn drove in deeper, twisting, the prongs at the sides tearing at flesh.

The screen said, MERRY CALLING.

I dropped the phone back in my purse.

"Who's that?"

At his question, I looked to my kid.

I did not lie to him. Lies were bad and I didn't want him to catch me in one and be disappointed or get the idea lying was okay (this was going to be hard to keep up if Trent and Peg actually pulled their bullshit).

I tried to give it to him straight. Sometimes I softened it. Sometimes I shielded him from things he really didn't need to know or was too young to know. But as best I could, I gave it to him straight.

This had led to us having some awkward conversations, especially the last year or so. He was growing up, as were the kids around him. Shit happened, was heard, seen, watched on TV, or caught in movies, and Ethan had been taught he could come to me with anything.

So he did.

And I gave it to him straight.

So when he asked the question that was simple to him but not to me, I did what I always did.

"Merry," I answered.

His brows went up. "Why didn't you take the call?"

He asked because he knew Merry was a friend. He knew this because, being a friend, we had occasions to be together outside me serving Merry drinks at J&J's, times when Ethan was around. Parties. Barbeques. Picnics. Basketball and football games Colt would organize with adults and kids. Hanging at the carnival at Arbuckle Acres during the Fourth of July. Heading out with Colt and Feb and their speedboat to a lake.

Merry was in his life. Merry liked kids, dug Ethan, and often passed a ball or Frisbee with him, teased him, shot the shit with him, ruffled his hair, squeezed the back of his neck, laughed when Ethan was funny, made Ethan laugh by being funny.

There was no reason Ethan could imagine why I would not take a call from a good guy who might not be a staple in Ethan's life but definitely had a firm foot in it.

"'Cause I'm with you at the grocery store and some stuff has gone down with Merry that's pretty intense, so when I chat with him next, I wanna give him all my attention."

This was the truth, thankfully.

Ethan's head tipped to the side. "What stuff?"

"His ex-wife got engaged to someone else."

Ethan was no less confused. "He still into her?"

That thorn drove deeper.

"Yep."

Ethan nodded like he was a one-hundred-and-fifty-year-old wise man with a twelve-foot-long white beard, sitting on a mountaintop, a pilgrimage destination for folks who wished to beg his wisdom.

"I see that," he muttered solemnly.

"You got an ex-wife I don't know about?" I asked, reaching for a bag of Funyuns as we made our way down the aisle.

"Three of them, actually," Ethan answered.

I swallowed a laugh and tossed the Funyuns in the cart. I still grinned at the back of his head as he grabbed a bag of Fritos Scoops.

"Too bad you didn't have a momma who taught you how to treat a woman right," I remarked.

"Nah, me that got rid of them, seein' as they didn't treat me as good as my momma," he shot back.

Suddenly, I needed to hold on to something because I felt weak in the knees.

My dad drank, slapped my mom around, then gave her the best gift he could: he fucked around on her with a woman he preferred, so he left us to be with her and then minimized contact in order not to deal with his responsibility, but it made it so we didn't have to deal with his garbage.

I didn't like school so I screwed around, graduating by the skin of my teeth, too young and too stupid to know one day I'd need it.

I liked wild because it felt good, so I found it everywhere I could find it and ended up with men so far worse than my father, it wasn't funny.

I ate shit because I'd bought it and I ate shit because that was life.

But in all that, I'd done something right. Something so right, it was the anchor of my life that kept me steady and whole instead of allowing me to get chewed to shit and spit out, bloody and beaten.

I'd made Ethan. I'd kept Ethan. And I made sure my boy knew he was loved right down to my soul.

Which meant he loved me that way right back.

"You know I love you, baby?" I whispered.

He turned his head and gave me a glare. "Jeez, Mom. Gag."

I couldn't help it, I burst out laughing.

The last couple of years, the love and hugs and cuddles I showered on my kid had had to dry up. He might allow it, in private and in moderation. But affection was not big on his hit list any other time.

"You done bein' gooey?" he asked through my laughter.

"Yep," I said, fighting that laughter back. "Just hit my weekly quota of gooey. But, just warnin' you, kid, next week I'll have to fit more gooey in somewhere."

He rolled his eyes, but his lips were tipped up again and those eyes were shining. He then headed to the Pringles selection.

We bought four tubes.

I found time in the pasta aisle to text Merry, *With Ethan. Talk later.*

I got back, *You on tomorrow?*

He could find out easily; my shifts at the bar were hardly a state secret.

Early, I replied.

Catch you there.

Fabulous.

He was going to lay it on me while I was at work.

Morrie had talked Feb into putting a few TVs in, which meant Sundays at the bar, always steady but not busy, became the last—busy. Good for tips. Bad to have a bunch of folks around while I had to take the hit that Merry was going to deliver.

But Merry thought I was a woman who "got it."

And I did "get it," even if I didn't want to.

So I'd take it, I'd understand it, and we'd carry on.

I just wasn't looking forward to it.

Three

GUARANTEE
Cher

"All right! We're rollin' out!" I called to the house, walking out of my bedroom.

It was the next day and we were on our way to my mother's so I could drop Ethan and then get to work.

In preparing, I'd managed to beat back the urge to go all out—or more to the point, *not*.

Part of me understood why Mia Merrick didn't make an approach to her ex-husband (a *small* part of me), this being he had so far from remained celibate since their break it wasn't funny. He'd tagged and bagged a lot of tail in the time I knew him, and although Mia rarely came into J&J's and definitely didn't attend any other events I'd been to when Merry was around, the amount of tail he'd hit in a town that small would be impossible to miss.

And I saw what he went for. Petite. Emphasis on hair. Talented hand with makeup brushes. Dressed like me, showing skin. They'd get their cling on, if not skintight, not much left to the imagination.

The difference was it was designer, expensive, not only the clothes but the hair. They didn't get their hair cut in their mother's kitchen and their color or highlights out of a bottle. They got it from folks who charged a lot more than my mom, who'd do it for a bottle of wine or me making dinner.

The extra cake spent on the entire package catapulted them from what I was considered—trash—to what they were considered—class—even if we were all going for the same effect.

I didn't spend money on clothes and hair, and my makeup was drugstore, Walmart, or Target purchased.

I didn't do this, because I had a kid.

This didn't mean I didn't have the odd piece in my closet that might show Merry I had that in me—class. The ability to turn a different kind of eye, maybe even his.

The thing was, it was the odd piece and those pieces were for hanging with my girls. They weren't for work. And I didn't want to say what it would say to Merry if I faced down the hit he was going to give me that day dressed in armor he'd take one look at and understand that I needed armor. I needed it because he had the ability to hurt me and that was because he meant more to me than I wanted him to know. Or, more to the point, he meant everything to me in *a way* I didn't want him to know.

Besides, it didn't matter. If he didn't know me and want me for me, then fuck him.

So I was in my usual. Tight jeans. Thick, black belt with a huge rhinestone buckle. Black tank with a deep racerback and a rocker cross on the front, studs abounding. Black lace bra that was sexy as all hell, straps showing, giving a hint of the rest of the goodness that was hidden. Spike-heeled, black suede bootie sandals with a slouchy top that my jeans were tucked into, my black-polished toenails and heels exposed.

Add big silver earrings, black leather studded cuff on my wrist, a tangle of necklaces falling down my front, big hair, and heavy makeup, and I was good to go.

This look was me, but it also had a bonus—it was good for tips.

I walked out of my bedroom as I threw on a droopy, loose-woven black cardigan and saw Ethan at the door with his backpack.

"You good?" I asked, going to my purse in the wicker bucket chair (the purse also black suede with silver studs and the addition of silver chain as straps).

"Yeah," he replied, opening the door and heading out.

I followed him, beeping the locks of my Chevy Equinox.

Not yet knowing he was criminally insane, I'd given my car to Dennis Lowe and he'd used it to cross state lines and continue his butchery. He'd dumped it along the way, and after all the bows were tied on the case, I'd gotten it back.

I'd then immediately sold it and used the rest of the money he gave me, plus the money I got from selling all the shit he gave me, to buy my now not-so-new, blue baby girl. She was big and roomy. She was my son's favorite color. She had a smooth ride. She was safe. She had an awesome stereo. And of all the things Denny Lowe did to me, I did not mind one single bit that his bullshit got me and my kid in a nice, safe car.

We deserved that. So I'd made it so.

I backed out of the drive and headed toward Mom's place.

Mom, like Ethan and me, lived in the 'burg proper. Not the old part where the houses were established, on big lots, graceful, and grand. Not the edges where the developments ranged from middle class to seriously upper middle class.

But the post-war middle part where the lots were big, the trees were tall, but the houses were small and there hadn't been a lot of time, effort, or money put in to throwing them up.

We hit the curb at Mom's and Ethan and I got out, moving up her walk.

Her place was not a rental; she'd bought it. Then again, she'd had a home to sell in Indy so she could. Property values, even for her 'hood in the 'burg, were higher than the not-so-great 'hood she'd lived in in Indy, so she didn't get much bang for her buck, but she liked it and had paid for it in full.

The layout was kinda like mine except more square. Living room to the front; kitchen to the back (not the side). Bedrooms down the hall, but there was a small study and the master bedroom was bigger and had its own three-quarter bath.

It had been a bit run-down, but we'd pulled it together with the help of Colt, Morrie, Jack, Colt's partner, Sully, Cal, Mike, and even on occasion, Merry. Precisely, I remembered Merry and Mike put in her new countertops in the kitchen and bath, and Merry re-skimmed the walls in the living room.

When we got to that living room Merry had re-skimmed, I saw Mom flat on her back on the couch.

"You best be up for movie day, honey-sicle, 'cause Gramma's pooped right out," she told the TV, then twisted her head back to look at us over the arm of the couch. "Or, you best be up for movie day *if* your homework is done."

I looked down at my mom.

She'd never graduated from waitress work. She'd done that before Dad left. She did it after. She did it now. She worked at The Station and she was good at what she did. She was liked so much, regulars asked to be put in her section.

She also made decent money. Like me, not rolling in it but not eating cat food either.

And she was fifty-six. She didn't look it. She took care of herself. She was on her feet a lot, so she got exercise, and she'd always taken care of her skin. She ate a helluva lot better than me. She gave a shit about how she looked, took care of her hair, dressed good. To that end, she dated. Even had a couple of men who hung around for a while, both of them treating her right, but she couldn't settle.

I got that.

Once bitten, two hundred times shy.

Her lying on the couch was bullshit. She was talking movies because she knew Ethan would be into that. Normally, she'd be working in her yard, deep cleaning the grout in the bathroom, or with her bitches, playing poker. Even though she looked great, was fit, and had lots of energy, she had ten years left of being on her feet, schlepping food to people. Then she'd use the meager retirement she'd saved to take the sting out of living below poverty level on social security.

I hated that for her. Just like I wanted more for my boy and went all out to get it for him, I wanted more for my mom.

And there was another part of why life sucked, knowing she'd never get it and I'd never be in a place to give it to her.

I'd put her through the wringer. My little girl years were not filled with Barbies and dreams of marrying whatever British royal was moderately hot at the time but instead listening to my father beat on my mother. Then I'd gone wild, pissed at the world that we didn't have a lot, that my dad was a dick who didn't give a shit about me or my mom and showed us just that.

Onward to shacking up with a junkie, letting him get me pregnant, and ending up as a stripper with a boyfriend who had about fifteen screws loose and wasn't afraid of using a hatchet.

Mom had loved me through it all, though. She'd been there for me, for Ethan, every step of the way.

And she still was.

Which meant she'd shown me the way. I might not have learned early, but the least I could give her was eventually getting there.

"Got homework," Ethan said, walking in and dumping his backpack on his gramma's coffee table. "But it'll take, like, ten seconds to do."

"We'll see about that," Mom murmured. "You do it, I check it."

"Jeez, Gram, I know the drill," Ethan returned.

"Just makin' sure you don't forget it," she replied.

Ethan did his favorite thing—rolled his eyes—then declared, "I'm gettin' a pop. You need more iced tea?"

The last was for his gramma.

"I'm good, sugar," Mom replied.

Ethan took off to the kitchen.

Mom looked to me.

"You good, Cher?" she asked.

"Good, Mom," I answered, moving in and bending low to kiss her cheek.

She had the softest skin imaginable. It was like she had a collagen facial first thing in the morning and the last thing at night every day of her life. Not many wrinkles, which boded well for me, but to top that, her skin had a softness that was surreal.

I loved it.

Always did.

Even when I was young, stupid, and being an asshole.

"Have a good day at work," Mom told me as I straightened away.

"Always do," I replied, and she knew I did. Being a bartender might not be like being a jet-set supermodel, but it was a fuckuva lot better than being a stripper.

"Kid! Your mom is hittin' the road!" I shouted.

Ethan came in with a can of Sprite in his hand, looking at me.

45

"Later," he said, mouth curved up.

No hug. No kiss.

I wasted several seconds of my life wishing I could turn back time, just a year, maybe two, when Ethan wouldn't let me leave without both.

When I didn't get my wish, I said, "Later."

I grinned at him. I grinned at Mom.

Then I took off.

I hit the bar and saw that Morrie was the one in to start opening. This was good. Colt might have told Feb what had happened with Merry and me, and she'd hesitate half a nanosecond in getting up in my shit about it.

"Yo," I called to Morrie as I hit the bar.

"Yo, babe," Morrie returned, at the cash register, putting in our float.

I went to the office to stow my purse and cardie, grabbing my cell to shove it in my back pocket, came out, and hit the back of the bar.

"Just so you know, I owe you five hundred dollars, seein' as me and Merry emptied that bottle of Talisker Friday night."

As I spoke, Morrie's eyes on me grew huge.

Now, Morrie Owens, he was cute. A big ole bear of a man with a protective streak, a great sense of humor, and a deep love of family.

"Say the fuck *what?*" he asked.

"Mia," I answered quietly.

His surprise left and he looked to the cash register, muttering, "Shit." His eyes came back to me. "Shoulda known."

"Merry did the bottle some damage, but I kept him company after closing and we emptied it. Not his choice. He was up for calling a taxi. So I'll catch you at end of shift with my tips and hit the ATM tomorrow before I come to work."

He shook his head, attention back to the register where he was closing the cash drawer. "That'll be me and Feb's contribution to the cause of Merry bein' a dumb fuck and not claimin' back his woman."

That pissed me off, and being me, I let it be known.

"All was fair in life, Mia Merrick would waltz her round ass in here and pay you that five hundred for being an even *dumber* fuck and not claimin' back her man."

Morrie looked back to me, and I might have worried about what he'd read in my words if I was the kind of woman everyone knew me not to be.

46

"Wasn't her whose mom was murdered in her own damned home when she was a kid," I carried on. "Wasn't her sister who was in that house and heard that shit go down. Wasn't her who had to live with that, grief buried deep, none of that family havin' the tools to sort out their heads. But it *was* her who had a man who lived that, and it was *her* who didn't stand by that man. So, far's I'm concerned, he's good that he's finally shot of her. Maybe next time, he'll find a better one."

And I hoped that to be true. It would kill, but I still hoped it would turn true. I'd be good with Merry happy. It would suck, but it'd still be good.

And anyway, that was life.

Or it was *my* life.

"You know, didn't think of it that way, but you're far from wrong," Morrie told me.

"No shit?" I asked.

He started chuckling.

"We'll share the load. I'll give you two hundred and fifty," I offered.

He shook his head as we heard the back door open, which meant Ruthie was strolling in.

"Glad you were there for him," he said. "I shoulda been there for him. Colt, Mike, someone. But I 'spect, what you just said, it's good it was you. Least I can do is cover the man's whisky."

It was cool of him to offer, and before this degenerated into a battle I couldn't win (because Morrie offering meant Morrie doing it), I decided to give in.

Bonus to that coolness, I wasn't out a wad of cash.

"Hey," Ruthie called.

"Thanks," I said to Morrie, then turned to Ruthie and called back, "Yo, bitch."

She grinned, shaking her head, and went to the office.

Morrie headed to the front door to unlock it.

Two minutes later, we had our first customer.

It got busy early. Once church was done and after-church big breakfasts at Frank's or big lunches at home were consumed, games were on and people hauled their asses out to commune with their fellow citizens and throw back some beers.

This was good for two reasons: more cash in my pocket, and being busy took my mind off the fact that at any second, Merry was going to walk in and deliver a blow he didn't know he was delivering.

I didn't get jumpy waiting for it. I knew better than that. I was resigned to the way of the world.

Jack came in, which meant me on the floor since he always worked back of the bar. I didn't mind this. I had candy bars and Funyuns to work off my ass, and tips were just as steady at the tables.

I was delivering some drafts when he came in. I felt him like a sixth sense, and this wasn't a new ability he'd instilled in me after fucking me. The minute I'd laid eyes on him and the months it'd taken me to get to know him and fall in love was when I'd gained that talent.

I looked his way, saw his eyes on me, face guarded, and I gave it to him right away. A big, cocky Cher smile.

He grinned, not quite hiding the relief, then looked to the bar, giving chin lifts to Morrie and Jack while heading around to the opposite end where all the cops hung out.

He did not take Colt's stool, the last one around the far curve. If there wasn't another choice, no one did. Colt's stool was his should he decide to saunter in, Feb there or not. It was just the way it was.

But Merry did take the stool next to it, one down from the hinge of the bar.

I dropped the drafts, took an order at a table on the way back to the bar, and wedged into the space between Merry's occupied stool and Colt's unoccupied one.

I'd bucked myself up before arriving so I was all good when I got there.

"Hey," I said to him.

"Hey," he said to me, eyes moving over my face, eyes that flashed in my head as a memory, heated and hooded, right before he came.

Shit.

"You get a break soon?" he asked.

"We're ordering in Shanghai Salon in a while," I told him.

"Let me take you to Frank's. I can call in our orders so they'll have them ready and I can get you back to work on time," he offered.

So he didn't intend to deliver the blow with me at work.

That was Merry—meaning, that was nice.

"Hang tight," I replied and looked to Jack heading my way. "Two Bud Lights and a Coors, bottle."

"Got it," Jack said, then looked to Merry. "Hey, son, you on?"

"Yeah, Jack. Can you shoot me a Coke?"

"Sure thing," Jack replied.

I got my bottles first and told Merry I'd be back as Jack was aiming the drink gun into a glass of ice.

I dropped the beers, did a walk-through of my tables, got no orders, and headed back to the bar.

I hit the opposite side of Merry this time, closer to the room and not the wall, and wedged in.

"No orders, have a second now," I told him.

"Then tell me what you want me to order you at Frank's and ask for your break," he replied.

"You on lunch hour at four in the afternoon, or what?" I asked.

"Things are slow, but yeah, Mike's doin' paperwork at the station, and shit goes down, I'll have to head out. Either way, I need to get back, so I don't got a lotta time."

That being the case, I moved into him, holding his gaze. "Right, then, do what you gotta do. Get Mike a sandwich and head back, because you know we're—"

I didn't finish because Merry looked from me to over my shoulder. His brows drew slightly together and he straightened a bit on his stool, so I looked over my shoulder too.

At what I saw, I fully straightened and mostly turned.

This was because Trent's wife, Peggy, was standing at the corner of the bar.

She looked so out of place it wasn't funny. Baggy, high-waisted mom jeans. A shapeless top that showed very little skin and attempted to hide the fact she hadn't taken off her baby weight, which was somewhat substantial, laying evidence to the fact it wasn't all baby weight. No muss, no fuss hairstyle for her brunette hair, which could have been Martha Stewart hair, in a good way, but she seemed allergic to a roller brush and teasing comb. No makeup at all. Sneakers that looked like they were Reebok aerobics shoes from the '80s, not kickass Chucks or cool Vans or neon Nikes.

And last, a pinched look on her face that said the last time she'd been in a bar was never and she wished she could have kept it that way.

"Cheryl," she said, and my name sounded forced out.

"Peg," I replied, turning fully her way even though I did not freaking want to, and not only because I did not want to be talking to Peg, but because Merry was right...freaking...there. Once turned, I greeted all friendly, "Hey."

She opened her massive purse, which looked like a diaper bag gone bad, and that was a feat since most of those things weren't the height of fashion, not to mention it was an actual *purse*, not a diaper bag at all.

Then she pulled out the envelope Trent had with him yesterday and slapped it on the bar.

It took a lot, but I managed not to recoil from it like it was a rattler she'd wrangled out, pissing it off and setting it on a trajectory to strike me.

I also could actually *feel* Merry's eyes honing in on that envelope in a way it was a wonder it didn't burst into flames from the laser beam precision.

She kept her hand on the envelope as she spoke.

"Trent made a mistake and took this with him after you guys talked yesterday," she declared. "I thought it was important to get it back to you straight away."

"Peg—" I started but didn't get any further.

"Also, just so you know, the arrangements he told you we were going to make for you and Ethan will start this week. We'll be mailing the first check on Friday."

I knew from her look and tone, which had always been friendly and now was not, that not only was Trent on her shit list for fucking up yesterday's conversation, he'd shared what I'd said and she was not happy with me either.

She also wasn't wasting any time putting her plan into motion.

That being they could share with a judge they'd scrimped, saved, and sacrificed to do right by me, but mostly Ethan, even after Trent had royally fucked things up, being a junkie loser who took off on his bitch and took her money with him.

I really wanted to tell her to go fuck herself. That all this shit was total bullshit, but her play, coming to me at my place of work when I couldn't make a return play, was jacked.

I couldn't do that. Too much was at stake. I had to be cool for Ethan but also because Merry was watching.

"Babe, I think it might be a good idea if we all found a time to sit down and talk," I suggested.

She scooted the envelope closer to me, replying, "You're at work, so I don't want to take a lot of your time. I think Trent made things clear yesterday. Now, I need you to take this envelope, Cheryl. You know, so I know what's in it is safe."

"Maybe—" I began, but she scooted the envelope sharply another inch my way and cut me off.

"You're at work and I have kids to get home to. If you'll take this, I'll know it's good and I can get home to my family."

Her words giving me no other choice, I reached out, and as I did, she quickly removed her hand so I could curl my fingers around the envelope and we'd not touch.

When I had it held safely in my hand, she nodded and declared, "We hope to see Ethan soon. Have a good day at work. See you."

With that, she turned on her aerobics shoes and walked out.

I stared after her, belatedly regretting my play of the day before.

I got pissed, which meant Trent got pissed and tipped his hand, which meant *Peggy* got pissed, and I wasn't sure Peg pissed was a good thing.

There was a reason Trent had come to heel. His kind of devotion to Peg could be won through reward or through punishment.

I was getting the sense right then it was punishment.

"You takin' a payoff right in front of a cop?"

Merry's voice, being Merry's voice (meaning Merry was there and had seen that, then said what he said, even though I knew it was a joke), tipped me over an edge I'd been riding for a long fucking time. But that weekend it was sharper, so it didn't take much for me to tip over.

Therefore I turned and snapped, "No it isn't a fuckin' payoff."

Merry's chin jerked down and his eyes narrowed.

"It was a joke, Cher," he told me.

"It wasn't a funny one," I told him, pressing the envelope to my stomach.

He looked down to it and then up to me. "Who was that woman?"

"No one."

At my answer, his ear dipped slowly to his shoulder before his head straightened and a look came over his face I'd never seen on him before.

But it was scary.

"What's in the envelope, babe?" he asked, his tone forced to casual, which meant it wasn't casual at all.

"Nothing," I answered. "Listen, I gotta—"

"What's in the envelope, Cher?"

"Nothing," I repeated. "Now, goin' back to what we were talk—"

He leaned an inch toward me and I was not a girl who was easily intimidated, but I had to admit, that inch was intimidating.

"What'd she give you? Who was that woman? Who is Trent? And what do they gotta do with Ethan?"

"Merry, straight up, this isn't any of your business."

That was when he leaned *two* inches toward me, and if one inch was intimidating, two was a threat.

This meant I should have known it was coming.

But knowing Merry, or thinking I did, thus thinking he wouldn't have what he was going to give me in him, I had no clue.

"Made you come for me," he whispered. "More than once. Straight up, Cher, it *is*. Who the fuck was that woman? Why is she passin' off cash to you? And why's it got you freaked way the fuck out?"

His words exploded in my head along with the knowledge he wanted to take me to Frank's to lower a boom he didn't know he was lowering to share, even after what we had, that we were *just friends*.

Therefore, so far beyond thinking about the right way to play it, I played it stupid, leaning forward and hissing, "Wouldn't think I had to educate you, Merry, but seems I gotta educate you. Thrusting your cock in a woman like me doesn't mean you own me."

He leaned back, which meant he straightened, and seeing as even sitting on a stool he was taller than me and I had to look up, that sucked.

Looking up meant he was looking down. Not his chin dipped, but he was looking down his nose, superior as shit, which was infuriating, and hot as fuck, which was intensely annoying.

His voice was a low, sexy as *all* hell drawl when he replied, "Wouldn't think I had to educate you either, baby. You know the man I am. You laid that shit out for me Friday night. But straight up, I thrust my cock in you, it means when some mom bitch shows at your work and freaks you out, I do what I gotta do to take your back."

"I can take care of myself," I snapped in another hiss.

His brows went up. "So you *do* got somethin' you gotta take care of."

Shit!

"Merry—"

I got no more out because his hand clamped on my upper arm and his head turned to the bar.

"Cher's on break," he growled.

"Uh…okay, dude," Morrie replied.

I got one look in to Morrie to see he looked as freaked as me, but for an entirely different reason, before Merry dragged me to the office.

Once he had us in, he slammed the door.

I yanked my arm from his hold, took two steps into the room, turned to him, and launched right in. "If it's okay with you, I'd actually like to use my break to eat something, Merry, not do whatever this shit is with you."

Merry ignored me.

"Who was that woman?"

"Not your business."

"Who…was…*that woman?*"

I shook my head sharply once. "Not…your…*business.*"

Merry kept at me. "Who's Trent?"

"Merry, Jesus." I planted my hands on my hips. "Let it go."

"What's in that envelope and why's she givin' it to you?"

I felt my eyes get squinty as the heat of shame and anger poured through me, not believing he'd think of me what it seemed he was thinking.

"You think I'm into bad shit?"

"Fuck no," he returned. "You're you, so that didn't cross my goddamned mind. But also, that woman would cut off her own arm before she'd fuckin' jaywalk. That doesn't mean she didn't freak you out. So tell me what's goin' down with her."

I shook my head, trying to find control. "Seriously, Merry, I get why you're here. Shit happened with us—you'd sustained a blow, we got drunk, it got outta hand. I get where you were and where we now are. It's good. We're good. Leave this shit alone, we'll *stay* good."

He crossed his arms on his chest. "Why won't you tell me?"

"Because it's not a big deal," I lied, not having a problem lying to Merry. I'd essentially been doing it, hiding my feelings for him, for years.

The anger seeped out of his features, gentle chasing in after it.

Shit, *fuck*.

God, he was so handsome, it *hurt*.

And that evidence right there, that he was a good man…

That…

It *killed*.

"Cher, babe, whatever's goin' down, you are not alone."

He meant to be nice. He meant to be cool.

But his words made the anger race right back because I wasn't; he was right.

And yet, I *so* was and I *so* would be, always and forever.

"You do not know what you're fuckin' talking about," I bit out.

"You got friends. You got people who'll look out for you," he returned. "Me bein' one of them."

"Yeah?" I asked sarcastically, and I was so angry, the wince of hurt that hit his face didn't touch me.

"Fuck. Yeah, Cher. Absolutely," he said softly.

I nodded. "Right. Okay. Good to know. So…" I lifted the envelope. "This is three and a half grand from my recovering junkie ex, who took off the day after I told him he'd knocked me up with Ethan, stealing all the money I had with me. Didn't see his ass again until he got clean and got himself a wife, Peg out there." I jerked my head to the door. "Now, you bein' a detective and all, you'd eventually put this together, but I'll save you the effort. See, Peg, she likes control. Peg, she likes to call the shots. Peg, she's a woman who knows how the world should be and how it *shouldn't*. So Peg's old man's got a kid from another bitch, a bitch who used to be a stripper and fucked a serial killer, and Peg's decided that kid needs to be in a good home, that bein' *hers*."

"Holy fuck," he whispered.

"Yeah," I spat. "So she's settin' it all up." I waved the envelope in the air. "Settin' me up to take me down. Do whatever she can to take the only good thing I did in this life away from me."

He took a step toward me, murmuring a gentle, "Cher."

And, God, that hurt too, the sting so killer, it injected poison in my bloodstream, having his gentle *Cher* but knowing I'd never really *have* it.

I turned the envelope his way to ward him off and he stopped.

I spoke.

"To fight her, I'll need to call on Colt. Again. Feb. Again. Jack and Jackie. *Again*. I'll need to explain *again* why I was taken in by Lowe. More will go down, askin' good people who look out for me to keep doin' it, all this takin' money I can't afford to fight it. But the bottom line is, Ethan'll be dragged through it. The Denny Lowe shit will resurface. Ethan might get it at school. He might lose friends. And straight up, my history is such a big pile of stinking crap, Colt could convince the president to come and stand as a character witness to my mothering skills and I'd still lose my kid. So yeah, Merry, I know I got friends. I know people will look out for me. I know you're one of 'em. But that does not mean I am not still very, *very* alone."

"Come here, Cher," he whispered, and I could see it, hear it, goddamned fucking *feel* it.

He wanted to comfort me. Put his arms around me and make it all better.

He had the power to do that.

He just would never use it because he didn't really want it.

"No," I said firmly, the poison activating, my insides melting, the pain extreme.

His head jerked and his gaze grew intense.

I continued talking.

"You don't get that," I told him. "You came here to get me to go to Frank's so you could tell me what went down with us was just a drunken fuck, no more. We don't change. Am I right?"

He didn't answer, so I answered for him.

55

"I'm right. So, you don't wanna be that to me, you don't get that."
I nodded my head. "I understand, the woman I am. I get it, Merry. No harm, no foul. But you don't get to pick and choose how you are with me, who you are with me, what you get to give me. I do. So you don't get that."

He said nothing, just stared at me with an alertness that was a little hot but also a little freaky.

"Now, you tell *anyone* about this shit, we're done," I told him, and his alert went into overdrive, charging the room.

I ignored it.

"I mean that, Garrett," I stated. "This is *my* business and *I'll* deal with it the way I see fit. If I gotta call folks in, *I'll* do it. You keep your mouth shut or what we got you wanna keep you'll lose. I'm not jokin' with you. I'm all kinds of serious."

Finally, he spoke.

"The woman you are."

"The woman I am," I confirmed.

"What woman is that, Cher?" he asked.

Was he serious?

He'd said it his damned self to Colt.

Woman she is, she knows...

"Don't pretend you don't know," I hissed.

"He played you," Merry declared. "A million other women would have bought his shit the same as you."

We were *not* doing this.

"Stop it," I spat.

"Goddamned truth," he pushed. "I know, babe, I'm in the business. Women buy shit like that all the time. The extremes may vary, but you are far from the only one."

I couldn't do this, and more, I wasn't about to.

So I put a hand to my hip, cocked my head, and asked, "Shit, darlin', two-for-one special? You give me five orgasms *and* heal all my emotional wounds? Shoulda signed up for that plan years ago."

His mood deteriorated instantly.

"Don't be a bitch," he clipped.

"Don't pretend you know fuck all about what's goin' on in my head," I shot back.

"Maybe, you let the door to that fortress you built around you open an inch, I can get in and you'll find I *do* know fuck all about what's goin' on in your head, I give a shit about you, and I wanna see you let it go and find yourself some happy."

"That doesn't happen for girls like me, Merry," I told him.

"That's bullshit, Cher," he told me.

I jabbed my hand with the envelope at him. "You do *not* know what it's like to live my life."

"Open the door an inch, Cher. I get through, we'll sit down and you can tell me."

"Fuck that," I snapped.

He rocked back on his heels, his eyes burning into mine, and murmured, "Right."

Goddamn it!

It was time to end this, and at that moment, I didn't care how much I was ending.

"You know, straight up, baby, I got a choice between Garrett Merrick, the guy I shoot the shit with, and Garrett Merrick, the man who gives phenomenal head, I pick door number two because you're good with your mouth, but you're better with your cock."

No hesitation, he returned fire.

"You give it good too, sweetheart. Best I had in fuckin' years. You're ready to go again, you give me a call and I'm there."

"Ethan's next sleepover, or the next time I gotta eat shit and send him to my ex and his bitch, you're on."

"Find out you held out on me, after shift you'll have a caller, and your mom can look after your boy while you're takin' my cock in my bed."

"You're on for that too."

His eyes continued burning into mine as he rumbled, "I'm not fuckin' with you, Cher."

"Back at you, Garrett."

"Then it's on," he announced.

"Oh yeah, baby. It's on," I agreed with enticing acid.

He lifted a finger my way and declared, "Then we got a deal. And you know how I deal, Cher. You *know* the man I am." He dropped his hand. "You're officially takin' my cock, I officially *take your back*. I won't say shit to anyone, but one goddamned thing happens with your ex and his bitch, you tell me. You don't, we got problems."

"Uh…think you forgot somethin', boss. I take your cock 'cause I want to. That's it."

He shook his head, his eyes still scorching into mine. "Oh no," he whispered, a sound that crawled over my skin in a way I couldn't figure out if it was good or bad. "I'm seein' you *think* you know the man I am, but you don't fuckin' know. Only way with me is *my* way. We made our deal. You got no choice now but to do it my way."

"Don't hold your breath for that to happen, gorgeous," I returned.

"Yeah, one of us is gonna be breathless, brown eyes, that's a guarantee."

He could absolutely guarantee that.

Absolutely.

And it hit me at that juncture that I was in the middle of negotiating with Merry a friends-with-benefits-*without*-the-friendship-part deal.

How the fuck did that happen?

"We done with this bullshit?" he asked.

"We are absolutely done," I answered.

"With this bullshit, you're correct. Other than that, you are not," he retorted, then turned and stalked out of the room, slamming the door.

I stared at it.

Then I sent voodoo vibes of evil I did not have the skill to accurately deliver (or any skill at all) in Peggy's direction for being whatever the hell she was and doing it with very bad timing.

After I failed at that endeavor and got my head together, I shoved the envelope in my purse and got back to work.

Garrett

Garrett stood on the tiny balcony of his shit condo and lit a cigarette as he listened to the phone ring in his ear.

He snapped the top of the Zippo closed and looked out at his stellar view of a parking lot that led to another building of condos, none of which were remotely pretty.

"Yo," his friend and brother-in-law, Tanner Layne, said in his ear.

Garrett exhaled and replied, "Yo, big man, you got a minute?"

"Sure," Tanner answered.

"Listen, I need a favor."

"This a favor that's gonna take a lot of my time, none of which I'll get paid for, or is this a favor that's gonna mean me pickin' up your mail 'cause you're headed to a beach?"

This was a valid question. Tanner was a private investigator, a good one. Garrett was a cop. Being a cop, there were rules. Being a PI, those rules were a lot looser. Garrett needed his brother-in-law when he needed loose, something that happened often, and he didn't hesitate to ask.

Tanner usually didn't hesitate to deliver.

Still, he bitched about it.

"Not a lotta your time, but it's important. You find it hard to fit in, I'll make it worth your while and pay your fees," Garrett told him.

Tanner said nothing.

This was also a valid response. Garrett had never offered this in exchange for services rendered.

Finally, Tanner spoke. "Jesus. What's the favor?"

"Need you to look into some people for me. Man's name is Trent. His wife's name is Peg. Don't know where they live. My guess is Indy but could be anywhere relatively close. Don't know their last name. Just know you'll probably find it, you look up the birth certificate of Ethan Rivers *née* Sheckle, seein' as Trent's his birth father."

"Fuck," Tanner muttered, then instantly jumped to the obvious conclusion. "Cher got some problems?"

"Yeah," Garrett told him, not giving that first fuck that he'd promised Cher he wouldn't tell anyone she had issues.

First, because Tanner would keep it on the down low. Second, because that stick-up-her-ass bitch was *not* going to get her hands on Ethan. Cher was *not* going to lose her son. The woman had been through enough. The time that she had headaches outside of the normal ones good folks had was over.

That was a decision Garrett had made the minute they'd had their conversation, and it wasn't because he'd fucked her.

It was because she was Cher *and* she was a Cher he'd now fucked.

"According to her," he continued, "Peg's not big on her husband's blood livin' with an ex-stripper or the rest of the baggage Denny Lowe landed on her."

"They goin' for custody?" Tanner asked.

"I get the impression, not yet. But I also get the impression that they're gearin' up for it."

"The impression?"

"Cher isn't feelin' like bein' super informative at this juncture."

Tanner again made no reply.

"She's freaked, though, in a big fuckin' way," Garrett told him. "Her history, she has reason. The way she's raisin' that boy and the love she's got for him, she shouldn't worry. But life she's lived, that won't be her first thought. She told me her ex is a recovering addict. She called him a junkie. I'm helpin' her out, hopin' you might uncover some ammunition in case they wage war."

"I gotta be in the office in the morning. I'll run some searches, get what I got to you, follow up if something opens up," Tanner offered.

"Be appreciated," Garrett muttered, dragging from his cigarette, then exhaling before he said, "Need you to keep this quiet, brother. You and me on this. And by quiet, I mean I don't even want Cher to know you're lookin' into this."

"Tough as nails, determined to look out for herself, not drag anyone into her shit," Tanner deduced.

"That's it," Garrett confirmed.

"I'll go quiet," Tanner told him.

"That's appreciated too."

"Never ends for her," Tanner observed. "The legacy of bullshit that asshole laid on her."

"Nope," Garrett agreed.

"Her ex had problems, we'll find somethin'," Tanner assured.

"I hope so," Garrett replied, then asked, "You and Rocky gettin' any sleep?"

This was also a valid question since his sister and brother-in-law gave him a niece, still a baby, though growing up, and she was a big fan of daytime naps, but she'd never been a fan of nighttime sleep.

"CeeCee's determined to be a night owl."

Thinking about his beautiful niece, Cecelia, and the fact that she was a product of the love Tanner and Rocky had for each other, Garrett grinned into the night as he took another drag.

"Listen, Garrett," Tanner continued. "Heard about Mia. Was deep in it with some work with Ryker. Didn't have time to seek you out. Called, but you didn't—"

Garrett interrupted him. "I'm good."

"Brother," Tanner said low, not believing him.

Garrett inhaled again, and on the exhale, he stated, "I'm good, Tanner. Did it smart, timed it right, threw a few back when Cher was on." He felt one side of his lips tip up. "She had a few words with me the only way Cher knows how. But the woman has wisdom."

Tanner still sounded disbelieving when he asked, "What'd she say?"

Since it all came out, the fact that the Merrick family was still dealing with the murder years ago of Raquel and Garrett's mom, Cecelia Merrick, that shit being ugly, nearly shredding Rocky, Garrett didn't hold much back from Tanner Layne.

Rocky would have come undone if Tanner, his mother, his sons, and his friend/mentor Devin hadn't held the tatters together. And it might not have happened—*a lot* might not have happened—if Garrett had given his sister what she'd really needed in the years since their mother was murdered.

He'd held back in the past, thinking he was protecting Rocky, doing what she told him she needed, looking after his sister, his family.

Tanner was family. Garrett and his father's silence about the demons that plagued the Merrick clan after Cecelia had been tortured and shot to death had nearly torn their family apart (again).

Shit had gone extreme.

Now he no longer made that same mistake.

So, right then, Garrett didn't hesitate in giving it to Tanner.

"Difference between you and Rocky and me and Mia is you got a shot at gettin' your woman back, you took it, and you stood by her when the bad hit. I have that same bad shit. A different way, but I got it. Mia knew it and didn't give that back."

"Fuck. Never thought to turn that table, but Cher's right."

She was.

For years, Garrett never turned that table either.

Mia was it. The one. Tormenting his mind. Owning his heart.

He'd been happy with her. She'd been happy with him. It had been good. Beyond good.

They'd had it all.

Then he'd ended it, and he didn't even know why he did it until Rocky came apart that day—Rocky, having done the same thing to Tanner years before, deep down into her bones terrified that happy would vaporize like it had the night Cecilia stood strong to protect her daughter, her husband's work, then lost her life doing both.

He also never would have guessed that the day he lost Mia for good was the day he'd see things for what they were.

Tanner and Rocky had it. Colt and Feb. Cal and Vi. Dusty and Mike.

Garrett might have it, he didn't know.

What he did know, now that Cher had pointed it out, was that Mia didn't.

Getting that knowledge from Cher, it was like he'd been yoked, that yoke heavy but also invisible. He didn't even know it'd hung around his neck, dragging him down.

And then it was just gone.

And now he was free.

"Good to know you're doin' okay," Tanner said.

"Yeah," Garrett muttered.

"Now, brother, CeeCee's down, so Roc and me got about five seconds of alone time and, no offense, I wanna spend that time with my wife."

Garrett grinned into the night again and replied, "Then I'll let you go. Later, Tanner."

"Later, Garrett."

They disconnected and Garrett stared into the parking lot, wondering what it would feel like to have an actual yard as he finished his smoke.

He turned and bent low to the crappy-ass, cheap, white plastic table that sat between two crappy-ass, cheap, white plastic chairs in order to stub out his cigarette.

He did this thinking back to if he'd ever smoked in front of Ethan.

Friday night, Cher had come out with him twice as they were getting hammered so he could have a smoke, standing in front of him on her high-heeled shoes, shifting from foot to foot in the cold, while he told her to get her ass back inside and she gave him all kinds of shit for smoking.

But Ethan? No. Garrett wouldn't do that. He'd never smoke in front of any of his friends' kids. Not when they were Ethan's age. Not when they hadn't already learned better.

He turned, pulled the sliding glass door open, and shut it behind him, intending to go to the fridge and get a beer.

He didn't get a beer.

He looked at the living room/dining room/kitchen part of his condo, all of it easy to see because it was condensed into as few square feet as a builder could design those three spaces.

He had crappy-ass balcony furniture.

The furniture inside was only a shade above crappy-ass, but it was still shit.

Immediately, his mind filled with what he'd seen of Cher's place.

He was not surprised that she lived in a house that looked like it was decorated by Janis Joplin's slightly more together sister. Stuffed full, dark at the same time bright with color, it had personality. It was unique. It held warmth that hit you the second you stepped foot over the threshold.

It was Cher.

The living room was good; her bedroom was better.

Her bedroom said anything goes. Her bedroom said your wildest fantasy could come true. Her bedroom said you were safe to be what you were, think what you want, do what you like, eat like a pig, drink like a fish, fuck like an animal, sleep like the dead, no worries, leave life at the door and just *be*.

And she'd delivered. They'd only had hours in that room, so she didn't deliver on it all, but the instant they fell to her bed, tearing at each other's clothes, she'd more than delivered.

On this thought, Garrett moved to his refrigerator, pulled out a beer, twisted off the cap, and turned to rest his hips against the counter, looking into his shitty condo, the eclectic warmth of Cher's pad not layering over what his eyes saw.

The feel of her, the smell of her, the memory of being with her in her bed was what filled his mind.

For years, he had stupidly tried to fuck Mia out of his head and his heart, knowing he was doing it and completely unable to stop himself.

And to make that shit even shittier, he'd done it by actually fucking Mia any time after their divorce that she came around to get a dose of his cock.

More often than not, though, when he sunk his dick into a woman who was not his ex-wife, Mia filled his head. Drunk or sober, it happened. It made him feel like an asshole. But he kept doing it.

With Cher, it did not.

With Cher, he was *with Cher.*

On a night when he was trashed and that shit was sure to happen, it didn't.

On a night where he never expected he could do it, he'd laughed. Not a little, a lot. His gut clenching with it. His eyes watering with it.

And he did that with Cher.

No, he didn't just do it with her, she *gave* him that.

You came here to get me to go to Frank's so you could tell me what went down with us was just a drunken fuck, no more. We don't change. Am I right?

She'd been right.

Garrett looked to the clock on his microwave.

It was just before nine thirty. Her shift that day was noon to eight thirty. She'd be home.

He engaged his phone, opened his texts, and shot her one.

Ethan got a sleepover this weekend?

He took another pull from his beer, thinking Cher's early shift was noon to eight thirty and her late shift was eight to three thirty. He knew that because he was a cop and he paid attention to everything, an occupational hazard, so he'd noted it just from being a regular at her place of business.

Those shifts meant, either way, on school days, she didn't have to rush Ethan to get ready. Even if she'd only had a few hours of sleep, she could make him breakfast, take him to school, not have to be anywhere but with him. Late shift, she could also go get him, get him home, make sure his schoolwork got done, make him dinner.

But even if they had time together, either way, that time was still fucked.

People did that kind of thing all the time, shift work that meant they had to get creative about who looked after their kids.

But those people didn't have Cher's history and a kid with a stick-up-their-ass stepmom who decided the way of the world and that her way was the only way. Garrett knew that was the way Peggy whoever-she-was was the minute he saw the bitch. Cher didn't need to lay that out. He knew she was trouble of one variety or the other before she opened her mouth.

Before he knew she was bringing Cher trouble.

Fuck, he hoped the junkie ex was dirty.

He pushed away from the counter, took his beer to the couch, and grabbed the remote.

He found a show right when his phone sounded.

He grabbed it off his coffee table and his mouth curled up when he read, *Kiss my ass, Merry.*

Using his thumb, he returned, *You want that, brown eyes, I'll work it in.*

She didn't make him wait and shot back, *Go fuck yourself.*

Now, sweetheart, you know that's not the way it works.

Then came, *We're done.*

He ignored that and sent, *Sleep tight. See you tomorrow.*

Tomorrow? she returned.

Have good dreams.

Tomorrow?

Garrett didn't reply.

Merry? Tomorrow?

Garrett again didn't reply.

Don't fuck with me, Merry. I don't need your shit.

Garrett grinned, but he didn't reply, and at that, Cher let it go.

He trained his eyes to the TV, not watching it.

He was thinking that he had absolutely no idea what he was doing.

The only thing he knew was that he was going to do it. And right then, as much of a dick as it made him, it was because Cher Rivers was the best fuck he'd ever had, bar none, including Mia.

After their showdown, where Cher showed him a different kind of fire than her normal—a fire he liked—and a vulnerability she'd never shown before—the kind as a cop and as a Merrick he couldn't ignore—he wanted more.

It was also because, when he was low, she took his back.

So now that she had the possibility of trouble, he was going to take hers.

If she wanted him to or not.

Four

Plotting My Murder
Cher

The next day, after I'd dropped Ethan at school, I was about to go out to the garage to get the storm windows when my phone rang.

I moved to my purse in the bucket chair, pulled the phone out, and saw a number I did not know.

I'd learned a long time ago never to answer those kinds of calls. I was careful to program in any numbers that I would need to know, including doctors, dentists, Ethan's school. I'd learned to do this, because if it didn't come up as programmed, they were either someone trying to sell me something or someone I absolutely did not want to talk to.

This being someone I didn't want to talk to, I dropped the phone on top of my purse and headed to the garage.

I had the windows out of the garage, stacked against the side of the house, the screen switched out in the front door, and was moving to the first window when I heard shrieked, "*You think I won't fuck with you?*"

I looked left and went still.

My next-door neighbor was cool—Tilly, an old lady. She was quiet. She was also private but friendly and happy to look after Ethan on the rare occasion I needed her. She did this because she was a good woman and she liked us, not because Ethan or I mowed her lawn and shoveled her snow whenever we did ours (which we did).

And she acted like the light of God shone down on her when her asshole son or her bitch-face daughter deigned to pay her a visit, bringing her grand-children. I was not in my house 24/7, but I didn't miss the fact that these pilgrimages back home to momma happened rarely. Ethan and I had lived there for over two years and those bastards had shown twice, collectively.

But the house next to Tilly's was a rental. Not one like mine, where my landlord gave a shit. One where the landlord didn't, so it was in visible disre-pair, which meant the rent was lower and the renters were of the same level.

I'd seen the new tenants. They'd been around a few months. In that time, they'd had one party that was loud, which I'd had closed down.

But they were around a lot, in and out a lot, and had a slew of visitors, so I had a variety of opportunities to see them.

Being a person who was quickly judged, I was not judgmental.

Still, the man had dickhead written all over him, and the woman was a sister in the way she'd convinced herself she couldn't do much better, so she didn't try.

Now she was on the stoop, red in the face, still in her shapeless night-shirt, hair wild, clearly, even from a distance, pissed way the fuck off.

He was in jeans and a jeans jacket, a few feet down the walk from her, his back to me, but his body language was easily read and he shared his woman's mood.

Since they were a house away, I didn't hear what he said. I just knew he replied when she kept screeching.

"*Fuck you! You don't change your mind, motherfucker. Carlito will learn* all *your shit!*"

At that, I knew it was time to go inside and do it quiet so neither of them would know I was outside and I'd heard what I'd heard.

This was what I did.

When I soundlessly closed my door behind me, I looked into my living room and hissed, "*Shit.*"

I didn't know Carlito.

But I worked in a bar that served booze to cops, bikers, and bankers. Hairdressers and lady doctors. Farmers, plumbers, and lawyers.

And at a bar, customers considered waitresses deaf to anything but drink orders.

Also at a bar, customers considered bartenders their own personal shrinks.

So I knew that the least of what a man called Carlito was was a low-life loan shark.

But considering I'd heard his name murmured on more than one occasion by Colt, Sully, Mike, Drew, Sean, Merry, and a number of other cops in that 'burg, I suspected he was more.

I did not need that shit on my block, but it was more.

I did not need that shit on the block where my kid lived.

I went to my kitchen to pour myself a travel mug, emptying the last cup of joe from the pot into the mug to take out with me when the coast was clear. I was standing in the living room, holding it in my hand and listening for my neighbors, when my phone sounded with a text.

Excitement and annoyance chased its way through me as I looked to my phone on my purse, wondering if the text was from Merry.

Last night, through texts, his games had begun.

I was trying to ignore this.

It was hard to ignore.

I put the mug down on the coffee table, grabbed the phone, and saw it wasn't from Merry. It was a text from Violet telling me she could pick Ethan up from school on Thursday when both Mom and I were working.

When I texted her back to confirm and give thanks, I saw I had a voicemail.

It was from that number I didn't know.

I didn't want to listen to it, but just in case the school got a new extension or some teacher was calling me from their own phone for some reason, I went to it, hit PLAY, hit SPEAKER, and heard, "Ms. Sheckle. This is Walter Jones. I would appreciate it if you could phone me back when you have a moment. Just so you know, I'll make it worth your while. I was a profiler with the FBI, currently freelance, and am researching a book I'm writing on serial killers of the last twenty—"

I set my teeth and hit DELETE.

Fucking motherfucker.

I jumped and turned when a knock came at my door.

I had a shit door that, even wearing my daintiest high-heeled sandal, I could kick through. It was two layers of thin, cheap wood with a small diamond window at eye level so you could look out.

And in that diamond window, I saw Merry.

Fucking *motherfucker*.

He'd texted *tomorrow*.

And it was tomorrow.

I stared at him through the window, but he did not stare at me.

He opened the door and walked right through.

Mental note: lock the damned door, no matter if you're inside just to pour a cup of coffee.

"Well, come on in, Officer," I greeted sarcastically, throwing out my hand with the phone in it. "Something I can get you? Cup of coffee? Late breakfast? Quick blowjob?"

He did not look amused. He did not look annoyed.

He looked ticked.

"You puttin' in your own storms?" he asked.

With the crap coming from my neighbors, Walter Jones getting my cell phone number and having no problem calling me, thinking he could ever in a million fucking years make it "worth my while" to talk about Dennis Lowe, and Merry waltzing into my living room, all in the expanse of ten minutes, I wasn't following.

"What?"

"Windows, Cher." He jerked his head toward the side of the house where the storm windows were stacked. "You puttin' in your own storm windows?"

I had no idea why he would care, but there was only one answer to that question, so I gave it to him.

"Well, yeah."

"Why doesn't your landlord do it?" Merry asked.

"Because he's seven hundred and twelve years old and my CPR skills are a little rusty, so I don't want him giving himself a heart attack switching screens out for storms when I can do it myself."

"It's his responsibility," Merry returned.

"I'd have to study my rental agreement, but I think routine maintenance is my responsibility, Merry."

"You study that agreement, you'd find you're wrong."

It had been a while since I read it, but I had a feeling Merry was correct.

I didn't share this feeling.

I said, "Then, considering the screens pop out, the storms pop in, and the doors only require little ole me to be able to turn a screwdriver, I'd rather just do it instead of calling him, waiting for him to come over, suffer a stroke while winterizing my house, thus scarring me mentally for life."

His eyes narrowed. "You this much of a smartass before I made you come for me five times?"

I waited for my head to swivel around on my shoulders while fire shot out of my eye sockets.

When that didn't happen, I snapped, "Uh...*yeah.*"

"Leave 'em," he ordered. "I'm done with my shift, I'll come over and put 'em in."

I didn't know how to react to that except allow my mouth to drop open, which I did.

Before I recovered, he asked, "You know Riverside Baptist Church?"

"Oh God. First you give me five orgasms, now you're gonna save my soul?" I asked back.

He crossed his arms on his chest. "Rein in the smartass, Cher. Don't got time to get you sweet, which means get you hot, so you'll give me what I want instead of bein' a pain in my ass. Answer the question: Do you know Riverside Baptist Church?"

That was when *my* eyes narrowed. "Get me sweet, which means get me hot?"

Merry became visibly impatient. "Babe, *focus.*"

"You want me focused, tell me why you're here, injecting cheer into my day," I demanded.

"Peggy Schott belongs to Riverside Baptist Church."

I snapped my mouth shut.

Merry didn't.

"She talk about that? Trent talk about it? Ethan come from them to you and talk about it?"

I felt my heart beating hard in my chest. "What I wanna know is why *you're* talking about it, and how do you even know that? How'd you even find out Peg's last name?"

"I told you I was gonna take your back and that's what I'm doin'," he returned.

That was what he was doing?

We'd had our previous fun-loving chat at four o'clock yesterday afternoon.

It wasn't even ten o'clock the next morning and he'd already learned about a church Peggy belonged to.

I had a bad feeling about this because I knew Merry, and once he got his teeth into something, he didn't let go.

And he had his teeth into Trent and Peggy, so my chances at stopping him from getting right up in my shit were minimizing by the second.

These thoughts made me throw up both hands in exasperation and snap, "It hasn't even been twenty-four hours!"

"Someone gives you a heads up they're thinkin' of fuckin' with you, you don't offer them a head start," he replied, then kept going. "Margaret Schott is the volunteer assistant director of a program run by Riverside Baptist Church called Faith Saves. The mission of this program is to send members to hang outside AA, NA, and Al-Anon meetings, as well as methadone clinics, approaching people who leave to seek recovery or guidance through the word of God."

"Holy shit," I whispered.

"Considering those programs are already significantly faith-based, the folks at Riverside either aren't that bright or not real good at hiding their recruitment tactics. Google Peg Schott's name; she's all over the church's website, tied to this program. Might be a jump, but doubtful—this is how she met your ex. You know anything about that?"

I shook my head.

"They take Ethan to church?" Merry asked.

I kept shaking my head.

"He's never mentioned it?" Merry pushed.

I continued shaking my head but asked, "This church bad news?"

"Haven't had time to dig deep. Jumped from that to some articles about a couple of community centers and other churches that give space to recovery programs that got together to call the cops to get Faith Saves off the pavement so they don't bother group members after meetings. But they stick to publicly owned space and they're peaceful, if irritating, so cops can't do jack. Haven't been able to follow it further."

72

I didn't have any time to sort through this information in my head before Merry kept talking.

"Trent Schott has priors."

I felt my lips part.

Merry continued to give it to me.

"Pulled over, suspected DUI, tests showed he was high. Weed. First offense, it was just pot, not much came of it. Got in a fight at a bar that rolled outside that the cops had to break up. His statement reported he was confronting someone who owed him money. They were both hauled in, but no property was damaged. He eventually dropped the charges, so did the other guy, so that slid. Then he was caught with a baggie of ice, not enough to make a big deal about it, so they didn't. He got community service. He was also suspected in a liquor store robbery, but they didn't have any security cameras and the clerk on at the time couldn't positively identify him."

I stared at Merry reeling this off, all not so good stuff that could be good for me, and I said nothing.

Then again, Merry wasn't done.

"Last one, strung out, he stole a lighter from a convenience store. Owner was behind the register, and he'd been having some not insignificant gang trouble and having that for a good while. Fed up, he bought a piece, tackled Schott, shoved the gun in his face, and made a citizen's arrest on the spot. Good news is, he also called the cops to make a proper arrest. Seein' as Schott only stole a lighter, security footage confirmed that, and he was able to hand that eighty-nine-cent item back to the owner, no charges were filed."

Before I could swallow it back, I made a noise that was half snort, half giggle before asking, "Trent was arrested by a convenience store owner?"

Merry grinned at me. "Tackled *then* arrested. And the owner was sixty-three at the time."

I made the noise again, my shoulders jerking with it.

Visualization of my imagination's version of this awesome event hit my head and I couldn't hold it back any longer. I busted out laughing.

I did it so hard, I squeezed my eyes shut and wrapped an arm around my stomach.

I sobered instantly when I felt a warm, strong hand wrapped around the side of my neck.

My eyes shot open and up to see Merry's face gentle, without humor, and he was looking down at me.

"There's my girl."

Uh.

No.

I stepped back, running into the bucket chair, so I had to skirt it to get out of his hold.

His hand dropped, but he stepped toward me.

I took another step back.

He took another step my way.

"Merry, stop moving," I ordered.

He didn't. He kept at me, I kept retreating, but he made his movements while talking.

"As hilarious as that is, Schott's inability to outrun a sixty-three-year-old man who has to clear a counter to get to him is not gonna go far with a judge. He might call a recess so he can go to his chambers to have a laugh, but no charges filed, it'll probably be inadmissible during a custody battle."

While he spoke, when I was about to run into my media center, I shifted and Merry shifted with me. I had to make another shift, rounding the room, and Merry did it with me.

"Merry, stop *moving*," I repeated.

"Not much in the rest," he continued like I didn't say a word. "Can't hide he used, so the DUI and ice won't be a surprise, and since he's in recovery and his record has been clean through that, might not get you far. The fight isn't good. Even if charges were dropped, you might be able to use that to prove he's got a temper and isn't averse to using his fists."

Through this, my leg hit an end table and I adjusted. We cleared the couch, I shifted again too soon, both my calves hit the coffee table, and my ass went down on it.

I looked up. Cell flat to the table, I braced my hands to push up, but Merry was there, chin in his throat, eyes on me, and when he spoke again, his mind was clearly on my location.

"Tried to get your mouth on me more than once when we tore at each other up last Friday, but I was in the mood to use mine. Lookin' forward to learnin' what you can do with yours, but like I said, baby, right now, don't got the time."

My only response that he couldn't twist was to glare at him, which was what I did.

"But got time before I go for a kiss," Merry informed me.

"Only kiss I'll give you is tellin' you to kiss *off*," I informed him.

"Who knew warm brown eyes like the ones you got could spark that kind of fire," he muttered as if he wasn't even talking to me.

"Step back," I demanded.

"No," he denied.

I continued to glare up at him, then I realized I was not the kind of woman who sat on her ass, glaring up at a man towering over her and pinning her in. So I stood, which put me smack in Merry's space, my breasts brushing against his abs and up his chest on my way.

They kept brushing when he didn't move back, but I didn't attempt escape, even to get away from the shafts of electricity this all caused at my nipples, shafts that headed south.

I glared at him from closer.

He stared into my eyes, his gaze moving down to my mouth then back up as one side of his lips curved.

He was getting off on this.

I didn't get that and I didn't want to get that.

I wanted this done.

"In the mood to play, Officer?" I whispered.

"Told you, sweetheart, don't got the time."

I shook my head but held his gaze. "Not what I mean. Single mom, all alone. Switch out her storms. Offer info to help her out of a jam. Been a while since I was in the know about these things, so tell me, what's the price for all that? You mentioned a blowjob. You got stamina, but I got talent. Balance that out, I'm thinkin' it'll take more than the usual ten, fifteen minutes. We'll give it twenty. So I can manage my time, is there more?"

I wasn't even done talking before I learned his eyes could spark fire too.

I also learned he *was* in the mood to play, that being, playing me at my own game.

And doing it better.

75

He dipped his face close, his voice low. "Storms get me the blowjob, brown eyes. I get the intel you need, that buys me sinkin' deep in wet pussy."

I felt my nipples get harder at the same time something else happened to me that, if he was of a mind to take his payoff right then, he'd get what he wanted.

I hid this reaction and asked, "You want this all in one go, or you wanna spread payback out for a while?"

"Keep plenty of time open, Cher. I intend to earn a fuckuva lot more and draw it out collecting."

I nodded, still keeping a lock on his eyes. "I get it. Girl like me, only payback expected for me to be able to give."

That didn't get me fire.

That got me ice.

"I hear you talk down about yourself one more time, Cher, shit will get extreme."

That made *me* ice over.

"Do not hand me that crap, Merry. You come into my home and got no problem talkin' about wet pussy right to my face tells me the woman you know me to be."

He dipped his face even closer, to the point it felt like if I blinked, my lashes would sweep his in a butterfly kiss.

"Do not hand me *your* shit, Cher," he growled. "That hang-up is yours, not mine. And how I know that is I made you come just finger fuckin' you and talkin' dirty in your ear, and it was the talk and not what my fingers were doin' that took you there. I like that, a woman who can let go and let me give her that without gettin' uptight and closin' down on me. You liked it too, a *fuckuva* lot more than me. So don't stand there handin' me your shit when I know you're wet for me now and I haven't fuckin' touched you."

I refused to reply to that because he was right and I had no intention of confirming that information.

But it was then he hit me with a verbal blow, the intensity of which, not in my whole shitty-ass life I'd ever received.

"Christ, if I didn't know you were worth it, I'd walk out the door and this would be done—all we got, over."

I could stand.

I could stare.

But I couldn't breathe.

Merry could.

He could also speak.

"Hope like fuck no one takes off with those storms while I'm gone. You think they will, move 'em into garage and leave the key under the mat. I'm switchin' 'em out, Cher. I come back tonight and they're done, I'll find you, and I won't be collectin'. I'll be dishin' it out, but you won't get it until you beg for it and do that shit for a really long time."

His words were lost on me.

I continued to stand.

I continued to stare.

But my lungs had started burning.

If I didn't know you were worth it...

"When's Ethan's next sleepover?" Merry bit out.

"Friday," I whispered. "But his friend's comin' here."

"Fuck," Merry clipped. "Find a time, babe. You don't, payback'll stack up and I'll have to take personal days and hole up in a hotel with you for a week. And there's not a doubt that stick-up-her-ass church lady your ex tied his shit to won't appreciate you bein' gone from your kid for a weeklong fuckathon."

That was kind of funny as well as hot.

I still said nothing.

Merry fell silent and stared at me.

Then he dealt the second biggest verbal blow I'd ever received in my life.

"Christ, you're pretty, even standin' there plotting my murder."

After that, he lifted a hand, grabbed me gentle but firm at my neck, yanked me up so my mouth hit his hard but brief, then he let me go.

"Later, babe," he said, strolling to my door. He stopped in it, turned to me, and bid his farewell by saying, "You touch those storms only to put them in the garage."

He closed the door on that.

I stood where he left me.

If I didn't know you were worth it...

What was I worth?

What was I worth to Merry?

I stared at the door, again breathing but not knowing what to think.

Not even knowing what was happening.

How had it gone from a drunken fuck, after which he was going to blow me off, to him investigating Trent and Peggy, demanding I find a time when I could offer his brand of payback, and him not only telling me I was pretty, but I was "worth it?"

It would seem me and Merry had to have a chat where we were not fighting or talking about my ex and his bitch's diabolical plans.

And I would suggest just that to him later, when he'd cooled down and when we were both far apart from each other.

I left the storm windows where they were. Merry wanted to put them in, at that juncture, I was not going to test his mood by going against his wishes.

Instead, I went to the laptop me and Ethan shared.

I powered that baby up.

Then I found Riverside Baptist Church and its program Faith Saves. I read every word.

Twice.

"Takin' my last break," I told Jack, who was behind the bar.

"Make it a good one," Jack replied.

I said nothing and went to the office.

Mondays during the day were not big days at J&J's. We had the odd drifter. Weather allowed, we had biker boys who knew J&J's was welcoming, so if they slid through town, they'd stop to play a couple of games of pool and throw back some brews. We had regulars with no jobs but the miraculous ability to buy drinks.

I was on early for the week, going nights next week, which was Feb and Morrie's way with scheduling to make sure Ruthie nor me took a hit from having to do all early.

Luckily, things looked up around five, and when I did early, I usually got my breaks and lunch out of the way when it was not after five because that was when the tips were made. I didn't need to be sitting on my ass, eating, when I could be making money.

Although cops had imprecise schedules, detective shifts were eight to five officially. If anything happened beyond that, the on call cop went in.

So unusually that day, I waited for my break until six thirty, when Merry was off. The autumn light was waning, which meant the storm windows were probably in before I phoned him.

He picked up on the second ring, greeting, "Hey."

"Hey," I replied, and it occurred to me that, although we had each other's numbers, I didn't think I'd ever phoned him.

We'd texted things, like him asking me, *You bringing that bacon potato salad to Vi's party?* (which meant, *bring it,* and so I always did), and me texting him, *Colts lost. You owe me twenty bucks.*

But I'd never phoned him.

"Cher?" he called, and I shook my head sharply.

"Looked up Riverside Baptist Church. That Faith Saves thing looks pretty legit."

"They're not gonna tell everyone on the Internet they're freaky-ass zealots intent on saving the world by kidnapping recovering addicts and brainwashing them."

My hand tightened on my phone, my mind thinking of Trent's devotion to Peg. "Holy fuck, Merry. Do you think that's what they're doing?"

There was humor in his deep voice when he replied, "Calm down, sweetheart. No. Just tellin' you as you look into the shit that I feed you, don't judge a book by its cover. We get it, we won't go surface—we'll look deeper. But I'll do the digging."

Okay, right, this was one of several things that had to stop, and to stop it, we had to talk.

"I have Wednesday and Friday off this week," I declared.

"Fuck, I just got the weekend off," he returned.

He was thinking I was planning payback time.

"Can we do lunch on Wednesday?" I asked.

"Mike and me bought a case this weekend, which means we're officially over our recommended caseload. Until we clear some, lunch is a memory for me."

I moved to the chair at the desk and sat in it before saying, "We need to talk, Merry."

"What're we doin' right now, Cher?"

"I'm on a break."

"So call me when Ethan goes to bed."

"That'll be late."

There was humor in his voice again when he replied, "Not like you aren't used to late nights."

"This talk we need to have needs to be face-to-face."

Merry had no reply to that, humor-filled or not.

I rushed to fill the silence.

"What we had…before…it was good. We fucked it up. We're still fuckin' it up, playin' these games. We should sit down, talk it through, get back to that good. It's the best thing for both of us, Merry, and we both know it."

He didn't agree. He didn't anything, so I rushed to fill that silence too.

"And Trent said they just wanted to see Ethan more. I didn't want to talk about it when he was in the mood to push it, and things went south from there. Before I blow it up with them, maybe I should sit down with Ethan and see how he feels about it. He likes his dad, Merry. He likes them both and he digs havin' a brother and sister. Maybe he actually wants more time with them too and doesn't want to hurt my feelings by tellin' me that."

He finally spoke, and when he did, it came gentle.

"Consider this, sweetheart. Maybe, this bitch has claws, and she's got more time to sink them into Ethan, that's not a good idea."

This was a concern.

But it was my concern, not Merry's.

"I still think that's my first step, talking to Ethan."

"I hear you. And maybe you're right. That doesn't mean you shouldn't do what you can to know what you're sendin' him into and if that's healthy or if it's not. Bottom line, your ex is a junkie. He's recovering, but that's still gotta give you pause. I know from the way you reacted that woman freaks you out, and she does that for a reason. Just find out what you're dealin' with before you make a deal with them that involves your boy."

"Okay, then, maybe I'll talk to Tanner about doing some legwork."

"Tanner's expensive."

This was true.

This was also my concern, not Merry's.

"Merry—"

"I'm on this."

"I don't want you to *be* on this."

"You didn't want me to put your storm windows in either, but they're in. I'll also point out that you spent your mornin' lookin' into the program your kid's stepmom is neck-deep in, not puttin' those windows in. I get you know how to go it alone, Cher. In this, you're just not going to."

"That's my call."

"Sorry you think that way, brown eyes, but the call's been made and it's not yours at all."

Shit, I was getting pissed.

"This is why we need to talk face-to-face, so I can explain to you I don't want you in my shit."

"You already did that face-to-face, and right now you're doin' it over the phone. But, babe, it needs to sink in we don't agree. I'm in. With your work schedule, mine, and the fact you need to spend time with your kid, we get face-to-face time, we'll be face-to-face with you on your back and me movin' inside you."

Shit. Now I was getting turned on.

"You had a window you could slide in there, gorgeous. You timed it right. Now Cher's closed for business."

So much humor was back, his reply of "Right" was shaking.

That meant I was no longer pissed or turned on.

I was *angry*.

"If you think with the life I lead I need some badass cop playin' games with me, you are very wrong," I told him bitingly.

He didn't miss a beat, returning, "Cher, with your life and the dry spell you endured, you need *a lot* of things and you're gettin' them all from me."

Of course, Lieutenant Garrett Merrick of the 'burg's PD didn't miss my dry spell.

Fuck.

"That shit's exactly what I'm talkin' about, Merry. I've been down a road where it wasn't my choice to be on. You think for a second I'm gonna be forced down a road I don't like where I'm at again, you think *wrong*. There is nowhere for this to go that's good and you know it, just like me."

"The only thing I know is, what's at the end of the road we're on is unknown. Along the way, I break through that fortress you've built around you and manage to extract your head from your ass, it'll be worth the trip."

"And then what, Merry?" I snapped.

"I don't know, Cher. That's the point. That's life. You have no clue what you'll get along the journey. But you won't get dick you stay in one place, spinning your wheels."

"If that place is a safe place for me and my kid, I'm good to spin my wheels for eternity."

"You may be safe, but are you happy?"

I added a heavy dose of sarcasm when I asked, "You gonna show me happy, Merry, outside of what you can do to me when you're fuckin' me?"

"No one can show you happy, Cher, unless you let them in to try."

"I open the door, is that what you want?" I asked, sarcasm mixed with disbelief now weighting my tone. "You want a shot at makin' me happy?"

"What I want is to make sure a woman I care about is solid with her kid. That they're safe. That the cloud of shit hovering in the horizon is not gonna rain down on them, covering them, because they've had enough of that. That's one thing I want."

His words meant so much to me, unable to hold my head up, I cast my gaze to the floor.

Merry continued talking.

"I also want to know how it feels when you wrap your mouth around my cock. And I want to wake up to you in my bed and look at you sleepin' to find out if the shit I saw Saturday mornin' was a dream or if it was real. That bein', you lookin' just as pretty as you look after drinkin' yourself stupid and bein' rode hard, which is the same as you look when you're standin' opposite the bar from me, pourin' a drink."

I kept staring at the floor, but I did it now breathing funny.

Merry kept at me.

"That shit is *not* right. No woman, not even Mia, could go head-to-head with me drinkin' *and* fuckin' and not wake up with mascara-caked, blood-shot eyes, a lipstick-smeared mouth, and a bedhead that is so far from sexy, it made me wonder why I hit that in the first place. Not you. You opened your eyes and looked ready to perform surgery, shake a martini, or ride my cock until we both found it, all a' that with a camera crew in tow, ready for your close-up."

Not even Mia?

No. Unh-unh. I didn't give a shit.

I tried to turn his mind from his thoughts, *and* me, by reminding him, "You learn that shit when you strip, baby."

"Then at least that line on your CV was worth somethin'; you got that outta it. Then again, *baby*, not complainin' about other skills you learned through your former occupation when you finally managed to climb on top, and I am not fuckin' with you on that. You're not hidin' shit from me, Cher. I don't know if you're tryin', but if you are, stop. You got your head wrapped around an idea, and I get that. I get why. I get there're a lot of folk out there who'd think that idea is spot-on. But they are not me. I do not mind, not even a little fuckin' bit, that I got you drunk, naked, and wild, givin' the lap dance to beat all lap dances, just as long as that's happenin' *to me*."

"You are so full of shit," I bit out.

"Jesus, fuck me, Cher. Seriously?" he retorted. "Due to biology being unbalanced, a session like that, I got one shot. We had one session. Seein' as it's clear you didn't pay close attention, when you get more, you'll know I liked what I got a whole fuckin' lot."

"So we *did* negotiate a friends-with-benefits deal yesterday. Is that what this is?"

"I don't know what it is, Cher. You want me to put a ring on your finger after fuckin' you once, I can tell you on that you'll be disappointed. What I know is, for years, I've had good times with you. Friday night, I had a *great* time with you. *Friday night.* The night Mia no longer was a possibility for me. Got a lotta people who mean a lot to me, but only one took my back, and you did that more than just fuckin' my cares away. You took my back *and* my side when everyone's been tellin' me to pull my head outta my ass about my ex-wife. You made me see it different. You made me think. You showed me what it meant to have a friend who had a mind to *me* and what I should expect from the bitch who owns my dick."

That meant a lot to me too.

But Merry wasn't done hitting me with the velvet blows of his honesty.

"What I want is more good times with you, Cher. I wanna fuck wild and I wanna laugh hard, and while we're doin' that, I'm gonna look out for you. More, I can't promise. That's not enough, then I'm still gonna look out for you. There it is. You gotta get off break, but before I let you go, you gotta know it's your play now. Make it."

With that, he hung up on me.

I dropped my phone to my lap and kept staring at the floor.

Merry wanted to fuck wild and laugh hard, having no clue my heart was involved.

He'd been tagging ass for so long with his heart belonging to another woman, he forgot that shit could happen, it did, and it did it all the time.

I knew two things.

I wanted to fuck wild and laugh hard with Merry.

But I didn't need the heartbreak that would lead to in my life.

I lifted my phone, hit the text button, and tapped in my play.

I didn't send it until hours later, when I was off shift, sitting in my running car, ready to put it in gear and go pick up my kid from my mom's.

I hit SEND, threw my phone on top of my purse on the passenger seat, my eyes so dry they stung, and I set my car on course to get my boy.

⌇⟶

Garrett

I'm happy spinning my wheels.

Garrett stared at the text.

Then he drew his arm back and let fly, the phone sailing through the air and embedding in the shitty-ass drywall of his living room.

He stared at it a beat before he walked out to his balcony to have a smoke.

Five

PROCEED
Cher

*L*ate the next morning, I was leaning over the basin in Ethan's and my bathroom, stroking on waterproof mascara, when my cell on the counter rang.

I looked down at it, and since I'd seen that number before, I knew who it was.

God, my life sucked.

I hit the screen to take Walter Jones's call.

I then immediately hit the screen to hang up.

I went back to stroking on mascara.

The phone rang again.

The motherfucker probably thought he lost connection.

I took the call and then hung up.

He called again.

I engaged and disengaged.

Done playing, I went in, blocked his number, and went back to finishing my makeup.

I walked into J&J's, surprised to see the place was deserted.

Then I saw Feb pop up from behind the bar.

Years ago, when I'd first met her, seeing all that was her did not do good things for my mental health.

There was a reason Dennis Lowe picked me, having obsessed on Feb and Colt since they were all in high school together.

Wanting Feb for his own, he'd found a replacement in me.

In other words, we looked a lot alike.

Obviously, we still did, both of us tall, built, blonde, and brown-eyed.

Though, there was more to it and it was uncanny.

Honest to God, she looked like my older sister.

For obvious reasons, these making me a target of an ax murderer, even when she turned out to be awesome, it had fucked with my head. Lowe had even called me Feb and February, saying it was a nickname because we'd met in that month, but doing it because that was who he saw in me.

He also told me his name was Alexander Colton and he was a cop, not what he was in reality—a geeky software guy who hid the batshit crazy.

Since she and Colt were looking out for me, I covered my reaction to our physical similarities and what that all bought me in my life, burying the wince every time someone said her name.

It took some time, but I finally pulled my head together, twisting my thinking process to what it should be.

Feb was gorgeous. She'd been in her early forties when I met her and was smack in the middle of them now. That shit had not faded. She was the kind of woman men would look at when she was sixty and they'd still think, *oh yeah*.

She also had an edge, like me. Hers had softened over the years since she got Colt back and they had their baby, Jack, but it wasn't totally gone. Lowe had also forced her life on a trajectory where she didn't want to be, and that had started decades ago, so it had lasted a lot longer than mine.

Her edge made her cool, however. It made the sweet she had in her a surprise, which meant it ended up feeling like a gift when she gave that to you.

And if she had all that and kept it, my big sister who wasn't of blood but was of a different variety, it boded well for me in the coming decades.

"Yo," I called.

"Hey," she called back.

I braced for her to start something with me about Merry, but she didn't. This was surprising.

Then again, I was surprised my cell hadn't lit up since Friday, not only from Feb but from all the hens in our coop.

"Darryl was last in last night and he didn't restock. I'm doin' that and takin' stock while I do. Need to get an order in. Can you take care of the bar while I do that? I'll help if things get busy."

Tuesdays during the day at J&J's were the same as Mondays, so watching the bar while Feb did her thing would not be tough.

Even if it was, for her, I'd break my back doing it.

"Sure," I said, heading to the office so I could dump my purse. "And I'll help with the restock."

"That'd be cool."

I went into the office thinking it wasn't surprising Darryl forgot the restock. If he was on alone on a weeknight, shutting down the bar, more often than not he forgot something. The only thing he never forgot to do was securing the money from the register in the safe.

Darryl could forget something you told him two seconds after the words left your mouth.

I didn't think this was because he was stupid (entirely). He was just one of those people who didn't have all their synapses firing. It took patience, but if you had that with him, he got where you needed him to go eventually.

I made it to the office, dumped my purse on the desk, and turned my mind from Darryl to the decision I'd made in my car on the way to work.

After I'd texted Merry last night, he hadn't texted back. With the games we were playing, that could mean anything.

But he seemed entrenched.

As for me, I needed to protect myself, and part of doing that was getting him out of my business, any business I had. To accomplish that, I had to sort out the Trent and Peggy thing, and considering I had a job and a kid, limited money, and no investigative skills, I had to call in help.

If I was going to be facing lawyer fees to keep Ethan, I also had to hoard my cake.

All this led me to one conclusion: I had to find someone who'd do the legwork for me and do it for a price I could afford to pay.

I dug out my phone, scrolled down to that name in my Contacts, and hit CALL.

Ryker answered on the third ring.

"What's goin' on with you and Merrick?" he asked as greeting.

I set my teeth, not surprised Ryker knew something was going on with Merry and me because Merry had dragged me into the office at J&J's. Morrie saw that, probably fifty other people saw that, and no doubt at least forty-eight (if not all fifty-one) of those people were talking about it.

I shared the minimum. "Something happened. One-time thing. We're movin' on."

"One-time thing?"

"One-time thing," I confirmed.

"You stupid?" he asked.

I decided not to answer that or react to it all, but I only decided that because I needed him.

I changed the subject. "I got a situation."

"No shit?" he told me.

Thinking he still was referring to what he didn't really know was going on between Merry and me, something I was done talking about, not to mention I had to get out and help Feb, I kept our conversation firm where I wanted it to be.

"Listen, I need a favor," I said.

"I play, you pay," he replied.

This was not a surprise. Ryker did nothing for nothing. You always paid. But I was speaking to him because he had three options he accepted for compensation: you owed him a marker, you gave him information, or you gave him money.

There was no marker he'd be willing to hold from me. And I didn't want to spend the money on an investigator, not one as good (or expensive) as Tanner Layne, not one who was probably shit but less expensive, and not Ryker.

But I worked at a bar and Ryker dealt in a lot of currencies, information being one that for him was most lucrative.

"My ex and his wife are making rumblings they might wanna take my boy from me," I shared.

"Sucks, sister," he muttered but didn't jump in to offer services for free.

"They may be happy just to negotiate more time with him. Before I sit down and do that, I wanna know, they get that time, he's goin' to good people. I need you to help me on that. And as a down payment to that shit, I'll tell you the renters two doors down from my place had a short but loud conversation I overheard and the name Carlito was mentioned."

I didn't know if Ryker had any interest in Carlito.

I just knew that Ryker had interest in anything, specific things being worth more, and those specific things he took an interest in was the kind of guy Carlito was.

Ryker was silent.

I opened my mouth to speak.

"*You at the bar?*" he barked, his tone so loud and severe, I automatically jerked the phone an inch from my ear.

I felt nastiness slithering up my neck into my scalp at the sudden extreme Ryker was aiming at me.

"Yeah," I answered hesitantly.

I got nothing in reply.

"Ryker?" I called but heard beeping, telling me the call ended.

I stared at my phone for a second, went to recent calls, and called him again.

He didn't answer.

Shit, that was not good.

I left a voicemail of "Call me," stowed my purse, shoved my phone in my back pocket, and headed out to help Feb.

"You need me to get anything from the storeroom?" I asked over the bar she was hunkered down behind.

"Took stock and grabbed everything I needed. Just gotta rotate it."

I went behind the bar.

There were four fridges back there. She was at fridge two.

I went to fridge three and dragged one of the boxes she'd filled toward me.

"Heard you took care of Merry after the Mia news made the rounds," she remarked casually.

Lying in wait.

Shit.

I knew I wouldn't get away with it. She was my big sister in *a lot* of ways.

I opened the fridge and pulled out the front bottles of Bud.

"Yep," I confirmed.

"That go okay?" she asked.

I looked to her. "We got drunk. We fucked. Shit got wrinkled. We're ironing it out."

Her eyes got big at the *we fucked*, but I ignored that and went back to the fridge.

"You two ironing it out…is that working?" she asked.

"Yeah," I answered her question, unsure if it was a lie, a semi-lie, or what I hoped it would be—the truth.

"Cher," she called.

I turned my eyes to her and there it was all over her face—that sweet that rode close to her edge, easy to get to if she gave a shit about you.

"It's cool," I assured.

"Shit like that goes down, a girl can get ideas."

I grinned and did it to hide the pain. I was good at it, so I was relatively certain she bought it.

"Not a girl like me."

The sweet didn't move from her expression. It also didn't hide the concern that started seeping in.

I twisted on the balls of my feet to give her my full attention.

"Listen, Feb, he's in love with another woman."

"I know that," she replied, the absoluteness of her words driving that thorn deeper. "I just don't want you to get hurt while he's workin' through that. And I know Merry's a good guy, but even good guys do stupid shit when they're workin' through hurt like that, as evidenced by the pile of stupid shit he's amassed while doin' just that for the last however-many years."

"I know the score," I told her, something she had to know.

It seemed she didn't when little wrinkles appeared between her brows and her head tipped to the side.

"What's the score?"

"He'll work through it, just not with me," I said the last quickly to reassure her. "He got what he's gonna get from me on that. And it was good, Feb. He needed it, and it was far from shit bein' there to give it to him. But that's done. If we can iron things out, we'll get back to what we had, keep that, and I'll be happy when he finds what he needs to get happy."

She didn't believe me and didn't hide the fact she didn't. It was right there with the sweet, the gentle, the concern.

She knew.

She knew I was in deep with Merry.

There was a lot I'd share with Feb, lay on her, lean on her to help me work it through, bitch at her just so I could get it out. Anything. Practically everything.

But not that.

"It's gonna be okay," I declared, doing it with finality so we could stop talking about it.

She nodded, hearing my tone, knowing what I needed and, being Feb, giving it to me.

With me helping, it didn't take long to finish the restock. When we were done, she grabbed the empty boxes and headed to the back to finish the stock take.

I went to the front to unlock the door.

I hadn't yet fully made it down the bar to round it when the door opened.

I turned and stopped when I saw Ryker prowling in, his eyes clamped on me, his big, motorcycle-booted feet bearing down on me.

The vision of this from Ryker would likely scare ninety-nine percent of the human population straight to the point of wetting themselves.

This was because he was huge. He was also wearing a black tank stretched across a massive chest, a black leather jacket hanging from his extensive shoulders, this hiding the two sleeves of tattoos adorning his arms. He had a large, lethal-looking knife sheathed at the side of his belt. He was bald and many would think he was ugly.

I was not a woman who thought that. Rough, tough, and scary didn't turn me off, and a man did not have to be conventionally attractive to get my attention.

Just looking at him, I knew Ryker could be a monster in bed and be that in a bad way.

He could be the same in a very, *very* good way.

Or he could shock the shit out of you and be all about you in gentle ways that blew your mind.

I suspected, depending on his mood, he was both of the last two. I suspected this because I knew Lissa, his woman.

She was a good woman, a hardworking one, a kind one, and not a stupid one. She would no sooner glance Ryker's way again if he didn't treat her right than she'd do harm to the daughter she adored. Definitely not have him in her bed and keep him there.

I also knew all about Ryker, including the fact he'd put a ring on Lissa's finger and officially adopted Lissa's girl, Alexis.

He loved his girls. And when the unimaginable threatened the 'burg and Alexis got caught up in it, nearly had her world obliterated by it, Ryker didn't hesitate after he went all out to make sure she was safe. He claimed both her and her mother, officially and legally, and covered them in his considerable protection.

So no, even if the man looked like a lunatic, he didn't scare me because he didn't hide who he really was, and the way he looked after the women under his roof said it all.

I put my hands on my hips and snapped, "You hung up on me."

I held my ground even as he got toe to toe to me, bowed his back, and put his mug right into mine.

"You did not hear whatever you heard from your neighbors," he growled.

My blood ran cold.

"And from here on out, woman, you do not even fuckin' *look* in the direction of that house. It does not exist for you. The people in it do not exist for you. You don't let your boy anywhere near that house or the people in it. Are you hearing me?"

Jesus, what was going on?

"Ryker—"

He got closer and his nose brushed mine when he barked, "*Are you hearing me?*"

"I'm hearing you, brother. Stand down."

He didn't stand down, but he did edge his face away half an inch.

"And you don't mention that shit to anyone, Cher. Not a fuckin' soul. Not Colt. Not Sully. Not pillow talk with Merry."

At the *pillow talk* comment, I screwed up my eyes at him. "Back off, Ryker. Now."

"I'm tellin' you 'cause you're one of the ten people I actually like in this world, do not say a *motherfucking* word."

"What's going on?" I asked sharply.

"That's not for you to know. You're smart, sister. Stay smart, keep yourself to yourself, and your mouth *shut.*"

"Jesus, Ryker, okay," I replied.

He scowled at me and I endured it, not happy at all with this turn of events.

Finally, he moved away, heading toward the door.

He stopped at it, hand on the handle, and turned back to me.

"Just so you know, we got you covered. Tanner briefed me. I'm all over the church lady," he shared.

My body locked in order to battle the sudden burn engulfing it.

His mood shifted and he grinned his maniacal grin.

"And just to weigh in, I'm feelin' all rosy, Merrick finally got his head screwed on straight and turned his eye to a decent woman worth his attention. Lissa's beside herself. She's been sayin' for years, he just shook off the ghost of that bitch, he'd see what's in front of his face. Good he finally took off the blinders that stupid twat locked on and looked. But this 'one-time thing' is fucked up, sister. Advice? Hook that boy. Sink those claws in deep."

And with that, he lifted a long-fingered, veined, humongous hand, gave me a salute, and disappeared behind the door.

His last declaration was lost on me.

The one before it had all my attention.

Tanner briefed me. I'm all over the church lady.

Tanner briefed me...

Tanner...

Merry had shared. Merry had promised right to my face he wouldn't tell a soul, and *he'd shared.* He'd told Tanner. Tanner had enlisted Ryker. Now they all knew and they were all up in my shit.

With intent, not allowing myself a moment to think better of it, I reached back and yanked out my phone.

I was shaking, I was so pissed, but I still managed to fire it up and get to my texts.

I found Merry, my last text to him hovering unanswered on the string.

Using both my thumbs, they flew over the screen.

Talked to Ryker. He's been briefed by Tanner. He's all over the church lady.

I was so pissed, I hit SEND before I was done.

That means you broke your promise to me. Right to my face, you promised. You lied.

I hit SEND again, even though I was still far from done.

You know what that means, Merry. You shared my shit. That means we're over in every way we can be over.

I hit SEND right when my phone started ringing.

I declined the call and finished up.

DONE, I typed and sent, my phone telling me that Merry was calling again. I declined that too.

Then I went in and blocked a second number that day.

I shoved my phone in my pocket and, with wooden movements, walked on my spike heels around the bar.

The door opened and our first customer came in.

That meant I did one of the few things I was really good at doing.

I hid the shit of my life, burying it down deep, plastered a cocky smile on my face, and called out a greeting.

Garrett

Garrett took the steps up to Tanner's office two at a time.

He slammed the door at the top, entering the reception area, and stalked to Tanner's office off the side.

His friend was standing by his desk, his eyes narrowed and on Garrett the minute he cleared the inner door.

"Jesus, brother, like that door the way it is. What the fuck?" he asked irately.

"Set Ryker on Cher's shit," Garrett ground out.

Tanner's chin jerked back before he confirmed, "Yeah. The deal I was workin' with him got sorted this weekend. Like Ryker, next day he comes in bitchin' about bein' bored. Learned things can be not good if he doesn't have some action, seein' as he's got no problem drummin' up action, and I don't have any action that I can involve him in. So I set him on Cher's shit."

Garrett lifted a hand and jabbed a finger Tanner's way, not giving that first shit that his friend's face changed, showing exactly how much he didn't like that.

"Told you, *brother*, you kept your mouth shut about that," he reminded him, dropping his hand.

"And I told Ryker to keep it quiet," Tanner returned.

"Well, he didn't. He told Cher about it."

Tanner's head twitched, his mouth set, then he forced through his lips, "Fuck, told him to keep quiet. Didn't tell him to keep it quiet from Cher. He probably thought she knew we were workin' it for her."

"Well, she knows now," Garrett pointed out.

Tanner focused more fully on him. "She pissed?"

Garrett spoke low, giving his understatement. "Oh yeah, big man, she's pissed."

Tanner folded his arms on his chest. "Talk to her, Merry. I know she's stubborn and wants it clear to anyone who might get close that she can look after herself, but bottom line, we give a shit about her and wanna help. She's gotta have it in her to see it that way eventually and settle in."

"You don't know Cher," Garrett shot back.

Tanner tipped his head to the side. "I do. Not as good as you, but I do. Though, I'll listen you wanna give it to me why you're all of a sudden so into her space, she throws a fit about people she doesn't want bein' in her shit, you're slammin' into my office to get in my face about it."

"I made a promise to her when I found out she had issues that I wouldn't share. I broke that promise for a good reason, but I did it thinkin' the man I broke it with would have my back on that and, by extension, hers. He didn't, and it isn't you who's gonna pay that price, Tanner. It's me."

Tanner's voice quieted when he asked, "What's the price, Garrett?"

"She and I are over."

His brother-in-law's brows flew up. "There was a Cher and you?"

Already pissed, Tanner's question made him more pissed because Garrett didn't buy his shit. From Darryl leaving Cher with him Friday night to Garrett strong-arming Cher into the office at J&J's on Sunday, word was flying around the 'burg. If Tanner hadn't heard it directly, Rocky heard it at work or Ryker had heard it, and one, the other, or both of them had shared.

"You been livin' in a hole since last Friday?" he fired back sarcastically.

"Rumor is flyin' but not confirmed," Tanner told him, finishing, "until just now." His gaze stayed intent. "You wanna share where that's at?"

"Right now, it's not anywhere, seein' as Ryker shot off his mouth and by that, Tanner, I mean the woman is done. I told you she was there when I was dealin' with the finality of losin' Mia, and she was there in a way that left somethin' to explore. I was makin' no headway with that but you are in the know that she means something to me, we're tight, and with Ryker's play today, that's gone. She's done with us any way she *can* be done."

"You were tryin' to make headway?" Tanner cautiously pushed.

"Fuck, you seen the Cher we're talkin' about?" Garrett asked.

Tanner grinned and mumbled, "Yeah."

Yeah.

Not a lot of men would look at the kind of pretty Cher Rivers had and not feel it somewhere, primarily in their dicks. Took a certain kind of man to see the barbs she surrounded herself with and give it a go. But there weren't many who wouldn't take it if a miracle occurred and she gave them a shot.

Tanner wouldn't take it because he had a wife, kids, and a happy life he worked hard to get.

But that didn't mean he didn't appreciate a good view.

"That's the package, Tanner. Found Friday night, wrapped up under it, what she's got blows the mind. I don't mean just the fact the woman is fuckin' outstanding in bed. You get that *with* the attitude, her sense of humor, and Christ, never laughed so hard with another being, man *or* woman. All that comes with her brand of loyal and protective, which is sharp, but that edge hides a warm so warm, you got hold on that, you'll never be cold."

"Jesus, Merry," Tanner murmured.

"Now," Garrett kept on, crossing his arms on his chest, "not lost on anyone in this 'burg, especially the ones with a vagina, any woman who gets my attention after Mia made the finality of our final obvious by accepting

96

another man's ring, that woman would be a rebound. And straight up, that's what I thought had happened with Cher the morning after. I needed to let go and she gave me that opportunity. Then I found she had a situation, and my reaction to that bore contemplation. I contemplated."

"And you wanna explore," Tanner surmised.

"I did. She doesn't. She's certain she's a rebound fuck, and she's certain of a lotta other things she was tryin' to convince me about in a way I knew I had my work cut out for me. One thing I knew, the way things are with me and the way she just fuckin' is, I could make no promises I couldn't keep. Not for her, so she didn't get in too deep. Not for her kid, who she isn't gonna drag into another situation that might go south. The last man she let in, turned out he was as bad as it gets. She doesn't need another man to make promises and shit all over her. But in all that, I'd made a promise. One promise. I broke it for a reason. Now she *really* doesn't wanna explore."

"I had no idea about any of this shit, brother, or my brief with Ryker would have gone different," Tanner told him. "I didn't expect he'd say shit anyway, but you know I wouldn't lay you out like that if I knew where your head was at with Cher."

Garrett drew a breath in through his nose and looked out the window.

"You really over Mia?" Tanner asked quietly.

Garrett turned his gaze back to him. "It's an uncomfortable feeling, kickin' your own ass for years, knowin' you let go the only woman you loved and knowin' you should've pulled out all the stops to get her back, then switchin' that on a dime to kickin' your own ass when you realize she wasn't worth that emotion."

"Yeah, I get that. That's a major shift, Merry. And, not tellin' you somethin' you don't know but gonna say it anyway 'cause it's important, you gotta *know* you made that shift before you explore dick with Cher Rivers."

Garrett locked eyes with his friend. "Happily stand at the town limits and wave the woman on her way to Bloomington. I'm dead serious about that. Our end did not happen Friday night. Our end happened five years ago. I drew out the grief of that, with her stringin' me along in ways I never shared because that was mine and hers. Seein' it through different eyes now, though, it wasn't mine and hers. It was hers, and it was shit."

"Stringin' you along?" Tanner asked.

"Mia likes games. Blinded by my feelings for her, never saw it for what it was, but she likes games," Garrett told him and watched Tanner's jaw go hard.

He wasn't a big fan of secrets between family or friends, but on this, he had to suck it up. Until Garrett wanted to make info like this Tanner's business, it wasn't.

Which meant only now, sharing this info about Mia was his business.

"Since Friday, had time to think about it," Garrett went on. "And what I think is that I held on to what I had with her so I wouldn't be open to what I *could* have with someone who didn't get off on yankin' my chain."

"Yankin' your chain?" Tanner prompted.

"We're not talkin' about Mia now," Garrett told him. "Time I gave her is done."

"Okay, brother. I hear you," Tanner muttered, then he asked, "You think you're where you need to be now?"

Garrett shook his head. "No clue. I just know I'm not where I used to be."

Tanner nodded. "Then you know—*you* of all people know, Garrett— from what didn't go down with Mia that turned out right to what you encouraged to go down with me and your sister, you know the way it is. And you know you gotta do one thing." He hesitated, drew in breath, and finished, "Proceed."

Garrett had given Tanner that same advice, and the road was bumpy, but the results were worth it.

Fuck.

The anger slid out of him, but it left frustration behind.

"Ryker made a difficult job a lot harder today, big man," Garrett pointed out.

"Dig deep and decide if it's worth the effort, Garrett. You make the decision—cut her loose or make that effort. Only you can decide," Tanner replied, then shook his head. "That last isn't true. She's a good woman. It's worth the effort. You wouldn't charge in here, pissed as shit, if you didn't know it. You just gotta know, for her sake and for her kid's, that your shit's together before you go for it."

Garrett drew in another breath, dropped his arms, and lifted his chin.

His message relayed about Ryker, with no reason to be pissed other than being pissed at himself, a ton of work on his desk, and a new problem with Cher to sort, he had no purpose being there.

"Gotta get back to the station," he muttered.

"On your walk, think about how Cher had occasion to have a chat with Ryker."

Garrett's attention turned acute on Tanner.

It came to him and he whispered, "Fuck."

Tanner laid out the realization that belatedly hit him.

"What I heard just now from you, she's thrown up her shields, fightin' you off. She knows you're diggin' in with her shit and she might've been lookin' for reinforcements to help her out with that so she could untangle you from it. So she's got no call to be pissed Ryker knew when she was gonna tell him herself."

Garrett grinned at his brother-in-law.

Tanner grinned back.

"Thanks, buddy," he muttered.

"Don't mention it," Tanner replied, turning toward his desk.

Garrett moved toward the door.

He stopped when Tanner called, "Merry."

He looked back to see the man sitting behind his desk.

"Rumors fly. Don't wanna piss you off, but just sayin', before some asshole asks and earns your fist in his face, and straight up, 'cause I'm curious, gotta know so I can shut it down before it blows: Word is, that rack she's got isn't all hers."

"Lots of gifts God gave Cher she doesn't recognize, that's one of them. If it isn't, her surgeon was a master. But, big man, if Cher ever had money to blow on somethin', she'd use it to give good to her boy. She wouldn't use it to get her tits done."

Tanner grinned again. "I'll take that to mean it's all hers."

"Don't give a fuck how you take it," Garrett told him. "Cher and me ever get down to sharin' medical histories, that in itself would be cause for celebration considerin' how things are right now. But, seein' as it's no one's business, you can warn every fuck who might open their trap to me or her about it to keep it shut or they won't be able to open it since their jaw'll be wired shut."

Tanner didn't miss a beat before he stated, "I'll take that as you already havin' your shit together about Cher Rivers."

Garrett shook his head and muttered, "Whatever."

He turned to leave again when Tanner called his name again.

He looked back.

"Jesus, brother, *what?*" he asked.

He asked it before he caught the look on Tanner's face.

He braced when he caught that look.

"It'd be good to see you happy. It'd be good to see you give what you got to give to a woman who deserves to get it. And it'd be good Cher's son has a man in his life who isn't an ex-junkie but is a staple and can offer him a shitload of things he needs to grow up and be a good man. That might not be the end for the three of you. But if it is, man, I'll be happy for you."

Garrett fought back clearing his throat before he asked, "You done?"

Tanner grinned yet again. "Yep."

"Rocky's made you soft," he returned.

"That is one thing your sister has never made me."

Garrett felt his lip curl. "Christ."

Tanner burst out laughing.

Not even close to that mood, Garrett muttered, "Later," and took off.

Cher

After my shift, I left out the back door with Darryl opening it for me to keep an eye on me on the way to my car (like he always did, or Morrie did, or Jack did).

I moved down the alley toward my Equinox.

I heard the door close and it did this earlier than Darryl would normally do it.

I knew why.

"Goddamned shit," I muttered under my breath, seeing Merry leaning against my driver's side door, his Excursion pulled in against the wall in front of my Chevy.

He didn't move as my heels clicked their pissed off staccato on the pavement. He just watched me come to him, ankles crossed, arms folded on his chest.

Shit, it totally, seriously *sucked* he was so hot.

I was five feet away when I snapped my question, "You lose the ability to read?"

The left side of Merry's lips curled up, but that was the only movement he made.

Asshole.

I stopped three feet in front of him.

"Move out of my way, Garrett," I ordered.

"So," Merry said softly, "considering Tanner set Ryker on your church lady, meaning he had things to do, I'm guessin' Ryker wasn't in J&J's to shoot the shit over a beer at high noon."

Oh fuck.

He'd figured it out.

How much—in other words, the Carlito business—I didn't know.

I kept silent.

Merry felt chatty.

"I'm guessin', in an effort to convince yourself of the bullshit you're tryin' to convince me of—that you're happy spinnin' your wheels, lettin' Denny Lowe interrupt your life for good and hunkerin' down in that fortress of yours until the day you quit breathin'—you made a call to the only man you know who could help you out and collect on his debt in a way you could pay."

How I got taken in by Denny Lowe telling me that he was a cop, I had no idea. Lowe might have had computer smarts and criminally lunatic genius that kept him free to chop his way through half the United States of America, but he was no cop.

Cops were far more intuitive and it took them no time at all to connect dots.

Then again, back then, I didn't know any cops.

Now I did.

Which meant I should have known *better.*

Crap.

"Move out of my way," I repeated.

"So," Merry said, "you were good to let him in on what was goin' down with you. And since you know Ryker's history and your shit involves shit that might be happenin' in a church, you knew you'd get him fired up. And since you are far from stupid and know how tight Ryker is with Tanner, firing Ryker up, you'd put it together that he'd throw every resource he had at gettin' what you need. So he'd fill in Tanner."

To be honest, I wasn't as smart as Merry thought. I didn't forget that the horrors that almost happened to Ryker's Alexis had originated when a con man infiltrated the Christian church in order to recruit girls for hideously nefarious ends. I just didn't put it together that if I mentioned a church being involved, Ryker would go all out. The only thing I was thinking was that I didn't have to ask for a favor I couldn't really repay.

He could scratch my back, I could scratch his.

I didn't share my train of thought with Merry.

I demanded yet again, "Move out of my way."

Merry didn't move out of my way.

He kept going.

"Which means you were good with sharin' your shit with Ryker and, by extension, Tanner."

That was enough.

"Yeah," I bit out. "*I* was. *I* was good with sharin' *my* shit with whoever I wanted. What I was *not* good with was *you* decidin' who to share *my* shit with, and I did not hide that from you, Garrett. I told you straight up the way it was gonna go. You made me a promise and you broke it knowin' the consequences. Now move...outta...*my way.*"

"You're right, I broke that promise. So, honey, now you gotta know just how pissed at me you should be, 'cause Ryker got a smell of somethin' he didn't like and it was somethin' he couldn't sniff out fully. So he pulled in Devin, and Devin decided he had to pull in Vera to get the job done right."

Devin was not only the crotchety, old-guy member of Tanner Layne's ragtag team of crazy people investigators, he was also Tanner's father-in-law, recently married to Tanner's mom, Vera.

In other words, as I suspected, Merry shared and my shit had spread, and it had done this *wide*.

In that moment, it occurred to me for the first time in ages that alley had seen the grisly murder of a woman who'd caught the edge of Dennis Lowe's ax.

So it was too bad someone was going to have to hose down the skull and brain fragments of my head exploding.

When this didn't happen instantaneously, I was able to force out, "Say *what?*"

Merry ignored my question.

"Now, diggin' deeper, Ryker got to the bottom and surface proved true—Faith Saves is what it is," he told me. "They got a mission, and while it might be irritating to some, they just wanna do good, even if not everyone agrees with how they're goin' about it."

Since I clearly had no other choice but to hear him out (because he wasn't giving me one), I planted my hands on my hips, beat back the urge to attack him with my purse, and settled in.

"I was also right about the fact that's where Peggy met Trent. They got to talkin' outside an NA meeting and things went on from there," he shared.

"Fascinating," I said acidly when he quit talking.

That left side of his mouth curved up again, but then his humor disappeared entirely in a way that I was no longer settled in.

I was worried.

"And you were right, sweetheart," he said softly. "She wants Ethan."

I swallowed, getting the sense that wasn't all of it.

I was right.

Merry kept speaking softly.

"Feelin' safe, sittin' in a park while her daughter's playin', cuddlin' her son, a nice, chatty lady sits with her, cuddlin' her grandbaby, Peggy Schott let fly. They got a problem with gettin' her husband's kid from his momma 'cause they don't have any money. Trent makes shit, so she's got a job that helps out but not much. She wants to be home full-time for her babies and so she can begin the work of raisin' her man's son right."

His last words were sticking in my craw, choking me, when finally he pushed away from the door of my car, but not to let me get to it.

To get close because he was going to lower the boom.

I stared up at him, heart slamming against my ribs, and waited for the blow to land.

"She's prayed to God to find the answer, brown eyes," he said carefully. "And according to her, He's given her the answer. She's got lotsa help back home with a big family, brothers and sisters, mom and dad, aunts and uncles. That means they just gotta find a way to get her man's boy away from his momma. Then they can take him down to Missouri, her family can find her husband a job, and she can stay at home, raisin' her brood in the God-fearin' manner they need."

"Fuck," I whispered.

"Do not send your boy to them, Cher," Merry whispered back. "Vera did not get good vibes from this woman. She's determined and she might not do what she feels she needs to do in a legal way. She might grab your boy, pack up her family, and *go*."

My legs were trembling, as was my repeated, "Fuck."

"Now, I know you're pissed at me," Merry said quietly. "And I know you got reason. I also know right now we got that, and if you'd waited to call Ryker in on it today and shackled him by not lettin' him gather the team the way it was needed, we wouldn't have it. Not ever. So I hope you got it in you to get past bein' pissed, because you know I did the right thing for you and Ethan."

I wanted to pull the anger around me to hold Merry back, but I didn't have it in me to do that while fighting back the fear.

I didn't know what to do.

Should I share this with Ethan? Should I break his heart that two people he'd come to care about, family he thought was his and would be forever, were plotting to take him away from me?

Should I get an attorney and confront Peggy and Trent with what I knew and warn them to back off? Negotiate something that would work for all of us, especially Ethan, in a way that was healthy?

And truthfully, was Peggy Schott even healthy? Did she know the God who was "giving her the answers" wasn't what it actually was, her deciding the way things needed to be?

Or should I sit down with Colt, report this, and ask for protection so nothing would happen to my son, and if it did, they'd know right where to look?

(Though, Merry already knew, so that last was rhetorical.)

"Cher," Merry called as his phone rang.

I realized I was looking at him but not seeing him. I focused to watch him pull his phone out of his back pocket.

Distractedly, I noted that since the last time I'd seen his phone, the screen had cracked.

"Shit," he muttered, sliding his finger on the cracked screen and looking at me. "Gotta take this, baby."

I didn't say anything. I might be focused on him, but my mind was still clogged with everything he'd told me.

"Merrick," he said into his phone.

My mind cleared when what was coming off him slammed into me in a way it was a wonder my body didn't jerk.

"*Where?*" he barked ferociously. "When?" he asked, only a little less sharply. But his voice deteriorated significantly when he asked, "How long?"

He listened. I watched him do it.

Then he said, "Fuck. I'm with Cher. I get her and Ethan sorted, I'm there."

He took his phone from his ear and ordered tersely, "In your car. I'm followin' you to your mom's, then I'm followin' you and Ethan home."

Oh no.

What now?

"What's goin' on?" I asked.

"In your car, Cher," he commanded, then moved. Starting in a prowl that fed into a jog, he went to his truck.

Sensing I needed to do what he told me to do, though I'd do that anyway because I needed to go get my kid, I got in my car.

I pulled out and headed down the alley. Merry's lights already on, he pulled out right on my ass.

He stayed on my ass all the way to Mom's.

I jumped down from my car and he was at my side.

"Merry, what's goin' on?" I snapped, hiding anxiety behind anger as he took my hand and yanked me toward the hood of my car, his attention not on me but on the night.

That was not good.

"Let's get inside," he ordered.

"Merry—"

He looked down at me, his face set in stone. "Fast."

Fuck, fuck…*shit.*

We got inside, fast, but I didn't have a choice since Merry all but dragged me there.

By the time he closed the front door, Merry had rearranged his features, but not by much.

Mom took one look at us and came right off the couch, face lighting up, mouth smiling, eyes darting to Merry, Merry's hand in mine, to me, then back to Merry.

"Well, Garrett, this is a lovely surprise," she declared.

"Yo! Merry!" Ethan greeted, jumping up from an armchair, his face just as surprised and excited as his gramma's.

"Grace," Merry muttered to my mom, letting me go to move in, bend down, and touch his cheek to Mom's. He turned to Ethan and stuck out a hand. "Hey, man."

Ethan stared up at him, his excitement at seeing his cool, grown-up, badass friend fading as he took in Merry's manner and he also stuck out his hand.

Merry shook it like they were adults and let him go.

Then he looked to Mom. "Grace, gonna get Cher and Ethan home, but before I do that, me and Ethan are gonna walk through your house, make sure windows and doors are locked. You got a back door light?"

Mom was also cottoning on to Merry's look and demeanor, so she just nodded.

Merry looked down to Ethan. "Check windows, buddy. I'll do the back door."

I knew Ethan wanted to ask. I also knew Ethan was a good kid. So, being a good kid, he didn't waste time asking. He took off to check windows.

"All my windows are locked, Garrett," Mom told him.

Merry turned back to her. "Let's just make sure."

106

He didn't even finish saying that before he moved toward the kitchen.

I made my way through the living room, pushing curtains aside and checking windows.

By the time Merry got back, I was done and Ethan was coming back into the room.

"Get your stuff, Ethan. We gotta get you home," Merry ordered.

Ethan went directly to his backpack by the armchair.

Merry looked to Mom. "Your front light is on, Grace. Keep it on. Okay?"

"What's goin' on?" she whispered, hands up at her chest, one folded over the other.

"I don't wanna alarm you but want you to be smart and safe." He looked to me. "You too, sweetheart." His eyes went back to Mom. "Man tried to rob the Shell station. He took off, evading officers. There was gunplay. He's armed and on foot. Men are huntin' him and I need to get in that hunt. But he was last seen in the backyard of a house on Fontaine."

Mom gasped.

Ethan's eyes shot to me.

I clenched my teeth.

Fontaine Street was two blocks from my fucking street, which was mere blocks away from Mom's fucking house.

"Should I warn my neighbors?" Mom asked.

"No need to alarm anyone, Grace," Merry told her. "But I want you to keep your lights on, curtains closed, doors locked. In this situation, a runner shies from light. He'll keep to the dark."

"I...okay," she nodded.

"We gotta go," Merry said.

Mom kept nodding.

Merry looked to me and jerked his chin to the door. "Hoof it, Cher. You and Ethan get in your car, lock it."

That was when I nodded.

I forced a grin at Mom, reached out, grabbed her hand, and gave it a quick squeeze.

"Be careful, Garrett," she called after us as we headed to the door.

"Will do," he muttered, moving behind Ethan and me, crowding us both.

I separated from my kid at the passenger side door but only because Merry was there, holding it as Ethan got in.

Demonstrating possible superhero powers, even after waiting for Ethan to pull himself in and close the door behind him, Merry still got around to my side and had his hand to my door by the time I'd hauled my ass to my seat.

"Lock," he growled, slammed the door and jogged to his truck parked behind us.

I locked the doors and put the key in the ignition, eyes to the rearview mirror, asking, "You okay, kid?"

"Merry and Colt and Sul and Mike'll get 'im," Ethan declared casually.

I glanced at him.

The cab was filled with the light from Merry's headlights.

"Go, Mom. Merry needs to get out there," Ethan ordered.

Shit, exactly when did my little man grow up?

I put the car in gear and went.

There was a repeat of what happened at Mom's when we got to my place, including Merry taking my hand as he rushed me and Ethan to the house.

Ethan and I checked the windows. Merry walked around, turning on lights, inside and all the ones I had out, and he did this also checking windows and doors.

This didn't take long before he was at the front door, ready to roll.

"Gotta go," he stated and ordered, "Lights on all night, Cher."

I nodded but moved quick when it seemed he was going to take off.

I caught his hand.

He looked down at me.

I repeated Mom's words quietly, but mine were shaking.

"Be careful, Garrett."

He held my eyes, looking like he was going to say something or do something.

He checked it and whispered, "I will, baby."

He gave my hand a squeeze.

Then he was gone.

Six

ETERNITY
Cher

I sat curled up on my couch.

The front light was on. The side light was on. The back light was on. The kitchen lights were blazing. And I'd left a lamp on in my bedroom.

The first time I'd checked, Ethan was in bed but awake. Same for the second and third.

The last, he was out.

So it was late, just me on my couch, the gun I'd bought the day after I hightailed my and Ethan's asses to Ohio when I found out who Lowe actually was was on the seat of the couch by my toes.

My phone was in my hand.

Obviously, I'd unblocked Merry.

And I'd opened my curtains, just a couple of inches, so I could see out.

As I watched, to occupy my mind, I found it fascinating in a vague way that our street went dead after midnight on a weeknight. Completely dead. No cars at all.

I also thought on the fact that I was lucky to have the next day off, since right then I was wide awake and in it for the long haul.

I hoped Merry would think of me and text or phone to tell me things were okay, they got the guy, he and all the boys and girls who worked at the station were all good.

But I was where I was only partly due to that.

Mostly, a man was out there who was desperate enough to rob a gas station (for fuck's sake) and, in more desperation, engage in gunplay with cops. He'd been seen in my 'hood. And my boy had only me to make sure we stayed safe.

So I was on my couch, awake, on the lookout, my son asleep, my gun close.

I caught light reflecting on the quiet, dark houses across the street and looked from the window across the room to my cable box.

It was one thirteen in the morning.

Maybe a neighbor just got off a late shift.

My back went straight when I found it wasn't a neighbor but instead Merry's Excursion pulling to a stop in front of my house.

Okay, I'd hoped he'd call or text.

But him showing in person was way better.

I jumped off the couch but kept an eye on him and saw him get out of his truck and round the hood.

I'd noted long ago the chief of police had no dress code for his detectives. Some, like Colt, wore jeans and sports jackets, making both look nice and professional just because he had that ability. Others wore nice slacks and jackets.

Merry wore suits, no ties. His suits were nice. They fit him well. They always complimented his coloring. They made the statement he took his job seriously. Even though he wore them extremely well, what they didn't do was make the statement that he was up his own ass and knew how hot he was.

And earlier, he'd been in one of them, a dark gray one with a midnight-blue shirt that didn't do much for him in the muted light of an alley, but I'd seen him in that combo before, and with good lighting, the shirt specifically did fabulous things for his eyes.

Now he was not in that suit.

He was in jeans, boots, a button-up shirt, and a leather jacket.

Apparently, you didn't go man hunting all dressed up.

I filed this away with the other useless but interesting information in my brain and headed to my door.

I had it unlocked and opened, the storm door the same, and I was holding it slightly ajar with my hand by the time Merry made it to my stoop.

Eyes to me, he pulled it all the way open.

I didn't hesitate to shift back.

He didn't hesitate to walk right in.

He kept his fingers splayed on the glass of the door to soften the noise it'd make in closing. Once it clicked, he turned his head so he could pay attention while he locked it.

I shuffled back further to give him room to clear, close, and lock the front door.

He did this and turned to me, dipping his chin down.

"They get him?" I whispered.

"Yeah. Marty tackled him behind the Dairy Queen."

Something about this made me want to laugh.

I didn't laugh.

I asked, "Everyone okay?"

"It's all good, sweetheart."

I nodded, letting the tension ebb out of me.

In the subdued light that stretched from the kitchen, I saw him look toward the hall.

His gaze came back to me. "Ethan asleep?"

I nodded again. "Had trouble findin' it, but he got there."

"Good," he muttered.

I stood there and Merry stood there. I stared up at him as his eyes moved over my face.

Then he looked over my head into the room as he asked, "You get any rest at all?"

"No."

His head jerked slightly and his eyes cut back to me.

"Please, fuck, baby, tell me that piece is registered."

"I bought it in Ohio."

His mouth got tight.

Ohio liked their guns and the easy ability of people owning them, and Merry obviously knew that fact.

"And, uh...Colt told me as long as I don't carry it, I'm good."

"Colt knows you got it?"

I nodded.

"He show you how to use it?"

I shook my head.

His mouth got tight again.

"Jack showed me," I shared quickly.

He sighed.

Suddenly it dawned on me this was weird, precisely the fact he was there at all.

"Are *you* okay?" I asked.

"No," he answered.

"Shit, what happened?" I asked, moving closer.

"What happened is, I got a call that reported an armed man was at large within blocks of your mom and your boy."

Oh God. Oh shit.

Damn it, Merry.

Automatically, I moved closer, putting my hand to his stomach.

"Merry," I whispered. Just that. I didn't know what else to say.

"Spending the night, Cher."

I felt my eyes get big at this declaration, but I didn't speak or move.

"With you in your bed."

Oh God.

"And if you don't lock that handgun away when you're not sittin' vigil to look after your kid, we'll be goin' to sleep after I make your ass red for bein' all kinds of stupid."

I felt my eyes get squinty and I spoke then. I also stepped back.

"You think I'd have an unsecured firearm in my home with my kid?" I snapped.

"Lock it up. You don't need yours out when I got mine."

Okay, we were back on rocky ground.

"Merry, I—"

Abruptly, he moved. Hooking me at the back of my head, his face was in mine, and at what I saw in his eyes, I stopped speaking and concentrated on breathing.

"Shut your mouth. Get your piece. Lock it up. And come to bed."

"I'm not real sure what's goin' on right now, gorgeous," I said carefully. "But my boy's in this house and—"

"What's goin' on," he cut me off to start and he didn't let up, "is tonight, you learn you got a man who gives a shit in your life, shit goes down in the night that more than likely would never touch you, but it's still goin' down and we both know shit happens, you don't sleep alone. You don't because he doesn't sleep alone. He sleeps where he knows you're safe. So get your fuckin' gun. Lock that fucker up. And come to bed."

I liked that. I wanted that. I wanted to learn that in a way it sunk so deep, I wouldn't even remember there being a time when I didn't have it.

And none of that was smart.

"Merry—"

"Now is not the time to fight me, Cher. I been out in the cold with a gun in my hand and a vest on my back, huntin' a man with my brothers. A desperate man, prowlin' through family neighborhoods. A man who demonstrated he's all right with pullin' a trigger. In a situation like that, anything can happen, to me, to one of my brothers, or to some random citizen who's in the wrong place at the wrong time. That's done, so right now there's one thing I need. And right now, I'm askin' you to shut your mouth and give me what I need."

What he needed.

Him sleeping where he knew I was safe.

No man, not one my entire life, needed that from me.

Or wanted to give it to me.

So what the fuck did I do with that?

"Cher," he growled an impatient prompt.

"All right, all right," I snapped, pulling my head from his hold. "Keep your pants on."

I moved to the gun. I grabbed the gun. I went to the kitchen and turned out the light. I walked to Merry, by Merry, and down the hall.

I felt Merry at my heels and he stayed at my heels until we hit my room.

I heard him close the door.

I went to my closet, shoved the beaded curtain that hid my shit aside, and reached high to my safe that was on a shelf.

Nothing was in that safe but Ethan's birth certificate and our social security cards, so I hadn't bothered locking it up after I got the gun. I shoved the gun in, locked it, and went back through the beads.

I stopped at the sight of a barefoot Merry, leather jacket on the floor, shoulder holster with gun lying on the nightstand, his hands and shoulders moving to shirk off his unbuttoned shirt.

There was a lot of goodness that was Merry that I'd discovered the previous Friday.

His body was definitely a part of this.

I knew he had sinewy forearms because I'd seen him in tees. Those sinews writhed with movement in a way that I had to guard against watching or it would put me in a happy trance I might never want out of.

This, I'd learned Friday night (or actually Saturday morning), was just a hint at the tall, lean mountain of goodness that was Merry without clothes.

I would struggle to rank my favorite parts (outside of one in particular, which was obvious). He had great everything—shoulders, chest, biceps, abs, the hip V, his thighs.

But however that list came about, special mention would have to be made to the dark hair he had on his stomach. Not a heavy mat across his chest and down. The hair started on the upper ridge of his abs, spreading out and down, sparse and enticing.

It got better as it gathered and thickened at the center of the second ridge, down more, more, more, like a line on a map with the arrow at the end, pointing at buried treasure.

And one could definitely say the arrow at that particular end pointed to serious buried treasure.

"Babe."

I started, my eyes darting from his crotch to his face.

Even though he caught me checking out his package, all he said was, "Tired."

I nodded and moved to him.

I was barefoot too, in my jeans, tank, and bra from work. I stopped a couple of feet from him, but he wasn't paying attention. He was twisted to turn out the lamp beside my bed.

I saw the range of his ribs cutting down from the swell of his lat before the room was plunged into darkness.

I undid my belt buckle, the button, unzipped my fly, and pulled my jeans down my legs.

I'd barely straightened when he hooked an arm around my waist. I swallowed a yelp, noting he'd thrown back the covers, because when we hit the bed, we were *in* bed.

Merry tossed the covers over us, rolling so I wasn't on top of him but we were on our sides, face-to-face. The roughness of his jeans gently scored the skin of my legs as he wound his in mine, leaned his weight in to me, his arm remaining around me, the other hand coming up to cup the back of my head.

He shoved my face in his chest.

It took a lot, but I didn't rub it there. I wanted to, feeling him, smelling him, knowing he was there for the reasons he was, wanting to believe that what he was giving right then could be mine for eternity.

He'd made it clear he wanted me to take hold of that.

I just doubted his ability to *really* give it.

Not in the way I needed.

Not in the way that needed to be for Ethan and me.

I heard his head move on the pillow, then I felt his quiet words stir the top of my hair.

"Like your room."

This surprised me.

For mental health purposes, I'd never allowed myself to consider the environs that would surround an at-home Garrett Merrick. But in that moment, I pictured lots of wood, some seascapes, a gun rack, and a very large TV.

"Don't believe in ghosts but evidence points to the fact that the spirit of Janis Joplin puked all over your pad."

I didn't have a lot of room to move, but I was me, so I managed to sock him right in his tight stomach.

He emitted a soft grunt right before I heard chuckling.

I shifted so I could press my hands into his hard heat, not to push him away but to absorb the feel of him right there.

Life had not given me much, so I knew to take what it gave when it offered me a boon. Since it had offered me a boon, I was taking it. Tomorrow, I'd face the consequences.

Now…

Well, this I was taking for me.

I got the sense that Merry knew I wasn't pushing away because he pulled me closer and leaned more of his weight into me.

I felt his hand tangle in my hair and I closed my eyes tight, taking that boon too, no matter how risky.

"You know I'm teasin'," he whispered. "It's cool and warm and all you."

God, he had to stop. If he didn't shut up, I'd start believing, and I'd believed before—twice—and except for getting Ethan, it had not lead to good things.

"I thought you said you were tired," I noted.

"Yeah," he murmured.

"So shut up and sleep," I ordered.

"Cher?"

"Callin' my name isn't sleeping, Merry."

"You shut up and listen for a sec, we both can get some sleep."

I shut up.

"No matter what, no matter how things go down—in life, with you and me—no matter I piss you off, no matter anything, sweetheart, promise me you'll never block me bein' able to get to you again."

My eyes flew open.

Merry went on, "I don't think I gotta convince you that you mean some-thin' to me. What I want you to know right now is, no matter the future, that'll never change. If I gotta know things are good with you or with Ethan, I just gotta know. In the world we live in, don't make it hard for me to get that information, baby."

"I unblocked you about two seconds after you left us, Merry," I whispered.

"All right. Good. But now I'm askin', don't block me again."

"I won't block you again, honey."

The arm he had around me gave me a squeeze.

Shit, I had to give it to him.

Shit, shit, *shit*, there was no choice.

"I was pissed and I had reason," I muttered into his skin, kinda hoping he couldn't hear me. "But you were right. Callin' in Tanner and the way he played it was what was needed."

I didn't get a squeeze at that.

He kissed the top of my hair.

He said no more. He didn't rub it in. He didn't push things to take advantage and gain more ground.

He just kissed the top of my hair and let it be.

God, he looked good, fucked great, liked my kid, liked my mom, liked me, was protective, smart, dressed well, drove an awesome ride, had a nice family, amazing friends, a solid job, was funny, thought I was funny, knew how to install countertops and skim walls, and he didn't rub it in when he was right and I was...*not*.

Was he perfect?

And was I crazy?

"You're not goin' to sleep," he noted.

"That's because I'm freaking," I shared openly.

"Tomorrow," he stated.

"It *is* tomorrow, Garrett."

I heard the smile in his voice when he said, "Right, then later *today*."

"You can't just turn off freaking, Merry."

"Okay, then shut up, relax, and go to sleep, or, seein' as your boy was probably tweaked at what went down tonight and isn't sleeping soundly, I'll need to haul your ass to my truck to fuck you until I exhaust you. And this doesn't work for me because it's had time to cool off, and a running truck on a street like yours is a curiosity. I don't need your neighbors checkin' things out and seein' me doin' you. That shit could get back to Ethan."

"I'm suddenly finding myself very fatigued," I announced, though it was a lie. I was suddenly finding myself not giving a shit if a running truck in my 'hood was a curiosity.

Merry chuckled.

That, just that, in my bed, in the dark, so close, might be the most beautiful sound in the world.

I drew in a deep breath and let it go.

Merry stopped chuckling and encouraged, "That's it, baby."

I drew in another deep breath and let it go.

Merry shifted his arm from around me but only so he could shove a hand up my tank and stroke the skin of my back.

At first, this caused a non-drowsy reaction since no man had ever touched me like that with the intention of relaxing me, and Merry's touch felt a particular brand of good.

But surprisingly quickly, it did what he'd intended, and melting into his heat, I fell fast asleep.

I was in the kitchen making dinner. Ethan was doing his homework in the living room.

We were waiting.

Waiting for someone we loved to come home.

"Brown eyes."

I went to the doorway of the kitchen. I knew he was home. I watched my son look to the front door. I turned my eyes there.

The door started to open. I felt my mouth curve into a smile even as I held my breath.

"Babe."

My eyes opened. I blinked away my dream. Then I slid my gaze to the side and saw Merry, dressed all the way to his leather jacket, sitting on the bed beside me, his hand curled warm on the side of my neck.

"Hey, sleepyhead," he whispered.

Sleepyhead.

Merry.

Cute.

I was still half asleep, but I wasn't out of it. I was there. Right there.

Hell, I didn't know if I'd ever been as *right there* as I was right then, staring at a gorgeous man who fucked good, liked my kid, my mom, me, looked after us, thought I was worth it, and called me pretty.

This filling my head, I pushed up, adjusting so I could put my hand to his abs, feeling the soft, thick cotton of his shirt and the tight muscle underneath, and I blinked again as I moved in. Eyes to the cords of muscle around the strong column of his throat, one of my many favorite parts of all that was him, I aimed and landed a kiss right there.

"Cherie," he whispered, his hand sliding from my neck up into my hair.

Cherie.

No one had ever called me that.

Not even my mom.

I liked it so much, it made me feel dizzy.

Or giddy.

Or both.

I didn't know, I'd never felt that feeling.

But I knew it felt good.

Riding that feeling, I slid my lips up, over his jaw, his morning whiskers scraping my lips in a way I felt in my clit. I kept going even as his head twisted, angled. My lips glided over his and locked on.

Then I kissed him, open mouths, sliding my tongue inside.

He let me, not taking over or anything.

He tasted like toothpaste and Merry, an awesome combination.

The last thing I'd had the night before was a Baby Ruth bar and a can of Diet 7UP, but I figured that had long since worn off and maybe I didn't taste so good.

I didn't care. I went for it, drawing him in, my insides contracting like they were caving in on an empty that had to be filled or I'd shrink to nothing, and the only sustenance it would accept was a healthy dose of Garrett Merrick.

So I fed from him, trailing my hand up his shirt from his abs to his chest, my fingers clenching in, pulling him closer to me and going for more.

Merry gave it and kept giving until his groan throbbed through my pussy, making it contract.

He pulled his lips away and landed a peck on the side of my mouth before he moved back minutely and looked into my eyes.

"I like how you wake up, baby, but you got shit timing. I have to get Ethan to school."

I stared up at him and slowly let his shirt go as I just as slowly turned my head to look at the alarm clock.

Ethan had to leave for school in exactly three minutes.

My alarm didn't go off.

What the fuck?

I looked back to Merry. "Ethan's ready for school?"

"Got up, got him up, got him doin' his thing. I made him breakfast. He's ready to roll. Just didn't want you to wake up and freak, so I woke you to let you know he's all good, I got him, and you can sleep in."

I could sleep in?

Merry made my son breakfast?

Merry *had* him?

A fog filled my head as this knowledge processed through me.

Since he was born, mornings with Ethan were *mine*. With my work history, they were the only times that were guaranteed, him and me. For breakfast. When he was a baby, a toddler, a little kid, for cuddles. On the weekend, for hanging together and watching cartoons. Before school, shooting the shit and making sure he was good to face the day.

That was mine.

No one got that.

Not even my mom.

When I worked late, she stayed at my place and either slept on the couch if she was tired or went home when I got home. If I had to count on Feb, Vi, anyone, I went to go get my kid, shuffling him out half asleep to my car, helping him drop into his own bed.

It might not be right, making a kid switch beds in the middle of the night, but my kid woke up in *his* bed with his mom there to take care of him.

And he did *not* wake up with some guy in the house that he knew but he did not know what that man was to his mother.

The world might think I'm a stupid, skanky slut.

But my kid did *not*.

And he was never supposed to get that first inkling his mom was that kind of mom, that kind of woman.

Not ever.

Not...fucking...*ever*.

"You got my kid up," I said to Merry.

"Yeah, babe, and now I gotta get him to school."

"You got my kid up," I repeated, and Merry's head jerked.

Then his eyes went alert.

I moved quickly, throwing back the covers and leaping out of bed. I snatched my jeans up, shoved a foot in then the other. Yanking them up, I looked to Merry.

"You don't get to do that shit," I hissed quietly, doing up my fly. "You do not get to make that decision, Garrett. He's *my* kid. *I* get his mornings."

Something flooded his face, a sweet something, but I was not done.

Not by a long shot.

"You shoulda stayed in bed, or you shoulda got me up and got out before he got up. You do *not* make the decision your own damned self about what my kid knows, what he sees, or who looks after him." I straightened and jabbed my thumb to myself. "*I do.*"

He stood, murmuring, "Cher—"

I got in his space, head tipped back, mouth still hissing. "You and I fucked once. Now you're jackin' my shit with your fucked-up head games, and that's okay. That's the way of the world. That happens to stupid bitches like me who do stupid shit like gettin' shitfaced and lettin' a man fuck her who's drownin' his sorrows because he's in love with a woman he cannot have."

Merry's expression changed again, but I was too far gone to take note.

"But my son *never* knows his mother's a stupid bitch like that. And he sure as fuck doesn't find out that shit from some asshole who gets his rocks off jackin' her around."

His entire long, lean body jolted like he'd been struck, but I turned on my bare foot and stomped out of the room, happy to see that I had to open the door in order to do it, which meant Ethan wouldn't have heard any of that.

I took a deep breath and another shallower one on my way so I at least had some of my shit together by the time I cleared the hall and came into my living room.

Ethan had his jacket on, his backpack on his shoulder, and when he saw me, he grinned.

"He told you, right?" he asked the minute he could get the words out. "Merry told you that Marty got 'im? Tackled him behind the freakin' Dairy Queen."

"Yeah, kid, he told me," I confirmed.

"Marty's so cool!" Ethan declared, saying words about Officer Marty Fink that only kids in that town eleven years old or younger would utter. "And get this, you know that waffle iron you bought at that garage sale that we used once and it conked out?" Before I could confirm that I knew the waffle iron he was referring to, he kept talking. "Merry opened it up, messed with some wires, and *now it works*."

God.

Ethan said that like Merry came up with the cure for cancer in his sleep, called the FDA, and got them on it, and already, statues around the world were being planned to be erected in his honor.

It was worse than I thought.

"He made you some too, Mom. They're in the oven, keepin' warm," Ethan told me.

"That's cool, Ethan. Now, do you have your homework done?" I asked.

He looked confused at my non-excitement to his excitement-filled morning and answered, "Yeah, Mom. You asked me that last night."

"Your gramma check it?"

"Yeah." He was getting impatient. "You asked me that too."

"Okay, warning," I declared, moving closer to him. "Last night a bad guy was on the loose, so I'm taking my quota of gooey for the week right now. I'm gonna hug you before you go and you're gonna have to put up with me tellin' you I love you."

My boy rolled his eyes, but I ignored it completely, getting close and taking him in my arms.

I hugged tight and went overboard, landing three quick kisses on his head, smelling the shampoo in his freshly cleaned, still slightly wet hair.

Christ, Merry also got him to shower. This was not big on Ethan's hit list in the mornings (or ever).

Ethan wound his arms around his mom, gave me a quick squeeze, and let me go.

I took my cue and let him go too, but after I did, I lifted up my hand and playfully shoved the side of his head.

"Love you, kid. Be good."

At this juncture, Merry came into play, opening the door and lifting his hand with his keys. We heard a faraway beep and I looked his way.

"Go on out, buddy. I gotta talk with your mom real quick, then I'll be out." He offered his keys. "You know how to start a car?"

My mouth got tight.

"Yeah! Sure!" Ethan lied, because he did *not*. Then again, he'd seen me do it often enough in his life and it wasn't hard.

"Start 'er up, keep her in park, but get the heater runnin'," Merry ordered.

"Right!" Ethan cried, grabbed the keys and looked to me. "'Bye, Mom."

"Later, kid."

He took off.

I watched, then looked again to Merry to see him also watching.

He turned to me only when the door on his Excursion slammed.

I opened my mouth.

Merry beat me.

"Any more shit gets found, Tanner'll call you direct."

I stood still and stared at him, the empty tone of his voice slamming into me as sure as if he was shouting.

"You should tell Ethan what's up with his dad and that woman," he advised, his voice still empty. "He should be in the know and aware if they try to pull anything."

Okay, right, I'd reacted and I was right to do so. Merry had made a decision that wasn't his to make.

But I was getting the impression that I may have taken my reaction a bit too far.

"Merry—"

"You like your head jammed right up your ass, Cheryl, have at it."

Pain stabbed through my midsection.

He'd never called me Cheryl. To my recollection, not even back in the day when I still *was* Cheryl.

"Not that this'll get through, but worth it to me to say it, so I'm gonna do that," he stated. "No way in fuck would I involve myself in your kid's life in the way I did this mornin' unless I was goddamned, fuckin' sure that I intended to be a part of his life and his mom's life in a way that was healthy

123

for all of us. May have jumped the gun with that, but there was a way to communicate that to me, and the way you did it was not that way."

Yeah.

I'd taken it too far.

Fuckin' sure that I intended to be a part of his life and his mom's life in a way that was healthy for all of us.

Shit.

I'd taken it *way too far.*

I took a step toward him, but a nuance of change shifted over his frame and I stopped.

"Merry," I whispered.

"You like it behind those walls in your fortress, Cheryl? Stay. I reckon it's cold as fuck in there, but I also reckon that don't matter to you. You're used to it. Enjoy it in there, spinnin' your wheels."

With that as his parting shot, he turned to the storm door, opened it, and strode right through.

It whispered shut on its hinge, banging at the last when I didn't catch it, but I did move to it.

And I stood in it, staring out as Merry got in his truck with my son.

Ethan looked to me and gave me a short wave.

Merry didn't look to me.

He just drove away.

I sat with my cell in my hand at my kitchen table.

I had a mug of coffee on the table in front of me.

Coffee Merry had made me. Coffee he'd made me, wanting me to sleep in on my day off and then get to take it easy.

My mind was at war.

All the ugly things I'd said to Merry that morning that he didn't deserve tormented me. I should have calmly explained how I felt about mornings with my kid. It should have leaked in that I was talking to Merry and he would cut off his own arm rather than give any impression to my son that I was less than Ethan thought me to be.

This and a lot of other things that had happened and had been said the last five days, not to mention the strong urging of my heart, made me want to engage my texts and send him the two short words that would tell him what I was feeling and give him what he deserved.

I'm sorry.

Another part of me—the dark, ugly part that kept me locked inside the cold, airless shell I'd created—thought this was good. It was over. It might *all* be over, everything Merry and I had, including our friendship, but that was okay.

I was safe from him and he was safe from me.

And I'd listened to my heart twice in my life.

I knew better.

Right then, it didn't feel that way.

Right then, it felt like if I didn't act immediately to fix the damage I'd inflicted on Merry and me that morning, I'd be making the biggest mistake of my life.

I lifted the coffee and sipped it.

It was very strong.

But it was good coffee.

Then I engaged my phone, my thumb moving over it.

I went to who I needed to go to and typed in a text to my mom.

Don't know if you heard. They got him. It's all good.

I hit SEND, took another sip of coffee, and stared out the window, my mind filled with Merry's low, deep, beautiful but hollow voice.

My phone sounded and I looked down at it.

That's good, sugar. And Garrett?

I pretended I didn't know what Mom was asking and sent, *He's fine. Everyone's fine. Marty Fink tackled the guy behind Dairy Queen.*

Within seconds, she returned, *Good to hear, Cher. But what your mother wants to know is why he was holding your hand last night or just why he was with my baby girl.*

I hated doing it, but I didn't want my mom to know just how incredibly stupid I was. She knew I could be stupid because I'd handed her a lot of stupid for twenty-five years before I started to get smart. She was now living in a world where her daughter was a little less stupid. She didn't need to think I was sliding back.

So I lied.

He was just tweaked, I sent. Then added, *He happened to be at the bar when he got the call. Worried that the dude was at large in our neighborhood. You know he's a good guy, Mom.*

I know that. I'm glad he's OK, she returned, and in her first three words, even through a text, I actually felt her disappointment that a good guy like Merry wasn't holding her daughter's hand in the way she hoped he would.

Then again, he was.

And I'd fucked it up.

Shit.

Two words. I knew Merry would accept them. Easy to type them out.

I'm sorry.

I turned my attention back to my phone, hit what I had to hit, and put it to my ear.

It rang three times before Vi answered, "Hey, babe."

"You got lunch plans today?" I asked.

"I do now," she answered. "Frank's? The Station? Feelin' like Chinese?"

"My pad," I told her.

"Cool," she replied. "What time?"

"Noon good for you?"

"Yeah. And hey," she went on, "Bobbie's got mums on sale for half off and I got my tradesman discount. You want some for your outside pots?"

"That'd be good. The usual. Purple and white."

"Hmm…not sure she has white. But she has cream."

"That'll work."

"Right. See you at noon."

"Yeah."

There was a pause before she asked, "Hey, you okay?"

"Not even close."

"Oh shit," she whispered, then asked tentatively, "Merry?"

"Just come at noon, Vi."

"I'll be there, honey."

"Later."

"'Bye."

I hit the screen to disconnect and tossed my phone on the table. I grabbed my cup of coffee, took a sip, put it to the table, and looked unseeing out the window.

I did this a long time, eyes dry.

When I finally snapped myself out of it, I realized I had just enough time to shower, slap on my makeup, do my hair, and get to the grocery store so I could make Vi a decent meal that didn't involve microwave popcorn, chocolate, or Funyuns.

But before I headed out of the kitchen, I turned off the oven, grabbed a potholder, and pulled out the plate of waffles.

They looked amazing.

I wanted to freeze them and keep them forever.

I threw them in the trash.

⌒

Violet Callahan sat across my kitchen table from me, silent. The sandwich of shredded, fake crabmeat, mayo, and avocado that sat next to a stack of Pringles on a plate in front of her was untouched.

Cal, her husband, had their kids, Angela and Sam.

Cal was a bona fide badass of the scary variety, regardless of how much he loved his woman, his kids, and her daughters from her first marriage to a man who, sadly, was murdered, or how easily he showed all that. He still was scary in a way that Ryker, who looked like the maniac he only partially was, couldn't be.

There was no way to explain it. If you met Cal, you knew that was just his way.

Which made it sweet as all get-out that he took their two very young children pretty much everywhere he went. They even had playpens and cribs at his office. It was crazy.

Then again, his first wife was a strung out junkie who didn't pay attention, and thus, his baby boy had drowned in a bathtub. So it wasn't that surprising he kept his kids close.

See? Life sucked. For everybody.

It was just that for some, they made their way to happy.

That just wasn't for me.

"Vi," I prompted when she didn't say anything. She'd barely moved, hadn't taken a bite, even though I'd been blathering for the last twenty minutes about all that had been going down with me.

Except for Ryker's warning about my neighbors, I didn't leave anything out.

"Vi," I snapped when she still didn't say anything.

"Quiet," she returned. "I'm trying to stop myself from slapping you upside your head."

Loved my girl.

Feb was my big sister and I loved her too. But Vi was my bestie, the best one I'd ever had, and I'd knock your teeth out if you said she wasn't the best friend there could be.

Even so, not real big on her telling me she wanted to slap me upside my head.

I narrowed my eyes. "Uh…*what*?"

"God, Cher!" she cried angrily, then leaned in to the table my way. "Why didn't you tell me any of this?"

"It isn't your problem."

She leaned back, glaring and speaking. "Yeah. That's the part that makes me want to slap you upside your head."

"I'm tellin' you now," I pointed out.

"You know," she started conversationally, then hit me with her best shot, and it was a doozy. "It doesn't feel real good when I got a BFF who'd race to my side at the drop of a hat if she got even the *inkling* that I need her—and I know this because *she's done that*—and she doesn't let me do the same for her. Of anyone, Cher, in all the shit that's gone down in this 'burg with people who mean something to you, *you know*, bein' a mom, *you freakin' know* it's no hardship when you're called on to look after somebody. It's an honor. I cannot imagine why you'd take that privilege from me."

I sat back in my chair like she'd slapped me.

"And yeah," she went on, "everyone's talkin' about you and Merry. *Everyone.* But we're not all sittin' around gabbin' about how Cher's caught herself up with a man who's in love with another woman or how Merry picked the one woman in the 'burg who he's gotta handle with care and no one knows if he's got that in him. We're *worried*. About *both of you*."

Before I could race out and buy a cat o' nine tails which I could use during my five-hour-long session of self-flagellation, she kept going.

"But Merry was right. You should tell Ethan about that crap his dad and stepmom are pulling. You should tell your mom. You should tell *everybody*. I can't believe you haven't done that already. He needs looked after and he's your kid. In anything, it's all hands on deck. This crazy lady thinks she can be a better mom and has got no problem taking your boy away from you all the way down to Missouri, that bitch needs to think again. Bottom line, Cher, any woman who thinks that way about another woman's kid is sketchy. I wouldn't let Ethan anywhere near her."

"Right," I whispered, though I'd come to that same conclusion myself already.

"And if her husband doesn't have the balls to set her right, he shouldn't get anywhere near Ethan either."

I pressed my lips together.

"As for Merry, you fucked up this morning, *big time*."

I looked out the window, my eyes so dry they hurt. "Yeah I did."

"And I hate to say this, because I want good things for you any way you can get them, but that might not be bad."

The change in her tone, her voice quieting, made me look back to her.

She put her hand on the table and slid it a couple of inches toward me.

"He never got over her," she said softly.

"I know," I replied.

"It's too soon after her getting engaged. Merry should have known better."

"I should have too, Vi. But this is far from a perfect world. Shit happens."

She nodded her head, her eyes now kind on me. "Yeah."

I picked up a Pringle, then I threw it back down.

"He's too good of a guy," she started, and I looked again to her. "He had reason to be pissed this morning, even if you were right. No way he should have woken Ethan and all that. You went off half-cocked, but a lot of shit is happening. He'll get that. He'll get it sorted in his head. Give it time. Give him time. He'll come back."

"I should apologize," I told her.

"You should and maybe you shouldn't," she returned. "He needs time about a lot of things. He needs to get over his ex. He needs to figure out where he's at and what he wants. In the end, you two will be friends again, of that I'm certain. The rest, it's him who has to be in the right place, and he's not right now, Cher."

"You're right. He needs to get in the right place, and when he does that, find the right woman."

Her brows drew together. "You say that, and I don't know for sure what you're sayin', but I think you're sayin' that right woman isn't you."

I flipped out a hand. "Vi, the cop and the stripper? This ain't Hollywood. A hookup like that doesn't go beyond just a hookup in real life."

She screwed her eyes up at me. "Now you're makin' me want to throw this awesome sandwich at you."

"Vi—"

She leaned into the table again and snapped, "Shut it."

I nearly burst out laughing.

Vi was as sweet as pie. She could hold her own, and she'd been through some serious shit, but she was sticky sweet.

Those two words were channeled from her badass husband.

"You're the best friend I've ever had and you're the coolest woman I know. Heck, half the time I'm around you I wanna *be* you."

I slammed back in my chair that time, I was so rocked by her words.

"Everyone thinks so, Cher. The first time I met you, you were in everyone's face, shouting *this is me*, which really meant *back off*, this coming from every word, deed, gesture, stripper shoe, and miniskirt. But the last couple of years, you mellowed out, found out who you really were, and came into you. You dress cool. You act cool. You're all…" She flicked her hand around in the air my way. "Edgy and shit."

I felt my lips quirk.

She kept semi-ranting.

"You hang with the cops at their end of the bar, *fuckin'* this and *motherfuckin'* that, and they act like you got a desk in the bullpen right next to theirs. You hang with the bikers at the pool table, and they watch your ass and stare at your rack like starvin' men who entered a room with a buffet. Morrie told

Cal straight up he, his dad, and Darryl always gotta keep one eye on you when the bikers are in the bar or they reckon one of 'em'll knock you out, fling you over the back of his bike, and spirit you away."

"That's bullshit."

"Why would I bullshit you? Cher, you're the shit and everyone knows it. That is, everyone *but you*."

"Feb's the shit in an edgy way. You're the shit in a sweet way. Rocky's the shit in a classy way. Dusty's the shit in a together way—"

"And we're all taken. You're the shit in a *Cher* way."

I took a page out of my kid's book and rolled my eyes.

She slapped her hand on the table and I rolled them back. When I saw her irate, pretty face, I nearly choked on the laughter swelling up my throat.

The laughter stopped right in my gullet and I felt a choking feeling for sure, but in a different way when Vi spoke again.

"He did what he did, honey. *He* did it. No one blames you. No one looks down on you. Everyone gets he did what he did and part of what he did he did *to you*. All they see now is a woman who had the absolute worst happen to her heart and you didn't give up. You kept going. You made your life better. You got better for your son. You're a good friend, a great mom, and an amazing woman. That's all anyone sees. I would not lie to you, Cher. What happened to you would destroy nearly anybody. You didn't let it destroy you. People don't look down on you. They *admire* you."

Swallowing hard past the lump in my throat, I looked back out the window.

"Please, honey, for all the people who love you, especially your boy and your mom, don't let him destroy you. Any part of you. Set the last bag of shit he left you aside and find some happy." My eyes drifted back to her as she finished, "Because, honest to God, you deserve it."

I stared at my best buddy, Violet Callahan.

She stared back at me.

This went on too long.

So I finally said, "Are you gonna eat that sandwich or what? That crabmeat might be fake, but it still cost cake and I'm not made of money."

She smiled at me, picked up her sandwich, and took a big bite.

I grabbed a Pringle and crushed it in my mouth.

"So, whatever eventually happens with Merry," she said with her mouth still full, and I looked to her as she swallowed. "You gotta spill. Is he good in bed?"

"Mind-blowing."

The smile she gave me then was a lot bigger.

"Way to break out of a dry spell, babe," she hooted. "Only you'd do it and make this big of a bang."

There were so many things about that that were funny, I burst out laughing.

My best buddy, Violet Callahan, did it right along with me.

Seven

NEVER
Cher

$\mathcal{M}$y day off was not as relaxing as I would have liked it to be considering the fact that I needed to take Vi's (and Merry's) advice, which meant phone calls to a variety of people to share what was happening with Trent and, especially, with Peggy.

These calls included one to Colt, whose voice got so tight over the phone, I knew he was about to blow a gasket.

However, even with a tight voice, he assured me, "No one is gonna do dick with Ethan that you don't want, Cher. So don't even think about it."

Of course, coming from Colt, who meant it and, if necessary, would make it so, that made me feel better.

As for Mom, since I didn't think it was right to share something like that over the phone or by text, and I didn't want to do it when Ethan was around (and he was always around unless he was at school), I hit The Station and waited until she had a break so I could tell her in person.

Needless to say, Mom was ticked. She wasn't Trent's biggest fan back in the day when we were together. She began actively hating him when he left me high and dry after knocking me up, this causing me to make the desperate but strategic career decision to become a stripper. And that hadn't faded over the years, so she wasn't all fired up that I'd let him back in Ethan's life.

As for Peggy, Mom declared, "Never could put my finger on it, but I knew that woman was a bad seed. Only been around her a coupla times, but each time she gave me the heebie-jeebies."

Hearing these words, I looked forward to the day when I would develop the mom sense my mother had (and most mothers had), but unfortunately, it seemed that sense would forever elude me.

I picked up my kid from school and set him on his homework while I went out to deal with the pots of mums Vi got us from Bobbie's Garden Shoppe.

Even if it was a rental, I planted flowers. Every spring I planted a border of alyssum along our walk. I'd also bought big pots to sit on either side of the stoop and had a hanging planter by the door. Along the front of the house, I'd planted a shitload of hyacinth, daffodil, and tulip bulbs so it was awash with color from early March to late April. I filled that in with purple and white impatiens or lobelia or petunias in early summer.

I was not a gardener like Vi (she was both by trade and the grace of God). It looked good, but it didn't look amazing. I liked doing it okay, but it wasn't my favorite activity.

What it was was just a little something to make our house look like a home, like someone gave a shit, and I wanted my kid to see that every time he walked to our front door. And since Ethan was intent on playing football for the Brownsburg Bulldogs when he got to high school, I always planted in the school's colors because I hoped he'd get what he wanted, and when he was dating cheerleaders and shit, I'd have to have the practice.

So I spent my afternoon yanking out dead bedding plants, turning mulch into the earth so it'd be ready to give me the goodness come spring, and planting fall mums in my pots and hanging basket.

But even with this innocent activity, life demonstrated how it could suck when I was almost done with the hanging basket (which meant I'd be all done) and I felt a nasty feeling glide up the back of my neck.

I looked left and saw my dickhead neighbor standing beside his mailbox at the street, letters in his hand, tattered jeans on his legs, skintight thermal on his torso, the makings of a beer belly straining the middle, his eyes on me.

He had his head tipped to the side, and I had enough experience to know, as I bent over my stoop to plant mums in the hanging basket, his attention was on my ass.

He must have felt my gaze because his head straightened, I saw the grin hit his face, and he lifted his hand to wave.

"Yo!" he called.

Shit, fuck, shit, shit, *fuck*.

I nodded to him, turned from him, pressed the dirt around the new plants, then hefted up the basket, walked up the steps, and lifted it to its holder.

I set it dangling, and without looking back, I walked into my house.

I still had cleanup, discarded plastic containers to toss, tools to clean and put up for the winter.

I'd do it later when the coast was clear.

But, being me—the way I looked, what I was—I knew, even having escaped, I'd just hit dickhead radar.

"To your left!" Ethan shouted.

I looked left, then I shot the shit out of the enemy.

"Good one. Okay, let's go over to that building over there," Ethan suggested.

"Lead the way, kid," I muttered.

We were on our couch. The remains of the frozen pizza, which had been our dinner, mingled with two tubes of Pringles and an open bag of super M&M's (a gift from the M&M gods—three times the chocolate in every piece) littering the coffee table in front of us.

It was after dinner and my kid and I were doing what my kid and I did a lot.

Playing a video game.

I followed my son's character around a building, we came under fire, we kicked ass, clearing the space, then I followed him through a deserted marketplace, keeping vigilant.

My vigilance took a hit when Ethan, hands clicking on his controller, eyes to the TV, asked offhandedly, "So, is Merry your boyfriend now?"

Fuck.

I still needed to have the talk with my son about his dad and Peggy. I was procrastinating, but I intended to do it before he went to bed (or, at least, I was telling myself I intended to do it before he went to bed).

However, I had hoped that he'd let the Merry thing slide.

As ever, my hopes screwed me.

"No, kid," I said carefully. "He just got tweaked that guy was in our 'hood. Your mom and Merry are just friends."

All right. Good. I got that out and none of it was a lie (ish).

"He was tweaked, so he spent the night?"

Fuck.

"Well, yeah," I said, going for casual and thinking I was pulling it off. "He likes us. He just wanted to make sure we were all right."

"By spending the night?"

God.

Maybe it wasn't good my kid was sharp.

I hit PAUSE on the game and looked to my boy.

He looked to me.

"Yeah, Ethan," I told him quietly. "He likes us a whole lot. It freaked him out that guy was in our neighborhood. There are men out there who don't like the idea of a woman alone with her kid with no man lookin' after them." I grinned at him. "We got ourselves covered, but Merry's that kind of man, you know?"

He nodded.

"Sorry it went down like that this morning," I told him. "Merry probably freaked you by wakin' you up. But he was tryin' to do your mom a solid, lettin' me sleep."

"He did the right thing," Ethan declared. "You don't get enough sleep, Mom."

And maybe it wasn't good my kid was so sweet. It made capping the gooey at one hit a week nearly impossible.

"And it sucks that Merry lookin' out for us and holdin' your hand and stuff doesn't mean he's your boyfriend," Ethan stated. "He's super cool. He's almost as cool as Colt."

And there it was again.

Ethan liked Merry, but more, Ethan liked Merry for me.

Honestly, there would never be a way to decipher the many varieties of how my life sucked. The suckage of my life was like pi—it went on endlessly.

"Yeah," was all I could say, because my son was right.

Ethan stared at me.

Then, without warning, he leveled me.

"You need a boyfriend."

I did a slow blink with the addition of a head jerk.

"It's, like...totally crazy you don't already have one," Ethan continued. "All my friends think so and I do too."

"Uh..." I pushed out, but Ethan was far from done.

"You're, like, the coolest mom on the planet. I have to dole out sleepovers 'cause all the guys wanna come over here." He gestured to the TV with his controller. "They can't believe you play video games with me. Brendon's mom only lets him play video games for half an hour *a day*. That's totally crazy. And she'd never play with him. No way."

"Perhaps she doesn't have your momma's awesome eye–hand coordination," I teased, lifting the controller in my hands.

"No. She's just got a stick up her butt," Ethan returned.

"Kid," I said quietly, liking he was sweet and sharp but not ever wanting him to be nasty. "Be cool."

"It's true," he replied. "Thirty minutes, Mom? That's just mean. And Everest's mom lets him eat sweets, get this, *only on a birthday*. His or his sister's or his mom's or dad's, and it's only ever cake. They have broccoli *every night*. Broccoli looks gross, smells gross, and tastes gross. But he has it, like, *every night*. He says he reckons if that keeps up, he's gonna turn into a broccoli."

At this news, I could see why Ethan's sleepovers were popular; I always laid out a spread for his friends. And I wasn't certain we'd ever had broccoli in our house since the day he was born.

I smiled at him, but the truth of it was, I should make my kid eat more broccoli and green beans and shit like that, and less Pringles, Oreos, and M&M's.

I wondered what Peggy would do if she ever learned how bad I let my kid eat.

Shit, maybe I should take a turn down the veggie aisle, and not just to pick up wonton wrappers for those sausage things I liked to make during football games.

"See why they wanna come here?" he asked me. "Because you dress cool and act cool and you don't make us put our pop cans on coasters and stuff. And if the Xbox acts up, you know how to get back there and wiggle the right cables to get it working. Teddy's mom makes us wait until his dad gets home because she doesn't know anything about the TV, *at all*. I mean, what kinda guy, kid or grown-up, wouldn't wanna be with a lady who's cool like you?"

God, he was going to make me cry and I wasn't sure my tear ducts even worked anymore. They'd dried up after Lowe fucked me over. If the water-works turned on again because my kid was being all kinds of sweet, it could be catastrophic.

In other words, I had to put a stop to this immediately.

In an effort to do that, I warned, "You're earning me exceeding my quota of gooey this week."

He turned fully to me, and I realized he was being very serious, or more serious than I'd realized he was being (and I'd already figured he was being serious).

He had something to say that meant something to him.

This meant I needed to shut up and listen.

"Well, whatever. Be gooey, I don't care," he declared. "But I'm not gonna be here forever, Mom. Five years, I'm gonna have my license and be on the football team. That means practice after school and conditioning and swimming on the weekends. And I'll have a babe and I'll need to take her out. I'll be gone a lot. Then what are you gonna do?"

"Ethan," I muttered, dreading that time, upset that he recognized that time would come and he worried about me.

"No, I wanna know," he demanded. "I'm almost eleven. You think I don't know how hard it is for you to look out for me? But you don't seem to know I don't need it. Okay, like, I get it that you can't leave me at home alone at night and stuff like that. But I'd be good during the day. I could even walk home from school so Gramma or Vi don't have to come and get me. It's not like that's crazy. Other kids do it."

Other kids might do it, but they only had a couple of hours to look after themselves before their parents got home. I didn't get home on early shifts until after eight thirty.

I was cool for a mom, I could see that, but that was too long for a kid Ethan's age to be by himself.

"That's not gonna happen for a couple of years, kid," I told him quietly.

"Right, but *you* know I'm good, even if you're not good with it yet, right?"

I could give him that for sure, so I did.

I nodded. "I know you're good."

"And, like, that's gonna be the way it'll be and then what for you, Mom? If I'm not around, who are you gonna be with? Who's gonna be around to make you happy?"

God, my eyes felt like they were growing in my head, pushing the boundaries of their sockets, and it hurt like crazy.

"That isn't something you need to worry about, baby," I said, and his head jolted.

"If I don't think about stuff like this, who will?" he asked. "Not you," he answered himself and kept going. "It's like you're all about me, and that's cool. That's part of you bein' a cool mom, you know, bein' into video games and things like that, but also how you are lookin' after me. But that's *all* you are, Mom. You, like...*work*, then you, like...*look out for me*. And that's it. I mean, Merry's a super-cool dude and I know he'd be totally into you, but he wouldn't think to ask because you're all about lookin' out for me. He knows he'd get shot down, so why bother?"

Yep, I was right. Even though he wasn't entirely correct, still, my kid was too sharp for his own good.

"And Merry's the only cool one left," Ethan informed me gravely. "He's really tall, and he's totally funny, and he wears suits like they're jeans. The girls at school who know him think he's hot for an old guy. I mean, there's Marty and he's all right, but he's also kind of a goof. And you deserve some-one like Merry, not a guy who's all right but also kind of a goof."

This was going on too long, and if it went on much longer, no joke, it might just kill me.

"You're about to get around six weeks of gooey," I returned, hoping to shut him up.

He knew what I was hoping and shook his head, exasperated. "You're just sayin' that to shut me up when you shouldn't because this is important." He leaned toward me. "I *liked* it when Merry woke me up this morning. He was funny and he showed me how that wire got disconnected in the waffle iron, so if it happens again, I can fix it. And we both were bein' real quiet 'cause you were sleepin' and he made that funny too. But I know we both felt good doin' it, knowin' you don't get a lot of sleep."

God, Ethan *really* dug having Merry around.

Damn.

"Ethan, honey—"

He threw his controller down on the couch between us and crossed his arms on his little man chest, interrupting me. "I just want you to be happy. I know Gramma does too. She worries. She's a mom, just like you, but I got you to look after me. She's a mom with a kid who doesn't have anyone who'll look after her."

And my kid was good at laying the guilt on too.

Shit.

"I'm an adult and I can look after myself, baby. I can look after both of us," I told him.

"I know you can, *Mom*," he declared impatiently. "But that doesn't mean you *should*. Not alone. Not when you're pretty and cool and funny and like football and should have a guy around who likes you just as much as Gram and me."

"I can't just order a guy off a menu, kid," I told him jokingly, hoping to cut through his serious vibe because it didn't sit real well that my son worried about me at all, but especially not feeling it this deeply.

It was the wrong thing to say, and I knew this when he set his little man jaw and turned his eyes angrily to the TV.

"You wanna look after me," I surmised gently.

He tightened his arms on his chest.

Okay, I had to do something.

But God, what I had to do was lie to my kid.

"I'll be happy someday, Ethan." There was the lie. Then I gave him a kind of truth. "You're right, you're gettin' older and I should let go a bit and

140

take some time seein' to me. I'll do that, promise." When he didn't look to me, I prompted, "Yeah?"

It took him a second, but eyes still to the TV, he grunted, "Yeah."

"I just love you a lot, baby," I whispered and watched his chin wobble before he got control of it. "You're the best thing I ever did and I don't want you to ever forget that."

He turned surly eyes to me. "I already won't."

"That's good news," I muttered.

He pushed it. "And I want you to promise that when I turn twelve, you'll let me walk home by myself so you or Gram or Vi don't have to come and get me."

"How about we talk about that when you're about to turn twelve," I suggested. "Deal?"

"Whatever," he mumbled, looking back at the TV.

I let out a sigh, then made a decision.

"Since we've already jumped headfirst into the intense, and you just laid it out to your mom that you're growin' up and I need to have a mind to that, there's somethin' I gotta talk to you about."

He couldn't hide his curiosity when he looked back to me.

"What?" he asked.

"Well…" I didn't know where to begin.

When I didn't speak further, my kid looked more curious, so I threw it out there.

"I had a not-so-happy chat with your dad not too long ago."

Ethan's eyes got big.

I kept giving it to him.

"I didn't like what he said a whole lot, so I'm thinkin' on things with him and Peggy. I know you like to spend time with them, but I'm gonna have to ask that you just talk to them on the phone for a while until your dad and me figure this out."

"What'd he say?"

Shit.

Here we go.

Okay, he wanted to be grown up? I had to let him.

Starting now.

See? The suckage of my life never ended.

I turned fully to him, lifting a bent leg and putting it up on the couch. "Okay, he said that he and Peggy wanna see you more and that kinda freaked me. But when I told him we'd talk about it after I had some time to think about it, he said other things that weren't real nice. Peggy wants you livin' with them full-time, and obviously, I don't want that. So your dad and me are gonna have to figure out some common ground while Peggy sorts her head out, because she's not gonna get what she wants."

There were not many reactions I would have guessed my son would have outside of being pissed this went down.

And I was right.

"Live with them all the time?" he asked, his cheeks getting red and his eyes starting to fire.

"That's not gonna happen," I promised firmly. "She just—"

"No, it's not gonna happen," he snapped, jumped off the couch and cried, "That's crazy!"

"Ethan, kid, calm down, honey," I said gently. "It's not happening. You're right. Okay?"

He leaned toward me and yelled, "That's *whacked*!"

"Kid—"

He didn't calm down.

He asked, "So, like, they wanna take me away from you and Gramma and...*you*?"

"Ethan, *it's not gonna happen*," I assured.

He stared at me.

"Baby, sit down, okay?" I asked gently. "We're good. This is fine. You know I wouldn't let anything happen to you that you don't want. It's gonna be okay. I'm just tellin' my little man what's been goin' down. Now I need you to cool it and talk it through with me."

He drew in a breath so big, his chest puffed up with it.

Then he sat down, eyes to the TV, and I gave him time.

Eventually, he looked at me.

"You know, I like him," he said. "Dad. He's okay. He can be funny. She's, like, a really good cook. Tobias and Mary are all cute and do stupid stuff all the time that's funny. But he's, like…*not* Colt. Especially with Peggy. Do you know what I mean?"

Did I ever.

"He's not Merry either," Ethan went on. "But in a different way because I never saw Merry with a chick. But, you know, Merry's *funny* funny, like he doesn't try. And Dad's weird funny because you can tell he's tryin'. But the Colt stuff, it's, you know, you can tell Peggy *totally* calls the shots. It's weird and a little freaky. I mean, it should be like Colt and Feb or, you know, like Mike and Dusty. Like, he's the dude and he's a real dude, but he doesn't walk all over her and she sure doesn't walk all over him." He focused intently on me. "Do you know what I mean?"

"I know what you mean," I confirmed.

"It isn't like I don't like 'em. It's just weird," he told me.

"Yeah, I bet," I agreed.

"But if I had a choice to be around a dude and his chick, it seems more right, the way it should be, bein' around Colt and Feb or, you know, like, Cal and Vi. Even if Cal is totally badass, Vi still doesn't let him walk all over her. Dad and Peggy, it's just…" He shook his head. "Freaky."

I loved this. I loved all of it, even Ethan laying it out that I needed to look after myself. I loved it so completely, it made me want to get up and shout at the top of my lungs.

I wanted to do that because this one conversation proved that somehow, against the odds, those odds mostly created by me, I'd still managed to raise my son right.

"This is good," he declared. "I could use a break. Dad asked if I wanted to spend next weekend with them and I was kinda wishin' I could say no. I'm gonna say no."

Well, that was a big honkin' relief.

"Okay, Ethan, I'm glad this works for you, because if you say no, he'll eventually come to me and then I'm gonna say no for you for a while. Are you good with that?" I asked.

He looked intently at me. "Yeah. And you want, you can tell them I don't wanna spend more time there and *definitely* I don't wanna live with them. He can't, like, walk into my life when I'm almost grown up and do stuff like that." He cocked his head and kept talking while studying me, offering, "If you don't wanna say that to him, I will."

"How about you keep things cool between you and your dad and let me do the talking for now? That work for you?"

He nodded but said, "If I gotta say it, Mom, I will."

Oh yeah.

Mental shout for joy.

My kid was smart. He was sensitive. He spoke his mind. He was strong. And he was brave.

I'd raised him right and I was only just over half done. I had more time to set that shit in stone.

That time wasn't enough, just because it would eventually end and I wanted it to last forever.

But it worked for me.

I nodded to him and replied, "Okay, kid. If you gotta say anything, you should say it anytime. In this situation or whenever. Just be cool about how you say it. You with me?"

"I'm with you," he muttered.

I tipped my head to the TV. "Now, are we gonna annihilate some more bad guys or you wanna help me clean the coffee table?"

"I'm not done with the M&M's."

Of course he wasn't.

Then again, I wasn't either.

I had a feeling I missed the boat on broccoli.

But he liked carrots, so I'd get some of those tomorrow.

"Right, you get the Pringles, I'll get the pizza, we leave the M&M's, then we kick some butt," I suggested.

He smiled. "Works for me."

He jumped off the couch as I pushed off it.

I waited.

He'd grabbed the Pringles and I was gathering up used paper plates, napkins, and the remains of the pizza, timing it just right.

I was still gathering when I called, "Ethan?"

"Yeah, Mom?"

I drew in a deep breath.

Then I told the pizza, "You're the absolute best kid on the planet and I love you more than breath, you hear me?"

"I hear you, Mom," he replied quietly.

I said no more.

We cleared up.

Then we ate M&M's and kicked video game bad guy ass.

After that, my kid went to sleep.

I sat cross-legged on my bed, one light on, dimmed by a scarf over it.

I was barefoot but otherwise still had on my jeans and tee, my makeup, my jewelry, everything.

I had my phone in my hand, my head tipped to it.

My texts were up, specifically mine and Merry's text string.

The last was from me.

DONE.

More evidence of my short fuse and me overreacting.

I closed my eyes tightly.

I opened them and allowed my thumbs to move over the screen.

I'm sorry. I was a total bitch this morning. It was out of hand. You didn't deserve it. Not a word. I lost it and I really wish I hadn't.

I stared at the text.

Then I hit BACKSPACE until it disappeared.

Ethan totally dug on you waking him up. He liked that you were looking out for me.

I studied the text for a while before I deleted it.

He just digs you. He thinks you're cool and funny and he was hoping you being with us meant you were with me.

My eyes blazed like fire, a sensation I was getting used to as I hit BACKSPACE until the words were gone.

I woke up liking that you'd looked after me too. Looked after us. I liked that a lot, Merry.

I erased and then typed.

Then I did what I'm really good at doing and screwed it up.

I made it gone and then made more.

145

But I'm in love with you and that scares me.

Quicker than the last, I got rid of that one.

I'm sorry.

I stared at those two words on my phone, my thumb hovering over the SEND button.

It moved and deleted.

I turned off the phone and tossed it on the bed, lifting both hands to press the base of my palms to my eyes, trying to soothe the fire.

That didn't work, so I unfolded out of bed and went to the bathroom to take off my makeup in order to start getting ready to try and get some sleep.

I knew this would be an impossible task.

And when I finally lay alone in the dark, I found I was right.

Garrett

Garrett stood on his balcony having a smoke, his head bent, his phone in his hand.

He engaged it, distractedly making note he needed to get a new one because that crack was fucking irritating.

His thumb sliding across the screen, he went to his texts.

Specifically his and Cher's string.

DONE.

That was her last.

Fuck.

He turned off his phone and looked to his view.

She was right.

When he woke early, he should have woken her to discuss how they'd play the Ethan thing. He'd jumped the gun, made a decision that wasn't his to make.

So she was right to be angry.

But she'd lost it, spewing shit that was completely out of line.

Which pissed him off.

He didn't hide it. She knew it, and it was written all over her by the time he'd walked out the door that she regretted it. And anyway, that was Cher. She didn't often hold back.

But since then…nothing. No apology. No Cher being cocky-cute or a pain in the ass in a good way to try to cover it up and move on.

Nothing.

The look of her waking up, the way her eyes were on him, the touch of her mouth to his throat, that fucking kiss, it all penetrated his brain.

He'd gotten in there.

You got somethin' worth fighting for, you fight for it. *You do not sit on your ass waitin' for it to come back to you.*

She'd been right.

But the way things were with them, she was also partially wrong.

She needed time. He needed time. Cher wasn't stupid. She paid attention. She knew she took it too far this morning. He knew before he even walked out her door that she wished she could take it back.

But he was pushing, and he was pushing at a time when any sane, logical woman who knew his history with his ex-wife would have the smarts to push back.

Cher was pushing back for more than just that, but there was also that.

He needed to cool it. He needed to give her some space. He needed her to know that he was moving on, and his decision to explore moving on with her, which meant with her and her boy, was a risk worth it for her to take.

Staring at the parking lot, Garrett made a decision.

He'd give her a week.

He took a drag, inhaled, let it go, and decided it was time to cut back in order to prepare to stop altogether. Ethan did not hide he dug having Garrett around that morning like he never hid he dug having Garrett or any of the men around.

It was over three decades ago, but he didn't forget what it was like to be a kid that age, drinking up all that was around you, storing it inside to let evaporate the shit you didn't need so the man you wanted to be could flood out when the time was right.

He didn't need to give Ethan the idea anything was cool that was not.

So the smokes had to go.

He was bending to stub it out when he saw headlights in the parking lot. With mild curiosity, he looked that way and saw a car driving through the lot to get to the other side of his building where the tenants and their guests parked their cars.

But he knew that silver Land Rover.

She could not be serious.

Christ, he thought this bullshit was over.

"*Fuck*," he hissed, scowling at the Rover while straightening.

He walked inside, slid the door closed, and secured it. He then moved to the kitchen bar and tossed his phone on it, not wanting to do that but instead wanting to call Cher, talk out their shit, and not go to sleep on it the way things were. Or, at the very least, text her something to let her off the hook thinking he was still pissed at her.

That wasn't giving her time, so he didn't do that.

Instead, he did what he absolutely did not want to do.

When the knock came at his door, he walked to it, looked out the peephole, and felt his jaw set.

He slid off the chain, turned the bolt, and opened the door.

He moved firmly into it and looked down at his ex-wife.

She was shorter than Cher by several inches. She had lots of red, wavy hair whereas Cher's blonde brushed just past her shoulders. She had green eyes that flashed with fire or humor, not Cher's dark brown that, even when she didn't know it and wouldn't want it, shone with warmth.

And right then, Mia Merrick was in the mood to play games.

"Go home, Mia," he ordered.

She looked up at him, eyes hooded, but he could read them. He'd had years of that. The woman couldn't hide anything from him.

She was angry.

And she was something else too.

"Haven't heard from you in a while, Merry," she said softly.

"Sorry. My bad," he replied. "Congratulations, babe. Wish you all the best," he told her with far less emotion than he'd spoken to Cher that morning, which meant his voice was a black void it was a wonder the bitch didn't disappear into.

Unfortunately, she didn't.

He watched a slow grin lift her lips.

She thought she'd read him.

She might have heard about him and Cher, it was doubtful she hadn't, but even if she did, she didn't know she'd lost the ability to read him six days ago.

She thought his words hid jealousy.

She leaned closer to him.

He swung back but did it studying her.

Pretty. So fucking pretty. A little minx. He'd thought she was *his* little minx. Got off on that. Bitch was wicked.

And he'd been wrong.

He couldn't totally read her because he was the asshole who didn't read for the five years they were apart that her wicked games were poisonous.

"Mia, go home," he repeated.

"You want me to go?" she asked, leaning further into him, pressing her tits into his chest.

He instantly pulled back.

Her eyes narrowed and she shot out a hand to cup his crotch.

She barely got her hand on him before he moved his between them. Wrapping his fingers around her wrist, he yanked it away, listening to her surprised cry when he used precisely the strength he intended, making the hold he had on her bite just enough to make a point.

"What the fuck's the matter with you?" he asked.

"Merry," she whispered, twisting her hand in his hold to try to get away, uncertainty in her features now.

He jerked her forward and she gave another surprised cry as he bent to get in her face.

"Listen to me," he growled. "You do not ever come here again. You sell that house. You pack your bags. You get your ass to Bloomington. And you forget I exist."

She looked into his eyes, the uncertainty gone, the training he'd given her that she owned his dick and could lead him around by it shining from them now. "You don't mean that."

"You have another man's ring on your finger," he reminded her.

"Like that means anything to you," she retorted.

"Fuck," he whispered, staring into her eyes. "Do you not know me at all?"

Her gaze dropped to his mouth. "I know you better than you know you, baby."

He used her wrist to give her a slight shake, and her eyes shot back up to his. "No, bitch," he bit out. "You don't. You wanna come and play and you made no promises that a man's countin' on to live the future he's got mapped out with you, that's one thing. This shit…it's another. You wanna be that cunt who fucks over her guy, have at it. But you're not usin' me to get you off playin' your games."

"If it's that big a deal to you, Merry, while you fuck me, I'll take his ring off," she offered.

Fucking bitch.

How the fuck had he not seen this before?

She came to him. It wasn't rare; it wasn't frequent.

But she came to him when she'd had a bad day…"and I just want to be with you, Merry." Or when she'd had a go 'round with her mom…"and no one will get it like you, Merry." Or when she felt…"we need to talk, Merry."

What she needed was to fuck, for someone to get her off like, apparently, no one else could, and it took her little time to talk him around to that mostly because she'd put her hands or mouth on him and they wouldn't talk at all.

He didn't comfort her. He didn't listen to her.

And most of the time, she'd be gone before he woke, or he'd lie in bed, watching her dress and listening to her say, "Gotta go, baby. I'll call you."

She wouldn't call.

But she also wouldn't hesitate to come back when she needed another dose of his dick.

He'd thought, one day, she wouldn't get up early and sneak out. One of those times, she wouldn't dress while he watched then leave, but instead come back to him and say shit like, "Dinner tonight. It's clear neither of us can let this go. Let's work it out."

He'd thought her coming at all said they weren't done. The door was open. He just had to walk through.

When that didn't happen, *he* felt like the asshole because he didn't ask for it, didn't push it, didn't point out that the finality of signing divorce papers was bullshit for the both of them.

She hadn't led him on. He'd fully participated and he was not a dumb fuck. He knew early what was going on.

That didn't mean he didn't feel she was leaving that door open.

Friday night, he thought she'd gotten fed up and closed the door.

It pissed him off more than Cher's rant that morning, not only that he'd been wrong but, with Mia's most recent visit, *how* he had.

The past few days, he'd been recognizing Mia's games for what they were, and it sat like a weight in his gut that information was confirmed.

He pushed her off, taking a step back and wrapping his fingers around the edge of the door. "Go home, Mia."

She shook her head like she was clearing it and her brows drew together. "Are you serious?"

He stared down his nose at her. "You know, woman, I'm not a cheat, on either side of that deal. How the fuck you got it in your head you could come here tonight, I don't know. But this is done. And just to make things clear to you, Mia, even if it doesn't work out with that guy, when I say this is done, I mean that any way it can mean. This shit is done because *we* are done."

She stared up at him, stunned.

"But...we're never done," she informed him.

"Never just became a fuckuva lot shorter," he informed her, stepped back and shut the door in her face.

He locked it and turned away.

She didn't knock again, and it was good she didn't bother because he hadn't lied.

They were done.

Christ, it sucked in ways she'd never understand that Cher didn't recognize the fucked-up mess they already had was a fuckuva lot healthier than the fucked-up mess he and Mia had become.

All of a sudden this thought made him smile, because if Cher was right there and he could've shared that with her, she'd bust out laughing.

Garrett turned out the lights and headed to the bedroom thinking, yeah, his brown-eyed girl had a week. That was as long as he was prepared to sit on his ass and wait for her to come to him.

If she didn't, she was ready or not, he was going to her.

Eight

A WEEK
Cher

Thursday Afternoon

My phone sounded with a text as I drove home from the grocery store, six bags of shit that had absolutely no nutritional value in the back of my car (plus four of those baby carrots snack packs).

In other words, I was good to go to keep my "cool mom" crown because Ethan and Everest were going to hit the better-living-through-chemistry food mother lode at about five tomorrow night when Everest came for his sleepover.

I'd also stopped by the bank and opened a new account with Trent and Peggy's thirty-five hundred dollars. It and anything else they gave me was going to stay set aside.

I didn't know why I did this, I just felt it prudent.

And if nothing came of whatever they planned to do but them giving me that money (as well as the hundred bucks every two weeks that they'd promised), then at least it was in a savings account earning interest until whenever I deemed it time to hand it over to Ethan.

I parked in my driveway and grabbed my phone.

The text was as I'd feared—not from Merry.

It was from Trent.

Call me. We need to talk.

I threw my phone back in my purse, got out, grabbed the bags, and took them in the house.

It was after I'd put everything away that I got my phone out again.

Just got back from the grocery store. I'm worried that my nutritional selections for my kid are preserving his body for science. So I bought carrots.

I stared at the text I typed in Merry's text string, the bubble hovering over it still declaring *DONE*.

Then I backspaced through the text, tossed my phone on my purse, and walked out of the kitchen.

Friday Evening

I moved through the living room with my phone in one hand, the snack-size four-pack of baby carrots in the other.

I saw my son and his buddy lounging on the couch, controllers in hands, twisting and turning as they hit buttons, eyes glued to the TV, the detritus of a feeding frenzy in front of them so extreme, it covered the top of the coffee table and leaked over all four sides.

I kept moving as I tossed the packs of carrots in the middle of it, causing a bag of half-eaten microwave popcorn to shift, littering popped kernels all over my carpet. It also caused an opened bag of bite-size Snickers to fall off and spray baby candy bars everywhere.

I didn't pause to clean up (though I did pause to snatch up a couple of Snickers for myself).

I spoke as I quickly negotiated the area in front of the TV so I didn't obstruct their view.

"Do me a favor and eat those, so when your parents sue me for putting you in a sugar coma, my attorneys can tell them I made a valiant attempt to cut through the crap with carrots."

Everest burst out laughing.

"You're crazy, Mom!" Ethan cried, doing it through a little man laugh that was part boy giggle, part man chuckle, eyes never leaving the TV, controller in hand shifting.

I had a feeling their reactions meant the carrots were going to be ignored.

I'd made that bed, so I also had a feeling I had no choice but to lie in it.

I hit my bedroom, climbed on my actual bed, and sat leaning against my collection of pillows that did, actually, look like something Janis Joplin would recline on for a *Rolling Stone* photo shoot.

I crossed my legs under me, made quick work of my Snickers, then lifted up my phone.

I went where I needed to go.

First attempt with the carrots was a fail, I texted Merry.

I deleted it.

Then I shared, *Two more day shifts then I'm back on nights. In a perfect world, I could give Mom a break and ask you to come over and hang with my kid while I work.*

I deleted that too.

Ethan would dig that. But I'd dig it more knowing that you were with my boy and he liked it.

Obviously, I got rid of that too.

Mostly, though, I'd like knowing you'd be there when I got home.

Quickly, before my thumb could hit anything on the screen that would be catastrophic, I deleted that too.

I jumped when my phone sounded in my hand, a text popping up.

Not from Merry.

From Trent.

Did you get my text yesterday? We need to talk. Call me.

Not a word from Merry, but my ex-loser texted me twice.

That was my life.

Of course, it was up to me to sort out the shit pile I'd created that stood between Merry and me.

But that wouldn't happen.

Eventually, he'd come into J&J's and give me indication he didn't totally hate me, though he'd probably be distant.

Over time, that would melt and he'd be cool with me again.

Finally, we'd get to joking and laughing.

Then, after a while, I'd watch him eye up some babe who did it for him. He wouldn't make the approach in front of me, not at first. He'd wait to get back to that after he knew we were back where we needed to be.

But he'd find his way to make an approach.

And then it would be done.

And we'd be where we were supposed to be.

Meaning, I'd be right back where I belonged.

Alone and skirting the edges, on the outside looking in to all the amazing that was Merry.

Garrett

Saturday Night

Garrett rode his bike under the covered parking spot he paid extra for every month so his Harley would be sheltered from the elements.

It was late.

He'd been riding all day partly because the weather would soon turn and he wouldn't be able to take out his Fat Boy again until March or April.

But mostly, he did it to find a way to clear his mind, keep focused, and not fuck things up by moving too fast with Cher.

As he rode in, he saw that he may have managed to get through another day without fucking things up with Cher, but he had another problem he thought he'd sorted, which, apparently, he had not.

He swung off the bike, but she was already out of her Rover and heading his way.

He didn't look at her when he started across the parking lot, but he felt her.

"This isn't happening," he stated.

"Merry, please," she begged. "Give me a second."

He kept walking.

"I screwed up," she declared.

She fucking did.

He made no reply, he just kept walking.

He felt her hurrying after him, her short legs no match for his long ones.

"I thought it was you. The way you'd ended us, I thought it had to be you," she told him.

At the foot of the ugly concrete steps, with their unattractive iron railing that would lead him to the concrete landing that would take him to his shitty-ass condo, not a pot of flowers in sight, nothing to make that place look like anyone gave a shit, he stopped and turned to her.

"Go home, Mia."

She stared up at him, her pretty face twisted and pleading.

"I gave you opportunity after opportunity," she whispered.

Oh no.

They weren't doing this before.

They sure as fuck weren't going to do it now.

"Go home," he repeated.

She reached out a hand, but when his eyes dropped to it, she halted its progress.

He looked back to her.

"I kept coming to you, but you never *did anything*," she declared.

So he'd been wrong the other night, right the rest of the time—that *had* been her game.

Regardless, it was fucked up and damaging, wasting time and causing harm when the bitch should have just *said something*.

At that point, however, it didn't matter. They were over, so going through this wasn't worth his time.

"Say it one more time," he warned. "Go home."

"I see now," she said quietly, eyes glued to his, imploring. "I made the first move. Kept making the first move, over and over. But maybe I should have made the second one too. Maybe you needed that from me. Maybe with…" Her eyes started drifting, but she put visible effort into forcing them back. "With the way things were with your family…" She rubbed her lips together quickly before going on. "With your mom, I should have had a mind to what was going on in yours."

Cher's words slammed into his head.

You got good, you don't let it go. It lets you go, you hold on. It slips through your fingers, you pull out all the stops to get it back. You got somethin' worth fighting for, you fight for it.

Mia was right.

It was him who had fucked them up.

But with his history, she gave that first shit about what they had, it was her who needed to make *all* the moves.

Now it was too late.

Before he could speak, she kept doing it.

"I'm gonna talk to Gerard. We have to…I need to be free, because you and I need to sit down and talk things out."

Garrett felt his brows go up. "You're gonna dump your fiancé to take a shot at me?"

Her body moved in ways that shared she was gathering the courage to say her next.

"I'm gonna do what I need to do to work with you to get us back to us."

"Thought I made it clear, Mia—there is no us."

Hurt moved through her features, right on its heels, chased by stubborn. There she was.

He'd always thought that was cute.

But Mia had a pain-in-the-ass mom who was a pain in Mia's ass because she was just like her daughter. They both had a man in their life, Mia's dad, who spoiled those bitches rotten. They'd been vying for his attention since Mia could cogitate.

But Justin McClintock loved both the females in his life and he had a lot of love to give. Through that, he'd taught his daughter if she wanted something, it would be hers.

She clearly now had decided she was serious with wanting Garrett back and wasn't going to fuck around with making that happen, and the way she'd been taught, she thought that would just be so.

He watched her smile, and he couldn't believe in their situation as it stood, at the same time he could because she was Mia, that her smile was smug.

"We're the 'burg's last Rocky and Tanner," she declared. "The last Colt and Feb. There never was an end to them. There'll never be an end to us."

"Gonna go bad for you, you believe that," he replied. "Now, go home."

Done with this shit, he turned and had moved up two steps before he felt her coming up after him.

So he turned back.

He looked down his nose at her and stated, "Right. This is not gonna happen. I told you to go home and I did that repeatedly. I told you we were done. I told you that you were no longer welcome here. You follow me up these fuckin' stairs, I'll slam the door in your face. You knock, I am not fuckin' with you, Mia, I'll open the door, cuff you, and arrest you for harassment."

He watched her eyes grow huge.

"I'll take you in myself," he continued. "You'll be booked. I'll press charges, woman. Not fuckin' with you on that either. And I do that, your man in Bloomington will know you came to visit me. Everyone will know the state of play between you and me, that bein' me makin' a very public statement that I'm tryin' to make now privately. We...are..." He bent slightly to her. "*Done.* Now, do not make me make a fool of you. I won't enjoy it. But I sure as fuck will do it."

He didn't give her a chance to react or reply.

He moved up the rest of the steps, walked to his condo, and let himself in.

He locked the door behind him.

He took off his jacket and swung it on the back of a dining room chair.

She didn't knock.

Finally, she was getting smart.

He took out his phone and checked it, just in case.

Nothing from Cher.

He felt his mouth get tight as he walked back to his jacket to pull out his smokes.

He needed one because Mia was in his shit, Cher was not, and he hadn't had one since he'd stopped for lunch in Brown County.

The autumn leaves were phenomenal.

But he wished he'd seen them from his truck with Cher and Ethan in it with him.

Cher

Late Saturday Night

It was ten to midnight when I made the call.

I was pissed. I loved "You Shook Me All Night Long." (Who didn't?)

But I didn't love it splitting the night on a continuous loop when my kid *and* me should be sleeping.

I turned on the lamp, grabbed my phone, and called the direct line that rang straight to the Brownsburg Police Department's dispatch.

"Brownsburg Police, Jo speaking. May I help you?"

"Jo, this is Cher," I told her.

"Hey, girl," she greeted. "Everything good?"

"I'm understanding the government's tactics with Noriega," I shared.

"Damn, another party?" she asked.

"Yep," I answered.

"I'll get someone to cruise by," she told me.

"I'd really appreciate that, babe. Your first beer's on me next time you're in the bar."

"We can't accept bribes, Cher, unfortunately," she said through an audible smile. "But, just so you know, noise violations are part of a cop's job."

"Good to know," I muttered, even though, with practice, I already knew that. I was just trying to be nice with my "bribe." "See you when you're back in the bar."

"Yeah, girl, see you."

She hung up.

I turned out my light.

Ten minutes later, the music stopped.

I did not pick up my phone to share all this without actually sharing it with Merry. I didn't type in the fact that I wished he was right there, because if he was, there would be no call to Jo at dispatch. He'd deal with it. And with all the neighbors knowing a cop was on their patch, the shitty ones would behave or just go, and it would all be good for me, my kid…and Merry.

No, I didn't text him that, even when I wouldn't send him that.

I closed my eyes and it took a while, but I finally found sleep.

Sunday Morning

I heard it from the bathroom as I was finishing up my hair.

It was a half an hour before we had to leave so I could drop my kid at Mom's and go to work.

Bad timing.

I knew from Ryker's warnings that I should ignore it.

But if I made the call I needed to make, that would alert Colt—and Merry—to shit happening on my block. Both of them (at least I thought Merry would still be in that space) would intervene.

And I had to live there.

They didn't.

Anyway, it wasn't about getting into my dickhead neighbor's business.

It was about taking care of Tilly.

So I knew I had to do it and was turning to walk out of the bathroom when this knowledge was confirmed.

Ethan was at the door, face pale, eyes on me.

"Mom," he whispered.

Fucking motherfucker was freaking out my son.

"I got this, kid," I told him, continuing to move.

He got out of my way and I went to the front door. I slid my feet in some flip-flops that were there that I should have taken to my closet a month ago but didn't. I just picked them up, vacuumed under them, and dropped them back whenever I cleaned.

When I finished doing what I had to do, I'd wear them to my room and put them away.

I put my hand to the door and turned to my boy, who'd followed me.

"Stay inside."

He stared up at me, nodding.

I opened the door, pushed through the storm, took a deep breath, and stalked down my walk.

"*Did you fuckin' hear me? I said come out here!*" I heard shouted. "*I know it was you, you old, fat bitch! You got a problem with me, you say it to my face! What you don't do is call the fuckin' cops!*"

I saw my dickhead neighbor at Tilly's door, banging and yelling.

"*Yo!*" I bellowed.

He stopped banging and swung my way.

I kept walking until I was in Tilly's yard but still far away from him.

He looked me up and down, dressed and ready for work, only in flip-flops and not the heels I planned to wear. I also hadn't yet put on my jewelry.

Some of the pissed went out of his face and something else came in it.

"This isn't about you, babe," he told me, suddenly friendly and calm.

Crap.

I put my hands to my hips. "I think it is, since you're shoutin' at Tilly when she didn't call about your party. I did."

His head jerked. The look of me, a full-on good-time girl, he was shocked it was me who made that call.

"Listen," I went on. "I have a kid. He needs his sleep, even on a weekend. It sucks I had to call it in, but I hope you get me when I say I need to look after my kid. No way I'm goin' over to your place in the middle of the night to ask you to have a mind to your neighbors. I had no choice."

He studied me for a few beats before he stepped down off Tilly's stoop and moved toward me.

I wanted to retreat step for step, but I stood my ground.

He could read me. We were of the same people. He knew I could look after myself.

And he knew, no way in hell I'd ever show a guy like him weakness.

No. Not ever.

With a guy like him or not, I'd *never* show a weakness.

I knew that too. I knew I had to show him every way I could that I was not weak. If I didn't, a man like him could destroy me.

And he would.

He stopped four feet in front of me.

"You're welcome to come over anytime, middle of the night or whenever," he offered.

Fuck.

"Thanks, but like I mentioned, I got a kid," I told him.

He looked beyond me, then back at me.

"Yeah. And he's cute."

I turned my head and saw Ethan standing just down the walk from our stoop.

Shit, shit, fucking *shit*!

I looked back at the dickhead.

"Yeah. I know. Anyway, Tilly's cool. She's a nice lady. You shouldn't give her shit. She's got two kids and a slew of grandkids who don't ever visit her, and that sucks. She lives quiet. She doesn't get into anyone's business. She makes awesome cookies at Christmas. You don't get in her face, brother, she'll make you some cookies, and trust me, it'll be worth bein' cool to her."

He grinned at me, his eyes shifting to my tits before they shot back to mine.

"I'll take that advice," he replied.

"Awesome. And sorry again I had to call it in, but just some advice, in case you haven't been in the 'burg for very long: cops keep a close eye on shit and neighbors look out for neighbors. You wanna party, you might wanna take it somewhere else."

That was taking it too far, and I knew it when hard entered his gaze and he declared, "Should be able to have a good time at my own fuckin' house."

I nodded. "I agree. It's just that if that gets loud, your good time fucks with other people." I tipped my head to the side, lifting my hand to give him the finger and thumb one-inch. "And worse, you came *this close* to ruinin' AC/DC for me."

He burst out laughing, doing it with his eyes twinkling appreciatively at me.

Shit, shit, fucking shit.

I took that too far too.

"Shame to ruin AC/DC," he said through chuckles.

"Yeah. Now, I got shit to do. We good?" I asked.

His eyes fell to my tits again, and he didn't lift them when he murmured, "Oh, we're good."

"Awesome," I muttered, fighting back a nasty shiver. "Later."

"Later, darlin'," he drawled.

Fuck, fuck, shit, shit, *shit.*

I lifted my chin to him, turned, and moved back toward my house, feeling his eyes follow me. I gave a jerk of my head to Ethan and he dashed up the steps of the stoop.

When I got closer, I saw him open the storm, and I also saw he had a baseball bat resting by the wall just inside the door.

My little man looking out for me (and Tilly).

I barely got the door closed when Ethan asked, "You okay, Mom?"

"Yeah, it's all good. He's gonna leave Tilly alone. It's fine," I assured him, hearing my phone begin to ring. It was in the bathroom and I made my way there, but I did it calling behind me, "We'll talk about you comin' out when I told you to stay inside after I see who that is."

"Not gonna let you go out there without takin' your back," he informed me.

That was cute. It was sweet. It was the right thing to do. It was also the wrong thing to do for a kid his age.

But I'd get to explaining that later.

I nabbed my phone, not thinking good thoughts at who the screen told me was calling.

I took the call and put it to my ear. "Ryker—"

"You get injected with a huge-ass dose of stupid since I last saw you?" he asked on a mild bark.

He was watching.

Why was he watching?

Fuck!

"Ry—"

"Told you that guy does not exist for you," he declared.

"I know, but Ry—"

"Won't let him do shit to the old broad. Anyway, the bitch went to church. She isn't even there."

I closed my eyes in despair.

Of course. Tilly went to church every Sunday. Then she went out with her girls for lunch. She wouldn't be home until at least two.

Shit.

"Now that you gave him an up close and personal, he's gonna live and breathe findin' a way to tag your tight, round ass," Ryker informed me.

"He has a woman," I informed him back.

"They're havin' problems, so she's gonna be history in about an hour, seein' as momma hot stuff two doors down, with a pair a' knockers made for squeezin' together and thrustin' a cock into is his key to tradin' up in a *big* fuckin' way."

Uh…

Gross.

"Ryk—"

"Don't know the games you and Merrick are playin', sister. What I do know is that if you don't cool your shit, I'm bringin' him in on this. And I know Merrick, babe. I know that brother better than you in ways he'll hide from you, even if you both stop dickin' around and sort your shit out. He finds out what's goin' down two doors from his bitch, he will lose his motherfucking *mind*. And Merrick's a maverick. Merrick keeps a loose hold on messy. And Merrick's brand o' messy makes *me* look adjusted. The only thing that would make Merrick lose hold on that is someone he digs bein' in a deep pile a' shit. Man'll stop at nothin' to dig you out, even if it buries him in the process. So listen up, Cher. Keep your ass safe. Keep your kid safe. And keep the man you're fuckin' around claimin' safe. Now we're done and this conversation won't be repeated. You don't get smart real fuckin' fast, you know where I'll go. And you'll know, it gets ugly, it's you made it that way."

He then disconnected.

I didn't move, one hand to my phone at my ear, the other one curled around the edge of the sink, holding on like it was a lifeline.

He finds out what's goin' down two doors from his bitch, he will lose his motherfucking mind.

What was going on?

Merrick keeps a loose hold on messy.

I knew that. I'd learned from a lot of experience, as well as making too many mistakes, how to read people.

The good ole boy Merry was surface. You could scratch through that using your fingernail and not a lot of effort.

Man'll stop at nothin' to dig you out, even if it buries him in the process.

I knew that too.

Shit.

All that, and Tilly wasn't even home.

"Mom?"

I drew in breath, dropped the phone from my ear, let go of the sink, and turned to see Ethan in the doorway.

"Don't be mad, okay?" he asked, shifting and eyeing me anxiously. "I was tryin' to do the right thing."

I drew in another breath and forced my body to relax when I let it go.

Then I told him, "I know that, Ethan. And it was the right thing in one way. There's nothin' wrong with you wantin' to look out for your momma. But it was also the wrong thing since I'd told you to stay inside."

He bit his lip.

I moved to him but didn't crouch like I used to. He was getting tall, not quite there yet, but he needed to learn to use what he had. What he didn't need was to learn how to put up with someone being condescending, crouching into him because he was a kid, even if they didn't mean to be.

"You're the man of this house," I told him and watched his chest expand with pride. "But, kid, you're also still a kid. Ask Colt, Sul, Mike—any of them will tell you a man's gotta know his strengths and his weaknesses. He's gotta learn to judge situations right. And they'll also tell you any kid who's still a kid, no matter it sucks, no matter the situation scares them and they wanna help, they gotta do what their momma says."

His shoulders slumped.

God, most of the time, being a mom rocked.

It was just times like this when it absolutely didn't.

Quickly, I continued, "In that situation, you shoulda got the phone and kept an eye on me through the window. You got a bad vibe, you could call Colt or the police or something. That way, you had my back but also did as I asked. But seein' as nothin' like that is gonna happen again, it doesn't matter. Life is life. You learn from it. Today, you learned."

Gazing up at me, he nodded.

"Right," I muttered.

"That guy kinda seems like bad news. Are you sure nothin' like that is gonna happen again?"

"I think your read on him is right. He's not a dude like the dudes we like to hang with, so both of us should keep our distance. But I also think his crap is his, so if we do that, it'll all be good."

He nodded again.

"Now, I gotta finish gettin' ready, honey. You good to go to your gram's?" I asked.

"Yeah, Mom."

"Right, let's get to that part of our day."

He grinned at me and got out of the doorway.

I took in another breath and headed to my bedroom.

Monday Night

Whether it was intentionally good timing or not, Trent phoned at the perfect moment, right before I was about to slide out of my car and hit work for the night shift.

He'd texted twice more since the first two.

I'd been blowing him off.

I needed to stop doing that so he'd leave me alone. He also needed to think on things and I needed to give him the things he needed to think about.

So I took the call with a "Hey, Trent."

"Texted you a million times, Cheryl," he exaggerated.

"I know. I'm sorry. Things were busy," I semi-lied.

"Ethan told me he's not comin' to see me and Peg this weekend," he shared irately.

I beat back a sigh.

"As you know, Trent, this gig is Ethan's," I replied. "He gets to decide when he wants to see you. He's back at school now so it's sleepover time, and the good stuff happens with his buds on weekends."

"He needs to spend time with his father."

Trent said the words, but they came right out of Peggy's mouth.

"All right, I gotta get to work in a minute, but you should know, Ethan and I had a talk about you and Peg wantin' to spend more time with him and he doesn't like that idea. He digs you. Your wife. Your kids. But he's feelin' the need to take things with you slow and that's his call. So if he needs space, you're gonna give it to him."

"He's a kid, Cheryl. He doesn't get to make those calls."

More Peggy.

"He's a kid, Trent, you're right. But he isn't five. He's nearly eleven. He knows his own mind, what he wants, what feels good to him. He's at a time where he's gotta explore makin' his own decisions and how that plays out. We gotta let him."

"He's too young to start that kind of thing. He needs guidance," father of the century Trent Schott educated me.

I sought patience (not my strong suit) and returned, "I'm not sayin' he doesn't need guidance. I'm just sayin' he needs some freedom and space."

"He can have all the freedom and space he wants when he's thirty. Now, bein' a kid, he needs his old man helpin' him learn to be a man."

And more Peggy.

But it would be Peggy teaching him to be a man.

The thought turned my stomach and I clenched my teeth to beat back my response to that.

This, unfortunately, allowed Trent to carry on.

"You need to tell him he's gotta come and stay with Peg and me. This weekend. We'll pick him up from your place at five thirty on Friday."

"That's not gonna happen, Trent."

"Then I'll tell him, and if he's not there, just sayin', Cheryl, that's a mistake you don't wanna make."

"Okay," I snapped, having had enough. "This is the deal—you got no rights in this situation, Trent. Not until a judge says what rights you got. You wanna drag my son through that, I can guaran-damn-tee you that you're gonna drive him further away from you than you already are, pushin' me with this shit. Now, we can avoid that and do right by Ethan if we calm down, sit down, talk somethin' through that'll work for all of us, and by 'all of us,' I mean it works for Ethan. But he's tellin' you right now he needs a break. That gives us a golden opportunity to sort shit out so when he's ready for more, we got it set up with an understanding between us how that's gonna go."

"Pushin' you with this?" he asked. "You tell him we pushed?"

We.

She wasn't even there when *he* pushed.

God, there *was* no Trent.

It was only Trent and Peggy.

Which meant there was only Peggy.

"I don't lie to my kid," I shared. "So yeah, I told him the good news that his dad likes hangin' with him, but that came with the bad news that his dad did not respect me by communicatin' that right. That is not my issue. *You* fucked that up."

"You're tryin' to turn my son from me. From me and Peg."

Me and Peg.

Barf.

"No, Trent, you don't see what's happenin' here. I'm tryin' to *tell you* that *you* are fuckin' this up, and I'm also givin' you advice on how not to do that. You decide not to take it, you bear the consequences."

"Peg and me show at your place Friday, Cheryl, my son isn't there, you'll hear from our attorney," he warned.

Like he had an attorney.

"Whatever, Trent. It isn't like you haven't put me through the wringer before. Not like he's a stupid kid and doesn't know the life he's led, I led, part of that bein' because of the choices you made. Do it again. You're such a dumb fuck you don't see I'm a scrapper, especially when it comes to my kid, and I always come out standing, your mistake. But to save you some time and gas money, my kid is not gonna be at my house on Friday at five thirty for you to pick him up. *Ethan'll* let you know when he's ready. Until then, last advice I give, wait for him to come around. You do, you'll be golden. You don't, you risk losin' him forever."

I disconnected, threw my phone in my purse, and hauled my ass out to go to work.

I did this hoping we'd have a busy night. I needed a ton of tips.

Because I had a feeling I might be facing attorney's fees.

Two hours later, I stared down at the end of the bar where Colt and Sully were bent over their beers, looking at each other, smiling and chuckling.

Feb was on. Jackie was looking after Colt and Feb's little Jack.

This happened. Colt liked to hang with his woman when she was on.

Then again, Colt just liked to be with his woman and they both liked to give their son's gramma time to be with her grandson.

Drew Mangold, another detective, had been in. He'd left fifteen minutes ago.

Mike had been there too. When I got there, he'd been sitting with Colt and Sully, shooting the shit, an after-work drink that led to two with cop bonding. But he'd left less than half an hour after I hit the bar for my shift.

No Merry.

He didn't come into J&J's every day.

But he was a regular. Once a week, more often two or three times, sometimes more.

It had nearly been a week since I blew things up.

He was avoiding me.

This scared me. He didn't seem the kind to hold a grudge. He was a straight shooter. He had a problem with you, he told you to your face and didn't delay (not that he'd ever had a problem with me, but I'd seen him have problems with other people and that was what he did).

He was not doing this with me.

He also wasn't living his life as he had so there was an opening for us to gloss over it and move on.

So it was safe to say I was worried. I'd not apologized. I'd not reached out in any way. There was no door open he could slide through so we could start the work to get back to the him and me that used to be.

My attention was called, a customer wanting a draft.

I pulled it, all the ugly shit that had come out of my mouth that I'd aimed at Merry slamming through my brain as I did.

I served the draft. The guy paid. I got a good tip that would probably pay for half a second of an attorney's time. I moved down the bar after a scan showed me some drinks needed refills.

I made drinks, notes on tabs, pocketing tips on those who paid outright and didn't open a tab.

Done with that, I glanced down at Colt and Sully. Feb was standing with them but twisted, her eyes on me.

She smiled a soft smile.

She'd noted Merry hadn't come in too.

I returned a cocky grin.

She didn't buy it, but she didn't act on that.

At that moment, Ruthie bellied up to the bar with an order.

I moved her way.

Early Tuesday Morning

It was four o'clock in the morning. Mom was snoring on the couch. Ethan was sleeping in his bed. I was in my bed, the room dark, my phone illuminated.

I fucked us up, I typed into Merry's text string.

I deleted it.

I fucked us up, I typed again, my eyes beginning to burn.

I deleted it again.

I miss you, I didn't tell him, typing it with no intention of sending it.

I backspaced through it.

I fucked us up, baby, and I'm so fucking sorry.

I didn't hit SEND, but I also didn't erase it.

Like it could just exist and he'd somehow get it without me giving it to him, I left it there, closed down my phone, tossed it on the nightstand, turned to my side, closed my blazing eyes, and did not sleep.

Garrett

Tuesday Night

Getting home after work, Garrett sifted through his mail at the kitchen bar, wondering how the fuck he got so many catalogs when he'd never bought a thing from a catalog in his life, and in the same time, he'd never made an online purchase.

Bills. Credit card applications. Life insurance offers.

And there it was.

"Jesus Christ," he muttered, staring at the handwriting.

Solely out of curiosity, he opened the envelope.

Upending it, an eight-by-ten color glossy slid out on his bar, face up. Stuck on it was a bright pink Post-it note in the shape of a heart.

It read, *I messed this up. I didn't work for it. I'm going to work for it, baby.*

He read the note and looked at the picture.

In it, he was sitting on a barstool in Vegas. Mia was in a clingy dress he'd liked a fuckuva lot, standing next to him, hanging on him. She didn't have to hang; he had his arm around her, holding her close.

On the bar was a three hundred dollar bottle of champagne. They were both holding filled flutes. They'd splurged because he'd just won seven thousand dollars at the craps table.

They'd taken a few sips before Mia had asked someone passing by to take that picture.

Then they took the champagne to the reception desk and did what they did. Not planning for a future, living in the now, doing it wild to pack in as much as they could, they blew almost all his winnings, got upgraded to a suite, and made short work of moving rooms.

The rest of the time they were in Vegas, three days, they didn't leave that suite. They got room service if they needed to eat. But if they weren't eating or sleeping, they were fucking, whispering, or laughing.

He'd never been happier.

And that was when it began. He felt it. He felt it their last night in Vegas when he laid on his back in the bed in that suite with his naked wife curled sleeping at his side.

He'd felt the fear.

They'd been three years in their marriage—three good, strong, solid years—and the minute they stepped foot off that plane onto Indiana soil, he'd started pulling away.

She'd let him. She hadn't fought it once. She'd been confused. Scared. Hurt. She'd let that show. It had killed him, seeing that, seeing what he was doing to her, but he didn't quit doing it. He didn't once cease in his efforts at driving her away.

And in those three years she hadn't once asked him what was in his head. What was making him drive a wedge between them. What was pushing him to kill their happy.

She hadn't even begun to put up a fight.

Eight years later, she decided to put up a fight.

Staring at that picture, all they had, all they were, all he'd wanted, all that had fucked with his head, all the harm he'd done to her, all the pain he'd caused surfaced and he gave it a second of his time.

Eight years.

Then Cher's bravery, smashing through that fortress she had every reason to build around herself to wake up that morning and look at him the way

171

she did, touch him the way she did, brush her lips against his throat, take his mouth, moved all thought of Mia aside.

Cher'd had it tough in a way that even in twenty years on the force he hadn't seen anyone fucked by life as much as her.

But it hadn't even taken her a week to break through the walls she'd built to guard her heart to start letting him in. It got fucked up, but she'd still done it.

Not eight years.

Not even a week.

That was all Merry needed.

He picked up the picture, tore it in half, in quarters, in eighths, then toed his trash bin and tossed it inside.

After that, he went to his fridge to get a beer before he went to his couch and turned on the TV.

It was Tuesday.

Tomorrow was Wednesday.

Which meant it had been a week.

Cher's time was up.

Ethan

Wednesday Morning

His mom's phone beeped.

He went to it and saw the text from his gramma telling them they needed to figure out a time to have a family dinner.

He opened his mouth to yell at his mom as he engaged her phone, punching in her password, going to her texts.

He closed his mouth when his mom's texts came up.

There was a line that said MERRY.

Merry, a cool guy, a cop, a badass—not an in-your-face badass like Cal, but still a badass who would be able to stop anything bad from ever happening to his mom. A cool guy, cop badass who looked all natural holding his mom's hand.

He knew he shouldn't, but he couldn't help himself.

He touched the line with Merry's name.

He read the string, scrolling with his finger, his eyes screwing up, not understanding.

Talked to Ryker. He's been briefed by Tanner. He's all over the church lady.

That means you broke your promise to me. Right to my face, you promised. You lied.

You know what that means, Merry. You shared my shit. That means we're over in every way we can be over.

DONE.

They were over?

There was something between his mom and Merry to be over?

She'd told him there wasn't.

But she hadn't told him the truth.

She was protecting him.

Again.

Ethan felt his heart beating real hard.

There were words in the message line that hadn't been sent.

I fucked us up, baby, and I'm so fucking sorry.

She called Merry "baby." She didn't call *anyone* "baby" unless she liked them a whole heckuva lot.

It said *I fucked us up.*

His mom and Merry were an us!

And they were fighting.

"Kid! You want hash browns for breakfast or what?" his mom called.

She was coming his way.

Ethan bit his lip.

Then he hit SEND.

Real quick, he typed in, *Don't text. If you forgive me, come see me.*

He sent that too.

Then, super quick, he moved to his gramma's text string just as his mom hit the kitchen.

Screen out, he waved her phone at her. "Gramma wants us to plan a family dinner."

"I'll get right on that after we get back from DC for the dinner the president and first lady are putting on in our honor."

Ethan burst out laughing.

His mom was totally funny.

And because of that and all the other cool that was his mom, Merry would come. Ethan knew it.

No texting. Merry was like Colt. He was a real dude. Ethan was sure he didn't play games. Ethan knew this because Merry hadn't messed around when he was worried about that guy who was running around with a gun in their neighborhood. Even if his mom was trying to play things cool for Ethan's sake, Merry kept close to look out for Ethan and his mom. So Ethan knew Merry wouldn't mess around with stuff like that. Not stuff that was important.

Stuff like his mom.

They'd talk. They'd make up. His mom could be stubborn, but Merry would break through.

They thought he was a kid. They thought he didn't see. They thought he didn't hear.

But he saw. He heard. He watched, because he sensed what he was seeing was how it should be and it felt good, being around the way they were.

That being that sometimes Feb could be stubborn too, and Colt broke through. So could Vi, and Cal always broke through too. Rocky was full of attitude—she was Merry's sister so he knew all about that—and Tanner always just thought it was funny, and when he laughed at her, Rocky didn't get ticked. Her face got all soft like she loved him even *more* because the way she was made him laugh.

Ethan's mom was super funny. She'd make Merry laugh all the time.

So they'd make up. Merry would see to that. Merry was in no way a stupid dude, and any guy would want a lady who'd make him laugh all the time. Ethan knew that *for certain*. He knew it because Colt did, so did Cal, Mike, Tanner. And when Ethan found his babe, that was what he would want too.

And after they made up, they'd stop hiding things from him so his mom could protect him like she did when that bad guy effed her over so bad.

Then...

Then...

Then Merry would be around all the time.

And she'd finally be happy.

Nine

Hangin' in There
Cher

Wednesday Morning

*I*was in my living room, vacuuming, an activity that for some reason in a house with only a thirty-four-year-old woman and a ten-almost-eleven-year-old kid living in it, had to happen more than once a week.

As was my way, to take my mind off something that was not my favorite activity, not to mention it was right then officially a week (and a couple of hours) since I'd let loose on Merry, fucked up everything between us, and I hadn't seen or heard from him at all, I had my music up loud.

I liked rock 'n' roll.

There was some guitar-twanging country that didn't drive me up the wall.

But my personal little secret was that I was a diva queen.

I certainly had a gift with banging my head to some Quiet Riot.

But with my vacuum in my living room, I was a goddess ready for the Vegas stage, belting it out with the likes of Aretha, Tina, Whitney, Donna, Linda, Janet, and Cher (the other one, who could actually sing).

And at that precise moment, I was killing it, accompanying the fabulous Celine in her version of "River Deep Mountain High."

The music was too loud with a dual purpose. First, I loved that song, and it needed to be loud so I could hear it over the vacuum. And

175

second, it drowned out my voice so I could kid myself about the fact that I could accompany Celine without sounding like a howling cat who would make the real Celine take off running on her two-thousand-dollar Valentinos.

I was preparing to let go of the vacuum in order to have both my hands free to do the air bongos (something that any living being should do when Celine's bongo guy lets loose on that track) when, suddenly, the sound cut out completely.

I looked to the receiver in my media center. Then my senses, no longer being interfered with by the brilliance of Celine, refocused and I whipped around.

Merry was standing by my coffee table, my remote in his hand, looking at me, mouth curled up in a smile, his tall, lean body shaking with silent laughter.

Fuck, I hadn't locked the door after I came home from taking Ethan to school.

Fuck! How had I forgotten to lock the damned door when I came home from taking Ethan to school?

Fuck! He knew my diva secret!

Fuck, fuck, fuck! He'd heard me singing!

I turned off the vacuum.

"Celine?" Merry choked out.

I stared at him.

"You, my brown-eyed girl, who'd see Tommy Lee lookin' at her rack and smack him across his face for bein' forward, causin' him to write a song that'd have millions of women throwin' their panties at him, listens to Celine fuckin' Dion?" he asked.

His brown-eyed girl?

Garrett Merrick's brown-eyed girl?

Me?

Garrett Merrick, estranged from me because I'd been a foul-mouthed, overreacting crazy lady, was standing in my living room calling *me* his brown-eyed girl?

I kept staring at him.

Then I whispered, "You're here."

The humor fled from him completely, his handsome face turned beautiful, and he replied, "Got your text, baby."

My insides convulsed.

My text?

Oh shit, had I somehow accidentally sent my text?

Before I could play my life in rewind to figure out how that might have occurred, Merry bent and tossed my remote to the coffee table and walked my way. When he got to me, he pulled the vacuum out of my hand, swung it aside, and got in my space, chin dipped into his neck to look down at me.

"Your apology was sweet." He grinned a small grin. "Your brand of sweet, considerin' you dropped the f-bomb twice givin' it to me. And I appreciate it, Cherie."

Cherie.

Not Cher.

Not the dreaded Cheryl.

He gave me back his *Cherie.*

A weird but not unpleasant warmth I'd never felt started to creep over me.

"I appreciate it, but you didn't need to give it," he went on, lifting his hand to cup my jaw and bending so his face was closer to mine. "I knew before I left that you were sorry."

I stared into his blue eyes that were looking into mine, communicating amazing things.

Somehow, that text got sent and there he was, in my living room, accepting an apology I didn't know I gave.

Here was another boon that life had thrown at me.

And before I could think better of it, I latched on ferociously.

"I overreacted," I blurted on a whisper.

The pads of his fingers dug into my skin gently. "I get that."

I held his eyes and gave a careful shake of my head so I wouldn't lose his hand on me. "No. Ethan and me…the way things have been…how our lives are…" My quiet voice dropped quieter. "I only ever get his mornings guaranteed."

"I get that, honey," he repeated. "I stepped over a line. It might not have been right how you communicated that, but that doesn't mean you weren't right to be angry."

I gave another cautious shake of my head. "No, I was totally out of line being that ugly."

"Cher, you love your kid and that's your time. Lots of shit is goin' down, not the least of which I was pushin' at a time when I should have been goin' gently. You're you. You reacted like you and like the mother you are. It happened. It's done. You apologized and I've admitted I didn't play that right. We're movin' on."

That was good. I wanted that. I wanted us to move on. I wanted the quiet understanding he was giving me. I didn't want him to be angry. I wanted him back in my life.

I also wanted to explore where his manner was saying we were going.

But what I needed was to get him to understand completely.

"It was ugly and it might have been right why I did it," I told him. "But it was also wrong. Ethan talked to me about it and he liked havin' you around." I saw a flare in his eyes I liked, but I didn't take time to let it register deep. I had to get this done, so I powered forward. "He liked you two doin' somethin' together to look out for me. He gets that I look out for him all the time and he's a good kid. He wants me to have that sometimes too. And he liked doin' that with you for me."

Merry didn't say anything, but he did glide his thumb along my cheek to edge the bottom of my lip and then back.

That meant he actually did say something, and what he said was unbelievably sweet.

I fought pressing my lips together or leaning in and pressing everything *to him*.

It was difficult, not only with his touch but the soft way he was looking at me. Another something from Merry I'd never gotten from another man in my life. And I was glad. I was ecstatic. Because staring into his eyes, getting that from him, if I knew that kind of thing existed and I went for days, weeks, years not having it aimed at me, I didn't know if I could keep breathing.

This feeling caused me again to blurt out more words.

"I texted you the next day."

I lost the look as his brows drew together in confusion.

"I didn't send it," I told him quickly. "I erased it. But I apologized. I explained. Then I erased it all."

The look came back, and in those mere seconds from losing it to getting it back again, I became a junkie, knowing down to my bones I'd do anything—any-fucking-thing—to get that look as often as I could aimed at me.

So I kept fucking talking.

"I texted you more. I told you I'm worried I'm not feedin' my kid right. I told you I tried to get him to eat carrots. I told you that didn't work."

Humor mingled with that look in his eyes and, fuck me, that was even better.

"I told you other stuff too," I shared. "I texted you all the time, without texting you."

"Glad you finally hit the right button, sweetheart."

I actually hadn't.

Or I didn't think I had.

I was about to explain that to him when a knock came at my door.

I looked that way, and unfortunately, Merry dropped his hand as he twisted to look too.

We were in a part of the living room where I couldn't see what was in the diamond window, and although the front curtains were opened, our angle didn't show my stoop.

But I knew who it was. A package had been delivered yesterday for my neighbor on the other side, Bettina. I'd put a note in her storm door. Bettina worked a job where she had occasion to have some weekdays off.

She was probably coming to collect.

"That's Bettina, my neighbor," I told Merry, and he looked back at me. "A package was delivered for her."

I tipped my head to the door where a thin but long and wide box was resting against the wall.

Merry looked, then returned his attention to me.

Another knock came at the door.

"I should give it to her."

"Yeah," he replied.

"Just be a sec," I muttered, moving by him, eyes to the floor, my mind belatedly realizing that I hadn't yet taken my shower that day.

My hair was good. My hair was always good. I had an expert hand with hair and knew the precise quality (but inexpensive) products to use that would make my hair look good, even if I didn't wash it for a week.

However, I did not have any makeup on.

And I had on a pair of supremely faded jeans that I'd owned since about a year after I'd had Ethan. They were so worn in and beat-up, they had splits at both knees, some up the front of one thigh, and one at the back just under the left cheek of my ass.

Bare feet. A seen-better-days cardie over a white tank. No jewelry. No perfume.

And Merry, looking awesome in one of his suits, was in my space, seeing me like this for the first time *ever*.

Shit.

I kept my eyes to the floor and only lifted them to aim my hand to the handle.

I opened the door and looked out, expecting to see Bettina, so I was surprised when it wasn't.

It was a man of average height. He was decent looking. Dark hair salted with silver and just slightly receding. He also had a thick goatee that was more liberally salted with silver. He was wearing very nice, dark wash jeans, a button-up shirt that had been ironed, and an attractive, expensive-looking sports jacket.

He also was not standing outside my storm door.

He had the storm door open and was holding it that way.

In other words, he had clear passage to get into my house with nothing protecting me from this stranger.

Considering I had no clue who he was, and he could've easily knocked on the storm door and been heard, there was no reason he should've felt comfortable eliminating that barrier. Furthermore, a storm door was also a security door, that was, making *me* secure from someone like *him*.

Due to this, I felt annoyance mix with the confusion, which caused an edge to my voice when I asked, "Can I help you?"

He nodded. "Ms. Sheckle."

My body snapped tight.

"I'm Walter Jones," he went on to declare. "I'd hoped to—"

He didn't get to telling me what he'd hoped, even though I knew what he'd fucking hoped, so he didn't have to tell me shit.

This was because I lost my mind.

"Are you fucking *shitting* me?"

My voice was loud.

His face set. "Ms. Sheckle—"

"No," I bit out, shaking my head. "Unh-unh. Man, when a woman does not take your calls, you need to get the hint no matter what reason you're makin' that call, and *especially* when you're makin' the calls you made to me, that you should leave it alone."

"As I hope you heard in my voicemail message, I intend to compensate you for your time," he told me swiftly. "I'm prepared to give you a thousand dollars to speak with me. If I could just come in—"

"Listen, asshole," I shot back. "For me to talk to some goddamned stranger who's lookin' to make money off the shit Dennis Lowe piled on me, a thousand dollars won't cut it. You could throw four fuckin' zeroes at the end of that and it *still* wouldn't cut it. Jesus, showin' up at my door..." My voice, already loud, was rising. "What's the matter with you?"

He opened his mouth to speak, but then his gaze darted over my shoulder, surprise hit his eyes and his body snapped alert.

I was so pissed, I didn't feel it.

When Walter Jones did that, I felt it.

And *it* was not good.

What *it* was was me learning the intensely uncomfortable feeling of the vibe Garrett Merrick gave off when he was about to lose his motherfucking mind. When he was about to lose hold on his brand of messy that made the likes of Ryker look adjusted. When he was preparing to get covered in a pile of shit in an effort to dig someone he cares about out from under it.

Slowly, even though I should have gone faster—his mood was so extreme, it made me move like I was surrounded in molasses—I turned to him.

I felt the vibe, but the look on his face confirmed it.

In fascinated, terrified awe, I saw that his handsome features now appeared carved from marble, and his eyes were glinting, wintry shards of blue ice that I could fucking *swear* lowered the temperature around us by thirty degrees.

I stood immobile, terrified, not that he would harm me, but that he was about to do something that might bring harm to him, and yet I was

181

so enthralled by the sheer menace he was exuding that was so far from the Merry I knew, it shook me and I couldn't move.

Merry was immobile too, for one beat…two…three…four…all of these feeling like eternity, nothing about him changing until finally I saw a minute shift in his expression and he stepped forward.

I braced to block his way so he wouldn't go apeshit on Walter Jones.

"Step off Ms. *Rivers's* stoop," he ordered, that smooth voice that hid the rough underneath a memory, his voice was vibrating with the rage he was not hiding.

"Sir—" Walter Jones started.

Merry shifted a hand, pulling back the dark blue suit jacket he was wearing to expose the butt of his gun in its holster at the side of his chest as well as the shiny badge clipped to his belt.

"Take…your hand…off *Ms. Rivers's* door…and step…the fuck…*off her goddamned stoop*," Merry growled.

I heard the storm door whisper, but it didn't bang into place because Merry moved quickly and caught it with his hand.

I moved to go after him.

He stopped and cast the blue ice of his eyes down to me.

"You stay in here, baby."

His tone was not gentle. It wasn't soft. It was a hard order he expected to be obeyed.

And the addition of "baby" was not meant to soften that order.

It was a communication to Walter Jones of who I was to Merry.

Thinking my best move at that point was to do what I was told, I nodded.

Merry pushed through the door. It whispered again as it closed and I caught it before it banged. Then I stood on the other side of it to watch Merry prowl the three strides that took him to Walter Jones, who was standing at the foot of my stoop.

When he stopped, he pushed both sides of his suit jacket back to plant his hands on his hips, again exposing his badge and gun, but also expanding his frame so he bested Jones in height and in width.

"So you been in contact with Ms. Rivers about Dennis Lowe," he stated unhappily.

"Can I ask your name, Detective?" Jones returned.

"It's lieutenant...Lieutenant Garrett Merrick of the BPD. Now, confirm. You been in contact with Ms. Rivers about Dennis Lowe?"

"I'm an FBI profiler—" Jones started.

"I don't give a fuck what you are," Merry cut him off. "What I want right now is to be sure I'm gettin' straight what's goin' on here. You been in contact with Ms. Rivers about Dennis Lowe. Yeah?"

"I'm writing a book—"

"I don't give a fuck about that either." Merry's tone was deteriorating. "I asked you, you been in contact with Ms. Rivers about Dennis Lowe?"

"Obviously, I have," Jones sniped in the face of Merry's interrogation, his patience waning too.

"And she made it clear that she didn't wanna speak to you," Merry stated.

Oh shit.

I hadn't actually done that.

"No, actually, she didn't," Jones spoke my thoughts. "Ms. Rivers didn't take my calls."

"No, actually, Ms. Rivers *refused* to take your calls, so she *did* make it clear that she didn't wanna speak to you."

That was a good twist.

And damned true.

"Lieutenant—"

"Then you found her address and showed *in* her door without notice."

"Her insight into—"

"Right," Merry bit out. "We'll start with this, and it shocks me I have to share this with you, seein' as you're in law enforcement—"

Jones interrupted him through tight lips, "At the present time, I'm not with the FBI. I'm freelance."

Not missing a beat, Merry stated, "Then it shocks me I have to share this with you, seein' as you're a former law enforcement officer, but you do not, under any circumstances outside havin' a warrant or probable cause, open the goddamned door to a dwelling. I don't give a fuck it's the storm door or the fuckin' front door. You don't do it and you know it. Unless you think doin' it'll intimidate the occupant of the dwelling into givin' you what you came to get."

"It's clear Ms. Rivers had some barriers to speaking to—"

Merry's head tipped sharply to the side. "So you admit it was clear Ms. Rivers didn't want to speak to you?"

Jones's mouth set.

Merry kept going.

"I'll continue. As a former officer of the law, you are very aware that Ms. Rivers made it clear to you that she doesn't wish to communicate with you, so right now you're committing the crime of harassment."

"As a former officer of the law, I know that calling Ms. Rivers on the phone and knocking on her door hardly comes close to criminal harassment," Jones retorted.

"As your intent was to discuss an episode in her life where she and her son were victimized by a serial killer, and you could infer from her refusal to take your calls that you were causing her alarm or even mental torment, this absolutely could be construed as criminal harassment. And I'll note that in these parts, it absolutely *would* be construed that way. Not to mention a credible threat to her safety, even if that safety is a threat to her mental health. So it *does* come close to criminal harassment. Ignoring her clear communication that she did not wish contact from you, then showing at her door and essentially helping yourself to her property by opening that door, that could conceivably add trespassing and even menacing."

"That's ridiculous," Jones spat.

"I disagree," Merry returned. "But you want a second opinion, be happy to call Lieutenant Colton and see how he feels about this shit you're pullin'."

Jones tried to check it but couldn't quite hide the fact he'd reared back.

That meant either Colt had already told him to go fuck himself (which was probably not the case, Colt would have warned me) or Colt's reputation had preceded him, considering the number of people before Jones he'd told to go fuck themselves.

Merry didn't miss Jones's reaction.

"I see. You think you're targeting the weak," he whispered disturbingly.

"As an officer of the law," Jones fired back, "you are aware that the study of the criminal mind is essential to understanding it, so that future incidences can either be avoided or the perpetrator can be tracked and caught before he or she causes too much damage."

"So," Merry took his hands off his hips and folded his arms on his chest, "you're writin' a criminology textbook?"

"No," Jones bit off. "I have a contract with a traditional publisher."

"Which means you're cashin' in on your FBI trainin' to make money off of misery," Merry deduced.

At that, Jones thankfully decided he was done.

I knew this when he stepped away from Merry and muttered, "I see that I'll need to find alternative avenues to understanding Lowe's psyche."

"How's this? The man was jacked," Merry told him.

At these words, Jones's face screwed up in a weird way that didn't seem right to me.

But Merry wasn't done talking, and as he kept going, Jones's face shifted back to annoyance before I could figure it out.

"And that shit was textbook. There wasn't anything new there, and you've got to have studied him so you know that's the straight up truth. What you intend to do is not a service to the community, man. Be honest with yourself. And you fuck with people's lives that they pieced together after that maniac ripped them apart, be honest with them that you're doin' this for cash in your pocket, book tours, and in hopes of seein' your name on a film credit."

That took Jones from annoyed and frustrated to pissed.

"Small-town cop who thinks he knows it all but doesn't know dick. I'll confirm you don't know dick since you sure as fuck do not know me," he clipped.

That didn't sound very FBI-like.

Then again, what did I know? I'd only met a couple of them and, thankfully, our associations were brief.

"Small-town cop in the 'burg rocked by Dennis Lowe's lunacy, and we've seen a lot of assholes like you," Merry returned. "You're standing outside the home of a woman Lowe fucked with that *you* underestimated, 'cause I'm tellin' you now, you're actually lucky you're dealin' with me. If I let her loose on you, she'd grind you to nothing. And that woman is my woman. So do not stand outside my woman's home and tell me what I don't know. I know you. I can see right through you. And all I see is ugliness and greed."

"This conversation is over," Jones murmured, beginning to move down the walk.

"It's about fuckin' time," Merry decreed.

Jones kept walking, but he looked over his shoulder to hurl, "Small-town cop, small mind, and too stupid to know it doesn't make him smart to have the last word."

To my shock, at that biting retort, Merry busted out laughing.

Then I got it.

Jones didn't leave the last word to Merry. He took it. Which meant he'd called his own damned self stupid.

I grinned.

Merry stopped laughing and stood, arms still on his chest, watching Jones walk to his rental car at the curb.

I stayed inside the door as Merry and I both watched Jones get in it, start it up, and drive away.

Merry turned his head to watch it go down the street.

I kept waiting.

Then he dropped his head and shifted to move up the steps of my stoop toward me.

I opened the door and opened my mouth to share with him how totally awesome he was, but I didn't get a word out before he lifted his head, looked at me and I saw the ice still in his eyes.

I held the door, unable to move until he put his hand on it and kept moving toward me, which meant I had to move out of his way.

The storm whispered then banged and Merry locked it.

Then he slammed my front door, and locked that.

But he slammed it, the unexpected noise sounding loud in my silent living room, making me jump then slowly, step by step, retreat.

He again turned eyes of blue ice to me.

"That happen to you a lot?" he asked.

His conversational tone didn't fool me, so I kept retreating.

"Stop moving," he ordered.

I stopped moving.

"That happen to you a lot, Cher?" he pushed.

I opened my mouth, but my movement was again slowed by his vibe filling the air so full, it weighed on me.

Suddenly, he leaned forward and roared, *"That happen to you a lot?"*

"Not so much anymore, Merry," I answered.

"Not so much anymore," he repeated after me.

"Sometimes," I shared carefully.

"Ethan open the door to that shit?" he asked.

"No," I answered and thankfully did not lie.

"They call?" he kept at me.

Slowly, I nodded but added verbally, "Not so much anymore with that either."

"Then, they don't get what they want 'cause you shut them down, they come to the door?"

"Yeah, but not so much," I reiterated. "Not anymore. Swear, Merry."

"Think they're targeting the weak," he stated.

"Maybe it starts like that, but if they make it to my door, I handle it and educate them different."

"You handle it," Merry again repeated after me.

"Merry," I whispered.

At the sound of his name, suddenly and without warning, he charged me. Automatically, I retreated and had to do it fast, so I tripped over my feet. Thankfully, that happened in a strategic place, so when I started to fall back, my shoulders slammed against the wall instead of me landing on my ass.

I could make no further move because Merry was so close to me, he was fencing me in.

Even if he wasn't, he grabbed my wrist, lifted my hand, and pressed it to the wall over my head.

I sucked in a sharp breath of surprise and held it, lifting my other hand toward his chest, not knowing if I intended to rest it there in an attempt to calm him or push it against him in an attempt to escape.

I wouldn't find out because he caught that wrist too, and then both of them were pinned to the wall over my head.

"Is there an us?" he asked.

My breasts brushed his chest as I started breathing heavily.

"Goddamn it, Cher, *is there an us?*" he clipped.

"I want there to be."

Fuck!

It came out because he was *freaking* me out.

Fuck!

"Then there's an us," he declared firmly.

Oh God.

He wanted that to be too.

That made me unimaginably happy.

And it scared the absolute fucking *shit* out of me.

"And there bein' an us, Cher, that means you're mine. Ethan's mine. Are you followin' me?"

"Merry—"

"Yes or no, you followin' me?"

I swallowed and it hurt that mid-throat it hitched because I needed way more than my normal oxygen in that moment and shutting my mouth to swallow meant not sucking in air.

"Answer me, sweetheart," he ordered.

"Yes, I'm followin' you."

He adjusted my wrists to hold them in one hand so he could rest his other hand at my upper chest, right at the base of my throat.

This did not mean he was calming down or about to let me go.

It meant something else.

I just didn't know what.

Yet.

"You're followin' me, which means you get me, which means from now on, any asshole phones you, you tell me," he commanded.

That was when it occurred to me that his motions were claiming.

Shit.

"Okay, Merry." I thought it sensible in his current mood to agree.

His hand at the base of my throat slid down, and suddenly, I wasn't uncertain about the situation.

Well, not true. My head still was, but my body was having a different reaction.

"They come to the door, you do not lose your mind on them. I'm not close, you shut the door in their face and call me immediately."

"Okay, Merry," I repeated.

His hand kept going down.

"You don't look after yourself. That's not your job anymore, Cher. You leave that to me."

Oh God, God, *God*, my eyes were burning even as the backs of my knees were tingling.

"Cher," he prompted harshly.

"Okay, honey."

"You don't go it alone, not anymore, not in anything, with assholes like that guy or anybody who tries to get to you, 'cause while we ride this out, you don't need that fortress. You don't need it because you got me," he declared.

I nodded, at that moment, his words penetrating, I was unable to speak.

His hand had slid between my breasts, down my belly, and his fingers shoved into the top of my jeans when he stated, "No one fucks with you, Cher. Not ever. But they sure as fuck do not show at your door and fuck with you."

Without my permission, my eyes fell to his mouth as I whispered in agreement, "No one fucks with me."

He undid the button on my jeans.

I drew in a soft, audible breath.

"Baby," he called.

My eyes drifted up to his the exact moment his hand shoved inside my jeans then my panties and his middle finger hit my clit.

Oh yes, Merry was claiming.

My lips parted, a gust of breath whispering through as my eyes floated closed.

He pressed his middle finger back, gliding it through the slick folds, murmuring, "So damned wet, barely touched you."

I tried to open my eyes but only got the lids up halfway before his finger moved again to my clit and started rolling.

Good.

So, *so* good.

"Oh God," I breathed.

"Gave you time, Cherie. You needed it," he whispered, his finger working magic. "You texting me sayin' you're sorry you fucked us up, tellin' me you want us unfucked, tellin' me you want to take a chance with me, that mean you done takin' that time?"

I hadn't intended to text.

I didn't even know if I *did* text.

But I couldn't think of that with what he was doing to me.

All I could do was confirm, "I'm done takin' that time."

He slid his finger back and filled me.

I bit my lip, my teeth gliding along the flesh as I pushed against his hold on my wrists so I could touch him while he was touching me.

"Be a good girl, baby," he urged, and my lids lifted a centimeter as a whimper escaped me.

He did a slow circle inside me.

"You gonna be a good girl, Cherie?"

"Yes," I panted.

He changed the rotation and shared, "Good girls get good things."

I wanted good things generally, but specifically, right in that moment, I wanted them from Merry.

"Merry, need more, baby," I whispered.

"How do you get what you need?"

He'd taught me that in bed when we were drunk but delicious fucking.

I tried to focus on him and gave him what I was taught. "Please, Merry."

"That's a good girl," he murmured, sliding his finger out and going back to my clit, giving me what I needed.

My hips jerked, pressed, working with him as I moaned, "Yes."

"Just so we're clear, good girls get good things, Cher. Bad girls get punished."

I was *so* going to be bad with Merry.

But right then, I was so far gone, I had to stick with good.

"Harder, Merry," I breathed.

"How you get that?"

"*Please*," I pleaded.

His mouth brushed mine. Then his tongue slid across my lower lip. I went for more and he pulled away, but he rolled harder with his finger, so I pressed my head to the wall.

"Yeah, honey," I encouraged breathlessly.

"Work that," he growled.

I worked it, rolling with him, helping him take me there, breathing erratically, my nipples hard and aching, brushing incessantly against his chest. I felt his mouth at my ear, sucking my lobe between his lips, his tongue touching the tip.

So little.

So much.

"Merry," I gasped, my hips now moving desperately, my nipples no longer brushing because he'd pushed into me, my breasts now pressed against the hard wall of his chest. I felt the edge of his teeth skim down the taut flesh of my neck and that was it. "Merry!"

Not even close to in control, my head snapped back into the wall before dropping forward to hit his shoulder and my body tensed from wrists to toes. His finger kept at my clit and I drew in repeated soft breaths in quick succession as I experienced the sweet release.

I started trembling as it took its wondrous time coursing through me. I turned my head and pushed my forehead into his neck, barely noticing his hand release my wrists. My arms floated down to round his shoulders and hold on as he reduced the pressure at my clit but kept rolling, guiding me through the last pulses of the brilliant orgasm he gave me. And as if he could feel it drift away, when it did, he cupped me.

I held on loosely, unable to latch on, my body like a rag doll. Luckily, Merry had shifted an arm around my back to keep me steady as I fought to even my breathing.

Merry didn't help with that as he gently slid his hand from my jeans, shifted slightly, just enough to get his hand between us, and I watched up close, my head still in his neck, his chin dipping down, as he slid his middle finger, wet with me, between his lips.

I spasmed in his arms.

He felt my reaction, and I knew this when he drew my finger out and his lips curved up in a sexy, cocky grin. He retraced his path between us with his hand, then obliterated any space by wrapping his arm around me, drawing me tight to him with both arms and turning his head.

I lifted mine marginally, catching his eyes, which didn't have even a hint of ice, before my eyes closed when his mouth took mine and he kissed me.

There was a vague taste of me on his lips, but the rest of it was Merry and I knew instantly, with a heady feeling, he would not give even a little control of that kiss to me.

It was wet, long, thorough, soft, and sweet.

He gave what he just gave, so that was all for Merry.

And it was a beginning that even me, who'd managed to read a lot of important things wrong in my life, couldn't miss.

When he released my lips, he stayed close, drawing his nose along the side of mine, our positions meaning our eyes had difficulty meeting.

But we managed it.

"How you doin'?" he asked quietly.

That made me want to laugh, the question was so damned crazy.

I was limp in his arms.

Hell, I was *in his arms*.

How did he think I was doing?

"I'm hangin' in there."

He found humor in my response too; I saw it light his gaze.

It sobered as he murmured, "My brown-eyed girl."

I sobered too, that feeling hitting my eyes again as I whispered, "Merry."

If I meant to say more (which I didn't know if I did or didn't), I couldn't when he gave me a fierce squeeze.

"Means a lot, you takin' a shot at this with me."

Oh God.

I had to give it to him.

I had to.

I couldn't fuck this up again. Not for him. Not for me.

"Means a lot to me too."

His sober eyes warmed.

"Like your boy, Cherie. Wanna get a chance to get to know him better when the time is right for you. But that's gonna wait. Right now, wanna know when you're next day off is 'cause just you and me are goin' to Swank's."

And it came again. Something I'd never had. Something I'd never felt. Something incredible given to me by Merry.

This time it was him asking me on our first date and telling me that date would be at Swank's, a fashionable, *expensive* restaurant in Indy.

This meant not a bullshit date.

This was a big-time, whole hog, in your face, this means something to me, we're gonna ride it out but we're gonna start that ride right date.

"Swank's?" I whispered.

"You got a nice dress?"

I didn't have one good enough for Swank's. But I'd steal one if I had to.

"Yes," I lied.

He smiled.

Oh God.

"Night off, babe," he prompted.

"Feb doubled me up. This week, Thursday and Friday."

"I'll get us in Swank's tomorrow."

Oh *God*.

He wasn't messing around.

"I'm scared."

There I was again with the blurting.

His smile died, but his arms got tighter. "I know."

We stared at each other without either of us saying more.

This lasted a long time and it was time I didn't want to end, standing in my living room in Garrett Merrick's arms.

It seemed, since he didn't move, he agreed with me.

But life was life, so eventually we'd have to let go of that moment.

And, not surprisingly, it was Merry who was the one who had the strength to do it.

"Wish we had time to talk shit out right now, but I gotta get back to work."

"Right," I said, making a move to pull away.

He didn't let me go, so I stopped and focused on him.

He lifted his head and I straightened mine but neither of us went far.

"For planning, you gotta know, Cherie, that you owe me."

I felt my eyes narrow in confusion. "I what?"

"Owe me, baby, and when we work out that debt, I'll want more than your hand down my pants."

My legs got wobbly.

"Right," I said again, this time breathy.

One side of his lips curled up and it was again cocky. "I'll get you home to your boy after Swank's, but just sayin', whoever's lookin' after him's gotta know you're gonna have a late night."

My still-sensitive clit gave a throb that was of a strength and enjoyableness I preferred to focus on, so I just nodded.

He kept the cocky grin as he watched me do it.

He apparently had enough time to continue looking smug and not let me go and go to work, which I started to find annoying.

"Would you like me to send a thank you note for my orgasm, or would me providing that gratitude verbally right now suffice?" I asked touchily.

"Prefer your gratitude to come in a different form than both, so I'll just wait until tomorrow."

I rolled my eyes.

He gave me another squeeze, and when my eyes got back to him, I saw he was out-and-out smiling.

"Call you to let you know when I'm picking you up," he told me.

"Okay, Merry."

He bent, touched his mouth to mine, gave me another squeeze, and then, to my despair that I hid totally, he let me go.

I stood where I was and watched him go.

He unlocked the front door, opened it, unlocked the storm door and had his hand on the handle before he looked back at me.

"We got a lot to talk about, Cher. We'll get that shit outta the way tomorrow at Swank's. But I don't want you dreading it, because, honest as fuck, we're gonna get through it and we're gonna get past it. I won't make you promises again that I can't keep. Swear that, babe. So when I promise right now that I know where my head is at with you and I want us both to give this the best shot we can give it, you can believe that."

God, *Merry*.

"You gonna give this the best shot you can give, sweetheart?" he asked when I said nothing.

I nodded.

He took in my nod, smiled a small smile, but pushed, "Promise me."

I wanted to hesitate. I wanted to think about it. I was scared out of my mind.

But in that moment, I did not want to give any of that to Merry.

I wanted to give him nothing but what he needed.

So I gave it to him immediately.

"I promise, honey."

His small smile got bigger before he said, "Later, Cher."

"Later," I replied.

His eyes drifted over me, his smile quirked, then he walked out the door.

I watched him do it.

Then I went to it and stood in it as I watched him walk to his Excursion at the curb.

This time, as he drove away, he looked to me and flicked out a hand.

I lifted mine and returned the gesture.

When he was gone, I closed and locked both doors. Then, before I allowed myself to have a nervous breakdown or to act all stupid and girlie and shout with glee while twirling or something (I hadn't been girlie in so long, I wasn't sure how to do it), I went to my purse and pulled out my phone.

I maneuvered right to my text string with Merry and stared at the last two texts.

I fucked us up, baby, and I'm so fucking sorry.

Don't text. If you forgive me, come see me.

The first one I typed in and left unsent.

Now it was sent.

The second one didn't even sound like me.

I closed my eyes slowly as it came to me.

Ethan.

My little man, he *so* wanted his momma happy.

I opened my eyes and looked at the texts again, not having that first clue what to do.

Ethan should not have done that.

And Merry needed to know it wasn't me who'd had the courage to take the next step.

But I didn't know how to handle either.

"Fuck it," I muttered, tossing the phone on my purse. I went back to my vacuuming, doing it with Celine, losing myself in rivers deep and mountains high, knowing when the time came to deal, if I did it right or I did it wrong, I'd still do it.

Because that was what I did.

It had always been what I did no matter what messes I got myself into.

I dealt.

For me.

For Ethan.

And now I'd do it for Merry.

Ten

THE SCORE
Garrett

*A*fter leaving Cher, Garrett walked up the back steps of the station into the bullpen, carrying two Mimi's coffees.

When he hit the top, he did an automatic scan of the space, seeing Drew and Sean in the office with the cap. Adam and Ellen, in uniform, were walking down the front steps.

And Garrett's partner, Mike Haines, was sitting at his desk, a desk that was butted front-to-front with Garrett's.

Mike had his eyes on him and Garrett moved that way, hitting Mike's desk at the side to put his coffee down before walking to his own desk.

"Get your business sorted?" Mike asked as Garrett set his coffee down and took his seat.

He looked to Mike. "Yep."

Mike eyed him, hand wrapped around his coffee still resting on his desk.

"Can't get a read on you," he noted after a few beats. "You either just got a late life offer from the Colts to be their starting tight end or you're planning to kidnap someone to torture them."

Garrett was not surprised Mike got this read. They'd been partners for a while.

"Accurate on both, seein' as things are good, as in real good, and I'm still pissed."

Mike took a sip of his coffee before suggesting, "Maybe we should start with the good shit."

"Takin' Cher Rivers to dinner at Swank's tomorrow."

Disappointment slid through Mike's features, his mouth went hard, and he sat back in his chair.

Mike could read Garrett, Garrett could read Mike. And his read was that this wasn't about Garrett not sharing with Mike how things were the last week and a half with Cher. Even if he hadn't said a word, Mike had definitely heard because everyone in town was talking about Garrett, Cher, and Mia.

But Mike knew him well enough to know that if Garrett wanted to talk it out, he'd do that. So Mike had let it go, waiting for Garrett to come to him if he needed him, or not.

No, his reaction was Mike knowing Garrett liked to get laid and him thinking that was what was happening here.

Garrett figured disappointment didn't slide through his own features, considering he didn't feel disappointed.

He felt pissed.

"You heard talk," he remarked.

"Impossible not to hear it unless I locked Dusty and me in a sound-proofed panic room the last two weeks," Mike returned.

"Well, I can confirm Cher and me hooked up."

Mike leaned toward Garrett's desk, starting, "Man—"

Garrett leaned forward too.

"It was that. Then it was not that," he bit out. "You know me, brother. I'm dumb enough to get drunk with a good woman who's a friend who means somethin' to me and fuck that shit up. I'm not that man who would do what you're thinkin' to Cher."

"You and Mia are—"

"There is no me and Mia."

At the strength of Garrett's tone, Mike did a slow blink.

"Straight up, Cher and me hooked up," Garrett carried on. "That's what I thought it was. Wasn't so drunk I didn't think she knew the score. She did. Problem was, I didn't."

"And what's the score?" Mike asked.

"The score is, when I went to J&J's after we'd had our thing to get us back on track, some trouble Cher was having walked into the bar with bad timing. I saw that shit go down, I asked her about it. But she's Cher. She's been fucked over so bad, she doesn't want anyone to think they can get at her just the same as she doesn't want anyone to think she needs them. She tried to shut me down." Garrett shook his head. "When she did that, what we had before and then what happened between us—havin' her, wakin' up to her—something in me, brother, it just clicked."

"It just clicked," Mike muttered, still studying him.

"Near on two weeks, can't get the woman off my mind."

Mike's eyes grew intent. "What'd you and Cher have before?"

"You ever known me to get to know a woman before I took her to bed?" Garrett asked. "I'm not talkin' dating. I'm talkin' spendin' years building a friendship with a woman and then takin' that further."

Understanding hit his eyes as he shook his head. "No, man."

"No," Garrett confirmed. "I know her, Mike. I know how she is with her kid. I know how she is with her friends. I can read her voice. Her eyes. Her movements. I know the depths of her loyalty. I know she'd take a bullet for her son. I know she's got a smart mouth because she's just fuckin' smart. She can hang with the guys. She's about givin' it all to her girls. She's funny as fuck. And *now* I know she has an unbelievable body, though I do not know how because I've seen the woman eat and that's impossible. I also know she's an outstanding lay. And I know she looks so pretty first thing in the morning, it's like a goddamned miracle."

"Jesus, Merry," Mike murmured.

"And I know when I found out she had trouble, that shit started eating at me instantly. Eating at me like shit would eat at me if I knew my sister had trouble. My dad. You. I wasn't concerned about a friend. I was all in *instantly.*"

Mike sat there, mouth shut, continuing to study him.

So Garrett gave him more.

"I also know shit is done with Mia, not just because she's engaged to another man but also because I've had time to think on things and I know now she was not the woman I needed in my life—not back then, not in the years we've been divorced, not now. She's not strong enough to handle my shit. She doesn't have the tools and she doesn't have it in her to find them. Might be wrong, but my take is Cher was born with those tools. But now, Mia wants to dump her man and try it again with me. I shut that down."

Mike's eyes slightly widened.

"Holy fuck," he whispered.

"Yeah. It's over with her because I got nothin' left for her, man. I dug deep, but it's just not there. And now I'm starting something with Cher and that's all that's in my head. Doin' that right. The way it started officially was fucked up, me gettin' hammered because of Mia. But the way we *really* started was totally fuckin' right, bein' friends and layin' that foundation so now we'll have a mind to each other as we take this shot."

Mike gave it a beat before he remarked, "This gets to Colt, you better have this speech down, Merry, because if he thinks you're not in this for the reasons you just gave me, then he's gonna lose his mind."

"Colt knows about the hookup and I'll explain shit now. I'll do it once, Mike. He doesn't know the man I am or the feelings I had for Cher even before this happened and know I'll have a care, then we got problems."

Mike nodded, muttering, "I'll take your back on that, brother."

Garrett didn't reply. He grabbed his coffee and took a sip.

"Now, the good stuff done, what's got you pissed?" Mike asked.

"You know if Colt gets any assholes up in his shit, writin' books or anything else to do with Denny Lowe?" Garrett asked back.

Mike straightened. "He and Feb used to. Think that's died down." His head tipped to the side. "Cher still got issues with that?"

"Former FBI profiler walked right up to her door an hour ago, offerin' her a grand to have a chat so he can write a book."

Mike's mouth went hard again.

"What a fuckin' dick," he clipped.

"It happens to her, Mike. Not frequent, according to her, not anymore. But it still happens. Phone calls and visits."

"She shut him down?" Mike asked.

"She started, I finished. But she's open to that. Wide open. She refused this guy's calls and he still showed. That ain't right for her, but she's got Ethan. She said he doesn't open the door to that, but it could happen. And that *really* isn't right."

"Agreed, but I'm not sure what can be done about it. It isn't a crime, and I don't wanna piss you off, Merry, but Cher's a single mom bartender and ex-stripper. Assholes like that'd think she's open season, not only because she believed Lowe's shit but because they think she needs the money. Colt probably doesn't get this 'cause, one, he's a cop, and two, he looks like he can break a man in half and would, they brought that shit into his life again."

"Yeah, that's exactly why she gets it and that's exactly why a statement needs to be made she's off-limits," Garrett stated, reaching into his jacket pocket to pull out his phone.

That was when Mike went alert.

"Brother..." he trailed off, but that one word was cautionary.

Yeah, he knew his partner.

"You can either take a walk so you don't hear this call or I can. Which one's it gonna be?" Garrett asked.

Mike studied him again.

Then he grabbed his coffee, nabbed a file, and took off.

Garrett engaged his phone.

He made his call and put it to his ear.

"Talk to me," Ryker said in greeting.

Garrett kept his eyes on the room as he replied, "There's a man in town, name's Walter Jones. Ex-FBI profiler who's writin' a book on Denny Lowe. He came at Cher. He was shut down. But he's here 'cause he needs shit. Thinkin' he knows not to go at Cher again, but she's got a mom and a kid. They also aren't the only ones in this 'burg who he could hit to talk about Lowe. Some might not mind talkin'. Most won't wanna be bothered. He needs incentive to get his ass gone."

"You know where he's stayin'?" Ryker asked.

"No clue," Garrett told him.

"A challenge," Ryker muttered.

Not a surprise, Ryker was on board.

"Can give you this clue—the make, model, and plate number for his vehicle," Merry told him.

"Text it to me," Ryker ordered.

"For this, you hold a marker or I give you cash. Think on it and tell me which way you wanna go. We'll talk after you get this done."

"Cher's a sister. This assclown came at her, not down with that. This is a freebie. But, bro, just sayin', don't get used to that."

Before Garrett could extend gratitude, Ryker disconnected.

When he did, Garrett typed out the car's details and a description of Jones, and he sent it to Ryker.

He didn't like doing it like that.

Not the part about setting Ryker on it. He didn't mind that.

The part that it wasn't him taking care of this business.

But he liked his job and he needed it to keep eating and to get out of his shitty-ass condo, because the time was ripe.

After the divorce, he'd left the house they'd lived in to Mia and he understood now a part of him was staying in his current place because he expected he'd be going back.

He also understood now why he'd saved up for a down payment on a place but then he bought a Harley. Same shit happened and he bought a speed boat. Same shit and he got a timeshare in Florida.

He'd never quit living his life for the now.

And he packed as much in as he could, eating what he wanted, drinking all he wanted, taking off when he wanted, fucking who he wanted, living how he wanted.

Just like his sister after their dad got drilled with five rounds from his partner's gun, the same night their mother was tortured and murdered by that partner when Rocky was hiding upstairs, Garrett lived with the poison in his mind that life would eventually turn. The happy family they had— their mom a beautiful, vibrant woman, their dad a good man in love with his wife and always showing it, Christmases, birthdays, some part of every day filled with all that was right about family—all in one night...gone.

So he'd lived in the now. He'd gotten rid of the only person in his life who wouldn't get it like his dad did, like Rocky did, but she was the person who would feel it the worst if something happened to him. After Vegas, he'd made it so Mia would never feel it when that day happened like the poison in his mind told him it was sure to.

He had no idea how he'd get past that with Cher and her son. If the worst happened to him on the job or just because life sucked, she deserved it even less if she got in deep with him and shit went down.

He just knew now that poison was in his system, and the woman Mia was, she didn't have it in her to help him work it out.

The woman Cher was, she did.

He'd sorted that in his mind, but that was the least of his baggage.

He not only needed to start conversations with Cher about what was happening, he needed to have a conversation with Mia.

She'd fucked things up since he left.

But he'd fucked things up, leaving her. She'd loved him. It was clear she still felt that. And bottom line, back then, he'd hurt her and he'd played his own part in continuing to do it.

He had to explain and apologize so they could both move on.

Mike came back, they went through their cases, decided where they were going to start their work that day, and they were getting ready to head out the door when Sully and Colt hit the top of the back stairs.

"Merry," Colt bit out the minute he made the room. "Interrogation."

Without another word, Colt stalked toward the side hall where the interrogation rooms were.

Garrett felt his jaw set and looked to his partner.

Mike's eyes were aimed at where Colt was disappearing. He felt Garrett's gaze and looked to him.

"Think he's heard about Swank's," Mike noted, mouth twitching.

"I see that didn't sit real good with you," Sully called to Merry. "But my advice, get in there or you're both gonna get suspended for brawling in the bullpen."

Not happy about it but knowing Sully wasn't wrong, Garrett got up and walked to the hall.

He found the door open to interrogation room one, Colt waiting inside, ass leaned to the table, palms pressed to the top beside his hips. Garrett made his statement by not entering the room but instead stopping in the doorway and leaning a shoulder against the jamb.

He further made his statement verbally.

"Not a big fan of being summoned, brother," he said quietly.

"Cher's made the calls," Colt clipped. "All hands on deck with her girls bringin' dresses to J&J's she can look over tonight and pick one for her date with you tomorrow at Swank's."

Fuck, he needed to call to get a reservation.

He made note of that even as he felt his lips curve at Cher doing what Cher did.

"I see that pleases you," Colt remarked, not sounding pleased, and Garrett focused on him again. "Probably please you more she made a date for a weekday sleepover for her boy at Meems's. So rest up 'cause you got all night to tap that *real* good, brother."

His tone was cutting.

His words were incendiary.

Garrett battled the burn as he pushed away from the door. "Watch yourself, Colt."

Colt's brows went up. "You're playin' with my girl and you're tellin' *me* to watch myself?"

"No, I'm takin' *my* girl out to dinner and I'm tellin' *you*, even though I know you're makin' a point, you need to watch your mouth when you're talkin' about her."

Colt's eyes went intense.

"Your girl?" he asked.

"Learned from her, not your business until she makes it. You two are tight. You and me are tight. For her, what she's got with you, that wins out. So she makes this your business, that's hers. What you need from me, respect to you as my brother, respect to you as the man who gives a shit about her, I'm havin' a care. You got my promise on that, Colt. Now, the rest of it, *you* need to have a care."

"I told you—"

"Her son's daddy and his bitch are thinkin' of makin' a play for her boy," Garrett cut him off to say. "I found that shit out for her so she could shut it down."

"She told me that, but—"

"This mornin', a man walked up to her door and offered her a thousand dollars to talk about Lowe."

That made Colt push up from the table.

"I shut that down too," Garrett told him. "This is not play. This is not a hookup. This is not about Mia. This is not dick but me and a woman I have feelin's for, explorin' what's goin' on between us. It's time she started her life again after Lowe interrupted it. She's doin' that with me."

He crossed his arms on his chest, held Colt's gaze, and kept going.

"I have no clue how this is gonna roll. I got shit I gotta deal with. She does too. But right now, we're lookin' at doin' it together. We can tough it out, I see good things. We can't, we can't. But that's ours. Not yours because you want to cushion her from any hits life might land. Not anyone's. I gave it time because I needed that time to know exactly where I was before I took it further. I gave it time because she needed to know I gave it that time for her and her kid. I'm all about doin' this right and that's also for Cher *and* for Ethan. That's said, so now you need to stand down, Colt. If not for me, wantin' me to have good in my life, then for her."

"You better—" Colt kept trying.

But Garrett was done with this shit.

"Don't say more. Don't threaten me. Don't warn me. Don't do shit, Colt," Garrett interrupted him again. "Not shit you can't come back from. You know I'm only givin' you what I just gave you because of what she means to you. You don't cut me some slack, we got problems, and straight up, man, I do not want problems with you when my attention needs to be on sortin' my shit so I can bust my ass to make a good woman happy."

Garrett knew he finally got to Colt before he watched his friend's eyes narrow as he asked, "Some asshole walked right up to her door to get to her about Lowe?"

Garrett nodded. "She says it doesn't happen much anymore, but it happens."

"He didn't call first?"

"He called. Cher didn't take his calls, so he decided on a face-to-face."

"*Fuck*," Colt hissed.

"Rumor's spreadin', seein' as this guy probably has a hit list and Cher was just his first, and Ryker's heard." Colt's face froze, but Garrett kept talking. "You know how protective Ryker is about the citizens of this 'burg, so I think Walter Jones might soon feel induced to find his way to the town limits."

"Shit, Cher's never learned, you got a problem, you court it gettin' bigger if you don't tell somebody. She could have told me about the calls and I could have had a chat with this moron over the phone and convinced him a trip to the 'burg would be a waste of his time. Instead, she didn't take his calls, you were there when he made his play, and now I don't know what's worse, whatever Ryker's gonna do to 'induce' this guy to take a hike or you bein' a bigger lunatic than Ryker because *you* know *he's* a lunatic and you set him on this guy."

"And you would have played it how?" Garrett prompted.

"My play would have been personal," Colt returned.

And *that* was why Colt and February didn't catch this shit.

"Yeah, and that gets messy. The cap, every one of your brothers, every man and woman in this county, and every judge at the courthouse would see your play because they'd play it the same way. Lowe spent decades where he existed only to destroy your life. He nearly succeeded in that. They'd get that. Me actin' for a woman I haven't even taken on our first date? Not so much."

Colt said nothing for a beat before he sighed.

That meant he saw Garrett's play.

"We done with our brief?" Garrett asked. "I got cases to close."

"We're done, brother," Colt muttered.

That also meant they were good.

Garrett nodded and started to turn away when Colt called his name.

He gave the man his attention.

"Would be good, you got some happy. Would be good, Cher did too. But you couldn't have picked a bigger challenge, Merry. I hope you know the work you got cut out for you, man."

"It's taken me nearly two weeks to get her to a place where I could even talk to her about a date, Colt. I think I know that."

Colt grinned.

Garrett shook his head. They were done. They were good. Time to get to work.

So he left Colt to do that.

But before he took off with Mike, he called Swank's, got the only reservation they had left, and texted the time to Cher.

He knew she was still on a course to surfacing, not retreating, when he and Mike didn't even make it to the bottom of the back stairs before his phone sounded with a return text.

Got it. And just so you know, I'm only going because I know you put out on the first date.

This meant Garrett Merrick walked out of the station laughing.

Cher

I walked down the hall into my living room.

My son, on the couch, eyes to the TV, looked at me.

"Whoa," he said. "You're ready way early."

I was.

This was due to the fact that I'd called Mom to ask her to come early because we had to chat. And because I'd called Feb and Vi to tell them I needed a dress for a date with Merry at Swank's. Since I didn't need to be spending two hundred dollars on a dress when my ex was threatening attorneys, I needed to borrow one, so I was hitting the bar early to do some dress borrowing in the office.

And last, because I needed to have a sit-down with my boy.

"Hit mute, kid, would you?" I asked.

He looked at me, then he lifted the remote from his thigh and hit MUTE.

I curled my leg under me as I sat on it on the couch, turned toward him.

"What's up, Mom?" he asked.

"Merry came to visit me today."

I'd practiced this. I didn't know how to begin, but I thought sharing that information and waiting to see how he'd react would guide my way.

How he reacted was how I figured he'd react with one addition I didn't expect.

That being his very first reaction was such extreme excitement, it was a wonder he didn't burst from the couch, propelled by its power.

Damn.

It hit him what I was saying and how Merry's visit came to be, so his first reaction was quickly dampened by panic mixed with guilt.

"Yeah, kid, I know you sent my text along with your own," I said quietly.

"Mom—" he whispered.

"Not good," I cut him off to whisper back.

His face was pale but his cheeks were red, and I knew when his eyes started shining that he was close to crying.

That was not what I wanted to do to my kid, ever, so I moved things along.

"First, I'll tell you that, with your invitation, Merry showed. We talked. Since you read my texts with him, you probably got the impression that something was goin' on between him and me. It wasn't, but it was. I didn't think either of us were ready to tackle that. Today, Merry convinced me differently."

The color came back to his face as the excitement came back to his eyes, but I had to keep going.

"We're goin' out on a date tomorrow. You're stayin' the night with Mimi and Al."

"Cool," Ethan said softly, clearly not sure how to play this because my tone was crisp and informative and not much else.

"I'll tell you that I'm glad me and Merry got the chance to talk, because I like him. I like that you like him. He's a good guy, and if things go okay, he'd be good for us. I'm a little bit scared of that, but I'm gonna give it a shot."

"I'm glad, Mom."

"What I don't like," I kept talking like he didn't, "is my son invading my privacy."

He leaned slightly toward me and started, "Mom—"

"No, son, listen. Don't talk," I said gently, but the tone was a mom tone that I didn't pull out very often because I didn't have to. I didn't think I'd used it in the last year. It could even be two.

He was getting it now.

"What you need to get from this discussion is that what you did might have led to good things, but it also might have led to bad things. It might have put your mom in a super uncomfortable situation with someone who means a lot to her. You had no idea what was goin' on. Merry and me are friends, and part of me bein' scared about startin' somethin' with him is because that friendship means a lot to me. That gets messed up, it's gonna hurt. You coulda messed that up at the get-go, not knowin' what was happening and doing what you did."

"But you and Merry—"

I nodded. "We talked it out. It's all good and that's important for you to know too so you don't beat yourself up about it too much. But I'm tellin' you now, you're almost eleven. In a few years, you're gonna have things in your life you wanna keep private. I figure then you'll look back at this and think about me bein' in your business and you'll get what you did is how it is. I'm gonna give you your privacy because I trust you and I trust you to do right. But nothin' is gonna erase the fact you invaded mine. It's gonna sting, kid, when you look back at it. Don't let it sting too much, but learn from it."

He bit his lip, eyes big and again shining, and I worried he'd lose it, so I had to keep going so he wouldn't do that.

"Now, like what happened with our neighbor when you did what I asked you not to do, this is the same. There's a lesson to be learned, Ethan, and all I want from this is that you learn it. But this is bigger than that. See, you aren't gettin' your own phone until you're at least thirteen. But you need to use my phone sometimes, and I don't wanna be givin' you passwords and changin' 'em only to have to give them to you again and change them 'cause I can't trust you. So, even though you did somethin' untrustworthy, I still gotta trust you. Which means I gotta make sure my point is made and you get how big this is. So, sorry, kid, but for the next two weeks, you got cleaning the bathroom and mopping the kitchen floor duty and you're not gonna get paid ten dollars when you do it."

He slouched back into the couch.

"You also keep the kitchen clean and the house picked up, all by yourself. I'll talk with your gram so she knows when she's around to leave you to that. You just got two weeks of it and then you're back to getting an allowance, you do more than your chores. But just need to hammer home you did wrong so you'll have a few times cleaning the bathroom and doin' the dishes on your own to think on that. Okay?"

"Okay, Mom," he forced out, sounding like it was not okay but definitely getting my message.

"Okay," I mumbled, happy that was over because, even if it had to be done, these were also the kinds of times when being a mom sucked.

I was about to push up but Ethan speaking stopped me.

"You told me you two weren't together," he said in a way that was like an accusation.

"Honey, straight up, I'm your mom and some stuff is just not your business, and that doesn't have anything to do with you bein' a kid and me bein' grown up. It's just not your business. But I'll tell you, at that point, I didn't lie. Things were kinda changin' between Merry and me and both of us wanted it, but I was tryin' to put a stop to it because I got more than just me to look after. Merry broke through and that was partly to do with what you did with those texts and partly to do with what you said to me the other night. But that doesn't make what you did right."

"Okay, then, you told me that Merry was hung up on his old wife. That was, like, a week ago or somethin'. How is he tryin' to be with you when he's into someone else?"

Shit, I did tell him that.

And, shit again, Ethan had been thinking on things.

And, more shit, he'd put things together in his little man way.

And the worst of that shit, I had the same question.

"And don't say that's not my business," Ethan continued, "because I like Merry and I'm guessin' you know that since I sent those texts. But now you're goin' on a date with him and you said that to me, and I gotta know my mom's goin' out with a guy who's into her, not some other lady."

"That's part of what we talked through today." I drew in a deep breath and hoped I was giving him the truth, a hope I had for him and for me. "He took time to have a think on things to know where his head was at, and he realized his head was with me. So that's why I'm goin' out with him tomorrow, because I like him more than just friends and I believe him when he says he wants to be with me."

Ethan stared at me, and he must have believed it too because he nodded.

I nodded back.

I had to do my last spritz of perfume and put on my shoes before Mom got there, then I had to chat with her and get to the bar, so I also had to get a move on.

I got up, about to tell my son we were all good, but as I was finding my feet, he spoke.

"I know I didn't do right. I know what I did was bad," he declared, looking up at me, right in the eye, face set. "I knew it then, but I decided I didn't care. But you gotta know I thought about it before I did it. I just didn't do it.

You also gotta know that if Merry makes you happy, I'd do it again. I don't care if it wasn't right. Because sometimes, Mom, you gotta take chances even if you might be goin' about it wrong, if what comes out of it is right."

"I could argue that logic, baby," I said softly.

"Then you'd be wrong," he returned. "'Cause I'm not stupid. I'm a kid, but I got eyes and I got ears and kids talk. So do parents. I know, Mom." His voice dipped. "I know you did some things even you thought weren't right to take care of me. But you did 'em because takin' care of me was right. So, in the end, they *were* the right thing, even though other people might think they were wrong."

Shit, he had me there.

"I'm thinkin' of tradin' you in for a kid who's a whole lot more stupid than you," I announced, and his face cracked, his mouth quirked, and finally he couldn't fight it anymore and grinned at me.

I started walking to my bedroom.

And I did it talking.

"Right, smart guy, when you win the Nobel Peace Prize, don't forget your momma in your acceptance speech."

"Whatever," he called to my back, but I knew he did it still grinning.

I couldn't help but grin too because that was done and I'd managed to get it done with my kid grinning.

I hit my room. I did the spritzing thing, strapped on my high heels, and grabbed my leather jacket.

I walked back out and was collecting my phone and grabbing a pack of Butterfinger Cups to throw in my purse (in case I needed a candy hit during work) when I saw Mom pull up to the curb.

"Okay, Ethan, I'm outta here. Be good for your gramma," I said as I went to the door.

"Lucky for you, you can take it easy at work since you don't gotta make as many tips because you got free labor since I did somethin' stupid that still got you a date with the coolest guy in town," he returned.

I wanted to be "severe mom" who put the kibosh on her kid being a smartass.

But the operative part in that was "smart" so I just shot him a smile before I walked out the door.

I met Mom halfway up the walk.

"Why'd you want me to come early?" she asked. "And where are you goin'?" She looked to the house and kept at me before I could even answer her first question. "Is Ethan okay?"

"I needed you to come early so I could tell you that Ethan's got additional chores, a deal we made because he did somethin' not right. He's got kitchen duty and needs to keep the place picked up. He's had dinner, but if you guys make a mess, it's up to him to clean it."

She looked back at me. "What'd he do?"

"Think that might be better it's between him and me for now, Mom," I told her quietly.

She'd been at my side with Ethan since I pushed him out, and during the pushing him out part, that was literally. This meant there were things she had with my boy, good and the odd times he was bad. I had the same things. Sometimes, Mom and me shared about those things. Sometimes, for Ethan, we did our own thing so the bad he did didn't spread and make him feel like a loser.

It worked for all of us.

So at that moment, without another word, she nodded.

"Also, before it flies through the 'burg like I know it's gonna do, want you to know I got a date with Merry tomorrow night."

In the shadows cut liberally by my front light, I saw her eyes get huge.

Now, my mom, even at fifty-six, with a life that didn't often treat her kind, had never lost hold on her girlie.

She demonstrated this right then, grabbing my hands and giving a little hop.

"Oh, my beautiful baby girl, that makes me so *happeeeeeeee.*"

It made me happy too.

But for me and my mom, since life didn't often treat us kind, she had to cool it with her expectations.

"Mom, it's just a date."

She leaned toward me, looking like a girl who just got her hand kissed by David Cassidy.

"With *Garrett.*" She leaned back. "He's very handsome."

"I've noticed."

"He's also very tall."

"I've noticed that too."

"Girl like you, you got length and you wear heels. Not easy for you to find a man who can top you, you're wearin' heels. Worried you'd find a boy and it'd be like Tom Cruise when he was with that pretty Kidman lady. They looked good together but never right. When you two walked into my house last week, holdin' hands, I thought to myself, that there *looks right*."

"Mom—"

"Quiet, baby girl, let your mom be happy," she whispered in a way I snapped my mouth shut.

She'd never met Dennis Lowe. Not my choice, he'd found excuses not to bury himself deep in my life. Excuses I should have seen as red flags to at least share the fact he was married if not that he was a whackjob.

And, obviously, me being with Trent didn't make her happy.

Garrett Merrick was the kind of man who'd make any mother happy.

If, of course, she'd never been around when he was keeping a loose hold on losing his motherfucking mind.

But my mother, I knew, could be around that and want him even more for me.

I gave her time before I whispered back, "Okay, be happy. I'm happy. I'm scared, but I'm happy. Just be smart too, Mom, because I got a knack for fuckin' shit up. Not gonna share, but I already almost blew it with Merry. So you wanna be happy, okay. Just do it bein' *cautiously* happy."

She shook my hands and replied, "I'll be cautiously happy, honey-sicle."

I nodded.

Then I went about finishing up.

"One more thing to tell you, and I'm sorry, Mom, but it isn't a happy thing, cautious or not."

"Oh crap," she muttered.

"There's a man in town, his name is Walter Jones. He's writing a book on Dennis Lowe." Her hands convulsed in mine so I held her tighter. "He stopped by, but he just happened to stop by when Merry was here, and Merry kinda…well…we'll just say that didn't make him happy."

Her eyes started to brighten with joy again.

Shit.

"Anyway," I went on, "I'm thinkin' he's not gonna stop by again, but just in case he thinks he can get somethin' from you, you gotta know. Don't talk to him and call me if he tries to get in touch with you."

That happened. Mom had been targeted. It was far more rare for her because many accounts of what had happened were already out there, even TV shows made about it, and it was known Mom had never met Lowe.

That didn't stop them all, though, especially them trying to use her to get to me.

I was not surprised when Mom skipped over all I'd said and honed in on one thing.

"Garrett took care of him for you?"

I sighed.

"I bet that was good," she muttered.

It was scary as shit.

And it was hot as fuck.

"I need to go to work," I told her.

"But you don't have to leave for half an hour," she told me.

Shit, fuck, shit.

Should I tell her?

I had to tell her. She was probably going to find out anyway.

"Merry's takin' me to Swank's and I don't have anything to wear, so I'm goin' in early to look through some stuff Feb and Vi are bringin'."

Her eyes got huge at the word "Swank's," and her face lit with so much glee, it was a wonder the dark didn't flee the night.

"Mom, *cautiously* happy," I warned.

"Right, right, *cautiously* happy about tall, handsome, last-good-one-standing Garrett Merrick takin' my baby to *Swank's*. I'll be *cautiously* happy about that, Cheryl."

"Whatever," I mumbled.

She smiled.

Huge.

I pulled my hands from hers. "Gotta go."

"Have fun," she called as I headed to my car and she headed to my door.

"You too," I called back.

She went into my house.

I got into my car and drove to the bar.

Wednesday night, with most of the other businesses on Main Street closed, the bar might be busy but not packed. I found a parking spot on the street two doors down.

I parked, hoofed it in, and saw the place was busy.

Good news.

Meaning good tips.

I also knew I was in trouble because Morrie was behind the bar, Colt was on his stool, and Cal was standing at the bar next to Colt.

This wasn't the trouble.

The trouble was, all their eyes came to me when I opened the door and Morrie grinned a my-girl's-gonna-get-herself-some grin. Colt looked like he wanted someone to tear his own fingernails out by the roots. And Cal looked like he was having trouble not busting a gut laughing.

Feb and Vi were nowhere to be seen, which meant they were in the office.

And the men knew about my date and what was going to happen in the office.

I made my way to that end of the bar and shoved aside the stool Cal was not sitting on so I could put my body there.

I looked up to him.

"How many shots do I need before I go in there?" I asked.

Very slowly, he grinned.

Staring up at him, those sky-blue eyes, the scars that perfectly marred what was once pure male beauty making a badass more badass, serious as shit, it was not the first time I wanted to walk direct from him to my girl Violet and high-five her for her score.

But I didn't do that because I heard a glass slam on the bar beside me and Morrie was there, pouring tequila.

"Feb isn't a big fan of drinkin' on the job," he stated. "You know I don't give a shit. But, officially, you aren't on the job yet, so I'm thinkin' what's in that office, you need about three a' those."

I didn't hesitate and slammed the shot.

I heard Cal chuckle.

I didn't look at Cal.

215

I looked at Colt.

"You gonna give me shit about goin' out with your brother in blue?"

"Gave Merry shit already," Colt returned, and my stomach clutched. "He shoved it back." My stomach unclutched and I beat back a smile. "Not sure which one a' you is more fucked in the head, him for takin' on your shit or you for takin' on his. Just know I'll kick either of your asses, you fuck the other over."

"You do know I'm a big girl, Uncle Colt," I shot back.

Cal chuckled again. Morrie joined him.

Colt started to look testy.

Or *testier.*

"Lotta people love you both, Cher," he said quietly. "Pleased as fuck you're takin' a chance on life and doin' it with the only guy on the planet I don't have to do an extensive background check on. But want you both happy. You give that to each other, I'll be over the moon. The opposite happens…" he trailed off.

Goddamned Colt, being his version of sweet.

Shit.

"Message received," I muttered.

"I see good things," Cal announced, and I turned surprised eyes up to him to see him already looking down at me. "He's a catch. You're a catch. That shit works, both of you are smart enough to know you scored and scored huge, and neither of you are stupid enough to forget it."

Joe Callahan thought I was a catch?

Morrie poured another shot. "Babe, hit that, then hit the office. Fortification, then you get the shit job done and you can look forward to eight hours on your heels, which'll be the best part of your night."

Morrie totally knew me.

One could say I didn't like shopping.

One could also say, unless there was a good deal of food to be consumed, the same with beverages, these being alcoholic, I didn't do your normal girlie-type things.

I didn't have money for manis and pedis and facials. I didn't have patience with crowds in order to hang out at coffee houses and shoot the shit or go to the mall and ask my bestie if my butt looked big in things.

No, I wasn't about that.

But I was the girl for you if you needed a wingman to go on the prowl, were happy to belly up to a bar and throw a few back while righting the worlds wrongs, if you liked to kick back and catch a game on TV, and I always had a dry shoulder to cry on.

Pawing through dresses with my girls around, giving their opinions about what would be *just perfect* for a date with Garrett Merrick, was not in the top two hundred things I would want to do.

And these men, who spent their free time bellied up to the bar or kicked back watching a game, knew my pain.

Fuck.

I looked to the office door.

I looked to the shot.

I grabbed the shot and slammed it.

Then I slammed the glass on the bar, looked through the men who were now all grinning at me, glad they were at the bar and not heading to the office with me, and I trudged to the office.

I opened the door and shut it behind me, thinking that Morrie knew what he was saying when he'd said I needed three shots.

He should have given me all three.

He also should have warned me.

This was because the office looked like the dressing room of a drag show and Feb and Vi weren't the only ones there. Mimi, Jessie, and fucking Josie Judd (who was more of a nut than Jessie, and that was nearly impossible) were there too.

"Please, God, tell me Raquel Layne is not about to walk through that door, 'cause I *know* my bitches wouldn't invite Merry's sister to come and offer me a dress to borrow to go on a date with him, a date where, at the end, it's a foregone conclusion I'm gonna get lucky."

They all laughed.

I didn't because not one of them assured me Rocky wasn't showing.

Finally, Mimi reached to nab my hand and dragged me further into the small space, saying, "Of course we didn't invite Rocky."

"How many shots did Morrie pour you before lettin' you in here?" Feb asked.

"Two," I answered.

"I thought he'd go for three," she muttered.

"Right, we got precious little time," Jessie snapped, glaring at me. "Only you would organize shit like this and give it fifteen minutes. That's insanity."

"Just pointin' out, I didn't organize anything," I returned. "I asked Feb and Vi to bring a couple of dresses. I didn't ask *you* at all."

She swung her torso back, eyes getting huge. "Well *pardon me* that I'd haul half my wardrobe here to make sure you gave Merry good on your first date."

"Bitch, you and I aren't even the same size," I shot back. "I like tight, but days where I let it all hang out are long gone and I only did that shit for money."

Josie, Mimi, and Vi laughed, Feb grinned, but Jessie narrowed her eyes at me.

"Okay, well, I wasn't supposed to tell you, Queen Attitude, but I *didn't* bring half my wardrobe. Feb called and I went shoppin'. We girls are all buyin' you a new dress to go on your first date with Merry because that's the way it should be. A girl should feel special when she's out with a good man who's into her, first shot she's takin' at gettin' somethin' good in a long time, first shot he's takin' at findin' somethin' good. We were just gonna say that you could keep whatever you picked 'cause we don't wear it anymore. But I got all the tags off everything in here so I can return what you don't pick and you in a knock-his-socks-off dress is on your *bitches*."

"Jessie!" Feb snapped.

But I stared, my eyes expanding in their sockets, so dry, they started burning.

"It isn't a big deal," Vi said quickly. "With all of us chipping in, it doesn't cost hardly anything."

I looked to the wall.

I looked to the floor.

They knew I had it bad for Merry.

All of them.

Of course they did. They were my bitches. From your bitches, your *true* bitches, you couldn't hide anything.

Even if you tried.

"Don't be mad," Josie urged. "We don't want you to be mad." I looked at her to catch her eyes slicing to Jessie when she finished, "That was why you weren't supposed to know."

"Coolest thing anyone's done for me."

After these words came out, five pairs of startled eyes shot to me.

"I mean, coolest girlie-shit-type thing anyone's done for me," I amended.

Mimi grinned at Josie.

Feb smiled at the floor.

Jessie sent an "I knew it" smile at me.

Vi just sent a sweet Violet smile at me.

I moved toward a jumble of clothes on the desk.

"Right, let's get this done. I got tips to make and some of this might require tryin' on, so we don't got a lotta time."

"Start with this one," Jessie commanded, throwing a green swatch of fabric at me. "It's perfect for your coloring."

"No, the red," Meems contradicted. "That's *hot.*"

"Green. Her hair, her eyes, it's gotta be the green," Josie put in.

I looked to Vi, then I looked to Feb.

None of us said anything.

But I had a feeling they knew exactly how bad my eyes were burning.

And they knew it hurt.

But they also knew that for a girl like me—a girl whose life turned to shit, but I made it through to stand in a small office in a small bar in a small town with women who had golden souls—that hurt felt good.

Eleven

No Pressure
Garrett

The next night, Garrett walked up Cher's walk and he did it with his eyes to her front door, the lights inside illuminating the diamond window and coming muted through her front curtains.

He felt something and looked to his left to see a man two houses over, moving down his walk.

His head was turned.

His eyes were on Garrett.

It was dark, the man didn't have his front light on, and there was distance so Garrett couldn't see him well. But he was also a cop, so what he saw didn't sit good in his gut.

It wasn't the way he was dressed. It wasn't the beat-up, rusted-out old Chevy truck he was moving toward at the curb.

It wasn't anything.

But it was something.

He looked forward to jog up the steps of Cher's stoop, glad that he knew Cher was a woman who would also feel that something vibe from her neighbor and keep herself and her kid well away.

He knocked.

She didn't make him wait.

She opened the door, and light behind her, front light on, he saw her top to toe.

And he went still.

"I'm ready," she said, opening the storm door and swinging it his way. His body jerked and he caught it before it hit him in the face. "Just gotta finish switching out purses."

She left him to open the door fully and disappeared inside.

Garrett stepped in, the door whispering then banging behind him, his eyes to Cher bending over the coffee table, ass pointed his way, switching shit out of a big slouchy purse into a small sleek one.

He barely noticed what she was doing.

His attention was focused on her ass.

Then it was on her legs.

After that, her shoes.

She straightened and turned to him.

That was when he got hit with all of her again, full-on.

Her dress was green. Not a bright green—kelly, emerald, shit like that. Not forest green either. It was dark, though, and the color looked great on her.

It was also skintight, from just above her knees all the way to the little sleeves that capped at the top of her arms. High neckline, a kind of gather or pleat at the side of her tits that gave them room to be there but held them up, somehow disguising them at the same time pronouncing them.

The dress gave nothing away while showing every-fucking-thing, every curve, line, swell, and angle, all the goodness that was Cher, subdued yet highlighted to extremes.

And he'd seen the back. The front was high, but the back dipped low to her bra strap.

So the dress had to be tight to hold her all in, especially her breasts.

Tight in good ways.

Her makeup was more than what she usually wore to the bar, deeper in a sexy way that would make her seem mysterious if he didn't know her and just clapped eyes on her.

Her hair wasn't the same as how she did it to go to work either, but he couldn't put his finger on how. It was down as usual. It was full as usual. But it looked like she'd done more with it.

Big gold earrings, lots of bangles on her wrists, a huge-ass ring on her middle right finger, her feet in sandals with a shit-ton of straps so thin, he had no idea how she could walk without them snapping. They were green but covered in tiny rhinestones that didn't sparkle, they just embellished, so they looked class not trash. The heel was tall and lethal, Garrett never meeting a woman who could go as high as Cher did and make it look like she was in flip-flops. But those she had on now were even higher.

He made the instant decision they'd stay on later when he fucked her.

Christ.

"Merry?"

He looked from her shoes to her face.

"You look phenomenal, baby."

Her body jolted so badly, that shit was visible, her head going with it, her hair swaying with the movement.

Then she seemed stuck, frozen, staring at him like she'd never seen him or any breathing male in her life.

When she stayed like that, it was his turn to call, "Cher?"

She seemed to force herself out of her stupor, and the instant she did, she was on the move.

Snatching up some wrap from her chair, she marched woodenly to the door, announcing tersely, "We gotta go."

She was out the door before he could say a word, and when he made it to that space, he saw her standing on the stoop, holding her storm door open for him, looking like she was fighting against tapping her toe.

He moved out, closing the front door behind him, and she charged in, shoving up against him to get in the space, key up to lock it.

Fuck, she also smelled good.

Real good.

"Cher," he said quietly.

"Let's go," she demanded, turning, skirting him, and hauling her ass down the walk before he could grab her hand, seeing as he had to use it to catch the storm door she'd moved out of because it was about to knock him off the stoop.

She made it to his truck well before him and Garrett decided to wait to unlock it until he was close.

He wasn't real big on how she stared at the door, not looking to him, as he stopped at her.

He hit the locks and she immediately went for the door.

His hand shot out to cover hers.

"Everything okay?" he asked.

Her gaze didn't leave his hand.

"Everything okay, Cher?" he repeated.

She looked up at him. "It's cold. You gonna let me inside?"

It was cold and he had a dick, so it was utterly impossible not to let his eyes fall to her tits to see that evidence straining her dress.

Fuck.

"Garrett," she prompted testily.

His hand over hers, he jerked open the door.

She pulled her hand away and climbed up.

After he closed the door on her, he drew in a heavy breath, rounded the hood, and angled in beside her, not a big fan of how this date was starting.

He'd clearly done something to piss her off. He had no clue what it was, but he reckoned she'd make it up if it didn't exist.

This told him the walls were going back up.

And this didn't make him happy.

More, he couldn't do the work he needed to do to knock them back down in a fancy-ass restaurant where he was gonna blow at least two hundred dollars not enjoying it and not being able to fully enjoy Cher in that fucking dress.

He started the truck and was just edging it from the curb, about to make the effort to clear the air on a drive that was not long but also wasn't short, in order that he might be able to salvage dinner and definitely be able to salvage the plans he had after dinner with her and her shoes.

She got there before him.

"Okay, I'm just gonna say this straight out, right now, so if you wanna turn around and drop my ass back at my house, you can do that without wastin' too much gas," she decreed into the cab. "It wasn't me who texted you that apology. It was, but I typed it in and didn't send it. Ethan got in my phone, not bein' a little shit, he just does that 'cause he doesn't have his own phone and anyway, I let him do it. He did it this time because he saw a text from his gramma. My guess is, he saw my unsent text to you and he likes you. He thinks you're gonna make me happy. He worries about me bein' alone, especially with him growin' up, so that's gonna happen more, and he wants to look out for me. So he sent that text. He also wrote the one tellin' you to come see me. So there." The last came out on a gush of breath. "There it is. I didn't have the balls to apologize. My ten-year-old kid had to have the balls for me."

Garrett concentrated on guiding his truck down her street.

He thinks you're gonna make me happy.

When he didn't reply immediately, she kept babbling.

"I typed it in, but I figure I don't get any points for that. When you came over, I thought I'd fucked up and sent it myself. I was gonna say somethin' about that, but then you got pissed as shit at Walter Jones and ended that with your hand down my pants. My attention got diverted. But I'm tellin' you now, straight away, so you know."

My attention got diverted.

He stopped at the stop sign at the end of her street, flicking on his blinker.

But even though the way was clear, he didn't turn.

"Garrett?" she called.

My ten-year-old kid had to have the balls for me.

"Merry," she whispered, the brusque out of her tone. She sounded scared.

At that sound, he shoved the truck in park and was just able to get that done before he burst out laughing.

He turned to her while doing it, hit the button on her seatbelt, and heard through his laughter her low, surprised cry as it zipped back right before she let out another one when he hauled her ass in his lap.

He managed to fight back the laughter just enough to lay one on her. He made it deep, he made it wet, and because she tasted good and she'd wound her arms tight around his shoulders, pressing her tits deep, he made it long.

When he finally released her mouth, he moved away only an inch and asked, "Is it too soon for me to put aside money for your kid's college education in order to thank him for helpin' me drag his mother's head outta her ass?"

He watched through the shadows as her face, soft from his kiss, screwed up with irritation.

He liked the soft.

But Cher irritated was cute and he liked that too.

"Yes," she snapped.

"Then I'll just have to give him a handshake and slip him a hundred dollar bill next time I see him."

"He got into trouble for that, Merry. You cannot give him *money*," she returned.

"Then when he suddenly has the cake to buy a couple new video games, just sayin' now, he didn't get it from me."

"This isn't funny," she retorted. "The ends don't justify his means."

"Cherie, sweetheart, your time was up. I was givin' you a week. It was Wednesday. It was a week. I'm pleased as fuck you apologized, you meant to send it or you didn't. But it wouldn't matter. You'd be in that fucking amazing dress in my truck on the way to dinner with me, Ethan sent that text or not."

Her brow furrowed. "You were givin' me a week?"

"You told me, you got somethin' worth fightin' for, you fight for it. You don't sit on your ass and wait for it to come to you."

He actually felt her draw in a huge breath.

But he wasn't done.

"In that circumstance, I had to sit on my ass and wait for what was worth fightin' for. I had to give her time. I had to make sure she knew I had time to think things through. So I decided on a week. I gave you that week. And here we are."

She said nothing, just stared at him seemingly unaware they were stopped at a stop sign, her round ass in his lap in his truck, her arms holding on tight at his shoulders.

He pulled her closer. "Now, your ass is in my lap and I like that. I like it enough, we're not even a block away from your house and I'm good to go

225

back so we can move forward on what it's doin' to my cock. But you look way too fuckin' good not to show you off. I'm gonna get to what's under that dress later. It'd be a damn shame that dress comes off this soon."

He brushed her mouth with his before he finished.

"And I'm hungry."

"I'm hungry too," she said softly.

"Right," he muttered, gave her a squeeze, then slid her off his lap and into her seat. "Buckle up."

He checked the road, hearing her seatbelt catch. It was still clear, so he made his turn. He accelerated, and as he did, it occurred to him Cher had it right.

If they dealt with the shit on the way to the restaurant, they could spend their time at Swank's enjoying it.

So Garrett took her lead.

"Okay, Cher, think you had the right idea puttin' shit out there right away, so I'll give you what I got so we can get it done and then just have you and me at Swank's."

He felt her eyes on him when she asked, "What do you got?"

Honest to God, he had no idea what her reaction was going to be to what he had to share. What he thought was that this might be a mistake, since it might be better if he could see her face in case she tried to hide any reaction.

Or it might be good that reaction was contained in the cab of his truck where she couldn't try to escape from him.

"Mia wants me back."

He didn't need to see her face.

He felt her reaction.

It was forceful, so he reached out his hand, found hers, and was not surprised when she resisted his hold.

He held tight, dropping their hands to her thigh.

"That's not gonna happen," he said quietly.

She didn't respond, so he quickly glanced her way to see her face was tight, eyes staring fixed out the windshield.

"That's not gonna happen, Cher," he repeated.

"Right," she mumbled disbelievingly.

"Been fuckin' her since we got divorced."

Her hand spasmed in his.

"She'd come to me," he went on. "She'd do it not frequent but regular. She says now that was her way of makin' the first move toward reconciliation. How she thought I'd catch that when she came to get a dose of my dick and most the time was gone before I woke up, I have no fuckin' clue. But she came again last Wednesday."

"Fuck me," Cher whispered.

"I turned her away."

Cher said nothing.

"Told her not to come back. She wasn't hip on that, went away, apparently thought on things, came back, and said she's been tryin' to sort our shit for years without doin' fuck all to sort it. Now she officially wants to give it a go."

Cher remained silent.

"I told her to get home, and when she pushed it, I told her she got anywhere near my condo, I would arrest her for harassment."

Her hand spasmed again in his.

He knew he had her eyes when she asked, "Say what?"

"You heard me," he answered. "But she's Mia, so she didn't back off. Sent me a picture of us before things went bad, sayin' she's gonna work on gettin' that back." He squeezed her hand. "That's what you gotta know. So I didn't go into this with you and fuck it up, I had to know I had my head right about her, and she fortunately gave me all I needed to get my head right about her which meant get her *out* of my head. In the end, wasn't hard since all I could think about was you and how it wasn't my favorite thing, sittin' on my ass, waitin' for you to either apologize or for your time to be up. But there it is."

"All you could think about was me?" She again sounded disbelieving, but it was deeper this time, not harsh, but still, it almost hurt to hear.

He pulled her hand to his thigh before he answered, "Yeah."

Cher didn't say more.

"Okay, baby," he started carefully, "you got that because you need it, for us startin' out and just because you need to know that went down. But also, you need to know that puttin' things into perspective with Mia meant I had to think on history. Bottom line, I fucked her over. I damaged what was us in order to end it because I had shit fuckin' with my head I didn't know how to sort. But I hurt her. Things got more out of hand after that and she participated in that, but it started with me burnin' her and our marriage. She's bent on attempting reconciliation. I need to make certain she knows that isn't in the cards so she can finally move on. I also need to apologize to her for fuckin' up what we had that's now lost in a way we can't go back."

"So you need to talk to her," she surmised.

"I need to talk to her," he confirmed.

"Mia and Merry talking," she muttered.

"Please don't go back there," he whispered.

He felt her eyes again on him, but she didn't say anything.

"You're here, and honest to fuck, it would pain me deeply, Cher, if you didn't think I was where I needed to be with you to ask you to find that dress, put it on, and haul your ass into my truck to take a shot with me. I do not wanna go back to havin' to prove it to you. What I do know with fuckin' up another relationship is that you gotta lay yourself out from the start. Right now, that's happening with Mia. You cannot hear it from someone else. And honestly?" It was a question, but he didn't wait for her answer. "I want you with me when I do it. Not with me, sittin' across from her. But with me so I can go to you after and lay on you what comes of that so I can let it go."

Again, Cher didn't speak.

He gave her time.

She said nothing.

"Am I back to provin' shit to you?" he pushed.

"No." Her voice was strange in a way he'd never heard from Cher. It was almost timid. "I'm here for you to lay it on me what comes of that, Merry."

Thank fuck.

That took a lot for her. He knew it.

And he was glad for it.

So as he drove, he lifted her hand and brushed her knuckles with his lips, feeling her fingers curl around his almost too tight as he did it.

He dropped their hands back to his thigh, glanced at her, and said, "Thanks, brown eyes."

"Don't mention it," she muttered.

He looked back to the road.

"Am I gonna have to take this bitch down?" she asked.

A Cher and Mia catfight.

Mia didn't stand a chance.

He grinned at the road.

"No."

"Things could get dicey in the dressing room of the strip club, gorgeous. All those bitches stealin' eye shadow and boyfriends and shit. It got ugly. So if she keeps sendin' you pictures and givin' you crap and you need me to take her out, you just call. I'm there for you."

"Good to know you got my back."

She'd been teasing.

She was absolutely not teasing when she stated, "You got mine, you get that back. Always, Merry."

He lifted her hand and kissed it again.

Her fingers didn't curl too tight that time, but they still held on.

When he had her hand to his thigh, she asked, "Is that it?"

"That's it."

"No high school girlfriend gonna come outta the woodwork that's gotta be dealt with?"

"I didn't have a high school girlfriend," he told her.

"Oh," she mumbled.

"I had seven."

He heard her sigh before she kept mumbling, "Why doesn't that surprise me?"

He smiled at the road.

"Just to note," she began, "you already know my boy is excited enough about us to send you text messages pretending to be me. But when I told Mom we were goin' out, she did a grab-and-hold stupid girlie hop."

Garrett started chuckling.

Cher kept talking.

"She called you the last good one standing." She let that hang, then finished, "No pressure, though."

He burst out laughing.

She squeezed his hand, then he smelled her perfume stronger before he sensed her closer, which was right before she touched her lips to the hinge of his jaw.

"Since we're layin' it out," she whispered in his ear, "you should know, I love it when I make you laugh."

He tightened his hand on the wheel as he felt a tightening in his crotch and the same in his chest.

"We're too far from home now, honey," he muttered. "Stop bein' sweet and sit in your seat like a good girl."

He felt her nose flick his ear before she did as told.

But she kept hold of his hand.

This was good since Garrett had no intention of letting her go.

Cher

I sat in Merry's truck, the best steak I'd ever eaten settled warm in my stomach with the rest of the best food I'd ever eaten, not to mention three glasses of champagne.

And we were on our way to his place after the best date I'd ever had, bar *none*.

With the shit out of the way on the road to the restaurant, the rest was just Merry and me the way we'd always been.

Except super-charged.

We talked. We laughed. He teased. I teased.

But the added element of us being a new kind of us, a different kind of together, a together that involved sex, having had it and going to get it, made the teasing *amazing*.

It was like two hours of the best foreplay imaginable, having it over good food, nice champagne, in a crazy-awesome restaurant, wearing fancy clothes with other people around, and yet it was just me with a handsome guy.

The last good one standing.

Having it, I felt lucky.

Not like the lucky I felt when I'd met Dennis Lowe, who was pretending to be Alec Colton, insidiously slithering into my life in order to shake it to its foundations.

A *genuine* lucky where the goodness was right there, not just within reach because, most of the meal when we weren't eating, Merry held my hand.

So I had a hold on it.

And it had a hold on me.

And all I had to do was not fuck things up and not let go.

"Nicest place I've ever been," I murmured into the cab.

"What, Cherie?"

I turned my head and looked at him.

God.

Could that be mine?

"Never been to a place as nice as that," I told him louder.

He glanced at me before looking back to the road. "Never?"

"Nope."

In the dashboard light, I saw his jaw weirdly go tight before he released it.

"Hand, sweetheart," he ordered, taking his from the wheel and holding it palm up between us.

I put mine in his.

His fingers curled around and he rested our hands on his thigh.

Yeah, I had a hold on it.

I just had to work not to fuck it up and never let go.

"Gotta catch up," he muttered.

"Catch up?" I asked.

"Givin' you the things you deserve that you already shoulda had."

Fuck, but I loved that he thought that about me.

I let that settle deep inside as I looked forward. "Need to take Ethan there. Maybe when he turns thirteen. Show him what life could be like if you're smart and work for it."

I was aiming for thirteen because I'd seen the prices on the menu, though it may take until Ethan was fifteen before I could afford it.

And I was still having difficulty processing the fact that Merry had blown that kind of cake on me.

"You're a good mom."

I loved that he thought that about me too.

"I'm a cool mom," I contradicted. "If I was a good mom, Ethan would eat broccoli."

Merry chuckled.

I smiled.

He flipped on his blinker.

I started paying attention to where we were going and I was surprised as Merry slowed to pull into an apartment complex that I'd driven by hundreds of times since moving to the 'burg but never really noticed simply because it wasn't the kind of place you noticed.

It wasn't a disaster, but it wasn't very nice either. There were far worse places to live, and I knew this because I'd lived in them.

It just didn't seem like a place Merry would live.

He had a nice truck. He wore nice suits. He had a Harley. I also heard he had a boat. And it wasn't only when he'd heard his ex-wife was marrying someone else that he ordered a shot of expensive whisky (though, he didn't normally order several of them).

So he had good stuff and he liked good stuff.

Then again, he was a cop and everyone knew they didn't get paid millions to put their asses on the line to solve crime.

Maybe to get his suits, his Harley, and his whisky, he needed to sacrifice other things.

This I could absolutely see.

He drove through the complex and I noticed his truck was by far the best vehicle of any.

And as he drove us through the complex, I was thinking that I didn't like this for Merry. I preferred to think of him in a home with a yard and a deck where he could barbeque, with decent cars in the drives of the houses around him, no one coming close to even thinking they could have a wild party that got loud and stayed loud.

I figured in this place, wild parties happened every weekend, even if a cop lived amongst them.

He parked. He got out. I opened the door and was almost out before he got to me, took my hand, and helped me the rest of the way.

He cleared me from the truck and slammed my door, beeping the locks, then guiding me to some stairs.

He was quiet. He seemed mellow.

I was mellow and that all had to do with good food, champagne, and Merry.

But as we walked, it started to wear off.

I was a sure thing. He knew I was a sure thing.

That didn't bother me.

But the last time we went at each other, I'd been out of my head drunk.

I'd liked it.

He'd liked it.

But still, we'd both been slaughtered.

I was not a girl who had too many hang-ups about sex. I went for it. I let the spirit move me. Sometimes I got good back. Sometimes who I was with didn't work for me.

Right then, the only sex I'd had in years was a shitfaced session with Merry and, before that, fucked-up sex with Denny Lowe. But never, not ever had I been with someone who'd *meant* something (except Merry).

Sure, I thought Lowe did. And I thought Trent did.

But now I *knew*.

So yes, fuck yes, I was beginning to feel panicky.

All this filled my head on the way up the stairs and it kept filling my head as Merry walked me down the landing. It continued to fill my head as he let my hand go and let us in his place, throwing the door open for me.

I walked into the dark, but it wasn't dark for long because Merry hit a switch and a not very attractive chandelier came on over a dining room table to my right.

Beyond that was essentially a galley kitchen, the "essentially" part because one side of the galley was not closed off but opened to the rest of the space, which was a living room. But it was still tiny.

The furniture was of decent quality, comfortable but sparse.

And I'd been right in my imaginings—Merry had a huge TV.

But other than a couch, a recliner, some end tables with lamps, a dining room table, some stools at the bar, and a media center, there was nothing.

No seascapes on the walls. No gun racks. No personality. No nothing.

Except some DVDs and CDs stacked in the shelves around the TV with three frames set amongst them.

Merry moved to a lamp in the living room and I moved to the only things that might give me insight into Merry.

On my way, I dropped my wrap and my purse in the seat of the recliner. I stopped at the first frame.

I saw, not surprisingly, that it was a photo of Merry, Rocky, and their dad, Dave Merrick. Dave was sitting. Merry and Rocky were leaning over his shoulders. I could see Merry's arm around Rocky. All of them were smiling at the camera.

He looked younger, so did Rocky. It was definitely before I'd met him.

And the only thing it gave me that I didn't already know was that Merry was hot ten, twelve years ago.

Not a surprise.

But he'd gotten better with age.

I looked to the other photo and it was a picture of Merry in a big, comfortable-looking chair, looking up at the camera, smiling beautifully, a wrapped bundle of baby held tight against his chest.

Merry and his niece, Cecelia.

Proud uncle.

I knew that too.

I moved across the front of the TV to get to the pictures on the other side.

This was a triple-frame spread across the shelf, the only thing in the space.

Center frame, a formal picture of Rocky and Tanner at their wedding, surrounded by Merry in his groomsman tux, Dave, Vera, Devin, and Tanner's sons with his first wife, Jasper and Tripp.

Right frame, Tanner and Merry, arms around each other's shoulders, far less formally posed but still taken by the wedding photographer in the same location as the middle picture.

The left frame, Merry in his groomsman tux and Rocky in her wedding dress. He held her in both arms; she'd wrapped hers around him. Her cheek was to his shoulder, their eyes aimed at the camera. Both of them were smiling, but Rocky looked like she was also crying.

I knew Rocky put that spread together for her brother. It was likely she'd framed the other pictures for him too.

And it shook me that all he had, all that was him in his pad, was his father, his sister, his niece, and his sister's extended family.

I was so deep in this thought, it surprised me to feel Merry's heat at my back, his hand touch my waist, and his lips at my ear, saying, "Best day of my life."

I stared at the photo, letting those words move through me, wanting to believe. Wanting to believe that was true and not that he felt that way about the day he'd married Mia.

"Finally, one Merrick had the guts to hang on to happy," he finished.

I turned, and he lifted his head as he took that opportunity to trail his hand along my waist so it lay light on the small of my back.

"It's cool your sister has that, Merry," I told him, and his lips curled up.

"More than cool for her, babe."

"Yeah, but best day of your life?" I pushed carefully.

He looked beyond me to the frame, then back to me as his left hand hit the other side of my waist.

"Lucky for me, I'm not dead yet."

I lifted my hands and rested them on his chest, curling my lips up as well.

"Right about now, that's lucky for me too."

His grin got bigger but only for a moment before it faded.

"You okay, sweetheart?"

He was reading me.

I drew in a big breath before I shared, "Ethan's at Meems's. Weekday sleepover."

His left hand slid to my back as his right one put pressure on.

My voice was weird, small, and trembling, as I admitted, "I'm givin' up a morning. She's gettin' him to school."

"You're givin' up a morning with your kid…for me." He said that, and the way he said it, I knew he knew how big that was for me.

Then again, I'd already taught him that lesson the hard way.

"So I got my brown-eyed girl all night," he murmured, his eyes falling to my mouth.

I slid a hand up to his neck and his eyes came back to mine.

With the movement of my hand, I meant to delay. I meant to get his attention. I meant to do this so I could say something.

But when he looked at me after the night he'd given me, and he'd already given me so much that I'd never had—taking me to a swish restaurant, telling me I looked phenomenal, kissing my hand in his truck, laying things out for me honestly, making me laugh, laughing with me—I couldn't say what I needed to say. I couldn't tell him how much this meant to me. I couldn't tell him I was the kind of girl who'd never dreamed because, even when I was little, I always knew I was the kind of girl who'd be stupid to dream.

I could never tell him that standing right there in his arms, in his personality-less living room, it was a dream I'd never dared to dream come true.

I couldn't tell him that.

So I said, "Thanks for dinner."

I watched something move through his blue eyes. Something beautiful. Something I instantly wanted the power to rewind life so I could hit pause and stare at it for as long as I pleased.

"You're welcome, Cherie," he whispered.

I stared in his eyes.

God, did he know?

Did he know that he was the dream come true a girl like me would never dare to dream?

I kept staring into his eyes, trying to see if that was the case, as I slid my hand up so I could stroke his jaw with my thumb.

He let me.

Then he shared he wanted other things.

"Wanna kiss you, honey."

"Then kiss me, Merry."

"No."

I felt my head give a slight twitch.

"No?" I asked.

"No," he repeated. "Need you to get this, Cher. I wanna kiss you. But right now, I wanna kiss you because you're standin' in my arms, lookin' up at me the way you're lookin' up at me. I definitely wanna kiss the girl who loves to make me laugh. And I wanna kiss the girl who put that dress on for me. I also wanna kiss you because after I kiss you, I'm gonna take you to my bed and I'm gonna fuck you. But you need to know, in this instant, I wanna kiss you because you're the girl you are right now, the way you are right now, lookin' up at me."

Oh God.

I wasn't hiding anything.

He knew.

"Merry," I whispered.

He bent his head and slid his nose down the side of mine, his lips a breath away, his blue eyes becoming my whole world.

"Wanna kiss you," he whispered back.

God, *God…Merry*.

"Then kiss me, baby."

I lost his eyes as he angled his head and kissed me.

It wasn't hard and rough and demanding, pushing me to go where he wanted me to be.

It wasn't soft and sweet and gushy, making our moment gooey instead of the beauty that it was.

It was wet and long and tender, the perfect kiss to end the perfect date with the perfect guy.

And when he lifted his head, I knew he was intent on keeping that perfect going when he let me go but took my hand and, without a word, walked me toward the hall that fed off his living room.

I followed him down the hall and into a dark room. I followed him through that dark room and I stopped with him, feeling his hand release mine.

He bent to turn on a light and I didn't take anything in.

I noticed the bed and that was all there needed to be.

He was turned to me and he was shrugging off the jacket of his dark gray suit, fully exposing the electric-blue shirt underneath.

I knew what to give him. I knew what men wanted. I knew where to go, how to lead him there with me. I knew it better than anybody.

And I was good at giving it.

So when his hands lifted to the top buttons of his shirt, I held his eyes and put my hands to the front of my thighs, curling my fingers in.

The second I did, his hands dropped from his shirt and he took the single step he needed to be in my space.

"No, baby," he murmured.

Again…

No?

He put his hands to my waist and slid them down, whispering, "I know you aren't gonna make me sit across from you in that dress all through dinner and then take away my opportunity to take it off you."

My breath caught and I felt a flood of wet between my legs.

I might know how to give it good.

But Merry knew how to give it better.

He slid his hands back up along my sides as he held my gaze. Then he bent in.

My lips parted in preparation, but his just brushed mine before they trailed along my cheek, my jaw. He touched his tongue to my ear, causing a shiver to tremble through me before he lifted his head and caught my eyes.

It was then he watched me as he glided his hands back to my waist, down to my hips. They didn't clench in. They pressed in, lifting up, taking the silky, stretchy fabric with them so it slithered up my legs.

Oh God. That felt good. Good enough that I had to hang on or I was going to go down.

Instead, I decided to concentrate on something, so I lifted my hands to the buttons of his shirt.

He dipped in again and gave me a short, wet kiss, a touch of the tongues.

I got one button undone and was down to the next as he slid my dress all the way up to my hips.

I was breathing heavier as I got the next button undone. That was when he moved his mouth to my neck, his hands back, down, up, and in the hem of my dress that was now at my ass. Then he pushed his hands down, and cupped my ass as his teeth nipped the skin of my neck.

Oh yes.

More good.

I gave up on the buttons because I had no choice. My legs were failing. I curled my hands in his shirt and leaned into his body, pressing my breasts to his chest.

He moved his mouth to my ear.

"Lift your arms, Cherie."

I uncurled my fingers and lifted my arms.

Merry drew back and slid the dress slowly the rest of the way, exposing most of me because I wasn't wearing a bra, though I had on a lacy black thong.

His eyes dropped to me as he tossed the dress aside. Then his hands came back at the sides of my upper ribs and slid down as his gaze roamed.

God, he didn't even need to touch me.

God, I'd never gone this slow. Never been this turned on, not with virtually nothing happening.

I'd never wanted something so badly.

No, *someone*.

"Merry," I whispered, and even I could hear the need dripping from his name.

His eyes cut back to mine and I couldn't beat back my gasp at the hungry blaze I saw burning deep before his fingers dug into my flesh, lifting.

I hopped up as he brought me to him, shifting. I curled my legs around his hips and he put a knee in the bed, his mouth coming to mine.

My back met bed as his mouth opened over mine and his tongue slid inside.

From then, it didn't go any less slow. Merry guiding, me following his lead, we touched. We kissed. We tasted. We trailed. I got his shirt off him. He separated long enough to rid himself of his shoes and socks. He gently dragged my panties down my legs. I went after his belt and held his gaze as he lay on his back in the bed and bucked his hips while I pulled his trousers and boxers down his.

Naked, it didn't go any faster. It wasn't about experience. Feeding the need. Taking what you wanted. Getting into your head and getting lost in the feeling.

It also wasn't exploring.

It was *memorizing*.

Basking.

Worshiping.

I was so into him, it was unreal. Listening. Watching. What a touch would do. The trail of my tongue. The nip of my teeth. The stroke of my hand.

I was dragging my lips along the crisp hair over the hard muscle of his stomach with a destination in mind when he pulled me up and showed me he was where I was.

That being, he was so into me, it was unreal. Listening. Watching. What his touch did to me. The trail of his tongue. The nip of his teeth. The stroke of his hand.

It might have been fifteen minutes; it might have been three hours. All I knew was by the time he was finally ready to give me what I needed, I was more ready to get it than I'd ever been in my life.

And even that he gave me in a way only Merry could give me.

He righted us in his bed, my head to his pillows, strangely proper, *powerfully* proper, like this time, our first time as an us, taking a shot at what we could be, he was going to do it right.

He reached toward the nightstand, his eyes never leaving mine.

I curled my legs around his thighs, careful of the shoes I was still wearing, not wanting to spike him with a heel, my arms gliding around his back, my gaze locked to his.

He kept it that way as his lips fell to mine and he murmured, "Take care of this for me, baby."

He found my hand and pressed the condom in it.

I didn't fuck around unwrapping it.

But when I brought it between us and found his cock, I took my time rolling it on.

I watched the hunger burn in his eyes and my erratic breathing became panting, feeling his thick cock pulse under my fingers.

When I got the condom to the base, he nipped my lower lip with his teeth.

Shit yeah.

I tightened my hold on him with my limbs, through all this our eyes connected. They stayed connected as I slid him through my wet, touching my tongue to my lower lip as his teeth sunk into his.

God, fucking, *fucking* Merry.

Just that…so hot.

I led him to my opening and he immediately pushed in half an inch.

I let out a soft gust of breath, sliding my hand away, across his hip, around, up his spine, into his hair.

When I had a hold, slowly—God, so unbelievably, *beautifully* slowly—Garrett Merrick filled me.

Connected with me.

Became a part of me.

I stared at him and felt it. Felt him inside. Felt his heat. His weight. Felt his arms wrapped around me. Felt my body wrapped around him.

I felt all that and I felt something else.

My eyes were not burning. No dryness. No pain.

They were wet.

Merry stared into them, the heat in his not waning but a new warmth joining it, before his head slanted and he kissed me.

Then he made love to me.

I was far from a virgin.

But that was my first time.

My first time ever.

My first time where a man thought enough about me to make love to me.

It was slow. It was tender. It included wet kisses. Eye contact. Silent communication. I touched him, clutched him, held him to me.

He drove deep and rhythmic, his arms wrapped around me.

It was there but it built, the slow, constant pounding of him against my clit, his cock inside me. When it started to come over me, I knew it was going to happen with just his cock and it was going to be bigger than anything.

"Merry," I whispered, my hand moving from his ass up to his hair, my fingers clenching.

He stroked in and, suddenly, it bolted through me.

"*Merry*," I gasped, his mouth hitting mine, his tongue touching the tip of mine, and I moaned down his throat.

The slow left him and he went faster, harder, driving into me, pounding deep, bodies connected, mouths connected, his tongue now as greedy as his cock thrusting inside, my orgasm swelling and hovering.

I kept hold on his hair, my legs curling tight around his thighs, my arm slanting across his back, fingers pressing in the muscle of his lat, anchoring him to me as whimpers escaped, filling his mouth, my body under his trembling.

When finally he broke the kiss but not the connection of our lips, his grunts mingling with my whimpers.

He planted his cock deep and groaned, "*Cher,*" before his body bucked and his growl of release filled my mouth.

After he gave me that, he tore his mouth from mine and thrust once more, hard and deep, while he moved to press his forehead into the side of my neck.

I felt it leave him as it left me and I began stroking him, running the tips of my fingers through his hair, tracing the defined lines of the muscles of his back, the rest of me unmoving.

Merry's arms gave me a powerful squeeze before he shifted to kiss my neck and then lifted his head.

He looked into my eyes.

I looked into his.

I kept stroking.

Merry took one arm from around me, wrapped his hand around my neck, and moved his thumb along my throat, up, sweeping it over my jaw, up, across my cheek, then over my lips where he left it gliding, back and forth, back and forth. A gentler kind of claiming, even though there was nothing left of me to be claimed.

If he wanted me, I belonged to Garrett Merrick.

All of me.

We stayed this way a long time. No words.

But they weren't needed. For once in my life, I hoped, I prayed, I *dreamed* that I was getting it right and this was what it seemed to be.

Without warning, but doing it gently, he slid out and rolled off, shifting me as he did so I was on my side.

He disengaged just as slowly, my legs automatically closing as they lost purchase on his hips.

He was at the side of the bed, through all this never losing eye contact with me. He lost it only when his gaze swept the length of me.

When it came back, he said quietly, "Don't move."

I nodded.

He got out of bed and walked to one of the three doors in the room.

The light went on inside it as he disappeared and I saw it was a bathroom.

He'd told me not to move, but with him gone, I realized I was in Garrett Merrick's bedroom, so I took that opportunity to quickly look around.

From what I'd seen of the rest of his pad, I wasn't surprised to see not much here either. Two nightstands. Two lamps on them. A tall, six-drawer dresser. A lamp on that. The bed.

On the nightstand that was right in front of me, there was change, crumpled receipts, a used pack of gum, a lighter, and not much else.

Looking over my shoulder to the other one and the dresser, there seemed to be more detritus of this type, an alarm clock, and not much else.

Except there were three trophies on his dresser, but not like they were on display. Like they'd been put there, pushed aside, or shifted when more room was needed. On the top of one was a man standing, rifle to his shoulder, eye to the sight. The top of another trophy that was not quite as tall (but still tall) had another man, same pose, but holding a handgun. The last one that was slightly shorter had a man on his stomach, his rifle aimed.

But that was it.

Just like the rest of his place. Functional and a lot of nothing else.

The one surprise was the furniture. Although there were no prints on the walls, no personality, the furniture in this room was really nice. Fabulous wood that was in a medium stain, not dark, not light. In the drawers on the dresser and nightstands, but in a far more spectacular way with the high headboard, the wood was set in a chevron design that was gorgeous, manly, but it was something I would not object to having for me.

The light went out in the bathroom and I lost interest in Merry's furniture when I saw Merry making his way back to me.

Yes, the hair on his stomach that pointed to what was not right then a buried treasure (but not long ago it had been a treasure buried *in me*) was awe-inspiring.

The treasure it was pointed to was just awesome.

Garrett Merrick had a beautiful cock, even now as it was, semi-hard after making love to me.

The length was perhaps just above average.

It was the girth that meant everything.

I lost sight of it, sadly, when the room went dark.

I felt the bed move, the bedclothes being whipped around. That stopped when I found my ankle in Merry's grip, and even in the dark, he made short work of unbuckling my sandal and sliding it off. He moved to the other one. That accomplished, the bed shifted again, then I found the covers over me about a half a second before I found myself wound up in Merry.

"Pains me to say this," he started after he'd settled us how he wanted us (and, to make it clear, how I wanted it to be, maybe for eternity). "But I ain't twenty anymore. You starin' at my dick like that, sweetheart, after what we just had, you're gonna have to give me some time." He paused before he finished, "Least twenty, thirty minutes."

I laughed softly as I pushed closer to Garrett Merrick in his bed, his naked body tied up in me.

He must have liked that because his arms tightened around me.

Suddenly, it all hit me with a power that made me wonder why it didn't blow me to smithereens.

Garrett Merrick had spent more than two hundred dollars on a dinner with me. He'd told me he wanted to kiss me, knowing what me kissing him back would mean. He'd made love to me, *made love to me*, me.

Me.

Me.

Me.

Eye contact throughout. Saying my name when he came inside me.

And now we were in his bed, naked, and he was holding me and teasing me.

"That wasn't fucking, was it?" I blurted.

It seemed his body further solidified against mine for a moment before he relaxed and slid his hand up into my hair.

He knew I'd never had that.

He now knew he was the first who ever gave that to me.

"No, Cher," he said gently. "That was nowhere near fucking."

Yes, straight up, burn it in my brain…

I could not fuck this up.

I couldn't.

He was the best thing that ever happened to me.

Not getting a goodness so good it was unreal after being stupid and getting knocked up by a junkie, the way I got Ethan.

A goodness I got because I earned it simply by being me.

Understanding that, as it seemed I was prone to do with Merry, I kept blurting.

"I want you to get to know my kid better. Tomorrow. He's got a sleepover with Teddy, but I'm droppin' him at the game. They're meeting there. Teddy's parents go to the game because their older boy plays. He's goin' home with them after. But before, we can take him to dinner."

Merry didn't say anything.

Shit, that was too soon.

"Or we can wait," I said quickly.

"I take you and Ethan for pizza, once we drop him off, do I get you at your place?"

Not too soon.

I closed my eyes slowly before I answered, "Yeah."

"You're on."

I snuggled deeper.

Merry kept his hand in my hair as he wrapped his other arm so tight around my waist, I felt his fingers skim the skin on my belly.

His warmth, his strength, my orgasm, his fantastic mattress, I wanted to stay awake and feel all that, but I couldn't stop myself from feeling drowsy.

And drowsy, sated, held close by Merry, my mouth kept running.

"Thanks for not fuckin' me."

I felt his body move with a chuckle that wasn't audible.

"Thanks for lettin' me not fuck you," he replied.

"Anytime," I mumbled, starting to drift.

"Cherie?" he called.

"Yeah, Merry."

Cherie. Merry.

Fuck, it was goofy as all get-out.

But it was also like we were meant to be.

"This is good. Proof. Truth. Remember this, honey. We hold on to this, what we just had, what we got right now, the night we shared, we don't fuck that up, we can stick it, you and me."

My throat closed.

My eyes started burning.

But I powered through it being me.

"Stop bein' gooey."

That got me more of his lean body moving in my arms, telling me he was laughing.

He got control of that, tipped his head so his lips were against my hair, and ordered, "Go to sleep, brown eyes."

"See you in the morning, gorgeous."

"Believe it, baby."

I believed.

Finally, I believed.

And for the first time in my life, held tight to Merry, it didn't scare the shit out of me.

Twelve

THE PLEASURE IS ALL MINE
Cher

I felt it shafting, tit to clit.

My eyes drifted open.

I saw shadows. I felt a nice mattress under me.

Heat behind me.

A hard cock pressed to my ass.

"Merry," I breathed as his thumb and finger at my nipple rolled again.

"This, baby," he growled, his voice gruff with sleep and the promise of an impending orgasm, "is gonna be fucking."

My hips twitched.

He shifted his and slid his hard cock through my sleek.

Shit yes.

"Baby," I whimpered, hardly awake, already there.

"Nightstand, Cher, fast."

I reached out to the nightstand carefully so as not to lose him as he glided his cock back and forth, his fingers still working my nipple, his other hand shoving under me, going over my belly, down, and in.

I gasped at his touch. Yanking open a drawer, groping blindly, feeling foil, I snatched up a condom and pressed back into Merry.

His hand left my breast.

I aimed the condom at it.

He took it.

I rocked my hips, rubbing him against me.

I felt the rumble in his chest against my back that became audible as I heard foil crinkling.

I lost his cock as he angled his hips away from me.

But I didn't lose his finger at my clit.

I ground into it.

I got his cock back, gliding, aiming, his lower body shifted down.

"Give me your mouth," he ordered.

I twisted my neck.

He took my mouth as his cock slammed into me.

With the force of the goodness of him filling me, I cried out, the sound swallowed by Merry as he rode me, I rode him, his finger manipulating my clit, his hand going back to my breast, curling around, thumb rubbing at my nipple.

He plundered my mouth, fucking me hard, working me, until it got too much and I pushed my head into the pillow.

He got my message and stopped kissing me, but his lips didn't leave mine, breathing, brushing, my harsh pants mingling with his rough breaths.

Then his grunts abraded my lips.

I liked that.

"Baby," I breathed.

"Yeah," he growled.

"Harder," I begged.

"Yeah," he grunted, powering faster, harder, riding me ruthlessly.

Brilliance.

"*Merry*," I gasped.

"Fuck yeah, baby," he groaned.

I came, rearing in his arms, my lips parted, my breath suspended in my lungs as it exploded in my tits, my clit, and my pussy convulsing, clenching and releasing against his driving cock.

His finger at my clit moved away as he shoved his whole hand in, his fingers separating around his still-thrusting dick, his leg hitching up, taking mine with it, the power of his drives mind-boggling. At the same time, his other hand left my breast and moved up, wrapping around my throat, then up more, around my jaw, holding my head twisted to him so I had his eyes in the dark, our lips whispering against the other's as he kept fucking me.

"That's it, Merry," I panted, still coming, but my climax was moving from me. "That's it, baby. Fuck me hard. I wanna feel you all day." I lifted my head and pressed my lips to his. "Want you with me all day, baby. Fuck me that way."

His hand tightened around my jaw as he grunted, "Beauty," then lost control, slamming into me again and again and again, his mouth leaving mine, his hand at my jaw shoving up, his face buried in my throat as he groaned.

Finally, he sunk into me, stayed planted, and I felt his uneven breaths coasting along my skin.

The pads of his fingers gave my jaw a gentle squeeze when he lifted his head, pulled mine down, and kept his other hand cupped to our connection as he took my mouth in a deep, wet kiss.

He ended it, dropped his forehead to mine, his eyes open, mine looking through the early morning dark into his, and he muttered, "Mornin'."

I lay there, Merry buried inside me, my clit, my tits, fuck, my entire body still tingling from him fucking me, and I stared at him.

Mornin'?

I burst out laughing.

While doing it, he released my jaw and I relaxed my head only for Merry to move his lips to my ear.

"For the record, I love makin' you laugh too."

Better than an orgasm.

Christ.

Merry.

I stopped laughing.

He kissed my neck below my ear and slid out of me.

I was in no way over suffering the loss of him when he shifted over me, arm at my waist yanking me with him like I was a human-size doll, and I found myself on my feet with Merry beside his bed. Naked.

He let my waist go, grabbed my hand, and I was being dragged across the room.

I opened my mouth.

"Shower," Merry said before I could start speaking.

I shut my mouth and hit Merry's bathroom, naked with a naked Merry, doing it grinning.

Forty-five minutes later, in my dress and shoes from the night before, hair wet, I walked up to my house.

Normally, I wouldn't care what this said about me.

Right then, seeing as Merry had my hand in his and was walking right beside me, I *really* didn't care.

We stopped on the stoop, and when I got my keys out of my clutch, Merry took them from me.

He shifted me out of the way of the storm door as he opened it, then he let us in.

The storm whispered then banged.

Merry closed the front door.

Then he took me in his arms and he kissed me.

I was hanging on tight, slightly breathless, when he lifted his mouth from mine.

"Be here to pick you and Ethan up at five thirty," he said.

"Okay, gorgeous," I replied.

He smiled at me.

I memorized that smile in a way I was certain never to forget it, not if I lived an eternity.

Then he gave me a squeeze, let me go, and moved to the door.

At the door, he looked back to me.

"Later, sweetheart."

"Later, Merry."

He lifted his chin and disappeared when he closed the door behind him.

I stood where he left me, in my dress and shoes of the night before, hair wet.

"I'm not gonna fuck this up," I told the door.

Right then, right there, after last night and that morning, I was as intent on that as I was on giving my son a decent life.

Absolutely.

I shrugged off my wrap and tossed it to the bucket chair. I pulled my phone out of my clutch and my clutch joined the wrap.

Finally, I bent my head to my phone, pulling up Merry's text string.

Best night I ever had. Thank you, baby.

I stared at it, thumb hovering over the SEND button.

"I'm not gonna fuck this up," I told my phone and my thumb hit the screen.

I let out the huge breath I didn't know I was holding, walked to the door, opened it, locked the storm, closed the door, locked it, then moved back to my bedroom.

I had my dress and shoes off, new undies and jeans on, when my phone I'd tossed on the bed sounded.

I snatched it up.

I'm glad, brown eyes.

I grinned and my thumb moved.

Best morning too, BTW.

I tossed the phone back to my bed and went to my dresser to choose a tee.

I was tugging it on when my phone sounded again.

I went back to it.

That's my good girl.

I didn't grin at that.

I shivered.

After I experienced that hint of beauty, my thumb moved again.

Stop turning me on and go fight crime.

I hit SEND.

I was making coffee when my phone sounded again.

Worth the wait.

I stared at Merry's text, my eyes feeling funny—not dry and burning, something else—before I lifted my phone and tapped it against my forehead like I could tap the words of his text into my brain.

I brought it down and my thumb flew.

Later, gorgeous.

Not long after, I got back, *Absolutely.*

I poured my coffee and after, turned my back to the counter and rested against it.

I stared at my awesome kitchen that was full of personality.

And I took that moment to revel in another of the boons life sent my way—boons that were coming far more frequently these days—this being the fact that I was facing the first day in a very long time, riding a quiet high of anticipation for what was to come next.

The day before had been fucked up by me being worried about what Merry would think about Ethan sending that text and not me.

This day, there was nothing to fuck it up.

Nothing.

It was all good and the forecast was strong it would only get better.

I'd never had that either, so I knew to appreciate it.

And that I did.

I heard the knock on the door, and right on its heels, "Mom! It's Merry! Can I get it?"

I was sitting on the side of my bed, zipping up my boot. I turned my head toward the clock on my nightstand.

Shit, it was five twenty-five.

Merry was early.

"I'll get it!" I yelled, hurrying with the zip.

"But it's just Merry!" Ethan yelled back. "I saw him from the window!"

Ethan wasn't allowed to open the door unless it was to his gramma.

"Right!" I returned, shoving up from the bed. "Get it."

I was halfway down our short hall when I heard Ethan's excited, "Hey, Merry!"

"Hey, man." I heard Merry say back.

I hit the living room to see them breaking their handshake.

Ethan whirled to me.

"Look, Mom! Merry's here!" he told me, something he'd already told me.

Suffice it to say, when I'd told my kid we were going out to dinner with Merry that night, he'd been in fits of glee.

In fact, he was so excited, he'd even told me he wanted to cancel plans with Teddy so we could all go to the game together and then get ice cream after.

Therefore, the first time in my life acting selfishly with my kid (but also because I didn't want to push things too hard too fast for Merry, thinking a quick dinner might be better than forcing him to spend hours with Ethan), I'd told him no.

Due to his exhilaration, I'd expected devastation.

But I'd forgotten in his childlike excitement that my kid was growing up. And apparently, part of that was him understanding that Merry and me needed some time just him and me, especially this early with what we were starting.

So Ethan had relented easily.

That didn't mean he wasn't jazzed about dinner.

Obviously, seeing as at that moment, he'd totally forgotten to hide his excitement and act the man of the house around Merry.

"I see," I muttered, moving in and looking to Merry, who stood in the open front door, watching and waiting for me to get to him.

Also watching and waiting for me to give him clues as to how to play this in front of Ethan.

I'd taught him that too, the hard way, and he'd learned, giving me what I needed.

God, *Merry*.

I moved close, lifted a hand, touched his chest, and held his gaze as I tipped back my chin.

He moved a hand to my waist and bent in, touching his lips to my cheek.

We broke apart.

"You can be gooey," Ethan declared, and both Merry and I looked to him. "Mom loves gooey. She'd be gooey all the time if I let her," he went on to share. "With me, she has to cap it. It'll be good to have another guy around so she can get more shots at bein' gooey."

I stared at my son.

Then I said, "Shut up, kid."

He looked at me, grinning wickedly. "Forget *that*, Mom." His eyes went to Merry. "I'm almost eleven," he announced. *"Eleven years*, dude, where it's been just Mom and Gramma and me. They're ladies. I've had no other guy around. They rock, but I'm *a guy* with *two ladies*. I think you get me. Now I've got a guy. That's a big thing for me. So, just sayin', I'm *so totally* spilling anything you need." He jerked his thumb at himself and completed his grand offer. "You wanna know, I'm your man."

I put my hands on my jeans-clad hips and repeated, "Uh...*shut up*, kid."

Ethan kept grinning. "No way. Girls stick together and I've had years of that. But guys stick together too. You're screwed."

I looked to the ceiling wondering, after dancing around for years in a G-string on a stage with a bunch of losers ogling me, if I had it in me to blush.

I found I didn't.

I also found Merry's hand at the small of my back.

I turned my attention to Merry for him to tell me immediately, "He's not wrong, babe. Guys stick together."

"See!" Ethan cried.

"How about you two *guys* go out for dinner and I'll stay home, knitting or something?" I suggested.

That was when Merry's hand slid along my back, his fingers curling around my side and pulling me into his side.

"You start knitting, you totally lose cool mom status," Ethan warned.

"What?" I asked him. "You mean your friends coming over and me using them to try on sweaters with penguins and crap on the front won't go over good?"

Ethan made a face.

Merry emitted a chuckle.

Vaguely, I heard a car door slam but felt Merry's movements, so I looked from my kid to him to see him looking over his shoulder through the storm door to see what had made that sound.

I also felt his body instantly get tight beside mine.

At his reaction, I looked beyond him and saw Peggy's minivan at the curb behind Merry's Excursion, Peggy clearly visible in the passenger seat and Trent was making his way around the hood.

Shit, I'd forgotten he'd said he was going to be here Friday at five thirty to pick up Ethan.

Of course, I'd told him Ethan wouldn't be here so he shouldn't bother.

But now Ethan *was* here, so was I, and so was Merry.

Damn.

Merry started to disengage from me as the room started to get heavy with his pissed off, badass vibe.

Shit *and* damn.

"Ethan, go to your room," I ordered swiftly.

"What's Dad doin' here?" he asked.

I looked to my son to see him staring confused out the storm door.

"Ethan, kid, go to your room. Please."

"I told him I didn't wanna come this weekend." His voice was pitching higher, almost whiny in a way I never heard anymore unless he was really tired or not feeling good.

He really didn't want to be with his dad.

And he really wanted to spend time with Merry and me.

"Ethan—"

"Man," Merry spoke over me, "help your mom out by doin' what she says, yeah?"

Ethan's eyes jerked to Merry, he nodded, then looked at me before he dashed toward the hall.

Another boon. Ethan looked up to Merry, so when Merry spoke, he didn't talk back.

On this thought, I heard the storm door let out its opening whisper and I looked that way to see Merry stalking out of it.

Badass unleashed.

Shit!

I moved to follow him, watching as Trent, nearly halfway up the walk, eyes to feet it weirdly seemed he was dragging, sensed another presence and looked up.

He got one look at Merry and jolted to a stop in a way that would have been funny if I wasn't worried Merry was about to go apeshit.

I dashed out the door and down the walk, listening to Merry order, "Turn around and go home."

"Who are you?" Trent asked.

"I'm the man tellin' you to turn around and go home," Merry answered.

Trent stared up at him, but when I hit Merry's side, he tore his eyes away and looked to me.

"Who's this guy?" he asked, jerking a thumb at Merry.

"Answered that," Merry bit out, and Trent's gaze shot back to him. "Now, get in your car and go home."

"Trent!" Peggy shouted from the car, not opening her window, opening her door. "What's goin' on?"

"Ma'am, remain in the car," Merry ordered loudly.

I watched Peggy register an order that went against what she wanted to do and I saw what she hid barely under the surface.

Apparently, no man but God told Peggy Schott what to do, that "God" being in her head, which meant *no man told Peggy Schott what to do.*

Instantly, she was visibly ticked.

"Where's my kid?" Trent asked.

I decided to try to take over. "I told you, Trent, he needs a break from you. And Ethan told you he wasn't comin' this weekend. I also confirmed that with you."

"And Trent told you he was." Peggy had decided to wade in. She was out of the minivan and hoofing it our way.

I looked to the back to the two car seats her kids were in.

"Mrs. Schott, your children are in your vehicle," Merry told her, and Peggy's eyes snapped to him at him using her name.

"You know me?" she asked.

"I know you," Merry answered, his voice low with more meaning than the possibility that I'd shared who Peggy was.

She made it to Trent and her head tipped to the side as she stared at Merry.

"You were there, at the bar with Cheryl," she decreed, as if this was news Merry was unaware of.

"I was," Merry confirmed. "Now, both of you, please return to your vehicle and go home."

"We're pickin' up Ethan," Peggy declared.

"You're not," I declared right back, and Peggy turned her screwed-up eyes to me. "And we're not doin' this now. I explained to Trent that Ethan needed some space. I also explained to Trent that while Ethan was gettin' that, we could sit down and talk about what the future might bring. But that's not happening now. That's happening at a time when we've all got our shit together and can talk about it rationally. In the meantime, Ethan's said he doesn't wanna spend time with you. If you wanna connect with him, talk to him on the phone."

"Ethan doesn't get to make those decisions," Peggy spat. "He's just a little boy. His *father* makes those decisions."

"I'm afraid he doesn't," I returned.

"And *I'm* afraid you're wrong," Peggy shot back. "Trent's his father. He's got rights."

"That's where *you're* wrong," Merry put in sharply, and Peggy's eyes sliced to him. "Trent Schott relinquished his rights when his girlfriend told him she was carrying his child and he cleared out after he *cleaned her out.* In this situation, Trent has no rights. In this situation, Ethan's mother makes *all* the decisions about where her son will be and with whom. She's made her decisions. She's communicated them repeatedly. Now, I'll say it again, return to your vehicle and go home."

"You don't know what you're talkin' about," Peggy snapped.

That was when Merry reached under the hem of his leather jacket and pulled something out of the back pocket of his jeans, that something being the badge he shoved into his belt at his front right hip.

"I know exactly what I'm talkin' about," Merry said lethally.

"You called the cops?" Trent asked, his voice high and even more whiny than Ethan's had been minutes before.

"I didn't call the cops," I answered.

"Well, he's a cop." Trent jerked his head Merry's way.

"I am. I'm also her boyfriend," Merry announced.

Trent's mouth dropped open, his eyes bugged out, and his torso automatically reared away from Merry.

Peggy's lips parted, but her eyes squinted so tight, they looked shut.

Trent looked to me and his voice was even higher when he asked, "You're seein' *a cop?*"

"She is," Merry answered for me. "And as her boyfriend, not a cop, I'm askin' you one last time to return to your vehicle. You make me ask again, that request will come from a cop."

All this went down, but it was lost on Peggy.

She was stuck back earlier in the conversation.

"Trent has rights," she declared, looking between Merry and me.

"That's simply not the case," Merry replied. "Not legally. Not informally. The only rights he has are those Cher grants him. And she's not granting him the right to see Ethan. This means you have no choice but to leave."

"It means we got no choice but to get Trent legal rights," she returned.

My heart clenched painfully, but Merry just shrugged.

"That's your call. But no judge is gonna rise up in a puff of smoke to appear in Cher's yard to grant them to you right now, so I'll say it again, turn around and go home."

No judge is gonna rise up in a puff of smoke…

God, I loved it when Merry was funny, especially when he was funny smack in the middle of Peggy being Peggy and Trent being his normal loser.

Peggy looked to me and threatened, "This isn't over."

I looked at her and retorted, "Yes it is."

"Get ready for the battle *of your life*," she warned.

"Already won that," I fired back. Then I gave her what she needed to try to find it in her to do the right thing. "You can work with me to help you build a relationship with my son, or you can work against me. You work against me, I won't have to do anything—Ethan will tell you, a judge, he'll shout it at the top of his lungs that he wants nothing to do with you. And if that's what my boy wants, that's what I'll get for my boy. If you care about him and want him in your life and as a part of your family, you have this window of opportunity to do that the right way. Don't fuck it up."

"No judge is gonna let a boy be raised by a woman who's got no problem usin' the f-word," Peggy sniped.

"No judge in this whole fuckin' country is gonna take my boy away from me," I returned.

"You're livin' a fantasy," she spat.

"I'm not the one who's willing to commit the crime of kidnapping," I said softly.

Her torso swung back, her eyes got wide, and even Trent was smart enough to separate himself from Peggy at this juncture, this bit of news being shared in front of a cop. He shifted away from her side.

"Yeah," I whispered. "You threatened me. I took action. I'll keep doin' that since I got friends who're good at findin' out shit, and I'll find out so much shit about you, about Trent, I'll *bury* you. Nothing…not…one… thing is gonna be forced on my kid that he doesn't want. I'll go to the mat for that, Peggy. I'll die for that. I'll do *anything* for that. Mark my words, you battle me, you will not win. I'll fight you every day of my life. I'll spend every dime I have. And I won't go down swingin' because I will not *ever* quit fightin'."

Only the barest hint of hesitation crossed her features before she leaned in and hissed, "He needs saved from you."

Shit, there it was.

"That, that right there," I returned instantly, "tells me precisely what kind of woman you are and what I gotta protect my boy from."

That seemed to confuse her.

"We're his salvation," she decreed.

Oh my God.

Was she crazy?

"You bring harm to his mother in any way," Merry entered our conversation, "he'll think you're sent straight from hell."

Trent got close to his wife again, grabbing her arm.

"Peg, let's go."

She stared at Merry. Then she shifted her eyes and glared at me.

"Peg, babe, kids are in the car. Let's go," Trent urged.

"Get an attorney," she warned me quietly.

"Whatever," I replied.

She kept glaring.

Trent tugged cautiously on her arm.

She turned her glare to him, tore her arm from his hold, and stomped her ass to their minivan.

Trent gave me an unhappy look. He gave one to Merry. After that, he followed her.

We stood where we were as they got in, but we didn't stand the way we were standing when they were with us.

Merry threw his arms around my shoulders.

That felt *great*.

I slid my hand around his waist.

He tucked me tight into his side.

I fit myself tighter.

And that felt even better.

We watched Trent fire up their minivan and we kept watching as they pulled away, our heads turning to keep them in sight as they drove down the street.

"Bad news, brown eyes. That church lady is fuckin' crazy," Merry muttered when the brake lights on the minivan lit at the stop sign at the end of the street.

"The Lord giveth great dinners with handsome cops, followed by fabulous orgasms and a mom gettin' to tell her boy he gets to eat pizza with a good man he looks up to," I replied, and as I did, Merry looked down at me and I looked up at him. "Then the Lord taketh away by sending a batshit-crazy church lady to stand in my yard, throw down with me, and, while she's doin' it, say words like 'salvation.'"

Merry started smiling.

"Not sure the Lord gave you those orgasms, sweetheart," he returned. "And He sure didn't pay for dinner."

"I hear you," I agreed. "That doesn't mean He wasn't shining His light on me the last twenty-four hours, save, of course, the last ten minutes."

Merry didn't quit smiling, it was just that his smile turned cocky.

"Guys!" Ethan shouted from the house, and we both looked over our shoulders to see him in the storm door. "What's goin' on? Why're standin' out there, starin' at each other, and not comin' in to tell me why Dad and Peggy are actin' all crazy?"

I stared at my son, who looked angry and worried.

This meant I sighed, which was a choice I made because the other one was losing my mind that Peg and Trent made my kid angry and worried.

The good part was Merry being there, being close, having a hold on me, and shifting me around so we could walk connected to my house.

The bad part was my kid was in my house and I had to explain to him his dad and Peggy weren't acting crazy, because, at least for Peg, she just *was*.

We made it into the house and Merry had barely closed the front door behind us when Ethan launched in.

"You don't have to tell me what went down." He lifted his chin. "You told me to go to my room. You didn't tell me not to open my window so I couldn't watch and listen."

He was right. I didn't.

I made a mental note should something like this happen again to do just that as I replied, "Then I'm not sure what there is to add, little man."

"You started whispering," he accused. "I didn't hear that part."

"And that's 'cause you shouldn't, buddy," Merry said carefully.

Ethan glared at Merry for a moment but only for a moment.

Then he declared, "Right," stomped to the phone, and jerked it out of its base.

I wasn't sure that was good.

"Ethan," I said warningly.

He turned his angry face to me, then he looked down and punched buttons.

"Ethan," I said again, moving his way.

He put the phone to his ear.

"Baby," I whispered, getting close. "Maybe you need to think about this. Don't act in anger. That can lead to bad things, things you might regret, and I don't want that for you, kid."

He looked up at me, his eyes sliding to the side as I felt Merry stop there behind me. Then Ethan opened his mouth.

"Yeah, Peg? It's Ethan," he stated. He waited. Then he said, "Dad's drivin'? Okay, I'll tell you. I wanna see you again never. You got that? I *never* wanna see you again. Not you. Not Dad. But especially not *you*. I heard what you said to my mom and that isn't right. Dad knows it isn't. *He knows*. Don't know why you don't. He left us all alone, he can't come back and be all stupid. And *you* can't do nothin' because you're nothin' to me."

He drew in a deep breath and I drew in one with him.

Then he kept giving it to her.

"I gotta tell you, this sucks 'cause I'm gonna miss Mary and Tobias. But it doesn't suck because I'm not gonna miss *you*. You bother my mom again, I'll tell you to your face. You push it, I'll say it to a judge. I'm never goin' with you. Not ever. You find a way to make me, I'll run away. I gotta look after my mom and you made me hafta do that by making it this way. So, later. You got it in you to be halfway decent, give Mary and Tobias a hug from me. Maybe when all of us are grown up, we can get together and talk about how crazy you are. But that'll have to wait until we're all grown up."

With that, he punched a button and tossed the phone to the couch.

He looked back to me. "Okay. Done. Now we got, like, *no* time to eat pizza. We'll have to snarf it down before I gotta meet Teddy at the game, which sucks, and I'm blamin' that on Peggy too." He looked to Merry. "I gotta get my bag, then we can go."

On that, he tramped from the room, Merry and me turning to watch him go.

"Just to say," Merry started softly, and my thoughts on my kid, worried, my eyes drifted up to him, "not sure how much better I gotta get to know your boy."

I felt my lips part, but he wasn't done.

He looked down at me. "Think I just fell in love, brown eyes."

I couldn't stop it, no way.

I swayed toward him.

He caught me in both arms.

And he still wasn't done.

"He's a good man, takin' care of his mom."

"Yeah," I whispered.

Merry smiled at me, soft and sweet.

Ethan stormed into the room, looked at us, and stopped.

"Okay, maybe I was wrong about the gooey, 'cause...*gross,*" he declared.

Merry didn't let me go.

Ethan threw out an annoyed hand. "We gonna get pizza or what?"

"We're gonna get pizza, bud," Merry said, dropping one arm but keeping his other around me to guide me Ethan's way.

"You okay?" I asked him as we moved.

"Uh...*no,*" Ethan answered. "Peggy's totally crazy and Dad just stood there and let her mouth off at you. All he cared about was that Merry's a cop. What's *that* all about?"

"Well..." I let that trail off, not sure I felt like sharing Trent's rap sheet and drug history and thus his natural aversion to law enforcement with Ethan at this juncture.

"It doesn't matter." Ethan lifted his chin again, eyes on me. "He's weak. I'm not weak. I'm like you. I can take care of myself. I can take care of you. And I'm like Merry, who's all, *get in your vehicle and go*, real angry-like but still patient when you just gotta take one look at him and see he so totally wanted to whale on Dad." Ethan looked to Merry. "I kinda wish you did, though Mom says hitting people is wrong. Dad needs some sense knocked into him."

Merry let out a sharp, startled bark of laughter.

I swallowed mine back and, once I managed this, said, "Ethan, honey, you need to calm down." He looked to me. "You need a shot of tequila?" I offered.

"Yes," he answered instantly.

"Well, you're gonna have to make do with the buzz of a two-liter glass of Coke at Reggie's," I returned.

He stared at me and suddenly the emotion that was controlling him shifted and I saw his jaw set, but he couldn't fight it.

His chin wobbled.

My heart skipped and the pain of it nearly took me to my knees.

"They're not gonna get me, are they, Mom?"

"No, baby," I answered quickly, firmly, but softly, holding back, wanting to rush to him and put my arms around him, but not wanting to mother him when he was going through a lot, holding it together, and doing it in front of Merry.

He looked into my eyes, nodded, and said, "Sorry, Mom, but he knows." He looked up to Merry. "You're police. You know the law. Are they gonna take me away from my mom?"

"Absolutely not, Ethan," Merry stated quickly, firmly, and not softly.

Ethan swallowed.

Then he nodded at Merry.

"Maybe we should cancel things with Teddy," I suggested, and Ethan's attention came back to me. "After pizza, we can all hang for a while."

"Only if Merry stays for waffles in the morning," Ethan decreed.

I tensed.

Merry didn't.

He said, "If it's cool with your mom, I'm here."

I drew in a deep breath and nodded.

Merry slid his arm around my shoulders again and stated, "Your mom and me'll go to the game with you and you can hang with your bud. Then we'll bring you home and we can all hang here."

The worry slipped away as Ethan's face lit when he realized he had me, Merry, pizza, the game, time with his friend, and together time at home. "Awesome! I hate to miss the 'dogs when they're playing at home."

"Then we got plans," Merry muttered.

"I'll take my bag back and call Teddy," Ethan announced, grabbed his bag and took off.

I turned to Merry.

"So, we fucked around for a week and a half getting to the zone where we'd start, then I catapulted you straight to hyperdrive with my kid, my life, and my problems. Does your hair feel like it's on fire?"

Merry smiled at me. "Nope."

"Well, that's good," I mumbled, looking at his shirt.

"Cher."

I lifted my eyes to his.

"That thinkin' I did was not about knowin' I wanted back in your pants," he stated. "I already knew that. It was about me knowin' I wanted to be a part of your life. I wanted this to happen, honey. It happens now, two days from now, two weeks from now, I wanted it. I got it early. I'm down with that. So stop worrying."

I glared at him. "*You* can stop being perfect. I'm getting a complex."

He again smiled at me. "You look good. There's no better ass in a pair of jeans in the entire county and it's mine to tap. You're a great mom. You put together a great pad, though I'm worried the ghost of Jimi Hendrix is gonna glide through at any second. You raised a great kid. And I get to make you both waffles in the morning. I'm thinkin' I didn't do too bad either."

God!

Merry.

"Ethan caps my gooey, I'm capping yours," I decreed.

He dipped his head to me, curling me closer, his tone telling me his thoughts on what gooey was were vastly different than mine. "How much I get?"

I opened my mouth to speak as I mentally told my spasming vagina to behave, but Ethan raced into the room and shouted, "Guys! Seriously!" so I didn't get to say anything.

I watched Merry smile again.

I liked it.

Then I watched him move away, and after that, I participated fully as I went out with both my guys and had pizza.

$$\smile\hspace{-0.3em}\frown$$

"She does this sometimes, passes out in front of the TV."

I heard that coming in a whisper from Ethan.

"I bet."

That I heard as a low rumble up close, coming from Merry.

"I usually shake her real gentle until she wakes up. Then I help her make sure the house is locked up, the lights are out, and we go to bed."

Again from Ethan.

"How 'bout you make sure the door's locked? I'll get the lights and get your mom to bed."

That was Merry.

Me?

I was realizing I was curled up on the couch, my head cushioned by something warm and awesome, but it was not exactly soft because it was Merry's thigh.

Shit.

I opened my eyes on a blink and saw Merry's stocking feet on my coffee table. I slowly shoved a hand in the couch and pushed up.

"I'm awake," I lied, poorly, seeing as the words were slurred.

"Right," Merry muttered.

I tipped my head back to turn sleepy eyes to him.

The grin he aimed at me was soft and sweet.

Shit.

Total junkie for that look, that grin.

Hell, I was just plain addicted to Merry.

"I'll do the door and the lights," Ethan said quickly. "'Night, Mom."

I turned my head, lifting a hand to shove my hair out of my face and seeing my son on the go. "'Night, baby."

He also aimed a grin at me as he switched out the light by the couch.

I felt Merry shift and looked his way to see him taking his feet right before he bent deep and took hold of me. He lifted me up into his arms in a bride and groom hold right in front of my kid.

I woke up a little bit more.

"Merry."

"I'll get her to her room and help you, bud," he said to Ethan as he negotiated the space between coffee table and couch.

"'Kay," Ethan replied.

Merry kept walking.

I put my hands to his chest. "I can make it to my bedroom."

"I'm sure you can," Merry said but didn't put me on my feet.

I rolled my eyes, which was about all I had time for before we were in my room (my house was tiny).

He put me to my feet by the bed.

"Get ready," he ordered when I tilted my head back to look at him. "I'm gonna help Ethan close the house down for the night."

"Whatever," I muttered.

He grinned at me.

I stumbled slightly and annoyingly as I headed to my dresser.

Merry chuckled.

I rolled my eyes again.

I felt his presence leave and the truth of it was, it was late, I was tired (I didn't get a lot of sleep on any kind of normal basis), life had been a roller coaster lately but we'd had a good night, the three of us, and right then, I was out of it.

So out of it, I didn't have it in me to dig through my drawers and accomplish the colossal feat of finding sleepwear sexy enough for the first time I wore it around Merry (both our times sleeping together, we'd done it naked) at the same time being appropriate for me to sleep in with Merry and with my kid in the house.

Since I likely didn't even own such a miraculous piece of clothing, I dragged out some drawstring pajama shorts, a tank, tugged off my clothes, and yanked them on.

I struggled out to the bathroom as Ethan was hitting his room.

"'Night again, Mom," he bid me.

"Sleep good, kid," I returned.

"You too," he said then, "'Night, Merry. Can't wait for waffles."

"Me either, bud. Sleep tight."

I glanced at Merry briefly, went into the bathroom, turned on the light, and shut the door.

I listed around doing my business, put zero effort in brushing my teeth (but I still managed to drag the toothbrush around), rinsed, spit, decided my makeup could stay on, and left the bathroom.

I hit my bedroom to see Merry getting up from the bed, shirt off, socks off, belt undone, and this made me partially rally.

The problem with that was he just grinned at me and walked out of the room, so his chest and the hair on his stomach with the arrow pointing to good things walked out of the room with him.

So I lurched to the bed, threw back my Janis Joplin covers, and did a face-plant in it.

I was snoozing when I felt the bed move, the dim of the lights on my eyelids disappearing completely because Merry turned out the light. Then he fitted the line of his lean, warm, hard body into mine, spooning me.

"Thanks for pizza," I muttered sleepily into the dark.

He hauled me close with his arm around my belly.

"Shut up, brown eyes, and stop thankin' me for everything."

I ignored him.

"Thanks for gettin' in Trent's face and bein' all cool even though you wanted to whale on him."

His body started shaking.

I kept mumbling.

"Thanks for bein' nice to my kid."

"He's easy to be nice to."

I knew that, so I ignored that too.

"Thanks for givin' up an awesome blowjob *à la* me to watch *Fast & Furious 6* with my boy."

"Just sayin', that's a debt you hold, baby, and I'll be findin' a time to collect."

I looked forward to that.

It seemed I had enough strength in me to use my mouth to speak. But not to suck him off, no way, especially with my kid in the house, which was a shame (the not-being-able-to-suck-Merry-off part; my kid being in the house was never a shame).

"Thanks for waiting for me to get my head outta my ass so I could take a shot on this, because so far, it's workin' great."

His arm at my belly got tighter and I felt his breath stir my hair when he tipped his head to me, but he said nothing.

"Merry?" I called.

"Right here, Cherie," he said softly.

"Thanks," I whispered.

He kissed the top of my hair and whispered back, "Go to sleep, sweetheart."

"Okay," I muttered.

"Just sayin'," he continued quietly. "You get it. You live with Ethan. You got that in your life. You get that goodness. You don't get it about you, but I'll get you there. But at least with half of it you know, the pleasure is all mine."

God.

Merry.

I snuggled back into him, closing my eyes tight.

He shoved his other arm under me and wrapped it around my upper chest.

"'Night, brown eyes," he murmured.

"'Night, baby," I murmured back.

Merry held me close, his body spooning mine.

And I fell fast asleep.

Thirteen

NEVER DARED TO DREAM
Cher

*M*y eyes opened and I saw my bed stretching out in front of me, the pillows next to mine dented with sleep.

They'd been dented by Merry.

That made me realize I felt warm and it wasn't the bedclothes that was doing it.

I listened but heard nothing. I lifted up and saw my clock said it was nearly nine thirty.

Merry, I was discovering, woke early, even without an alarm clock.

Ethan, on a weekend, slept as long as he could.

Curious as to what Merry might be doing in my house with no one awake, I pushed the covers back, threw my legs over the side of the bed, got up, and headed straight out of the room.

In the hallway, I saw Ethan's door was open.

Interesting.

Walking down the hall, I heard it. Voices murmuring. Being quiet.

They didn't want to wake me.

My two guys in the kitchen, my son up early because Merry was there, being quiet in order not to wake me.

I'd never admit it to anybody, but that made me feel warm too...*and* squishy.

My feet silent on the carpeting, I headed to the living room through it, the murmurs becoming more distinct, but I couldn't hear much of anything.

Until I hit the doorway of the kitchen. I heard them. I saw them.

And my knees went weak.

Ethan was in his jammies at the table, hair a mess, shoveling waffles in his mouth.

Merry was at the counter, jeans on, shirt on but untucked, feet bare, standing next to the waffle iron but taking a sip off coffee, his mouth curled up, his eyes on my boy.

Oh yeah. Shit.

Warm and squishy.

"So I was all, 'kiss my butt,' and they were all, 'whatever,'" Ethan was saying.

I had no idea what he was talking about, but whatever it was, Merry found it amusing.

I liked this. I liked Merry making my kid waffles. I liked the fact he could do that at all, considering I'd paid three bucks for that waffle iron and it'd only worked once, so I was glad he'd fixed it. And I liked my kid having a guy in the house to babble guy shit to, getting up early to do it on a Saturday morning.

I leaned against the jamb and instantly got two pairs of eyes, my brown ones in my son's face and Merry's blue ones in his beautiful face.

"Mom! Cool! You're up!" Ethan cried. "Waffle time!"

"Seems you started without me," I noted.

Ethan smiled. "I was hungry."

I looked to Merry. "How many has he had so far?"

Merry was still grinning but now doing it at me. "Three."

"I'm a growin' boy," Ethan decreed.

"You're definitely that considering I'm soon going to have to sell my plasma in order to keep you in Oreos," I returned.

"I'll sell mine too so we can double up on America's finest cookie," Ethan offered.

I shook my head, doing it smiling, and moved into the kitchen. I went straight to my son and didn't push my luck with gooey. I just reached out and shoved his head to the side, but I did it tousling his hair just a little bit, hoping he wouldn't notice.

He noticed and I knew this when he muttered, "You're a goof, Mom."

"Whatever," I muttered back and moved to Merry.

He watched me and I watched him, thinking he looked right at home in Janis Joplin's kitchen.

I got close, put a hand to his abs, and lifted up to kiss his jaw.

"Mornin', baby," he said quietly.

I pulled back my head but stayed close, looking him in the eye, trying to decide if him making my son waffles in my kitchen was a better "mornin'" than the one he'd given me the day before.

It was an impossible decision. I was just going to have to equally enjoy all the boons he was giving me.

I didn't suspect this would be hard.

"Mornin'," I replied.

"Want waffles?" he asked.

"Want coffee," I answered, shifting away. "After teeth brushing," I went on. "Then waffles after coffee," I finished, wandering out of the room.

"I'll get on that, princess," Merry said.

I gave him a look as I hit the doorway.

"Mom!" Ethan cried again like I wasn't five feet away from him.

I turned in the door and lifted my brows.

"Teddy still wants to go to that movie we were gonna see today. If I call him and his mom's still up for takin' us, can I go?" he asked.

Could my son go to a movie, taking him out of the house for a few hours on a day that Merry had off and I might be able to spend that time with him?

"Sure," I answered.

"Awesome!" he near-on shouted. "I'll call Teddy after I finish eating. If his mom needs it, can you drop me at their place?"

"Sure," I repeated.

"You're good with it, you can be lazy today and I can do it," Merry offered.

Ethan's eyes got big with excitement.

"Then it's a pajama day for me," I declared, though it wasn't since I had to work that night, but at least during the day I could make it that way.

Unless Merry came back and my pajamas were history.

"You set it up, bud, I'll drop you," Merry said to Ethan, then looked at me. "I'll come back."

My knees got weak for another reason, and I shot him a very different kind of look before I took off to go brush my teeth.

I did this for the first time in my life, leaving two guys who meant the world to me in my kitchen.

Two of them.

A dream I'd never dared to dream.

And shit, that dream coming true made me feel warm and squishy.

I was still in my pajamas.

I was also on my knees.

Merry was in his jeans, his shirt, but he was sitting on the side of my bed with me kneeling between his legs.

And I'd finally got my mouth around his dick.

My kid was at a movie. Merry had dropped him off.

Then he came back to me.

His cock was wide, Jesus, and the veins protruding, catching against my tongue, making me want to trail the tip along them (something I did, repeatedly), the head thick and broad. Amazing.

I couldn't take him all—he more than filled me—but that didn't mean I didn't try.

I did.

I gave it my all.

And then kept giving.

Honestly? I didn't know who liked it more, Merry getting his dick sucked or me giving it my all, trying to take him deep, hearing the noises I was making him make, feeling his powerful body tense around me.

I felt his hand on my head shift, so his fingers clenched in my hair as he bit out, "Christ, Cherie."

I took him as far as he'd go and lifted my eyes to his.

His hungry gaze was on me, and the instant he got mine, his started burning.

"*Fuck me*," he growled.

I slid him out and lifted up, beyond ready, whispering, "Okay."

He was ready too. I knew when he shifted immediately, eyes still on me, hand going to the back of his jeans as I yanked my pajama shorts and panties down.

He was still rolling the condom on when I climbed up, knee to the bed, swinging the other leg over.

He had himself ready for me, one hand guiding his cock, the other hand sliding along my side to my back and lower until he cupped my ass.

I felt him where I needed him and drove down, taking him completely.

I watched his head drop back, the cords of the muscles at his neck straining, the column of his throat bared.

Right there. That was mine. All for me.

I went in.

Trailing my mouth along something I'd wanted for so long, it was not funny, while riding the cock of a man I'd wanted so badly, it was scary, all this on my bed in my house, I felt my pussy start convulsing.

Merry felt it too (obviously) and righted his head, dislodging my mouth from his throat, his free hand coming up to grip my hair.

"Do not come," he ordered.

"Okay," I breathed, moving, doing it fast, taking him deep, slamming down on him hard.

"Cherie." His tone was thick with sex and warning. "Do not fuckin' come."

God, that pushed me closer.

"You might hafta ride this one out when I'm done, baby," I gasped, getting closer.

"Slow it down," he growled.

That only made me speed it up.

"*Fuck*," he grunted, watching me take him. Then his hand in my hair slid to the back of my neck and curled around firm, just as his hand at my ass moved so he could circle my waist with his arm.

Having a hold on me, he held fast and stayed me before a downward glide, so I just had the tip.

Torture.

"Merry," I whispered, my voice needy.

"Be a good girl," he ordered.

Fuck, seriously.

"Merry." That was pleading.

"Wanna watch you fuck me like I got off watchin' you blow me," he shared gruffly. "So slow it down."

I bit my lip, straining against his hold.

"You gonna be my good girl?" he asked.

His words and, well...*everything* pushed me closer and my entire body tightened, fighting to drive him deep.

Something changed in his eyes that sent me spiraling.

"You're gonna be bad," he whispered.

"Baby, *please.*"

He held me at my neck, but his arm went away from my waist.

I thought he was letting me loose.

He wasn't.

His hand landed on my bare ass and the sound of the smack rent through the room as it scored straight from my ass right to my clit.

Oh yeah. I liked it like that.

"Gonna be good?" he asked.

"No," I whispered.

He gave me what I wanted and spanked me again.

My thighs jerked, my eyes stayed locked to his, and my clit started buzzing.

"Gonna be good?" he repeated.

I shook my head.

He spanked me.

Fuck...*yes.*

"My brown-eyed girl likes to be bad," he murmured, his heated eyes now on my mouth.

I licked my lips.

His hand landed on my ass.

"*Merry,*" I breathed.

His fingers at my neck grew light and he ground out, "Fuck me, baby."

I fucked him. Fuck yes, I fucked him hard and fast, coming on the third stroke, the orgasm so huge, I started bucking, winding my arms around his shoulders, clenching my fist in his hair, ramming down on his big, thick cock.

"*Merry.*" It was a near cry as the orgasm engulfed me.

My head shot back, my back arching, and my body kept moving, partially me, partially Merry's arm again around my waist, slamming me down.

I heard his noises as I rode out my orgasm, driving deep until finally his arm around me tightened, keeping me down, full of him, and he buried his face in my tank at my breasts and groaned as his body shuddered under me.

I dropped my head so my lips were at his hair and allowed my climax to leave slow, sliding out of me while I sat on Merry's big dick and held him to me.

I only moved my head when he moved his, trailing his lips up my chest, my neck, my jaw. Both his hands moved as his head did, coming up to rest on either side of my head.

He tipped me down and I thought he'd take my mouth, but he didn't.

He stared into my eyes, not moving.

I read what was in his gaze.

He liked that. He liked me being his good girl. He liked me being bad. He liked that we had that. He liked that I got off on it. He liked that I gave it freely. He liked that he could take it from me. He liked we were right there, my ass red, his cock buried inside me, as close as we could get in so many ways, him and me.

On this thought and the fact I liked it too, totally, both his thumbs slid out and he traced my cheekbones.

"Leavin' you," he whispered, and I felt every inch of me lock. But Merry didn't waste any time sharing he wasn't taking himself away. "You got less than an hour, honey. Shower. Get dressed. I got your pussy all over my jeans. Gonna go home, hit the shower. Change. Be back and I'm takin' you to Frank's for lunch."

I was still full of waffles.

I would eat three of Frank's fried tenderloin sandwiches to get what Merry was giving me.

He was not fucking around. Date. Meet the kid. Show nearly the entirety of the 'burg he was with me by strolling into a Brownsburg Bulldogs home game, holding my hand.

Now taking me to Frank's so the rest of that entirety of the 'burg would see it or talk about it, and the fullness of that would go beyond since they'd eventually (but soon) hear about it.

I slid both my hands to the sides of his neck, but I didn't say anything.

"Get you home by the time your kid gets back," he finished.

I nodded.

His gaze dropped then lifted.

"Good with your mouth," he muttered.

I gave his neck a squeeze and said nothing.

"Don't know which I prefer—my good girl or when she's bad."

I felt my lips curl up as my eyelids lowered.

He didn't miss it.

"She likes to be bad," he said softly and approvingly. "Gonna test that, Cherie."

I again made no verbal reply, but he felt my shiver and that was when his lips curled up.

His hands left my head so he could wrap his arms around me as he declared, "You're right."

Finally, I spoke.

"About what?"

"This is workin' great."

I could actually feel myself melting in his arms, and I knew it was melting even though I'd never done anything like that in my entire life.

"Merry," I whispered.

"You're all I said you were *and* you give great head?" His lip curl turned into a cocky smile. "Definitely workin' great."

I sighed in fake annoyance. "A man and his blowjobs."

"Babe, the act? Awesome," he stated. "You grabbin' my hand practically before I could get in your door and draggin' me to your bedroom so you could shove me on your bed and get your mouth on my dick?" His hold on me tightened slightly. "*Awesome*."

"You have a great cock," I shared.

His hips shifted and his smile didn't get any less cocky. "It likes you too."

"Thank God," I muttered.

He kept smiling, but he did it gently pulling me off him.

He put me on my feet as he straightened from the bed.

"Gonna use your john, then I'm gonna go," he said. "After that, less than an hour, Cher."

I nodded.

"Dig Ethan, like spendin' time with him. But I want my good girl and my bad one all to me again. While I'm away, want you to think on finding us that time and soon, you hear me?"

I nodded again, back to feeling warm and squishy because he was wasting no time letting me know he wanted more of me.

He shifted and I knew he was adjusting his jeans even as he ordered, "Now kiss me."

I got up on my toes, leaned in, hands to his chest, head tipped back, and I kissed my guy.

It was wet but short.

When he was done, he bent, nabbed my pajama shorts and panties, and handed them to me.

But after I put them on and before he walked out of my room, he bent to touch his lips to my nose.

God.

Merry.

"Less than an hour," he said softly, then I watched him walk away.

I did it thinking that was mine. All that tall, lean handsomeness. His big dick. Him making my son (and me) waffles. Him wanting my ass in a booth with him at Frank's so he could show the whole 'burg he was claiming me.

That was all mine.

Forty whole hours, that had been mine.

And I hadn't fucked it up.

A record.

A record I was going to keep breaking.

Maybe for eternity.

Garrett

Garrett's phone started ringing before he let himself in his apartment after taking Cher out to lunch at Frank's, going back to her place and hanging on her couch (mostly making out) until her kid got home, then hanging with Ethan and her until she had to start getting ready for work.

He left her to it.

That didn't mean he wasn't hitting J&J's later that night for a drink.

He pulled his phone out on that thought, doing it smiling.

He took the call still smiling.

"Yo, Rocky," he greeted his sister.

"So, let me see," she said in his ear. "Swank's Thursday night. A freaking *Bulldogs* game on Friday. Frank's four hours ago."

He tossed his keys on the bar and started to shrug out of his jacket. "Apparently, 'burg's buzzing."

"'Buzzing' is not the word for it. They haven't had anything this juicy since…" she trailed off, probably trying to think about when they'd had something that juicy.

But he already knew. "Since you and Tanner sorted your shit."

"Well, really, since Dusty got shot by that kid, but that isn't the good kind of juicy that this is," she replied, but her voice turned hesitant when she asked, "It is, isn't it, Merry? You and Cher, it's the good kind of juicy, right?"

"I like her, honey," he shared. "Like her, her kid is great. So yeah, it's the good kind of juicy."

She was silent a moment before she said, "I'm glad." More hesitant when she asked, "Mia?"

"Mia's done."

Even though he gave her that firm, he knew she was chewing on it because she was silent again.

She broke it, saying, "I think that's good. Cher...she's a fighter. Mia... not so much."

She got it.

Rocky got it better than anybody.

"Yeah," he agreed.

"So, you bringing her over to meet your niece, say, tomorrow?"

He nearly burst out laughing. "She already knows Cecelia...and you. But I get you. Though, what I get, still gotta tell you that we had our first date two days ago, Raquel."

She amended her question.

"So, you bringing her over to meet your niece next weekend, but you're getting your ass over here tomorrow before CeeCee forgets what her uncle looks like?"

She wanted him to come and spend time with her daughter.

She wanted more for him to come and spend time with his sister so she could see for herself that he was edging toward happy.

He grinned. "I'll come 'round. Catch a game. Remind that baby girl I exist."

"That'd be good."

"And I'll talk to Cher. We've jumped in with both feet. Maybe it'd be good we take some time to get used to the waters we're in for a while before we hit more rapids."

"I hear that."

And again, she got it. She and Tanner had hit so much white water, it was a wonder they weren't crushed against the rocks.

They weren't and Garrett was pleased as all hell they'd finally hit smooth.

"Have a feeling you'll be meeting her and Ethan in a different way soon, though," he told her.

"That'd make me happy."

What would make his sister happy was knowing her brother was happy.

And he was happy. Cher putting on that dress for him. Cher giving him all she gave in the variety of ways she gave it the last two days. Seeing all she made in her son—funny like her, a smartass in a good way like her, a scrapper who doesn't take shit just like Cherie, and loyal, so fucking loyal, it was beautiful.

Yeah.

Garrett was happy.

He just hoped he had it in him this time not to turn it to shit.

"Right, seein' as I got plans tomorrow to spend time with my niece, I'm gonna spend some time with my girl while she's at work," he started. "Lettin' you go so I can get at least fifteen minutes of some football in so I don't start gettin' the shakes before I get behind the wheel of a vehicle."

"Best let you do that," she muttered.

"Rocky?" he called.

"Yeah, Merry?"

"Love my little sister," he said.

That got him silence again before she gave it back. "And love my big brother. See you tomorrow, Merry."

"See you then, honey."

They disconnected.

He'd thrown his phone on the bar and was heading toward his couch when a loud banging came at the door.

He hadn't been home for ten minutes, but he knew from the insistent sound, not to mention the 'burg buzzing, who was standing outside on the landing.

He didn't want to head that way, but he did because it had to happen eventually. He reckoned he might as well get that ball rolling now.

He checked the peephole and saw he was right because outside was a woman who was pissed for what Garrett considered no reason, which made him pissed, even though he knew he should keep a lock on it.

He didn't.

He opened the door.

"What? Do you have cameras on me?" he asked, knowing that was not the way to lead, but he was angry Mia was not getting his message and he was not a big fan of her banging on his door.

He wasn't surprised when she shoved in, taking two strides into the room before turning on him.

She threw out her hands, face full of rage. "Are you serious with this shit, Merry?"

He closed the door, using that time to pull himself together, and turned to her. "We gotta talk."

"Yeah." She took those two steps back to him and shoved his chest with one hand, doing it hard enough, his shoulder rocked back. "We fucking do."

He wasn't big on her shoving him either.

"Take a breath," he demanded, forcing his voice to quiet just as he was forcing himself to remain calm and not lose it.

"I don't *need* to take a breath. I cannot *believe* you're humiliating me this way," she snapped.

They weren't going to do this.

Not now, not ever if it came out angry.

"This is not the time or the place," he stated. "Like I said, we gotta talk. But it's not happenin' now when you're pissed and I'm not feelin' like bein' pushed into a bad mood."

"Well, fuck that," she bit out, shoving him again, this time with both hands so his whole torso swung back.

He took a step to the side and warned, "Watch your hands, Mia. I don't want them on me again."

She tipped her head to the side. "You don't? Oh. I would guess you don't, considering you got the good stuff direct from *a professional* all weekend."

He took a deliberate step away from her before he purposefully locked his body.

After he did this, he dragged in a breath that was supposed to be deep and calming, but it came in shallow and did not one thing to ease the fury he felt building.

"Watch your mouth," he whispered.

"Fuck you," she shot back. "Swank's was bad enough. *Swank's*. That woman *and you* at fucking *Swank's*. But a football game? You took *her* to a fucking *football game*? In *the 'burg*? For *everyone to see*?"

"You need to leave. Now," he returned. "I calm down, you calm down, we'll talk."

"About what?" she asked. "How you're testing me? How many tests do I have to pass, Merry? I mean, you shit all over our marriage. You shit all over our future. Then you shit all over me *for years*. And now you're dating the town *slut*, rubbing that in my face when—"

He advanced, she retreated, and neither stopped doing it until he had her pinned against the living room wall.

He didn't touch her and kept his distance, but she felt him. He knew she knew she'd pushed too far. He knew this because she pressed against the wall and didn't move.

"You ever fuckin' talk to my face or I even *hear* you spewed shit like that about Cher again, Mia, so help me God, the over we're already over will be history. You won't even be a memory, good or bad. I'll erase you so completely, I see your fuckin' face, you'll think I have no clue who you are."

"Merry," she breathed, eyes big, his name coming out pained.

"I wanted to sit down and talk about this, but you're here and you're like you are, which means I'm not big on seein' you ever again, so this is happenin' now," he declared.

Then he gave it to her.

"I fucked up. I fucked *us* up. You're right. I shit all over our marriage. I did that and I own that. It sucks I hurt you because…once, I loved you. Once, you meant everything to me. But I was fucked in the head. I fucked us up because I was terrified of what it would do to you if somethin' happened to me and you lost me. I've felt that loss and know it's an empty that never gets filled and I didn't want that for you. I should have talked that out with you. I should have worked that out with you. I didn't. And that was my fuckup."

"I—"

He didn't even let her get started.

"I've had a chance to think and as shit as that was, me doin' that to you, and as shit as it was, me continuing to fuck you even after I made us over, you didn't have it in you to deal. You *don't* have it in you to deal. You lost me in a way you could've gotten me back. You knew it, fuckin' everyone knew it, but you didn't do it. So I fucked up. You fucked up. We're even and we're movin' on."

"But I want us—"

"I don't give a fuck what you want, Mia. I made this plain. I wanted us to sort our shit so we could move on without it fuckin' up the memory of what we had. I told you we were over. I start somethin' important with a woman who means a good fuckin' deal to me and you come to *my* home, shovin' me and gettin' in my face, sayin' jacked shit about that woman. So now that memory is gonna stay fucked. And not because I made it that way." He lifted a hand and jabbed a finger toward her face. "*You* did."

He stepped back and to the side but kept his eyes locked to her.

"Now get the fuck outta my house and do not ever come back. We are done, Mia."

She didn't move an inch, not even her gaze from his.

"I love you," she whispered.

The last five years, he'd lived for her to say those words.

Now they meant nothing.

He shook his head.

She had no clue.

"Love is facing head on somethin' that threatens it and not bending, sure as fuck not breaking, when that thing leans on you to let go. You don't have that. In your way, I know you loved me. My way of lovin' you was just as fucked up. We screwed that up so badly, there's no goin' back. At this point, the best we got is not jackin' our shit again with someone else. I got every intention of not makin' that same mistake twice with what I'm starting with a good woman who means somethin' to me. I'm pissed as hell at you right now, but I hope you find you got it in you to do the same with your man. The one thing I'm certain about is that there's nothin' left between you and me."

"I refuse to believe you mean that," she replied earnestly.

He stared at her.

Yeah, she had no clue.

And at that point, he had no options, so he put his hands on his hips as he looked to the floor.

"Merry," she called.

He lifted his head. "Get out."

"But...Merry—"

He leaned her way and clipped, "Get...the fuck...*out.*"

She studied him, and when his body shifted, she said quickly, "Maybe we should find a time to talk when we've both calmed down."

"Fuckin' shit," he muttered and moved, taking the only option she was giving him.

He went to his jacket and shrugged it on. He grabbed his phone, shoved it in his pocket, and nabbed his keys.

He then went to the door and looked back to his ex-wife, who had only moved a few feet from the wall.

"I'm goin' out," he shared. "I don't got much I give a shit about, though it'd suck havin' to buy a new TV. Now you can either get out so I can lock up and keep that TV, or you can stay until you finally catch my drift. All I ask is you close the door. If you're here when I come back, I'll go to a hotel. What I am not gonna do is spend more time with you. You got five seconds. What's it gonna be?"

"Merry, you can't just…"

She kept talking, but Garrett didn't listen.

He counted to five.

Then he walked out, closing the door behind him while Mia was still talking.

Garrett got fast food for dinner, trying to calm down before he hit J&J's.

He would find he didn't succeed when he opened the door, his eyes going behind the bar to see Cher there with Jack. She took one look at him and her face shifted from the grin that was starting into a freeze.

She began walking down the bar.

He moved in, taking it in.

It was relatively early on a Saturday night, but the place was in full swing. Darryl was there and Dee was working the floor.

Jack and Cher had the bar.

But the stools at the end were all empty, waiting for the men who usually claimed them. None of them were there mostly because all of them had women they preferred to be with on a Saturday night, so they wouldn't be at a bar unless their women were with them.

Except Merry.

Like Colt, his woman worked there.

He hit a stool and she was right in front of him.

He barely had his ass on the seat before she remarked, "I'd say this was a nice surprise except you look like you wanna kill somebody."

"Mia's heard about us."

She stared at him before she turned and reached to the top-shelf whisky.

Yeah, they knew each other. This wasn't just starting out. They'd laid the foundation. They'd just added fucking fantastic sex and expensive dinners and him getting more of Cher's smart mouth.

And her sweet.

"Baby, aim lower. I got a taste for the good stuff, but my budget's bein' revised," he said.

He saw her body jolt, she gave him a look over her shoulder, then she reached lower.

As she poured him his drink, he took in her tight red top, her ass in her jeans, and her high heels. Finally, he felt himself calming.

"Good news is, the talk me and her had to have is done," he shared.

She set the bottle aside and leaned in to her forearms. "Yeah?"

"Not the way I wanted it to go," he said.

When he took a sip of whisky and didn't elucidate, she prompted, "Talk to me, gorgeous."

Garrett shrugged slightly.

"Said what I had to say," he told her. "Seein' as she came in pissed as all hell, thinkin' me goin' out with you was me testin' her, not sure she heard. She said a few words. I returned a fuckuva lot more. Not thinkin' she got me seein' as I told her to get her ass out, but she didn't leave, so I did. She might still be at my place. Or, alternately, she left, leavin' my pad wide open and I'll get home later to find I need to go out and buy a new TV."

As he spoke, he watched her eyes get big, and when he was done, she asked, "You left her there?"

"Yeah. Closed the door on her, she was still talkin'."

"Holy shit," she whispered.

"She wouldn't leave and I was done, so I had no choice."

Her lips twitched.

He might be calming, but he found not one thing funny.

"It wasn't the way I wanted it to go, Cher," he reminded her.

"You walked out with your ex-wife in your place," she stated.

"Couldn't strong-arm the bitch," he pointed out. "She was okay with shovin' me, but man's any man at all, he's got it in him to check it even if he's itchin' to shove back."

Her lips were no longer twitching.

"She shoved you?"

"Twice."

He saw that he might be calming, but Cher was not.

"You're fucking *shitting* me," she spat.

No, she was not calming, and as cute as she looked, preparing to turn into a hellcat for him, it was time to focus on calming her.

"It's done. May take a while, but if the words don't sink in, my actions will. Only thing I gotta worry about now is hittin' my place later and findin' it cleaned out. I got a plan to take my girl's boy out with her and her mom to celebrate his birthday at Swank's. Won't be able to do that if I gotta drop two large on a TV."

That did it. All the anger vanished when he talked about taking Ethan to Swank's for his birthday.

But her lips parted when he talked about dropping two grand on a television.

"Two large?" she asked, her eyebrows going up.

"Gotta get a new one, not gonna fuck around. Trade up. Eighty inches."

"Your media center won't fit an eighty-inch TV," she noted.

"Then I'll also have to buy a new media center."

She stared.

Then she busted out laughing.

And that was it.

All that he needed.

Cher was laughing.

Garrett was calm.

He reached out and nabbed her hand.

She didn't pull away.

More for the 'burg to chew on and he felt the eyes. He knew that he and Cher were the latest meal.

He didn't care. And even if he did, he'd care less when her hand latched on to his and she leaned deep across the bar.

"Silver lining, gorgeous, your to-do list is one lighter," she said, still laughing.

"Yeah," he agreed.

She held his hand and hers tightened as the humor slid from her.

"Sucks, baby," she whispered. "Wish it didn't go down like that for you."

He did too.

But at least it was done.

He just had to hope his message finally leaked in so Mia would stop her shit.

Then again, he was going to look for a new place (another reason to hope his TV was there when he got back; he didn't need that outlay lightening his down payment). Eventually, he'd move and she wouldn't be able to find him.

Or he'd have her ass arrested for harassment.

One way or another, the message would get across.

He looked into Cher's warm brown eyes as they looked into his, assessing to see if he was okay.

To show her he was, he asked, "My good girl find time for just her and me?"

Those eyes went soft and her fingers stayed firm around his when she replied, "Batten down the hatches, Merry. Had a chat with Mom. Family dinner is set for Thursday with your ass in a seat at her table."

"Terrific," he muttered, and she smiled.

"But I got Saturday off and Ethan has a sleepover at a friend's, so I'm all yours."

"I'm on call."

"Fuck," she whispered.

"On call doesn't mean on a desk," he told her. "Just means I might have to leave, but it also means I can come back."

Her eyes brightened. "That works, honey."

It did. It was his life. And if he didn't jack it up, it could be hers. So it was good she could work with it.

"Now, you gonna let that whisky sit forever, or are you gonna rinse away the shit and get loose with me while I'm workin'?" she asked.

He gave her his answer by letting her go, grabbing his glass, and taking another sip.

She approved by smiling.

"Gotta make sure things are covered," she told him. "But I'll be back."

"I'll be here."

She liked that. He knew because she didn't hide it.

And he liked *all* that.

Yeah, they were working and doing it in a way he knew deep into his gut that wouldn't quit.

Unless he jacked it up.

"Go easy," she advised as he let her hand go. "That shit only costs ten bucks a go, but a pissed off ex-wife left at your pad, you might be dealin' with more than a boosted TV."

"Way to kill a calm, baby," he muttered but did it grinning.

"Just bein' real, makin' sure you don't get blindsided," she returned and leaned back in. "But, just sayin', the bitch trashes your place, you can catch your shows at mine. The spirit of Jerry Garcia likes company."

That was when Garrett busted out laughing.

Which was when Cher knew it was safe to leave.

She did, making drinks, filling Dee's tray.

But she came back. Jack also came over to chat. And Dee stopped by to shoot the shit.

When they were gone and sometimes when they were there, he had Cher.

A night at J&J's with his woman who worked there.

No other place he'd rather be.

Fourteen

FUCKING HAPPY
Cher

Mom wants to know if there's something you don't eat.

It was Sunday, late morning, and Merry had a day planned at his sister's house to commune with family and play with his niece.

I had a day planned watching football with my kid before having to go to work, both of us eating ourselves sick, our every-Sunday plans when football was on.

I was at the stove frying sausage.

It was almost done when I got a text back.

Onions.

Gotcha.

And tofu.

I grinned.

Knew that without you telling me. Red-blooded. No way you eat sissy excuse for meat, I told him.

Damn straight, he replied.

I looked back to my sausage.

I ate tofu.

But, then again, I ate anything.

I drained the sausage, mixed it with the other shit, and poured it into the wonton wrappers to put in the oven to bake.

Then I texted my mom so she'd know not to serve onions or tofu for dinner on Thursday.

Ravens lost. You owe me 20.

That came from Merry later that afternoon and I read it with a grin.

As I was reading it, another came in.

Bears are gonna lose. Another 20. I'll take it in trade.

I felt my grin turn naughty.

Bears aren't gonna go down, I told him.

They are, then you are, he told me.

That gave me a shiver.

I nearly bobbled my phone when Ethan asked, "You textin' Merry?"

I looked to him lounged in the bucket seat. "Yeah."

"Tell him Browns lost. He owes me ten bucks."

I stared at my son.

Then I looked to my phone and texted Merry.

Ethan says Browns lost. You owe him ten bucks.

I sent that, then immediately typed more.

You betting with my kid?

Within seconds, I got back, *Babe, he's the commissioner of the fifth grade fantasy league.*

That was when I stared at my phone.

I had no idea my son ran a fantasy football league.

How could that even be?

I didn't look at my kid.

I kept my eyes to my phone while I made a big decision.

Ethan and I had our things, just Ethan and me. Mom and Ethan had their things, just Mom and Ethan.

And Ethan had shared something with Merry that he hadn't shared with me.

I had no idea if running a fantasy football league at age ten (almost eleven) was good or bad. I just knew, unlike any other man I'd let into my life, Merry had a moral compass. If he thought it was bad, he'd say something and not the way he'd just said it.

So the big decision I made was that I was going to let my son and my man have their things, just Ethan and Merry.

Well good, I texted and sent. Then, *I'd hoped he'd be an engineer, but Vegas bookie is just as sweet.*

To that I got, *Stop making me laugh when I can't kiss you.*

Which made me grin again.

"Yeesh," my boy muttered, disgusted. "Merry's not even here and you're all gooey."

That didn't make my grin die.

Not even slightly.

Though it did make me throw one of my many awesome, mismatched Janis Joplin pillows at him.

Ethan caught it and threw it back.

On Monday morning, after I'd dropped Ethan at school and hit the bank to deposit my tips (and the stupid one hundred dollar check that Trent and Peggy sent me, putting that in Ethan's new account), I heard the text sound from my purse in the seat next to me as I was driving home.

I decided driving home safely was priority one, considering my life no longer sucked and I wanted to live it fully, so I left my phone in my bag (something I always did, considering, even when my life sucked, my kid was awesome, so being safe was always priority one).

But once I was in my driveway, I dug it out and was throwing open my door, looping my purse over my arm, and reading it at the same time.

It was from Merry.

Ethan get to school okay?

Not having him for years and falling in love with him more and more every time I saw him or even thought of him, I never would have thought, if the impossible happened and I got him, there would be farther to fall.

I was dead wrong.

I was moving my thumb over the phone as I hopped out of my car, nowhere near done with my text, when I started to shift out of the door to close it and ran into something.

I jerked in a turn and stared at my dickhead neighbor who was right there, in my space.

Okay, apparently, even when most of your life stops sucking, some of that suckage remained.

"Hey," he said.

"Hey," I replied, forcing myself not to look around to see if I could find Ryker watching.

"Sorry, baby." He moved back half a step. "Thought you saw me."

I got out of the way of my door, slammed it, and put space between us as I beat back a lip curl at him calling me "baby."

I also did all this as I answered, "I was texting."

"Yeah," he said, taking a step toward me, and I held my ground even though I didn't want to. "Listen, know you got a kid but thought you might wanna find someone to look after him and go grab a beer sometime."

I looked to his house.

I saw the beat-up Chevy truck I knew he drove.

I did not see the run-down Ford Fiesta his woman drove.

Not good news.

I looked back at him. "It's cool you askin', but just to say, I got a kid and I also got a man."

His face changed and it was not a happy change.

"Black Excursion?" he asked.

He'd been watching me.

Now I was the one who was not happy (or less happy, considering I wasn't happy at all he was in my space).

"Yeah," I told him.

He moved closer to me.

Shit.

"Dude's not your style, darlin'," he said in what I expected was his come-on voice.

It did nothing for me for more reasons than the fact the asshole didn't even know my name, so he couldn't know what my style was.

Unless he made assumptions about me.

Which pissed me off.

However, I could not engage.

And that sucked.

"'Fraid you're wrong," I replied, stepping away.

"That guy's too clean-cut," he declared, taking another step toward me. "You seem like a woman who likes to have fun, let it all hang out." His gaze dipped to my tits. "And you can feel free to do that with me, baby."

He was right. I was that kind of woman, and I was good doing that with Merry because my dickhead neighbor read Merry wrong—Merry was also that kind of man.

"Think we can have good times, you and me," he stated, looking into my eyes again and taking yet another step toward me.

"Think my man wouldn't be too happy about that," I returned an understatement. "But you gotta know, I *am* happy with my guy, so no offense to you and your offer, but I'm good where I'm at."

"You sure you wouldn't wanna take a shot at better?" he pushed.

Him? Better?

He'd been watching but had he actually *seen* Merry?

"Got a good thing," I said softly, hoping to get through and get this asshole away from me. "Been waitin' for it a long time. It's good for me. It's good for my kid. No way I'm gonna fuck that up. You with me?"

Not that I'd even consider it with him.

Then again, I wouldn't consider it with anybody...but Merry.

He studied me.

I let him.

When I was about to quit letting him, thankfully, he nodded.

"I'm with you, babe. I hear that. But I'm two doors down, you know? Shit happens with that dude, he doesn't look after you, there's always a cold one waitin' for you just down the street."

I had a feeling he didn't know what looking after a woman meant.

And I was never going to find out.

"Thanks, that's sweet," I lied.

He smiled.

He had good teeth, but I knew that was all that was good about him.

"You ever need anyone to look after your boy, I'm around a lot." He kept smiling. "And I like kids."

And *that* was *never* going to happen.

"That's sweet too," I lied again.

"Just so you know, in case shit goes south, I can be all kinds of sweet."

How was he not getting the hint?

"Noted," I murmured.

He kept smiling. "Later, babe."

"Right. Later."

He did a slow turn, doing it watching me.

I did a quick turn and hoofed it to my house.

Once I got inside, I finished my text to Merry and hit SEND.

Ethan's all good and you're all kinds of sweet.

And that was no lie.

The second after I sent that, I went to my Contacts and found what I needed.

I put my phone to my ear and got Ryker's voicemail.

I waited for the beep and shared, "My dickhead neighbor just asked me out. He took no for an answer, but that didn't stop him from pushin' it and bein' chatty. Since it's flyin' through the 'burg, you gotta know Merry and me sorted things out. If you don't want Merry breathin' down your neck on this, or wadin' in and committing felonies when the badass is unleashed, you need to do whatever it is you're doin' and you need to do it quick. My neighbor is watchin', that watchin' he's doin' is *watchin' me*, and if Merry cottons on to that, all holy hell is gonna break loose."

I got a beep to tell me I got a text before I finished my message, so when I was done, I went right there to see the text from Merry.

Late lunch. You and me. Frank's. You good for 2:00?

I had early shifts that week.

But I'd go to the moon at any time he wanted to have lunch with Merry.

In other words, I was good with anything.

You're on, I told him.

Text me with your order sometime between then and now. I'll call it in before we go so you'll get out in time.

He thought of everything.

Thanks, baby.

Anything, brown eyes.

I drew in a deep breath.

Yeah.

Fuck yeah.

I had a good thing.

⟶

Sit tight. Be smart. And don't jack shit up.

That text was not from Merry.

That text was a poorly timed incoming from Ryker while I was sitting across from Merry at Frank's with a breaded tenderloin sandwich in front of me.

Get a move on, but now, shut up. I'm with Merry, I returned.

"Who's that?" Merry asked, lifting his Reuben and the inevitable happening, considering it was a Reuben *à la* Frank, shoved full of corned beef and sauerkraut, which meant a huge glob of it fell out before Merry even got it to his mouth.

I tossed my phone in my purse and ignored his question.

"You should know this, actually *bein'* from the 'burg and all, but you gotta eat a Reuben *à la* Frank with a fork," I educated him.

"Women eat sandwiches with forks," he replied to me. "Men make a mess and don't give a fuck."

I couldn't argue his point, so I didn't. I took a bite of my sandwich.

I did it hoping Merry wouldn't press me about who was texting me.

I also did it uncomfortable because I was no relationship expert, but one thing I did know: a surefire way to fuck one up was keeping something important from the other person. In fact, I was pretty sure keeping *anything* from the other person wasn't a good thing.

Merry might not need me to share every piece of information about myself.

I just knew if he asked, I should be open to sharing.

Including whoever texted.

Especially if it was about some trouble Ryker was involved in that was happening right on my street.

I'd felt Merry gearing up to go apeshit. That feeling let loose where he actually lost it, that would be a bad thing. So I knew Ryker was not wrong.

I just hoped whatever he was up to, he'd deal with it and do it in a way so Merry never knew I even had an inkling.

And worse, didn't share.

"It good, babe?" he asked.

I focused on Merry and not my thoughts. I did this chewing and realized he was asking about my sandwich.

"Yeah," I answered before I asked, "You gonna let me buy lunch?"

"Women argue with their girls about who's buyin' lunch," he stated. "A man takes his woman to lunch, he pays."

I was glad he seemed to have forgotten about the texts.

But I was still uncomfortable about it.

I lifted my brows. "Is that a badass rule?"

"Nope. One of the commandments," he returned immediately.

"You sign those in blood?" I asked.

"Yup," he answered. "Though not ours. The man whose ass we kicked to earn membership in the brotherhood."

"Sorry I missed the initiation ritual," I said through a smile before taking another bite.

"It was quite the show, baby."

I chewed and did it still smiling.

Merry took another bite and lost another quarter of filling.

I swallowed so I could laugh without choking.

I did it thinking, *this is how it feels...happy.*

Outside many miraculous moments with my son, which were all about lucking out by having a kid as awesome as Ethan, I had no clue.

I had no clue just sitting across from the guy who did it for you at a booth in a diner could make you so...fucking...*happy.*

But it did because that was what I felt, sitting with Merry, trading smart-ass back and forth, and eating fantastic sandwiches.

Just that.

And that's all I felt.

Fucking happy.

"Shit."

It was Wednesday evening. Darryl was behind the bar with me. He was yanking out the bins full of recyclables in order to clean them out.

When he cursed, I looked to him to see he was bent to his task but his head was tipped back, his eyes were at the front of the bar, and his face was set to displeased.

I looked that way and felt my body get tight.

She'd timed it meticulously. I was a chick so I knew that to be true. Just after six on a weekday, the bar was full of patrons who wanted to get loose after their day by throwing back a drink.

She was there at that moment because she wanted an audience. She wanted people to know she'd thrown down with me. She might even be wanting to save face.

And if she thought Merry was testing her, she wanted that shit to get back to Merry.

As for me, I was pissed she was there. I was pissed she was there with her eyes locked to me and her expression telling me where this was going. I was pissed she was bringing this to my place of work.

But I was also curious.

Not only at what she was going to say but because Tanner Layne was there to witness it. Tanner was sitting at the end of the bar in what looked to be a debrief work huddle with his buddy Devin.

They'd both been in since things with Merry and me started officially (and even when it was unofficial). I knew they both knew what was going on, Tanner probably more than anybody.

But in that time, they hadn't treated me any differently.

Tanner liked me. We were buds.

That said, I knew Tanner had pushed Merry to get back with Mia. And he was too good of a guy to let me know to my face that he thought Merry was making a mistake with me.

Now, if that was the case or if it wasn't, if Mia forced something, whatever that was might be unleashed.

"Cheryl." I heard snapped, and I stopped thinking all this and focused on Mia, who'd positioned herself at the bar where there were two vacant seats.

As I did this, I noted I wasn't the only one focused on Mia at the bar. The entire place was almost silent because *everyone* was focused on Mia at the bar.

"*Cher.*"

That was growled angrily from behind me.

I twisted my neck and looked up to see Darryl right at my back.

"I'm good, Darryl," I told him.

Just his eyes shifted down to me.

"And I'm good standin' right here, makin' sure you're good," he returned.

Seriously, Darryl was all right.

"Fine," Mia bit out, and I turned my attention back to her. "*Cher.*"

I moved closer to her at the bar and decided to start out by playing dumb.

"You need a drink, Mia?"

"No, I don't need a goddamned drink," she spat. "I need you to leave my man alone."

I sighed.

Definitely making a statement she wanted to get back to Merry.

"And I need you to know I'll fight for him if you make me," she went on.

"Listen, babe, I'm at work. Can we not do this here?" I requested, then added, "Or, say, at all?"

"You need to understand the way things are."

That meant no.

I still could not engage (even if I wanted to).

"Okay, I understand," I told her. "Now, do you want a drink?"

At that, she seemed confused, probably because she was expecting a different response from me.

"Woman, this is a bar," Darryl entered the conversation when she hesitated one-point-five seconds. "You're in here, you drink. You don't drink, you're not in here."

"No offense," Mia said to him. "But I'm not talking to you."

"Don't care if you are or if you aren't," Darryl returned. "Fact remains, you're here, you drink."

"I have a few things to say to *Cher*," Mia retorted.

"You said 'em," Darryl shot back. "Now order a drink or gonna hafta ask you to leave."

Mia decided she was done with Darryl and looked to me. "Everyone knows he's mine. The whole town knows. They don't want the likes of you for him. They want him *for me*."

Shit, now she was making me mad.

"The likes of me?" I asked, though I shouldn't have. I was keeping it together. I didn't need to give her the ammunition to make me lose it.

She looked me up and down. "You know what you are."

Yeah, she was making me mad.

With effort, I beat it back and nodded. "I know what I am. I know Merry likes what I am. And I really don't give a shit what everyone knows or wants for Merry. Merry wants me and that's good enough for me."

"Merry doesn't know what he wants," she fired back.

Christ, she was annoying.

"He doesn't?" I asked sarcastically. "Weird. He seemed pretty sure Thursday night. And Friday morning. And Saturday."

As I meant to do, I got in there. I knew it when her admittedly pretty face twisted and she didn't look so pretty.

"I'm sure he did," she hissed. "What you forget is you weren't the first he was *sure* he wanted, though I bet with all your on-the-job experience, you gave it good."

That wasn't annoying.

That was infuriating.

I moved closer to the bar. Darryl moved closer to my back.

But in the back and forth, we'd missed the fact that another player had hit our scene.

"Before more shit comes outta your mouth you're gonna regret, Mia, you need to end this and go."

I looked to the left to see Tanner standing there.

"This doesn't have anything to do with you, Tanner," Mia replied, but she wasn't done. Sliding a catty glance at me, she turned back to Tanner. "Though, I'll say I'm surprised it seems you don't want better for Merry."

"Doesn't mean shit what I want for Garrett," Tanner stated, and I felt that in not good ways, seeing as it wasn't a ringing endorsement or a throwdown for me. "What does is what Garrett wants for Garrett," he went on.

"And Raquel didn't want you for seventeen years, but you both knew better," she returned.

I watched Tanner's mouth get tight and I thought that was him conceding the point.

I was incorrect in this assumption.

Very much so.

"I am not Garrett and you sure as fuck aren't Rocky," he bit out. "This is not about that. This is somethin' totally different. You want it, I'll give it to you. You're right. I do want better for Merry. I want my brother to be happy. And I know him. I know no way in fuck he'd be happy with a woman who'd spew the shit you just spewed to a good woman anytime, but sure as fuck not waltzin' in her place of business to throw down with her in front of everybody."

"This has to be said," she returned, lifting her chin even though a hint of uncertainty hit her expression.

Tanner shook his head. "You're intent to make your statement clear after five years of fuckin' around and doin' not one thing to get back your man. Advice? Wake up. You dicked around too long. It's done. You lost him. And just a heads up on that, Mia, this town *is* talkin'. And while your women might be fillin' your head with shit to keep you on a path that is no longer righteous, the rest of the 'burg is glad Garrett finally found a woman who's got it in her to stick."

Okay, right.

That was a ringing endorsement and definitely Tanner throwing down for me.

Suddenly, I wasn't angry.

Suddenly, I grinned.

"He's mine," Mia told Tanner, her voice weakening but only in the face of his words. It did not reflect her resolve. I had a vagina. I saw the look on her face. I knew that as fact.

Shit.

I quit grinning.

"Heard about it. Reckon I don't know shit about it," Devin stated, also now there, leaning in to the bar over an empty stool, looking at Mia. "But what I heard, seems to me he's never been yours."

"I don't even know you," Mia said to Devin.

"Well, little miss, I know about you," Devin replied. "And since you seem to be puttin' a lotta stock into what everyone thinks, thought I'd share straight from the mouth of a member of the peanut gallery." After Devin delivered that, he looked to me. "Now, I *am* here to drink, so I'd be obliged if you'd get me a fresh one. I'm half parched, waitin' on this ridiculous drama to play out."

It had lasted less than five minutes.

Then again, Dev could put away some booze.

"I'll get on that, Dev," I muttered.

Before I could, more muttering happened and this came from Tony Mancetti, who was sitting on the closest barstool to our drama.

"Need a fresh one too, Cher. And, just addin' from my seat in the peanut gallery, I'd put money down on you."

Oh fuck.

More warm and squishy.

I couldn't help but smile at him. "Well, look at you, Tony. Who knew you could be sweet?"

"Figure you could, seein' as I tip twenty percent."

"Oh, right. In case I haven't shared the gratitude for that, brah, you got it now."

"I'd be grateful to get another drink," Tony said.

"I'm first," Devin declared.

"On it, Dev," I said.

And I decided to get on it.

But first...

It was a faulty play that didn't go well for her, but that wasn't my problem. She brought it, and since she was there, I had one thing to say.

I looked to Mia to see she was preparing to slink out.

"One thing, Mia," I called, and she looked to me. "You throw a hissy fit again, go to Merry's pissed you're not gettin' what you want and you shove him, *repeatedly*, he's not gonna do dick to you because he's not that guy."

We might have been losing folks' attention since the scene was petering out, but with my words, we got it back.

Though, I had drinks to make and tips to earn, so I wasn't up for a show and, therefore, quickly finished.

"*I* find out you cornered a good man like that again, *I* got no problem shovin' back."

Her eyes narrowed. "Are you threatening me?"

I held her gaze direct and my one word had deep meaning. "No."

She glared at me. Then she glanced around, belligerence etched in her face. I didn't take my eyes off her, but I suspected she did not get back what she thought she would see, people siding with her after I made my promise.

She got something else after folks learned she'd put her hands on Merry.

I knew it when her face started to get red, she darted another glare at me, and took off.

I didn't watch. I got on those drinks, feeling Darryl leave my back.

I made Dev's drink. I got Tony his.

Then Tanner caught my attention by coming close to the bar where the altercation happened and not going back to his seat where Devin had returned.

I looked up at him. "Need another one, Tanner?"

"Need you to call Merry, Cher," he said quietly, then slightly lifted a hand. "I get you roll with life, darlin', take your hits and keep on rollin'." He tipped his head to the door. "But that shit's gonna hit his phone and fast, it hasn't already done it. And he's not gonna be real happy if one of the first calls doesn't come direct from you."

My brows shot up. "Relationship advice from shit-hot PI Tanner Layne?"

His lips curled up. "I get it regular, Cher. You want some a' that for you, listen to a man who's got it goin' on."

He had a point.

And he was totally good with me being with Merry.

I nodded with my lips curling up too and reached to my back pocket to get my phone.

"And I'll take a fresh one," Tanner finished.

I got his fresh one, then I got Darryl to take the bar while me and my phone hit the office and I hit go on Merry's contact.

I barely had my cell to my ear before Merry answered.

"You okay?"

He'd heard.

"Who called?" I asked.

"Lore," he told me. "Man didn't hear what went down, just knew Mia showed and threw down."

Loren Smithfield. Resident player. He was right then playing pool at the same time scanning the joint for ass to tap.

"I'm okay," I assured.

"Got some things I gotta finish up with Mike, then I'll be in for a drink."

I'd take that because we'd been texting since lunch at Frank's two days before, but I hadn't seen him.

Though, I didn't want him to think he had to come in for me.

"I'm really okay, Merry," I told him.

"I know you are. That's you. You're not okay, you find a way to be. That doesn't mean I'm not pissed as shit my ex is bein' a stupid bitch and draggin' you into that. So I'm gonna be in to make sure you're okay, and I'm gonna be in so I can be with you and not go find her and rip her a new asshole."

"Best play you got, seein' as I'm not sure she'd feel a new asshole," I muttered.

Merry's next sounded disbelieving. "Lore said Tanner waded in. He didn't set her straight?"

"I don't know. I don't think like her, but I got the impression she's all in and Tanner mighta delivered a few hits, but she's feelin' the need to prove something, so she's gonna get back up and keep fighting."

"Fuck," Merry muttered.

I had no response because I didn't know what to say. Not only had I never been in a situation like this, it was true, I didn't think like Mia. I had no idea what she was planning and how those plans would be carried out.

And worse, if they might wear Merry down.

"Somethin' you should know," he said in a way that told me it was something I should know, but it was something I didn't want to know.

"Hit me," I replied, even though I wasn't big on taking another hit that evening.

"Drew and Sean had the occasion to be in her development yesterday. Said the FOR SALE sign on her house is down."

"She sell?" I asked hopefully, knowing that was stupid.

It was always stupid for me to hope.

"Don't know. Don't care and don't wanna give the impression I do."

That was a good play.

I again said nothing.

"She doesn't have it in her," he said quietly.

"Mm-hmm," I replied.

"Babe, not feelin' dick about this except supremely pissed she had a go at you and equally pissed my hands are tied. I got no moves except ignoring her ass. Not a man who likes to be cornered, but there's nothin' I can do. I confront her, she'll take that as attention and time I'm givin' her and read it wrong. There's no move but wait it out, play it smart, and give her nothing. She doesn't have it in her to stay the course. She's gonna give up."

"Merry, I'm at work," I reminded him. "Darryl's back of the bar. He can pull beers and uncap bottles but a mixed drink is a crapshoot. I gotta get back out there."

"Cherie," his tone was now soft, "sorry as fuck she did what she did, but I'll be sorrier, her doin' that shit puts thoughts in your head that I'm not where I'm at with you, which, it's important to note, is where I wanna be."

I drew in breath.

He kept talking.

"I'll be there in an hour. If you're down with it, follow you home and hang with you until Ethan goes to bed."

That'd work for me.

"That's a deal."

"Right, lettin' you go. See you soon."

"See you soon, Merry."

I was about to hang up when he called, "Cher?"

"Still here," I told him.

"Last coupla days, slowed things down," he stated. "You were right, we hit hyperdrive. But you need to settle into this in a way you believe. And you also got a kid. He's had you and he's had *all* of you for eleven years. He digs me and doesn't hide it. I like that. But I don't need to all of a sudden be in

your space and in his face every second of the day. Once, I went about winnin' a woman. Never tackled the feat of winnin' a family. Need you to know
I'm in this with you and it's a place I wanna be. Same time, need your boy
to know that, you got me, he doesn't lose you. He just gets me too. We take
that time to do this smart, which means I give you and Ethan space along
the way, I don't want you to use that space to let shit fuck with your head."

Winnin' a family.

God.

Merry.

"All right, baby," I whispered.

"Don't wanna sound like a dick but also don't wanna be assurin' you
constantly about where I'm at." His voice dipped. "You need to believe in
this, Cher."

It was hard for me to believe. For years, along with the rest of the 'burg,
I'd lived the whole Mia-and-Merry-need-to-get-back-together thing.

But he was right.

I'd made a decision to give us a shot. I'd promised him I'd give it the best
one I had. And I'd promised myself I was not going to fuck this up.

And it had just been days and I was falling down on that job.

"Roger that, boss," I replied.

"I'm spoutin' important shit, she gives me the smartass."

"It's me."

"It is."

He didn't make it sound like it was a bad thing.

"Are we gonna talk for the next hour so you're only gonna be here for
fifteen minutes before I get to go home to my kid and my guy? Or are we
gonna hang up so you can get your shit done and come see me?"

Merry didn't reply.

He hung up on me.

Which was too bad since he couldn't hear me laughing.

Fifteen

Don't Let Go
Cher

*E*than nearly knocked me off the couch when he shot off it to get to
the door.

A second earlier, he'd looked through the break in the curtains.

I looked to the cable box.

It was Thursday night, ten to six, and Merry was there.

I turned my head left and saw Ethan throw open the front door and
unlock the storm.

He waited a beat...two...three...all while I suspected Merry was walking up the walk.

Then he shouted, "Hey, Merry!"

I studied my son, wondering if Merry read the situation with him
right.

Ethan had totally been down with Merry hanging with us and watching
TV the night before.

And he was totally down with Merry walking up our walk and going to
his gramma's for a family dinner.

It didn't appear Ethan needed space.

It appeared Ethan was like me and just needed Merry.

"Hey, man." I heard Merry's voice, and that was when I pushed out of
the couch, grabbing the remote.

I was turning their way at the same time switching off the TV when Merry walked in and gave Ethan a man-to-man handshake.

They'd let go when Ethan informed him, "Gram's makin' her meatloaf." He lifted a hand and shook it in a don't-be-disappointed gesture. "I know it sounds like it sucks. But it doesn't. Gram's meatloaf is the *freaking* bomb. It's like a huge hamburger baked with ketchup on top. She usually puts onions in it, though she won't do that tonight."

"Sounds good," Merry told him.

"Then she makes this tater tot casserole to go with it. It's *crazy* good."

Merry grinned. "Sounds like it's a good thing I'm hungry."

Merry's comments did not deter Ethan from his information sharing. "And fried corn."

"Can't call yourself a Hoosier unless you got fried corn stuck in your teeth at least once a week," Merry replied.

Ethan burst out laughing.

"Okay, kid, now that you've broken down the menu," I said, moving toward them. "Maybe we can get to your gramma's and eat it."

Ethan quit laughing and looked at me. "You just want me to shut up so you can be gooey with Merry."

"That and I'm hungry," I returned.

"Whatever," he muttered to me and looked to Merry. "While you get gooey with Mom, can I go out and start your truck?"

As an answer, Merry tossed Ethan his keys.

"Right on!" Ethan shouted after he caught them.

He wasted no time rushing to the bucket chair to grab his jacket and then he raced out of the house.

The storm door whispered and banged.

I looked to Merry.

"Get over here and give me gooey," he ordered.

The essence of hotness: a badass capable of uttering the word "gooey," doing that shit and making my clit tingle.

I wasted no time either.

Merry met me halfway probably with a dual purpose, the second part of that being we were not in the door where Ethan could see when Merry took me in his arms, bent and laid a wet one on me.

When he was done I was wishing we had all kinds of time to be gooey.

Since we didn't, I warned, "Don't let Mom steal you away with her tater tot casserole. Just so you know, I have the recipe."

Merry held me close in his arms and smiled at me.

My kid. My guy. My mom. Her tater tot casserole. And Merry smiling at me.

There it was again.

Fucking happy.

"This is delicious, Grace," Merry told my mother.

We were sitting at Mom's kitchen table.

Ethan was shoveling his gramma's food in his mouth like he'd been told he was getting nothing but C rations for the next year after that meal.

I was freaking.

This was because somewhere between leaving my house and sitting at Mom's table, something had happened to Merry.

Something extreme.

Gone was the mellow, funny guy he gave my kid. Gone was the thoughtful, gentlemanly guy he gave my mom. And gone was the teasing, hot guy he gave me.

He was quiet to the point he was distant, like he was there but he didn't want to be.

Worse, he wasn't hiding that.

At all.

Those four words were the first he'd spoken since conversation had awkwardly died when both mom and me sensed Merry retreating.

"Thank you, Garrett," Mom replied. "I'm glad you like it."

He nodded to her once, didn't further engage, just turned back to eating.

My heart sank to my stomach.

That was so *not* Merry.

Mom looked at me and I instantly saw that her enthusiasm at having a new addition to her family dinner, this being a good guy who was into her daughter, had died.

She wasn't freaking like me.

She was disappointed.

Then again, she didn't go all out for dinner, cleaning her house, even putting out flowers Merry would most definitely see and know that was an outlay Mom didn't splurge on often (her doing it to show Merry he was making the right choice of possibly wanting to be a part of this family) to have him act like the last place he wanted to be was there.

I had nothing for my mom, nonverbally and definitely not verbally, to explain what was going on with Merry.

What I wanted was to kick him in the shin, this my way of telling him to snap out of it at the same time asking him what the fuck was his problem.

That was the Cher way of dealing with things.

But after nearly blowing it with Merry, I needed to learn not to do shit like that. I couldn't react, mouth off, or do something stupid and then face the consequences later. Not without risking fucking us up, and I'd promised myself I wouldn't do that.

But this wasn't Merry. Not even a little bit. I'd never seen him like this. Even when Tanner and Rocky were on the bumpy path of their reunion, something neither Merry nor his dad hid was just as bumpy for them, he didn't get like this. Not when he had a shitty case he was investigating that took time and effort that, in the end if he closed it, only allowed him to give a small measure of relief to the people who'd had their lives irrevocably altered when the shit of life buried them under the stink.

"I hear you have a boat," Mom noted, attempting to snap Merry out of it by engaging him in conversation.

"Yep," he told his plate.

He said no more.

Well, that didn't work.

"You got a boat?" Ethan piped up excitedly.

That got him. Merry looked to my son, the blankness leaving his face, and it softened.

"I do, bud," he said quietly. "But, just to say, it's for sale."

I stared at him because I had no clue he was selling his boat. I'd actually never been officially informed he *had* a boat.

I didn't do healthy relationships until now (arguably, especially at this moment), but that seemed like something to share, say, when he was hanging at J&J's having a drink. Or perhaps when we were making out on my couch and feeling each other up last night after Ethan went to sleep. Or during dinner at Swank's, waffles at my place, lunches (plural) at Frank's, or in one of what I was now seeing were the not-very-informative texts he'd sent me.

"Why are you selling it?" Mom asked.

Merry looked to her. "In the market to get a house. Got a realtor; she sent some listings. Looked through eighteen of 'em. Didn't like what I saw except for two, both outside my price range. To make 'em in my price range, I gotta liquidate some things for the down payment."

I kept staring at him, because selling your boat might not be something that you'd share with the woman in your life but buying a house definitely was.

I wanted to be smart. Not get ticked or more freaked but instead twist that to something happy.

First, Merry out of that crappy apartment. Second, the idea he was doing that now, after he'd decided to take a shot at an us with me.

But the way he gave Mom that information, void of emotion, didn't sit well with me.

Mom didn't care about the void-of-emotion part.

She went straight to the twisting.

"You're in the market for a house?" Her voice was an octave higher, filled with hope and excitement.

"Yeah, Grace. Don't live in a great place. Time to move on," Merry answered, no inflection in his tone at all.

Mom gave happy eyes to me.

Ethan declared, "A boat is better than a house."

"You don't have my view, buddy," Merry replied.

"View is always better from a boat," Ethan informed him.

Finally, one side of Merry's lips curled up. "Can't argue that."

"Have more corn, Garrett," Mom urged, seeing his plate almost clean and picking up the bowl of corn.

"Prefer seconds of that casserole, Grace," he returned.

She dropped the corn so fast it clattered and nabbed the casserole.

With Merry reengaged (sort of), the rest of dinner and dessert went okay.

Not great.

Just okay.

And okay was so...*not*...Merry.

After we were done, Mom shooed the boys out so the women could do the dishes, something she'd normally never do because she wasn't about "women's work" unless that work involved pushing out babies, which was only women's work due to biology.

Which meant she wanted to be alone with me to hash out what was going on with Merry.

The guys hit the living room and I hit the sink, wanting to hash out what was going on with Merry too. The problem with that was, in this scenario, it was me who had to provide the information and I had no clue.

Mom got close with the meatloaf platter and a Tupperware container.

"Garrett's being strange. Are you two okay?" she asked under her breath, seeing as her house was nearly as tiny as mine and they were in the next room.

I thought we were.

For the life of me, I couldn't imagine the way Merry was at dinner had one thing to do with him and me.

I just couldn't think of what it *did* have to do with.

"Yeah," I told her.

"He wasn't him..." She paused. *"At all."*

"Yeah," I repeated.

"Except with Ethan," she revised.

At least there was that.

"You need to talk to him, honey-sicle," she advised.

I looked from filling the sink with soapy water, to my mom.

"Maybe I should let this slide," I suggested.

Her face started to go mom-like, so I rushed on.

"We're new, Mom. Still feelin' each other out. It's only been a week since our first date. Not your fault, I was all for it, but maybe dinner at the mom's house was too soon."

This was a possible option of what was going on with Merry.

But even as it came out of my mouth, I didn't buy it.

"He's sat at that table before, Cheryl," she reminded me, swinging her hand to the kitchen table. "I fed him and Mike when they helped out with my house, and I fed him lunch when he was takin' care of my walls. He filled his plate with food from that table when I had Ethan's ninth birthday party. Stuffed his face from that table at last year's Christmas party. He is not a stranger to this house. He's not a stranger to me or Ethan. But he was a stranger tonight."

She was right.

I looked back to the water filling the sink and turned it off. I was shifting to go to the table to grab plates, but I stopped when Mom's hand caught my forearm.

I gave her my eyes.

"Whole town's watchin', you know that," she said quietly. "Whole town's waitin' to see what comes of you and Garrett Merrick. Figure most of 'em are rootin' for you two. Same's I figure most of 'em think you're gonna go down in flames, that bein' you who ignites that blaze or, due to history in this scenario, more likely it bein' him."

Her hand left me, but she didn't quit talking.

"I know my girl. I know you want everyone to think you don't care what they think. But I also know you care about that man in there."

She jerked her head toward the wall on the other side of which was her living room.

She then kept going.

"It is no secret Tanner Layne had his hands full beatin' back the demons that plagued the woman he loved, demons that drove her away from the only man for her and she knew he was just that. She still let those demons win, sugar. Story told so often in this town, I know. Everyone knows. And what we know is Tanner made one mistake in all that. In the beginning, he gave up. But Raquel put up a hell of a fight to make him quit and they were young so neither of 'em knew better. You and Garrett are not at that place."

I opened my mouth to tell her she wasn't wrong, and more (something *I* had to chew on), Mia's fatal mistake was giving up too.

But Mom wasn't done speaking.

"Like I said, I know my girl. So I know my girl's a fighter. Now, don't you make the mistake of doin' somethin' you're tellin' yourself is right, givin' him space and time to sort his own self out, when you know it's wrong. Garrett Merrick didn't sit at my table tonight, honey. And you need not to waste any time findin' out what took him away from that table, which meant he took himself away from *you*."

"There's a lot goin' on that you don't know, Mom," I shared.

I shared it and it was lame.

"I know this," she returned instantly. "I know he knows he sat at my table as the man who brought my two babies in his truck to my home to eat my food with the possibility he'd be at that table a lot in future. He knows me, but he knows what tonight meant. So he would know not to mess that up, no matter what's goin' on."

"He was just quiet," I told her.

"He wasn't quiet, Cheryl. Half the time he wasn't even *here*."

She was right and she was also telling me not to fuck this up.

I was just so good at fucking things up, I didn't know another way to be.

And the biggest part about that was, Merry's retreat scared the shit out of me.

Mia Merrick didn't have it in her to fight for her man and I had no problem pointing that out.

Faced with just a taste of what she'd had shoved down her throat, the acid of it burned.

And if I let my head go there, the scary it was would be terrifying.

"Talk to him," Mom urged on a whisper. "I'll tell you this, baby girl, that happened tonight at my table and you have to deal. Because that man's got a woman in his life now, a woman with a son. And he's lookin' for a house. And that says *other* things. I'm not tellin' you to get things straight with him because I want my girl's hooks in a good man. I'm tellin' you to get things straight *for* him because *I* know what he's got with you. *I* know what my grandbaby will give him. *I* know that man is far from stupid. *I* know he deserves good in his life. And *I* know he'll kick his own behind and *not* bounce back from that, he lets *you* slip through his fingers."

I loved my mom. I'd fucked her over like I'd fucked a lot of shit in my life.

But I loved her because I did all that and she still said what she just said, which meant she loved the hell out of me.

I looked into her eyes. Then I nodded.

After that, I headed to the table to get the dishes.

It was a school night, so even though we had some time to visit after the dishes were done, we didn't have a lot.

And through that time, Merry again gave Ethan what he needed but only what he had to give to Mom and me.

This meant she gave me a telling look after the hug we exchanged before we left. But she pretended like it was all good with the warm hugs and good-byes she gave Merry and Ethan.

Ethan chattered on the way home. Ethan chattered when we got home. And Ethan didn't hide his disappointment when I shared it was bedtime.

He didn't fight me, though, because it actually wasn't bedtime. It was half an hour after bedtime, so he knew he'd already gotten a reprieve.

What freaked me (further) was that Merry took Ethan's bedtime as his opportunity to leave rather than what we did last night after Ethan went to bed—taking time, being together, whispering to each other, laughing quiet so we wouldn't wake my kid up, and making out.

He gave Ethan another man-to-man handshake.

He gave me a distracted kiss on the cheek.

Then he took off.

The only good part about this was that my son was growing up and there wasn't a lot he didn't notice. But he wasn't grown up enough to know that a man like Merry didn't kiss his woman good night like that.

Obviously, I didn't educate him.

I got him to bed and then I sat on my couch with my phone in my hand.

I started a dozen texts.

I couldn't figure out which words to use, so I erased everything.

I looked at the clock, then I turned my head and looked at the wall, well beyond which was the house that Tilly lived in.

And Tilly was a late-night talk show girl.

"Started the habit with Johnny Carson, honey, a habit that's hard to break," she'd told me.

Before I could talk myself out of it, which would mean talking myself into fucking things up with Merry, I pulled my boots back on, grabbed my purse, my jacket, and my keys, and headed out.

Tilly's house was quiet and dark except for the flickering light of a TV coming from her curtains.

I knocked not too loud but also called out, "Tilly, it's Cher."

The door opened almost immediately and I looked down at the round woman with curly hair that was an equal mix of black and steel, who had big blue eyes in a face as round as her body.

"Is everything okay, Cher?"

"Listen, I know this is askin' a lot, but I need to ask if you'd go over and stay with Ethan. He's sleepin', but I…" Shit, shit, fuck, fuck, *fuck*. "I don't know if you heard, but I'm seein' Garrett Merrick and there are some important things I gotta talk about with him. We couldn't do that with Ethan around, and Merry went home before we got to it. It's not stuff you can talk about over the phone either. I know this is selfish, but I can't sleep, Till. I gotta go over to Merry's and talk things out."

"I'm in my slippers, hon. Let me get my shoes," she said instantly.

Totally a good neighbor.

And she'd so totally heard about me and Merry.

She got her shoes.

I followed her over to my house and sat in my car until I saw the door close behind her. Then I sat in it until I saw my curtains flickering with the late show on TV.

After that, I backed out.

I hit Merry's complex, and before I could turn tail and do the easy thing rather than doing what I'd promised him I would do and give us the best shot I could give, I got out of my car and hauled my ass up to his place.

There was a window in his apartment that faced the landing. No light.

I knocked as loud as I could without being obnoxious to him or his neighbors.

It took too much time (probably ten seconds) before dim light came from the blinds at his front window. I heard the locks go and the door was opened.

Not opened.

Hauled open.

"Fuck, Cher, is everything okay?"

I looked up at his face, lit by the outside lights on his landing, and saw distant-Merry was not with me.

He looked worried.

But he smelled like cigarettes and it hit me it'd been a while since I'd smelled that on Merry.

"I don't know, baby, is it?" I asked carefully.

"Where's Ethan?" he asked in return, his gaze flicking beyond me.

"Tilly's at the house keepin' an eye on things until I get back."

Merry's eyes narrowed when they came back to me. "Babe, it's nearly eleven."

I knew that. I just didn't know why he was telling me that. He couldn't be so far gone he didn't know why I was there.

Could he?

"We have to talk," I told him.

"About what?" he asked.

"About you checkin' out at dinner tonight."

There it was. I saw it happen and it freaked my shit *right* out.

The door closed on his soul and that was written all over his face.

"I didn't check out at dinner tonight," he lied.

"Merry—"

"I had my ass in a seat, eatin' tater tot casserole, and you were right there with me."

"That's not what I mean."

His brows snapped together. "You mean to make problems that aren't there?"

Seriously?

"Merry, *you checked out.*"

He shook his head at the same time he sighed. "Get back to Ethan, Cher."

I lifted a hand. "Merry—"

"It's late. Get back to your kid."

"Dammit, Merry," I snapped. "Talk to me."

"About what?"

"Boss, you are not talkin' to a princess who could climb on top of a mattress, feel a pea, and bitch about that shit. You're talkin' *to me*—a real woman who knows what's important," I snapped. "And you *checked out tonight*. Now, you gotta know that I know, like every-fuckin'-body knows, a Merrick checks out, you don't dick around with checkin' him *back in*."

His face went hard. "We'll talk about this on Saturday."

So there *was* something to talk about.

And he wanted to wait until Saturday. Two whole days for him to retreat further from me?

"We'll talk about it now."

"Listen, Cher, I do not need another woman at my door wantin' a chat with me when I do not want that shit."

A low blow, pairing me with Mia to push me away.

I stared at him.

Then I pushed right in.

"Fuck," he muttered.

I went to the back of his couch, threw my bag and keys in the seat, and turned to him, yanking my jacket off.

"Know this play too," he stated. "Not in the mood to chat and not in the mood for a woman to fall on my dick, thinkin' that says everything."

That was an *outrageously* low blow.

Shit.

Okay, I needed to hold it together, not go batshit crazy and mouth off, saying something I'd regret.

I took in a deep breath and draped my jacket over the back of the couch to give myself time to do that.

Only then did I look at him.

"What triggered it?" I asked quietly.

He stared at me before he threw the door to, turned back to me, and crossed his arms on his chest.

But he didn't speak.

"What's fuckin' with your head, Merry?" I pushed.

"Right now, you," he returned.

"Did I do something before?"

He shook his head, murmuring, "Jesus, Cher."

317

I kept at him.

"Ethan?"

He stopped shaking his head and just looked at me.

"Mom?" I continued.

He didn't answer.

I took him in. Still in his nice button-up shirt, this one navy, perfect for his eyes, perfect for his coloring. Dark jeans that fit good. A fantastic belt. Nice but casual boots. That thick, dark hair that, even though I knew he was in his early forties, had not even a strand of silver in it. Set features in a strong, handsome face.

Five hours ago, all that was mine.

Now he was withholding it from me.

I wanted it back.

I closed my eyes, opened them and whispered, "You mean the world to me."

His tall, lean body jerked only slightly, like he caught it and tried to check it before the movement gave him away.

But I saw it.

"For a week, I've been happy," I told him.

"Cher—"

"I got a good mom. I got a good kid. I got good friends. It's not like I've never been happy. But with you, havin' you, I've been *happy*."

His voice gentled as he said, "We'll talk about this Saturday, Cherie."

"There is no way in fuck, Garrett, that I'm givin' you two full days to lock yourself away from me," I replied. "Ethan's asleep. He's good. Tilly's with him. And now I'm here, askin' you to *talk to me*."

"I'm fine," he declared. "We're fine. You're makin' a drama out of nothing."

"And you're standin' there, lyin' to me."

Any gentle I'd gained took a hike.

"You know me, but you don't know me enough to say shit like that to me."

"Talk to me," I repeated.

"You need to go home, babe."

"What tripped it?" I asked.

318

"Cher, won't say it again. You need to get your ass home."

"What took you away from me tonight?"

"We're not talkin' about this."

I threw out both arms, leaned toward him, and lost it.

"*What took you away from me?*" I shrieked.

I took an automatic step back and hit couch when he leaned my way, his face twisted in a way the feeling it expressed hurt *me*, he slammed his fists to his hips, and roared, "*Flowers!*"

I stood still, finding myself suddenly breathing so heavy, my chest was actually heaving.

Because I just witnessed Merry going from gentle to pissed to impatient to *destroyed*.

Staring at that look on his face, I had no fucking clue what to do.

And that look scared the living *shit* out of me.

"Flowers?" my mouth whispered for me.

Merry studied me. Then he moved jerkily, prowling toward the dining room table, lifting his hand and tearing it through his hair, moving like a caged animal, until he stopped and turned back to me.

"*Fuck*," he snarled.

I didn't move an inch except to follow him with my eyes.

"Flowers, baby?" I prompted.

"Fuck," he repeated.

"Flowers, Merry."

"Fuck," he whispered.

"What do you need?" I asked quickly.

He looked to the side and I saw his jaw tight, his cheek ticking.

"Merry, what do you need?"

He looked back to me and announced, "I'm a cop."

"I know that," I told him carefully.

"You get that?" he shot back.

I thought I did, but the way he was speaking, I wasn't sure. So I just nodded.

"You need to get that, Cher," he stated roughly.

"I get that, Merry."

"You don't."

"I do," I promised, even though I wasn't sure I did.

"We eat, we do it in front of the fucking TV."

His abrupt subject changes were bizarre, and even if I was getting him (which I wasn't sure I was), with the quickness of those changes, I wasn't keeping up.

"Okay," I said hesitantly.

"No fuckin' flowers."

"No flowers, Merry," I agreed.

"Your mom wants me back, I'll eat at her table. But you tell her that shit—no flowers."

I nodded.

He said no more.

"Why no flowers, baby?" I asked quietly.

"Cecelia liked flowers."

I shook my head.

His baby niece liked flowers?

"I—"

"My mother, Cher."

I shut my mouth.

Shit.

Shit.

Fucking shit.

"We Merricks aren't real good at sittin' down with family."

"Your mom liked doin' that," I whispered.

"Every night. No fail. And either Dad bought 'em or she got 'em herself, but in our house, there were lots of flowers."

God.

God, Merry.

"Weak," he grunted, that one word sounding torn from him in a way so extreme, it also ripped through me.

"What?" I asked, knowing we were now somewhere else. I wasn't keeping up, but it was essential that I did.

"This shit. I'm fuckin' forty-two and still not over it. It's weak."

Was he crazy?

"I dread it," I told him.

"Bet you do," he said like he knew what he was talking about.

Maybe he did.

I told him anyway.

"The day I lose her...I dread it. She's been there. Always been there. I fucked up, Merry. You know I did. But it was worse when I was a kid. Christ, when I was a teenager, I fucked up, but she was always there. She held my hand when I pushed out Ethan. She looks after him just as much as me. She's always there and I love that. I love *her*. But I know she's gonna go. It's the way it is. And I dread it. I know I'll never get over it. It'll be like a piece was torn from my heart and it'll never beat the same way again. I know that. And I also know feelin' that feeling is so far from weak it isn't funny."

Merry didn't move, not even his mouth.

"Lord forbid it happens anything like the way you lost yours. Won't be in my power however it goes down. But the way you lost your momma, Merry...*God*." I shook my head, feeling moist in my eyes. "The beauty you are, standin' right there? I don't know how that could be. I'm breakin' my back to give Ethan good and I'm doin' it with fingers crossed, hopin' he grows up half the man you are. You lost your momma and you're all that." I swung a hand to him. "You're fuckin' straight up crazy if you think any of that is weak. Love is not weak. Grief is not weak. Lovin' her so much you're givin' that to her decades after she's been gone and you're still standing? Baby, seriously, how the fuck can you think that's weak?"

"Come here, Cher," he ordered.

"No," I denied, thinking I needed to sort his shit out. "Answer me."

"Come..." he drew in a breath that didn't work and I knew it when the next was growled, "*here, Cher*."

I looked into his eyes.

Then I walked there.

Four feet away, he lunged at me, hooked my waist with his arm, and I was flying through the air. My surprised cry stuck in my throat when my back hit the dining room table with Merry bent over me.

He kissed me, hard and wet and brutal, his hands tearing at my clothes.

I tried to get to his.

He broke the kiss and ordered, "Arms over your head, Cherie."

"Baby," I whispered.

"Do it," he grunted.

I lifted my arms over my head, staring into his blue eyes, panting.

He dropped his mouth to mine and took it in another savage kiss.

Then I kept my arms over my head as he pulled off my top.

I kept them over my head as he yanked off my boots.

I kept them over my head as he tore my jeans and panties down my legs.

I kept them over my head as he tugged the cup of my bra down my tit and went at me, tonguing, sucking, biting.

I kept them over my head (but did it squirming) as he went after the other tit.

And I kept them over my head when he lifted his head and watched me as his hand dove between my legs.

"Bein' good," he muttered thickly.

"Give you what you need," I panted back.

Emotion rolled over his face, God, so much of it, it was a wonder it didn't drown me.

He drove two fingers inside and found my clit with his thumb.

"Give that back," he growled.

Fuck, he did. He gave that back. So good. So hot. I forgot what was going on in my need for him and I shifted my arms so I could touch him.

"Baby."

My eyes had closed, and when he said that, his fingers stilled, so I opened them.

I settled my arms over my head again.

He went back at me.

I arched, driving down into his hand, begging for more.

He gave it.

I rode it.

"Don't you come, Cherie," he ordered.

I tried to focus. "Merry."

"You come when I got my dick in you."

He kept at me and I whimpered.

He was asking the impossible.

But I was going to do my all to give it to him.

He dipped in and his mouth brushed mine. "Give me what I need."

"Okay, honey."

He stayed close but tipped his chin down to watch what he was doing to me.

God.

Hot.

"Need your cock, baby," I begged.

"Give me more."

I gave him more, writhing on his dining room table as he toyed with me.

"Need you, Merry," I gasped. "And wanna hold on when you fuck me."

He looked from his hand between my legs into my eyes.

"You gonna give me what I need?"

I stared into his eyes and whispered, "*Always.*"

On a groan, his mouth took mine as his hand slid away.

That was when I moaned in disappointment against his tongue.

But I felt him working between my legs and then I lost his mouth when my neck arched, my head turning to the side, as he drove in and filled me.

"Arms around me, brown eyes," he grunted, plunging hard and fast.

I wrapped my arms around him and lifted my knees high.

He pounded in deeper.

"Fuck yeah," I breathed.

Merry's fingers curled around the back of my knee, sliding down to my ankle. He swung it in at his back and kept it there.

His other arm braced under me, he lifted up slightly, and watched my body jolt on his dining room table each time I took him.

I slid my hands up, both of them diving into his hair and clenching as other parts of me started doing the same thing.

"Hold on, Cherie," he grunted.

"Yeah, baby."

He knew it was happening when my body tensed around him, under him, my pussy grasping when he repeated, "Hold on tight, Cherie."

I held on tight as I came hard, and I kept holding on tight as he took me harder, driving himself to his own orgasm and taking me along for the ride.

It *way* didn't suck, feeling mine hovering while I also felt Merry get his.

It took its time and left both of us, but we didn't move. We didn't speak.

So Merry's face was in the side of my neck when, minutes later, he yet again repeated, "Hold on."

I squeezed him with everything (which meant *everything*) as I pointed out, "I am holding on."

"No," he whispered against my neck, and the way he said it, it was my heart that squeezed.

He shifted his lips to my ear.

"No," he said again.

He lifted his head and I righted mine so he could catch my eyes.

He did and he was looking deep when he finished.

"Don't let go."

When he said that, that was when everything I had didn't squeeze.

It spasmed.

We stared at each other and we did it awhile before I lifted my head from the table, touched his nose with mine, then dropped back.

"No flowers," I whispered.

He closed his eyes slowly.

I held on.

He opened them.

"You're never gonna get those from me, baby."

"I can live with that," I replied instantly.

"My job...anything can happen."

"I can live with that too."

"We go the distance, Ethan's gonna be it, Cher. Don't want kids. Never did. I see your brown eyes in his face. He's a great kid. That works for me."

This was shocking.

It was also a bummer.

Because if we went the distance, I wanted to see his beautiful blue eyes in our kid's face.

But if he felt he needed to protect our child from the loss he suffered by not having one, I could get that.

Still...

"Is that a bottom line deal breaker, or is that open to discussion at a later date?" I asked.

He started to close down. "Baby—"

324

I held on tight.

"Merry, I get you need to know I'm where you need me to be. And I promise to do my best to be where you need me to be. But I also gotta know you're gonna do what you can to be where I need *you* to be. And there's a lotta things I like about you, gorgeous. And high on that list is your eyes. You got mine times two. Don't close the door on me gettin' the same thing."

"Even if we made a kid, you couldn't be sure he'd get my eyes," he pointed out.

"Your eyes are so beautiful, Merry, it'd be worth the shot."

Those eyes flashed as his lips grunted, "Jesus."

"Just sayin', he or she doesn't get yours, they'll get mine, so you'd get that times three."

Something else flashed in his eyes, surprise and unease.

I'd know why when he asked, "She?"

"I know you're a badass, babe. But so is Tanner and he made three, one of 'em a girl. And Cal's one too. He's made three…so far…and repeat on the girl. It happens. Even a badass's swimmers can make girl babies."

"We need to stop talkin' about this."

I didn't let go as I asked, "Why?"

"'Cause I'm bent over my dining room table with my dick inside you, your kid's at home bein' watched over by an old lady, and you're talkin' about girl babies. I watched Cal endure the torture of helpin' to raise Keira before she caught Jasper, and Jas didn't manage to calm her ass down. He just managed to give her a man at her back while she was goin' wild so she didn't court too much trouble. And Vi's sweet as pie. You gave your mom shit. *You* get a girl, karma's gonna bite you in the ass and *I'd* be that girl's daddy. It's been a rough night. You took care a' that. Now you're practically guaranteeing nightmares."

I grinned at him. "I'll take it from this that the door is open to discuss babies at a later date."

He looked over my head, muttering, "Fuck me."

"Merry?" I called.

He looked back at me and lifted his brows.

"You mean the world to me," I whispered.

His eyes flashed again, the emotion rolling over his face, and his hand, still at my ankle holding it around him, tightened.

"I'm not gonna let go," I promised. "I'm not gonna let you push me away. I'm keepin' you with me."

He didn't answer.

Verbally.

He pulled out, lifted me from the table, and carried me to his couch.

He set me in it and threw an afghan over my naked body before he strolled from the room.

I tucked it around me and watched him disappear down the hall.

I held it around me as I stared at the mouth of that hall until he came back.

My head and body moved to keep my eyes on him as he went to the dining room table, gathered my clothes, and brought them to me.

He dumped them in the couch before he grabbed me again and sat in it, hauling me and his afghan into his lap.

He lifted his hands to my head, using both at either side to slide my hair back before he used both to press my face into the side of his neck.

Only when he got me there did he take one hand away to wrap his arm around me.

"I said some dick shit to you tonight, Cher."

I pushed closer. "That's okay."

"It isn't," he returned. "It isn't, baby. You can give me a lot, but do not let me be a dick to you no matter what we both get is happening."

This was good advice, so I nodded.

"Gonna apologize to your mom."

"I think she gets it, Merry."

"Gonna do it anyway."

I drew in breath.

Then I nodded again.

"You wanna take a shower here?" he offered. "Or are you good and you wanna get back to Ethan?"

I pushed against his hand on me so I could catch his eyes.

"As long as I know one of my guys is good, I gotta get back to my other one."

326

He didn't break contact. "I'm good, Cherie."

I studied him.

He looked like Merry. That was it. Maybe a little sexier since he'd come. Maybe a little tired because it was late (and he'd come). And definitely a little bit of cute-Merry was leaking in because he was tired.

Other than that, he was just Merry.

So he was good.

"Then I better get home."

He nodded, then dipped in to give me a light, sweet kiss.

After that, he lifted me up as he got out of the couch and put me on my feet.

He stood close as I dressed, and when I was done, he took me into his arms to give me a harder, longer, just as sweet kiss.

He also held my jacket for me to put it on.

And last, he walked me all the way down to my car and stood in the spot I'd backed out of as he watched me drive away.

I texted him that I was safe and sound after I'd walked Tilly home and I was behind closed, locked doors, sitting on my bed, ready to get in my pajamas, brush my teeth, and go to sleep.

Good, he texted back.

I put my phone to the nightstand, got in my pajamas, and went to the bathroom to take off my makeup and brush my teeth.

I was in bed and tossing my earrings to the nightstand when my hand hit my phone, the screen illuminated, and I saw I'd missed a text when I was in the bathroom.

I grabbed the phone and read it.

You mean the world to me too.

Moist hit my eyes again.

Good, I texted back.

I'd just turned the light out when I got more from Merry.

Don't forget that. But more, baby, don't let me forget it.

I closed my eyes tight.

Then I texted, *I won't.*

Now get some sleep, he ordered.

I would if my guy would stop texting me.

He took that to heart, obviously, because I didn't get a return text.

For some reason, this bummed me out.

I lay in the dark thinking that, which meant sleep eluded me.

Ten minutes later, I heard my phone sound.

I snatched it up.

The world, baby.

I closed my eyes tight again, sucking in a deep breath.

I opened them, reminding myself I was not that woman. She was not me. That shit just wasn't the way it was.

Then again, I had also not been the kind of woman who felt warm and squishy.

But I couldn't help it. I couldn't stop it.

I had to do it.

So I did it.

I typed fucking *xoxoxoxoxoxo* and ended that shit with a kissy-face emoji.

I hit SEND.

Merry didn't respond.

Regardless, he'd said what he'd said.

So I fell straight to sleep.

It wasn't until the next morning when I was home from taking Ethan to school that I got the texts.

The first, *Ethan get to school okay?*

That came from Merry every day.

If he checked in about my kid that he wasn't around to make sure got to school okay every day, he was *so* going to make babies.

I just hoped like crazy he'd make them with me.

Merry's babies: awesomeness.

Giving Ethan brothers and/or sisters: nirvana.

Yep. All good, I replied.

Right, Cherie. And just saying

That stopped right there and I thought he'd hit SEND early.

I'd find he didn't when he finished in his next text.

You give me any of that softass xo shit and smiley crap again, I'll know I lost my bad girl and this won't make me happy.

I stood there staring at his text, torn between giving in to a shiver and busting a gut laughing.

I picked door number two.

Then I texted, *Message received. Have a good day!* and I finished that filling his screen with smiley faces, hearts, and a few rainbows.

My phone rang seconds later, and I answered it because it was Merry.

When I did, I found he was a lot more generous than me.

Because when I put my phone to my ear, what poured into it was Merry laughing.

Therefore, happy.

A happy I gave him.

Which made me happy.

And even more determined not ever to let go.

Sixteen

ALREADY THERE
Garrett

"You alive in there?"

At Mike's question, Garrett started and turned his gaze from the computer screen he was staring at across the expanse of their desks to his partner.

"What?"

"Haven't moved in ten minutes, man," Mike told him, studying him closely. His head tipped slightly to the side. "You okay?"

Garrett shifted in his chair to fully face his friend.

"Nearly fucked things up with Cher last night," he told Mike bluntly. "Family dinner at her mom's, I closed down. Serious. Blanked Cher almost entirely, mostly blanked Grace. Only gave attention to Ethan."

"Shit," Mike muttered, continuing to study him.

"Cher came over to my place after, snapped me out of it."

"Well, that's good," Mike said carefully.

Garrett shook his head. "Been seein' her a week, shit's already happening."

"It working?" Mike asked.

"Cher snapping me out of it?"

"No, you and her."

"Spectacularly."

He said it. He meant it. It still scared the fucking shit out of him.

Mike nodded, a small smile curving his mouth. "Then hold on to that, man."

"Mia and me worked spectacularly too, Mike," Garrett pointed out. "And Rocky and Tanner worked spectacularly."

"I hear you, but everyone's young and stupid during their lifetime, Garrett," Mike returned. "Part of life is figuring out how to grow up and not still be stupid."

His words were wise. They were also funny, so Garrett let out a chuckle.

While he was doing that, his phone rang. He looked to his desk and was surprised to see it was a call from Cher.

She texted; she rarely called.

Concerned it was something urgent, he nabbed his phone and took the call.

"Baby, all good?" he asked.

"In the world at large, as far as I know, yes. Outside continued war and famine. The men who rule can't seem to sort their shit out enough to sort *that* shit out, of course," she responded and she didn't shut up. "A woman had that job, shit would be smooth. But we bitches are too busy tearing each other down to worry about war and famine."

She was being a smartass.

All was good.

Garrett sat back in his chair, grinning at his desk as she continued.

"In my world, also yes. I'm at work. Some guy is retiring and decided his party fare would be liquid, which means we got twenty-five people here and most of 'em are good tippers," she shared, then carried on, "But in Ethan's world, it isn't, seein' as Mom was supposed to take him and his bud to the game tonight, hang with them there, and bring them back to my pad for some gaming before I take Teddy home. But there's a waitress sick at The Station and they've asked Mom to do a double shift. That's time and a half plus tips, and in our world, you don't turn down time and a half plus tips. Vi's busy. Feb's workin'. Meems has already got a sleepover with six boys she's dealin' with. Dusty's bustin' her hump gettin' ready for that show she's got comin' up and—"

Garrett interrupted her. "You want me to take Ethan and his bud to the game."

"Jessie can watch him," she told him quickly instead of confirming. "But she's declared she's not goin' to a high school football game unless she's got at least one of her girl posse with her and no one is available. And Ethan might spontaneously combust if he misses a 'dogs home game. So, yes…"

She paused and he knew she was pulling up the courage to go on, something unusual for her, when he heard the hesitancy in her tone as she finished.

"I know this is a lot and it's early with us, with you and Ethan. I probably shouldn't even ask. But I like to give my boy as much as I can give him. And—"

He cut her off again, saying quietly, "Cherie, I can take Ethan and his friend to the game."

There was another pause before, "Are you sure? You can say no. You can be honest. Anytime. With anything. I can talk to Ethan and—"

Again, Garrett interrupted her. "Cher?"

"Yeah?"

"Shut up."

She surprised him again and did as told.

"Gonna stop by J&J's, get your keys," he told her. "You need me to pick him up from school too?"

Now Cher was talking quietly. "Yeah, honey, if you can. I was gonna get him and make him sit in the office here, but you lookin' after him would be a lot better. When he has to sit in the office, he doesn't bitch, but I can tell he's not a big fan of being cooped up there. Is that gonna be a problem with work?"

"No, but he's gonna have to hang with me and Mike in the bullpen for a couple of hours."

Another pause, then, "Prepare to be freaked, but you do that, he'll love you forever. And I mean *forever*. He might demand his best man mention you during his wedding reception speech, with the possibility of *you* being that best man, that kind of forever."

Garrett grinned again at his desk. "And that's supposed to freak me, why?"

"If you don't know, not gonna tell you," she muttered, then louder, "After I get off work, I'll meet you guys at the game."

Garrett felt his brows draw together. "Do you wanna go to the game after a shift at the bar?"

"It won't be long. And anyway, I wanna relieve you from duty. I also gotta get into my house and you'll have my keys," she answered.

"Watchin' the Bulldogs play ball is hardly 'duty,' brown eyes," he informed her. "Go home. Put your feet up."

"Merry—"

He rolled back from his desk, leaned down, elbows to his knees, eyes to the floor, focus now entirely on his girl so he could reassure that girl.

"Guys' night out," Garrett said softly. "I got Ethan. We'll talk man shit and I'll feed him and make sure he and his bud are good. I'll get them home. You finish your shift, go home, relax, unwind, prepare, 'cause I want my girl rested and ready for our Saturday."

Cher said nothing.

When this went on too long, he called, "Baby?"

He heard her clear her throat before she told him, "I have a spare set of keys in my junk drawer in the kitchen. Ethan can show you. Could you drop them by J&J's sometime before the game so I can get in while you guys are out?"

"Absolutely."

She again didn't reply.

So he asked, "You okay?"

"No."

It was a whisper and his focus sharpened.

"No?" he asked.

"No," she said. "Ethan's gonna love this. Guy time. Man talk. Showin' you off to Teddy. And I love it, knowin' I don't gotta say he can't have somethin' he wants because I gotta work and I can't find anyone to give it to him. So no, Merry, I'm not okay. This is not an okay feeling. This feelin' is me bein' fucking happy."

His throat closed, his chest tightened, and his first reaction was to disconnect the call. But at the same time, his gut had warmed because it felt so damned good just giving Cher that emotion and also doing it knowing she hadn't had a lot of it in her life.

He powered past his first reaction and told her, "I'll walk down to the bar in a few to get the keys, babe. Yeah?"

"Yeah, gorgeous. See you then."

"Later, Cher."

"Later, Merry…and thanks, honey."

"No problem."

He disconnected, straightened in his chair, and rolled back to his desk. He felt Mike's gaze, so he lifted his to his friend's.

"Take it we got a ten-year-old for ride-along this afternoon," he remarked.

"If that's gonna be a problem for you—" Garrett started.

Mike shook his head. "Ethan's a good kid. We're in doin' paperwork, so he's not stopping us from doin' shit we need to do. And not like he hasn't hung with the guys before."

That was true. It hadn't happened often, but on occasion over the years when Cher needed him because there was no one else to help, Colt had brought Ethan in.

Garrett looked across the room.

Colt was sitting at his desk, grinning at something Sully was saying, Sully sitting across from him.

She hadn't asked Colt.

She'd asked Garrett.

That felt great.

And it made him uneasy.

"Kid's a good kid," Mike said, and the change in his tone caught Garrett's attention. "Woman's a good woman. I believe in you, brother. Sittin' across from me is a man who hasn't had it all. A man who thought he did and lost it but learned different. Who's watched his friends make poor decisions and bounce back. Who now has a shot at gettin' it all and is old enough not to be stupid."

That meant a lot, coming from Mike.

But Garrett wasn't going to share that.

Instead, he grinned and gave him shit.

"You should be a therapist, Mike. Open your own clinic. Call it 'Don't Be a Dumb Fuck Treatment Center.'"

Mike grinned back, returning, "You bein' my first client, thinkin' of adding, 'How Not to Be a Smartass.'"

"That might be a tougher addiction to kick," Garrett told him.

"You might be right. Though, this line of work, run into a lot more dumb fucks than smartasses."

"Truth," Garrett muttered.

Mike's phone on his desk rang.

He turned his attention to it, so Garrett quickly called, "Yo."

Still going for the phone, Mike's gaze swung back to him.

"Thanks, brother," Garrett said low.

Mike lifted his chin.

Then he answered his phone.

Late that night, standing at her door, Cher in his arms, Garrett broke the kiss that had started five minutes ago as a good-night kiss and became a make out session.

He caught her eyes through her half-mast lids and whispered, "Late, baby. Gotta get home. Let you get to bed."

Her hands slid down from his hair to rest on his chest as her lips went slightly pouty.

It was cute.

But it was more sweet, her pout saying she didn't want him to leave.

"Okay," she muttered but didn't move out of his arms.

"You dropping Ethan at his friend's at five thirty tomorrow?" Garrett asked.

She stayed in his arms and nodded.

"Be here at six to take you to dinner. Be prepared to spend the night at my place," he ordered.

She grinned in a way that was not cute or sweet but something a fuckuva lot different.

Before that grin made him hard, he gave her a squeeze and said, "It was a good night, baby."

She continued to look into his eyes as she pressed closer. "Yeah?"

"Yeah," he confirmed, because it was.

Ethan was a good kid. Ethan liked him. And Cher had not been wrong. He'd soaked in guy time, man talk, and he didn't hide the pride he felt having Garrett around and showing him off to his bud.

It did not suck.

It felt fucking great.

Which, at the same time in his fucked-up head, was fucking terrifying.

Because if he fucked this up, it wouldn't be fucking over Cher, which was bad enough.

It would be fucking them both.

Again, he powered past that feeling and offered, "You need me anytime to step in with Ethan, if I can do it, I'm there."

Cher didn't respond except to drift a hand up his chest to wrap it around the side of his neck and rub her thumb gently along the column of his throat.

That said something, though.

And her eyes said something too.

They were warm and happy.

He put that there. He gave her that.

And that felt fucking great too.

Just as it was downright terrifying.

He focused on her look.

He focused on her touch.

He focused on her soft body pressed to his.

He focused on the night he had with her boy, which moved on to a night spent with her, her boy, and his friend.

He focused on how he and Ethan and Cher were getting comfortable with each other. How Garrett liked the way she teased her kid. How he liked the way Ethan's friend looked at Cher like he wished he was twenty-five years older and could slide a ring on her finger. How natural it was for her to balance having her man there with giving her son and his bud their kid time, all this while giving Garrett attention, Ethan attention, and ribbing Teddy, giving him attention.

And focusing on all that, he reminded himself not to be a dumb fuck.

Finally, she spoke.

"I think, you're down with it, we should discuss another waffle morning. Maybe next weekend," she suggested.

He gave her another squeeze. "You're good with that, you think Ethan's good with that, we'll do that."

She pressed closer and smiled.

He dipped his head and kissed her again. Another good-night kiss that turned into a five-minute make out session.

With effort, he ended it, touched his lips to her jaw, lifted one hand so he could slide his fingers along where he'd touched his mouth, and let her go.

"'Night, brown eyes," he murmured.

"'Night, Merry," she replied.

He turned and pushed out the storm door. Once out, he twisted to see her in it, watching him go.

He gave her a look.

She rolled her eyes and did what his look told her to do. She locked the storm, stepped back, closed the front door, and he heard that lock go.

Only then did Garrett start down the walk.

Instinct made his head turn.

When he did, he saw the guy he'd seen the night he'd come to take Cher on their first date. He was standing in his drive, leaned over a car that was running, arms on the roof of the car, attention to the driver's side window.

Two men were in the souped-up muscle car. Nissan GT-R.

Big-ticket car for that 'hood.

And a late-night discussion in the cold.

The man could be saying good-bye to friends who were leaving after coming over and having a few beers.

But it didn't look like that and Garrett had been a cop a long time, so he knew it wasn't that.

And he didn't like the feeling his gut told him it was.

Garrett kept watching as he made his way to his truck at the curb.

The guy must have felt eyes on him because he lifted his head.

There was eye contact through the dark and Garrett didn't break it.

The guy did when he pushed back, looked down, said something to the driver, slapped his hand on the roof, and moved away from the GT.

Garrett beeped his locks, rounded the hood, opened his door, and swung into his truck.

He took his time with firing up his vehicle and putting it in drive.

The GT backed out.

Garrett memorized its plate.

Cher's neighbor stayed in his driveway like he was planted there. The GT was pulling away and the guy didn't move.

It was a statement.

This was his turf, he could do whatever the fuck he wanted, and he wasn't big on attention.

Garrett hit the gas, keeping his gaze on Cher's neighbor as he did, making his own statement. This meant he saw the neighbor watch him as he pulled away.

He was forced to break contact when he lost sight of him.

He stopped at the stop sign at the end of Cher's street, saw it was clear, and made his turn.

He did this thinking he'd get a plate on the guy's truck, the number on his house, and run him and the owner of the GT on Monday when he was back at work.

Saturday Night

Cher drove down on him and he had no choice but to close his eyes, losing the sight of her, naked and riding him, her back arched, arms up, hands lifting up her hair, just like he'd ordered her to ride him.

He clamped his fingers into the flesh of her hips to pin her down as he grunted and exploded, shooting hot and deep into a fucking condom.

She ground into his cock as he kept coming, and only when it started moving from him did he feel her tits hit his chest before the warmth of the rest of her pressed close, her face in his neck, her lips nuzzling his throat.

Garrett was still coming down when he released his hold on her hips and trailed his hands in then up her back. He slid one around her at her shoulder blades and glided the other one into her hair, gathering it gently in his fist to keep her where she was because he liked the feel of her lips at his throat.

"You good?" he asked, his voice thick from sex and gruff from taking most of her weight.

It was a question he knew the answer to. She was good because she'd come before him, and from the looks of it, even if his orgasm had been phenomenal, hers was better.

Fuck, but she got off on the way he liked to play.

He liked control. He wanted what he wanted and enjoyed dominating the situation so he'd get just that.

Most of the partners he'd had liked it too. But they were often hesitant or skittish, locked in their heads, hung up on shit that took time or training to get them past.

He didn't mind the time or the training, but considering none of them were women he intended to keep, both were eventually a waste.

Cher let loose. Gave it all and gave it up readily. She was with him all the way from the start.

He wanted to spank her ass, she took it, pushed it, came hard for him. He wanted to finger her on his dining room table and watch, she kept her arms over her head and gave it to him. He wanted her to perform by riding him with her body on display, hands in her hair, she took his cock and gave him the best show he'd ever had.

His to toy with.

His to dominate.

Just his.

His.

On that thought, he felt that unease again sour his gut even as his arm around her tightened.

She lifted up her head and caught his eyes. "I'm good, honey."

Looking into her face, sated, soft, happy, his hand drifted out of her hair to cup her jaw.

"Thanks for dinner," she whispered.

Fuck, his brown-eyed girl.

The unease loosened when warmth started to invade.

"Stop thankin' me for everything," he ordered.

Her lips tipped up. "Thanks for a fuckin' awesome orgasm."

"You did all the work," he pointed out.

She ignored that completely. "Thanks for bein' shit-hot in bed."

He shook his head on the pillow and felt his body start shaking too.

"Would suck, you bein' tall, gorgeous, and knowin' how to skim walls but a terrible lay," she remarked.

His shaking turned to audible laughter.

Through it, he asked, "'Knowin' how to skim walls?'"

"That's definitely big points on the guys-that-are-worth-it test."

He kept laughing even as he asked, "Seriously?"

"Absolutely," she answered through her smile. "Though, awesome orgasms are bigger points." She pressed closer, tits to his chest, hips into his. "*Much* bigger."

"Just to say," he started, "wasn't me who put on the show tonight, honey. You took yourself there. I was just along for the ride. Or I should say, I seriously got off on a great fuckin' ride."

She was still smiling, but he saw the pleasure of his compliment hit her eyes as she returned, "If you think straddlin' you, ridin' you, and watchin' how much you like it didn't have a part in takin' me there, you think wrong."

Automatically, his hips bucked slightly into hers as he growled, "Fuck. I'm forty-two, haven't banged a woman minutes after a woman banged me since I was in my twenties, and now I'm gettin' hard again when I didn't even go soft."

Her brows shot up. "Is this a complaint?"

"Fuck no," he answered. "But it is me tellin' you to get off my dick. I need to go to the john and get rid of this fuckin' condom so I can bang you again."

She grinned and took her time sliding off of him, which meant she took her time sliding him out of her.

Fuck.

Cher.

Spectacular.

He touched his mouth to hers, rolled off the bed, and headed to the bathroom.

When he hit his bedroom again, he saw she'd tangled herself in his sheets, leg and hip on display, most of her tits too, her hand up to her chest with the sheet barely covering them. All this on her side, body curved, head resting in her other hand, elbow in the pillow, eyes to him.

Or to his cock.

With his age and experience, it wasn't lost on him that women appreciated what God and genetics had endowed him with.

It was just that Cher didn't try to hide or be coy about the fact she particularly appreciated it.

He liked the confidence that showed. She was who she was. She liked what she liked. She didn't fuck around communicating that.

He also liked the look of her tangled in his sheets in his bed.

He memorized that vision instead of standing there and savoring it, because he knew he'd like the feel of her tangled in his sheets *and* him even better. So Garrett's dick lost her attention when he slid into bed and pulled her to him, tangling himself up in sheets and Cher.

When he captured her gaze, he asked, "Where we gotta be for me to ditch the condoms?"

She looked confused but answered readily, "Uh…right here, right now."

"You on birth control?"

She nodded.

"Babe," he started. "You had a dry spell. I didn't. You sure you're good with that?"

"You been careful?"

That was when he nodded.

"So, right here, right now," she decreed.

She trusted him.

Completely.

Fuck…his girl.

"Sweetheart…" He gathered her closer. "How 'bout I have my annual physical a coupla months early and add a test?"

She made no response.

"Cher—"

She interrupted him with a whisper, her eyes dropping to his lips then his throat.

"Take care of me."

Garrett didn't know if that was an observation or a demand.

He again cupped her jaw and put light pressure there so she'd lift her gaze to his.

When she did, he felt no unease. No sour. No tightness.

Nothing but awe at what he saw in her eyes.

So much awe, his body went solid experiencing it, like he was locking it in so he'd never lose it.

"Thank you."

She was still whispering.

"For what, Cherie?" he whispered back.

"For making me happy."

Fuck.

His brown-eyed girl.

He slid his fingers back into her hair, grunting, "You're killin' me, baby."

"I'll stop," she returned instantly. "If I kill you, you can't bang me again."

He smiled as he rolled into her, giving her his weight, moving his hands on her, and gave it to her straight. "Makes me happy to make you happy."

"Good."

Since she deserved it and he needed to let it loose, he kept giving it to her straight. "And it scares the fuckin' shit outta me."

She slid her hands along his sides, to his back and down to curl her fingers in his ass, all as she held his eyes.

"I'm holdin' on."

He felt his mouth quirk. "Yeah. To my ass."

He watched her eyes heat even as her lips curved up, and she did both as she opened her legs, his hips fell through, and she wound her calves around his thighs.

"Better?" she asked.

"Oh yeah," he murmured, his attention shifting to her mouth.

She dug the fingers of one hand in his ass as she moved the other, gliding it up his spine, asking, "You gonna do me or what?"

Garrett dropped his head, trailing his lips from the corner of hers across her cheek to her ear.

"Yeah, I'm gonna do you," he whispered there.

"Well, get on with it, boss."

He slid a hand over her hip, along her thigh, and hitched her leg up so it was curled around his ass, instructing, "You better hold on tighter, Cherie."

"Goodie," she breathed, running her nose along his jaw.

Garrett grinned.

Then he commenced in giving his girl reason to hold on.

And do it *tight*.

Very Late Saturday Night

Cher was up against the wall, her face filled with fear, the gun pointed an inch from her nose.

The blast made everything go black.

There wasn't even a scream.

Garrett opened his eyes to the dark. The length of his body stretched taut, he could feel the sheen of sweat on his chest, the wet gathering in his groin.

He blinked at the ceiling.

It was then he felt Cher curled into him, calf thrown over his thigh, cheek to his chest, arm around his gut.

He drew in a deep breath and concentrated on relaxing his muscles on the exhale.

It took him four breaths.

Then he moved and he moved his woman as he did. Shifting her around so he had her back to his front, he curled into her and wrapped his arm around her belly, drawing her close.

"Merry," she mumbled.

"Here, Cherie."

She said no more.

She was out.

Garrett stared into the dark.

Terrified.

Sunday Morning

Garrett sat at a stool at his bar, watching Cher shuffle around his kitchen in one of his tees, opening and closing cupboards, having announced she was making him breakfast. As he did this, he was also sifting through the Sunday paper and clicking through his laptop.

"Most of my kitchen is garage sale, and still, my shit is better than yours," she grumbled, straightening from a base cupboard while closing its door.

He looked from the listing his real estate agent had sent to him that he'd been considering to her. "I'm a bachelor. I don't need good shit in my kitchen."

She turned to him, skillet up and pointing his way. "Half the Teflon is scratched off this."

"So use oil," he returned.

"Merry, this is actually a health hazard," she informed him.

He burst out laughing.

As he did, he heard the skillet hit the stove and she said, "No. Seriously."

"Bullshit," he replied. When her face screwed up with mild irritation, he gave her a white lie. "Been usin' that skillet awhile, and as you can see, I'm fine."

She pointed to the skillet. "You use that skillet?"

"Yep."

"How often do you cook?"

He grinned.

She had him.

"You got me."

She turned to the stove. "Gonna hit some garage sales next weekend. Get you a decent skillet. And if it's Teflon, get you some plastic utensils so you don't scratch it to shit."

"Cherie, waste of time and effort. That skillet is just for show in order to get Rocky off my ass after she gave me this same lecture about havin' shit in my kitchen seein' as then, I didn't have *anything* in my kitchen. But it was a waste of money, even if the shit I got is shit. I don't cook."

She turned back to him. "You get a wild hair to fry a burger, you're covered, and it'll only cost a dollar or two."

"Babe, I don't cook," he repeated.

"Then, right now, you gonna take me to Frank's for breakfast?" She pointed to the stove. "Because I'm not cookin' eggs in that skillet."

"You want eggs, then yeah, I'm takin' you to Frank's," he returned. "Seein' as you don't like my skillet, not mention the fact I don't actually have eggs since *I don't cook.*"

She put her hands on her hips, the mild irritation no longer mild.

"We go to Frank's, I gotta get dressed. Then we gotta head out, drive there, park, order, wait, and eat, and I'll have to pick up Ethan right after. And that would mean I can't make breakfast for you, amazing you with my culinary brilliance, which you have yet to experience, after which you'll have plenty of time to bang my brains out again and *then* I can go get my kid."

Garrett grinned at her. "Okay, then I'll toast you a bagel since I got those, cream cheese, and a toaster that works. We make a deal that our next sleepover happens at your place and you can amaze me with your culinary brilliance then. But now, while I'm toasting, you look at this listing I got up on my computer. After we eat, I'll bang your brains out, then we'll go get your kid. That a plan?"

Her eyes dropped to his laptop and she didn't confirm she was down with his plan.

She asked, "Listing?"

He slid off the stool, ordering, "Come here. Look. I'll toast bagels."

She headed his way as he headed hers.

And he knew he had better, even if it was not lost on him that he already had seriously fucking good, when she copped a feel at the same time he copped a feel when they passed each other.

He grabbed the bagels right when he heard her soft gasp.

He turned to her.

She was staring at the computer, eyes wide, a look of wonder on her face the likes he'd never seen anything close to before from Cher.

That was also cute.

Cher Rivers had never been cute.

But now she was giving him that.

He liked it.

"I take it you like it," he noted.

"I…are…" She lifted her gaze to his. "Are you seriously thinking about gettin' this place?"

"Yeah. Though I haven't viewed it yet, it's still a front-runner."

She looked down, reached out, and he heard her clicking.

He turned to the toaster.

He put a bagel in, and turned back to her, leaning his hips against the counter and seeing she was now bent, her face closer to the screen, her finger still clicking.

"So what do you think?" he asked.

She lifted slightly up, again giving him her gaze.

"This price can't be right," she told him.

"You saw the bathrooms," he told her.

Her eyes flicked down then back to him.

"Yeah, they suck. But Merry, that price? This is a lake house." She straightened entirely. "Okay, so maybe it's a really big pond, but that pond is *big* and it's still waterfront property. The kitchen is amazing. The floors are incredible. And it's a *lake house*. The views are…" she trailed off.

"Needs a new roof," he shared when she said no more. "A new furnace. New windows. It's got no air conditioning, so the summer is gonna suck if that isn't put in with the heating. And, babe, everything they did was cosmetic— that kitchen, the floors, paint. They didn't get to the bathrooms. There're two and a half of them, they're fuckin' ugly, and gotta go and those'll cost a whack. They've had four offers fall through after inspection. In the shape it's in, it's been on the market nine months and they've dumped the price twice. Now they're gettin' smart with a new price. But still, they gotta dump it even more for me to be able to cover the mortgage and do the work needs to be done."

"It'd be worth it," she stated immediately.

He again grinned. "You're that sure?"

She looked at him, looked to his laptop, reached out, clicked, picked up his laptop, and turned it to him.

On the screen was a picture of the property, a view from the porch that pointed lakeside. In the shot, there were the edges of the arms and seats of two Adirondack chairs, the white wood planks of the porch floor, the vibrant green of healthy grass, and the calm, deep blue of a small lake.

Listing pictures usually sucked, but that one could be on a postcard.

"I'm that sure," Cher confirmed.

He looked from the laptop to her and grinned again.

"It has three bedrooms," she told him something he knew. "And a study. And I can see you with a kickass grill on that porch. You got a kickass grill and you wanna fry a burger, you don't need a skillet."

She shut up, turned the laptop her way, and again started clicking.

After a couple of seconds, she muttered, "I like thinking of you here."

Garrett stopped grinning.

"This place isn't home," she went on, attention still to the computer. "It isn't you. This…" She lifted her eyes to him, turning the computer back his way. "*This* is you, baby."

On the screen now was the living room. It was huge. Beamed ceilings. Big TV mounted over a gray stone fireplace. Wood floors. Thick rugs. Leather furniture.

His mind's eye conjured visions of her curled in the couch and Ethan with a controller in hand, sitting in the armchair.

And his gut got warm just as it went sour.

He liked the vision.

But it activated and he saw Ethan's head turning to the door. Cher getting up from the couch and walking that way.

There were uniforms outside, waiting to give the news, create the hole that'd never be filled, lay down the hurt that'd never go away.

The vision blurred and focused.

The door opened and uniforms were outside.

But it was Garrett getting the news. Garrett and Ethan.

"Merry?"

He focused on her.

The bagels popped up.

He turned to the toaster, grabbed a plate, opened a drawer, and looked inside.

None of his silverware matched. He didn't even remember where he got it. He left everything they'd had in the home he'd shared with Mia. When he rebuilt his life after Mia, he'd picked up whatever to make-do.

It didn't matter. He didn't cook. He didn't hang out at his place unless it was to watch TV, and all he needed was beer and chips to do that.

He had his Harley.

He had his boat.

He had his truck and a life with no strings, so if he wanted out, a break to take off, to live life, he did it.

And came home feeling empty.

Hell, he was already empty.

The fuck of it was, he had no clue if it was better to stay empty or get filled up, get used to that feeling and endure losing it. Losing it to a fight that leads to a breakup. To stupid shit that leads to a breakup. To something tragic that leads to heartbreak…and more empty.

He knew the answer to that getting shot of Mia.

It felt worse being empty. Having no one to be with. No one to share with.

Nothing to live for.

Still, the thought of the loss paralyzed him because he'd felt it before.

He put these thoughts aside, nabbed a knife, and was about to turn to the fridge to get the cream cheese when he saw Cher's hand setting it on the counter by the plate.

Then she fit her front to his back, wrapped her arms around his stomach, and pressed her cheek to his lat.

She said nothing.

She just held on.

He opened the cream cheese, dug in with the knife, and started spreading.

"This place sucks," he muttered.

"Yeah," she whispered, holding on.

"A mortgage might suck more," he told her.

"Don't know, never had one," she replied and pressed closer, held on tighter. "Just know you're too good of a guy and you work too hard to live in a place like this. You deserve more, Merry. You deserve to go home to a place that kicks ass. That's all I know. It might not be that house. It might be another condo but a better one. It might be somewhere else. It's just not here."

He made the decision to lighten the mood, stopped smearing, put the knife on the plate, and turned in her arms.

He took her in his.

"I'm gettin' from this you don't like my pad," he teased.

She grinned up at him, rolled up on her toes, and slid her arms from around him to his front, gliding them up his chest to hold on to his shoulders as she leaned her weight into him and he leaned his to the counter.

But even through her grin, her eyes were serious.

So were her words.

"You deserve better."

Her words aimed true, like an antidote to fight the poison congealing in his gut.

It was fast-acting.

Instant.

And losing that sick just because she gave him three words, Garrett decided the bagels could wait.

He was making love to her now.

Which was what he did, dipping his head and taking her mouth before he took her back to his bed.

He didn't bang her.

He took his time. He concentrated solely on giving it to Cher, building it for her, stopping her when she tried to give back, giving her more to turn her attention, only going along for the ride.

It was lazy. It was slow. It was tender.

And when they were done, everything she had wrapped tight around him, she gave him that look she'd given him the night before—soft, sweet, warm, cute...loving.

He locked it inside again.

They got dressed and had to hurry to go pick up Ethan on time.

So they ate their bagels in his truck.

* * * * *

Sunday Afternoon

Garrett stood at the window by Raquel and Tanner's dining room table.

His eyes were aimed outside.

Tanner was standing out there on their porch. The underground pool that took up most of the yard he'd put in for his wife was covered for the winter. His daughter was at his hip. His yellow lab, Blondie, was bouncing around three feet away from his legs, her eyes glued to CeeCee.

349

This was because CeeCee had Blondie's tennis ball.

She threw it, which meant she mostly dropped it. It bounced on the cement a couple of inches from Tanner's feet.

But Blondie, being a great dog, bounded toward it and made a show of grabbing it like CeeCee threw it thirty feet.

Cecelia watched this and Garrett heard his niece's peal of laughter.

Blondie dropped the ball in Tanner's hand. When he got it, with a sharp sidearm throw, he quickly sent the ball sailing thirty feet.

Blondie took off after it.

CeeCee let out another peal of laughter.

"It get better?" he asked the window.

"It gets better, Merry."

At his sister's answer, he turned his head to see her sitting at the dining room table, her eyes on him.

"It go away?" he asked.

She held his gaze a moment before she nodded.

"Yeah, honey. It goes away," she said softly.

"Totally?" he asked.

Her gaze was soft. There was pain.

There was also hope.

"Not totally," she whispered. "But it's just a sting, Merry. You get it. You feel it. The big thing is, you *understand* it. Just what it is. And since you do, you can move on."

"I'm fallin' in love with her, Rocky," he whispered back.

Slowly, his sister's lips curled up in a smile as her eyes got bright.

"I can't turn this to shit," he told her.

"You won't," she replied.

"It's her. She deserves to be happy. She hasn't had that and she deserves it. I'm givin' that to her and it feels great. But it's also her kid. Ethan's fuckin' amazing, Raquel. He wants good for his mom, but he deserves good in his life too. For both of them...I cannot turn this to shit."

"You won't," his sister repeated.

He looked back out the window.

CeeCee had the ball again. And again, she threw it right at her father's feet.

Blondie retrieved it.

Tanner took it and let it fly.

Blondie chased after it.

"How?" he asked.

"How what?" his sister asked back.

"How's it go away?"

She didn't answer, and he was about to look at her again when he felt her fingers sliding into his as she got close to his side.

She held his hand and they watched what was happening on the porch. Blondie in the yard, retrieving the ball. Tanner looking down at his baby girl. CeeCee's blue eyes tipped up to her daddy, her mouth moving. She had only a few words in her arsenal, so that meant she was mostly babbling at him. But it was clear Tanner didn't mind by the way he was smiling down at his little girl.

"I'm pregnant again, Merry."

Garrett's head snapped around as he looked to his sister.

"That…" She tipped her head to the window. "And this…" She put her hand to her belly. "That's how it works."

"Cher wants kids," he told her.

"You both get to that place, give them to her," she returned.

He shook his head as he looked back out the window and pulled his hand out of her hold. He lifted his arm, catching his sister around the neck and tugging her to his side.

He kept his eyes aimed out the window as he turned his head and kissed the top of her hair.

For Rocky's part, she'd wrapped both arms around his middle.

"Pleased as fuck for you, babe," he muttered.

"Me too," she replied.

They held on and watched the antidote to Raquel's poison hold his daughter and play with their dog.

"Falling in love should be good," she said gently. "It should make you happy. It should make you hopeful. It should make you look forward to the future and savor what's happening in the now. I want that for you, Garrett, but it's not only that. It's the way it should be."

"I hear that. But bein' fucked up, destroying havin' that with Mia, on edge that I'll do that shit again, that's just not where I can be with Cher."

351

She gave him a squeeze. "Nothing's going to happen to Layne. Nothing's going to happen to you. Nothing's going to happen to me." He looked down at her. "But even if it does, Merry, I have this. This moment with you. What's happening outside. The baby girl I gave my husband. The baby he gave me that's growing inside of me. We can't live crippled by what we're scared might happen. We have to live in the moment, happy with what we have."

"I hear that too," he told her. "I just got no clue how to get there."

"Your problem, honey," she started softly, "is that you aren't recognizing you're already there. You just won't *let* yourself *be* there."

Garrett stared down at his sister, his throat starting to burn.

"Jesus," he muttered.

Rocky smiled. "Be in the now, Merry. The now would make you happy if you just let it be."

He tightened his arm around her neck. "Sucks, but you were always smarter than me."

"Yes, but you were never afraid of spiders."

A sharp chuckle bolted out of him.

Fuck, his sister was crazy.

"I see I got the upper hand here—you're smart as a whip, but I can kill spiders without freakin' out," he remarked.

"You live a life in Indiana terrified of daddy longlegs, then we'll discuss it."

He had to admit, she had a point there.

He grinned at her.

She gave him a squeeze.

They both looked back out the window.

Blondie was running.

CeeCee was babbling.

Tanner was smiling.

His sister was pregnant.

He felt it.

He held on to it.

Because, in the now, all was just as it should be.

It was happy.

Seventeen

TOUGH CHICK
Cher

Monday Evening

Mom was in my house, kicked back and watching TV with Ethan. I was in the Equinox, backing it out in order to head to work but wishing I was going to Merry's.

We'd had our awesome Saturday night and Sunday morning, and Merry had hung with me and Ethan before he'd taken off to spend some time with his sister.

And as we'd rushed toasting some bagels before getting my kid, we'd agreed that we'd find time to meet for lunch that week and I'd arrange it so one of my nights off, it was just him and me; the other one, it was family time.

Family time.

Merry hadn't used those words. I hadn't either.

But I liked thinking of it that way just as much as it freaked me out.

It was all going good.

No, it was going great.

I hadn't fucked anything up yet, not a thing.

I was happy. Merry was happy. Ethan was happy.

It was a miracle.

That freaked me out too.

Even so, there were bummer parts to it.

Specifically not seeing Merry more often. A lunch here, a night there, lots of sex when we could squeeze it in.

As great as it was, it wasn't working for me.

I wanted more.

There was no denying it.

I wanted *more*. And I didn't know how that had happened. How I went from being a woman who'd lived a life never having what she wanted, now having what I wanted, and still wanting more.

I should be happy with what I had.

Now I had the feeling that being happy just made you jones for *more* happy and that was where you fucked up. A *new* kind of fuckup. Not being content with what you had.

I needed just to let myself be happy without freaking out about it and not fuck shit up.

(I still wanted more.)

I hit the street and shifted to drive. I started motoring when I caught something in the light of my headlights off to the left.

I kept driving but did it staring.

Then I did it glaring, anger flaring fast and rocketing straight to fury.

He gave me big eyes. Then he gave me hand gestures.

I ignored both, kept driving, stopped at the stop sign at the end of the road, made my turn when it was clear, and drove two blocks before I pulled over and yanked my phone out of my purse.

I jabbed at the screen and put it to my ear.

My friend Ryan, who right then was sitting in a car across the street from my dickhead neighbor's house, answered on one ring.

"Cher—"

"Do not speak," I hissed. "Meet me at the bar…*now*."

"I kinda can't leave my—"

"Ryan, what'd I say about speaking? Get your ass to the bar."

"But the guy who hired me for this job is kinda scary."

Oh yeah.

I was *ticked*.

"Trust me, right now, Ryan, I'm scarier."

Ryan said nothing.

"You gonna meet me at the bar, like, in two seconds?"

"I'll meet you at the bar, Cher," he muttered.

I disconnected.

Then I jabbed at my screen again.

After I did that, I put my phone to my ear.

It rang a long time, then I got Ryker's voicemail.

"Your surveillance guy just quit. And you're off my Christmas card list. And if you come into J&J's and I'm the only bartender on, you aren't gonna get a drink. And if I didn't totally dig your missus, I'd never fucking speak to you again."

After I said all that, I hung up and drove to J&J's.

I stormed in, and being me, I didn't bother hiding how pissed I was.

This made Feb, who was standing at Colt's side of the bar seeing as her husband had his ass planted on a stool there, widen her eyes at me.

Colt saw his wife's face and twisted on his stool.

He got one look at me and let out an audible sigh before begging, "Please, fuck, tell me Merry isn't the asshole who's makin' you look like that."

"No, Merry *isn't* the asshole who's making me look like this," I returned, stomping toward the office.

"Who's the asshole makin' you look like that?" Feb called as I opened the door to the office.

I turned to them. "Ryker," I spat.

Neither of them looked surprised.

This was likely because Ryker didn't have a habit of making people look pissed off.

He'd made it an art.

I went into the office and stowed my purse, slamming drawers as I did it, this not making me feel any better.

Me slamming the office door when I left also didn't help.

Further not cooling me down, I felt something coming off Colt as I tramped his way.

I looked at him and stopped when I caught the expression on his face.

"You wanna tell me why Ryan just slunk in here, lookin' like a whipped dog, and made his way right to the back where I can't see him or whatever the fuck that moron's got goin' down?" he asked.

Colt knew Ryan. Back during the manhunt for Denny Lowe, Ryan had led them to me, and both Ryan and I had given them lots of information to figure out just how many screws Lowe had loose (in other words, *all* of them). That information might have even helped them (a little bit) to track him down.

Unfortunately, Denny had managed to wound three men, one woman, and murder three more victims before they stopped him.

But we'd helped (maybe…and not altogether willingly, but the last part only because Ryan was tweaked and I was pissed off I was fucking an ax murderer).

I knew Ryan because he was a regular at the strip club.

He was a nice kid, geeky, not real good at being social, and unbelievably smart. But smart in that bad way that made him geeky and not real good at being social.

He'd had a crush on me. He'd made it clear. It was sad and cute at the same time.

He also gave me money. It wasn't a lot, but back then, when Ethan was much younger and every time I turned around he needed something—new clothes because he was growing, medicine because he got an ear infection, food because he was human and had to eat—I needed all the money I could get.

It didn't feel good taking Ryan's money, but I consoled myself (poorly) by being his friend.

One of the only ones he had.

Sadly, this led to Denny meeting him, learning Ryan might work at Radio Shack but had many other skills, and Denny put him to work, spying on Colt and Feb. This meant he'd gotten Ryan to plant cameras everywhere—in Feb's house, on Colt's street—and Ryan had taught Denny how to do it, so Denny planted cameras in J&J's.

Ryan then kept an eye on the feeds because Denny was paying him.

And because of me.

This meant it was me who got Ryan caught up with a serial killer, hauled in, questioned, and scared out of his mind.

I held guilt about this, obviously. In the end, I'd wanted to give Ryan a bunch of the money Lowe had left me to pay him back for all his kindness and then never see him again.

But Ryan had told me that would hurt worse than any of the other shit that befell him because he'd been unlucky enough to cross paths with me.

So I paid him back the way he wanted me to.

By continuing to be his friend.

This was not a hardship. He wasn't real good at being social, but he was a good guy, he could be funny, and he'd always been a good friend.

Eventually, I got over what I did to him and the reminder he always was of what Denny did to both of us.

I did this because I cared about him a lot.

However, even with all that had happened, Ryan had not learned not to be stupid regardless of how smart he was.

Which meant Colt had had occasion to brush up with him, and not just when Ryan came to Ethan's birthday parties or when I had everyone over to watch a game.

To Colt's question about Ryan being there, I jerked an agitated finger to my face and asked, "Pissed off look?" Then I answered myself, "Ryker and also Ryan."

Colt sighed audibly again.

"I'm handlin' it," I declared.

Colt's attention on me deepened even as his mouth warned, "This better be shit you can handle without Merry gettin' a pissed off look, Cher. 'Cause you pissed off gives me a quiver. Merry pissed off might mean I'm in the dark with a shovel and a flashlight, coverin' a brother's ass by buryin' bodies."

That gave *me* a quiver.

I ignored the quiver, nodded to Colt, and called to Feb, "Got somethin' to sort. Be right back."

"We're slow. Take your time," Feb returned.

I didn't take my time.

I marched quickly to the pool table area where, as Colt said, Ryan was around the wall, sitting at a back corner table that was not even close to being visible from the bar.

I went right to him, stopped, and planted my hands on my hips, glaring down at his pale face, which had luckily lost the pimples he used to have when I'd met him, though some of them had left marks.

"Have you lost your mind?" I hissed.

He leaned toward me but kept his seat, "Cher, it's a big job and the guy who hired me trusts me to do it right."

I.

Was.

Gonna.

Kill.

Ryker!

"Is the guy who hired you gonna console your momma when you get dead doin' this big job for him?" I asked.

His face got even paler, but he didn't answer.

I read this to mean he knew the danger.

I didn't know the danger.

But I knew it was significant.

And I knew that if Lissa and Alexis wouldn't be upset that daddy didn't come home, I'd go to the nearest gun store, buy a baton, find Ryker, and beat him unconscious.

I threw out my hands, leaned toward him, and repeated, "Ryan, have you lost your mind?"

Suddenly, his head twitched and his brows shot together. "Do you know what the job is?"

"I know I don't want you doin' it," I returned.

He seemed to relax before he replied, "I'm a big boy, Cher."

"You're my friend, Ryan. You've had my back a lot over a lotta years. It's not about you bein' a big boy. It's about me givin' a shit about you. And part of that givin' a shit about you is wantin' you to be safely sellin' extension cords at Radio Shack and not sittin' in your car outside a house two doors down from mine where I know a dickhead lives and is likely into dickhead shit that makes you unsafe. And part of this unsafe is that you're surveilling a house two doors down from mine, doin' it stupid by," I leaned deeper, "*sitting in your car outside that house.*"

Ryan sat back hard in his chair when I leaned into him. "It's my job to keep an eye out."

"I got that," I returned. "And even though that job is *over*, heads up, you don't do that *sitting right outside* a house you're *staking out.*"

"I got ears in that house, and when I put them in, I didn't have time to use the good stuff. The feeds don't range too far. I gotta be close."

At the news Ryan had actually *broke into* my dickhead neighbor's house and planted bugs, I rolled my eyes to the ceiling, wondering if it was possible to feel your blood pressure spike since I was pretty sure I was experiencing that.

I rolled my eyes back just in time to see Ryan's gaze shoot over my shoulder. He jolted in his chair before he froze, his eyes wild, his body strung tight.

This would lead me to believe Colt had joined our huddle.

However, I knew the feel of the man who had entered our space while I was too busy reading the riot act to Ryan to notice.

And that feel was not Colt.

Shit.

"Ryan's surveilling a house two doors down from yours?"

Merry asked that question and he did it in a voice that was low and tense, an indication that he was about to go apeshit crazy.

Slowly, I straightened, and even more slowly, I turned to my man.

I looked into the blue shards of his glittering, pissed off eyes.

Yep.

This close to apeshit crazy.

Needless to say, Ryan doing stupid shit (repeatedly), not to mention being a friend of mine, he was well-known by the entirety of the BPD.

"Merry—" I started.

I didn't finish because he moved and he did it fast.

Lunging toward Ryan's table, he slammed a fist down on it so hard the table jumped. Ryan also jumped. But Ryan didn't otherwise move because Merry was still moving, this time so he had Ryan's sweater in his fist and his face in Ryan's.

"You got a job two doors down from Cher?" he growled.

"D-d-dude—" Ryan stuttered.

"*Answer me!*" Merry barked.

"Y-yeah," Ryan whispered.

"Who put you on that job?" Merry asked.

"Merry—" I tried again.

"Shut it, Cher," he clipped, his eyes not leaving Ryan. "Who put you on that job, Ryan?"

"I...I...n-n-no disrespect, Merrick," Ryan stuttered, "but the dude who has me on the job would lose his mind, I shared that with anyone."

Merry stared into his eyes, then pushed him off and Ryan's chair tipped up on two legs. Ryan threw his arms out, wheeling them as his feet kicked so he wouldn't slam to his back. He seemed suspended until his chair tipped forward and he was safe.

But I was not.

Because Merry had turned his attention to me.

"You know who's got Ryan on this job?" he asked.

"Merry—"

"My name is not an answer to my fuckin' question, Cher," he bit out. "You know who's got Ryan on this job?"

I looked into his eyes, my heart taking that moment to kick in, beating too fast.

This was me fucking things up.

I should have told him.

Merry this pissed off was a good deterrent to open sharing about things such as these, though, and if he gave me the opportunity to defend myself when he was calmed down, I would tell him that.

But the fact remained, he was Garrett Merrick. He was a cop, but he was just *that guy*. That guy who would want to know if someone he cared about was close to something not good. And he was definitely that guy who would want to know if the woman he was seeing and her kid were close to something not good.

Shit.

"Cherie..." he prompted on a sinister whisper.

I drew in breath.

"Ryker," I told him.

His face turned to stone.

I moved closer to him, though not too close (his face was stone, but he was breathing through his nose in a way that was scary as shit).

I put my hand light to his abs and started talking.

Fast.

"I don't know anything, honey. I just know Ryker warned me to stay away from the guy. And since he did, when I saw Ryan outside his house tonight, I lost it and called him in to give him a safety lecture."

"You think, Ryker warned you to stay away from this guy, maybe you should tell your man the likes of Ryker told you to stay away from this guy?" Merry asked.

Okay.

There it was.

Relationship-wise, even though I'd failed the relationship test spectacularly (twice), I still knew right then that where I was with Merry was *not* a good place to be.

"Well...uh..." I began, carefully starting to pull my hand away from his abs.

I got nothing more out and didn't even get my hand back because Merry's shot out. His fingers curled around my wrist, pressing in so my palm was flat against his hard abs.

Normally, I'd enjoy the feel of his hard abs.

His blue ice look, which was freezing me from the inside out, curtailed my enjoyment of his hard abs.

"You're seeing Merrick?"

This came from Ryan, and we both looked his way to see him staring in shock at me.

I thought his crush was over, what with me leading him to a whackjob serial killer whose chosen weapon was an ax, the resulting blood, gore, horror, computer confiscations, and police interrogations (etc.).

The look on his face said that I'd thought wrong.

"Ryan—"

"Geez, Cher, you might wanna pick up a phone sometime," he snapped. "It's not just on Ethan's birthday and when the Colts make the playoffs that I like to hear from you. You get a decent guy in your life, the least you could do is share so I could come over and we could toast it with a beer or somethin'."

Whoa. Wrong again.

I blinked at Ryan.

He glared at me.

Okay. Right.

Was he seriously giving me shit about being a bad friend while Merry was about to lose his motherfucking mind?

"You mind if I have a go at her now?" Merry asked Ryan.

Shit.

"Sure," Ryan magnanimously answered.

Shit!

"Good, then, to finish up with you, the job you're on just ended," Merry declared.

Ryan got pale again. "But—"

"The job...you are on..." Merry said slowly, enunciating each word clearly, "just...*ended.*"

"Right," Ryan mumbled.

"Go get a beer," Merry ordered.

"Right," Ryan repeated on a mumble, shoved back, got up, and scuttled away.

Leaving me with Merry.

That was what I got for being a shit friend who didn't call her geeky mastermind buddy to share that her love life had taken a turn for the better.

"Cher," Merry called.

My eyes drifted from Ryan's back to my guy.

When I caught his, I whispered, "Merry, don't be pissed. It wasn't—"

"You make me happy."

I shut my mouth, my feeling of being freaked about how great things were going as well as being worried Merry was right then ticked at me and I was messing everything up instantly mingled with a feeling that was as giddy as it was warm and squishy.

"I gotta learn to live in the now so I can feel that happy and not think about shit that might or might not happen that'll fuck with that happy," he declared.

"Oh…kay," I said softly, slowly, cautiously, thrilled he seemed to have made a breakthrough with crap that was screwing with his head but wondering why we were on that subject now.

He slid my hand from his hard abs up to rest against his beating heart.

I held my stance and my breath when he dipped his face close to mine.

"Do not do anything stupid that will take away our happy," he said quietly.

Oh.

Now I got him.

"I worried it wasn't right, but Ryker—"

"Ryker does not love you in his tee in his kitchen, bitchin' about his skillet. He does not love to make you laugh. He does not love it when you make him laugh. He might think your kid is the shit but not as much as I do. He probably wouldn't give a fuck that you've decorated your pad for the sole purpose of making Jefferson Airplane comfortable on the off chance they pop by, but I think it's hilarious and it's you and I love that too. I could go on. I won't. What I'll do is finish by sayin' it's best you don't worry about Ryker when you should be *talkin' to me.*"

"Point taken," I said quietly, all he'd said making me feel giddier, warmer, and squishier.

Merry kept hold of my eyes a beat before he nodded.

"You don't know anything about this guy?" he asked.

I shook my head but belatedly laid it out. "Just that he's bad news. Ryker told me to steer clear. I heard him and his woman shouting, and she'd mentioned Carlito. And, well, uh…" I trailed off.

Merry pressed my hand harder against his heart.

He said nothing, but I got his gist.

"He asked me out," I finished.

Merry stared at me, muttering, "Of course he has."

"Well, until recently, I *have* been a dickhead magnet," I explained.

"No, babe. You're fuckin' pretty, you dress great, and you got a fantastic body. Pretty much any guy who has a functioning dick would take one look at you and want in your pants. *That's* why he asked you out."

And Merry gives me more.

"That's a nice thing to say," I murmured, even though it wasn't.

It was a bunch of amazing, awesome things to say.

"I take it you said no," he noted.

"I'm kinda seeing someone."

His brows shot together. "This was recent?"

I nodded and added, "He hasn't been living there very long."

His head tipped slightly to the side. "He hit on you and he's got a woman?"

"I think they broke up."

"Mm…" he muttered strangely but said no more.

"Are you gonna go apeshit on me?" I asked, feeling hopeful that, since he hadn't yet, he wouldn't.

"No," he answered.

Good news.

"Are you gonna go apeshit on Ryker?" I went on.

"Absolutely," he answered.

"Good," I mumbled, dropping my eyes to my hand on his chest. "I'm pissed he pulled Ryan into whatever he's got goin' down. He deserves scary apeshit-Merry."

"Babe."

I lifted my eyes back to his.

"We learn a lesson?" he asked.

I was not a big fan of him asking that question with the nuance he thought I was a little girl who needed the big man to educate her.

That said, I'd definitely learned a lesson.

Not to mention, I knew better.

The minute Merry and I became an us, I should have stopped keeping things from him.

"I'll answer affirmative to that only with the warning that if any future communications hold a nuance of condescension, especially full scale of the same, they will be responded to with knee action requiring hours of ice downs and render our sex life moot for a week," I declared.

"You got trouble living two doors down," Merry fired back. "You essentially knew about it. Didn't tell me about it, even though two seconds after we became an us, the first thing I told you was that you laid that shit on me. And you're makin' threats because you think I'm being condescending?"

"Yes."

He studied me.

Then he grinned as he moved my hand from his heart, curling it around his side as his other arm curled around me, drawing me close.

"It's good you're fuckin' pretty and I've been in your pants and liked what I go so want to go back for more or you might get apeshit."

It seemed like the crisis was averted, which was a relief.

At least for me.

Ryker was another story.

But I figured he could handle himself.

"I need to get back to work," I told him. "Or to work at all, seeing as I didn't even start. Ryan showed and I just let 'er rip."

"Then I best let you go so I can find Ryker and tear him a new asshole."

"Tear him a bigger one for me."

He shook his head before he dipped it and touched his mouth to mine.

On the upswing, he muttered, "Came in for a drink with my girl."

"You're in luck. I'm a bartender and can see to that," I replied.

"Can't have a drink and go out and rip Ryker a new asshole."

"Do that and then come back and hang with me."

"She's bossy even after she fucks up huge."

I shrugged, being cocky, only because I could.

And again with the happy.

Because I'd fucked up huge; it was true. Merry wasn't a big fan of me doing that; this was true too.

But it seemed he was big enough to get beyond it.

Or better, he liked me enough to get beyond it.

Or both.

So I could be cocky.

But I also felt happy because this said a lot about Merry, about me, about the relationship we were building. A fuckup like that could have led to a fight that could have torn down some of what we'd built, paving the way for us to tear down more.

Instead, we'd ended it like we'd started it.

Just us.

So yeah, I could be cocky.

And happy.

He studied me as I had these thoughts, ending them with my lips going up in a small smile.

Seeing that, he shook his head again, gave me another mouth touch, then murmured, "Get to work. I'll be back."

He started to walk away and I started to follow him, but then he stopped.

I did too.

He twisted to me. "Steer clear of that house, baby."

Something in his face freaked me.

Shit. Did he already know something was going down at that house?

I didn't ask. I nodded.

He nodded back, turned around, and kept walking.

Only when he tipped up his chin did I notice Colt leaning against the wall that delineated the pool area from the rest of the bar.

I walked right to Colt, who didn't move, and stopped.

"Did you call him?" I asked.

"Nope," he answered. "You barely rounded the corner to get to Ryan when he walked in the front door. I just told him where you were."

Bad timing.

"Though," Colt went on, "you plus Ryan equaling disaster, or just Ryan bein' a dumbass on more than a rare occasion equaling disaster, Merry showin' saved me from makin' the call I was just about to make."

"Traitor," I muttered, only slightly joking, and made a move to pass him and finally get to work.

"Cher."

I stopped at his side and looked up at him, raising my brows.

"You mean a lot to me. The pain-in-the-ass little sister I never had," he announced.

Shit.

More warm and squishy, even with the pain-in-the-ass part.

"Sayin' that to soften the blow of sayin' this," he continued.

Fuck.

"Take your big brother's advice," Colt stated. "You're a tough chick and we all get that. But you hooked your star to a guy who makes a living providing protection. That is not a job. It's a calling. Do not take that away from him. I don't give a shit if it's somethin' you think is stupid, like fightin' over who takes out the trash. But definitely shit like this, Cher. You gotta let him have shit like this or you're not gonna keep him."

Apparently, Colt had been our audience for a while.

"I thought I was protecting him," I explained.

"You got that job, babe. Definitely. But when you do that, actually do it. And you aren't doin' it, keepin' anything from him."

I had noted late in life, after getting Colt in that life, that having a big brother rocked.

Except in times like these when he shared badass wisdom and relationship advice and it compounded the feeling of being an idiot I already felt.

It sucked to admit it was lucky for me he did. I'd already come to this conclusion about how to proceed in a relationship with Merry, but his added wisdom wasn't entirely unwelcome.

Just mostly unwelcome because it compounded the feeling of me being an idiot.

I powered past that because I had no choice and because the jig was up, and since it was, I had to see to my part of the protection deal with Merry.

"Ryker's got somethin' goin' on with that house, Colt, and I'm not thinkin' Merry's gonna be too happy when he finds out what it is."

"I'll talk to Mike. I'll talk to Tanner. We'll have his back."

That made me feel better.

"Thanks," I muttered, again moving to pass him.

"Cher," he called again.

I stopped on an audible huff and gave him big impatient eyes.

I knew by his dancing he was going to give me shit, but I had no clue how the kind of shit he was going to give me would make me feel.

"You ask anyone else other than me to give you away at your wedding, it's gonna piss me off."

All the oxygen evacuated my body. Gone. I couldn't breathe. And when you can't breathe, you can't move. So that's what happened. I stood there, immobile, not breathing, staring at Colt, thinking of walking down an aisle in a church toward Garrett Merrick.

Since Colt got me and got me good, he smiled huge, moved into me, tossed an arm around my neck, and forced me out of my statue state to walk tucked into his side toward the bar.

"Holy crap, what'd Merry do to her?" Feb asked as we got close.

"Nothin'. I just called givin' her away at her wedding," Colt declared.

I wheezed.

Feb grinned.

Then she put in her two cents. "I think Ethan should do it." She looked to her husband. "Merry'll want you to stand up with him anyway, babe."

Ethan giving me away.

How perfect would that be?

"Are you serious?" Ryan snapped. "Shit, how long you been seein' Merrick?"

"My count, officially, they been together just over a week," Colt shared helpfully.

"Are you *serious*?" Ryan repeated on another snap, his eyes aimed at me getting squinty. "A week? And you're getting married? The dude's a good guy, but *are you crazy*?"

I pulled my shit together and snapped back, "We're not getting married. Colt's just bein' an asshole."

Ryan looked somewhat relieved but mostly confused.

I felt Colt gearing up to say something else, so I pulled out of his hold and ordered, "Everyone, shut up about Merry."

Colt didn't shut up about Merry.

He declared, "I'm beginning to see how this whole Merry and Cher thing is gonna be fun."

I shot him a look.

He burst out laughing.

I rolled my eyes.

Luckily, everyone else shut up about Merry.

And I finally got to work.

Garrett

Garrett stood, leaning back against the front of his truck, his eyes to the door of the bar, his phone his ear, wishing he had a goddamned cigarette.

Since he'd quit, he didn't.

The bar wasn't J&J's. It was a bar in Clermont where Ryker liked to do business.

But he knew Ryker wasn't there because he'd done a walkthrough of the inside and didn't spot him. He'd also asked the bartender, who wouldn't say shit on a normal occasion, but she said he hadn't been around all day and Garrett believed her. And the biggest clue, his Harley wasn't outside the bar.

Ryker was hardcore. Even in winter, if the roads were clear, the forecast was good, and Ryker had to go somewhere, he was ass to his bike.

Right then, no bike.

That meant no Ryker.

With not a small amount of annoyance, he listened to his phone ring.

It was late. Not too late, but late.

Still, Tanner would be up.

"Yo, brother," he answered.

"Yo," Garrett returned. "Need a few minutes."

"You got 'em."

"You know where Ryker is now?" Garrett asked.

"Nope," Tanner answered.

"You two workin' any jobs together?"

"Yep."

Garrett drew in a breath and then asked the question he needed answered right or he'd be going apeshit on his brother-in-law.

"One of those jobs gotta do with a man called Jaden Cutler?"

"Nope. Never heard of him."

Garrett relaxed. Slightly.

Jaden Cutler was Cher's neighbor.

Then he asked about the owner of the GT. "How about Robert Paxton?"

"Never heard of him either."

Good.

"Been lookin' for Ryker for a coupla hours, big man," Garrett told Tanner. "Called him twice. He's not pickin' up. He's not at any of his known hangouts. Got any advice on where I can find him or what he might be doin'?"

"You wanna tell me why you're lookin' for him?" Tanner asked.

That was when Garrett gave him what he knew from what he'd run that day at the station about Cher's neighbor and his bud in the GT, some of which Cher had confirmed that night.

"Jaden Cutler's got a rap sheet about fifteen pages long. Assault. Theft. Possession with intent. His known associates read like a who's who of the scum of Hendricks and Marion counties, but he's new to the 'burg. He's done community service. He's also done six months for a B and E. Got off on a technicality on another arrest when an IMPD officer accidentally contaminated some evidence. Got off on yet another charge when a witness recanted their testimony. And he's now livin' two doors down from Cher and Ethan."

"Fuckin' shit," Tanner clipped.

"Robert Paxton visited Cutler Friday night in his GT-R that probably costs as much as Cutler's rental house," Garrett continued. "Paxton's rap sheet isn't as long, but with what's on it, it just means he's smarter than Cutler about gettin' caught. He's not 'burg related at all, until now. All his activity has been in Marion County. Made a coupla calls to some of my boys in IMPD and both names are well-known in Indy. Both of them also got a known associate. A man someone we know knows real well: Carlito Gutierrez."

"*Fuckin' shit*," Tanner bit out, and Garrett could tell he was on the move, probably to get out of hearing distance of Rocky.

"Ryker's got somethin' workin' in regards to Cutler," Garrett shared. "I know this because I walked into J&J's tonight to hear Cher rippin' into Ryan, who Ryker tagged to surveil Cutler's place. Cher saw him doin' it and lost her mind. Ryker's also warned Cher to steer clear of Cutler, but she's heard Cutler talkin' about Carlito. She might be steerin' clear, but, until tonight, she didn't tell me Ryker gave her that warning and Cutler isn't feelin' like steerin' clear of her. He's asked her out."

"Even if this is all a surprise, Garrett, gotta say none of it is actually a surprise. As stupid as Ryan is, he's a genius at monitoring and surveillance.

If Ryker's got a job he wants done, he's gonna go cheap and he's gonna get the best he can for bottom dollar, which is part of why Ryan is so stupid, seein' as the guy's got the talent to charge a fuckuva lot more. And, brother, it's 'burg lore that Ryker and Carlito got a beef."

"It absolutely is," Garrett agreed. "Problem with that is, no one knows how that beef started, which means no one knows why it's so strong, it's lasted for years. Those two give each other a wide berth, Tanner, and those two don't give *anyone* a wide berth."

"I'll have a conversation with Ryker," Tanner said.

"No, brother, *I'll* have a conversation with Ryker."

"Okay, Merry, give you that and set it up, but I'm gonna be there."

He could do it, and to keep his shit sharp, he should.

"Set it up soon," he agreed.

"On it."

"Right," Garrett muttered, pushing away from his truck to head to the driver's side door. "Not findin' Ryker, so gotta go have another chat with my woman."

"Right. Later, man. I'll call when I touch base with Ryker."

"Thanks, Tanner. Later."

They disconnected and Garrett swung up into the cab of his truck. He drove to J&J's. He parked. And he hit the bar to see Feb still there but Colt gone, likely at home, looking after their boy. Ryan was also gone. Business had picked up, but on a Monday night, not by much.

Feb was clearing glasses at the pool area.

Cher was behind the bar.

Garrett kept his eyes to her as he walked the bar and watched her walk it too.

He got to the end and slid his ass on the stool next to Colt's empty one.

"Beer or whisky, baby?" she asked quietly.

"Beer," he answered.

She went to the fridge and nabbed a bottle of his favorite brew.

She uncapped it, set it in front of him, and leaned into her forearms on the bar.

"Find Ryker?" she asked.

"Nope."

"That must be why you don't have blood on your clothes."

He grinned at her before he took a slug of the beer and lowered the bottle to the bar.

It was then he gave it to her.

"I don't like this. I don't like that guy. Seen him twice when I've been comin' or goin' to your place, and even before knowin' he's got business that links him to Carlito, didn't like the feel of him. So, you got somethin' you got two nights to chew on, Cherie. Either I start hangin' at your pad a whole lot more, that bein' me bein' there when you and Ethan are there as much as I can be, including spending the night, or you and Ethan have a long-term sleepover at my condo."

Her eyes went huge before she leaned deeper into her forearms.

"Honey, the dude is my neighbor. He might be into bad shit, but he's just my neighbor. You think that might be a bit of an overreaction?"

"I got a bad feeling, sweetheart."

"And I got a kid, Merry. It wouldn't be too smart to give Ethan the wrong messages about stuff like that, and I mean that in a lot of ways. It's too damned fast, for one. And he digs you and we're just startin' out. If it doesn't work, we *all* crash and burn."

"You don't think that crossed my mind?"

Cher shut her mouth.

"Two days, Cherie," he said softly. "Think about it. You can say no. I just won't like it."

It took her a few beats, but she finally nodded.

The lights were dim. It was a bar.

But Garrett still saw the look in her eyes.

"Takin' care of me," she whispered.

"Yeah," he whispered back.

"Takin' care of my kid."

He didn't reply.

She reached out a hand and wrapped her fingers around his forearm.

He twisted his arm and moved it so he could wrap his fingers around hers.

"You kiss my hand in J&J's, you're gonna deliver a hit to my rep as the 'burg's resident tough chick," she warned.

He hadn't intended to kiss her hand.

When she was done talking, he lifted her hand and kissed it.

"Aw, that's sweet," Feb declared as she walked behind him to go around to the back of the bar.

Cher rolled her eyes.

Merry grinned.

The front door opened and she looked over her shoulder toward it before she pulled her hand from his.

But she didn't do that until after she gave his fingers a brief squeeze.

"Be back," she murmured.

He lifted his chin.

As Feb transferred spent glasses to the sink and spent bottles to the bin, Cher moved down the bar and called out to the new patrons, "Yo."

The 'burg's resident tough chick.

It was true. She'd taken a beating and there she was, just keeping on keeping on.

But she wasn't made of steel.

And Garrett didn't lie.

He had a bad feeling.

He took another tug from his beer and watched Cher serve the newcomers a couple of drafts, trying to assess if he was actually overreacting due to her history, his history, or if his gut was telling him his tough chick was facing a viable threat.

He watched her smile as she pocketed her tips and moved back his way, making eye contact with other folks who had asses to stools to see if they were good.

She had to stop to mix a drink.

And while she did, Garrett decided he didn't give a fuck if it was an overreaction or if his gut spoke true.

With her history and his, he hoped she picked door one or door two, either of them meaning Garrett had access so he could look after Cher and Ethan.

Because he didn't want to take any chances.

Eighteen

IT'S JUST MERRY
Garrett

Early Wednesday Morning

$\mathcal{G}$ arrett woke up to his phone ringing.

On his stomach, alone in his bed, he reached a hand to his night-stand and tagged it.

He looked at the cracked screen, made another mental note to go out and get a new one, and took the call.

"Yo, Mike," he greeted.

"Sorry, man. Call out." Mike sounded just as drowsy as Garrett, meaning he'd been woken too. "Homicide."

Fuck.

Garrett pushed up and reached out to his light.

Homicides in the 'burg were rare.

Death happened all the time. Accidents. Disease. Old age. Suicide.

But homicide, not so much.

The 'burg was too small to have units dedicated to specific crimes. This meant the 'burg's detectives bought cases on rotation no matter what they were.

Garrett had been on the job a while. All the men in the bullpen had been on the job a while.

But he felt it was safe to say none of them had been on the job long enough where they took a homicide in stride.

It wasn't the gruesomeness of death.

It was that his job was not the kind of job that at the end of the day, you were filled with joy. Or energy. Or anything.

Except, if you closed a case, you got a high off of your part in bringing justice.

Luckily, those highs were huge and they made the job worth it.

Homicide didn't give you that. Not ever. Not even if you caught the killer.

It was too final. There was no going back. No coping.

It was just done.

The bad guy had to be caught. He had to be punished. You busted your ass more than any case you had to see to that.

But the only thing a successful takedown offered was closure to those left behind.

And that didn't mean shit.

"Meet you at the scene," he muttered unenthusiastically.

"Text you where," Mike replied in the same tone.

"Right."

"Later."

They disconnected and Garrett's phone sounded again the second his feet hit the floor as he pulled his ass out of bed.

He looked at Mike's text and texted back his ETA considering shower time, dressing, and getting to the location.

He was there before Mike even though Mike's house was closer. Then again, Garrett didn't have a woman in his bed to slow things down, even for a morning kiss.

This reminded him that day was the day Cher's time was up on making a decision.

Ryker was MIA. Even Tanner couldn't get a lock on him.

This did not make Garrett happy and it made Tanner worried.

Without Ryker to explain, none of them had any idea what Jaden Cutler had to do with Carlito Gutierrez—Ryker being their usual informant on all things Carlito—or what Robert Paxton had to do with either of them.

And Colt having a conversation with Ryan the day before didn't shed any light on the situation either. Ryan had been on the job for approximately two hours before Cher spotted him. He'd planted his bugs but hadn't heard anything since Cutler hadn't returned home.

A mystery.

And cops didn't like mysteries.

But all this going down on Cher's street, Garrett *really* didn't like this particular mystery.

He approached the address Mike texted and saw uniforms at the scene, crime tape already up. Marty, plus Marty's new partner (a rookie), Abe, and Adam were milling around. Ellen, Adam's partner, wasn't, which meant she was likely talking to a witness somewhere.

It was early. School and work traffic hadn't even started, so the scene was deserted except for police presence.

And the scene was right at the mouth of a cul-de-sac in a lower-middle-income development that had been so hard hit by the recession the country was just pulling itself out of, half the houses in the development were abandoned, and they looked it, or they were for sale, and that didn't look much better.

Empty was empty. There was a feel to it, and no matter what it was that was empty, it didn't feel good.

Garrett parked, got out, gave a chin lift to Adam and Abe, then moved toward Marty, who had seniority over all the uniforms, and he was closer to a blue Ford Fiesta, the lone car parked on the street. Also the scene of the crime.

"ME's on his way," Marty announced when Garrett got near. "Ellen's inside with the lady who called it in. Mike comin'?"

"Should be here soon," Garrett muttered, his eyes on the driver's side of the car. "Fuck," he whispered.

It was a woman.

He hated homicide because he was a human being.

But he hated it worse when it was a woman.

This one young. Too fucking young.

Then again, they always were.

"Far's I can see, she took three. The one to the throat did it, though," Marty said.

He was right. She had a bullet hole in her thigh, one in her chest, but the one in her throat had left a stream of blood down her chest—so much blood, it had pooled in her lap.

GSWs meant blood, obviously, but not that much blood.

The shooter hit an artery.

Good news, she bled out in seconds.

Bad news, she bled out at all.

Shooter also did her from above. She was a mess, but he could see the angle of all the entry wounds. She was in the car, the shooter either standing outside it and he was tall, or he'd shot down from another vehicle.

Her seatbelt was on, but her car was wheels to the curb like she'd parked, not like she'd been done on the go.

"Shot through the window," Garrett muttered, observing the glass littering her hair and clothes.

"Yup," Marty said.

His eyes scanned the interior of the car and Garrett saw her purse on the floor, stuff that was supposed to be in it not, since it was on the floor and on the passenger seat. He also saw the key in the ignition.

That meant she hadn't had time to get the belt off. Window up, she hadn't rolled it down to chat with someone she knew in the early morning dark.

Either she was coming to this location or going, but the purse told him whichever way it was, she was doing it in a hurry. Either she threw the purse in and the shit inside scattered or she was driving fast and erratically and the shit inside scattered.

Garrett heard a car approach and twisted to see Mike pulling up.

He lifted a hand to Mike and turned back to Marty.

"Got an ID?"

"Yup, though haven't touched anything," Marty told him. He jerked his head to the house the Fiesta was parked in front of. "Woman in there is her sister. Says vic's name is Wendy Derian. Didn't get more from her 'cause she was freakin' out, shoutin', carryin' on. Ellen's with her, hopefully calmin' her down."

"You catch anything from her?"

Marty shook his head. "Nope. Except a lot of cursing and 'I knew its.'"

Garrett felt his spine straighten. "'I knew it?'"

"Yeah, that's why I'm hopin' Ellen's calmin' her down so she can explain what she knew."

"Fuck, a woman," Mike said as he approached.

Garrett looked to him to see his partner's eyes on the car.

"Sister's inside, Mike. She called it in. Take in what you gotta take in, then we'll go talk to her," Garrett said.

Mike nodded, moved closer to the car, and Garrett gave his attention back to Marty.

"Crime scene comin'?" he asked.

"Yup."

"Neighborhood's gonna wake up. Not much population but word travels. Might be a good idea to get another cruiser out here," Garrett instructed.

Marty nodded and turned to Abe. "Yo. Get dispatch to send another cruiser."

"Gotcha," Abe replied quickly, immediately jogging to their vehicle, having been keeping his distance from the Fiesta.

Garrett eyed Abe a beat, trying to remember when he started and what had gone down since.

His first homicide.

Abe was a gung-ho guy. Not even twenty-four years old and raring to go. Couldn't wait to put his mark on beating back crime in the 'burg. Was always volunteering for everything, was there early for his shift, happy to work late. Marty thought he was hilarious, which was Marty's way of not finding him annoying.

He was not gung-ho now. With a dead woman in a Ford Fiesta, he was subdued, watchful, quiet, and helpful.

That was what homicide did to a rookie. Knocked the cocky superhero shit right out of you.

"When he's done callin' that in, Marty," Garrett said quietly to the veteran cop. "Might be a good idea you start him canvassing. See if anyone saw anything. Heard anything."

Marty nodded.

"I'm good," Mike said. "Let's go in."

Garrett and Mike moved to round the Fiesta, both of them turning their head to watch as the ME van pulled up.

They didn't stop walking. They made it to the door of the house, Garrett knocking even as he looked around the cul-de-sac.

One house, windows boarded up. One house, lawn hadn't been mowed all summer, obviously deserted, bank notices of foreclosure still posted to the door. One house in decent shape, FOR SALE sign out in front of it.

This house, the only one occupied.

Ellen opened the door, jerked her head to the side to indicate they should come in, but she didn't speak.

Garrett opened the storm and he and Mike went through, following Ellen into the living room.

As he went, he took in as much as he could.

The place was nice. Clean. Furnished a helluva lot better than Garrett's condo.

Pride there.

Pride in taking care of a house that the owners were probably so upside down on, it'd take decades to get right side up.

Pride in the travels the occupants had taken to Disney World, Atlantic City, the Sears Tower, and more, these declared through the snow globes, plastic banks, and other cheap souvenirs displayed throughout the home.

Also pride in family. Framed pictures everywhere and more shoved into the edges of the frames or propped up against them. Pictures that held the image of the woman pacing the room. Some men. Other women. Relatives. Friends.

And pictures with the woman sitting dead in a pool of her own blood in a compact car at the curb.

Garrett took in the woman pacing. She was still in her pajamas. The family resemblance was unmistakable. Dark hair. Curves. Olive skin. Fine features. But definitely older, at least by a decade. Wendy Derian appeared to be in her late twenties; this woman was in her late thirties or even having hit her forties, and she took care of herself like she did her house.

She didn't stop pacing when they hit the room.

She also didn't stop muttering. "Knew it. Fuckin' knew it. Knew it with that dickhead. That dickhead douchebag. That dickhead douchebag asshole *loser.* Fuckin' *knew it.*"

She might know whatever it was she was muttering about, but she had no clue Garrett and Mike had joined her and Ellen, that was how far she was in her head.

And her anger.

Which meant the grief hadn't hit her yet.

This was unusual. It had to have been over an hour since she called it in. Grief was mighty. It typically powered through the initial anger easily... and quickly.

This was also good. It was difficult to get statements from sobbing, hysterical people.

Angry people let it all hang out.

Garrett looked to Mike to see Mike's eyes on him.

"Ms. Derian," Ellen called. The woman jerked to a halt and turned narrowed, pissed off eyes on Ellen. "This is Lieutenant Garrett Merrick and Lieutenant Mike Haines of the Brownsburg Police Department. They're here to ask a few questions about this morning." Ellen turned to Garrett and Mike. "This is Marscha Derian."

"Thanks, Ellen," Mike muttered.

Garrett caught Marscha Derian's dark brown eyes, held them, and communicated with his own.

So when he said unemotionally, "We're sorry for your loss," even though it didn't sound it, she might understand he meant it.

"Yeah," she spat. "Me too."

She didn't understand he meant it. Nothing was penetrating her rage.

"Would you like to sit down? Get a cup of coffee? If you don't have a pot going, we can make one," Mike offered.

"No, 'cause, see, got three brothers, another sister, and my mom and dad, which means I got a shit-ton of calls to make today and I'm not lookin' forward to any of 'em," she bit out. "So I just wanna get this done and want you to get that shit," she tossed a hand toward her front window, "outta here."

That shit.

Nope, the grief hadn't hit her yet.

Either that or she and her sister weren't the best of friends.

Garrett and Mike exchanged another look, then both of them pulled out their notepads and pens.

"Okay, then, Ms. Derian, we'll get to it," Garrett started, flipping his open. "Officer Fink says you called it in. Did you—"

"Heard the gunshots but didn't know what I was hearin'," she cut him off to declare. "Never heard nothin' like that. Was sleepin', it woke me up, and I just laid there. Just fuckin' laid there, wonderin' what the fuck that was." She shook her head. "Nothin' happens around here anymore. Only got four neighbors left on this street, so things are quiet. Couldn't figure out what that noise was. So I just laid there."

Garrett and Mike didn't move even as her last declaration made her face change, her entire demeanor change.

Anger leaking out.

Shock coming in.

This would be followed by the pain.

"You here alone, Ms. Derian?" Garrett asked quietly.

She shook her head sharply like she was shaking herself into shape, and she focused on Garrett. "Yeah."

"You give Ellen a name of someone she can call so you got someone you trust close?" Garrett asked.

"I'm good," she declared.

Mike entered the conversation. "Please give Ellen a name of someone she can call so you got someone close."

Marscha Derian sucked her lower lip between her teeth and bit it.

Then she looked at Ellen, who was hanging back, and gave her the name and number of someone to call.

Ellen took notes, and the minute Marscha was done talking, she stepped out of the room.

"You heard the gunshots," Garrett prompted quietly.

"Shoulda known," Marscha declared.

"Known what?" Mike asked.

She looked to Mike. "Wendy, she likes the bad boys. Always did. Got suspended from high school *twice* because of shit her boyfriends were into.

And yeah, I said boyfriendzzzzz." She emphasized the *z*'s as well as her statement even though neither Garrett nor Mike questioned it. "Went from one loser to another. Not only never learned, they just got worse."

"Are you saying you're aware that your sister was associating with someone you considered dangerous?" Mike asked.

"Uh…*yeah*," she answered with heavy sarcasm. "She was *associatin'* with a lot of fuckwits that I considered dangerous. So did my brothers. My other sister. Our mom and dad. All her decent friends. And by *associatin'*, I mean suckin' their dicks and takin' their shit."

Christ.

"Maybe we should get to the gunshots you heard. Then we'll move on to the people Wendy spent time with," Garrett suggested.

"Nothin' to say about those shots since I'm a goddamned idiot. Heard that shit. Just laid there. Just laid there while someone was shootin' my sister outside my goddamned house."

"If you haven't heard the sound of gunshots before, it isn't unusual that you wouldn't immediately know what they were," Mike assured.

"I shoulda known," she retorted.

"Because the company Wendy kept?" Mike pressed.

"Because the company Wendy kept," Marscha spat.

"Outside the gunshots," Garrett cut in. "Did you see anything? Hear anything?"

She looked to him. "I heard bang. Bang. Bang. *Bang*. Four times. I heard 'em all. They were loud. Woke up laid there. Then it hit me, got up, went to the window, looked outside. Saw Wendy's car, the lights on, nothin' else. She'd been out all night. Didn't tell me where she was or when she was comin' home. Just told me yesterday she was goin' out and then she left. Saw her car and it finally hit me what those sounds were. Ran out there. Saw her sittin' there, starin'. Car was on. She was in it. Just sittin' there, bleedin' and starin'."

Marscha Derian was now shaking.

Garrett edged slightly closer, urging carefully, "Think you should sit down now, ma'am."

She needed no further encouragement. She shuffled back until her calves hit the couch and she plopped onto it.

Garrett looked toward the entryway and saw Ellen there. She nodded.

A friend was on the way.

"We're sorry to make you go through this," Mike said. "But we have to get all this down."

Marscha was staring at the carpet. At Mike's words, she slowly tipped her head back and looked at him.

She was losing focus. The pain was pushing through. It was going to hit any second.

They needed to get everything they could before she succumbed.

"At this point, what did you do?" Mike asked.

"Stupid," she whispered.

"What was stupid?" Mike pressed.

"I turned off her car," Marscha answered.

Fuck.

"Did you touch anything else?" Garrett asked.

Her head slowly swiveled his way and then she shook it.

"Ran inside, called nine-one-one," she told him.

"You go back out?" Garrett queried.

She shook her head again. "The operator kept me on the line. Told me to stay inside."

"Good," Garrett muttered.

Mike took over. "Is there someone in particular she was associating with that you have concerns about?"

"That'd be a long list," she shared. "Though, most recent, even though he'd ended things with her a week ago or whatever, is Jaden Cutler."

Again, Garrett's spine shot straight, but this time his stomach also turned just as Mike's gaze cut to him.

It took a lot, he tried, but he didn't succeed in keeping the harsh out of his voice when he turned back to Marscha and asked, "Jaden Cutler?"

She was way too far gone to process the harsh in his voice.

"Most recent dickhead douchebag asshole loser that Wendy *associated* with. Also the worst of the lot. Totally. And it was *him* that broke up with *her.* Kicked her ass out. She was livin' with me but also livin' in hope he'd take her back. Can you believe that shit?"

"Outside of disliking him, do you have any reason to believe he was a danger to your sister?" Mike asked.

"He's just a *danger*," she declared. "Mean as a snake when he's in a bad mood. Up his own ass, thinkin' he's God's gift when he *is not*. Man doesn't work, but he's got money. How is that? How do you not have a job and have money?" she asked.

"I know several ways, Ms. Derian, but do you *know* this Jaden Cutler was involved in anything that might lead to what happened to Wendy this morning?" Mike pushed. "Did she say anything to you? Did you hear her say anything to anyone else, for instance, on the phone? Did Cutler say anything in your presence?"

"No. But you got the experience I got with Wendy and her parade of losers, you just know."

She had nothing.

Fuck.

"Did Wendy ever talk to you about Cutler, his acquaintances, or the people they spent time with?" Garrett asked, hoping like fuck she'd mentioned Carlito Gutierrez.

She hadn't.

"No," Marscha stated and tossed out a hand in irritation. "This is all I was to my sister—a crash pad when she ditched one of her losers, or when one of her losers beat her up or cheated on her and she thought she'd teach him a lesson by takin' off only to go back, or when one of them decided it was time to move on so they dumped her. She was dumped, she didn't take a lot of time finding a replacement because, apparently, she couldn't exist without a healthy dose of asshole in her life."

Garrett braced when she finished her litany and instantly looked to the front window.

It was going hit.

Now.

"Guess she couldn't," Marscha whispered. "Couldn't live without it. Couldn't live with it."

It was then the tear fell. Just one, down her cheek to hit her pajama top.

Then she dropped forward. Face in her knees, her back bucked in a way that looked painful, and her sob tore through the room with such force, it felt like a physical thing.

They'd get no more and both Garrett and Mike had long since learned that when it hit, two cops hanging around, watching or attempting to ease a pain that had no relief other than time, was unwelcome and unwanted.

Their job was to catch the bad guy.

Garrett was already on the move.

Mike was too.

"You'll stay with her?" Mike muttered to Ellen.

"Yeah, Mike," Ellen muttered back.

"Favor, Ellen," Garrett said. "She's got any info on Wendy's friends—names, numbers, anything—get those down. We'll also need access to the rest of the family after Marscha gives them the news. Yeah?"

Ellen nodded.

They exited the house, but Garrett did it with his hand inside his jacket, going for his phone in his pocket.

"Need two minutes," he said to Mike as he moved off the front walk into the yard and not toward the vehicle at the curb, which was now surrounded by five cops, the ME, and Jake, their crime scene guy, who was taking pictures. There were also neighbors. They were hanging back on a sidewalk across the street, but they were there.

"Bet you do," Mike murmured, moving down the walk toward the scene.

Mike, obviously, was in the know about Ryker, Ryan, and Jaden Cutler.

Garrett stopped in Marscha Derian's yard, engaged his phone, and slid his thumb on the screen, vaguely annoyed that today would not be the day he'd have time to get a new phone.

But most of his attention was on what he was doing, not his phone.

It was also not on the beginnings of a homicide investigation.

He put the phone to his ear.

She was busy getting her kid ready for school. The phone not close. Whenever he called, or even texted, if her phone was close, she answered right away.

This time, it was answered after four rings.

"Uh…boss, school doesn't start for an hour," Cher said in greeting, her voice warm and filled with humor. "Can't confirm I dropped my kid off safely just yet."

"Get somewhere that is not close to your boy," he ordered.

"What?" she asked, no longer sounding warm and amused.

"Get somewhere where Ethan can't hear this discussion."

She didn't reply and he knew she didn't because she was doing as she was told.

He also knew she was there when she asked, "Is everything okay?"

"Wendy Derian was murdered this morning, shot three times."

Cher said nothing for a beat before she said softly, "I don't know who that is, Merry."

"She's Jaden Cutler's recently ex- and very recently deceased girlfriend."

"I don't know who that is either."

"Jaden Cutler is your neighbor, two doors down."

"Oh fuck," she whispered.

"Pack," he grunted. "I'll go to the grocery store. I'll buy a fuckin' skillet. But you and Ethan are in my condo until whatever the fuck is happening is done."

"Merry, I think—"

Garrett cut his eyes to the Fiesta. "Dead in a pool of her own blood in a goddamned Ford Fiesta sitting at the curb in front of her sister's house."

He actually felt her emotion through the phone—horror, a vague sadness for a woman she didn't know, concern about Merry—before tentatively, "Did this…Cutler guy…have anything to do—"

"Unknown."

Her voice was a lot less hesitant when she reminded him, "He's just my neighbor, Merry."

"He's a threat, Cher."

"I—"

"You move in with me, or you move in with your mother, or you move in with Colt and Feb or Vi and Cal. Strike that, your mother's off the list. It's me, Colt, or Cal. Pick."

"Maybe you can come by the bar tonight and we can discuss—"

"Me at the bar with you while Ethan and your mom are two doors down from this guy?"

She didn't say anything.

"Pick, Cher," he demanded.

She still didn't say anything.

"Pick, baby," he pushed.

"You," she whispered.

Thank fuck.

"Pack," he ordered.

"You're bossy when you're freaked out," she muttered.

"I'm bossy all the time," he returned. "*Pack.*"

"All right," she said, but it came out as a grumble.

Garrett drew in a deep breath.

It didn't release the feeling.

The sour. The fear. The poison.

"Don't worry about the skillet. I'll bring one," she told him.

He closed his eyes and dropped his head.

The fucking skillet.

That was what he needed.

The sour. The fear. The poison. Gone.

"I got shit to do right now. Get you a key. We'll sort it out later," he told her.

"Okay, babe."

"Glad you picked me, Cherie."

"You think this is it?" she asked.

He didn't get it. "What's it?"

"The end of the suckage that seems to infest my life, this time even when I'm not making stupid decisions that fuck up said life and totally have nothing to do with it."

He lifted his head and put his hand to his hip. "Don't know, sweetheart. Just know with this particular suckage, I'm gonna be there to make sure you get through."

She sighed. "Unfortunately, you're right. I'm a dickhead magnet and I'm a life suckage magnet. This means, that asshole's just my neighbor, but since I'm in close proximity, whatever his shit is would find some way to stick to me."

"Lucky you're not gonna be in close proximity. You're gonna be in a crappy-ass condo four miles away."

Some humor was back when she said, "Yeah, lucky."

"Got a homicide to investigate, brown eyes. Gotta let you go."

"Okay, honey. Do that shit quick and make my 'hood safe. The Mamas and the Papas are slated to come to dinner this weekend and I'm not sure they'll dig your pad."

It was painful, but he had to do it.

So he bit back the laughter that left a different ache in his gut.

"Not a rule, but definitely frowned on to bust a gut laughin' while standin' in the yard of a grieving sister whose curb has become a murder scene," he informed her.

"Oops, sorry," she muttered. "I'll curtail my comic genius until a more appropriate time."

"How about startin' that now?" he suggested, turning his back on the street so no one could see the smile he couldn't beat back.

"Right."

"Get Ethan safe to school," he ordered.

"Definitely. 'Bye, gorgeous."

"Later, brown eyes."

He disconnected, turned, and headed across the yard to his partner, his colleagues, and a dead woman in a compact car.

Forty-five Minutes Later

Before Garrett got in his truck to leave the scene and meet Mike at the station, he stood outside it, watching the ME van rolling away with Wendy Derian in a body bag in the back at the same time their tow guy was hooking up the Fiesta.

He did this with his phone to his ear.

He listened to it ring and he kept hold of his shit as it kept ringing until he got Ryker's voicemail.

"By now, you've probably heard that Jaden Cutler's girl took three. She just rolled away in the back of the ME's van. You also probably get that this does not make me happy. And I'm guessin' you get that your continued disappearing act is making me less happy. You know dick about this, Ryker, you better fuckin' come forward. You got friends. They give a shit.

They'd cover your ass on a lot, and you know this because we've already done that. But now a woman's dead." He drew in breath and finished, "I think you get me."

He disconnected.

Then he swung into his truck.

Cher

I sat across from Ethan and watched him wolf down three soft-boiled eggs crunched in with saltine crackers, a touch of butter, and some salt and pepper.

Something my mother made me eat when I was a kid that I detested.

Something that I'd tried on my kid when it became clear he liked everything that could be considered food, as long as it had only so much nutritional value.

He loved it. He called it my "breakfast specialty."

I could make it, but once made, I could barely look at it.

"Kid," I called.

"Yo," he said, eyes to his bowl, mouth full and getting fuller since he was shoveling bright yellow, slimy cracker goo in it.

I made a face.

He looked to me.

"What?" he asked.

We had important shit to talk about. I had to get past the egg goo.

"You remember that conversation we had not too long ago about you growin' up and me needin' to have a mind to that?" I asked back.

He slouched in his chair, fleeting panic racing across his face as he said, "God, Dad. What'd he do now?"

I quickly shook my head. "No, kid, it's not your dad. I haven't heard from your dad since all that went down on the front walk. And like I said then, your dad is not gonna do anything you don't want him to do, I'll see to that. But I do have something to talk to you about, and it'll require me trusting that you actually are growin' up and I can tell you what's gotta happen. Then we can talk it out however you need to do that."

He came right out of his slump, straightening his shoulders and keeping eye contact.

My little man.

"Hit me," he ordered.

I wanted to laugh or at least grin, but he was being serious and I had to give him that.

"Right, okay, you know that guy who lives down the way that gives off a bad vibe, the one who was bangin' on Tilly's door?"

Ethan nodded.

"Well, somethin' is goin' down. I don't know a lot about it, but Merry doesn't have a good feeling about him and he's a cop, so his feelings are usually smart to pay attention to. Until he figures out what's going down, he wants us to stay with him. So, today, we're goin' to his place where we're gonna stay for a while."

Ethan just sat there.

I did too.

"Is that it?" he asked.

"Well, yeah," I answered.

He went back to eating, but before shoveling in another load of egg mush, he muttered, "Cool."

Cool?

"Uh, is that it?" I asked his question.

He looked to me. "Is what it?"

"Do you have any questions?"

"Like what?"

"Like, how long we're staying with Merry? And the answer to that is, I don't know, but hopefully not long. Just until that's sorted."

"Okay," Ethan said, then went back to his bowl.

I stared at the top of his head.

Then I asked, "Are you worried about anything?"

He looked at me again. "Like what?"

"I don't know. Anything," I told him. "Merry and me haven't been seein' each other very long, but this isn't like we're moving in with him. And that guy freaked you out. I don't want you to hold back if something's bothering you or you have a question you want answered."

Ethan tipped his head to the side. "Are you and Merry dating?"

I thought that was a weird question because he knew the answer.

Still, I gave him that answer. "Yeah."

"No, Mom. I mean, are you dating or are you boyfriend and girlfriend?"

It kind of freaked me out my ten-almost-eleven-year-old son knew the difference.

I couldn't focus on that right then. I had to focus on his question.

Merry and me hadn't officially had the conversation, but I did feel it was accurate to answer, "We're boyfriend and girlfriend."

"So, that guy is bad news. Merry heard about him. His woman is livin' on the same street, and we're movin' in with him until he deals with it," Ethan declared. "It's not a big deal. It's just Merry."

I stared at my kid again.

Ethan must have misinterpreted my stare because he went on to explain, "If that guy lived close to Feb before Colt married her, Feb would move in with Colt. Same with Vi and Cal. Merry's like them. So..." He shrugged. "Whatever."

"Whatever?" I asked.

My son didn't elucidate.

He asked, "Does Merry have a nice place?"

I told him the truth.

"No. It sucks."

"Bummer," he muttered.

"It has a decent TV," I shared.

Ethan shoveled egg mush in his mouth and asked through it, "Can we take the Xbox?"

"That and a skillet," I confirmed.

Ethan mouth scrunched to the side in confusion. "A skillet?"

"Merry's been more interested in riding his Harley and catching bad guys than buying a decent skillet."

Ethan grinned an egg-saltine-salt-and-pepper-mush grin.

My little man but still my boy.

God, I had the awesomest kid in the universe.

"You're the awesomest kid in the universe," I declared.

His eyes narrowed. "Are you gonna get gooey?"

"No. Except tellin' you you're the awesomest kid in the universe."

He shoved his spoon into his bowl and scooped up more mush, muttering, "Already knew that."

I grinned.

Then I grabbed my phone.

I texted, *Ethan's good with the extended sleepover as long as we can bring the Xbox with our skillet,* and hit SEND.

Considering my man was embroiled in a fresh murder investigation that involved a woman I'd seen once, in her nightie, having an argument with my dickhead neighbor, I was not surprised his reply took an hour and a half.

When I got it, it was, *Xbox affirmative. He get to school okay?*

Seriously.

Totally.

If we went the distance, I *so* was going to be able to talk him into more kids.

Yes, boss. FYI, we've been accomplishing that difficult maneuver since the third day of kindergarten when he quit pitching a fit because his momma was dropping him off with bitches who made him take naps, I returned.

Whatever. Come by the station. Need to give you keys. Leave the Xbox by the TV. No one touches my TV but me. I'll deal with it when I get home. Be home before you go to work so I can see to Ethan.

I stared at the text, wanting to take a screen shot of its awesomeness, print it out, frame it, and put it by my bedside so I could read it every day.

Since I didn't want to be a whackjob who would do something like that, I just experienced another boon Merry gave me.

That being, me, now a woman who had a man in her life who was a man who was *in her life*. Being there. Taking care of her. Being a partner. Being a part of her kid's life. Taking care of her kid. Liking that. Wanting it. Going for it.

After I let that goodness sift through me, I called my mom and explained the situation.

Needless to say, Grace Sheckle was pretty fucking happy my kid and I were moving in with Merry. So much, she didn't care there was a possible homicidal boyfriend living two doors down from my house.

Not even a little bit.

I packed my bags. I packed Ethan's. I disconnected the Xbox. I packed some groceries. I grabbed a skillet. I loaded this all in my car. I went to the station, got the keys, and stole a quick, distracted kiss from my man who was on the phone the entire time I was there.

While there, I also got a lot of greetings from a lot of friends, all of whom were busy, so I didn't dally.

I took our shit to Merry's and put things away as best I could.

His extra room was a junk room, not a guest room.

I'd deal with that tomorrow.

I went out to go to the grocery store to add to the seriously meager supplies Merry had in his kitchen, something I needed to do before I went to go get my kid from school.

And I left the Xbox on the floor in front of the TV.

Garrett

"Nothin' here but girl shit," Jake muttered.

Garrett and Mike stood across the table in the basement were Jake did some of his work. Scattered on it were Wendy Derian's purse, the contents of the same, and the contents of her car.

"Yeah, except there's no cell," Garrett replied.

Jake looked up to him. "Nope."

"We went through the room she was stayin' in at her sister's. Not one there either," Mike noted.

Garrett looked to Mike. "Twenty-eight-year-old woman's gonna have a cell phone."

Mike looked to the table. "Shit."

Woman in a hurry to get where she's going.

Cell gone.

Not good.

"Got stuff to process, guys. You need anything else?" Jake asked.

"No, man, thanks," Garrett answered.

They moved out of the room, but they didn't move to the stairs to go back to their desks. They moved to the stairs to exit the building in order to do legwork. They had a list of friends and family to hit.

But Garrett knew where they were gonna start.

"Cutler's?" he asked as he pushed the door out to the back parking lot.

Mike nodded.

They moved to the unmarked sedan they used on the job and didn't speak, not even to discuss who drove.

They'd been partners a while. They had that down.

They took turns.

Today was Mike's turn.

Garrett folded into the passenger side.

Mike set them on their way.

Cher's house was quiet, her Chevy not in the driveway, when they hit her street and parked outside Cutler's.

They got out. They went to the house. They knocked.

No answer and his truck was not in the drive or on the street.

"We'll come back," Mike said.

Garrett nodded and they took off. They went down the list and hit what they could—Wendy Derian's employer and then her friends at home, some at work, ending with going back to the family.

Most were home. They'd gotten the news and news like that translated to an instant personal day.

But they got the same from everyone, which was the same as what they'd gotten from her sister.

Wendy was well-liked. She was funny. She was sweet. She was a decent worker (she wouldn't win awards, but she showed and got the job done).

But she was stupid. Picked the wrong men. Never learned. Kept doing it.

No one liked Cutler. Friends were wary of him. Family detested him.

Even with that, there was a lot of shock. She might've picked the wrong men, but however bad they were for her, no one thought she'd end up shot three times because of it. Maybe banged up. Even beat to shit.

Not dead.

This read that whatever the men she picked did—whatever Cutler did—she wasn't involved.

She went to work. She spent time with her friends. She did not exit her life for her man or to cover up whatever he was wound up in or the fact she was tied up in it too. She didn't seem to be hiding anything or retreating from life, work, friends, or family.

She just kept getting mixed up with the wrong guys.

Mixed up so much with Cutler, the only thing friends and family did get was her demeanor during the time after their breakup to her death.

She was cut up by it. Told everyone who would listen that he was "the one," the breakup came out of the blue, to her they'd been happy, and Cutler didn't give her even a hint of a clue why he ended things.

That's all they got. Including them coming up empty with the fact that she'd told no one where she was going the night before. No family member, friend, coworker, not a soul. The only person she'd mentioned it to was Marscha when she left, but she gave no detail.

At five fifteen that night when they went back to Cutler's and found no truck with no response to their knock, they had dick. No witnesses to what went down in the cul-de-sac. No one liking Cutler enough to spend too much time with him to know anything about the other side of his life that he couldn't show them with Wendy. And Jake coming up with nothing outside Cutler's prints in the car, which were expected since she'd been living with him.

"Not got a good feelin' about this," Mike murmured as he headed them back to the station.

"Nope," Garrett agreed.

"We got dick," Mike told him, something they knew.

"I wanna hit that house again later when he might be home," Garrett replied.

"We can hit her hangouts in the meantime," Mike said. "I'll tell Dusty it's gonna be a late one."

They hit her hangouts, which were not surprisingly the perfect places to pick up the wrong guy.

This meant that no one said jack outside expressing their shock and sadness at the death of a sweet gal that everyone knew but no one knew who might want to kill her.

She also had not been to any of these hangouts the night before nor did any of the regulars know where she'd gone.

And at a quarter to eight, when they went back to Cutler's, there was still no truck and no lights on in the house.

"We'll try tomorrow," Mike said.

"Right. Gotta get home so Cher can get to work and I can look after Ethan."

Mike grinned at the windshield. "Domestic bliss already?"

"Don't know, but you'll be the second to know when I do."

Mike chuckled.

They went back to the station, did what they had to do to end their days, and Garrett got to his place just in time for Cher to give him a kiss and rush out to work.

Taking one look at Ethan on his couch, he shrugged off his suit jacket and installed the Xbox.

Ethan went for it with some video game, but he did it jabbering to Garrett about his day. The sound of the TV and Ethan talking made his condo seem a lot less crappy-ass than it always did.

Garrett listened as he went for some food, finding he had more of it in his kitchen than he'd ever had in his life, including the part of his life that he shared with his ex-wife.

He made a sandwich.

And later, he and Ethan polished off one of the three bags of Oreos Cher had stocked, doing this while watching sports talk shows before they both hit the sack—Ethan, because he was a kid and was supposed to go to bed early; Garrett, because he'd been woken up early by a murder and was glad to put the day behind him.

But before he turned out the light, he made one call.

"Was pissed at you. Now pissed that I'm worried about you," he told Ryker's voicemail, then ordered, "Call me, Ryker."

He hung up, hit the lights, and stretched out in bed.

He fell asleep.

Ryker did not call.

He approached the car.

It wasn't a Fiesta.

It was a blue Equinox.

He didn't want to approach, but his feet kept moving, taking him there.

He stopped outside the driver's side door.

Shards of glass in her hair and on her clothing, sitting in a pool of her own blood, her top drenched with it.

Cher.

Garrett's eyes shot open as his body jolted.

He stared at the dark, feeling cold because of the dream and the slick of sweat on his skin.

"Fuck," he whispered, lifting his hands, pressing the pads of his palms to his eye sockets, forcing stars to shoot through his eyes in order to obliterate the residue of that dream. "Fuck," he repeated.

He got it.

Finally, he got it. He understood.

His poison was different from Rocky's.

He thought it was the same.

It wasn't.

Now he understood.

He just had even less of a clue what to do about it.

But he knew who did.

⟊⟊⟊

Cher

At quarter to four in the morning, I let myself into Merry's.

I shrugged off my jacket and silently put it and my purse on the dining room table.

The Xbox was not on the floor but in one of the shelves that had been empty, but now was not, under Merry's TV.

My kid was sleeping on the couch.

It was a pullout that Merry had pulled out and put sheets and a thick blanket on.

But it was still a couch.

Something had to be done about that, but Ethan didn't look uncomfortable.

He looked out.

Tomorrow.

I moved down the dark hall and saw Merry standing outside the door to his bedroom.

A near-to-four-in-the-morning welcome home.

Nice.

I said nothing.

He said nothing.

But when I got close enough, he hooked me with an arm around my waist and pulled me into his room.

The door catching barely made a noise.

Merry shuffled me back as I lifted my hands to his chest.

"Need to get my kid a bed, baby," I whispered.

"I'll talk to the guys. See what we can arrange for tomorrow."

I nodded.

"Catch a killer?" I asked.

I saw his grin even in the dark.

"Not yet."

My legs hit bed, then Merry and me hit bed, him on top.

His mouth went to my neck.

"You tired?" he asked.

"Yeah," I answered.

His hand slid up my side, taking my shirt with it. "How tired?"

I shivered the good kind of shiver. "Not that tired."

His hand slid over my ribs and started going up.

"Can you fuck quiet?" he asked.

My hands slid down his bare back until they encountered pajama bottoms.

Soft.

Flannel.

Nice.

"Absolutely," I answered.

His mouth came to mine and I felt his smile before he kissed me.

We fucked hard. We fucked quick. It was great.

And we managed to do it quiet.

Nineteen

HOPING I WAS WRONG
Cher

Thursday, Early Morning

*M*erry's bathroom door was closed.

I was at the sink, hands to the basin, eyes to the mirror.

Merry was at the sink too, hands to my hips, eyes to mine in the mirror.

And I was taking his cock.

Watching him, his muscles straining, his gaze burning into mine, his fingers digging into my flesh, his body moving with his thrusts in time with feeling his cock drive hard and deep, in order to stifle a whimper, I dropped my head.

One of his hands slid up my spine, caught my hair, and pulled my head back.

He wanted me to watch.

And when he was banging me, Merry always found a way to get what he wanted.

Fuck.

Hot.

"Don't turn me on too much, baby," I warned on a whisper.

In answer to that, he dipped his knees and drove up so deep, he had to have hit my womb.

Amazing.

"That isn't helping," I moaned.

And to that, he gave a gentle tug on my hair that felt like he was driving me down on his dick.

My head back, my neck bowed, Merry kept thrusting as he grunted, "Arch your back for me."

I did and watched his eyes drop to my tits.

"More," he growled.

I gave him more.

At that, he growled again, eyes glued to me in the mirror, and he fucked me harder.

Shit, I could see that being a turn on for a guy because it was a turn on for me.

I braced my hands on the basin and started rearing back into his dick.

"Fuck yeah," he groaned, moving his hand from my hair to my shoulder and driving me back even harder.

"Merry," I breathed.

He curled his torso over me, his cock still pounding, his other hand moving from my hip up my belly. He caught one of my breasts and watched himself tug hard at my nipple.

But I watched the raw hunger on Merry's face as he did it *and* I felt what he did, and it shot from my nipple to my pussy, detonating. My head flew back and I clenched my teeth, driving my moan back down my throat where it felt like it was vibrating along with my orgasm against my man's plunging cock.

I wasn't done yet when he pulled out, turned me, lifted me, planted my ass on the edge of the vanity, then tipped and lifted it. His mouth to mine, he thrust back inside.

"Close," he grunted.

I knew what he was saying.

I raised my knees, pressed them to his sides, and took his cock as I slid my hands into his hair and panted into his mouth while he grunted quietly into mine.

"Now," he groaned, planting himself deep, and I yanked his head down, his open mouth to mine.

I slid my tongue inside so I could fully experience the orgasm he was growling down my throat.

I kissed him through it and I kissed him as he came down.

He took over the kiss when it left him.

Mine had been hot.

Merry's was sweet and soft and long.

Both were fantastic.

But it had to end, so he ended it, lifting his head as he slid a hand up to cup one side of my face.

His eyes roamed my features for a long time.

"Fuck, it's like you're at your prettiest first thing in the morning," he muttered.

God, I liked that.

"You're just saying that because I let you wake me up at a God-awful hour and fuck me," I teased.

He looked into my eyes. "Beat me to the punch, Cherie. That was my next compliment. You're the best fuck I've had first thing in the morning… or ever. But I'm not bullshitting you when I say a good part of that is first thing in the mornin' fuckin' someone as pretty as you."

To beat back the warm and squishy all that made me feel, I pressed myself tighter to him, my hands roaming his hair, his neck, his shoulders, murmuring, "And I thought it was my excellent lovemaking skills."

He grinned. "*I* make love to *you*, honey. My girl *fucks*. And she does it… day or night…lookin' *pretty*."

I straightened in his arms. "I can make love too. You just won't let me."

I wasn't sure this was true. I'd never tried it.

"We'll test that when we got time in my bed where we don't have to be quiet 'cause your boy is on my couch."

Shit.

My eyes shot to the closed door.

"I should check on him," I muttered.

"He didn't hear."

I looked back to Merry. "You sure?"

"I can't see through walls and don't got a dog's hearing, but I've been a ten-year-old boy. It's not even six in the morning. He's out of it. He didn't hear a thing."

"He's in unfamiliar surroundings."

"He's with his mom and a guy he trusts. He's fine."

That was true.

"I should still check on him."

One side of Merry's lips tipped up. "Can I slide my dick outta you before you do that?"

I gave him a look.

Then I said, "Yeah."

He gave me a very different look before he dropped his head and kissed me as he slid out of me.

When he was done, he pulled my ass off the vanity and put me on my feet. Merry went to the toilet. I went to my discarded panties and pajamas.

I tugged them on and moved out of Merry's bathroom and bedroom, closing the door behind me.

Slowly, quietly, I walked down the hall.

I barely reached the living room when I saw my kid, arm flung over his head, blanket tangled in his legs, pajama top having ridden up his belly, totally out.

I smiled.

Then I slowly, quietly made my way back down the hall and into Merry's room to find him naked and in his walk-in closet.

I hit the door and leaned against the jamb.

"He's out," I shared.

"Told you," he muttered to a suit on a hanger he was jerking across the rung.

"Shower time," I said.

Merry looked to me.

I pushed away from the jamb and walked to the bathroom, discarding my pajamas and panties as I did it.

I made it to the bathroom first.

But it was Merry who turned on the shower.

⌒

I was at the sink in Merry's kitchen.

"Is this your culinary brilliance?"

Merry asked that question and I turned in order to answer him.

But when I turned, I didn't even open my mouth.

I stopped dead.

Because on one side of the kitchen was Merry, leaning against the counter in suit pants, a nice shirt, bare feet crossed at the ankles, a plate held up in front of him holding the eggs, bacon, hash browns, and toast I'd made him and my kid. And on the other side, my boy was leaning against the counter in jeans, a long-sleeved tee, bare feet crossed at the ankles, hair wet, his own plate held up in front of him.

"No, her culinary brilliance is her egg crackers," Ethan answered for me.

"Egg crackers?" Merry asked my kid.

"She'll make it for you tomorrow," Ethan offered my breakfast services on a mutter, shoving hash browns in his face. Still chewing, he finished, "It's her specialty."

I pulled myself together and announced, "It's gross."

My kid looked at me. "You'd think that way. You're a chick. It's dude food."

Dude food.

My son was funny.

I grinned at his funny.

But I said, "Whatever."

Ethan looked to Merry. "Since Mom's on lates, so she can go back to bed and crash, can you take me to school?"

Oh shit.

Even if it was his choice (or more aptly, demand), we were up in Merry's space and in his face.

We didn't need to be crashing in on his life too.

"Yeah," Merry answered unhesitatingly, and looked at me. "Days off tomorrow and Sunday?"

I nodded.

Merry nodded back and turned his attention to his food.

"We gonna have my birthday party here, or we gonna move it to Gram's?" Ethan asked.

Shit. His birthday was next week. And the party invites had gone to school with Ethan three weeks ago. They stated the party was at my pad.

But we weren't at my pad.

Fuck.

"You can have it here," Merry said.

"We'll talk to your gram," I said at the same time.

Merry looked at me. "When is it?"

"Next Saturday."

Merry looked at Ethan. "Thought your birthday was Wednesday, bud."

Ethan beamed at Merry because he remembered his birthday.

Since he was busy beaming, I answered for him, "Birthday's Wednesday. Party's Saturday."

Merry, eyes to me, asked, "Feb's got you scheduled off next Wednesday, yeah?"

I nodded.

"Your mom?" he went on.

I nodded again.

"Right, then I'll make reservations at Swank's."

Ethan's voice was pitched high when he asked, "Say what?"

Shit.

I hadn't talked with Ethan about Swank's yet.

Then again, I hadn't expected Merry and me to make it far enough to get to Swank's without me fucking things up in some way.

But here we were.

Thankfully.

"It's a nice restaurant, kid," I said quickly. "Steaks and—"

"I know what it is!" Ethan cried excitedly. "Brendon's parents take them there New Year's Eve every year. He says you can cut the steaks *with your fork.*" My son looked to my man. "You're takin' us there?"

Merry was grinning at him. "You want that, yeah."

"I want it!" Ethan practically yelled, and looked at me. "This is *so* cool. I can't wait to tell the guys. Brendon is a good guy, but he can also have a stick up his butt 'cause his folks are loaded. He's always talking about stuff that Teddy and Everest and me'll never do 'cause Teddy lives in a double-wide and Everest's dad is a douche. I'm still, like, top of the heap because my mom doesn't make me eat broccoli. But Brendon's breathin' at my neck 'cause he's got a cable premium package *and* Netflix *and* Amazon Instant

Video *and* Hulu. This'll put me over the top. *Way* over the top now since my mom's boyfriend is a badass cop with a killer SUV who lets me hang at the station and takes us for steaks you can cut with a fork. So this…is…*awesome.*"

I didn't know whether to be thrilled to my soul my son was so happy or scared out of my mind that I would undoubtedly someday soon do something to fuck everything up with Merry and me, considering Ethan was in this deep with what Merry and me meant to his place in the middle-school-boy hierarchy.

Before I could make up my mind, Merry got right in there and made it worse.

"Even fearin' spontaneous combustion, bud, you should know I got Netflix and Hulu. I also got the premium package that includes NFL Sunday Ticket."

Ethan's eyes went huge and he breathed, "*NFL Sunday Ticket?*"

"Yep," Merry confirmed.

Breakfast forgotten, slowly, my kid swung his eyes my way.

Yeah, Merry just made it worse.

"Eat," I ordered. "You'll need as much fuel as you can get to rub it in to your friends how awesome you got it. But, just warnin' you, I've been reconsiderin' your diet. That might not mean broccoli, but I see vegetables in your future." I looked to Merry. "That means yours too."

"Mom!" Ethan cried.

"I like vegetables," Merry muttered, and went back to his plate.

Ethan immediately stopped bitching and turned contemplative eyes to Merry.

At least there was that. I didn't know if Merry's proclamation that he liked vegetables would hold sway when Ethan was actually confronted with the real article. But at least it made him think.

"Eat," I repeated my order. "Then you gotta wash up, get your shoes on, and get your stuff so you guys aren't late."

They ate, both my boys leaning against opposite counters in the kitchen of my boyfriend-of-two-weeks' house where we were currently living.

Merry finished first and helped me do the dishes.

Ethan finished next, rinsed his own plate (the plastic kind you got in those sets at Target that cost nearly nothing, looked like shit, and felt like you were only one step up from eating off paper), and put it in the dishwasher.

Merry seriously had to learn the beauty of a yard sale.

"I'll be back," Ethan declared before he dashed to the bathroom in Merry's hallway.

That was when I got in Merry's space.

"Babe, gotta get my shoes and jacket," he muttered even as he rested a hand on my hip.

"You do know you can never—not ever, not *ever*—break up with me now, no matter how I manage to fuck this up, because you just told my kid you have NFL Sunday Ticket," I hissed.

First, Merry's head jerked.

Then he stared down at me.

After that, both his arms closed around me so hard I slammed into his body and lost my breath as he busted out laughing.

I liked the sound. I liked the feel.

But I couldn't breathe.

"Merry, you're squeezing the breath out of me," I gasped.

He instantly let me go. Then, just as instantly, both his hands framed either side of my head and his face was in mine.

"A spectacular early-morning fuck. A long shower. Damned fine eggs and toast. The promise of dude food, whatever the hell that is. And the first time I've laughed before eight o'clock in the morning since I can remember. Cherie, sweetheart, if this is you fuckin' up, keep on doin' it."

Shit, he had to stop.

"God, I'm feeling warm and squishy again," I bitched.

Merry started laughing again.

"Gross! Are you two bein' gooey?" Ethan called with disgust from the living room.

"Yeah," Merry answered, sliding his hands from my head to wrap his arms around me. "Your mom is funny. That deserves gooey."

I stood in Merry's arms, feeling a lot of good things, most of them about what Merry'd said, coupled with his hugs and laughter.

Then I stood and felt other things as I watched my son arrest, just standing there, his face slack, his eyes on us, but they were working.

And then I watched him grin.

Whatever just occurred to him, he intended to keep it to himself, and I knew this when he bounded to the couch I'd told him to fold up (and he did), plopped on it, and reached for his shoes.

"I gotta do the same," Merry said, and I looked to him to see he was looking down on me. "Give me more gooey before I do it."

I slid my eyes to my kid.

He was yanking on his sock.

I slid my eyes to my man.

He was looking at my mouth.

So I rolled up on my toes and gave him gooey by touching my mouth to his.

Merry's eyes were happy and smiling when I rolled back.

Okay, maybe I could do this without fucking it up.

Maybe we could *all* do this without fucking it up.

That thought made me smile back.

This got me a squeeze from my man before he let me go.

He strode out of the kitchen on bare feet, came back in shoes while shrugging on his suit jacket and looking hot, and called out to my boy to get his shit for school and say good-bye to his mom.

Ethan already had his jacket on and was tossing his backpack over his shoulder, calling to me on his way to Merry and the door.

They both smiled and waved at me before they went out. They did this in different ways—Merry's wave was low and cool, his smile handsome and hot; Ethan's wave was high and goofy, his smile warm and sweet.

The door closed behind them.

Honest to God, watching all that, I knew it didn't get warmer and squishier.

It just didn't.

And I couldn't imagine it ever would.

But for the first time in a long time, I was hoping.

Hoping hard.

Hoping I was wrong.

Garrett

Garrett sat in his truck outside Ethan's school, watching the kid bounce toward the building in that way kids walked before they learned cool. Ethan was doing this twisted back toward Garrett, hand up, waving.

Smiling, he lifted his own hand and did a salute.

When he lost sight of Cher's boy as he crawled along in the line of the cars of parents who'd dropped off their kids and were waiting to exit the school, he yanked out his phone and sent her a text.

Ethan's good.

Then he sent another text, this one to Mike.

Gotta do something before I come in. Be there as soon as I can.

He got a text back from Cher as he was sending the one to Mike.

Thanks, baby.

After that, she put a bunch of *x*'s and *o*'s intermingled with some flowers and ended all that, for some strange and hilarious reason, with an emoji of a ghost and one of a flashlight.

This meant he was smiling when he made the call he had to make and put his phone to his ear.

"Yo, son, heard you caught that homicide," Dave Merrick said in greeting.

His father was a retired BPD detective. In other words, with a son on the force and just because he was who he was, he kept in the know.

"Yeah, Dad. Listen, you got some time this morning?" Garrett asked.

"I'm retired, Garrett. What else do I got but time?" Dave answered.

"Gotta swing around," Garrett told him.

"You had breakfast?"

"Cher filled me up."

Dave was silent, which reminded Garrett that in the last few weeks, he had not had a lot of time for his old man.

It was highly likely Dave had heard about Garrett seeing Cher.

But he hadn't heard it from Garrett.

On this thought, the woman behind him in a BMW and a hurry honked. Still crawling with the traffic in front of him, he looked in his rearview mirror to see her gesticulating at him irately, as if he alone was holding up the proceedings.

He started to say something to his dad, but within two seconds, when he didn't make the nine cars in front of him vanish by magic, she honked again and he saw her mouth moving in a way that wasn't hard to lip-read as she continued to gesture. Half a second later, when she caught his eyes in the rearview mirror, she honked at him again and threw both of her hands up in angry exasperation.

He looked to his right to see kids heading into school, some on foot, some parking their bikes on a rack outside, many of them turned to watch the woman.

Seeing this, he put his truck in park, asking his dad, "You gonna be there, I swing around?"

"Yep, son. I'll be here," Dave replied.

"Great. Be there in ten, maybe fifteen," he told him as he threw his door open.

"See you then."

He disconnected as he angled out of his truck, his phone beeping with a text from Mike that Garrett glanced at and saw said, *Gotcha.*

He moved toward her car, and the woman stopped gesticulating and stared at him as he looked beyond her to gesture to the cars waiting to swing out and pass them in order to keep traffic flowing.

He then shoved his phone in his inside jacket pocket, which gave him the opportunity to push his jacket back, exposing his badge on his belt as he dropped his hand and put it on his hip.

He made it to her side of the car and tapped on the window.

It whirred down and she looked out.

"Sorry, didn't know you were police," she muttered, cheeks pink, eyes hidden behind expensive sunglasses even though the sun had barely risen.

But her expression was easily read, showing irritation at the further delay, something she was not going to share to his face, and embarrassment because she'd been caught by a cop who could do something about her being an impatient bitch.

"It make a difference I'm police or not?" he asked.

"I've got an early meeting," she explained. "Dropping off Asa, I'm late for work."

"That might be so, ma'am, but, and I hope you agree with me, you honkin' and behavin' like that in front of a bunch of nine-, ten-, and eleven-year-olds does not teach good lessons. Makin' it worse, nothin' anyone can do to make the drop-off go faster, seein' as there's nowhere anyone can go until it's open to go there. So think it's best you keep your hand off your horn and wait your turn like everyone else."

"They should do something about this," she snapped, flicking a hand at the cars slowly passing them, a long line to get in, the line crawling to get out. "It's like this every day and it's ridiculous."

She was not wrong.

He didn't share he agreed with her.

He stated, "That's not the issue. The issue is, I got a boy in that school and he's of an age where there're a lot of ways he's learnin'. And I don't want him to see folks actin' like you and thinkin' it's okay when it's not. He's gotta learn to be patient, workin' with his fellow citizens to get on in life. If this situation doesn't work for you, take it up with the school or the town or suck it up like everyone else. Don't take it out on other parents who got the same goal as you to get their kids to school safe and get on their way. Yeah?"

"Yes, Officer," she mumbled.

He nodded. "Thanks for your time."

She nodded back.

He walked to his truck, thinking that there was not a lot of joy in his job.

Except when he got to do shit like that.

He got in his truck. It took him all of three minutes to crawl to the exit of the school and pull out.

Then he went to his dad's.

He pulled in the driveway, got out, and made his way up to his dad's house, the house Garrett and Raquel grew up in, the house their mother was murdered in.

He never got why his father didn't sell it before Rocky and him moved out, and he definitely never got why he didn't after.

He also never questioned his dad about it. The Merricks didn't do shit like that.

Which might be one of the reasons why they were all, in their own ways, fucked up.

Dave didn't meet him at the door. It was cold and cold could fuck with Dave and the injuries he'd sustained that had healed okay but not completely when the man who'd murdered Garrett's mother shot his father full of holes.

But when Garrett hit the front door, he found in the time between his phone call and now, his dad had unlocked it.

He went in and called out.

"Kitchen, son!" Dave called back.

Garrett headed to the kitchen and found his old man at the coffeepot.

"Joe?" he asked the pot.

"Yeah," Garrett answered.

His father poured him a cup like he liked it—no milk, two sugars—and Garrett waited to see where he took it—kitchen table, the bar or if he was good to stand, drink and talk.

Garrett knew the cold was fucking with him when his dad took it to the table, handing Garrett his mug on the go.

They sat. Dave stretched out his bad leg and did it almost without wincing.

Watching that, Garrett felt the sour hit his gut. But this was a different kind of sour. One he'd lived with a long time.

"So, seein' Cher Rivers," his dad muttered, lifting his coffee to his lips.

"Yep," Garrett answered, then sipped his own, swallowed, and lowered his mug. "Been busy. No excuse. Since it's serious with Cher, should have found time to connect with you."

Dave's mouth quirked. "My son's finally got a woman in his life with staying power, not sure I'm priority."

Garrett held his eyes. "Like I said, it's serious, Dad."

Dave didn't break eye contact. "Had Devin here a few days ago, drinkin' my bourbon and tellin' me Mia staked a public claim that's no longer hers to stake, doin' it blindsidin' your girl at work. You not there, Tanner took your back...and hers. So, from that, already got it's serious, Garrett."

"She's a good woman."

"Know Cher," Dave returned on a firm nod. "Know that. Know she's got a good kid and Ethan's good 'cause he's got a good mom. Just glad you finally got your head outta your ass, seein' as every time she got anywhere near you, she ratcheted up the tough broad, smartass, cute routine with the sole purpose of makin' you smile at the same time hidin' she was doin' it 'cause you caught hold of her heart."

At his dad's words, his heart clenched.

He didn't know that.

Or, more accurately, he hadn't noticed that.

The Merricks were about family loyalty and being nuts, managing to do those closed off emotionally, which was only part of them being nuts. But Dave was an ex-cop. So not for a second did Garrett doubt what his dad was saying about Cher was true.

"No shit?" he asked quietly.

"This would be the part where my son's head was up his ass, you didn't notice. Think probably the whole 'burg did. But you didn't."

Fuck.

"No one said anything," he noted.

"Boy, Cher's had it bad for you for years. Don't know why no one else said anything. Just know why I didn't. And I woulda said somethin' if I thought you were in the place to do somethin' about it without breakin' her. But I thought you were still tied up in Mia." Another lip quirk before he lifted his coffee mug in a pseudo-toast Garrett's way. "Seein' as you're not, I'll repeat, I'm glad you finally got your head outta your ass."

"Things have not gone smoothly with Cher, and Mia's only part of that," Garrett shared.

Dave shook his head knowingly. "Things that're worth it never do. You got a woman where it goes smooth, you get rid of her. There's no passion in smooth. There's no challenge in smooth. You got smooth, that mean's she's bustin' her ass so you can sail along without a hitch in the road, which in turns means she's all about lookin' after you rather than gettin' what she needs out of the deal. Man's no man at all, he doesn't meet his woman's needs. Woman's no woman at all, she doesn't got it in her to look after gettin' what she needs. That might not make sense to you until you live it, so I'll just boil this down, son. Smooth is boring."

Garrett grinned at his dad. "I wouldn't know. Not sure I've ever had smooth."

His dad shook his head again. "Rough road you've been travelin' wasn't about that. Journey you took with Mia…" He kept shaking his head as he trailed off, then he grinned back. "But a woman who throws down in a bar full of people when she hears your five foot three ex shoved you, that's the good kind of bumpy."

Garrett hadn't heard that. "Cher threw down with Mia because she shoved me?"

"Oh yeah."

It was then, Garrett shook his head but he did it still grinning.

"Lucky for you, you've already proved you're a hardass, so Cher defendin' you at J&J's isn't a hit to your cred," his dad teased.

"She thinks she's the 'burg's tough chick," Garrett told him.

"She's not wrong. Then again, life is life, so in this town, she's got a lot of company."

It felt good to know his old man liked Cher.

But he had to get to work and he had something he needed to get from his father, so he had to get down to it.

"I'm dreamin' about her, Dad," Garrett shared.

Dave's grin turned to a smile. "Now, son, not sure your old man is up for hearin' detail on that."

"No," he said low. "I'm dreamin' her dead."

Dave straightened. He paled. And he shut his mouth.

Garrett straightened too. "Now is not the time to close down on me. I thought I had this mess in my head like Rocky had it in hers—worried, me bein' the man in the situation, the cop, that someone I loved would lose me like she worried Tanner's occupation would take him from her. She was there when what happened to Mom happened, so her mess was compounded by guilt she wasn't able to stop it."

When he mentioned his mom, he saw his father's mouth get tight.

But he didn't quit.

"I'm seein' from these dreams I'm not worried someone will lose me. I'm worried somethin' I do will put Cher in danger."

"Like I did to your mother," Dave forced through tight lips.

"Like what happened to Mom," Garrett returned. "You didn't do it to her. It happened to her."

"Because of what I did."

"Because of what was happening," Garrett said firmly. "You didn't do dick, Dad. Except your job."

Dave stared at him, then shifted irritably in his chair. "You wanna tell me why you're here, goin' over this with me?"

Garrett stared back at his dad, not believing he even asked such a fucked-up question after what had happened when Rocky broke down and Tanner justifiably lost his mind on both his and his father's asses.

Then he said, "Thought that was obvious. I'm here because I'm fallin' in love with a good woman and I wanna hold on this time. She's got a kid, a kid I'm fallin' in love with right alongside her. And she wants more kids, Dad. *My* kids. Unlike Rocky when she was twenty-one years old and she blocked Tanner from her life, not mature enough to deal with all the shit screwing with her head, I'm forty-two and realize I have issues. So I need to find the tools to deal with them so I can make my woman and her son happy. Not tear them apart."

"You're aware of it, just do it," Dave stated.

"The first dream, she was against a wall with a gun in her face—a gun that exploded," Garrett declared.

His father's body gave a small jerk.

That was how his mother had died.

After she had been tortured, that was.

Garrett kept pushing. "Second one, she was like the vic's body I saw yesterday—in a car, covered in blood. You okay with your son havin' those kinds of dreams?"

"See a doctor," Dave clipped. "That helped your sister."

"I don't wanna see a doctor. I want to talk to my dad."

Dave's head twitched before he said, "I don't have those tools to give you, Garrett."

"Yes, you do," Garrett returned.

"If I did, I'd hand them to you."

"You don't hand them to me, if my time comes, how am I gonna hand what I learned to a kid me and Cher make? Ethan's birth father is a moron, the kind he's not gonna turn that around. If this is what I think it is with Cher, the best Ethan's gonna have is me, and gotta tell you, the more I get to know that kid, that honor would be mine. But I gotta do that right. And if there's a time in his life he needs me to be strong for him, teach him how to be that himself, how do I do that if I don't even fuckin' know?"

414

Dave's face twisted.

Garrett leaned toward his father.

"Just tell me it's gonna be okay," he whispered. "Tell me I got this. Tell me I can do my job and keep her safe. I can do my job and keep Ethan safe. What happened to our family is not gonna happen to the family I make. All I need, Dad, is for you to tell me it's gonna be fuckin' *okay*."

"Nothing's gonna happen to you," Dave whispered back. "Nothin's gonna happen to Cher. Fuck, Garrett, you lived your whole life thinkin' that?"

"Right alongside you livin' your whole life feelin' guilt it was your fault that somethin' happened to you. Mom and you. I love you. You're my father. I felt that pain and guilt right with you. And I felt my own pain and guilt bein' powerless to take yours from you. So, shit yeah, Dad. I lived my whole life thinkin' that. No. Not thinkin' it. Emotionally paralyzed because I was terrified of it."

Dave held his gaze, pain and guilt in his eyes.

Fuck.

It never ended.

"Mia, boy...cute. So cute," Dave started.

Garrett did a slow blink as his chin jerked back.

What the fuck?

"Not sweet. Sharp," Dave carried on. "Girl's sense of humor like a razor. Made you happy, oh yeah. She did. Loved seein' my boy happy. But even with that, knew she was wrong. Good-time girl. When bad times came, I knew she didn't have it in her. Your mother woulda put up with her, but she'd never really like her," Dave declared.

Garrett sat back, stunned at hearing shit he'd never heard.

Dave kept going.

"And I was right. She didn't have it in her. She wanted smooth, like her daddy gave to her, which meant you had to bust your ass givin' that to her. You didn't have that in you and that is not a weakness. That's a real man. Like no woman should do that for her man, no man should hafta do that for his woman. And no woman should expect that from a man. A marriage is a partnership. *Both* of you gotta hold on to weather any storm, boy. I was not surprised Mia didn't go the distance. It hurt seein' you hurt. But when you lost her, I wasn't surprised."

415

He stopped speaking and Garrett didn't start. He had nothing to say and he didn't understand why his father was sharing this now when it should have been shared years ago.

Regardless of that, it was beside the point.

Mia was gone. Everyone now got why, and annoyingly, it seemed a bunch of them, including his father, got why a long time ago.

Discussing her did not have dick to do with holding on to Cher.

"Cher Rivers," Dave continued, hopefully getting to the point, "that's a different story. You know it. If you didn't, you wouldn't give a shit about your *issues*. You'd be just as blind, makin' the same mistakes you've been makin' for years and not givin' a shit. If you didn't know she's a different story, you wouldn't be here, askin' an old man who has no idea how to deal how to deal. And the reason I don't have any idea how to deal, Garrett, is because I learned real good how to weather a storm. And how I learned that is that I could face anything, your mother at my side. When I lost her, I lost that ability. I didn't get it back. Any time I tried, it reminded me how much I missed her. So I quit tryin'. I don't know how to tell you how to keep your head together or how to quit havin' those dreams. All I know is that I'd have those answers if your mother was sittin' at this table with me."

Through his dad's words, Garrett felt his throat close.

He also watched his father's eyes get bright and felt wet hit his own.

He didn't move.

He also still didn't speak.

Dave Merrick cleared his throat, sniffed, and kept talking.

"Last thing I gotta say to you is to repeat, Cher Rivers is a different story. You're worried about these issues you got. You're worried you can't get past them. What you don't see is that you got your hands on a woman who knows how to weather a storm. So what you got is a woman who knows about your issues. This means you don't have to do shit, Garrett, except count your lucky stars you're able to hold tight to your woman so you can weather...the goddamned...*storm*."

He knew Dave was done.

Then again, he actually *was* done because, fucking finally, he'd given Garrett just what he needed.

And it was just plain done because he needed his father to point out that Cher had already given him what he needed. And she did this days before, not putting up with the shit he'd pulled at dinner at her mother's house.

But Garrett still couldn't speak because his throat was still closed and he was having trouble with his breathing.

This meant he cleared his throat and sniffed, just like his dad.

"Now, your sister's pregnant again, which fills me with joy," Dave declared. "But she's forty, so I'll be havin' words with Tanner about another go with that because, more time passes, it's gonna start bein' dangerous for her. And anyway, this kid makes four for Tanner and four is enough for any man, for God's sake."

Garrett smiled.

"But I'm not done with grandchildren," Dave kept on. "Lived empty except for you two kids after we lost Cecelia. Time you two did what you can do to fill me up. Cher's young, got a lotta baby makin' in her. But you best get on that because you're no spring chicken and I ain't either."

Garrett stopped smiling even though what Dave said was funny.

He also whispered, "Love you, Dad."

"I know you do, son, and love you too. You make a kid, you'll know just how much," Dave whispered back.

He knew that. His dad didn't say it often, but he didn't shy away from it.

Since Garrett could remember, before his mother died and after, Dave Merrick always showed it.

Talking low, Garrett stated, "You're not to blame about Mom."

Dave didn't reply.

"You aren't, and Rocky and me never blamed you," Garrett went on.

The guilt and pain sat in his dad's eyes where it had been for years, never leaving, never even dulling.

"Mom wouldn't either," Garrett finished. "And you know it."

Surprisingly, his dad spoke then.

"I know it."

At least there was that.

Dave Merrick said no more.

And Garrett had said what he could. Whether his father took it in, that was his choice.

But he'd said what needed to be said.

Father and son sat at the kitchen table, where his mother put flowers as often as she could, and they just looked at each other.

It took a long time to say it and now there was nothing more to say.

But Garrett learned something else right then at that table.

With anything important, it was better late than never.

"I got a homicide to solve," Garrett eventually told his old man.

Dave tipped his head to the table. "Then I got a cup a' joe I best be pourin' in a travel mug."

They got up. His dad poured his coffee in a travel mug. He also walked his son to the door.

"Want Cher and her boy here for dinner, Garrett," Dave ordered. "Soon's you can work that out."

He stopped and looked at his dad, muttering, "You got it."

He moved in, wrapped an arm around his old man, and slapped his back twice.

He got three back.

That was his father; he always bested on the back slaps.

Grinning, Garrett let him go, lifted the mug, and took off out the door.

"Careful out there," Dave called.

"Always," Garrett called back.

He got in his truck and drove to the station.

Count your lucky stars you're able to hold tight to your woman so you can weather the goddamned storm.

Fuck, he missed his mom.

And he had a great dad.

On the way up the back stairs to the bullpen, his phone sounded with a text.

He pulled it out and read, *Eggs and toast are not culinary brilliance. Dinner tonight will be. Warning, I'm introducing vegetables to my kid's diet. Before hitting your pad, please secure an adrenaline shot in case he goes into shock.*

Shit, Cher. Damned funny.

And she had been that way with him since he knew her.

She gave that to everyone else.

But looking back, he'd definitely had his head up his ass. She'd pulled out all the stops to make him laugh, to give him the impression she was just one of the guys but with tits, which meant hiding the fact that he was not like Colt to her. Or Sully. Morrie. Mike. Cal. Tanner. And not because he wasn't married.

Because she was into him.

Shit.

...weather the goddamned storm.

He texted back, *What time you need me home?*

He gave Mike a chin lift as he walked to his desk.

He was seated at it, ready to brief with Mike before they took on their day, when he got back, *It's not me fighting crime. You tell me when and dinner will be ready.*

Will do. But later. Good? he texted back.

You got it, boss, she replied.

"Everything okay?" Mike asked.

He looked to his partner.

"Yes," Garrett answered. That word was solid because he meant it in many ways, not all of which he was going to communicate right then. "You know where I can get an extra bed? Need to convert my second bedroom to an eleven-year-old kid's room."

Mike's lips twitched. After years of his partner being the town player, he thought this was hilarious.

"Nope," he answered. "But I'll ask Dusty. Maybe Rhonda has something."

Garrett nodded and reached out to turn on his computer.

He didn't get there.

"You hear from Ryker?" Mike asked.

"No," Garrett answered.

"Time to try and hit Cutler again?" Mike asked.

"Absolutely," Garrett answered.

Mike got up.

Garrett got up without even turning on his computer.

They went to the sedan.

And that day, Garrett drove.

Twenty

MATCHMAKER
Garrett

In the bullpen, Mike stood three feet from the whiteboard, staring at it. Garrett sat on the side of his desk, also staring at it.

Sean and Drew stood close, staring at the board too.

At the top was a long horizontal line, short vertical dashes on the line.

Close to the right edge and under a dash, on three lines, it said, *4:30 a.m. gunshots heard, time of death.*

Next to that, under a dash, two lines said, *4:39 a.m., 911 call.*

The space between those times and the time Wendy left work as well as the space after those times was empty—except for question marks.

Stuck to the board, there were driver's license photos of Wendy Derian and Jaden Cutler. There were also crime scene photos of her, her Fiesta, and four shell casings on the pavement outside her Fiesta.

Marscha had heard it right; Wendy had been hit three times. Jake found another bullet lodged close to the gear shift.

Either a warning shot or a miss.

In the top right-hand corner, it said, *Cell phone?*

Other than that, there was nothing.

Dick.

Their trip to Cutler's that morning bought them the same. He still wasn't there.

"Fuck, we got dick," Mike muttered.

"You got dick," Drew confirmed.

They all stared at the board.

"Seriously," Drew kept on. "I don't think I've ever seen a board so empty."

Garrett watched Mike turn annoyed eyes at his colleague.

"Can't go to Carlito 'cause no one mentioned him," Sean remarked, eyes still to the board. "Can't go to any of Cutler's associates because no one has mentioned them either."

"Not like those guys aren't used to fishing expeditions," Mike returned, turning his eyes to Garrett. "They're known associates. One of their own lost his girl. We're just looking for any information we can find." He tipped his chin up to Garrett. "Game?" he asked just when the phone on Garrett's desk went.

Game to possibly stir up a hornet's nest they had no idea what was buzzing around it?

"Fuck yeah," he answered Mike, looking at his phone. The display said it was reception. "Just a sec. It's Kath," he said, and took the call. "Merrick."

"Uh…sorry, Merry," Kath replied, for some reason sounding like she was talking under her breath. "But Justin McClintock is here and he says he wants to talk to you."

Garrett stared unseeing at the phone.

He could not believe this shit.

"I'm in the middle of a murder investigation, Kath," he told their girl downstairs something she knew.

"I explained that, but Merry, he demanded to have a word, he didn't back down when I shared that tidbit, and he seems kind of…perturbed."

Goddammit.

He did not need this.

And what this was, was Mia's dad coming to Garrett's place of work to get in his face in an effort to give his daughter what she wanted.

Eyes to Mike, Garrett said into the phone, "Reiterate to him I've got important shit I gotta see to in order to solve a murder. I'm comin' down, but he's only got five minutes."

"Will do," she replied, and disconnected.

Garrett put his phone in the cradle. "Mia's dad's downstairs and Kath says he's 'perturbed.' I gotta give him five minutes, then we can go."

Now Mike was perturbed.

"Her dad? Jesus, how old is she?" Mike asked.

"You spoil a kid like McClintock spoiled his daughter, I'm findin' she never grows up," Garrett replied, straightening from the desk, snatching his suit jacket from the back of his chair, and shrugging it on as he headed to the stairs that led down to the reception area.

He saw McClintock pacing just inside the front doors.

Both of Mia's parents were height challenged—her mom Mia's height, her dad about five foot five.

In life, this gave Justin McClintock something to prove.

It had served him well, because in business, the man took no prisoners. He wasn't completely loaded, but he was far from hurting. He drove a Lexus. His wife drove a Jag. They still lived in a big house in a nice development even though their daughter and two sons had long since moved out.

And he gave his daughter a piece of jewelry, the like Garrett learned early he could never compete with, doing that every year, birthday and Christmas.

In the beginning, Garrett had given her other things. He'd made her laugh, made her happy. They were living the good life and he was a part of that, so this wasn't a problem; if they had that, he didn't care if her father gave her jewelry.

But in the end, they'd fought about it because he'd used something he didn't care smack about to drive the wedge he was building between them deeper.

Mia had never asked her dad to lay off, though. She took the diamonds. The emeralds. The tennis bracelets. And she did it with glee, right in front of her husband, even after he'd laid it out—no matter how fucked up it was or how false—that he hated that shit.

Christ, but it seemed he hadn't paid attention at all.

Walking down the stairs, watching Mia's father turn angry eyes to him, and all he felt was relief that Cher's father wasn't in the picture.

And that he'd finally started paying attention.

He glanced at Kath as he walked by her, giving her a look that said he'd rather not have an audience for this.

She read his look, gave a short nod, grabbed some papers off her desk, and hurried toward the copy machine.

Garrett looked to McClintock. "Justin. Sorry, you picked a bad time."

Justin puffed up his chest and skewered Garrett with his eyes. "Don't give a shit if it's a bad time, Garrett."

His tone was antagonistic.

Garrett stopped three paces from him.

"Right. I'm down here outta respect but also to share we're not only not gonna do this now, we're not ever gonna do this."

His tone was steel.

McClintock took a step toward him. "You think that, you think wrong."

"Okay, then, Justin. How about after I wrap up a homicide investigation, I go to your office and we have whatever this is out on your turf?" Garrett suggested sarcastically.

"You fuck with my daughter, you don't get to fuck with me. *I* fuck with *you*," McClintock snapped.

Garrett crossed his arms on his chest. "I see Mia's told you some tales, so I'll give this the time it takes to set that straight. Your daughter and I divorced five years ago. I'm now in a serious relationship with another woman. Mia's not in my life and hasn't been in my life in any kind of healthy way for half a decade, so she doesn't get any say about who *is* in my life. That's it. There's nothin' more to it."

"Mia's shared how you've been stringing her along in a *very* unhealthy way. Those're the 'tales' she's been telling, Merrick," McClintock returned. "Now, are you saying my daughter's a liar?"

If Mia shared that kind of thing with her father, it was clear that the fucked-up non-relationship he'd had with his ex for five years after their divorce wasn't the only unhealthy relationship in her life.

"I'm saying the relationship we have is none of your business," Garrett shot back. "It wasn't when we were married. It wasn't after we were divorced. And the absolute lack of one now is the definition of it being none of your business."

"I beg to differ when my daughter has quit her job, taken her house off the market, as well as broken off her engagement with another man all because she's committed to helping her husband get his head sorted out. And while she's committed to that and has shared that with you, you're not only spending time with the town slut, word is, you've moved her in with—"

McClintock didn't finish.

This was because Garrett moved and did it aggressively, backing McClintock up until he hit the connected bench of chairs that ran the front of the reception area. And he did this with such speed, McClintock's ass crashed into a seat.

Looking up at Garrett, his face paled with fear before it reddened with bluster and he opened his mouth to speak.

Garrett leaned so they were nose-to-nose and beat him to it.

"Have you met Cher Rivers?" he growled.

"I don't need to—"

"If you've never met her, you don't know fuck all about her. So you sure as fuck don't talk that kind of trash about her."

McClintock was shifting in his seat, all bluster now, demanding, "Step back, Garrett."

He didn't step back.

Garrett declared, "It's a sad thing to say about a woman her age, but the God's honest truth is, your daughter is a spoiled-rotten brat."

He lifted a hand and jabbed his finger an inch from McClintock's face, savoring the flash of fear he saw before the bluster shot back when his eyes narrowed.

On his jab, he went on.

"*You* created that. The woman is in her late thirties and her daddy is still out bustin' his ass and makin' himself look a fool to get her what she wants. Since she hasn't already done it, the time is now for her to grow the fuck up and learn to take care of herself. Even more, she needs to learn to take care of the things in her life that mean something. The age she is, Justin, if *she* doesn't do that shit, she's gonna lose those things and you can't do jack to get them back for her, case in point, Mia not fighting for her marriage and only deciding she's willin' to do that when it's way too fuckin' late."

"You need to step back," McClintock spat.

Garrett straightened, but he didn't step back. This meant McClintock had to get out of the seat while shifting to the side to avoid hitting Garrett's body. He did that and Garrett turned to him just as his phone in his jacket started ringing.

He wanted to take the call. With his work and a woman in his life, that woman having a son, he might even need to take the call.

He unfortunately had to get this done, so he didn't take the call.

"We'll see what your captain thinks of you assailing a citizen right in the reception area of the goddamned station," McClintock threatened.

"As it's a *police* station, we have cameras. Those will show I didn't touch you. I also didn't demand to speak to you. I didn't show at your place of business, interrupt your pursuit of doing that business, and do it uttering slurs against a woman who means something to you. Feel free to discuss this with my captain. He'll give you the respect of listening to you without laughing to your face. Then he won't do dick."

Garrett's phone stopped ringing.

McClintock's enraged look turned nasty. "I cannot believe I'm looking at the man I happily walked my daughter down the aisle and gave her away to. She's hurting...because of you. Her life's in a shambles...because of you. She—"

Garrett took a step back and planted his hands on his hips, interrupting, "Listen to yourself, Justin. I did not give a ring to another woman, then go to Mia with what amounts to a dare to win her back or lose her forever. I didn't find out she became involved with another man, *happily* involved, and seek her out to share I was ready, after five years, to try and resurrect our marriage. After repeated warnings that all between us was good and dead with no hope of resurrection, I didn't go to her man's place of business and cause a scene."

As Garrett spoke, McClintock's face got tighter and tighter.

He might spoil his daughter, but he wasn't stupid. As Garrett gave him the words, he was realizing Mia had made her own bed.

But Garrett wasn't even close to done.

"*She* quit her job to move to Bloomington to start her life with another man. *She* took her house off the market and ended her engagement; I didn't ask her to. It might be way too late for her to learn lessons you never taught

425

her, but I found out just this morning, when it's important, it's better late than never. You gotta let her sort out her own mistakes. If you don't, she'll never learn."

It seemed like his words had been sinking in, but his advice hit a brick wall. McClintock might not be stupid, but he was when it came to his daughter. Garrett knew this when he saw the stubborn set in McClintock's jaw.

Not his problem.

But it was time to sum up.

"The only thing I know right now is, no matter what you say or do, your daughter and I are done. I've moved on in a way there is no going back. So, however this gets sorted, Justin, don't drag me into it because, like Mia, the problems she's created for herself have fuck all to do with me."

"So much for 'to have and to hold, for better or for worse, until death do you part,'" McClintock sniped.

Garrett sighed, not about to get into explaining the concept of divorce to a stubborn man.

He was done.

"If that's all you got, Justin, I got a killer to catch."

"When you come to your senses, Garrett, and try to get my daughter back, do not expect me to be your champion," he warned.

Garrett very nearly rolled his eyes, and he didn't think he'd rolled his eyes since he was about twelve years old.

"Consider me informed," Garrett muttered.

They stared at each other and Garrett did it with his face set studiously blank.

He did this to hide the fact that he didn't like this because he'd always liked Mia's father.

He spoiled the girls in his life, but he was a good guy. Funny. He told a great joke, was usually in a mood that could only be described as jovial, and he'd liked and accepted Garrett easily. His continuing to spoil his daughter when she was Garrett's wife was marginally uncool, but it wasn't heinous. And when the marriage finally disintegrated, he'd only sought Garrett out once to have a chat with him, hoping his intervention might get Garrett's head out of his ass.

That chat had gone entirely differently than this one.

Garrett hadn't relented then when McClintock had shown him patience and respect.

He didn't relent now either, and it wasn't because McClintock had not shown patience or respect.

It sucked that the vague but benign ending to Justin McClintock being in his life had turned malignant.

But it was what it was, and frankly, the way father and daughter were behaving, he didn't give a fuck.

His phone beeped with a message and Garrett decided the staring contest was over.

"Be well, Justin," he muttered, turning as he reached into his jacket to pull out his phone.

He'd taken one step away from McClintock when the man called his name.

Garrett drew in a calming breath and turned back.

"She loves you," McClintock said quietly. "Loves you like you wouldn't believe."

Out of respect for a decent man, just a shit father, he replied quietly, "If she did it the way we both needed it, Justin, she would have weathered the storm."

McClintock flinched.

That got in there.

Yeah, he wasn't stupid. He'd raised a weak daughter. One who had no idea how to fight her own battles. One who had no idea how to hold on.

Not all McClintock's fault. Mia was an adult.

But he hadn't helped.

"Like I said, and I meant it, be well," Garrett repeated, then he turned and jogged up the steps so McClintock couldn't suck any more of his time.

As he went, he saw the voicemail was from Tanner. At the top of the steps, he slid his thumb across the cracked screen as he glanced toward Mike, lifting his chin to say he was ready to roll.

He put the phone to his ear, moving to his desk to nab the car keys.

"Merry, brother, don't know what you're doin' but need you at my office as soon as you can get here. Found Ryker, or I should say, Ryker found me. He's got company. They've all got a story to tell and these stories are ones both you and Mike are not gonna wanna wait too long to hear. Give me a call and then get your ass over here. They don't got a lot of time and you need to hear it before that time runs out and they take off."

While listening, Garrett had stopped not only because he got the news that the vanished Ryker had resurfaced and all the other things his brother-in-law had shared, but because Tanner's voice sounded strange.

It sounded like he was close to laughing.

He took the phone from his ear and looked to his partner.

"Ryker's at Tanner's office," he told Mike.

Up from his desk, ready to go, Mike's brows rose. "No shit?"

"They've got someone with them and Tanner said we need to get there ASAP."

"Then let's go."

They headed to the front stairs, Garrett texting Tanner, *On our way.*

"Things go okay with Mia's dad?" Mike asked as they moved down the steps, both their eyes scanning the area at the bottom to see Kath back at her desk and Justin McClintock gone.

"No. But it went," Garrett answered.

Mike didn't reply. Then again, there wasn't much more for Garrett to say.

On the sidewalk, as they hoofed their way down the block toward Tanner's office, they had a brief discussion about the fact that they'd be swinging by Mimi's to get a coffee on their way back.

This being after Mike and Tanner hopefully successfully stopped Garrett from going apeshit on Ryker.

They hit the door next to Mimi's that had a brass plaque next to it that read TANNER LAYNE INVESTIGATIONS. The door led right to a set of stairs. The stairs led to a landing and one door, that door belonging to Tanner's offices.

They pushed through, moved through the reception area, walked into Tanner's personal office situated at the front of the building, and both of them stopped dead.

Even though he felt the pulse of alertness beat off Mike, Garrett reckoned it was only him whose vision went blurry with rage.

This was because Ryker's long, beefy frame was lounging negligently in a chair in front of Tanner's desk and he was eating a Hilligoss powdered sugar, chocolate-buttercream-filled donut. The donut wasn't his first, seeing as his lips were lined with sugar and that sugar liberally dusted the front of his black tank as well as the lapels of his leather jacket.

He looked like he just got back from vacation and they were all there to check out his pictures, not like Garrett had been looking for his ass for days and in the meantime a woman who was linked, however loosely, to his shit got dead.

But this wasn't it.

Along with Ryker and Tanner, who was sitting behind his desk, there were two people Garrett had never seen before in the room. A man and a woman. They were both in suits. Both trim and fit. And both, without a doubt, Feds.

The woman was at the window farthest from Tanner's desk, looking out. The male Fed was in the middle of the office, standing close to the final occupant in the room, which was the last part of what pissed Garrett off.

Jaden Cutler.

"What the fuck?" Garrett whispered.

"Stay cool, brother," Tanner warned, but when Garrett tore his eyes off Cutler to look to his friend, he saw Tanner's eyes were filled with humor he was barely able to hold back. "And just to say, you're gonna wanna lose it even more than you do right now after you hear what you're gonna hear. It's just that you'll eventually find it amusing. Trust me."

Garrett ignored Tanner and looked to Ryker.

"Been lookin' for you," he said.

"Know that, bro," Ryker replied casually through donut dough and buttercream.

Garrett turned his attention to Cutler. "Been lookin' for you too."

Cutler did not look like he'd been on vacation. As Garrett pushed through his anger, he saw Cutler looked wrecked.

But he said nothing.

The male Fed entered the conversation. "Lieutenant Merrick…Haines, I'm Special Agent Jeff Harleman." He tipped his head to the woman. "That's Special Agent Tiffany Faria. What we're about to explain is need-to-know. Since you're investigating the murder of Wendy Derian, you need to know. However, it would be a significant blow to our investigation and strain relations between our organizations if you speak to anyone about what we're about to tell you. That said, our hope is that you won't have to keep this confidential for long."

"We got relations between our organizations?" Mike asked a pertinent question.

"Not exactly," Agent Tiffany Faria put in. "Though, we do have relations with IMDB and they're in communication with your captain. So, although the Brownsburg Police Department isn't a partner in this investigation, those who need to know are aware of what needs to be known."

Garrett kept a lock on his irritation at the ridiculousness of how the Feds were communicating.

Instead, he focused on irritation he was practiced at controlling, thinking about their captain.

The man had become more politician than policeman. The fact that the Feds were operating even minutely on their patch and he hadn't shared it with his officers was not a surprise.

It was fucking annoying.

But it wasn't a surprise.

This was because if he shared it with his team, he couldn't claim total responsibility for whatever bust went down, even if the only thing he did was pick up the phone and listen to the Feds tell him to steer his officers clear of any part of the investigation they were pursuing.

Yes.

Fucking annoying.

"Seein' as clearly something that has to do with something you're doin' got Wendy Derian dead on BPD's patch, how about you make us aware of what needs to be known," Garrett clipped.

He was speaking to the agents.

But it wasn't lost on him that anytime Wendy's homicide was mentioned, Cutler, who was seriously unhappy, looked unhappier.

Both Faria and Harleman nodded, but it was Harleman who spoke.

"We currently have a large RICO investigation going against Carlos 'Carlito' Gutierrez."

Fuck.

Carlito worked a wide area and only a small part of it was Hendricks County, a lesser part of that the 'burg. The Feds would follow all leads but focus on the largest part of his operation, which was in Indy.

"This investigation has been ongoing for a year and a half," Harleman continued. "We've made allegiances with a variety of players and one of those players is Mr. Ryker, who's acting as a confidential informant."

Garrett cut a glance to Ryker, but this was not a surprise.

Ryker did not consider himself a rat and he'd probably rip your face off if you even suggested it.

As his profession, Ryker sold information and everyone was in the know about that. If you didn't want him in your business, you did everything you could to keep him out. It was just that he had an uncanny talent for finding ways in.

If he liked you, though, he protected you and kept what he knew about you close. He'd never breathe a word, not even under torture.

Ryker didn't like many people.

And as far as Garrett knew, the person he hated most was Carlito.

"As Gutierrez and Mr. Ryker are not the best of friends, and Mr. Ryker has a special skillset of which I'm told you're aware, he's been a significant asset in our investigation," Harleman shared. "We were getting close to an arrest, and in order to dot some *i*'s, we needed Mr. Ryker to secure someone closer to Gutierrez's operations. Mr. Cutler works with Gutierrez. However, he owed Mr. Ryker a variety of markers. Mr. Ryker acted as go-between, striking this deal for us that Cutler inform from the inside."

Garrett's gaze cut quicker back to Ryker. "You're workin' with this guy?"

"He's a fuckwit," Ryker replied. "But he's also a means to an end."

"Fuck you," Cutler spat.

"Don't turn my stomach with dirty talk like that when I just ate five Hilligoss, assclown," Ryker returned.

"Gentlemen," Faria murmured warningly.

"Obviously, no love lost between you and Cutler," Mike noted to Ryker. "But maybe you'll explain what end you're lookin' for."

"Not a big fan of Carlito," Ryker grunted.

"Not askin' for shit I know," Mike returned. "You haven't been a big fan for years, Ryker, and those years runs longer than your deal with the Feds."

Ryker leveled his eyes on Mike. "Done dickin' with him. It's time he went away."

"This mean now, at long last, you're gonna share your beef?" Mike asked.

All attention, especially that of Tanner, Mike, and Garrett, none of whom knew what went down with Ryker and Carlito, which meant all of whom were curious, turned acute on Ryker.

"He dicked with me," Ryker stated. "You are in the know, bro. You dick with me, I dick back."

Shit.

That gave them nothing.

Mike wisely decided to let that go. Whatever went down between them for Ryker to get in bed with the Feds would stay where Ryker wanted it to stay until he was ready to share.

Buried.

So Mike turned to Jaden Cutler.

"It's clear you're aware, Mr. Cutler, that your ex-girlfriend was murdered yesterday," Mike noted carefully.

"Yeah," he grunted.

"Do you believe Ms. Derian's death has anything to do with your dealings with Carlito Gutierrez?" Mike asked.

Cutler's face got red.

And it shocked the shit out of him when Garrett saw the pain.

"It don't got shit to do with Wendy the way you think," he bit out. "Good through and through, my Wendy."

His Wendy?

Garrett looked to Mike.

Mike looked to Garrett.

Garrett then turned his eyes to Cutler. "It's our understanding you had ended things with Ms. Derian."

"Well, yeah," he drawled sarcastically. "Seein' my ass is in a sling with all this shit with Carlito. Feds up in my shit. Ryker up in my shit. If Carlito found out I'm a rat, no tellin' what he'd do, just know that shit would be jacked up and it'd hit wherever the fuck he wanted it to hit." He turned wounded, angry, narrowed eyes to Harleman. "Just like it hit."

"That was unfortunate," Harleman muttered uncomfortably.

Garrett felt that in his throat and turned to look at Mike, who had his brows raised and his eyes locked to Harleman. Then Garrett turned his attention to Tanner, who no longer looked amused and was shaking his head at Garrett.

"Yeah. Fuckin' *unfortunate*," Cutler fired back in a way that made Garrett return his attention to him. It was also in a way that Faria moved closer to him and Tanner rolled his chair to the side, alert, in case Cutler lost it.

"At the risk of this guy losin' his mind, which, from what I'm gettin' from this shit, he's got the right, you wanna explain what the fuck is goin' on?" Mike asked.

"Stay cool, Cutler," Tanner warned.

Cutler glared at Harleman. Then he turned his head and glared at Tanner.

After that, he stood down, doing that by dropping his head to stare at his feet.

Garrett studied him, thinking if anyone had told him he'd ever feel sorry for that guy, he would have told them they were crazy.

But at that look of sorrow, helplessness, and defeat, he felt sorry for the guy.

"We're unaware of exactly what Wendy Derian had to talk with Carlos Gutierrez about," Harleman began to explain. "We have Cutler and another informant inside his operation, some bugs, and eyes on Gutierrez and his men. Even with all that, we were unable to hear what was said. We just know that Ms. Derian spent quite a bit of time hitting various players in Gutierrez's operation late Tuesday night through early Wednesday morning until she was able to secure a face-to-face with Gutierrez. Their meeting lasted just over fifteen minutes. She left and did it in a hurry." Harleman's eyes slid to Cutler as he finished cautiously, "Clearly, whatever she had to say displeased Gutierrez. It's our belief, at his order, one of Gutierrez's soldiers followed her and wasted very little time taking care of what had become a problem."

At the last, Cutler's head came up, his jaw hard, a muscle jumping in it as he pierced Harleman with his stare.

"You didn't follow her?" Mike asked Harleman with annoyed disbelief.

"Ms. Derian was not a part of our investigation." Harleman's eyes again slid to Cutler briefly before he finished, "Part of the deal. She knew nothing of importance. She stays out of it. She stays uninformed. She lives her life untouched by this mess."

"That didn't work." Mike's words were now just annoyed.

Harleman gave him an aggravated look, but his stance remained uncomfortable.

They'd fucked up.

Huge.

Everyone knew it. It was time to move on.

"You know what she talked to him about?" Garrett asked Cutler.

Cutler looked to Garrett. "I disappeared. I broke shit off when we were good. She didn't want that. I didn't want that. She didn't know any of this mess was happenin'. She knew I worked for Carlito. She was probably just tryin' to find me," Cutler answered.

"And Carlito ordered a hit on her for trying to find you?" Garrett pushed.

"Yeah, man, *'cause I disappeared.* Carlito likes to know where his boys are." He jerked his head Harleman and Faria's way. "Assholes yanked me. Carlito no doubt got tweaked. Doin' Wendy coulda been a message or he figured I shared and thought she knew somethin'. She's sweet, but she can be not so smart. She coulda even made some fucked-up play, thinkin' she could scare Carlito into tellin' her where I was. Doesn't matter though, does it? My woman is dead."

It did matter. The cop in him had a need to know.

But the man in him looked into Cutler's eyes and decided not to push further.

He turned to Harleman.

"Do you know which soldier?" Garrett asked.

Harleman shifted, alert to Cutler but eyes on Garrett. "We know which ones were unaccounted for, so we have our suspicions."

"You gonna share those with us?" Garrett pushed.

"Not at the present time," Harleman answered, and both Harleman and Faria became more alert as they faced a room with a pained and pissed Cutler and two cops investigating a homicide with uncooperative Feds not handing over crucial information.

"With chatter we've been hearing since Ms. Derian's death, concerns we had that led us to yank him have been confirmed—Mr. Cutler is blown,"

Faria told them. "He's emphasized that he did not share with Ms. Derian he was working with us and we're apt to believe that because, before Ms. Derian even sought an audience with Gutierrez, Gutierrez hired a man I believe you know named Ryan Danvers to surveil Cutler."

Jesus, Ryan wasn't working for Ryker?

Shit.

Ryan had never said he was working for Ryker. Cher had. Ryan had just said he was working for a scary guy who he didn't want to give up.

And Carlito Gutierrez was a scary guy. Unless you had a solid deal with the Feds or a beef with him and were capable of laughing in the face of death like Ryker, you didn't give him up.

"Right now, Gutierrez is scrambling," Faria carried on. "We're coordinating our men to make arrests before that scrambling takes anyone to Mexico. In the meantime, we need to get Mr. Cutler into protective custody. This is something that's being arranged as we speak. And when the arrests are made, something we hope will happen this afternoon, we'll turn over what we know about who may have killed Wendy Derian."

"As you can see, we're up to our necks in it. Lots of shit to do and not a lot of time to do it. So this, right here, is a courtesy," Harleman added, pointing to the floor to indicate the meet. "With that, we're askin' you to return it and curtail your investigation until this afternoon."

"A courtesy," Mike muttered irritably.

Garrett was irritated too.

However, he, like Mike, was aware that the RICO case took precedence and there was no way in hell their cap would let them push the homicide at this juncture. But it didn't matter. They wouldn't do it anyway. Especially not when their suspects would be hand delivered within hours.

So he didn't focus on that.

He looked to Tanner and asked, "How is any of this funny?"

"None of that is," Tanner replied.

"So what's funny?" Garrett asked.

"Bro, serious as shit, you were hung up on that ex-twat of yours and takin' way too long."

This came from Ryker, and it was so out of left field considering what was being discussed, Garrett braced.

"Come again?" he asked Ryker, who was looking up at him from his chair, mouth wiped clean but powdered sugar still all down his front.

"It was drivin' Lissa crazy," Ryker said in answer, an answer that wasn't an answer.

"Explain, Ryker," Garrett clipped.

"Two birds." He tipped his head to Cutler. "One stone."

"Come..." Garrett bent slightly toward Ryker. "*Again?*"

"Right, son, Cher's so into you, the minute you hit that bar, it was lit up in neon, right there in front of your face for everyone to read," Ryker declared.

Garrett's body got tight.

"Everyone but you," Ryker carried on. "You were so hung up on your ex, completely fuckin' blind. Finally, that woman tags another guy with her ball and chain, you pull your head outta your ass long enough to tap Cher's. Problem is, after, you two start fuckin' shit up. Lissa got worried. So when Cher called me and she heard shit comin' down the way from someone I got on a string..."

He shrugged, threw out a hand, and said no more.

Garrett clenched his teeth.

Tanner urged helpfully, "Think the man needs more, Ryker."

"Fuck, gotta spell it out? Okay," Ryker muttered impatiently.

He straightened in his chair and looked back up at Garrett.

"I made a big deal of it, but it wasn't a big deal." He tossed a beefy mitt Cutler's way. "He's an assclown and he *was* part of Carlito's operation before and after he turned rat. But that didn't have shit to do with shit. I made a big deal of it, freakin Cher out, thinkin' once you got wind of it, *you'd* make a big deal of it and swoop in to the rescue. Don't know what the fuck happened with that 'cause it took you a long time to get wind of it. Doesn't matter. I'll point out now I wasn't wrong, seein' as shit went down and now she and her kid are livin' with you. This means *both* your heads are outta your asses and my job is done."

Garrett stared at Ryker.

"Lissa's over the moon, which translates to more blowjobs for her old man, and seein' as my baby's got unqualified talent in that arena, I'm thinkin' this matchmaking shit is gonna be my new gig," Ryker finished.

"You lied to Cher in order to freak her out, which you hoped in turn would tweak me so I'd protect her and Ethan?" Garrett said low.

"Merry, brother," Tanner put in calmingly, and Garrett could hear him straightening from his chair, but he didn't take his eyes off Ryker. "You give this a second, you'll see this is the amusing part."

Garrett didn't give it a second.

"You lied to Cher in order to freak her out," he stated.

"Dude, heard you saw to this, but in case you didn't get it through to her, your bitch needs to learn to share. No way I'd be down with Lissa keepin' somethin' like that from me, even if I'd lose my motherfuckin' mind, I knew what it was. There's a firmer foundation in a relationship if there's open communication," Ryker advised.

"You are sittin' right there, giving me relationship advice." With his remark, Garrett's voice was not just low, it was vibrating.

Ryker's brows went up. "You get laid last night?"

Garrett stared at him.

"This morning?" Ryker pushed.

He felt Mike close to his side.

"Yeah," Ryker muttered, grinning a lunatic grin, eyes locked to Garrett. "I woulda bet with her dry spell, Cher likes it like that. Catchin' up."

In a blink, Garrett had shoved Mike off and was leaning over Ryker, who he had pressed to the top of Tanner's desk, Garrett's fist in his tank, both of Ryker's hands wrapped around Garrett's wrist.

"Stand down, Merry," Mike warned.

"You played head games with my woman?" Garrett whispered.

"Dude, get off me," Ryker whispered back.

"You played...head games...*with my woman*," Garrett growled.

"Brother, calm down," Tanner ordered.

"Lissa likes you both," Ryker told him. "She wanted you happy. She wanted you happy with each other. And I want my woman happy. So I did what I did to make her happy and you and your woman got what you deserved outta that. Now, with all that, what the fuck's your problem?"

"Did you tell that guy to hit on her?" Garrett asked.

"Fuck yeah," Ryker answered. "*Hello?*" he called sarcastically. "You were *taking too long*. Fuck, after you nailed her the first time, it took you over a fuckin' week to take the bitch on a date."

Garrett drew in a sharp breath through his nose.

437

"Let him up, Merry," Mike urged.

He stared Ryker in the eye, knowing if Ryker wanted to throw down, things would be messy and no way could Garrett pin him to the desk for this long.

He didn't need messy.

He was not close to finding this amusing, but he had culinary brilliance to look forward to that night and he didn't want to do it through cut lips.

He straightened, pulling Ryker with him.

He let him go and stepped away.

Ryker gave him a scowl, then looked down to smooth his tank.

His head shot right back up. "Fuck, why didn't anyone tell me I got powdered sugar on my tank?"

"For fuck's sake," Tanner muttered.

Garrett looked to Cutler. "You broke it off with Wendy to keep her safe."

Cutler was not enjoying the show. Cutler wasn't looking forward to going where he was soon going to go. Cutler was undoubtedly eventually going into WITSEC so he'd soon stop being Jaden Cutler in order to start being another guy in another town, starting from scratch and hoping like fuck Carlito never tracked him down. Cutler was also not looking forward to doing what he undoubtedly made a deal to do—testify against Carlito.

And Cutler was grieving the death of a woman he cared about.

"Didn't work," he grunted.

Garrett eyed him.

Then he muttered, "Sorry for your loss."

"Sorry I fucked with you and your woman," Cutler returned, his eyes sliding to Ryker then back to Garrett. "But you get in deep with *that* motherfucker, you gotta suck up whatever markers he calls."

After he said that, he lifted his hands to indicate the room, which clearly said the state of play with the Feds and him was all Ryker.

"Ride's here, Jeff," Faria announced.

"We done?" Harleman asked, his gaze swinging between Mike and Garrett.

"We'll have a chat with our cap and expect a phone call later this afternoon," Mike answered.

"Hope you'll get one, which means we'll be done," Harleman murmured, looked to Cutler and said, "Let's go."

Cutler moved, not surprisingly, without handing out hugs or heartfelt good-byes.

Harleman moved with him.

Tanner, Ryker, Mike, and Garrett watched.

Faria dragged her heels.

They heard the door to the offices close behind Harleman and Cutler and then they saw Faria stick her head back through Tanner's office door.

She looked to Garrett.

"You won't find this amusing either, but that doesn't mean it's not interesting. Name you're gonna get on who did your vic is a name you ran four days ago. We couldn't say it so Cutler wouldn't know it. We only lost track of one soldier Wednesday morning. It was Paxton who did your girl."

With that, she took off.

"Fuckin' hell," Garrett muttered.

"Not that I give a shit," Ryker started, and Garrett swung his attention to him to see the big man looking at him, "but Lissa'll be pissed if she's uninvited to Ethan's birthday party. We good?"

"We aren't," Garrett answered immediately. "But I'll suck it up and pretend so Ethan can have whatever present Lissa buys him."

"Good call. She's generous," Ryker muttered.

"I know," Garrett muttered back.

"What I wanna know," Mike stated at this point, eyes to Ryker, "is how you got the balls to buy Hilligoss prior to a meeting and not bring enough for everyone?"

"Place ain't closed. You want a donut, go buy a donut," Ryker shot back.

"It's common decency, man," Mike returned.

"I ain't common and I ain't decent," Ryker decreed.

No truer words were spoken.

"Just sayin', we all got shit to do, so how 'bout we all go our ways and do it?" Tanner suggested.

"Good idea," Garrett agreed.

He and Mike headed to the door.

As they did, Garrett made no reply and just kept on walking when Ryker called out, "You can thank me later, sport."

They were in line at Mimi's when Mike started chuckling.

"Don't start," Garrett warned.

"Jesus. Ryker, a matchmaker," Mike murmured, the words shaking with humor.

As they hit the front of the line, Garrett lifted his chin to the girl behind the counter, who had blue hair, and said to Mike, "He sucks at it."

"Don't know, Merry, you get laid last night?"

Garrett turned to Mike.

"This morning?" Mike asked.

Garrett said nothing.

Mike watched his partner be silent a beat.

Then Mike burst out laughing.

Garrett had the door to his condo open barely an inch before the smell assaulted him.

He didn't even have to eat it to know it was brilliant.

He pushed through, saw Cher in his kitchen, Ethan on his couch, and two sets of bright, happy brown eyes turned his way.

One set smiled.

The other did as well.

But the mouth under it shouted, "Merry! Guess what?"

He grinned at his woman, then turned that grin to her son.

"What, bud?" he asked, throwing the door closed behind him and walking to the dining room table, shrugging off his suit jacket.

"One hundred percent on my geography test," Ethan declared, turning on the couch to get on his knees in order to share this exciting news facing Garrett fully.

He threw his coat around the back of a chair but didn't take his eyes off the boy.

"Right on, Ethan."

"Give me a mountain range," Ethan ordered.

"Andes," Garrett said, moving toward Cher.

"South America!" Ethan cried. "Another one."

"Alps."

"Europe! Another!"

Garrett made it to Cher and slid a hand from her waist to the small of her back, but he didn't take his attention from her kid. "Himalayas."

"South Asia!" Ethan yelled. "Now give me a hard one."

Fuck, he didn't know a hard one.

"Ural," Cher muttered under her breath.

Someone had helped her kid study.

He pressed his hand in and called to Ethan, "Ural."

"Russia!" Ethan shouted.

"Impressive, buddy," Garrett declared.

"One hundred percent, impressive," Ethan decreed.

Garrett chuckled before he requested, "Mind if I say hey to your mom?"

"Sure," Ethan allowed, twisting back to land on his ass on the couch. "Just not too gooey."

He was still smiling when he turned to Cher.

That smell.

Her right there in his kitchen, looking pretty.

Her kid giving him the best welcome home he'd had in years, even though he hadn't even said hello.

All that, Garrett wanted to give Cher more than gooey.

Ethan right there, he couldn't.

But with what he did give her, he managed to touch his tongue to hers briefly before he lifted his head.

"Hey," he murmured.

"Hey, gorgeous. Good day?"

It had been a good day.

He'd had an important conversation with his father that settled his soul and maybe, he hoped, neutralized the poison in his gut for good—or at least made it so he could manage it.

He'd discovered his woman and her kid were never in any danger, but now they were really not in any danger with Carlito and his crew picked up and being processed on RICO charges.

And it was looking good that Wendy Derian's killer was behind bars with the RICO haul. The gun in the suspect's possession was the caliber that did Wendy, had been recently discharged, and Robert Paxton didn't have a firm alibi for the time of her murder. He was also in possession of her cell phone.

Jake still had to run ballistics, but during interrogation, Paxton gave Mike and Garrett indication he may roll over on a variety of things, including being ordered to carry out the hit on Wendy, doing this in order to make things tougher for Carlito but easier on him.

He didn't tell Cher any of that.

He said, "Yeah. More later."

She studied him a beat before she nodded.

"You gonna tell me what that smell is?" he asked.

"Garlic cheddar chicken, buttered noodles, fresh rolls from Kroger, and…" She dipped her voice quiet. "Green beans."

"I heard that," Ethan called.

She smiled up at him, not having moved from the curve of his arm, not an inch.

And he saw it. There in her face. That look he had memorized. That look, part of which she'd given him over and over for years and he'd been too blind to see.

That look now he'd never forget

She was happy. She was safe and happy.

And the part that had been his for a long time and he didn't notice.

She was in love with him.

He lifted his free hand to slide it into the side of her hair as he took that look in.

He was wrong.

She wasn't prettiest first thing in the morning.

She was at her prettiest any time of the day when she was looking into his eyes.

And hers were happy.

And in love.

Ethan

Ethan looked from the TV to his mom and Merry in the kitchen.

They were being gooey, standing close, staring into each other's eyes, Merry's hand in his mom's hair by the side of her face.

Totally gross.

Even after witnessing the gross, when Ethan looked back at the TV, he did it smiling.

Twenty-One

OVERACHIEVER
Cher

Late Thursday Evening

*I*n my cami and pajama bottoms, I sat cross-legged in Merry's bed, facing Merry.

He had his back to the headboard, his body stretched out, his chest bare, the covers pulled up to his hips.

And he'd just shared his day.

For once in my life, I was at a loss for words.

But, being me, it didn't take long before I found some.

"That BMW bitch...she have dark hair cut short and look-at-me-I'm-loaded sunglasses?" I asked.

"Yeah," he answered.

I knew her. She'd honked at me too. More than once.

"I've seen her wear those glasses during a thunderstorm," I shared.

Merry said nothing, just kept looking up at me with half his mouth hitched up like he thought I was cute or something.

"You got outta your car, flashed your badge, and gave her shit?" I asked.

"Yep," Merry answered.

So...totally...*fucking*...*loved* this man.

"You do something like that with me around to witness it, straight up, a month of blowjobs at your command," I announced. "Any time. Anywhere.

Swear. You give the word, I'll drop and suck you off better than you've ever had it, baby."

His hand, resting on my knee, slid down the side of my thigh as he shifted down the bed and slightly to his side. He caught me at my hip and gave a tug.

I fell forward even though I could have righted myself. I knew what he wanted, so I didn't.

I uncurled my legs and stretched out on top of him.

We ended with one of his hands on my ass, the other sliding up my back, both of mine trapped between us on his chest.

"You've already given me that, Cherie," he muttered.

I'd given him the best head he'd had?

Awesome.

"Then I'll give it my all to give better," I vowed.

He smiled, his hand sifted into my hair, and he pulled me down for a short, hard kiss.

He released the pressure and I lifted my head.

"You got no reaction to that Ryker shit?" he asked quietly.

I did.

I found it mildly annoying.

I also found that Ryker, the most up-front guy I knew, was full of shit.

Yes, sure, Lissa was a sweetheart and she wanted the best for the people she cared about.

But Ryker didn't do the whacked-out shit he'd done to make Lissa happy.

He did it because he liked me and he liked Merry.

And because, under all that muscle and crazy, he was a romantic.

This meant I had fodder *for years* to give him shit.

Which I did not find annoying at all.

"I've decided for my peace of mind to jump right from mildly annoyed to amused," I answered.

"Probably a good call," Merry murmured. His hand moved from my ass so he could wrap his arm around my waist as he said, "All that shit taken care of, you're good to go home tomorrow."

As crappy as I thought Merry's condo was, this was disappointing.

I didn't share that.

I just said, "Yeah."

"That's why I didn't arrange a bed for Ethan. After tonight, he'll be in his own," Merry told me.

I nodded.

"Though, thinkin' of cleanin' out that junk room and setting it up," Merry stated. "Just in case."

More sleepovers.

And my kid was invited.

That made me giddy.

I hid it and just smiled, though I had a feeling my smile was super huge because it hurt my face.

Merry's gaze dropped to it, his lips quirked, his eyes fired, and his arms gave me a squeeze.

Because he was Merry and pretty much perfect, he didn't rub it in, but instead let it go and looked back to my eyes.

"During that talk with my dad today, he mentioned he wants us all over for dinner."

I knew Dave Merrick. I liked Dave Merrick.

I liked it more he wanted me and my kid to come over with his son for dinner.

A whole lot more.

"Okay," I whispered, cleared my throat and suggested, "Maybe he'd like to come to Ethan's party."

"No maybes about that."

Oh yeah, I liked that. A possible grandpa for Ethan.

I liked that a whole lot.

"When we go to Dad's, we'll get Rocky and Tanner, invite your mom, and make it a family thing. You think Grace'll be up for that?" Merry asked.

My mother might literally be up for that if she could manage to make a miracle and walk into Dave Merrick's house, doing it how she was feeling—floating on air.

"Think I can talk her around to it," I muttered.

Merry smiled at me.

I didn't want to take that smile away, but I had to ask.

"You okay with Mia's dad's surprise visit?"

446

His fingers at my waist started stroking the skin there. "Not really. But he's not as hardheaded as she is. I think he got my message. Whether he's able to get it to sink in for her, no clue."

I hoped he could. Except for the unknown of whether Peggy and Trent had something up their sleeve, or if they'd actually smartened up and were giving Ethan some space, Mia was the only wildcard we were dealing with.

"You think all the crap swirling around us will settle and we'll find out what it's like to be together when it's just normal?" I asked.

"Wouldn't know. Never had normal. But my guess is, normal is probably really fucking boring," he answered.

That was a good answer because I wasn't sure I had it in me to be normal. I'd also obviously never experienced it. But my guess, too, was normal was probably *mind-numbingly* boring.

I used my thumb to trace the beautiful column of his throat, saying softly, "Good you had that talk with your dad."

"Yeah," he replied softly, his blue eyes warm, but I could see it there. Actually, I saw it the minute he got home that night.

Something was missing, but something else had replaced it. And what was gone was bad, but what was in its place was not.

Now I knew what all that meant, what I saw in his eyes.

Relief and maybe even a little bit of contentment.

Like everything, Merry wore it well.

"Maybe good your dad had that talk with you too," I suggested.

His fingers at my hip stopped moving and curled tight. "Not sure he's ever gonna let go of the guilt, brown eyes." He kept hold of my hip and my gaze. "But I am sure I now get why he won't."

My thumb stilled on his throat.

Was he saying…?

"Merry," I whispered.

"He loved her. He lost her. He misses her. He took risks that meant the end of her life. He didn't end it, and I think in some part of his head he gets that's not his fault. But he couldn't hold on to her as tight as he's still holdin' if he ever let that go. And I get that. I get that love he has for her. I get that need to hold on. I get it now."

He got it now, holding me, staring at me.

Holy fuck.

"But yeah," he kept going. "Even with that, you're right. It was good for him we had that talk too."

I didn't push the other part, the part that made my heart pump fast, doing that shit still making it feel lighter.

I told him something I knew for certain.

"No matter how many years pass, it means something to a parent when their child needs them. At first, kids need you so much, all you want them to do is grow up so they can do things for themselves. Then you learn. You learn you should have savored every time they reached for you or called your name."

Merry was still staring at me, but the look in his eyes had changed. There was a sweetness there that I liked a lot but had never seen.

Oh yeah.

If this worked, I was *totally* going to be able to talk him into kids.

Me, being me, not perfect but wanting to give Merry everything he needed, I didn't push that.

But I did keep talking.

"You quit needing your dad in any real way a long time ago, honey. So I know for certain you going to him about something important meant everything to him."

When I finished, his look turned darker but warmer, just as his arm tightened around my waist and pulled me up so our faces were closer.

"Ethan was pretty jazzed about that test and you pullin' out the pistachio ice cream sundaes to wash away green bean residue," he surprisingly remarked, considering I thought his look and movements were leading somewhere else. "Thinkin' he's out, but his sleep may be light." He tipped his head on the pillow and the look that hit his eyes I felt in my womb. "Early morning date for the bathroom?"

Okay, so he *was* going where I thought he was leading.

It would just happen hours from now.

I forced my other arm from between us, shoving it around him so I could get closer, and replied, "Oh yeah."

His hand in my hair twisted gently.

"Liked comin' home to you and your boy, Cherie."

Oh God.

God, God, *God.*

I liked that.

"Liked you doin' it, Merry."

And I did.

It was a dream come true, nearly literally, except in the dream I'd had, we were at my place.

But I had a feeling I was going to get that dream too.

"We'll get you and your boy home tomorrow. But let's set that up to happen more often, sweetheart," he suggested.

Oh yeah.

I was going to get that dream too.

"Okay," I agreed readily.

"Now, give me some gooey and we'll get some shut-eye so I can wake you up early and fuck you."

I melted into him and gave him the gooey. It turned into a mini make-out session, but neither of us pushed it far because my boy was probably sleeping lightly down the hall.

Merry turned out the light, I got under the covers, and we curled into each other, safe in his bed in the dark in his crappy condo.

But even if you'd offered me the world as a choice, I wouldn't have wanted to be anywhere else.

⌒

Early Friday Morning

I bit the flesh of Merry's shoulder when I came.

His deep groan sounded against the skin beneath my ear, driving down my neck, my chest, and right to my clit when he did.

Eventually, he dropped my leg that he was holding around his hip and I again felt the water hitting us.

Right. We were in the shower.

As my leg fell, he slid his cock out of me but kept his arms around me.

I turned my head his way to say something cocky or smartass, just to see him smile.

I didn't get it out.

Because, early morning fuck in the shower done, my man felt like kissing me.

So I let him.

⌒⟶

I stared at Merry and my kid leaning in to the counter on either side of Merry's bar. Ethan was up on a stool on the outside; Merry was on his feet in the kitchen. Both were bent over their bowls, shoveling bright yellow, egg-cracker goo in their mouths.

And Merry was not gagging.

In fact, it appeared he liked it.

This fact made it clear that crap actually *was* dude food.

This was surprising enough.

The rest of what was happening shocked me silent.

"So, talk to your buds. Get their parents' permission. Be ready at quarter to six. I'll get you, swing 'round to pick them up, take you all for some grub, to the game, and drop them home after," Merry stated.

"Cool," Ethan grunted, shoving more egg goo in his mouth.

They were making a date.

Merry looked to me. "Before your shift, you wanna go to dinner with me and the boys?"

I was an afterthought.

Why did I think that was so fucking *awesome*?

"How 'bout I trade my own Merry time later for you havin' a guys' night tonight?" I suggested.

"Works for me," Ethan said to his bowl.

Merry winked at me.

It worked for him too.

He turned away and recommenced eating.

"You on call this weekend?" Ethan asked his bowl.

"Nope," Merry told his bowl.

"Waffle morning tomorrow?" Ethan asked.

I held my breath.

Merry's gaze slid to me.

I nodded once.

His attention went back to his bowl before he answered, "Yup."

"Cool," Ethan grunted.

I watched and listened, my eyes feeling funny. They were stinging, but not because they were dry.

Merry straightened from the counter. "You finish that, bud. We gotta hit the road, yeah?"

"Yeah," Ethan replied, scooping the last bite out of his bowl.

Merry headed my way.

I started to pull my shit together.

Since I was standing at his sink but was busy pulling my shit together, I didn't move even as he got in my space, *right* in my space, looking down at me as he reached around and put the bowl in the sink.

I heard the bowl hit as his face dipped to mine.

"Dig dude food, brown eyes," he said.

"You give me an egg-goo kiss, I'm gonna barf," I replied.

He burst out laughing, but lucky for me, he stepped back before he did it.

I watched, enjoying every second.

Merry gave me a grin before he turned and strode through the living room, muttering, "Best go brush my teeth."

Ethan jumped off his stool, declaring, "I'm gonna do that too."

I blinked, then stared at my son.

He brushed his teeth by his own choice…never. Like I had to ride him to take a shower, I had to get on his ass to brush his teeth.

It seemed having Merry around wasn't only good for orgasms and getting a variety of different kinds of warm and squishy.

It was good for a vast number of other things.

Fifteen minutes later, after getting a toothpaste-flavored good-bye kiss from my man and two different style waves from both my guys, they were gone.

I turned to the sink and cleaned up dude food.

Friday Evening

I walked into J&J's for my shift and knew I was in for it.

This was because Colt was on his stool. Cal was standing by it. Mike was sitting on the stool next to where Cal was standing. Ryker was hanging close to Cal and Colt.

And Benny Bianchi was standing, leaned into the bar next to Mike.

Benny Bianchi was Joe Callahan's cousin.

They might be cousins, but they were tight so they were more like brothers, and them being family couldn't be missed.

Cal was sheer male beauty, marred by the hardness and heartbreak of the life he'd endured and the scars on his face. Though, both of these made him even hotter than he probably was back in the day before all that had happened.

Benny was just sheer male beauty. *Very* male. *Very* beautiful.

Like a movie star.

But better because he was real.

He was also taken, married to my girl Frankie, who'd lived in the 'burg for a spell, and when she'd lived there, we'd become friends.

She'd moved back to Chicago to be with Benny, who lived up there and owned a pizzeria.

His pizzeria was the bomb. I knew this because, since Frankie had moved away, I'd taken Ethan up there for several weekends, stayed with them, and discovered this fact.

Ben worked the pizzeria; Frankie had a sweet job where she made a shit-ton of money.

She also had the job of popping out babies for Benny. In their time together, which had not been much, they'd already had one and she was heavily pregnant now.

I knew this before I walked into the bar because she'd called me six months ago to tell me.

I knew this right then because the only good part of my current scenario was that she was also there, around the curve of the bar, in a girl huddle with Vi and Dusty. All three of them were on the outside of the bar, Feb and Dee were on the inside.

The chicks would take my back.

But the reason I knew I was in for it was because in all the years I had it bad for Merry, the only person who called me on it was Benny.

In fact, he'd done it the first night I'd met him.

He, Frankie, and me had gone out to have drinks. Merry had showed. Benny had sussed things out. They took me home, Benny walked me to my door, and he'd laid it out.

He was cool about it. He wasn't a dick when he told me to soften up, and if I did, I'd open up enough to let a guy in, that guy being Merry.

I hadn't taken his advice.

In the end, I didn't need to. Merry and I finally got there, and looking back, even though Benny's advice was solid and he'd given that advice to me a couple of years ago, years some might consider were wasted, I believed in my heart it had to happen this way.

Merry needed that time to travel his path how he needed to travel it.

I was just crazy-lucky it led to me.

But I knew, walking in the bar that night, that Benny knew I'd scored Merry.

And he had a dick, so no doubt he was going to give me shit about it.

"Do not say a fuckin' word," I warned the instant I got close to the gang.

His handsome, white smile got huge as his hand came up to his broad chest. "Me?"

"Just shut it," I ordered.

"Cher!" Frankie cried, just having seen me.

She popped off her stool and rushed to me.

I stopped glaring at her husband and smiled at her, moving her way.

Frankie was one of those bitches who had the ultimate power—she could look all class showing skin, and for her, the tighter the dress, the higher the heel, the better.

She obviously didn't change when she was pregnant. Great figure, big, beautiful belly, all encased in a long-sleeved, skintight dress that showed cleavage and had a skirt that hit her three inches up from her knees. And on her feet, six-inch platform stilettos.

She looked amazing.

We hugged.

"Cher hugging. Already, gettin' laid regular is makin' her a girl," Colt remarked.

I let Frankie go and turned on Colt.

"I hug bitches I haven't seen in months. Get over it." I gave both Benny and Frankie a look. "And you guys have shit timing. Ethan's birthday party isn't until *next* weekend."

"We know," Frankie said. "We brought him a present. But I've still got that work thing I told you about happening next weekend, so we had to come down and celebrate Vi and Cal's news this weekend. And anyway, we had to come to cut the crazy since Vinnie and Theresa are here too. The good news with that is that they're lookin' after the kids. A night out with my man, reconnecting with our posse in the 'burg, there is no bad news."

Vinnie and Theresa were Benny's parents. The whole family was Italian (or, in Frankie's case, her being a mutt, only the dominant parts of her were Italian), so they could find a reason to celebrate the sun rising.

Even so, Vi was my girl and I had no idea what news they were celebrating.

But I could guess.

I looked her way and guessed.

"Are you knocked up again?"

Vi smiled and shrugged.

I did not give her shit for not telling me. I understood she was giving me time with Merry.

And anyway, this wasn't big news. The bitch was always pregnant.

I looked to Cal. "Jesus. How many do you need?"

"One more after this," he stated.

"No more after this," Vi snapped.

Cal looked to his woman and grinned.

Vi looked to the ceiling.

Merry had told me his sister was also pregnant.

It was like it was contagious.

I turned my attention to Dusty. "You knocked up?"

"Not yet," she said.

They were trying.

I figured Mike had the mojo the rest of them had, which meant he only had to look at his woman, think dirty thoughts, and she'd be carrying his kid. Thus, I figured that joyous news would be celebrated next week.

I looked to Feb.

"I love my little Jack, but I got a four-year-old, a dog, a cat, a bar, and an alpha male on my hands. I think I'm good," she decreed.

My eyes went to Dee.

"I got two and Morrie, which makes it like I actually have five. I'm definitely good," she shared.

"When are you and Merry gonna start?" Colt asked.

"Kiss my ass," I said as answer.

I got girl smiles and man chuckles to that.

Whatever.

"A brother can be in a nursing home and make babies. Not you, sister, so you best be gettin' the lead out."

This advice came from Ryker.

I turned my attention to him.

Everyone went silent.

That meant everyone knew about Ryker's matchmaking too.

I said nothing.

Ryker said nothing.

I won our staring contest when he prompted, "You just gonna stand there and stare at me?"

"I'm not standing here staring at you. I'm waiting for you to grow wings and hover over us with your golden bow and arrow," I returned.

Ryker grinned his scary grin. "As you've experienced, I kick fuckin' ass with my golden bow and arrow."

"Just to say, the 'burg can do without your version of Cupid," I remarked.

"I can wait for the gratitude," Ryker declared magnanimously. "You and Merrick can name your first kid after me."

"Dude, *Merry* and *me* got our shit together. Your bullshit coulda fucked us up," I shared.

"Tell yourself that," Ryker replied.

My eyes narrowed. "How thick *is* your skin?"

"I'm half reptilian," he returned. "The alligator kind."

"Okay, how thick is your skull?" I kept at him.

"Not as thick as yours, you wasted years before you fell on your man's dick," he retorted.

I shouldn't have even started this.

So it was time to end it.

"I'm feelin' like making tips tonight, not cleanin' up blood," I decreed.

"Like you could cut me," Ryker scoffed.

"Don't underestimate a pissed off woman," I warned.

"That's why I got sugar in my bed, not spice. Don't ever need to worry about that shit," Ryker stated.

This was going nowhere.

"I need to get to work," I muttered, turning to the office.

"Cher," Ryker called.

I sighed and looked back to him.

"Lissa's over the moon," he shared.

That might be true, but it was Ryker who was happy for me.

"You're all soft under all that crazy," I replied.

He grinned a grin that many children would witness and have nightmares for decades.

"Don't tell anyone."

I rolled my eyes and walked to the office to get rid of my purse. When I walked out, Dee was out on the floor with her tray, which meant I was back of the bar with Feb.

I got the lay of the land, made some drinks, then hit my posse at the end.

"You ready for your show?" I asked Dusty.

She made pottery. It was awesome pottery, but I didn't get it since she also made a shit-ton of money off it. Apparently, some people really liked pottery. Enough to spend hundreds of dollars on just one piece.

"Yeah," she answered. "And I've set a piece aside to give to you and Merry for your wedding."

I narrowed my eyes at her. "Don't you start with that shit. You're a chick. You're supposed to have my back."

"It's more fun to mess with you," she returned.

Damn.

I should have seen it coming.

Dusty was a lot like me. She had some girlie in her but not much. Mostly she was a straight shooter who had it completely together.

I lifted my hand and did a sweep of the far end of the bar, declaring, "I think Feb can cover you all with drinks."

"Weak," Cal grunted.

"I need to be in a good disposition to earn tips," I retorted.

"Why?" he shot back. "You been earnin' tips for years not in one."

He had a point.

"You can kiss my ass too," I returned.

"Lame," he muttered.

He was not wrong.

God, with Merry giving me the warm and squishy, making me happy, I was losing my edge.

I wasn't proud of continuing the lameness, but I actually *did* have to earn tips.

So I muttered back, "Whatever," and wandered down the bar.

The night wore on and it was Friday at J&J's. Time to herald in the weekend and do it right by going out, throwing a few back, and communing with your 'burg brethren.

So I was busy.

And it was much later when the opportunity was afforded to him.

Being Benny, he took it.

Cal was deep in conversation with Ryker and Colt, Vi at his side, his arm curled around her neck, holding her close. And Mike, Dusty, and Frankie were gabbing with Dee, who was standing with them, carrying a full tray of empties.

Benny was in on the Cal conversation, but he made himself free to catch my eyes when I was forced down their way to nab a bottle of beer that was in the fridge closest to them.

"Happy?" he asked quietly, just for me.

"Yeah," I answered quietly, just for him.

"Good," he replied and gave me the flash of his white, movie star smile.

He was wrong.

It wasn't good.

It was beautiful.

But I didn't correct him.

I looked to his pregnant wife, then back to him.

He knew what beauty meant.

I shot him a return smile.

Then, before anyone noticed our moment and gave me shit about it, I ended it and got back to work.

⟨⎯⎯⟩

Saturday Afternoon

I slid my lips up Merry's throat as the last tremors of my orgasm drifted out of me.

I could tell the last of Merry's were still with him at the thick gruffness of his voice when he murmured, "Seems my brown-eyed girl *can* make love."

I smiled.

My kid was at a friend's house, hanging out.

And I was at Merry's condo, trying my hand at giving as good as I got. Seemed I'd succeeded.

I slid my lips to his jaw.

I was on top, Merry still inside since we'd just finished, his arms around me tight. But as my lips drifted, his arms loosened so his hands could float light and sweet over the skin of my back.

"Got the reservation at Swank's, baby. Six thirty. That good?" Merry told me.

"Yeah," I told his jaw, wondering what I was going to wear and hoping one of Ethan's two dress-up outfits still fit him.

"And got a lock on tickets for the Colts' next home game. Need to know from you if I should get two or if Feb can make it so you can come with us."

At his words, my head shot up and I looked in his eyes.

"What?"

"Colts versus Saints. Sunday after next. Can you get Feb to arrange that day off?"

"You're buyin' tickets?" I asked.

"Uh…yeah. Just said that, babe."

"Colts tickets are expensive, Merry."

"Maybe, Cherie, but Ethan told me he'd never been to a game."

I shook my head. "He hasn't, but…Swank's…" I let that hang since that said it all.

And what it said was that he was a cop, not a Rockefeller. Dinner at Swank's for four could easily set him back close to five hundred bucks. I'd never been to a Colts game either, so I didn't know how much tickets cost. But I knew they didn't give them away.

"Yes, that's his present," Merry confirmed. "Steak you can cut with a fork *and* a Colts game."

I stared down at him, totally uncertain what to do.

Because in all the boons Merry had given me, straight up, this was the one that was the most amazing.

It was also one I had to control.

"Gorgeous," I started carefully, "I love the generosity, but you'd break the bank if you try to give him all the things he hasn't gotten in life."

"Brown eyes," he returned, sounding like he was being careful too, "he's already gotten all the important things he needs to get in life. He's smart, so he knows that. And since he's smart and knows that, appreciates it, and shows that by bein' a good kid and lookin' after his mom and grandma, he should be rewarded for being the good kid he is by being able to go to a Colts game."

"You're lookin' at buyin' a house," I reminded him.

"There's always gonna be houses. But there'll only be this one opportunity to take a newly-turned eleven-year-old boy to his first Colts game."

That feel hit my eyes, and when it did, it hit simultaneously in my throat and my belly.

Merry's face warmed.

He knew what I was feeling.

And he knew me, so he didn't say shit about it.

He asked, "So, you gonna ask Feb for the day off?"

"Yeah, I'm gonna ask Feb for the day off."

His hands stopped drifting on my back and he wrapped his arms around me. "Then I'll get three tickets."

I shoved my face in his neck and muttered, "That'd be cool, Merry."

We lay there together, connected, a girl who never allowed herself to dream, lying on top of a dream come true.

When it was time, Merry slid me up to slide himself out of me. He shifted us. He shifted the covers. He went to the bathroom to deal with the condom. And he came back, shifting us so I was exactly where I'd been before he'd moved me.

Lying on top of a dream come true.

"Why Rivers?"

Merry asked that, and hearing it, I lifted my head to look at him again.

"Why what?"

"Rivers, baby. You could have picked any last name you wanted. I like it. It's cool. But why'd you pick Rivers?"

I shrugged, dropped my head, and nuzzled my face in his throat again while giving him the simple answer.

"I like water."

"You like water?"

I nodded against his neck and gave him more.

"Mom's always been a waitress. Dad's always been a deadbeat. She couldn't give me a lot, but she tried to make sure every summer we went on vacation. Without any money, we didn't go far and we didn't have much. Shitty motels. Diner food. But she did her best. And she always found water. Driving us to some lake. Putting our asses on a Greyhound down to Florida and hitting some seedy hotel, but one that was on a beach. We didn't give a shit it was seedy or cheap. I was an asshole to her, but not on vacation. We had fun. We relaxed. We forgot life sucked."

I lifted my head to look at him and kept talking.

"Good times. The only really good times probably for the both of us that weren't clouded by the shit of life or my bent to be a pain in her ass. So I like water. Maybe it's because I just like water. But I think it's because Mom busted her ass to give me those times and it means something to me because my mom means something to me. And because it reminds me she gave me the most important thing I ever got—all I need to be a good mom to the kid I got. I couldn't call myself Cher Lake or Cher Ocean or Cher Beach. So I picked Rivers. It works."

"Yeah," he said. "It works."

But the way he said that, my attention on him sharpened.

And when I saw what I was pretty sure I saw, I accused, "You're plannin' a vacation for you, me, Ethan, and maybe even my mom somewhere near water, aren't you?"

The faraway look in his eyes vanished and he smiled at me.

"Caught," he whispered.

God, it had happened.

No, it *kept* happening.

I'd hoped. For the first time I'd hoped—hoped I was wrong that life couldn't get better.

And he kept proving me wrong.

"You're never gonna get a new house at this rate," I warned.

"Yeah, I am," he replied. "Shower sex with you is fantastic. Sink sex with you is out of this fuckin' world. But you only got one bathroom in your pad and your boy is right next door to that and right across the hall from your room. And when you and Ethan come for sleepovers, I'm good with getting creative but not a big fan of having my options limited. So at least one of us needs a house that offers me options. Since it's doubtful you can even disassemble your tribute to the flower generation and reassemble it in a new place, much less wanna do that, it's up to me to find it. And a man will go to great lengths for options, which include the possible option of future vacation sex."

"You're gonna break the bank in order to secure fuck options?" I asked.

"Am I a man?"

"Yes."

"Then do you realize that's a stupid question?"

I started laughing. "Yes."

"So I won't bother answering it."

I gave in to laughing.

As I was doing it, Merry joined me at the same time he rolled me so I had his weight and heat covering me.

When I was done, I slid a hand up his chest to cup his jaw.

"Prepare for gooey," I warned.

His eyes were still lit with humor, but with my words, one side of his lips tipped up.

"Sock it to me."

I didn't delay in socking it to him.

"You don't just make me happy, Merry. You keep making me happier."

His face got warmer and more beautiful than ever.

"That's the goal, brown eyes," he whispered.

"You're an overachiever," I whispered back.

He didn't reply.

He kissed me.

Then it was his turn to make love to me.

And there it was again.

Merry making me happier.

⌒

Garrett

Monday Morning

Garrett slid the pancakes he'd made in front of Ethan, who was sitting at the table.

He headed back to Cher's stove.

Cher was at the countertop, bent over it, the ball of one foot resting on top of the other one, her eyes to a pad of paper on the counter.

"You're still into the *Star Wars* theme?" she asked the paper, her question directed to her son.

"Yeah, Mom," Ethan answered his pancakes, slathering butter on them.

"R2-D2 cake?" she went on, scribbling on the paper.

"Yep," Ethan confirmed.

"Chocolate?" she kept going.

"Affirmative." Ethan was now soaking his pancakes in syrup.

No.

Submerging them.

Watching that, Garrett felt his lips tip up before he turned his gaze to his woman. "How many pancakes you want, babe?"

"Two," she muttered distractedly, still scribbling. "Thanks, gorgeous."

He turned to the griddle and poured batter.

He was putting the bowl aside when he heard a noise like someone was shoving air with their tongue through clenched teeth.

462

He cut his gaze to Cher.

She was still bent over the counter but twisted to look down her side at him, her lips pressed together, eyes big, and she jerked her head.

He had no fucking clue what that was about.

He was going to learn.

She twisted back to look at her boy.

"Haven't heard from your dad, kid." She drew in breath and then offered, "You want me to give him a call? You've never invited him, Peg, and the kids, though they know about your extravaganzas and probably would wanna come. You think this year's the year?"

That was what it was about. She needed him alert and at her back when she introduced something that might be tough to talk about with Ethan.

Or, more to the point, she needed him alert for Ethan.

Fuck, that felt good.

"Don't call. Don't care he comes or not," Ethan muttered, shoving pancake in his mouth.

She gave it a few beats before she suggested, "It's been a while, honey. Maybe you should give him a call."

Ethan, chewing, looked to his mom and swallowed.

"It's been a while, yeah. You think that's long enough for him to learn not to be a loser?" he asked.

Garrett saw in profile as Cher bit her lip.

That meant no.

"Right," Ethan said, and looked back to his pancakes. "Don't care he's not at my party. *Really* won't care if *he* doesn't give *me* a call. It's not *his* birthday that's comin' up. He's missed a bunch of mine. His choice whether he's gonna miss more."

"You did tell him you didn't want to see them again," she reminded her boy.

"If I told you that, would you leave me alone forever and ever?" Ethan returned.

Cher bit her lip again.

That time it meant not a fucking chance.

Yeah.

Ethan Rivers might be only nearly eleven, but he had his head screwed on straight.

Cher opened her mouth, but Garrett said quickly and quietly, "He's right, baby."

She twisted to look down her body at him again.

"If Schott wants a part of Ethan's life, he's gotta make the effort," Garrett finished.

She took Garrett in. She twisted back and took her son in.

Then she said, "Right," and looked at her pad of paper.

She was blowing it off, but it was pretend. He saw the tense line of her shoulders.

She was worried about her kid, but she wasn't going to baby him. She was going to let him make his own decisions.

It was a good call. It was time for her to give Ethan that and for Ethan to learn how to do it right.

He'd touch base with her later, after he dropped Ethan at school, to make sure she was good.

Garrett turned back to the stove and flipped the pancakes.

Then he felt it, so he turned back.

Ethan was looking at him.

He had a weird look on his face. Suddenly, his shoulders came up really high, almost to his ears.

He mouthed, "Thanks," quickly dropped his shoulders, and gave his attention back to his food.

Garrett looked back to the griddle.

In his line of work, Garrett had seen it time and again.

As much of a loser as Trent Schott was, any boy felt the absence of a father straight through everything that he was.

Everything.

With a good father who wasn't perfect but gave it his best shot, Garrett didn't know if it was better to have that hole go unfilled than to have some moron make a half-assed attempt to fill it. And with Dave as his dad, Garrett would never know the answer to that.

He just had to hope that one day Ethan would find him and share it so he could do whatever he could to help him get past it.

On these thoughts, Garrett felt a burn that he could only extinguish knowing they had a reservation for Swank's and he had an envelope on his bar at home with three Colts tickets in it.

He flipped a pancake, calling, "You gonna want more, bud?"

"Yeah," Ethan answered. "One, maybe two. Thanks, Merry."

"Whatever you want, kid," he muttered to the pancakes.

He said those words and felt it again. Ethan's eyes on his back. Maybe even Cher's too.

He didn't turn.

He made his woman and her son pancakes.

Wednesday Evening

"I thought he was full of it," Ethan declared before he lifted his eyes from his plate. "But Brendon did not lie." He raised his fork, which had a chunk of steak skewered on its tips. "You *can* cut these steaks with your fork."

"It's a miracle," Grace muttered, all dolled up, looking nearly as pretty as her daughter in part because of the happy smile she was aiming right then at her grandson.

But she was wrong.

It wasn't a miracle.

It was a prime cut of beef that cost fifty-three dollars.

It was also worth every penny. And Garrett knew that to be true as he watched Ethan shove the chunk of steak into his mouth, his eyes going round with marvel.

He felt something slink up the leg of his trousers and looked to his woman at his side.

Now *he* was wrong.

Grace looked pretty.

But all done up for their night out, Cher was fucking *dazzling*.

She was also looking at him.

And her look told him she loved him. It also told him she loved what he was giving to her son.

So yeah.

Absolutely.

A fifty-three-dollar steak was a damned expensive steak.

But it was worth every fucking penny.

Thursday Afternoon

Garrett stood on the porch, looking out to the water.

He'd finally had time to schedule the viewing.

And there he was.

The bathrooms were in worse shape than he'd thought.

The rest of it was better than he could've imagined.

Especially the view.

His real estate agent stood with him.

"I'm not sure they're going to accept that offer, Garrett," she remarked.

"The place needs work," he told her, something she knew.

"They're aware of that, which is why they've dropped the price seventy-five K."

"Comps show my offer is not an insult," he returned.

"Maybe so, but the market is reviving."

He turned to look at her. "Make the offer. Be cool about it so they don't shut us out. There's room to move."

"You might need a lot of room. They give the impression they're entrenched."

He looked back to the water.

I like water.

"I gotta get back to work," he murmured, then turned again to his agent, leveling his eyes on hers. "Make the offer. I don't care you gotta make magic, Diane. Get me this house."

"Okay, Garrett," she replied.

He nodded.

He then took another look inside the opened door at the big great room, its fantastic kitchen, its phenomenal hearth, all the warm and welcoming space.

He turned the other way and took a last look at the water, which could be seen from the kitchen. The living room. The study. The room that could be Ethan's. The master suite, which was all the way on the other side of the house from the study and other two bedrooms.

And with one last glance at his agent, he went to his truck and got back to work.

⌒

Saturday Morning

Garrett was on his way out the door to head to Cher's to help her with Ethan's party when his phone rang.

After glancing at the screen, he took the call.

"Hey," he greeted.

"I made magic," Diane said.

Garrett smiled.

Twenty-Two

On Top
Cher

"I'm sorry, we don't have more tiki torches."

"How can you not have more tiki torches? This is a party place. We're having a luau. A luau is a party. Which is why I'm shoppin' at a party place. And you can't have a luau without tiki torches."

"Sir, it's October in Indiana."

"So?"

"We sell down stock of tiki torches after summer in order to make room for Halloween, Thanksgiving, and Christmas items."

"You should be ready for every occasion."

"We pride ourselves in being that. That's why you currently have twelve tiki torches here. But I'm afraid we don't have more right now. And just a suggestion, next time, should you want something in high quantities, if you give us a call beforehand, we'll be happy to order it for you."

"Twelve isn't a *high quantity*. It's a perfectly reasonable quantity unless you need *twenty*, and I need *twenty*."

"Again, I apologize. We just don't have twenty."

"I *barely* have enough leis and grass skirts. And, just to say, neither are very high quality."

"I'm sorry you think that as well, sir. But—"

"*Yo!*" Merry barked.

I jumped at the sound, pulled from my focus on my extreme annoyance at being an audience to this sheer ridiculousness when Merry and me had a ton of *Star Wars* and other party shit in four collective baskets, a cake to pick up, decorating to do, and later, merrymaking to achieve for my son.

Plus, my mother was at my house with my kid, helping me get ready by doing what she called "light cleaning." This meant she was going to move shit around to where *she* thought it should be, which was what she always did when she jumped at the chance to do some "light cleaning" before some event I had at my house. This also meant it'd take weeks to find the shit she moved, something which was nearly more annoying than the selfish, thoughtless, in-a-hurry human population you encountered when you were out running errands (but just nearly).

Needless to say, I didn't have time for an asshole on a tiki torch mission in Indiana for a luau he was giving in fucking October.

I looked up at Merry to see he agreed.

He'd also shoved his jacket back on both sides and had his hands on his hips.

There was no badge on his belt, seeing as he was off-duty.

Thus, I wondered how this would go.

That said, Merry was tall and lean and badass. The guy with the torches was not tall and was kinda doughy, so I had high hopes it would go well... and, hopefully, *fast*.

"You wanna move this along?" Merry suggested, though it didn't come close to sounding like a suggestion.

"It's my turn at the register," the man in front of us sniped. "You'll get your turn."

"I'll get it a lot faster, you give it up about tiki torches you aren't gonna get, seein' as this guy can't conjure them from thin air," Merry returned, shifting his torso to the side only slightly to indicate the line that had formed behind us, which had at least three other customers waiting to check out. "You do that, you can get on your way so the rest of us can get on our way."

This was a faulty strategy.

He'd called out to the man's civility.

Since the man had none, that was totally not going to work.

"I hardly need your attitude on a day where I'm looking forward to hosting a luau," the man retorted.

There it was. I was right.

He didn't give a shit that he was affecting *all* our days with *his* attitude about fucking tiki torches.

"Ditto, turkey," the woman behind us snapped.

Surprised, I looked back at her to see a blue-haired, sharp-eyed lady with a basket filled with *Frozen*-themed party plates, cups, like-colored streamers and balloons, and a second basket filled almost to overflowing with bags of fake snow.

"My granddaughter got one year older today and I obviously am not getting any younger, especially waiting in this line," she declared irately. "I'm not really looking forward to watching Princess Anna's demonstration of sisterly love for the seven millionth time. But I'd rather do that than expire, waiting at the cash register of a party store, watching a grown man pitch a fit over tiki torches."

"Yeah," agreed the lumbersexual guy at the back of the line who had shaggy hair, a long, scruffy beard, was wearing a plaid shirt, and holding an enormous bouquet of pink and silver balloons with some Mylar ones mixed in that said, *Sweet Sixteen.* "Buy your tiki torches and go."

The guy in front of us got red in the face, shoved the torches and baskets filled with leis and grass skirts toward the clerk, and snapped, "I'll get them elsewhere."

"Good luck with that," Merry muttered.

The guy shot him a filthy look before he stormed out.

"Next," the clerk said, dumping the unwanted luau items behind him to clear the register area, doing this with practiced nonchalance, gazing expectantly at Merry and me like all that hadn't happened.

Then again, he probably had twelve situations like that every day.

This made me glad I was a bartender. People tended to kiss bartender ass to get what they wanted. You didn't, your ass got ignored and your glass stayed empty.

On these pleasant thoughts, we got our *Star Wars* stuff. We took it out to Merry's car. Then Merry headed us toward Marsh to pick up the R2-D2-shaped chocolate cake.

"Just to say, you totally get a blowjob for even going to a party store with me," I declared as Merry pulled out of the parking lot. "You get another one for gettin' in that dude's face. But you didn't flash your badge and scare the bejeezus out of him, so the month of 'any time, anywhere head' is yet to be earned."

"Baby, can't flash my badge at a party store to get some guy to stop bein' an asshole."

I looked to him. "You did it with the BMW bitch."

He glanced at me before he looked back at the road. "That was good timing. My badge was already on my belt. Today, I'm off duty."

I turned to face front again. "I need to take you grocery shopping with me when you're on duty."

"They kinda frown on that too, sweetheart, the me-on-duty part being operative, seein' as they actually want me to work when I'm on duty, not go grocery shopping."

"Whatever," I muttered, but I did it grinning because he was funny when he was being rational.

"Gotta say, it's good to know I got two blowjobs in store, so I probably shouldn't point this out and give you ideas, but you don't seem to hesitate goin' down on me, even if I haven't done something to earn your mouth."

"Good point," I kept muttering (and grinning).

"Though, the promise, brown eyes? Sweet." Now Merry was muttering.

"Glad you think so."

He drove.

I sat in his truck, grinning.

"Cher?"

"Yeah?"

"You're an overachiever too."

I felt my chest depress.

I turned my eyes to him.

He was also grinning.

"Fuck," I groused.

"What?" he asked.

"Making you happy makes me even *happier*."

"You say that like it's bad."

"It is."

He glanced again at me then back at the road, his brows drawn, his face dark. "How is that bad?"

"Because it means you're always one-upping me on the happy. I can't make you happy without you making me happier because I'm making you happy. It's a vicious cycle where you're always on top. And that's bad."

"I know some times when you're on top that make me a fuckuva lot happier than you are."

His words and the memories they invoked gave me a nice shiver.

And experiencing that, I shared, "I'm not sure that's true."

"Trust me, baby. When you ride me, I watch you come, but I *feel* what you give to me."

"I *feel* what you give to me too."

"You come harder on your back. That's when I'm givin' it to you. When you're on top, you're givin' it to me."

This was definitely true.

"So there are times when you're on top with the happy in more ways than one," he finished.

I faced forward again, mumbling, "That makes me feel better."

Merry reached out and nabbed my hand, holding it.

And more happy.

"Glad I could be of service," he murmured.

"Stop being perfect," I ordered.

He chuckled.

"And awesome," I went on.

He kept chucking.

"And funny, smart, sweet, and hot," I finished.

His hand squeezed mine hard as he burst out laughing.

And there it was.

I was on top.

⟨——⟩

"Is there something I can do, Cher?"

A bunch of people were stuffed in my kitchen with me, one of them being Rocky, who'd just asked that question.

It was time for cake.

But it was also a birthday party with fifteen kids and twice that many adults paying homage to my boy for being awesome (and turning eleven), so there was always something to do.

"Yeah, babe. Can you grab the ice cream?" I asked, unearthing R2-D2 from his flat, white box.

"Absolutely," she murmured, pushing her way to the fridge.

I felt a hand warm on the small of my back as I saw another hand offering me two boxes of candles, one box of blue, one black.

"Need a light?" Merry's voice rumbled into my ear.

I twisted to look up to him. "Yeah, gorgeous. And can you grab the plates and forks and get everyone in the living room?"

His hand slid down to the top of my ass, fingers curved around my hip, and gave a squeeze. "You got it."

He dropped the candles on the counter by the cake, dug in his jeans pocket, pulled out a lighter, and tossed that on the counter too. Then he bent and kissed my neck briefly before he took off.

"Everyone in the living room," he announced as he went. "Time for cake."

"My big brother...domesticated," Rocky remarked.

I looked to her to see she had a tub of ice cream in her hand and her eyes aimed where Merry was herding people out of the kitchen.

She turned to me and her smile was big.

"Looks good on him," she declared.

"Your brother always looks good," I replied.

Her big grin got bigger.

I dipped my head to her middle. "Congrats, by the way. Merry told me."

She balanced the tub of ice cream in one hand in order to put her other to her belly. "Thanks."

I turned to the cake and snatched up the candles.

Rocky got close.

"You want some?" she asked.

"Want some what?" I asked back, shoving candles in the cake and feeling weird doing it. R2-D2 was also my favorite *Star Wars* character and shoving candles in his middle (even if that middle was pure frosting) felt like stabbing my favorite teddy bear.

473

She put the ice cream on the counter and took some candles from me, starting to help.

"Some kids," she explained.

Rocky and I weren't tight like Vi and I, Feb and I, Frankie and I, or even Dusty and I were. We knew each other. We liked each other. But I was closer to Tanner.

But she was my man's sister.

It was time.

"Yeah," I said softly.

"Cute baby girls with your brown eyes," she replied softly.

I looked to her. "Cute baby boys with his blue ones."

She smiled again.

This one wasn't huge, but it said a whole lot more than both the others had and all it said was good.

"We need help in here?"

Rocky and I turned to the door to see Dave walking in.

"Yeah, Dad, go in the living room and pull the curtains so we have dark for the candles," Rocky ordered.

"Gotcha," Dave said. He gave me a grin and turned right back around.

"And make sure people have their cameras ready!" Rocky bossed right before he disappeared through the doorway.

He lifted a hand to indicate he'd heard and was gone.

"I'll get a knife," she muttered. "Ice cream scoop?"

"That drawer there," I said, jerking my head.

I finished with the candles and grabbed the lighter to start lighting.

"Baby, ready?"

I twisted again and saw Merry had six packages of *Star Wars* plates held sandwiched in one of his big hands, a package of plastic forks in the other. The living room beyond him was dimmed. All was ready.

"Ethan in place?" I asked.

"Yeah," Merry answered.

I smiled. "Then yeah, honey. All ready."

He smiled back, turned, and stopped dead.

I stopped dead too.

This was because there was a loud banging on the door.

Very loud.

And from that loud, you could definitely read angry.

Very angry.

What the fuck?

Merry glanced my way, then tossed the plates and plastic silverware aside and prowled out.

With a quick look at a perplexed Rocky, I tossed the lighter aside and hurried after him.

I hit the kitchen doorway to see forty-seven people crammed into my not-very-big living room, a room draped in black-and-blue streamers; black, blue, and silver balloons bunched and stuck in corners and around the ceiling light; and black plastic Darth Vader head-shaped trays and white plastic Stormtrooper head-shaped trays filled with Chex Mix, M&M's, honey-roasted peanuts, or Fritos littering every surface available.

And all of those people were silent as the angry knocks kept coming.

I also saw my son's confused face turned to the door. Merry was struggling his way through bodies to get to it, but Colt was already there.

Colt opened it.

"Stop knocking," he bit out when the knocking didn't stop because whoever was doing it was doing it on the storm door.

"I demand to see Cheryl!"

Fuck.

Peggy.

I looked to Ethan, who no longer looked confused.

His face was pale and his eyes were on me.

"It's cool. Everything's cool," I said to the room at large but turned to the closest adult, who happened to be Dave. "Do me a big favor, Dave. Can you get my son in the kitchen?"

"Sure thing, honey," Dave muttered.

I pushed through bodies, eyes to the door where Merry now was with Colt.

But he was pushing through the storm.

And he was pissed.

Colt was following him.

And he was pissed too.

475

Shit, this was happening outside.

I looked back at Dave, who was halfway to my kid.

"And, uh…shut the blinds in the kitchen, would you?"

"Mom!" Ethan cried.

"Give me and Merry a second, baby," I requested.

Bad choice of words, especially with all these folks around.

"I'm not a baby!" he snapped.

I made it to the door and focused on him. "I need a second, kid. Merry and me need a second. You know we'll give it to you when we know what's going down. Just let us see the lay of the land first. Okay?"

Dave had his hand on Ethan's shoulder. Feb was close too. Vi was pushing their way.

Ethan was glaring at me.

Then he bit out, "Fine."

"Go with Dave and Feb, you with me?" I asked.

"Whatever," he muttered, getting up from his seat on the floor by the coffee table, which had been cleared for cake placement, candle blowing, and ice cream scooping, the edges of the table and the floor around it littered with presents.

All ready for the good stuff.

Fucking Peggy.

I set my teeth, gathered my wits, tamped down my fury as best I could, and stormed out of my house.

Merry and Colt had managed to get her halfway down the walk.

I didn't know what was happening. I just saw through the two men's bodies she had one arm gesticulating.

She also had her daughter in a stroller and her son on her hip.

And my son was right then being hustled into our kitchen just before he was supposed to get cake, ice cream, and spoiled rotten by people who loved him, all because Peggy was having whatever fit Peggy was currently having.

In other words, I might have succeeded a little bit in tamping down my fury.

But I didn't hold tight enough to the reins.

I rounded Merry, did it with velocity, but got no further when his fingers caught the back waistband of my jeans and I came up short.

I didn't need proximity. I wasn't going to belt a bitch who was holding a baby.

I had the use of my mouth.

So I used it.

"Are you fucking *out of your mind?*" I asked.

She turned to me, face contorted with what appeared to be more rage than I had.

"Where's my husband?" she bit back.

"I don't fucking know," I answered.

"Refrain from cursing in front of my children," she ordered.

"Get your kids outta my yard and I won't have to," I retorted.

"I want to talk to my husband," she demanded.

"Then find him wherever he is and talk to him, something you're not gonna be able to do here, seeing as *he* isn't here," I returned.

"He's stopped going to meetings," she declared on a toss of her hair.

"I don't even know what you mean, but whatever you mean, I don't care," I replied.

She bent my way. *"Meetings,"* she hissed. "To keep out *the devil.*"

"My guess, NA," Colt waded in to explain.

Oh crap.

"And he's also stopped *coming home,*" Peggy went on.

Shit.

I took a small step back as what was happening here penetrated.

And what was happening here was not good.

"Is he here?" she asked.

"Like I said, Peggy, no," I answered far more calmly. "I haven't heard from him in a while."

"He hasn't been home in over a week," she informed me, like this was my fault.

I said nothing.

She kept the information flowing. "He also hasn't been to work."

Oh man.

She was screwed.

"It's his son's birthday party. I was certain he'd be here," she declared.

It was my turn to share some information.

"Then you don't know Trent, Peg, because he doesn't give a shit about his son."

"He's his father," she snapped. "A father goes to his son's birthday party."

"He hasn't been to one yet," I reminded her.

"That's because *you*," she leaned toward me, "wouldn't let him."

I drew in breath.

I had to hold on and not get mad again. She was up shit's creek. She knew it but was denying it and looking for someone to blame or take it out on.

But in the end, she'd go home to betrayal and abandonment.

When she was gone, I'd go into my house to watch my kid eat cake and open presents, my man at my side and everyone we loved who loved us back crammed in my little Janis Joplin living room.

So I could find it in me to be patient.

"That's because Ethan wasn't comfortable with it," I explained, something she well knew.

"That's because *you* weren't comfortable with us being a part of your son's life," she fired back. "Trent wanted more."

"Peg, seriously, think about it. *You* wanted more."

"Trent wanted it," she hissed.

"Trent is the guy who knocked up his girlfriend. That's it. Even with the minimal effort he put into winning his son, all of it at your demand, so all of it really for you, he's always just been the guy who knocked up his girlfriend."

"That's not true," she snapped.

"He's the guy who knocked up his girlfriend," I repeated quietly. "He's only been playing at being a father because it made you happy." I glanced swiftly at her kids. "And I think that hasn't changed."

She lifted her chin and reiterated, "That's not true."

I looked at her with her kids in my yard and saw bravado.

She was giving it her all.

But she couldn't hide it.

Her husband, a recovering addict, had disappeared. She had a part-time job and two young kids.

She was terrified.

I knew that feeling.

Something moved over her face.

I braced.

"He emptied our bank account."

Oh shit.

"Peg—" I began.

She tossed her hair again and spoke over me. "He was angry about the last visit we had here. We fought. He told me I was pushing too hard with Ethan *and* with him, whatever that means. How can you push a father too hard to *be a father?*"

It sucked that in that moment, I cared that it sucked for Peggy she was getting this wake-up call.

"He told me I needed to cool it because you were dating a police officer," she kept going. "Then he became distant. Then he was just…" She threw out a hand. "Gone."

I drew in breath.

Before I could speak, Merry did.

"It's Ethan's party. Your husband isn't here. I completely understand how his recent behavior and him not coming home is concerning you, but as unkind as you might think this is, it's Ethan's day and we need to focus on Ethan. We're all sorry that you're going through this, but it's highly unlikely your husband will show up here or contact Cher or Ethan. However, if he does, the only thing we can give you is our promise we'll notify you. Other than that, your problems are yours, Mrs. Schott. You need to take them elsewhere."

I thought that was kind of harsh, though it was all true and someone had to say it. And it was cool that Merry made it so it wasn't me who had to be the bitch to get her gone so we could get back to my kid.

But as he said it, Peggy stared up at Merry. The instant he was done talking, she looked to me.

The bravado was gone.

The fear was everywhere, all over her face, in the line of her body, even shimmering in the air.

Her little boy felt it and started fretting.

479

"He might be using," she whispered to me.

"Addicts do that," I said carefully. "They mess up. But he's been clean a long time, Peg. Maybe if you find him, you can get him back on the right road."

"People at church are helping me. We've been trying. Looking everywhere. Where he used to go. Where they know people go. Talking to people who know where people are. We can't find him," she shared.

"I—" I began.

"Mrs. Schott," Merry cut me off. "We got an eleven-year-old's birthday party happening in that house. I'm sorry, but we need to get back to Ethan and you need to be on your way."

She looked up at Merry, bouncing her boy up on her hip. He was about to lose it and start bawling, I could tell.

"But my husband has left me," she told Merry.

"Do you have family? Friends?" Colt asked.

She looked to Colt. "Of course."

"Then go home and call them."

She looked beyond Colt to my house. "I was sure he'd be here."

It was sad—those two kids of hers—tragic, even.

But she'd been married to him for years and she didn't know Trent at all, which meant Merry was right.

Her problems were hers.

"I gotta get back to Ethan, Peg, but I'll help you get the kids in the car before I do. Okay?" I offered.

Her eyes drifted to me.

They were brimming with tears.

Shit.

"We got her. You get in there."

I turned my head and saw Dusty and Rocky moving our way.

Cal was in the yard not too far from Merry and Colt. Mom, Tanner, and Mike were standing on the stoop. Ryker was also in the yard, arms crossed on his chest, looking grouchy. Ryan wasn't too far away, looking like he was trying to keep some distance from Ryker but also be close to me should I need him.

Rocky went right to Peg's son on her hip.

Dusty went after the stroller.

And I took that moment to glory in another boon. Not one Merry gave me. One I'd earned myself.

I had really fucking awesome friends.

(Yes, even Ryker.)

"Now, let's get you in your van," Rocky urged.

"Go," Dusty ordered me, commandeering the stroller and turning it down the walk. "Get on in there. Light up the candles. We'll have our cake when we get back. But save opening the presents. That's always the best part."

I nodded, the movement feeling weird, wooden. At first, I didn't know why.

Watching Rocky bounce Trent's possibly now fatherless son on her hip while she guided a lost Peggy to her van, following Dusty, I figured it out.

I knew her fear.

And I wasn't Peg's biggest fan, but I wouldn't wish that on anybody.

I looked up at Merry and opened my mouth.

He got in my face.

"Do not go soft on me," he ordered low.

I closed my mouth.

Just a look. That was all it took.

Jeez, when did he get to know me so well?

"Her bed she made," he stated.

"But—"

"Monday, I'll make some calls, do some searches, ask around. If I hear anything, I'll tell you and you can tell her. I don't hear anything, I'll talk to some buds. They'll keep their eyes peeled. Anyone sees him, they'll tell me, I'll tell you, and you can tell her. That's what I'll do for Ethan. He's gonna worry. And since I'm doin' that for Ethan, I'll be doin' it for her. But that's all I'm gonna do, Cher."

"I'll take it," I replied immediately.

He nodded and muttered, "Let's get your kid some cake."

"Yeah," Ryker boomed. "It's time for fuckin' cake." Then he uncrossed his arms and stalked through Mike and Tanner on my stoop, into my house.

I took one last look toward Dusty, Rocky, and Peggy.

With so many people at my party, the van was down a ways. Rocky and Dusty were strapping in her kids. Peggy was standing on the sidewalk like she didn't know where she was.

Merry's arm went around my neck.

He turned me and guided me toward the house, repeating, "Don't go soft."

I looked up at him. "You think she can get home?"

"She's a mom. When she gets behind the wheel, that'll kick in."

I knew that was likely true.

Time to focus not on Peggy but on my kid.

"Super stoked you didn't let me talk you out of the Colts tickets, babe," I declared. "After this shit, Ethan's gonna need something awesome to turn his mind."

This did not make Merry feel any better. I could tell by his jaw going hard, his cheek ticking, and his angry gaze slicing to Colt, who was walking back to the house with us.

Colt also didn't seem to feel relief that scene was over.

Then again, Colt was a new(ish) dad and Merry was a very new dad-like figure.

I'd been a mother for eleven years and three days.

If something threatened to turn my son's day to shit, that day was important or not…

No problem.

I had this.

(But the Colts tickets were gonna help.)

(Huge.)

"I wanna talk about it now," Ethan demanded.

The partygoers were in the living room save me, Mom, Merry, Colt, Feb, Cal, Vi, and Ethan's seemingly now ever-extending family through Merry—Tanner, Rocky, Dave, Mike, and Dusty.

Little Jack was in the living room with big Jack and Jackie.

482

Cal had a hold of his daughter, Angela; Mimi had Vi and Cal's son, Sam, in the other room.

And Tanner had Cecelia in his arms.

I'd noted all this distractedly, seeing as this growing family of friends was literally *growing* and it was mine, meaning it was Ethan's, and that was a birthday boon he wouldn't really understand, but it was his all the same.

But mostly, I was about my kid.

We'd all come into the kitchen after Rocky and Dusty got Peggy on her way. Though, obviously, the rest of us got there first since Rocky and Dusty were getting Peggy on her way.

It was just that Ethan was a little freaked.

Which was making him stubborn.

"I get that," I replied. "But you got a bunch of people in the other room who wanna watch you open presents, and I, for one, got a craving for R2-D2's innards."

I was trying to make a joke, lighten the mood.

Ethan saw through it right away.

"Was Dad there?" he asked.

"Kid, come on," I replied softly. "We'll talk after the party's over."

"Mom, that's crazy, her bangin' on the door like that. Who does that?" Ethan asked me.

A woman whose husband vanished.

"Son—"

Feeling sudden movement, I turned to see Merry, who'd been standing beside me in my face-off with my kid, was now crouching.

"Look at me," he ordered after he got low.

Ethan stopped scowling at me to look at Merry.

"You can hack it?" Merry asked.

Ethan's back straightened, but his gaze on Merry didn't waver.

"I can hack it," he announced.

Merry looked up at me.

I sucked breath in through my nose.

I had not shared all of Trent's problems with my son. For instance, he didn't know his father had used drugs. So he obviously didn't know how much he had used them either. He also didn't know his dad had been in trouble with the law. Not once, not several times.

He just knew the things I couldn't hide—Trent was absent, and when he wasn't, he was a loser.

I didn't know what Merry intended to say to my kid.

I just knew I trusted him.

So I nodded.

Merry turned back to my boy.

"Your dad wasn't there, Ethan. Your dad has problems. He's got to keep a tight handle on those problems or they'll get the better of him. He left Peggy without telling her what's happening with him and she doesn't know where he is. We can't know, but this gives indication he's lost hold and his problems got the better of him. She's worried, trying to find him, and she thought he would be here. He isn't, so we couldn't help her. There's not much we can do to help her, but I'll see about doin' what I can when I'm at work again."

He shuffled forward, reached out, and curled his hand around the back of my son's neck.

Then he kept talking.

"It's important to point out these are not your problems, bud. These are Peggy's problems. They're your dad's problems. Life works out in crazy ways sometimes and it seems your dad gave you and your mom one good thing: when he took off, you guys learned how to manage on your own. So when trouble hits for him, you just keep on rollin'. Now, your mom needs you to keep on rollin'. Can you do that for her?"

"He did to Peggy what he did to Mom, just later, didn't he?" Ethan asked Merry.

"We don't know. We just know what I told you," Merry answered.

"He did to Peggy what he did to Mom," Ethan muttered.

Merry gave his neck a visible squeeze and light shake, swaying Ethan gently.

"You gonna keep on rollin'?" he asked quietly.

Ethan looked at Merry.

Then he tipped his eyes up at me.

"We're done with him, Mom. That's it," he declared. "He does that to you and me, then he gets Mary and Tobias and does it to them. And even if Peggy is crazy, he did it to her too and that isn't cool. So even if he does try to come back some day, we're done. We don't need him."

"Your call, honey," I said softly. "It's always been your call. And it'll be your call if something happens and you change your mind."

He stared at me a beat before he turned back to Merry.

"I'm ready to keep on rollin', Merry," he stated.

Merry gave him a grin.

"That's my boy."

My heart fluttered.

My son's chest visibly swelled.

I heard Mom clear her throat.

"Right, I'll grab the ice cream," Rocky said.

"Everyone back in the living room," Dave ordered.

People moved. Merry straightened.

I kept my eyes to my kid.

He felt them and looked up at me.

"You good?" I whispered.

Ethan nodded.

"Let's go, buddy," Colt called.

Ethan looked at Colt.

Then he followed his uncle into the living room.

"Holy cramoly!" Ethan shouted, yanked what was inside the envelope out, turned his eyes to Merry, lifted his hand straight into the air, waved it around, and screeched, *"Colts tickets! Holy cramoly! I can't believe it! That's sooooo awesome!"*

He popped up and raced over legs and laps, pushing through bodies until he made it to Merry.

Once there, he threw his arms around Merry's middle and gave him a big hug.

Even now a big boy at eleven, he didn't let go and only tipped his head back, my little man smiling huge up at my big man.

"Thanks, Merry! The greatest present ever!" he yelled.

Merry grinned down at my kid and ruffled his hair.

"Glad you dig 'em, bud," he muttered.

Ethan jumped up, seeming to forget he was still attached to Merry, which meant his jump jolted Merry. This made Merry's grin turn into a smile.

Then he let go and whirled my way.

"Mom! Isn't this awesome?" he asked me, waving the tickets.

"Totally, kid," I answered.

"Ready to ruuuuuuuumble!" Ethan shouted before he shoved his way back to the coffee table, the dissected R2-D2, and more presents.

I was squatting close to my boy, taking notes so Ethan could write thank-yous, shoving spent paper and bows in a trash bag, and finishing up my piece of cake.

I was also allowing myself to enjoy the latest boon.

This being, when life threatened to knock my kid sideways, it had always been me and mom who had to scramble to make sure it didn't knock anything in him he couldn't get rid of. Anger. Bitterness. Sadness. Regret.

I looked to Merry to see him watching my kid tearing into his next present, and he had the look on his face that he sometimes had when he looked at me, but modified.

Even modified, it was soft and warm and perfect.

That was my boon.

Because my man dug my kid.

And me and my mom had another member on our team to make sure Ethan didn't get knocked sideways.

And he was a ringer.

Twenty-Three

PEOPLE LIKE THEM
Garrett

Thursday Afternoon

"Yeah. Thanks, man," Garrett said into his phone. "Later."

He disconnected.

Colt and Sully were standing next to Mike's desk, talking to him about a case they were on.

But when Garrett got off the phone, all eyes came to him.

"That was Roy from northwest district," Garrett said to their unasked question. "Had reason to be chatting with one of his sources. Trent Schott is on the street, scoring."

"Fuck," Colt muttered.

"You got a vicinity, you offer Ryker a marker, he'll find him for you," Sully suggested.

Garrett looked at Sully. "Schott isn't my job. His wife isn't my job. Cher and Ethan are my job. Promised them I'd ask around, but Ethan wants nothing to do with him. We know he's using. If Cher wants, she can tell Peggy. Anything else is up to her."

Sully grinned. "You just don't wanna owe Ryker a marker."

"There's that too," Garrett muttered.

That was when they all grinned at him.

Garrett ignored them and reengaged his phone.

He called his woman.

He gave her the news.

He found out while having a drink as she worked that night that she'd told Peggy. She'd also told her kid. She reported that Ethan cared but pretended he didn't.

Garrett decided to keep an eye.

And as he did that and the days slid by, he found both mother and son did what they did.

They just kept rolling.

Three Weeks Later

Garrett was sitting at his desk when he got a phone call from Devin.

"Woman packed up. Moved out. On her way to Missouri. Good call, seein' as her man has spent about thirty hours of the last three days not high, and that's only 'cause during those hours, he's been passed out," Devin declared. "FYI."

With that, he hung up.

Merry grinned and tossed his phone on his desk, not surprised that Devin had been looking into things. He was a lot like Ryker, but his gig was disguising the fact he gave a shit behind being a crotchety old man, not a huge-ass, scary biker.

Schott using again did not make him grin.

Ethan would be okay.

Cher wouldn't care, but she would be focused on making sure Ethan was okay.

But, crazy church lady or not, Garrett didn't like the idea of Peggy Schott having to find a way to raise two kids who were suddenly without their dad.

Missouri was a good call.

He waited until he was face-to-face with his woman to share that news.

She looked relieved.

And regardless of how fucked up the situation was, Cher relieved made Garrett happy.

With Peggy Schott gone, Mia quiet, and no threat on Cher's street, all this meant Garrett was seriously looking forward to testing out normal with his brown-eyed girl.

⌒

They weren't going to get that.

It just wasn't what life had in store.

Not for people like them.

Twenty-Four

On Board with That
Cher

Early Saturday Morning, Late November

The alarm went.

Merry stirred.

I stirred.

Merry turned it off.

I cuddled into him.

He wrapped his arms around me and gave me a squeeze that felt half-affectionate, half-like he was using the movement to wake himself up.

"I got 'im," I mumbled.

"I got 'im," he mumbled back.

I pressed closer. "You caught that case last night and got home late. You sleep. I got 'im."

"Babe."

I turned my head, touched my lips to his throat, and whispered, "Merry. You gotta let me take care of my kid once in a while. And just sayin', let me do the same with you too."

A beat passed before he gave me another squeeze that was all-affectionate.

Then he let me go.

I slid out of his bed, lurched out of his room, closed the door behind me, and walked the short distance down the hall to the other bedroom.

I knocked and opened the door.

In the early morning dark, I saw my kid's form under the covers in a new double bed. There were nightstands. There were lamps. There were posters of Colts players on the wall.

Although most of it had been thrown away or carted to Goodwill, there was still junk, but Merry had shoved it in the closet.

We were on a sleepover.

They happened these days. It wasn't frequent, but it happened.

What was frequent was Merry sleeping over at our place. In fact, these days, that was nearly every night.

Unless we were at his.

"Yo, kid. Wake up," I called. "Time to get ready. Gotta get you to Brendon's and we can't be late."

"Umma, gumma, mumma," Ethan mumbled.

I should have known it wouldn't be as easy as calling out to him. It was just six o'clock on a Saturday. He was eleven. Hell, I was thirty-four and I wasn't real hip on being up at that hour.

I moved to his bed and put a light hand on his shoulder.

"Not my idea to have a full-scale birthday blowout at my dad's cabin in the middle of nowhere that you gotta drive two hours and then hike through a forest to get to," I said. "Wasn't my idea to say yes to that crazy invite either. Since you said yes, you gotta get your butt outta bed and get ready or you're gonna be late. You don't want to miss the crazy-train to fishing in the middle of nowhere in November."

Ethan rolled to his back.

"I'm stupid," he muttered.

"Hmm…" I replied noncommittally.

"Brendon's stupid," he went on.

"Assessing stupidity at this moment, kid, is not gettin' your butt outta bed."

He made an unintelligible noise as he threw back the covers.

I moved to the door and, with practice, waited at it as he slumped my way.

I got out of his way and watched him go to the bathroom in the hall, turn the light on, and close the door.

That was when I knew he wouldn't relapse and face-plant back in bed. So I returned to Merry's room.

When I'd closed the door behind me and tiptoed to my bag through the dark, he muttered, "He up?"

"Yeah, gorgeous. Go back to sleep."

"Sure you don't want me to take him?" Merry asked, kinda slurred, definitely sleepy, also hot, and last, cute.

"I got him," I said. "Go back to sleep."

"Give me gooey before you go," he ordered, still kinda slurred, sleepy, but definitely cute and hot.

I changed from my pajama bottoms and cami into a bra, jeans, sweater, socks, and boots.

Then I made my way to my man in the bed.

He didn't move as I put my hand on his hip and leaned in to brush my lips against the stubble of his jaw.

But he did mumble, "Naked when you get back in bed with me."

Oh yeah.

I could do that.

"Right," I whispered. "Be back."

"Later, baby," he told the pillow, rubbed his face in it and turned his head the other way.

Yeah, again.

Cute.

I did my thing with my kid, making sure he brushed his teeth, was dressed appropriately, had layers just in case the weather changed, and all he needed packed for a cabin-in-the-middle-of-nowhere sleepover. I also made sure he had Brendon's card and present, and I got a breakfast bar down him.

The last was likely unnecessary. Brendon's parents had money. For his weekend-long birthday extravaganza in some woods somewhere fishing that had to start at oh-dark-thirty, no doubt they had a catered breakfast buffet waiting at their house.

If it was me, I'd have two dozen Hilligoss donuts. But considering they felt their son's diet should consist of more than sugar and chemically enhanced colors and flavoring, I figured they probably hadn't had a donut in their house since…well, they *bought* their house.

Which was too bad. If they had them, I could have swiped a few for Merry and me.

Instead, I decided to swing by Hilligoss on the way back.

My kid and I got in my car. I took him to Brendon's. I walked him through the early morning dark to the big house on the Heritage, the 'burg's fancy-ass housing development.

Brendon's parents asked me in.

To my shock, they had Hilligoss. Not two dozen. *Five.* Brendon's parents did not provide this blessing. Brendon's uncle did.

They offered me coffee and a donut. I only accepted the donut. When I mentioned Merry, Brendon's mom packed four for me (probably hoping to get them out of her house as fast as possible). Obviously, I didn't hesitate to accept.

I made sure I had phone numbers for Brendon's parents and the other two guys who were going with them to look after the boys.

One number was Brendon's uncle, the one who brought the donuts. He was also the one I noted with the attention of a woman who had it good at home (which meant absently) was on the upper scale of seriously good-looking. Not to mention he had a strong hint of badass to him, which made me wonder (also absently) what he did for a living.

Brendon's mom walked me to the door, saying, "Ethan says you're seeing someone."

I turned my head to look at her.

We weren't buds.

She was nice and all, but she lived on the Heritage. She was a stay-at-home mom. She went to yoga classes. She didn't shop in Indy; she went up to Chicago to get the *really* good shit. But she did go to Indy to drink martinis (probably—I didn't know this for sure, I just knew she never came to J&J's).

I was a bartender who lived in a boho-decorated crackerbox house.

This alone wasn't conducive to us being buds.

Therefore, I looked at her in surprise, because being nice and all never included anything personal.

"Yeah," I replied.

"That's too bad. Jay just filed for divorce. I was thinking of fixing you two up."

I stopped and stared at her.

Jay was her hot brother-in-law.

And that was life. A dry spell for years after hooking my star to a psychopath, I finally get someone—someone awesome, someone *perfect*—and some bitch suddenly wants to fix me up with a hot guy.

"Kinda taken," I muttered.

"If that doesn't work out, you've got his number. He saw you picking up Brendon a couple of weeks back and asked about you. He doesn't do that kind of thing and not just because he recently filed for divorce. He never did that kind of thing, before her or the last year they've been separated. This means he's interested. So my take, he wouldn't mind hearing from you."

I looked down her wide hall with its gleaming wood floors to the tall guy at the end of it wearing khaki cargo pants, a pullover army-green fleece with a half-zipper at his throat, three days of thick stubble, and a seriously attractive smile on his face that he was aiming down at Ethan's bud Teddy.

He might be fun.

And that was life.

Because I hoped I'd never know if he was or not.

I looked back at Brendon's mom. "Nice to know. But things are kinda serious with my guy."

She shrugged and smiled. "Just in case."

Whatever.

I returned her smile and took off.

I drove back to Merry's, parked by his Excursion, and hoofed it up to his condo. And I used the key he'd given me the same night he'd given one to Ethan (something he didn't make a big deal out of, but it was another warm and squishy moment, a huge one) to let myself in.

The condo was dark.

I considered making coffee and taking a cup to Merry with the donuts on a plate so we could scarf them down, doing this to give us both energy to do other things on a lazy Saturday when neither my man nor I had to work and my kid was off in the woods and wouldn't be home until late tomorrow afternoon.

I went to the bar, dropped the bag of donuts on it, and decided we could come out and make coffee and snarf down donuts later to carb up for a second round.

This meant I peeled off clothes on my way to Merry's room. By the time I got there, I had my jacket off. My sweater, boots, and socks, all gone.

So I opened the door wearing nothing but jeans and a bra.

What I saw was an empty bed and I could see that clearly because of the light coming from the bathroom.

I moved that way and felt my mouth water when I caught sight of Merry in his navy flannel pajama bottoms and nothing else leaning into a hand on the basin. His hair was a sleepy mess. His stubble was dark against his jaw. And he had a toothbrush in his mouth.

I grinned as I experienced a nice private shiver and moved his way.

Still brushing, he turned his head toward me as I walked into the bathroom.

His blue eyes instantly dropped to my bra.

My eyes dropped to the triceps bunching in his arm braced against the basin.

They moved to his lateral muscle. From there, they drifted down to his ass.

I went where my eyes beckoned and shifted behind him, pressing in. Hands to his waist, I slid them up to his ribs as I bent in and touched my lips to his spine.

I heard him spit out toothpaste foam.

I slid my lips up as I slid my hands in.

The tap went on.

I slid my tongue out and my hands down.

I felt the hair on his stomach.

God, I loved that hair.

I engaged my nails.

Merry's ab muscles contracted.

The tap went off.

I glided one hand up, flat against his pec. I also glided one hand down, tracing the arrow of hair, going for buried treasure.

I heard a low rumble come from him and he shifted his ass back into my hips.

Oh yeah.

I pressed into him as I bared my teeth, scraped the skin of his back, rubbed my thumb across his nipple, and dove in, pushing into his pajamas and finding treasure.

His thick cock was rock hard.

Fuck yeah.

His body tensed.

"Jesus, Cher," he growled.

I held tight and stroked.

"*Fuck*," he grunted, pushing his dick into my hand.

Fuck yeah.

I stroked harder.

"That's it, baby," he encouraged gruffly.

I licked, kissed, and lightly scraped his back as my free hand roamed his chest and my busy hand worked his dick.

"Wanna feel your tits," he ordered, voice thick, ass again pressed deep into my hips, letting me do all the work.

One-handed, I undid my bra. I slumped a shoulder so it would drop off. It did and I let it hang on the wrist of the hand engaged in giving my man the good stuff.

I wrapped my arm back around him and pressed my tits into his back.

"Fuck yeah," he groaned.

I kept at his cock with one hand as my other moved to the waistband of his pajama bottoms at the side. I looked down as I shoved down, watching as I exposed his skin, his muscle, his fine ass.

My legs trembled.

"Baby," I breathed.

"Knees," he rumbled.

No hesitation, I let his cock go and dropped to my knees.

Merry turned and shoved his pajama pants down, kicked them aside, and reached to my head.

He didn't have to guide me. I reached to his hips, latched on, shifted, found the head, and sucked deep.

"*Fuck yes*," he said on such a deep groan, I felt it rumble down my throat.

He was right.

Fuck yes.

I sucked him off, giving it everything I had, then giving in when Merry took over, holding my head, fucking my face.

One hand tight to his ass, the other hand tight around the back of his thigh, I took it. I loved it. Fuck, I was thinking I'd come getting it. And when a moan slid up my throat and sounded against his driving dick, he pulled out.

Then I was up, and before I knew it, I was facedown on his bed.

My whole body jerked after he reached a hand around, made light work of my fly, and yanked my jeans down.

My panties went with them and then my hips were up.

"All fours," Merry growled.

I pushed to my hands.

Merry thrust into my pussy.

My head flew back.

He fucked me harder.

I twisted my neck and looked back at him, panting, *gone,* but still able to encourage, "Give that to me, baby."

He pounded deep, eyes to my ass, his cock thrusting inside me, grunting, "So fuckin' gorgeous."

I dropped my head, rearing back, gasping, "Yeah, Merry. Please, baby. Keep givin' that to me."

He did and he didn't have to do it for long. I was so primed, I exploded, my arms dropping down, my head flying back. I was trembling even as I was burning—so beautiful, all Merry.

He thrust in, stayed planted, and pushed so I came off my knees, going forward. My legs spread-eagled to accommodate him, flat on my front, he got me in position and resumed moving, driving hard.

My orgasm shifting out, wanting another one, I started to lift up to get my forearms under me in order to drive myself into him.

His hand came to my neck and he gently pushed, grunting, "Baby, stay down."

My eyes flew open. My mouth went dry.

And my mind blanked.

I wasn't there.

I wasn't anywhere.

Not anywhere.

It came to me that I felt my body being fucked.

I was wet. So wet.

Wanting it. God, I wanted to get fucked.

I tried pushing my forearms under me again.

The hand at my neck tightened and I heard, "Stay down."

Stay down.

I stayed down.

The cock thrusting into me kept doing it. I heard the grunts of effort. Flesh hitting flesh. Then his hand at my neck tightened further as he drove deep, stayed put, and groaned.

I stared at the comforter.

It took a while, a long while, then there was gliding. Slow, sweet, gentle.

Had he been sweet?

He'd been sweet.

But not to me.

Never to me.

To who he wanted me to be.

I felt lips touch my shoulder.

That felt sweet.

But he wasn't sweet.

I knew sweet.

Now I knew sweet.

It wasn't him.

"Be back."

He slid out. I felt covers flipped over me. The bed moved.

He was gone.

I threw the covers back and bolted. On my feet, beside the bed, I saw my jeans and panties.

I didn't bother with the panties, I yanked on my jeans.

Where was my bra?

Fuck.

I couldn't find my bra.

Fuck it.

I needed a top.

"Cher?"

I saw my bag in the corner.

That's where I'd find a top.

I ran to it.

"Cher."

I dug through.

Who packed this? There was nothing there. Makeup. Deodorant. Socks. Jeans. Some panties.

I needed a goddamned top!

"Baby, what the fuck?"

I felt a hand light on my back.

I whirled viciously, swiping it away.

"Jesus."

"Don't fuckin' touch me," I bit out.

"Cherie—"

"Do not *ever* fuckin' touch me," I clipped.

I saw a hand come my way, aiming at my jaw, and heard a soft, gentle, sweet repeat of "Cherie—"

I attacked.

Savage.

Wild.

I hit. I kicked. I clawed. I bit.

I heard grunts. I heard curses.

I nearly got caught but leapt away and kept fighting.

Verbally.

"You hold me down, do you see her?" I asked, my voice grating with fury.

"See who?"

"See her. See her. *See her!* When you hold me down, face in the bed, motherfucker, do you see her? The woman you wish you were fucking?"

"Cher, that's—"

"*Do you?*"

"Baby, it's only you."

"Fuck you!"

"It's only ever been you."

"*Fuck you!*"

The two words rent the air. They weren't a crack. They weren't a slice.

They were a *slash*.

They went through me.

I felt them.

I just wanted them to go through *him*.

Leave him bleeding.

Leave him.

Destroy him.

Get him out of me for good.

I had to go.

Fuck.

I had nothing on up top.

I didn't care.

I turned and ran.

I didn't make it out the door. I was caught with an arm at my waist.

I started fighting again.

I was shifted to the side, pressed front against a wall, nearly immobilized, only able to kick back.

But I wasn't hitting anything.

"Calm down." The growl came at my ear. "Talk to me. What the fuck's the matter with you?"

"No more. No more of that shit. Hold me down so you can't see me. Fuck me. Think of her."

"Have you lost your goddamned mind?"

"You think I don't know?"

"You don't know."

"I know."

"Jesus, Cher. If you knew, you wouldn't say this shit. You wouldn't even think it. It's you, for fuck's sake. Been you since the beginning. Never her. Christ, woman, I'm in love with you. Mia does not factor."

I stilled.

Mia?

"You gonna calm down?"

I stared at the wall.

Merry's wall.

Merry's wall in Merry's bedroom in his crappy condo.

I'm in love with you.

The words should have given me something else.

Instead, they opened me up for it to come.

And it came.

Oh yeah, it came.

The pain.

The pain of shame.

Fast. So fucking fast. No way to hold it back. It tore through me in a way I *couldn't* hold it back. Not anymore. I couldn't bury it. I couldn't stop it overwhelming me.

My legs buckled under the weight of it and I slid down the wall.

I didn't hit the floor.

I heard, "Jesus, baby," and I was up.

I curled into him, and when we were down and my ass was in his lap, I *burrowed* into him.

Through this they fell.

The tears.

Uncontrolled.

Choking me.

Drowning me.

They felt strange. Hot. Ticklish. Shameful.

Hateful.

"I'm right here, Cherie," he murmured, one arm holding me tight, the other hand stroking my hair. "Not goin' anywhere. I'm right here. Talk to me. Where'd that shit come from? What's goin' on, honey?"

I tried to suck in breath.

Through the sobs, I barely got any in.

I burrowed closer like he could give me oxygen.

"Okay, sweetheart," he whispered. "Just hold on and get it out."

I did as told.

I held on and let it go.

He held on too. He stroked me.

And he absorbed it.

This went on for what felt like years before I started to quiet.

He said nothing. He didn't push. He didn't ask.

He just kept holding me, stroking me, and letting me let go.

Just like Merry.

Perfect.

"I should have known," I whispered into his skin.

"Shoulda known what, brown eyes?" Merry whispered back.

"He did me on my stomach. Hands and knees. Only those. He never let me look at him. I thought it was his kink, but I should have known that wasn't kink. It was sick. I didn't know that if he let me look at him, he would have seen me. *Me.* And he wouldn't have been fucking Feb."

I wheezed as Merry quit stroking and both his arms tightened so hard, I couldn't breathe.

Just as quickly as he did it, his arms loosened.

But not by much.

"I triggered a memory," he muttered.

He did.

"Yeah," I whispered.

"Fuck."

I pushed even closer. "Not your fault."

He was silent a second before he urged gently, "Give it to me."

I took my moment of silence before I said softly, "In the beginning, before I learned, learned what he didn't like, he held me down and would say it. 'Stay down.'"

"Fuck," he repeated.

"Not your fault, Merry."

"We'll avoid me fuckin' you on your belly in the future. And definitely those words."

I closed my eyes tight. "No."

"Cher—"

It took a lot to pull my shit together and give him my puffy eyes, my red face, any ability to look at me at all after that scene.

But I did it and I did it because he was Garrett Merrick.

I looked at him.

He wasn't freaked. He wasn't disgusted. He wasn't angry.

He looked troubled.

And he looked upset.

For me.

Yes, that's why I could look the way I looked after what had just given me that look and give the evidence of it all to Garrett Merrick.

"He doesn't get that," I told him.

Merry put a hand to my face, rubbing his thumb through the wet on my cheek. "Whatever you want."

"All that was going down, us getting together, my neighbor, your ex, Trent and Peggy, I didn't..." I trailed off but finished, "You were my first... after him. I should have guessed I'd need to keep a handle on it. I didn't guess."

Merry didn't reply. He just watched his thumb slide across my cheek.

"You think I'm a girl," I muttered.

His thumb stilled and his eyes cut to mine. "What?"

"Freaking out. Falling apart. Sobbing in your arms," I explained.

His face froze and his body under mine got tight.

And his voice sounded weird when he noted, "Honey, you *are* a girl."

"Yes, but—"

"And I'm pretty fuckin' glad you're a girl."

He would be.

"Of course, but—"

"And seriously, you havin' it totally together with this relationship thing was fuckin' with my man mojo. Takin' on my shit. Balancing me and your kid. Building two relationships at the same time—the one we got, the one you gave me with Ethan. Weathering every storm like it's nothin' but sprinkles. Not a big fan of you losin' your mind in my bedroom after I fuck you. But there are far worse things than bein' there for my girl while she cries in my arms and lets go of some serious shit that's burning a hole in her soul. It means something to me that you trusted me with that. It means something that you trusted me to be strong enough to handle it."

I stared at him.

"Though, don't make it a habit. My brown-eyed girl is a girl, but she's also a tough chick," he went on.

That was a tease. He didn't mean it.

I could cry in his arms every day of my life and he wouldn't give a shit. (Though, I'd never do that.)

I kept staring at him, doing it for the first time since it all went down with Dennis Lowe, feeling safe, *being* safe, totally safe to let it go.

But as I did it, my eyes filled with tears again.

I felt one break free and slide down my cheek.

Merry watched it go.

I started talking.

"I was so stupid."

Merry looked back at me.

"So stupid," I repeated. "He didn't want to meet my mom. He never asked us to his place. I never met any of his friends. His bullshit in bed was fucked up. Even if it was kink, I should have had more self-respect than to let him do that to me. And it wasn't that I didn't see it, Merry. It wasn't that I didn't put it together. It was all textbook at the very least for him being married but also him bein' possibly fucked in the head. So it wasn't that I couldn't put it together. It was that I *refused* to see it, because after my dad, after a bunch of shit guys treated me like crap, after Trent, I needed so badly to believe. To believe I could find some happy. So I refused to see. And that's bad enough just for me. But I exposed Ethan to that. I exposed my baby boy to that kind of crazy just because I wanted us to have a little bit of happy."

"You weren't stupid, Cherie."

"I so was."

He gave me a squeeze. "In all their years together, how many signs do you think Lowe gave his wife?"

"I know, but—" I tried to cut in.

I failed.

"I never met her," Merry spoke over me. "But every word said about her was that she was nice, people liked her, and no one said she was dumb. Men like him, it's part of the sickness, sweetheart, finding the skills to hide he's sick. He needed something from you and he turned on the charm to get it, by that time having had years to hone his skills at manipulating things to get what he wanted to feed the sick at the same time hide it. He played you, Cher. That's all he did. The reasons why were worse than the usual player who uses those skills to get you in bed or a con man who does the same to orchestrate his score. But in the end, that's all it was. And you are far from the first person, woman or man, mother or not, who trusted someone enough to get played."

I was staring at him again because something about the way he laid that out felt like a knot was being untied inside me. It had been tied together to hold back something important, something crucial, and whatever that was, it finally was let loose.

Or maybe it was that *and* freaking out on him, attacking him, and dissolving into a sobbing mess in his arms.

Whatever…that knot loosened, that thing inside me untied, it loosened something else.

My mouth.

Thus, I blurted, "I love you."

"No shit?"

I didn't stare at that.

I blinked.

Then I asked, "I say, 'I love you,' and you say, 'no shit?'"

"Babe, had my head in my ass, bein' my own brand of stupid, so I didn't see it. But when I looked back, I saw it." His lips quirked. "So yeah. No shit. Seein' as you been in love with me a long time."

Oh fuck.

He'd figured that out.

"I have not," I lied.

"Liar," he called me on it.

I started to push away.

His arms got tighter.

"Cherie, I love you too."

He sounded like he was struggling not only against me pulling away but also laughter.

Regardless of the fact that I totally…*fucking*…loved hearing those words directed at me from Garrett "Merry" Merrick's beautiful mouth, I was me.

So I stopped pushing and glared at him. "I know. You shared that when you had me pinned against the wall."

"Honey, you drew blood *and* nearly got me in the balls…*twice*. It was either pin you or let you have at it and then go to the emergency room."

I felt my eyes get big. "I drew blood?"

"Back," he grunted. "Nails. It's nothing."

I stretched to try and see his back. "Let me see."

"It's nothing."

I glared at him again. "Let me see, Merry."

"Not right now. Later. Now, one thing we gotta get straight—"

"I'll talk to Doc," I stated, guessing at what he wanted to get straight. "Ask him if maybe I should talk to someone about PTSD or something so you can fuck me on my stomach, because pre-ax murderer, I liked it like that."

Merry grinned at me. "Baby, you put up a helluva fight and you were seriously *gone*, but if you can be glib about therapy for PTSD for the sake of not losin' a sex position, I think you're good."

I hoped so because Feb and Morrie had good insurance, but I had no idea if it covered psychological shit and I had an extra name on my Christmas list now, an important one, and I was already giving up my candy and makeup habits (not all of them but some) in order to save to give it to him good. I didn't need therapy bills.

"Okay, so if you weren't gonna get up in my face about seein' someone to sort my shit out, what do we gotta talk about?" I asked.

"The fact that you clearly think it's weak to show emotion and to describe 'weak' you refer to bein' a girl. Showing emotion isn't weak. Showing emotion takes a lot of courage. Trusting someone to give shit to that you can't hold inside anymore isn't weak either. I know this because a wise, pretty, brown-eyed woman told me this not two months ago. And if we have girls, I don't want you teachin' them that they can't be girls however they wanna be girls and that anything girl-like is weak. 'Cause that shit ain't right."

I was staring again.

Then I was weeping again.

Finally, I was blurting again.

"If we have girls?"

"You want more kids?"

"Yes," I whispered.

"Then that can happen, fifty-fifty chance, and if they like butterflies and flowers and have no interest in bein' tough chicks, gotta know you're on board with that."

I was on board.

So on board.

Still whispering (and blurting *and* weeping), I said, "I love you."

Merry was whispering too when he replied, "Love you too, Cherie."

"Can I look at your back now?" I asked softly.

He fell back, doing it twisting.

When he had me back to the bed and him pressed into me, he said, "After I fuck you again."

My arms around him tightened as my brows went up. "Not concerned about another episode?"

"This time I do you, I'll be lookin' in your eyes."

I liked it like that.

Enough to lift my head and press my lips to his.

He pushed back so my head was to the pillow and opened his mouth.

Our tongues tangled at the same time.

Merry didn't do me looking in my eyes the whole time.

But it was me who lost eye contact when he made me come.

I would find out later I did draw blood on his back. Two lines, one deeper than the other along his shoulder blade.

I was careful as I washed them in the shower. I gooed them up with Neosporin before we snarfed down donuts.

But the ointment ended up on Merry's sheets.

What could I say?

We had the whole day.

We were young, healthy.

We loved each other.

And that was worth a repeat.

We loved each other.

I loved Merry and *Merry loved me.*

Life was good.

For once.

With a hopeful forecast for the future.

Finally.

So it was time to fuck.

"Babe?"

I was nearly asleep, fucked out and cuddled into my man.

"Mm?"

"Keep an eye, open communication, it happens again, you got shit messin' with your head, we talk. You need it, we take you to Doc."

I opened my eyes.

My man took care of me.

I closed them again.

"Whatever you want," I whispered.

He pulled me closer.

"Love you, brown eyes," he murmured.

Yeah.

Life was good.

"Love you too, Merry," I replied.

Not long after, snuggled to Garrett Merrick, I fell asleep.

Garrett

Cher was in a certain mood.

That mood was moving her to taste him, slow and light, everywhere.

He liked it a fuckuva lot, but they'd been busy. He had news he hadn't shared.

"Baby," he called.

"Mm?" she murmured against his abs.

"Come up here," he ordered.

She lifted her eyes to him. "Headed in a different direction, honey."

He grinned. "Come here a sec."

She studied him a beat before she slid up until they were face-to-face. She rested her chest against his.

"What?" she asked quietly.

"There were a lot of variables, wanted to make sure it all went down— the inspection, what I asked to be fixed, what I was gonna suck up—so I didn't tell you just in case it fell through. It all got worked out. Now I can tell you. Got an offer on the condo coupla weeks ago, took it. Sold the boat. I used that and savings as the down payment. Closing is set for Thursday on the house."

She stared into his eyes. "What house?"

"Lake house," he told her. "I close on this place in three weeks. Get that money, use some of it to do some updates. But I'm gonna have to live there while they get done."

"You're closing on the lake house."

"Yeah."

"That house you showed me on your laptop?"

"Yeah."

"You're closing on that."

He grinned again. "Yeah."

"You're gonna live there?"

His grin got bigger. "That's what I said."

"Ethan and me get sleepovers?"

They'd start with that.

They'd end with him having a lake house that looked like Jim Morrison bought the place, not Garrett.

He rolled her and answered, "Oh yeah."

She was now on the bottom, staring up at him.

She did this awhile without speaking.

Then she declared, "For a housewarming, I get to buy you a kickass grill."

He'd let her do that.

"You're on."

"And twenty tiki torches."

Garrett burst out laughing.

When he was done, he saw she was smiling.

His brown-eyed girl…happy.

He knew a way to make her happier.

And he was on top.

So he dipped down and set about doing that.

In the end, he succeeded.

Twenty-Five

NO ROOM FOR TEARS
Cher

Thursday Morning, Mid-December

"We should do Christmas here," Ethan said to Merry and me while sitting at the breakfast bar in Merry's awesome new house, shoveling in some of Merry's pancakes. "We can open presents, then go out and ice skate on the lake or something."

"Kid, it hasn't even snowed," I reminded him. "There's about a half a centimeter rim of ice that runs the edge of the lake and that's it."

He shrugged. "Maybe we'll get a deep freeze between now and then."

"We don't have ice skates," I went on.

"That would be why we'd go out *after* we open presents. And just sayin', ice skates are a big fat no. Hockey skates, though..." He let that hang.

And there it was. Shared with all the finesse of a hammer.

My kid wanted hockey skates for Christmas.

This did not fill me with joy. Hockey skates might lead to hockey lessons and hockey probably cost a mint. I didn't have a mint nor would I ever.

But if my kid wanted hockey skates then hockey lessons, I'd find a way.

I just wished he'd turn his attention to Frisbee. A Frisbee champion needed functioning limbs and a plastic disc. Ethan luckily already had functioning limbs and I figured even the most expensive Frisbee you could get cost less than hockey skates.

On this thought, Merry spoke.

"Bud, don't have any decorations and your place is already all set up, seein' as we spent twelve hours straight decorating it a week ago and now it looks like Santa vomited all over the joint."

Ethan busted out laughing.

I turned and glared at Merry.

Merry, not sitting but bent over his plate at the bar opposite Ethan, turned his attention from his plate of pancakes to me.

"What?" he asked, one side of his lips tipped up.

"I like Christmas," I snapped.

"I can tell," he replied.

Ethan kept laughing.

"I got a kid," I stated. "You decorate for Christmas when you have a kid."

"Mom, I quit believing in Santa Claus when I was six," Ethan reminded me of the dire day he imparted that information on me, information he'd learned from some snot at school who had an older brother and sister, both of whom had big mouths as did Ethan's snot friend. "Now I'm nearly twelve. I'm totally over the over-the-top Christmas stuff."

"Yes, you did stop believing in Santa when you were six," I confirmed. "You also quit getting presents from him when you quit believing in him. Think about *that* for a second, smart guy."

The look on Ethan's face told me he was thinking about it and I'd made my point.

I didn't rub it in.

But I did keep at him.

"And you're not *nearly* twelve. You're eleven and two months. That isn't even close to nearly twelve."

I was right, of course. It wasn't.

But it was more that I couldn't think of my kid as "nearly twelve." This meant, after that, he'd be nearly thirteen and then nearly fourteen and then nearly out of the house, off to college, then getting married to some bitch who better treat him right or I'd cut her.

So no.

I couldn't think of Ethan being nearly twelve until he actually *was* nearly twelve.

"Just sayin', babe," Merry started, and I looked down at him. "Dudes and chicks are different. Women spend most of their lives denying their age. Men spend theirs living for retirement."

This was true.

And it sucked.

"That's because chicks stop bein' hot at around thirty-five and men can be hot for, like, ever," Ethan declared, and I turned my now-far-more-intensified glare to him.

He was impervious and I knew this when he kept talking.

"I mean, look at Colt. He's, like, borderline old guy, and he still totally has it."

"And Feb doesn't?" I asked.

My kid looked to me. "She's an exception."

"You do know I turn thirty-five in two months," I reminded him.

He grinned at me. "You're an exception too."

"You totally are," Merry muttered.

My head whipped Merry's way. "You could help here, you know."

Merry looked to my son and said as if by rote, "Ethan, women are attractive at any age."

Ethan grinned at my man and replied, "Right."

I decided Merry would get another blowjob around the time Ethan turned twelve.

But I had a lesson to teach, so I'd deal with that later.

"So, prior to your twelfth birthday, I'll tell Feb, Rocky, Dusty, Frankie, and Vi you think they're all past it," I declared. "And before your gramma goes out for the big stuff for you for Christmas, I'll tell her you think she's *totally* past it."

"They're all exceptions too. Even Gram. I wouldn't know, obviously, but Teddy's grandpa said she's a looker," Ethan returned.

"So who *isn't* an exception?" I asked.

Ethan looked like he was thinking about it.

Then he broke into a big grin and stated, "Maybe I spoke all hasty."

"See, baby, you got a smart kid. You give him time, he'll get to it," Merry said.

"You both are annoying me," I announced, though this was really a lie. I thought they were pretty hilarious. Annoyingly hilarious but still hilarious. I reached out to grab Ethan's empty plate. "And it's time for work and school, so you can quit annoying me by gettin' on the road."

I grabbed my own plate too, turning toward the sink, hearing Merry talking. "Your mom's right, buddy. Let's hit it. Teeth. Backpack. Coat. And grab a scarf and gloves. It's cold out there. Yeah?"

"'Kay, Merry."

I turned on the tap to run water over butter and maple syrup residue, completely unable to continue even pretending to be annoyed after hearing Merry tell my boy to grab a scarf and gloves.

I watched Merry's hand put his plate on top of the other ones in the sink as I felt his other hand light on my hip.

"Easy to get a tree, grab some cheap ornaments, and put it up. I'll even get one of those big blow-up snowmen for the front yard, you and Ethan wanna do Christmas here," he said in my ear.

"I can't do Christmas unless Santa has anointed my house with Christmas vomit," I told the sink. "You up for that?"

I heard his chuckle and felt the heat of him come closer as his hand slid from my hip to my belly.

"We'll get an air mattress. Ethan can sleep on that in one of the extra rooms. Grace can sleep in Ethan's room. Everyone comfortable. Do presents here, breakfast, then later, go to Rocky and Tanner's. Dad'll be there. Vera and Devin too. Jasper and Tripp as well, Keira attached at Jasper's hip, like usual. Big family thing when we do Christmas dinner."

Big family thing.

A big family thing that Merry wanted.

But he wanted that family thing to start here, in his house, with what we were building.

I closed my eyes.

Ethan had a room at Merry's and it was definitely his room. Not a junk room. Nothing was in the closet but some of my kid's clothes. Shampoo, toothpaste, toothbrush in the crappy bathroom Ethan used that Merry was going to gut after Christmas and redo.

The roof, furnace, AC, and windows had been first, obviously, and Merry hadn't fucked around with those. He had us there and he had that frequently, he'd told me, so he took care of that right away. Right away, as in, he had work scheduled to start practically the day after he moved in.

I had clothes in Merry's closet and doubles of all my stuff (except makeup—that required an investment, but I had bits and bobs, so I was getting there) in his crappy master bath.

We were all but moved in.

And now—Merry's house being so big, the great room a place where we could all be together, Ethan liking showing off its awesomeness to his buds so sleepovers continued to be frequent (they just happened at Merry's), and Merry pretty much taking over the care of my kid when I was at work nights or evenings—we were mostly here.

We might sleep at my place once or twice a week.

But Merry's place was becoming home.

This was intentional. He gave both of us sets of keys the day he'd closed on the house. The first night we stayed over, which was the first night he was in the house since we'd helped him move, we found he'd bought an Xbox so Ethan would have all he needed to feel at home. And he told me to pack us both and make it so we weren't lugging bags back and forth all the time.

"Settle in, baby. You and Ethan," he'd whispered to me in the dark that first night in his house. "I think we're all past the idea of sleepovers."

I was. Definitely.

My kid would go to the ends of the earth for Merry, so I figured he was too.

I just didn't know Merry was at that place.

But I was glad to know.

And the next day, I settled us in.

Right then, however, I knew just what place Merry *actually* was in.

And it was even better.

I turned in his arm at the sink, looking up at him.

"You want Christmas," I whispered my guess.

"Yeah," he replied. "Didn't wanna say anything, but since Ethan mentioned it and seems he's good with it, there it is."

"Then we'll have Christmas here. I'll talk to Mom."

He smiled down at me and I saw excitement in his face that made my badass Merry into my badass Merry who could be cute.

"Thanks, baby," he murmured, bent in and touched his mouth to mine. When he lifted up, he said, "Since you're off today, I'll go get a tree and we'll decorate it tonight. You got time to go out and get some ornaments? Lights? Whatever else we need?"

Did I have time for Christmas decoration shopping during Christmas shopping season, when the population at large should be at its best but was undoubtedly at its worst, doing this for a tree for Garrett Merrick's awesome new lake house?

I *totally* had time.

"I have time," I confirmed.

He looked like he was fighting laughter, which was telling me I wasn't hiding my enthusiasm for that day's chores, when he said, "Cheap shit, babe. Just to get us by. I have a feeling next year I'm gonna have more Christmas crap than anyone needs by a long shot."

My exciting new plans for the day flew straight from my head.

"What?" I asked.

Merry didn't repeat his feelings about what would happen in the next year, which, my guess, included Ethan's and my Christmas stuff being at his awesome new lake house.

Instead, he got bossy.

"Go to Bobbie's. Ask Vi if you can use her discount. Get those plastic tubes of ornaments, the ones that are twelve for a buck. Get a couple. And some lights. But don't mess around with the lights, babe. You should always invest in good lights. Next year, we'll find a way to use the extras."

I blinked, what Merry said earlier going straight from my head.

"Twelve-for-a-buck ornaments? Only a couple tubes?" I asked.

"How many you need?" he asked back.

"I don't know. Are you buying a proper Christmas tree or a Charlie Brown Christmas tree?"

His head jerked back like that question was an affront.

"First Christmas here with you, Ethan, and Grace, I'm not gonna get a shit-ass tree."

That was nice.

However…

"So what you're saying is, the good part, the part *I* like, you want twelve-for-a-buck ornaments, two tubes of them, but you're gonna get a nice tree and you want me to go whole hog on the lights because you have a dick and lights have a plug and that's the way of the world."

Merry was no longer affronted.

His lips were twitching.

"You want three tubes of ornaments? Knock yourself out."

Thirty-six ornaments on a full Christmas tree.

Not gonna happen.

"I'll get what I get," I declared.

Merry's face again lost its humor. "Serious, Cher, we'll have your shit here next year and we don't need decorations for two trees."

I was back to thinking about Merry's plans for the upcoming year.

"We'll have my shit here next year?"

"Yeah."

I waited for him to say more.

He didn't say more.

"Did I miss the invitation to move in with you?" I asked.

His humor yet again returned. "No."

I waited for him to say more.

Again, he didn't.

"Are you gonna *steal* my decorations so you have them next year?" I asked.

His amused face got close.

"No, baby. I'm gonna put in two decent bathrooms. Then I'm gonna buy better furniture because my shit sucks. After that, after we're all good and used to each other and I got a nice home to offer my woman and her boy, a real home, a comfortable home, I'm gonna invite them to move in with me. When they accept, I'm gonna have to accept all her shit. There's a lot of it and it includes fifteen boxes of Christmas crap. And don't deny you got fifteen boxes, sweetheart, because Ethan and I lugged every one of those fuckers out of your garage, and when we did, we counted them."

He said the last quickly because I'd opened my mouth.

He also didn't stop talking.

517

"So, to end, we'll have your shit here next year, so we don't need expensive stuff for the tree we have this year."

"The master is pretty big, gorgeous," I said quietly. "We could put a tree in there next year with our new decorations."

His expression got more amused. "Jesus, Cherie, no one needs a tree in their bedroom."

"But I want one."

"Then get what you want to decorate this year, and next year, we'll put a tree in our bedroom."

I stared into his eyes.

That came right out. No hesitation, it came right out. Right out of Garrett Merrick's mouth.

I told him I wanted a tree in the bedroom; he told me to get what I want.

A girl who didn't dream sure as hell was smart enough never to want. She took what she could get and that was that.

And just like that, no hesitation, I wanted something silly.

And Merry gave me what I wanted.

"You want us to move in with you."

My voice was funny—quiet, husky.

His voice was not quiet or husky. It was deep and kind of incredulous, like he couldn't believe I hadn't figured it out yet.

"Of course I do, brown eyes. I bought this house for you."

My throat suddenly felt tight.

He…

What?

I kept staring as I forced out, "What?"

"More house than I needed at a price higher than I wanted. But you liked it. You like water. Ethan's got his space. We got ours. We got together space. We got expansion space. So I bought it."

I kept staring at him, but something happened while I did.

He watched me a beat, saw that something happen, and said, "Fuck, you're gonna cry again, aren't you?"

I slapped his shoulder and snapped, "I've cried once with you, Merry. *Once.*"

"Well, this time I don't have time to get you through it. I gotta get Ethan to school."

I gotta get Ethan to school.

He took my kid to school every day. Every day. Unless he was out on an early morning case, which was rare, it was no fail.

Every day.

Mornings were now *our* thing, the three of us, but the school run was Merry and Ethan's thing.

I felt wet hit my cheek.

"Shit," he muttered, watching the tear fall.

"Stop making me happy," I whispered.

His eyes came back to mine and his were dancing.

But when he replied, he was whispering too.

"Not gonna happen."

"You need to be annoying on a more regular basis," I demanded softly.

His body started shaking and his voice was doing it as well when he stated, "That's not gonna happen either."

"Okay, then you need to go because I have a lake house Christmas theme to plan and execute and that's not gonna happen when you're standing here being awesome."

He audibly started laughing, and in the middle of it, he kissed me.

His laughter tasted great on my tongue.

The best.

"Okay, guys," Ethan shouted. "Are you done with the gooey? 'Cause I been waitin' in the hall, like, *forever.* I might not wanna get to school, but I'm cruisin' toward perfect attendance third year running, which includes *not* being tardy, and, you take much longer, you're messin' with that mojo."

Merry broke the kiss, and when he did, my tears had subsided.

This was because Merry's kiss, as ever, was a good one.

It was also because my man and I were standing in his kitchen in his lake house, which would soon be *my* kitchen in *our* lake house, and we were staring at each other, laughing at my kid.

And I was finding I had a life that was filled with a lot of that.

Laughter.

So now, for a different reason, I had no room for tears.

I stood in Bobbie's Garden Shoppe in her enormous Christmas section that was renown throughout the Midwest. It was this because it was so huge, she had to dedicate half her shop to it *and* half her parking lot, seeing as she had massive heavy-duty, heated tents where more of her Christmas crap was displayed.

I was there and had been for forty-five minutes.

But I found what I was looking for.

So there I stood, staring at a Christmas tree, and I was pretty certain I was going to buy the whole damn thing as it was—ornament by ornament, garland by garland—and resurrect it in Merry's awesome new lake house. It was boho to the max, colorful with lots of berries and crystals and differently sized and shaped ornaments, very cluttered, stuffed full, totally awesome.

There was no other tree in Bobbie's whole shop like it.

But I'd had a look at a couple of the ornaments, and even with Vi's discount, to recreate that tree would cost a thousand dollars.

It was perfect for Merry's pad, so I did not care.

Okay, that wasn't true. It was perfect for me (I still didn't care).

What I cared about was something else.

I whipped out my phone, jabbed my finger on the screen, and put it to my ear.

"Hey, babe. What's shakin'?" Vi asked in greeting.

"Do you think Merry would lose his mind if I bought pink and purple Christmas tree ornaments?"

"How many?"

"A lot."

"Okay, then, one hundred percent affirmative on him losing his mind."

"Shit," I muttered, already kind of knowing that was the answer.

"Say one ornament that you put on the inside of a branch close to the trunk that's mostly hidden and he can't see, you might get away with that. But more than that? No go."

I stared at the tree. "What about canary yellow? And teal?"

"Negatory and negatory."

"Lace cutout stars?"

Her voice was getting shrill either with hilarity, disbelief, or both when she asked, "Have you met Garrett Merrick?"

"Shit," I muttered again.

"I thought you guys already decorated."

"We did. My house. But we decided this morning we're doin' Christmas at Merry's. So I need a whole new tree."

"Ooo, sweet. Christmas by the lake. Awesome."

She was not wrong.

"Fake tree?" she asked.

"I don't know. He said he'd get one. That could mean anything."

"He's a guy. If he says he'll get one, that means it'll be real and you'll be cleaning up pine needles until February. You'll also have a time of it talking him out of going somewhere and chopping one down himself just so he can chop down a tree. My advice, babe? Focus on those things, primarily talking him into a fake tree so you don't have to vacuum pine needles for two months, not wasting time talking him into pink ornaments. Trust me on this. You got a badass in your bed, you learn to pick your battles."

I had a badass in my bed. I loved him. I wanted to keep him there. So I should listen to Vi. She had a lot of experience. She'd married a badass in the making when she was eighteen, and he'd grown into a full-blown one who unfortunately got dead way too soon. She'd then married an even bigger one who kept knocking her up when she wanted to concentrate on hoping her second child didn't get knocked up by her own badass boyfriend at the same time keeping an eye on the fact that her oldest daughter had begun dating a badass cop in Chicago.

Yes, I should listen to Vi. She lived and breathed badass.

Whatever you want.

Merry said that a lot.

To me and to my kid.

I stared at the tree.

Not only would it be awesome this year, it'd be even *more* awesome in the master suite next year. Our tree. Merry's and mine.

Whatever you want.

"Bobbie gonna give me your discount?" I asked Vi.

"You're buyin' pink ornaments, aren't you?" she asked back.

"Merry likes me to have what I want," I told her.

"Yeah," she said softly. "That's why I have my new lavender bed set that Joe said he'd sleep on over his dead body. Then again, that's also why Joe's got his next kid in my womb."

"Yeah," I replied, feeling squishy she had that and now I did too. Decision made, I muttered, "This tree is gonna cost a mint."

"I'll call Bobbie. See what she can swing for you."

"Thanks, Vi."

"No probs, babe. See you later."

"Later."

I shoved my phone in my purse and moved to the baskets under the tree. I was filling my cart with boho Christmas when Bobbie wandered up to me.

She looked to the cart then to me. "Shit, I was gonna offer you thirty percent instead of Vi's twenty-five, but you goin' whole hog like that this late in the season, I'll give you forty. Just tell 'em at the register you're Vi's friend and Bobbie says forty. They give you shit, make them page me."

With that, she wandered away.

But I was grinning because forty was brilliant. It didn't make this doable. I still had a grill to buy (housewarming). I also had a phone to buy (Merry's screen was cracked and it drove me crazy in a way I didn't know how it didn't drive him crazy, so I was doing something about it, and what I was doing was for Christmas).

But for boho Christmas at Merry's new lake house, for the first time since I'd clawed my way out from under it, I'd carry a balance on my credit card for a month (or two).

I'd also continue to cut back on the candy. The makeup was a wash since I was setting up my stash at Merry's. Our first Christmas with Merry and spoiling my man, though, I'd sacrifice my candy.

Totally.

I got the tree stuff for me. I got the expensive lights for Merry. And I got some matching garlands to put on Merry's mantel because, if you had a mantel at Christmas, it had to be decorated and I was pretty sure I could talk Merry into believing that.

But even I knew I was pushing it (but couldn't stop myself) when I bought Christmas kitchen towels.

I was loading all of this in the back of the Equinox when I heard, "You do know you ruined my life."

I stopped loading and looked to Mia Merrick, who was standing by my cart, holding a potted poinsettia curled in each arm.

Shit.

Why?

Really.

Why?

Why couldn't I just have an *excellent* day?

A day where I woke up in Merry's arms, my kid safe and snug and warm under his roof in his new awesome lake house that had new double-paned windows and a new furnace.

A day where Merry made us pancakes and teamed up with my kid to give me shit, which I would for eternity (if I had the shot) make them think annoyed me when I secretly loved every second of it.

A day where Merry said he wanted Christmas and he wanted us to move in with him.

A day where I could buy a bunch of Christmas crap that (best case) Merry was going to think was hilariously me or (worst case) Merry was going to hate. For the former, he'd just tease me, and if it was the latter, he'd still let me have what I want.

Why, from the parking lot of Bobbie's Garden Shoppe, couldn't I go to the grocery store, buy a tube of premade Christmas cookie dough (cookie dough was not candy, so it didn't count) and some Pringles (because we were low), go home, make Christmas cookies for my boys, and decorate a tree my man (and maybe my kid) were gonna hate?

Why?

Why couldn't all that just *be* without anything fucking with it?

"Mia, really, today's been a good day and I'm not—" I started.

She got closer to me (something I liked even less than her being there at all) and cut me off. "Today's been a good day? Has it, *Cher?* Has it been a good day for you? Well, how lucky you are. Because today and yesterday and the last three months have been *shit* for me…" Her face twisted before she finished, "Because of *you.*"

No wonder Merry scraped her off. She was a pain in the ass.

"If you think I'm lucky, babe, then—" I tried again.

I didn't get far.

"Do I think you're lucky?" she sniped. Her gaze cut inside my car and back to me, and her voice degenerated significantly when she asked, "Merry needs Christmas decorations for his new house?"

Okay, right.

I was done. I didn't need this and I wasn't going to have it.

So I was going to end it.

"If you've deluded yourself into thinking I'm the cause of all your problems, that's your gig, Mia. It has nothing to do with me. Take it elsewhere," I stated.

"Deluded?" she asked, coming even closer. "Isn't it *you* who's fucking my husband?"

"No. It's *me* who's fucking Garrett Merrick, who *isn't* your husband. Now, step back," I demanded.

She didn't step back.

"He'll come back to me," she declared.

"Whatever," I muttered, grabbed the handles of the last bag in the cart and put it into my car.

"He will. He'll come back. It's him and me and everyone knows it," she pushed.

"Really? Are you that deep in the fantasy? How sad."

I didn't say that.

My head turned at the new voice.

And when I saw who was behind it, I stopped dead.

I did this because, joining our tableau, was Susie Shepherd.

And her catty, bitch-from-hell eyes were aimed at Mia.

I didn't know Susie. Not at all. She never came into the bar partly because she was Colt's ex, partly because she was kidnapped by Denny Lowe and shot by him during her time as a hostage, and partly because everyone in town knew she'd sold her story, which made the residue of Lowe's journey of lunacy last a lot longer.

She was also known 'burg-wide as a soulless, selfish, spoiled bitch.

This was evidenced by the fact that she and her partner in crime, Tina Blackstone (who *did* come into J&J's, regrettably, since the bitch didn't tip), wreaked havoc countywide in a variety of ways they were committed to to the point it seemed like a mission.

These included targeting married men with their charms (and unfortunately, since Susie was very attractive, she was successful with this). They gossiped viciously with the few friends they had, spreading that gossip as far and as wide as they could, even if it was all lies. And they threw down easily and frequently whenever the spirit moved them (even to the point of Susie going at it with Vi right in front of Cal, who Susie had fucked, a fact she'd shared with Vi *right in front of Cal*).

Everyone in town hated her.

I only knew her because I'd seen pictures of her in conjunction with reports about Lowe's mayhem and I'd seen her around town here and there.

But in the grand scheme of things in the 'burg, I knew one thing for certain: if your day was filled with happiness and light or it was the worst kind of crap, Susie Shepherd could darken it exponentially.

Shit.

"Your input isn't needed here, Susie," Mia snapped.

"*You* aren't needed here, Mia," Susie snapped back, then looked at me, throwing out a disgusted hand. "I mean, seriously. Normally? Rude. But it's Christmas." She shook her head. "Some people."

I stared at Susie in shock.

Mia didn't.

She turned fully to her and shared, "I was having a private conversation with Cher."

"You were staking your claim to Merrick. *Again*. I don't get it, Mia. The man's so over you, it's embarrassing. I mean," she jerked her head to me, "she's all but shacked up with him, in Bobbie's parking lot with a trunk full of Christmas decorations they're gonna put on a tree in his new house and probably fuck under, and you get in her face." She shook her head and concluded, "It's not embarrassing, it's plain sad."

I watched this all going down with some fascination at the same time I made a mental note to find time to fuck Merry under our new boho Christmas tree.

"Your opinion is unwanted," Mia shot back.

"Just trying to help a sister save face," Susie said with false concern. "I mean, why you haven't left town yet, I do *not* know."

"*You* are asking *me* that?" Mia retorted.

Susie shrugged. "Yeah. The words did come out of my mouth two seconds ago."

Mia decided she was done, declaring this fact by saying, "Just go away. This is none of your business."

I braced when Susie suddenly took two steps forward, getting right in Mia's space and face, and hissed, "It *is* my business." She lifted a hand and jabbed a finger my way. "She's happy. He fucked her over, but now she's finally happy and you're in a goddamned parking lot fucking with that. So it is my business, Mia. Stay out of her face or you'll find mine *all* up in yours. And, baby girl, get me. Your kitten claws might sting, but you tangle with me, I'll *shred* you."

Holy fuck!

Susie was throwing down.

For me.

"So you two are Denny Lowe sisters, is that it?" Mia bit back.

"Yeah," Susie whispered. "Yeah we are. We don't wanna be, but we are. And, just in case you aren't getting this, because we are, you don't fuck with us."

Whoa.

Susie was totally throwing down.

For me.

I was attempting to process this and how I felt about it when I braced again. This was because Susie's eyes lifted from Mia and she tensed.

Visibly.

Susie visibly tensed and I watched the blood drain clean from her face.

Then she started backing up.

Her mouth moved.

It moved again.

No sound came out.

"What?" I asked.

Her mouth moved, and again, no sound came out.

"Susie, are you okay?"

She looked to me.

Then she screamed, "*Run!*"

And that was when the gunshots exploded.

Garrett

"Pink."

Garrett turned in line at Mimi's Coffee Shop to see Cal behind him, his baby son asleep and strapped to his chest, his little girl in front of him in a stroller, the key fob to Cal's truck half an inch from Angela's face, a clear object of fascination.

"What?" he asked.

"Pink," Cal repeated, looked to Mike at Garrett's side, his eyes fucking *alight* with humor.

Shit.

"And, I hear, some purple," Cal went on.

"What are you talkin' about?" Garrett asked.

"Vi reported in. The ornaments for your tree. Brace, man. Cher's testin' you," Cal told him.

Pink Christmas ornaments.

Did they even *make* pink Christmas ornaments?

"They do that," Mike muttered.

Garrett turned to his partner. "They do what?"

"Test you," Mike said.

"Now what are *you* talkin' about?" Garrett asked.

"Pink ornaments. Purple sheets. Shit for the kitchen you do not need," Cal answered the question he asked Mike. And he wasn't done. "Wait until you get in a discussion about who's gonna pay what bill. Vi gave it her all to unman me with that one, brother. Cher sinks her teeth in you, you give in even a little on that, she'll have your balls and *she'll* be payin' *your* mortgage."

Fuck.

"And toss pillows," Cal kept at it. "So many toss pillows, it's borderline insane. They got some for summer. Then, for some Godforsaken reason, they switch them out for winter. They add some for Halloween. Thanksgiving.

Christmas." He shook his head, but his eyes were still full-on amused. "They use this shit to test you. See how tight a hold they got on your dick."

Garrett stared at him.

Angela whirled her dad's key fob in the air and shouted, "May-May!"

That meant Merry.

He grinned down at her, bending to touch the tip of her nose with his finger. "Hey, sweetheart."

When he straightened away, she twisted to try to see her father. "Want May-May!"

Cal bent over the stroller. "Merry's workin', baby. Today, you got Daddy."

"Daddeeee!" she yelled, a big grin on her pretty face, clearly not too cut up she couldn't have Garrett.

"Just let it go, man," Mike advised to Garrett, and he turned to Mike as Mike moved forward in the line. "And by that, I mean the pink ornaments. Just let her have them."

Cal inclined his head toward Mike. "That's the way. Suck it up. Take the hit. You fight over pink ornaments and purple sheets, she may let go of your dick." He grinned. "And you don't want that."

"Cher's got beads acting as a door to her closet," Garrett told Cal.

Cal nodded sagely, still grinning. "Mm-hmm. You're in for it, brother."

"What I'm sayin' is, who gives a shit?" Merry asked. "She's it. Got over the wrong one; got my hands on the right one. So if she wants pink ornaments and I got no preference of Christmas ornaments except havin' 'em, then who cares? If it makes her happy…" he trailed off on a shrug.

Cal's brows drew together like he couldn't comprehend what Garrett was saying to him.

Garrett grinned at him as his phone rang.

He pulled it out, looked at the screen, decided tomorrow he was fucking *finally* going to go get a new phone, and he took Sully's call.

"Yo, Sul."

"Merry, brother, call just came in. Shots fired. Parking lot at Bobbie's Garden Shoppe."

Garrett froze.

Not because there were shots fired.

Because of the tone in Sully's voice and the fact that Cher was going to Bobbie's that day.

"Sul," he whispered, his insides freezing.

"Shits me to say this—shits me—but gotta say it. Calls came in reported the shooter abducted Cher."

He turned sharply and headed to the door.

"You with Colt?" he asked Sully.

"Merry," Mike called.

"We're headed that way," Sully told him. "Colt's a little…" He didn't finish.

He didn't have to.

Garrett knew what Colt was.

He was that too.

Except she was *his*.

She was Colt's friend.

But Cher was *his*.

And she'd been abducted.

Fucking *abducted*.

So what Colt was, Garrett was more of it.

"We're headed that way too," Garrett told him, shoving out the door.

"Merry, dammit, what the fuck?" Mike clipped.

"You got any more?" Garrett asked Sully.

"Nothin'. Call just came in. Pandemonium at Bobbie's. Got units goin' out there. If I get more before you get there, I'll call," Sully answered.

"Later," Garrett bit off, standing on the driver's side door of their service sedan. He looked to Mike, who was rounding the hood. "Keys," he demanded.

It wasn't his day to drive.

"Garrett, what's goin' on?" Mike asked tersely.

"Shots fired at Bobbie's and preliminary reports say that the shooter took Cher."

"What?" Mike asked, stopping short by Garrett.

"What?" Cal growled, and Garrett spared a glance to the sidewalk where Cal and his kids were.

He looked back to Mike. "Keys."

"You aren't drivin', brother," Mike replied quietly.

Garrett leaned his way. "Give me the goddamned keys."

"Round the car, Merry. I drive," Mike returned.

They faced off.

For half a second.

Then Garrett jogged around the car so they could get to Bobbie's.

⟜⟩

Cher

From my place, lying in the backseat of a car, hands zip-tied behind my back, I stared at the profile of Walter Jones, who was driving.

"You're not ex-FBI, are you?" I whispered.

He said nothing.

"You're not ex-FBI. You're one of those sick fucks who gets off on all things Dennis Lowe," I guessed.

"Shut the fuck up."

He was.

God.

He was.

And he had me.

"I got a kid. I got a mom. I got a man. I got a life. I'll repeat, *I got a kid*," I told him.

"Shut *the fuck* up."

"He's eleven."

I rolled to the floor when he suddenly stopped the car, pain shooting up my shoulder and across my hips, both of which hit first.

By the time I twisted my head to look up, he was leaned around the driver's seat, pointing his gun at me.

"I said," he whispered, "shut the fuck up."

I shut the fuck up.

He waited.

Then he turned back around and drove.

⟜⟩

Garrett

"She didn't run."

Garrett stood in the parking lot of Bobbie's with Colt, Mike, and Sully, listening to Susie Shepherd talk, Mia standing next to her but not close. Both of them were visibly freaked right the fuck out, but surprisingly, it was Susie who had it together to report what had happened.

He tried to stay locked on Susie, but he couldn't.

His eyes wandered to the back of the Equinox. The hatch up.

She'd been loading bags when Mia confronted her. Interrupted by his fucking ex-wife, then abducted by an unknown man with a weapon.

Six shopping bags he could count.

Fucking *six*.

She was excited for Christmas. Christmas with him and her boy.

Pink ornaments.

"It was too late, though. He was right on her. Snuck up the side of her car. She didn't see him because she was dealing with Mia, and I didn't see him because I was too. Cher didn't have time to run," Susie finished, and Garrett looked back to her.

"Merry," Mia whispered.

Abe ran up. "BOLO out on the vehicle. They're settin' up roadblocks. Everyone's been called in." His eyes fell on Merry. "Everyone, dude. Everyone's out lookin'."

Even though the man had shot three rounds into the air to make his point, everyone getting that point and scattering, Susie had managed to have it together enough to see what car the man took Cher to. Make, model, but she got no plate.

Now they had a BOLO.

"Merry," Mia whispered again.

"Describe him again," Garrett clipped at Susie.

"Dark hair. Receding. Gray in it. Same with his goatee," she described. "Good clothes. Blue shirt, nice jeans, nice leather jacket. He had some heft, but it worked on him." She glanced at Colt before she returned her attention to Merry. "You know my type, so just to be helpful, I wouldn't fuck him. He's too short, he wasn't all that, and he's clearly a psychopath, shooting gunshots in the air in a fucking garden shop parking lot."

Garrett turned to his partner. "Find Ryker."

"You got something?" Mike asked.

"Just find Ryker."

Mike nodded and stepped back, pulling out his phone.

He looked to Colt and Sully. "Call Warren. Nowakowski. Find out if Walter Jones was FBI."

"Jesus, Merry, you think—?" Colt started.

Garrett looked back at Susie. "You said his vehicle looked like a rental?"

She nodded. "I saw a decal. Didn't see it clearly, but it didn't say dealership. It said rental. Just didn't see which company."

Garrett turned to Colt. "Description matches, Colt."

"I'll call Nowakowski," Sully murmured. "You call Warren."

They pulled out their phones.

"Merry," Mia whispered.

Hearing her repeat his name, he felt it snap. It was a twinge right at his heart, small but not insignificant, seeing as it reverberated through his frame, exploding in his brain.

Compelled by the explosion, Garrett turned to her and roared, "*Not now, Mia!*"

Her pale face turned ash.

"You love her," she kept whispering.

"Jesus, fuck," Garrett clipped, turning to put distance between himself and his ex, not to mention get to the goddamned car so he could look for his woman, doing this while ordering to a hovering Marty, "Get that bitch away from me."

He could not go apeshit crazy. He had to keep it locked down. If he lost his mind, he couldn't use it to find his woman. And when he found her, he'd be in no place to be there for her.

He had to lock it down.

"Uh…Mia, if you'd—" Marty started.

"I'm gonna go out and look for her."

Garrett turned back at his ex-wife's words.

"I'm gonna look for her," she declared again.

She lifted her chin and caught hold of Susie's hand.

Mia Merrick, spoiled rich girl, holding fucking Susie Shepherd's hand, Susie being spoiled *bitch* girl.

"Me and Susie. Me and Susie are gonna go look for Cher," she kept at it.

Susie yanked her hand away and looked down in disgust at Mia, demanding to know, "Have you lost your mind?"

Mia looked up at Susie. "You said you were sisters."

Cher and Susie, sisters?

"We are, but I'm not doin' shit with you. *I* got nothing to prove. And anyway, might be a good idea you let the people who know what they're doing do it without *you* in the way," Susie returned, and looked to Garrett. "Are we done?"

"Keep your phone close," Garrett told her.

She nodded, glared at Mia, and stomped away.

"Well, I'm gonna look for her myself, then," Mia declared.

"You impede this search, I swear to fuck—" Garrett started.

"I want to help," she returned.

She wanted to make a point. She wanted to make a play.

And now was *so* not the time, it wasn't fucking funny.

"Then how about you shut up and go home," Mike asked, phone still to his ear, irate eyes on Mia.

She looked with surprise at Mike then to Garrett.

"Okay. Maybe I'll just go home," she decided hesitantly, watching Garrett closely.

"Good call," Colt muttered.

She looked to Colt then again to Garrett.

She had no traction there, no support, no one giving any indication they thought there was anything left of Merry and Mia. Or that they even *liked* Mia, with or without Merry.

And she got not one thing from Garrett.

So finally, he got what he was expecting.

It was too much for her, she was giving up.

It was written all over her face. An expression he'd seen a lot over a lot of years and missed repeatedly.

He didn't miss it then.

He just didn't care.

"I just…I hope she's okay, Merry," she said.

"Whatever," he muttered, turning away.

The minute he did, she was out of his head.

He moved as he bit out, "Mike."

Mike looked his way. Phone still to his ear, he moved with Merry.

Garrett pulled out his phone and called his dad.

"Yo, Garrett, son," Dave answered, talking quickly. "Ernie heard it. Tanner phoned me just after Ernie heard it. Tanner's out. I'm out too. So's Ernie and Spike. Don't you worry. We'll find that car."

His father and his retired BPD cronies were not unwanted additions to the search.

But he needed something else.

"Shit gets around, Dad. It's still early, school's not out for a while, and I appreciate you lookin' for Cher. But I need someone to deal with Ethan. Ethan and Grace."

He stopped at the car and looked over the roof to see Mike still had his phone to his ear, but he beeped the locks.

"I'll call Rocky," Dave told him.

"Rocky's in class."

"She'll sort somethin' out, Garrett. You need men on the streets, not me holdin' Grace's hand."

His dad was right.

He needed men on the streets.

He needed that car found.

He needed Cher found.

Fuck, his head hurt.

"Call Rocky, Dad," he ordered as he yanked open the door and folded into the car.

"You got it, son."

He was taking the phone from his ear to disconnect when he heard his father call his name.

"Yeah?" he asked when he put it back.

"We'll find her," his father said quietly.

They would. They absolutely would.

They had to.

For Ethan. For Grace.

For Garrett.

They had to find her.

He couldn't think of it another way.

He couldn't think of her not behind the bar at J&J's when he walked in. He couldn't think of her not there, pretending she was annoyed her kid and him were giving her shit over pancakes. He couldn't think of losing her brand of sweet. Never seeing it again, when she could be cute.

He couldn't think of not waking up to her pretty every morning.

He couldn't think of never having that look from her, that look that said she loved him.

He couldn't think of losing what his father lost how his father lost it, in other words, in a way he'd never get it back and the child she made who he loved wouldn't either.

He couldn't think of that.

If he did, his head would explode.

Or his heart would stop.

And if that shit happened, he couldn't help find her.

"Yeah, Dad. Got calls to make, shit to do. Later, yeah?"

"Later, son."

He took his phone from his ear as Mike backed out of their spot. "Ryker's not answering."

"Fuck," Garrett muttered.

"Called Tanner. Tanner's been tryin' him too. Incommunicado."

Not unusual with Ryker.

Just irritating because they needed everyone they could get.

"He didn't report back on Jones," Garrett told Mike. "Don't know where he found him. Don't know where he was stayin'. Don't know what he did to get him gone. Just know he disappeared and Cher didn't hear shit. Until now."

"We don't know this is that guy, Merry," Mike pointed out.

They didn't.

He had not gotten sick-fuck vibes from Walter Jones. He hadn't gotten any read on him except ex-cop.

In truth, until they pulled Bobbie's camera feeds, they had to go forward thinking it could be anyone. It might not have anything to do with Dennis Lowe. It could be someone losing it at Christmas because they lost their job and couldn't afford presents. Or they cheated on their wife and she threw them out and they were messed up and wanted to make some woman pay. Or they had some fucked part of their head get more fucked and they went to the parking lot of a goddamned garden shop and abducted a woman.

It could be anyone.

Anyone who had Cher.

His blood started to burn.

He lifted a hand and pressed his middle three fingers to his forehead, and he did it hard.

"She's tough, brother," Mike said softly.

Garrett pressed in harder.

Chatter was coming from their radio. Men and women out, reporting in. Checking parking lots. Driving down streets. Off-duty officers from Avon, Danville, Plainfield were all mucking in. Shots fired. A woman abducted. She belonged to a cop. The brotherhood was closing in.

"I love her," Garrett told his knees, pressing harder into his forehead, holding back the rage, keeping it contained, trying not to fly apart.

"I know you do, Merry."

"Gonna make babies with her," he told his partner.

"Yeah, you are."

"Give Ethan brothers and sisters."

"Yeah, Merry."

"Never wanted that. Not with anyone, Mike. Never wanted any of that with anyone but Cher."

"Stick with me, brother. Yeah? Stick with me."

Garrett pulled in breath.

He would not see a burgundy Ford Taurus with his eyes to his fucking knees.

He dropped his hand and lifted his head.

His phone sounded with a text.

He pulled it out and looked at the cracked screen.

Out looking. You got time to tell me, Vi wants to know if Ethan's covered. Cal.

He's covered. Grace too. Rocky's got them, Garrett texted back.

Someone needs to get Ryker's head out of his ass. He's not answering. He needs in on this hunt, Cal returned.

We're on that, Garrett replied.

Cal sent no more.

Mike drove.

Garrett scanned the streets and listened to the reports coming in at the same time he sent a text to Ryker that Cher was missing and they needed him to report in.

After he sent it, he backed out of his texts with Ryker and went to the string under Cal's.

He opened it.

Ethan's safe at school. He reports we're almost out of Pringles. You're out, you wanna get on that?

Him to Cher.

Your wish is my command, then a half dozen *x*'s and *o*'s, another half dozen hearts of various colors, ending with a shamrock and the head of a chicken.

Cher to him.

Garrett closed his eyes tight as pain spiked through his brain.

Then he opened them and scanned the streets again.

Cher

"I need to go to him."

"You fuckin' do shit I don't tell you to do, you'll be lyin' beside him."

I stared at Ryker's big, powerful, scary biker-dude body prone on the floor.

Wet hit my eyes.

Blood had pooled around him on the linoleum.

A lot of it.

Too much.

Too much of Ryker leaking all over my goddamned kitchen floor.

Garrett

He took the call from Colt.

"Got Nowakowski," Colt stated. "Walter Jones was a profiler for the FBI. Now he's freelance. He's also right now pissed as shit that Nowakowski called and interrupted his vacation golf game on some course in Arizona to make him pissed as fuck by telling him some guy is impersonating him in Indiana."

"Fuck," Garrett whispered.

He should have checked. He should have looked into that shit.

Then again, the man who had Cher had done his homework. Preliminarily, how far would anyone dig before they let him get his foot in the door?

Still.

Fuck.

"Only two rental car agencies around Indianapolis International got burgundy Ford Tauruses in their fleets. Got folks checkin' those that are out and who's got 'em. They got LoJack, we'll get positions of the vehicles that are out. Still checking other agencies not at the airport. I'll report back on that," Colt continued.

"Right," Garrett muttered.

"Jake went through the footage of Bobbie's parking lot cameras. They got an image of this guy. Isolated him. Jake's doin' what he can to give us somethin' we can use. He'll send what he's got to your phone. Let us know if this is the guy who visited Cher, sayin' he was Jones."

"Gotcha."

"And Feb wants you to know she, Jackie, Vi, and Dusty are with Rocky at Grace's. Rocky decided it's best that she took Ethan out of school. Since Jackie is on the list with the school to pick him up, she helped with that. She says they're all hangin' in there," he finished.

Garrett thought of Ethan.

He thought of Grace.

Another spike of pain in his head.

"Thanks, Colt," he forced out.

"More when we got it. Later."

Colt hung up.

"They're sending an image of the guy," Garrett told Mike as they drove.

"Good," Mike murmured.

A minute later, Jake emailed him an image.

It was the man who'd told them he was Walter Jones.

He confirmed that to Jake. Connie in dispatch confirmed it to everyone on the hunt. Jake sent out department-wide emails with the image.

Now they knew he was not the man he'd said he was.

And they had to hope he didn't know about LoJack in rentals or how to disable it. Though, if he did his homework on the ex-FBI agent he was impersonating, he'd know LoJack.

So, other than knowing he was not who he'd said he was, they didn't know dick.

Primary to that being where the fuck he was.

Which was where Cher was.

And where Garrett needed to be to take care of his brown-eyed girl.

Cher

"What's wrong with him?"

"Shut up."

"He's bleeding a lot. What's wrong with him?"

Walter Jones stopped frantically opening and closing my kitchen cupboards and turned, shaking his gun at me.

"Shut *up*."

"He's my friend," I chanced the whisper.

"He's an asshole," Jones returned. "You don't want me in your town, you ask nice. You don't come and get up in my shit. You get up in my shit, I get up in yours." He pointed the gun at Ryker's body on the floor before returning it to me. "What's wrong with him is I got up in his shit. And that means he's got three bullets in him."

Oh fuck.

Oh no.

Ryker.

Lissa.

Alexis.

Fuck!

"Let me go to him, please," I begged, doing it not knowing what I would do even if he let me.

I just needed to be with Ryker.

I just needed to do that for Ryker.

And I needed to find out if he was still alive.

Jones resumed opening and closing cupboards. "Just shut up."

I shut up and looked from the chair at my kitchen table that Jones had planted my ass into to Ryker.

I was too far away. I couldn't see if he was breathing.

I jumped when something crashed.

Jones was shoving all my stuff from my shelves to the ground. Bowls, plates, pitchers, everything crashing on the floor, breaking, the shards flying everywhere, hitting Ryker.

Years of yard sale finds, estate sale finds, garage sale finds, antique shop finds, my kid's cereal bowls, the plates Merry always chose for when he made us waffles or pancakes.

My life crashing to the floor, the jagged shards hitting my brother Ryker.

Fucking motherfucker.

"What are you looking for?" I snapped.

"Cameras," he grunted.

What the fuck?

"Cameras?" I asked.

He turned on me. "That little weasel plant cameras?"

"What are you talking about?"

"That weasel. No, not a weasel. A rat. Did he plant cameras?"

It hit me.

"Ryan?" I asked hesitantly.

"Yeah," Jones bit out. "The rat. The rat who led them to Denny. *Him.* He likes to watch. He'd like to watch you. Did he plant cameras?"

I stared at him, breathing hard. "Is Ryan okay?"

"He's as okay as that guy there." He jerked his head to Ryker.

Oh fuck.

Oh no.

Ryan.

My eyes got wet.

"You shot him?" I whispered.

"Dead."

Dead.

Ryan.

I stared at Walter Jones.

The tear fell.

I should have known.

I should have known, with my life.

I should have known there would always be room for tears.

Garrett

His phone rang.

He looked to it.

It was Rocky.

He drew in breath and took the call. "Honey, unless this is about Ethan, now's not a—"

"Merry?" Ethan interrupted.

The pain spiked, scoring into his brain.

"Hey, buddy."

"Rocky doesn't know I'm usin' her phone. I swiped it. But I had to…I had to…" He drew in an audible breath. "Can I go to the station? Maybe Tanner can come and get me. I just…I just wanna…sit at the station."

Fuck, he sounded scared.

His boy sounded scared.

Pain skewered Garrett's brain as he beat back the fury.

"Prefer you where you are right now, kid," Garrett told him.

"I know, but—"

"Ethan, bud, I gotta be doin' what I'm doin'. Tanner's helpin'. Mike. Cal. Colt. Sul. My dad. Everyone. So I got no one to look after your gramma except you. Need you to look after Grace. Can you do that for me now? Look after your gramma?"

"Yea—" His voice broke and Garrett's vision blurred. He listened to Ethan clear his throat before he said, "Yeah. I can do that. I can look after Gramma."

"Good, bud. See you soon, yeah? I'm gonna see you soon, buddy. You hear me?"

It was weak and nearly inaudible when Ethan replied, "I hear you, Merry."

"Suck it up, Ethan," Garrett ordered gently. "Need you strong, okay? Before you go back to your gramma, suck it up for me. Go back to her strong. She's probably scared. You need to take care of her, yeah?"

Ethan didn't reply.

"You with me?" Garrett prompted.

He heard Ethan clear his throat again and his voice was a lot stronger when he said, "I hear you, Merry. Gotta get back to Gram."

"Yeah you do. See you soon. See you both soon."

"'Kay, Merry."

"Love you, son."

A sniff, then, "I love you too."

"Right. Later."

"Later, Merry."

They disconnected.

Garrett drew a sharp breath in through his nose and kept scanning.

"You did right, Garrett," Mike said softly. "Gave him strength, direction. Something like this happened when Jonas was Ethan's age, a time he's just beginnin' to figure out what kinda man he wants to be, he wouldn't wanna look back and remember himself fallin' apart."

"Right," Garrett bit out.

"He needed a mission."

"Right," Garrett repeated.

"You did right."

Garrett said nothing.

Mike drove.

Garrett's phone rang again.

He looked to the screen.

It was Cal.

If Cal had something to say that wasn't important, he'd text.

He was phoning.

Garrett took the call.

He didn't say a word before Cal spoke.

"Burgundy Taurus, man, right in your woman's goddamned driveway."

The pain spiked.

He looked to Mike. "They're at Cher's."

Mike turned on his blinker.

"You got eyes?" he asked Cal.

"Walked by. Sheers closed but movement in the kitchen," Cal answered. "Otherwise, made no approach."

"Distinct movement?"

"Yeah. One person. Couldn't tell much. But it wasn't Cher."

It wasn't Cher.

"Stay clear," Merry ordered. "We're on our way."

"Got it."

Garrett disconnected and ran his thumb over the screen.

"He took her to her own fuckin' house?" Mike asked.

"Cal says car's in the driveway and there's movement in the kitchen, not Cher," Garrett answered as he made his call and put the phone to his ear.

"Yo," Colt answered.

"Cal reports burgundy Taurus in Cher's drive. You and Sully. Mike and me. And I'm calling Tanner. We go in soft with no one else there to fuck this shit up."

"You're too close to this, brother. Let me call Drew and Sean there. Adam and Ellen," Colt replied. "We'll take care of her."

"If I'm too close, you're too close," Garrett gave him the truth.

There was a pause, then, "Fuck."

Colt knew the truth.

"You call cap," Garrett ordered. "Tell him what we're doin', but do not let him throw everything we got at this so fifteen squads from all over the county roll in hot and tweak this guy to do somethin' even stupider than abducting my woman. We don't know what we're dealin' with here. We go in easy."

"You got it. I'm on it. Meet you there."

"Our ETA, five."

"Ours, seven. But we'll shave off two."

They disconnected.

Her own fucking house.

He called her number. It was the fourth time he'd called since he'd heard. She didn't answer.

Then he called Tanner and gave him the news.

"Okay, keep your shit, man, but if this is about Lowe, her bein' Lowe's and now you bein' hers, this could be about you. Goin' to her place, he could be drawin' you there," Tanner warned.

"That thought crossed my mind," Garrett replied.

"We'll get her, brother," Tanner assured.

They would.

They had to.

Because he definitely could survive losing Mia.

He could even survive losing his mom.

But he wasn't sure he was capable of waking up and not seeing Cher's pretty.

Cher

"You're breaking all my shit," I bit out.

He was also near to dislocating my shoulder, jerking me around while he shoved the gun in my shelves in my media center and knocked shit off, not to mention tore pictures off the wall.

"Ratted on him. Got him caught. Weasel fucker," he muttered.

Things had turned.

He had turned.

It was like I wasn't there. He was so focused on finding cameras that didn't exist, I was an afterthought.

And I was fucked.

There was nothing I could do. My hands were still zip-tied behind my back.

I couldn't run and get shot dead, making my son fatherless *and* motherless.

I couldn't fight to try and get the gun away from him.

I couldn't think of Ryker on my floor, hopefully still breathing.

I couldn't think of Ryan at all.

I couldn't do anything but get extremely pissed off that my life sucked so fucking *bad*.

I should have known.

Never hope.

Never want.

Certainly never dream.

Never.

If this guy made me dead, he'd set my kid on a path where he could learn that.

And I wouldn't be there to set him straight.

Fucker.

Fucking *fucker*.

"Please let me go," I whispered.

He didn't let me go.

His head came up and he jerked me around so quickly, my head snapped on my neck.

I saw him stare at the door.

My eyes shot to the door.

Was someone there?

Should I cry out?

"You ratted too."

His words in that weird whisper made me look to him.

He was looking at me.

"I wanted to make a video for them. A nice video they'd like. A video of you on *his* camera. A video of me cleaning up Denny's business."

Oh God.

Please let someone be out there.

"You," he kept whispering, "the slut-stripper whore and the weasel. You got him caught."

"He was murdering people," I replied.

"In the name of love."

I stared at him.

Fucking *fuck* this guy was *whacked*.

And there it was. Just my luck. Just the suckage of my life.

I missed it.

Again.

"It's time," he said.

Oh no.

Shit.

Fuck.

"Time for what?" I asked.

"Time for it to end."

He jerked me to the door. He opened the door. He kicked the storm and the glass shattered.

He put the gun to my head and walked me out, our feet crunching on glass.

He held me in front of him like a shield.

I could feel the cold metal against my temple.

But all I could see was Merry standing in my yard.

His gun was up, his eyes on me.

He was there.

Of course he was there.

He took care of me.

"Lower your weapon!" I heard Mike shout.

It was just a flicker of movement, but I knew Merry's eyes were now on Jones.

"Lower your weapon and step away from Ms. Rivers!" I heard Sully yell.

"Her first," Jones shouted to Merry. "Then you."

Gun still up, Merry's eyes stayed locked to Jones.

"You got a bead?" I heard Tanner ask.

I swallowed.

He'd take care of me. He was there. Right there. In my yard.

He loved me.

We'd finally found happy.

He'd take care of me.

I had to believe.

He was Merry, my Merry.

I had to believe.

I stayed focused on Merry.

Merry stayed focused on Jones.

His head barely moved, but it did.

In an affirmative.

I braced.

"Hold on," Merry said.

That was for me.

And I did what I was told.

I held on and believed.

Jones shifted minutely.

"Take the shot!" Colt roared.

Merry's gun exploded.

I screamed when the blood spatter hit my face.

Jones fell.

Twenty-Six

PEOPLE LIKE US
Cher

*M*arksmanship trophies.

Oh yeah, my man was badass.

"I love you," I called, standing on my stoop, a dead man at my feet.

Merry lowered his gun.

"No shit?"

I pressed my lips together because that was the least romantic thing a man could say in this situation (or any situation), just as it had been the last time he'd said it.

But still, I was *this close* to crying.

Because I was alive to hear him say it.

(Not to mention, he'd just shot a man in the head for me.)

I controlled the tears.

Then I turned and raced into the house.

"Cher!" Colt called.

"Ryker! He's been shot!" I shouted back while I sprinted through my living room.

I hit my knees on a slide right through a puddle of blood toward Ryker in my kitchen. When I stopped, I twisted, doing it awkwardly to get my hands, which still were tied behind me, on Ryker to see if I could find a pulse.

"Please have a pulse. Please, badass motherfucker, have a goddamned pulse," I begged, searching for it.

"Man down. Send paramedics to our position. GSW," Merry said.

I looked to him to see him moving swiftly into my kitchen, his phone to his ear.

"Three," I told him. "Three of them."

Merry's eyes flared.

"He's been hit three times," he said into his phone. "Unconscious. Significant loss of blood."

I lost sight of Merry behind me. Then my wrists were lifted, I heard the snap of a knife cutting through plastic, and my wrists were freed.

I turned, going back for Ryker's pulse as Merry shifted, crouching across from me, shoving my hand aside and reaching in himself.

Colt, Mike, Tanner, Cal, and Sully came into my kitchen.

"Shit," Sully whispered, eyes to Ryker.

Colt got close and crouched.

"Pulse. Weak," Merry muttered. "Cher, get some towels."

Pulse.

Weak.

Thank God.

I moved out. Mike moved in. By the time I got back with towels, they had Ryker on his back.

Men nabbed towels from me, went for a wound, and pressed.

I felt a hand on my arm and looked up at Cal.

He had one of my kitchen towels. He turned into me and his eyes watched his hand as he wiped blood off my face. He didn't take a lot of time doing it before he caught my chin with his fingers and looked into my eyes.

"You good?" he asked.

I nodded.

He studied me.

Then he grinned. "Tough chick."

"You bet your ass."

He shook his head and dropped his hand.

I started to move to Ryker, catching sight of Tanner as I did.

There wasn't a lot of room, especially with Ryker's big body sprawled on my floor, but Tanner was pacing what was left of it, eyes glued to his bud, movements agitated, face set in stone.

They were tight, Tanner and Ryker. And don't ask me how I knew, I just knew that Tanner was fighting the urge to drill the body on my stoop with more holes.

I went to Ryker's head and got to my knees. Lifting his head gently, I slid my thighs under it to act as a pillow.

"Merry?" I called.

Merry looked from Ryker to me. "Yeah, Cherie?"

"Jones said he shot Ryan."

Merry's mouth got hard and he looked to Colt.

Colt looked to Sully.

Sully pulled out his phone and stepped out of my kitchen.

I turned my attention to Ryker.

"You're good, brother," I told him, curling my hands around his neck. "You're good. You have to be. Alexis is boy crazy and someone has to protect her from teenage pregnancy, and you are the walking, talking anecdote for any boy who wants to get in a girl's pants, if that girl's your daughter, that is."

Ryker, unconscious, said nothing.

My fingers curled in tighter.

"You're good, brother," I repeated. "You've gotta be good. You got sugar in your bed. What man in their right mind would leave that?"

Ryker just lay there.

It wasn't right. It wasn't Ryker.

Ryker didn't just *lay there*.

He annoyed.

He got up in your shit.

He threw back drinks and spouted inappropriate crap that made you want to smile and punch him at the same time.

I leaned over him as far as I could get.

"You gotta be good, brother. People like us, Ryker…people like us, we can't give up. We gotta show the world. We gotta show our kids. We gotta show 'em it's okay. We gotta show our babies we can do it if we don't give up. We gotta show 'em it pays off, it comes to you if you got it in you to wade through the shit. You'll get the good if you don't give up. You can live it if you just dare to dream."

I heard the sirens.

I bent even further, my forehead to his.

"You got it all, brother. You finally got it all. Don't give up," I whispered.

Ryker said nothing.

He just lay there in a puddle of his own blood on my goddamned kitchen floor.

Ryan

He was trying to open his eyes.

All he saw was fuzzy. Blurred.

But he smelled weird stuff. Like he was in a hospital.

He felt nothing.

He blinked slowly, the only way his eyelids would move.

The blur was still there when he was done.

But he felt something.

His hand was squeezed.

Then he heard it.

"You're good."

Cheryl.

She was there.

As crazy as it was with all the shit that had happened to them, she was always there.

The best friend he'd ever had.

"You're good, Ryan," she whispered. "Rest, brah. Yeah?"

He tried to nod.

He didn't succeed.

He fell back to sleep.

Garrett

Three Days Later

"Well, fuck yeah, of course. Because I *am*," Cher declared loudly.

Garrett stood at the door, shoulder to the jamb, and watched his woman move away from the hospital bed. She rounded it and gave Lissa a hug. She went to the chair Alexis was curled into, bent, and kissed her cheek.

Then she moved to Garrett.

Garrett nodded to Lissa, smiled at Alexis, and looked at Ryker in the bed.

When he caught Ryker's eyes, Ryker lifted his hand, tubes stuck in it.

It took him time, but he finally executed his badass salute.

Lissa ruined it when she grabbed his hand on its descent and tucked it to her belly.

Ryker shook his head on the pillow.

Garrett bit back laughter.

Then he mouthed, *I owe you.*

After which Ryker did not mouth, "I know."

That was when Garrett shook his head.

Cher made it to him, grabbed his hand irately, and yanked on it.

He took that and the fact she didn't stop moving as indication she wanted him to follow.

He held tight to her hand and followed.

He also bit back his smile as they walked and he watched her annoyed profile.

"What are you?" he asked.

She looked up at him. "What?"

"What are you?"

"What am I?"

"You said to Ryker, 'of course I am.' Of course you are what?"

She rolled her eyes and faced forward, still moving.

He tugged her hand and stopped.

She had no choice but to stop with him.

"What are you?" he pushed.

"Mom and Ethan are at your place. It's been three days. I bought ready-made Christmas cookie dough. I gotta bake that shit, then we got a tree to decorate. But before that, we're going to the fucking phone store. I'm getting you a new phone and no back talk. It's your Christmas present. You can use it between now and the big day. I'll swipe it Christmas Eve, wrap it, and… surprise."

He ignored all that, though they definitely were hitting the phone store on the way home. Cher just wasn't buying his new phone. She could buy him something else for Christmas that didn't cost hundreds of dollars.

Instead, he kept at her.

"What are you?"

She looked at him a beat then looked away. "Colt has a big mouth."

He tugged her hand again. "Cher."

Her eyes came back to him. "It was that dare to dream stuff," she snapped. "Colt told him. Ryker thinks it's hilarious. He called me a girl."

He gave another tug on her hand until his girl was close enough to let her hand go so he could wrap his arms around her.

"And I am," she declared. "I am a girl."

"Thank Christ," Garrett muttered, feeling one side of his mouth hitch up.

She lifted her chin.

"I'm also a girl who's moving into your house. Invite or not. Crappy bathrooms or not. We can use my furniture, which *is* comfortable, even if half of it's from a garage sale. If you say no, we're moving in with Mom. But no way am I makin' my kid egg goo in a kitchen where Ryker nearly bled out on the floor."

"Babe, have you been anywhere outside my bed, my house, or my sight unless you're at work for the last three days?"

"No."

"You think I'm gonna let you make dude food in a kitchen where Ryker nearly bled out on the floor?"

Her lips started curving up. "No."

"Why?" he asked.

"Why?" she asked back.

"Why wouldn't I do that?"

It didn't take long for the answer to come to her.

When it did, she melted into him.

"You take care of me," she said softly.

"Yeah. And Ethan. So yeah. Ask for time off. We'll pack up all Janis Joplin's shit that lunatic didn't smash and move it to my place. But first, tonight, we're putting fuckin' pink ornaments on our first Christmas tree."

She drifted her hand from his chest up to curl around his neck and rolled up on her toes.

She did this, staring into his eyes.

"Thanks for shooting a man in the face for me," she whispered, her brown eyes dancing.

It hurt a fuckuva lot, but seeing as they were in a hospital corridor, Garrett managed to force his roar of laughter down to just a chuckle.

"You're welcome, Cherie."

"I love you, Garrett Merrick," she told him.

"I know you do and I love you too, but just to repeat during this gooey moment where you might think you can get in there, Ryan is *not* recuperating in our guest room."

The warmth in her brown eyes turned partially flinty at the ongoing argument they were having about her friend who was recovering in a hospital in Indy.

He'd lost a lot of blood.

He'd taken shots to worse parts of his body.

And he'd been left longer.

He'd also been taken off the critical list that morning.

"His mother is a ball-breaker," Cher told him.

"So are you."

He had her there. It was written all over her.

It took her a few beats, but she finally found her comeback.

"She's not the good kind."

And she had him there.

He tried a different tack. "Babe, I don't have a bed in either guest room."

"You will if we use my old one."

Fuck.

She had him again.

"Right. I don't want a geek genius in our house, playing video games with Ethan, possibly teaching him geek-genius stuff, which would not be bad, but also teaching him Ryan-stupid shit, which would absolutely not be good."

"Hmm…" she murmured.

It was a good call to pull the Ethan card. She wanted Ryan to teach her son to be stupid less than Garrett did.

So he dodged the bullet.

This, and looking forward to store-bought-but-home-baked Christmas cookies and pink ornaments, made him pull her even closer.

"It happens," he replied.

"What happens?" she asked.

He dipped closer and held her tighter.

"It happens," he repeated. "For people like us, baby. It happens, eventually. Just as long as we hold on."

She liked that. She showed it with her pretty brown eyes. She showed it by pressing closer. She showed it by wrapping both arms around his neck.

Finally, she showed it by rolling up further and taking his mouth.

And he liked that.

So he showed her too.

While she was taking his, he took hers.

And with that—as they did and as they'd continue to do—together, Cher Rivers and Garrett Merrick successfully weathered yet another storm.

Epilogue

SUCH A GIRL
Feb

May

I walked into the living room to see my son tossing treats to my cat, my husband with him, holding back our dog by his collar.

Seeing this and it annoying me, I planted my hands on my hips, asking, "Are you serious?"

My husband's eyes came to me.

They grew dark as they dropped to my dress and his face assumed an expression I felt in my womb.

My son's eyes also came to me.

Since we had somewhere to go, I decided to focus on Jack.

"What, Momma?" Jack asked.

"Baby boy, the vet said Wilson's too fat," I told him, resuming walking into the living room so I could get to my purse in the kitchen.

"Daddy says the only eggerzize Wilson gets is runnin' 'round for kitty treats," Jack replied.

I glared at Colt as I walked by him, and I did this mostly because he hadn't lied to our kid—Wilson was lazy as hell—so I had no retort.

For his part, Colt grinned at me as I walked by him.

Years he'd had to become impervious to my glare.

That was annoying too.

557

I hit the kitchen, asking Colt, "How many have you given him?"

"Three," Colt lied.

"Eelehben," Jack told the truth.

I again glared at Colt, who had followed me into the kitchen.

"We need to get goin'," he stated. "Not have our three thousandth argument about Wilson's cat treats."

Unfortunately, he wasn't wrong.

"Scout taken care of?" I asked about our dog, who had likely gotten his treats earlier but forgotten that had happened, which was why he was now skulking into the kitchen, straight to his bowls.

I took my clutch from under my arm so I could transfer stuff from my purse, which was lying on the kitchen counter, into it as Colt answered, "Yep," while fitting himself to my back. He then bent in to kiss my bare shoulder before murmuring in my ear, "Like this dress, baby."

I lost some of my annoyance, feeling my husband's heat. I lost more at the touch of his lips. I lost more at his words.

I lost it all when I caught sight of something out of the corner of my eye.

I loved silver. Because I did, I wore a lot of it.

And every day, no matter when I got home—if it was eight at night or three in the morning—I took my silver off at our kitchen counter.

I dropped it in a pile wherever it hit.

The next time I saw it, I'd see that my husband had organized it. Bangles in a bundle. Rings lined up. Chains straightened. Earrings stacked, one on top of the other.

Sometimes I saw him do it, so I knew it wasn't about him keeping it neat.

When he did it, his touch was reverent, like the jewelry was still on me.

I didn't know why he did it. I never asked. I just let it feel nice, thinking of his fingers touching my silver, something that I loved, something that touched me.

After losing decades, we'd now been back together for years.

I took off my silver every day in the kitchen.

And my husband straightened it every day for me.

It was now straightened.

And I felt each touch it took Colt to straighten it right on my skin.

I loved it that I had that like I loved it that I had him.

And no woman could be annoyed when she had that.

I finished with my purse and turned.

Colt shifted to allow the movement, but then he shifted back in, wrapping his arms around me.

I lifted my hands and rested them on his shoulders, my eyes scanning my man.

"You don't look so bad either," I noted.

He grinned, dipped in, and touched his mouth to mine.

"Can we go?" Jack asked.

We both looked to our son, who was also now standing in the kitchen.

"I wanna play with Ethan," he explained his impatience.

Jack loved Ethan like Ethan was his big brother.

Ethan gave that back.

Colt gave me a quick squeeze before he let me go and moved to his boy.

He picked him up and set him straddling his hip, Jack wearing his little man suit pants and shirt that was a close match to the suit pants and shirt his daddy was wearing.

"We're gonna go, but remember what we told you," Colt said, walking them out of the kitchen. "It's a big day. Ethan's gonna be busy."

"But he'll be able to play, right?" Jack asked.

"Yeah, I reckon after a while, he'll be able to play."

Jack smiled at his father.

Colt returned his smile as he nabbed his suit jacket from the back of a dining room chair as well as Jack's, which was lying on the table.

As for me...

I smiled inside.

I did that a lot these days.

Then again, I did it a lot on the outside too.

I grabbed my clutch and moved toward the kitchen door, giving my dog a scratch while I did.

I walked out. My husband and son walked out behind me.

Colt put Jack down so he could lock the door and I took my baby boy's hand. My baby boy who was growing up and not so much of a baby anymore.

We walked to Colt's truck.

We climbed in.

And Colt took us to Ethan.

For a wedding by a lake that was going to be catered by my brother at a grill and a table groaning with potluck chips, dips, and salads—the only thing wedding-esque being the flowers and decorations the bridesmaids insisted on putting up (something we all got up early to do that morning) and a beautiful wedding cake the mother-of-the-bride demanded she provide—the wedding party was enormous.

Vi as maid of honor, me at her side, Dusty, Rocky, Mimi, Jessie, Josie, and Frankie.

On the other side, Tanner as best man, Mike, Colt, Sully, Cal, Sean, Drew, and Ryker.

Yes, Ryker.

The bride had insisted.

That said, the groom hadn't protested.

So there stood Ryker, grinning like a lunatic and fidgeting in his suit.

And while folks stood around in the green grass beside a quiet lake outside an awesome lake house, the bride made her appearance.

She looked amazing.

Simple, form-fitting, strapless white lace dress that hit her at her knees and had a dusty-rose satin ribbon wrapped around the waist; a thick bunch of silvery-pink Indiana peonies in her hand that she'd cut herself that morning from the bushes that edged the entire house.

Mother at her left.

Son at her right.

They hit the edge of the lake where we were all fanned out, the bride having expertly managed to negotiate the entire trek through the grass in strappy, spike-heeled sandals while one of Morrie's buds played Pachelbel on his guitar.

Cher also managed the entire trek with her eyes glued to Merry.

The procession stopped.

Pastor Knox asked, "Who brings this woman to be wed?"

Ethan's shoulders straightened as he called out loudly, "Her mother and I do."

I felt my eyes get wet and I nearly lost it when I caught Cher's profile, her cheeks dusted rose with blush, shimmering with a powder she'd fanned over the color, pinker now, as were her eyes, as she fought back her own wet.

Cher didn't cry. Not ever. Not that I'd seen.

Unless her son was giving her away to the man she'd loved for five years, only just recently letting him know it.

Cher kissed and hugged her mom. She did the same with Ethan.

Merry came forward and kissed and hugged Grace. He offered to shake Ethan's hand, but Ethan decided he wanted something else and he hugged Merry's middle.

Merry hugged him back.

Vi made a choked noise.

I cleared my throat.

Ethan grabbed his mom's hand and offered it to Merry.

Merry accepted.

They turned to the preacher.

After that, Garrett Merrick and Cher Rivers got married.

Colt

He stood with his wife's front tucked close to his side, his arm curled around her shoulders, her arms wrapped around his middle, watching.

And not getting it.

He bent to Feb's ear.

"Why are they laughing?" he asked.

She caught his eyes.

Her brown ones were dancing.

"I have no clue," she answered.

They both turned back to the front porch of Merry and Cher's lake house where the new husband and wife were having their first dance, Merry swaying Cher, both of them held close in each other's arms, both of them straight up busting a gut laughing, doing all this to Celine Dion's "My Heart Will Go On."

No, Colt didn't get it.

But watching two people he cared about so fucking happy…

He didn't need to.

Cal

July, Three Years Later

Cal stood at the back of the church.

Tony's bud had just escorted Vi down the aisle.

It was time.

Fuck, where was Kate?

He caught movement at the corner of his eye and turned to watch Keirry rushing up to him as fast as she could, considering she was wearing her long bridesmaid gown and she had her little sister's hand in hers.

Angie was rushing right alongside Keira. Then again, his baby girl would follow his big girl right to the mouth of hell.

Fact.

He just had to hope Keira didn't lead her there. Keirry was a magnet for trouble and Cal thanked God she hooked her shit to Jasper Layne, who'd die for her.

He watched them come his way and he did it feeling his jaw get hard.

He'd put his foot down about those fucking bridesmaids dresses.

And, as usual, his girls had rolled right over him.

It showed too much cleavage.

And it was too fucking tight.

It was also too late.

The other bridesmaids started filing out behind her.

So this shit was going to happen.

Fuck.

"Daddy!" Angie shouted, breaking free from Keira and rushing to him, looking pretty in her flower girl dress.

He bent and caught her.

Swinging her up in his arms, he murmured, "Hey, baby."

"Hey, Daddy," she replied on a big grin and an assessing look that reminded Cal of her mother. "You look handsome."

He kissed her neck. "And you look even more beautiful than your normal beautiful."

Her smile got bigger.

Keirry made it to him and grabbed his arm.

"Joe, Kate wants to talk to you."

He looked down at her. "Come again?"

"Kate wants to talk to you," she repeated.

He looked to the doors of the church that had been closed after Vi was escorted down. They were supposed to open so Kate's friends and sisters could walk down the aisle before Kate marched down it to get married way too young to a Chicago cop who Vi, Keira, Angie, Sam, and Ben all adored but Cal fucking hated.

He looked back to his girl. "Keirry, now's not the time for a chat."

She reached to Angie and pulled her sister out of his arms. "Then you better hurry."

Jesus, maybe she was having cold feet.

That would be the best news he had all day.

Though it would make her mother lose her mind.

He growled.

No words came out, he just growled.

Then he prowled through the vestibule and around the corner where the girls got ready.

He stopped dead when he saw Kate standing in the hall there.

He also stopped breathing.

"Hey, Joe," she whispered.

Fuck, his girl was beautiful.

Not his girl.

But still.

His girl.

She moved to him.

She hadn't gone big, not Kate. No humongous skirt. No humongous price tag.

He and Vi would've given her a wedding on the moon if she'd wanted it.

She wanted what she was getting.

Easy. Elegant.

Kate.

Now, Keira's was gonna mean selling a kidney, and Cal could say that even being loaded.

Juggling her bouquet, Kate reached for his hand.

The instant she touched him, his fingers curled around hers.

"I gotta say something, Joe," she whispered.

Oh no.

They weren't gonna do this.

He could barely handle what was happening that day.

They sure as fuck weren't gonna do this.

"You don't gotta say it," he whispered back.

Her fingers tightened in his. "I gotta say it."

"Katy—"

"Joe."

He shut up and held on to her hand and her gaze, giving in.

As usual, with his girls.

She spoke.

"No one on earth I'd wanna be right here, right now, but you."

Christ.

"Baby..." His voice was so rough, that word grated his throat coming out.

"No one, Joe."

Cal swallowed and pulled her closer.

"He's with me. He's always with me," she told him. "So I'm glad I get to be with you too."

"He'd be proud of you, Kate."

She nodded, her eyes getting bright. "I know."

"So fuckin' proud, honey."

"I know, Joe."

"You're so beautiful, baby, it hurts lookin' at you," he told her.

Katy pressed her lips together.

He wasn't done.

"And it is no lie that this is the proudest moment of my life, gettin' to walk you down that aisle."

She made a noise.

He yanked her in his arms.

He held on. He did it tight.

Because it was the last chance he'd get.

After a while, Kate tipped her head back. "I probably should go get married."

Cal grinned at her. "Yeah."

He took her arm and turned her around.

They both stopped.

Keira was there, close, Angie to her hip.

Her eyes were bright too.

"Get over here, dork," Kate ordered.

Keira rushed to them.

And Cal walked down the hall and through the vestibule, Kate on one arm, his other arm around Keira's shoulders, Keira's arm full of her sister.

He had to let two of his girls go so he could walk one of them down the aisle to give her away to the man she loved.

Five minutes later, he did that.

He didn't lie.

It was the proudest moment of his life.

And it hurt like a bitch.

⌒

Violet

I held Ben in my lap.

Sam was in a little boy tux up at the altar, leaning against Tony's best man's legs, swinging his ring bearer pillow, his father's son, totally bored out of his skull.

Angie was standing by Keira, Keira's mini-me with her father's eyes, staring with rapt attention at her big sister getting married.

My husband had his arm wrapped around my shoulders.

He gave me a squeeze.

I turned to look up at him.

He dipped down and touched his forehead to mine, his nose resting along mine.

I held my breath.

Then he pulled away just as Ben shifted, jerked, pushing out of my arm and launching himself at his dad.

With ease, Joe caught him and settled him against his chest.

I watched.

Our little guy had this thing. It was weird and it was wonderful.

Any time he hit his dad's chest, he just calmed. Even when he'd been teething. Even when he'd fall and scrape something. Like all he needed was evidence of his father's solidness, his strength, and he could just let go.

I knew how that felt.

This was what he did then, curling in, cheek to his dad's chest as Joe tucked him close, Ben resting his hand light against his father's lapel, his eyes shifting sideways so he could keep them on one of his big sisters, all of whom adored him, all of whom my baby boy adored right back.

Joe's eyes were on Kate.

I returned mine to my daughter.

I knew what the forehead touch was. I didn't need to ask. Joe didn't need to explain.

It was his way of saying I'd unbalanced our scale…again. The scale of our life, where he gave and I gave, and it was supposed to go back and forth, staying balanced.

He thought I unbalanced it all the time with the way I gave.

He was wrong.

I didn't even have to look at him with our son on his chest. I didn't have to think back fifteen minutes ago to how I felt watching him walk my girl down the aisle with that look on his face. That look that said he didn't want to be anywhere but there at the same time he wanted to pick her up and carry her the other way, taking her to a place where they never grew up and you never had to let them go.

No, I didn't need any of that or any of the million other things Joe had done since that evening he shoveled the snow from our driveway.

I lived with the knowledge Joe had forever unbalanced our scales because I was sitting at my daughter's wedding due to the fact that Joe had killed a man so I could.

He'd saved my life.

He'd given me his love.

He'd given my daughters his love.

He'd given my girls and me more babies, a big family.

There was no way I unbalanced our scale.

Which I supposed meant our scale actually stayed balanced, him thinking I sent it crashing, me knowing he did.

I snuggled closer in his arm.

He tightened it around me.

Balance.

I felt my lips tip up.

And I watched my beautiful girl get married to the man she loved, a man who reminded me a lot of her father.

And a lot of Joe.

A man Joe totally hated.

Because he took his girl away.

Layne

June, Four Years Later

"You did good all this time, managing not to knock Keirry up," Tripp said to his brother.

Jasper looked to Tripp, grinning, but doing it also muttering, "Shut it, Tripp-o-matic."

"I'll second that, seein' as that means you nor me got dead 'cause Joe Callahan lost his mind you put your hands on his girl," Tanner Layne added.

"Cal wouldn't lose his mind, Dad. He totally digs me," Jasper told him.

Luckily, this was true.

"I can guaran-damn-tee you that Cal is in total denial about that whole part of you bein' with Keira," Tripp shared. "Even now, you have babies, you might wanna think of declaring them immaculate conceptions."

"He can be in denial," Jasper returned logically. "Means it was what it was and now I'm still breathin' for it bein' what it's gonna be."

"To that end…" Rocky's voice came from the top of the stairs.

Layne aimed his eyes over his shoulder to see his wife look amongst them in the loft area, which used to be a workout/office space when Layne had lived there with his boys.

Now that his boys were gone and his house was filled with girls, Layne worked out at the gym and the loft was an alternate television area because Cecelia and Annabel could never agree on what they wanted to watch.

So now he and his boys weren't lazing on workout equipment like they used to.

They were lounging on a massive sectional.

"I think we should probably go so we can get to the church on time," Rocky finished.

And this meant they were lounging on a massive sectional while wearing tuxes since Jasper was marrying Keira that day.

"Shit," Tripp muttered, planting a hand in the back of the couch and throwing his body over it, landing on his feet. "I gotta go pick up Giselle. Meet you there."

He took off but didn't pass Rocky without stopping and giving her a kiss on her cheek.

Rocky accepted it, and as Tripp bounded down the stairs, she looked to her husband folding out of the couch. Then she looked to his son who was doing the same.

After that, without a word, his wife walked down the stairs, leaving Layne with Jas.

He turned to his boy.

"You screwed me, bud," he stated.

Jas's head jerked and he abruptly stopped moving.

"What?" he asked.

"Knew what you wanted. Found what you wanted. Took care of her. Did right by her. Fell in love with her. Took your time to get to this place. You have your shit together. Keira has hers together. Now you're movin' on. That means I don't get to do what fathers are supposed to do. Got no fatherly advice to give. Got no warnings. Got no guidance. Got nothin'."

Jasper grinned at him.

"Nothin' but love and pride," Layne added.

Jasper's grin faded and his gaze grew intense on his old man.

"You and your brother are the best sons a man could hope for, bud. Love you and so fuckin' proud of you, it hurts," Layne finished.

Jasper moved to him. Layne caught his son at the back of his neck and pulled him to his chest.

Jas wrapped his arms around his dad.

He gave Jasper's neck a squeeze.

Jas pounded him on the back.

They let go.

They cleared their throats.

Then Layne said, "Let's get you to the church."

His woman leaned deep into his arm and he felt her lips at his ear.

"We have a problem," she whispered.

Yeah, they had a problem.

The boys' mother was sitting in their pew.

Due to her attitude, her relationship with both her sons was strained and had been for years. She was invited because Jasper was a good man. And no matter how strained things were with his mom, he was also a good son and he wanted her there.

But Gabby was not happy to be sitting in a pew with the ex-husband she hated and his wife, who she detested, and, being Gabby, she wasn't hiding it.

Which pissed Layne off.

It also pissed off his mother, Vera, who was right then sitting in the pew behind Gabby, staring daggers at her.

Devin had Vera's hand clamped tight in his, which indicated to Layne that Vera had said something that made Devin feel he needed to contain her.

And Layne did not want a catfight at his son's wedding.

He glanced over his shoulder to make sure Devin was containing her.

Devin gave him a look, then he used his free hand to reach into his tux pocket to pull out a flask.

He unscrewed it one-handed and took a hefty tug.

Vera turned while he was doing it and snapped quietly, "Devin!"

His mentor, best friend, and now stepfather turned to his mother. "You don't act up, I won't feel the need to get liquored up."

Vera huffed and sat back in her seat, resuming her glare at the back of Gabby's head.

Devin returned the flask to his pocket.

Layne caught only a glance at a tight-faced Gabby, who was completely ignoring them (luckily), when he looked to his wife.

"Kinda get that, sweetcheeks," he muttered.

"I'm not talking about Gabby," she whispered back. "We're all used to Gabby. I'm talking about the fact that both CeeCee *and* Bel have a crush on Jack Colton."

Layne looked beyond his woman to his two daughters sitting in the pew next to her.

Right then, neither of his babies cared about Jack Colton. Both CeeCee and Bel had their eyes glued to the door at the side of the church where they knew their brothers were going to walk out very soon.

They were getting along for Jasper's big day.

This wasn't unusual and not just his girls being good for their beloved big brother. If they weren't fighting, they were doing each other's hair, giving equal time to both endeavors.

Layne didn't get it.

He didn't try.

Rocky got it.

Layne got to spoil two daddy's girls.

Rocky got to raise two daughters and share all the goodness she had with them.

So it worked.

"None of them but Jack are in double digits, Roc. I'm not sure we gotta be worried about that yet," Layne replied, casting his gaze to the altar.

"Okay, well, if you don't think so, then you don't know Angie Callahan also has a crush on him," she returned.

Shit.

He looked to his wife. When she caught his eyes, she lifted her brows in her nonverbal, *See?*

"How 'bout we get Jasper tied to Keira before we worry about another love tangle with the Callahans?" he suggested.

Rocky grinned.

The side door to the church opened and Jasper, followed by Tripp and then several of Jas's buds, stepped out.

A few minutes later, Layne stood in a church, watching his son watching Keira Winters walk down the aisle.

Rocky was watching something else and he knew it when she leaned deep into his back and again found his ear. "Every time Cal walks one of his girls down the aisle, why do I take one look at his face and wanna burst into tears?"

Layne tore his gaze off his boy to glance at Cal.

Then he looked back at Jasper and he saw something that was different but all the same on his son's face.

So he pointed out the obvious.

"'Cause that's the look of love, sweetcheeks," he whispered back.

She found his hand. "Yeah."

He curled his fingers around hers.

Cal gave Keira away.

Jasper accepted her.

Layne's throat hurt through it all.

But when he watched his son kiss his bride, the pain released.

And all he felt was his wife's hand in his…

And happy.

Mike

September, Seven Years Later

"Um…baby, I think we have a problem."

Mike looked from shuffling through the mail on the kitchen counter to his wife.

He knew that look on her face.

"Please, Angel, do not tell me my daughter is pregnant again."

In the six years since they'd been married, Reesee had published eight books.

She and her husband, Fin, had also given Mike three grandkids.

His daughter was happy as a clam on her farm with her husband and her brood.

Mike could coast through the goodness of life because Dusty gave that to him. His grandkids gave that to him.

But with his daughters, he was not happy.

This was because Mike had another girl, Mandy, who was much younger than her big sister.

This meant this kind of torture—his baby girls making babies—would be drawn out, prolonged.

Never ending.

Christ.

Dusty grinned, moving toward him.

"No, gorgeous." She stopped close to him. "Rees isn't pregnant. Though I'd never describe an impending grandchild as being a problem. *This* is problem. Or at least it might be in the beginning."

"What?" he asked.

"Just going to say, I've made the call and preliminarily tamed the wild beast," she declared.

This wasn't an answer. Though it did make him mentally brace harder.

"What?" he repeated.

She reached a hand toward the counter, nabbed her tablet, looked down at it, sliding her finger on the screen, and finally her eyes came up to his.

"Brace," she whispered.

"Fuck," he muttered.

She turned the tablet his way.

His eyes dropped to it.

On it was an online entertainment news site.

And the headline was, "Jonas Haines of Broken Bird Marries Model Adriana Rivera in Vegas."

"What the fuck?" Mike murmured, pulling the tablet out of his wife's hand and reading it.

Jonas Haines, known as "No," lead singer, lead guitarist, and founder of the chart-topping rock band Broken Bird, yesterday reportedly married his on-again, off-again girlfriend, bathing suit model Adriana Rivera, in Las Vegas.

Haines, 31, and Rivera, 20, have dominated the gossip columns for the last two years with their stormy relationship. This includes Haines's brief incarceration for charges of assault and battery when he located a crazed fan of Rivera's who was stalking his lady love. Charges were later dropped through a plea bargain arrangement for Alfie Birk, who pled guilty to criminal harassment and menacing and received a reduced sentence.

It's reported that Haines's best man was a woman. Stella Gunn of the Blue Moon Gypsies, the established rock star who gave Haines and Broken Bird their break, asking Broken Bird to open for the Gypsies before they'd even signed a record deal, stood with the rocker.

In turn, standing up for Rivera was a man. Kai Mason, Gunn's husband and the head of an elite security agency in Los Angeles, the agency used by Broken Bird as well as Rivera personally, stood with the model.

Neither Haines's nor Rivera's spokespersons are confirming the nuptials except for Broken Bird's team stating that at this time, Haines and Rivera's relationship is "definitely on." It's been alleged that confirmation is being delayed in order for the bride and groom to inform their families that the wedding took place.

It's unknown where the newlyweds are at this time; however, social media sites have lit up with witnesses at Las Vegas and Los Angeles airports stating they've seen the couple and also reporting they've boarded a Fiji Airlines flight bound for those islands for what could be nothing other than their honeymoon.

Finished, Mike looked at his wife.

"Hunter is not happy," Dusty noted, something Mike did not need her to note.

Hunter was Dusty's best friend's husband.

He was also Adriana's father.

And last, Hunter had not been a big fan of this situation for more years than No and Addie had been together. In fact, it had been since the first time he saw his daughter, at thirteen, gazing with love-struck eyes at No, who was with his band playing at his sister's wedding.

"But I talked him down," Dusty finished.

"Have you heard from No?" Mike asked.

She shook her head. "I called. Reesee called. Even Fin called. He's not answering." Her mouth quirked. "Probably because he's a day ahead of us on Fiji." She paused, then added, "And he's busy."

"This isn't funny," Mike informed her.

He watched his wife's lips continue to quirk.

"Angel," he warned.

Her lips stopped quirking. "Addie's been in love with No since she was thirteen."

Mike had nothing to say to that because it was true.

"And No's been in love with her since the second they bumped into each other again two years ago," she continued.

"She's not even old enough to drink," Mike stated.

"She's old enough to fall in love," Dusty returned.

"She's old enough to *think* she's in love."

"Baby," she whispered, moving closer. "You were here at Christmas with those two. I get you're worried. But there's no way you could watch them and not see they're completely, desperately, crazy *in love*."

Fuck, he couldn't say anything to that either.

Because it was true.

Mike wrapped an arm around his wife and he pulled out his phone.

He held her as he slid his thumb over the screen.

He put it to his ear.

Jonas answered on the third ring.

"Dad."

"Got some news for me, No?"

Apparently, he didn't because there was silence.

"Jonas," Mike prompted.

"It's her, Dad. She's young, but I don't give a fuck. It's her. It just is."

"Yeah, neither of you hid that from your family last time we saw you and you haven't been hiding it from the population at large, the crazy shit you've both been playing out publicly."

"You know Addie. She's about drama."

His son sounded like he liked that.

Then again, he married it, so he did.

"That isn't the issue," Mike said. "The issue is, I read about it on a god-damned tablet."

"It was a spur-of-the-moment thing," Jonas muttered.

"I figured that part out," Mike told him.

"We're gonna have another ceremony when we get back," No assured him. "One we'll have with our families."

"I can do without going to another wedding, No. What I'm not a big fan of is reading something like this rather than hearing it direct from my son. You're famous. I hear a lot about you that's truth and a lot that's lies. But when it's important, when it means you're happy, I wanna hear it *from you.*"

"I'm happy, Dad," No said quietly.

Mike drew in breath.

"I'm glad, son," Mike replied quietly.

Dusty pushed closer.

"She's happy too," Jonas told him.

"I'm glad about that too," Mike replied.

"We've been dodging calls because we've been busy and because I wanted you to know first. You know now, so I gotta call Rees."

"Yeah, your sister can bust your ass for depriving her of a celebrity wedding."

"Last five books on the *New York Times* list. I'm not the only celebrity in the family."

"Lucky for me, she's got someone in her life who keeps her grounded, not someone who busts up hotel rooms."

"Addie broke a vase. It was blown out of proportion by the media."

"She broke it throwing it at you."

"She's excitable."

Mike did not want to go there.

"Call your sister," he ordered.

"I will," No said, a smile in his voice. "And Dad?"

"Yeah, Jonas?"

"Love you."

Mike sighed.

Then he said, "Same. Give our love to Addie. And hope to see you both soon."

"Love back to Dusty, Mandy, and Austin."

"Right. Later, son."

"Later, Dad."

They disconnected.

Mike threw his phone on the counter.

Dusty snuggled closer.

"All good?" she asked.

"He sounds happy."

His woman smiled.

"Really happy," he whispered.

"Then it's all good," she whispered back.

He looked into her eyes.

She was happy too. Happy because she was happy, and happy because his son was.

"Love you, Angel," he murmured.

"Yeah, gorgeous, it's all good," she replied and rolled up to her toes.

Mike took her mouth.

Their daughter Amanda at a friend's house, their son Austin at basketball practice, the house was empty.

So after Mike took his wife's mouth, he took her hand and led her to the bedroom.

Then he took something else.

Benny

December, Two Years Later

Benny turned to his wife, who was sitting on the edge of the hotel bed, strapping on a high-heeled sandal.

"Come again?" he asked.

She tipped her head, her thick, dark hair sliding down her back, and gave him her eyes.

"That's what Vi told me over coffee this morning."

"Angie is dating Jack Colton," Benny stated.

Frankie bent down to finish with her shoe, confirming, "Yeah. They live across the street from each other. They grew up together. They wrestled in the grass at barbeques when they were kids and they've been dancing around each other at parties with the grown-ups now for years. Vi didn't miss it. I didn't. No one did but Colt and Cal. It's like Colt and Feb, part two. Except hopefully without the heartbreak."

"She's not old enough to date," he told his wife's bent head.

When she straightened and looked at him, she was grinning.

"She's seventeen," she reminded him.

"That's not old enough," Ben declared.

Francesca burst out laughing.

Then she pushed up from the bed and walked on her high-heeled shoes, in her skintight dress, his way.

Ben watched. Fuck, they'd been together seventeen years, she'd given him three kids, and still, watching his wife strut his way, he wanted to bag this wedding, put the DO NOT DISTURB sign on the door, and spend the afternoon fucking his wife.

She fitted herself to his front.

And he wanted that even more.

He wrapped his arms around her and stopped thinking about his cousin's daughter.

"How bad you wanna go to this wedding?" he asked.

Her eyes got hot, her face got soft, but her mouth said, "You miss your nephew's wedding, Carm is gonna lose her mind."

She would.

His sister would do that.

And they'd flown all the way to California to do this, so they should probably do it.

Frankie fiddled with his collar. "And you know, just on the heels of Violet's news about Angie, you should prepare. Because Ales told me she has it on good authority from two sources that that Rio boy, who plays wide receiver on the football team, is gonna ask her out."

Ales was *his* daughter.

Which meant he had a say.

So he said it.

"Ales definitely isn't dating," Ben declared.

"Baby, she's fifteen."

"Exactly. Way too young."

Frankie smiled at him.

"And she's absolutely not dating a kid named Rio. What the fuck kind of name is that?" he asked.

"I think it's cool," Frankie remarked.

"You're wrong," Benny returned.

She slid her hand to his neck, her lips tipped up. "You're hot when you get all irrational-dad."

"And you're hot all the time. If you don't stop touchin' me, lookin' like you do in that dress, with your tits pressed to me, we're gonna be late to my nephew's wedding."

Her eyes dropped to his mouth.

"Can't have that," she murmured.

His hands dropped to her ass.

"Babe," he warned on a squeeze.

She lifted her gaze.

"Let's get the kids, make sure they haven't torn apart their room, and go do this," he said. "Ma and Pop'll be cool with bringin' the kids back. We'll come back early and we'll have our own celebration."

"Works for me," Frankie agreed.

Good.

They had a plan.

He bent in and touched his mouth to hers.

She lifted up on her toes and made the light kiss hard.

When she rolled back, she again caught his eyes. "Love you, Benny Bianchi."

He gave her ass another squeeze, this one reflexive.

"Love you too, Frankie Bianchi."

She smiled at him and moved out of his arms.

"Gotta grab my tie," he told her, wanting to let go of his wife in order to grab a tie like he wanted water torture.

"I'll start rounding up the kids."

He watched her ass as she moved to the door.

Then he called, "Babe?"

She turned back to him.

"Not jokin' about that Rio kid thing. Ales doesn't date until the time is right," he declared.

She gave him a look he felt in his dick.

"*So* hot when you're all irrational-dad," she whispered, then strutted to the door.

Fuck, Frankie would rally Ales, and with both his girls using their different ways, he was gonna cave.

Shit.

He got his tie.

He bunched it up and shoved it in his pocket, not about to put it on until he absolutely had to.

He then saw his wife's purse on the bed.

He grabbed it and their key card.

After that, he walked out of their hotel room to help his wife round up their kids so they could meet up with Cal, Vi, and their brood and they all could go watch his nephew get married.

When they got that done, he could come back.

And celebrate with his wife.

Garrett

May, Four Years Later

"Serious as hell, brown eyes, someone should outlaw this shit."

Cher turned to him and he lifted up, taking his mouth from her ear to catch her eyes.

Those brown eyes he loved were bright with unshed tears and she was also moving like she was about to throw up.

He knew she wasn't going to vomit.

And she also wasn't going to cry.

She might shed a tear but only if she didn't manage to swallow back the laughter she was fighting.

Their chairs pulled close so he could throw his arm easily around the back of hers, he curled her to his side.

She made a choking noise.

He dipped his mouth again to her ear.

"Hold it in," he muttered.

"You're not helping, Merry," she wheezed.

"You can't bust a gut laughin' during the best man's speech. Especially at this wedding."

"Just let me deep breathe," she forced out.

"You're not breathing at all."

She turned and whacked him one on his arm.

He smiled down at her.

She glared at him.

That was one way to get her not to laugh.

He knew a better way, and to keep her from laughing, he employed it, leaning in and taking her mouth in a hard, sweet kiss.

When he was done, she lifted her hand and rested it on his neck, her thumb stroking his throat.

He kissed her nose.

She melted into him and turned in his arm, giving her attention back to the best man.

Garrett didn't give his attention to the drunken best man, who was totally fucking up his speech.

He looked at the groom.

When he did, he saw Ethan looking at him.

Garrett held his boy's eyes, grabbed his glass, and lifted it his way.

Ethan dipped his chin.

His drunk friend quit jabbering and managed to slur out his request for everyone to toast the happy couple.

They did.

This meant, thankfully, the fool was done and conversation began to resume. Ethan stood and took the microphone from his bud.

Conversation stopped when he spoke into it.

"I have a few things to say."

Cher's attention perked up.

So did Garrett's.

Ethan looked to his bride.

"I'm a lucky man today," he said softly into the microphone.

Cher pressed closer.

Ethan's woman's face flushed with happiness.

"Thank you, baby, for saying yes," Ethan went on.

His new wife put her hand to her mouth, and even though her new husband stood at her side, she blew him a kiss.

"So sweet," Eve whispered.

Garrett looked to his right, seeing his daughter leaned into her elbows on the table, watching her brother.

He looked beyond her and saw his eldest girl, Shelby, doing the same except not with her elbows on the table.

He and Cher got two and two.

Shelby had her mother's eyes.

Eve had her father's.

Garrett looked to the wedding party and saw Matt up there with his brother.

And Mathias's eyes were blue.

Garrett looked to Ethan when he again spoke.

"I need to say what I gotta say, and I need to say it now with everyone in this room who means something to me, to my wife." He looked down at her again then back at the room. "And I need to say it so you all know. Because you all should know, today of all days. You should know I made some vows in a church. And they mean something to me. I signed a legal paper. And that means something to me too. But I'm gonna make some vows right now that mean everything."

He stopped talking and he looked right at Garrett.

And witnessing the expression on Ethan's face, Garrett felt his chest depress.

"Right now, in front of all of you, I'm gonna make the vows my dad showed me you should make when you fall in love with a woman."

"Oh shit," Cher murmured.

Ethan turned and looked down at his bride. "I vow to take care of you. I vow that every day you'll feel safe because you know that down to your bones, seein' as I'll be breakin' my back givin' it to you. And I vow to give you shit when you're bein' a wiseass."

Laughter filled the room, but Ethan was not done speaking.

"I also vow to take your shit when I'm bein' one. I vow to make sure you got what you want as often as I can give it to you. I vow to love the children we make, spend time with them as often as humanly possible, and knock myself out to make them feel safe. I vow to guide them to the right paths in life, showin' them I'm proud they're mine, they're *ours*, even when they don't do anything special to make me feel that way."

His voice dipped before he went on.

"And most importantly, green eyes, I vow to make you laugh at least once every day for the rest of the beautiful life I also vow to give you. I vow to make you do it hard. I vow to give it from the heart so I can make it come from your gut, and you'll never forget how happy you make me because I vow to bust my ass to make you the same. I love you, baby, and I cherish you, and that's what you're gonna get from me until one or the other of us stops breathing."

"*Oh, Ethan!*" his girl cried, surging out of her seat, throwing herself in Ethan Merrick's arms, and shoving her face in his neck.

He wrapped one around her and kissed her hair before he turned to the room, raised his glass, and finished.

"So toast with me, with my bride, to what real love means—care and safety and laughter and givin' your baby shit when she's bein' a wiseass."

Laughter and applause hit the room as Ethan lifted his glass.

Everyone lifted theirs.

Ethan shifted slightly, aiming his glass and his eyes at Garrett.

Garrett jerked up his chin.

His boy, now a man, now a husband, drank.

So did everyone else.

Then Ethan turned to his woman and kissed her.

Garrett did not drink.

Neither did Cher.

Because, while others were drinking, he was putting his hand to his woman's jaw and turning her face his way.

Damn.

Pretty.

Even bawling.

His gaze roamed her wet cheeks before it caught hers.

"You're such a girl," he whispered.

"I know," she whispered back.

He smiled at his wife.

Then he bent and took her mouth.

This concludes The 'Burg series. Thank you for reading.
The gang from J&J's sends their love.

Made in the USA
Monee, IL
07 September 2022

13459443R00343